Jātaka Tales of the Buddha
An Anthology

Volume III

Retold by

Ken and Visakha Kawasaki

Illustrations by

N.A.P.G. Dharmawardena

PARIYATTI PRESS
an imprint of
Pariyatti Publishing
www.pariyatti.org

ISBN: 978-1-68172-312-9 (Print)
ISBN: 978-1-68172-364-8 (PDF)
ISBN: 978-1-68172-373-0 (ePub)
ISBN: 978-1-68172-363-1 (Mobi)
Library of Congress Control Number: 2017956359

First Pariyatti Edition, 2018

Table of Contents

Volume III

189
The Value of Friendship
Mahā-Ukkusa Jātaka

It was while staying at Jetavana that the Buddha told this story about having friends.

Once, a layman, the son of a genteel but impoverished family of Sāvatthī, sent a go-between to propose marriage to a young woman of the same class. In return, the young woman asked the go-between, "Does the young man have any reliable friends who can, on occasion, act on his behalf?"

"No, madam," the go-between answered. "I don't believe that he has any close friends at all."

"Well," she declared, "before I can consider his offer of marriage, he must make some good friends!"

The young man followed her advice and introduced himself to the four city gatekeepers. After he got to know them quite well, they introduced him to the town wardens. Gradually, he became friends with some of the nobles, with the king's advisors, with the commander-in-chief, and even with the crown prince, who introduced him to the king. After some time, the king gave him a position of trust, and the young man became known as Mittagandhaka, the man with many friends. Moving in these circles, it was not long before he became acquainted with the eighty great disciples, and

1

Venerable Ānanda introduced him to the Buddha. The Buddha established his entire family in the Three Refuges.

The second time the young man proposed marriage, the woman unhesitatingly accepted. The king himself arranged for his wedding feast to be celebrated under royal patronage and presented the couple with a fine house. Everybody in the court also sent them gifts. Because of their regard for Mittagandhaka, all the inhabitants of Sāvatthī held his new wife in high regard and felt close to her.

On the seventh day of their wedding celebration, the new couple invited the Buddha and five hundred bhikkhus. After the meal, the Buddha gave them a blessing, and they both attained the first path.

Later, in the Hall of Truth, all the bhikkhus were talking about this. "Friends," one of them said, "it is remarkable that, because Mittagandhaka followed his wife's advice, he became a friend to everyone and received great honor from the king, and both husband and wife attained the first path."

When the Buddha heard what they were discussing, he said, "Bhikkhus, this is not the first time that this man has received great benefit because of this woman. Long ago, her good advice saved their family." Then he told this story of the past.

Long, long ago, when Brahmadatta was reigning in Bārānasi, there was a large lake in the jungle. On the southern shore of the lake lived a male hawk, on the western shore lived a female hawk, on the northern shore lived a great lion, and on the eastern shore lived a huge osprey. On an island in the middle of the lake lived a turtle.

When the male hawk asked the female hawk to become his mate, she asked him directly if he had any close friends.

"No, I don't." he replied. "Most of the time, I just keep to myself."

"That won't do," she declared. "If we are to live together, we need to have some reliable friends who can help us if trouble arises and defend us in case of danger. You must find some friends."

"Who should I make friends with?" he asked.

"Well," she replied, "you could get to know the osprey king, who lives on the eastern shore of the lake, and the lion king, who lives on the northern shore. You might also become friends with the turtle, who lives on the island in the middle."

The hawk took her advice and sought out these neighbors. Soon, they were well acquainted and became good friends.

The female hawk agreed to be his mate, and they built a nest in a kadamba tree on an islet in the lake. In time, they had two babies.

One day, while the babies were still fledglings, some hunters from a nearby village were foraging through the jungle, looking for game. Late in the afternoon, they arrived empty-handed at the lake. Not wishing to return home without anything to show for their day's labor, they tried to catch a fish or a turtle. Failing even at that, they swam to the islet and rested under the shade of the kadamba tree. Flies, gnats, and mosquitoes so tormented the men that they built a fire to drive the insects away.

As the smoke from the fire rose through the branches of the tree, the baby hawks began crying.

"Do you hear that?" shouted one of the men. "There are birds in this tree! Look! There's the nest! Stoke the fire! Let's roast some fowls and have our supper!"

When the mother hawk heard her babies and saw the blazing fire, she cried, "Husband! Quick! Those men want to kill our young ones! They have built a fire to roast our babies! Fly over, and tell the osprey of the danger! Ask him to save our children!"

The hawk flew swiftly to the eastern shore and gave a sharp call to announce his arrival.

"Hello," said the osprey. "Why have you come? Is there a problem?"

"Oh, great king of the birds," answered the hawk hurriedly. "I have come to beg your help. Some villagers have built a fire under our kadamba tree, and they plan to eat our little ones!

"Have no fear!" said the osprey. "The wise make friends for unforeseen occasions, and the good must help each other in times of need. Of course, I will help you! Now tell me! Have the churls climbed the tree yet?"

"No, not yet. They are still piling wood on the fire," the hawk told him.

"Good!" the osprey replied. "Then go back, and comfort your mate. Tell her I'm on my way."

The hawk returned, and the osprey flew toward the kadamba tree to survey the scene.

As soon as the men started climbing the tree, the great bird dived into the lake, filled his mouth with water and soaked his wings. Then, as he flew over the islet, he opened his mouth and flapped his wings. The water he had brought rained down and completely quenched the fire.

Startled, the men climbed down and kindled another fire, but the osprey put it out in the same way. The men refused to give up and built a new fire every time the osprey extinguished the flames. Soon, it was quite dark, and the great bird was exhausted from hauling so much water.

"Husband," the female hawk said to her mate, "the osprey is in distress! Go and ask the turtle to come and relieve him."

"Friend," the hawk said to the osprey, "thank you for your help. You have done us a great service! My wife is concerned, however, that you are wearing yourself out on our behalf. Please rest a while! You've done more than enough!"

"Not at all!" the osprey vehemently exclaimed. "A true friend must do all he can for his friend, even if he dies doing it!"

"We certainly appreciate that!" replied the hawk. "But please rest awhile." The hawk quickly flew off to visit the turtle.

"Hello," said the turtle. "What brings you out tonight?"

"Our children are in danger!" the hawk replied. "Villagers are building fires to roast them. The noble osprey has been working for hours to put out the fires, but now he is worn out. Would you please come and help protect our nestlings?"

"One who is virtuous gives food, help, and even his life for a friend. For you, dear hawk, I will do whatever you need."

When the turtle's son heard what was going on, he cried, "Let me go, Father! Your friend is my friend. I'll save those baby hawks!"

"That's very good of you to offer," the turtle said to his son, "but, when those villagers see me, fully grown, they might leave the hawks alone."

The great turtle sent the hawk back and promised to be there shortly. He dived into the water, collected some mud, and swam to the islet. Crawling ashore, he threw the mud onto the fire and quenched the flames.

"What's going on?" shouted one of the men, surprised not to see the osprey flying by. He looked down at the fire that had just been put out and cried, "Look at the size of that turtle! He's huge!"

"There's enough meat for all of us! Why bother with these baby hawks? Let's roll that cursed turtle over, kill him, and enjoy turtle soup!"

The men scrambled down from the tree as fast as they could. Some began tearing strips from their clothes, and others collected creepers. They tied them to the turtle's legs, but, struggle as they might, they could not roll him over. The mighty turtle was so strong that he kept crawling toward the water and dragged the men through the mud.

The men refused to let go until they were in such deep water that they realized they were in danger of drowning. Finally, they gave up and clambered back to shore, where they collapsed, gasping and coughing up water.

"What a mess!" one of them cried. "Half the night, a miserable osprey kept putting out our fire, and then we were almost drowned when this turtle pulled us into the lake!"

"You're right," said another, "but it's too late to go home. Let's build another fire and dry off. In the morning, we'll catch those little hawks and have some breakfast."

As they noisily gathered dry sticks for yet another fire, the female hawk said to her mate, "They are determined to devour our babies. Go and talk to our friend, the lion."

The hawk flew to the northern shore of the lake and landed in front of the lion's den. "Hello," said the lion. "What brings you here at this time of night?"

"Great king of the beasts" the hawk began, "our little ones are in danger. Men have been trying all night to catch them. The osprey and the turtle have repeatedly put out their fires, but they have just built another one. Since you are our king, I have come to ask for your help. Would you please come and save our children?"

"For you," the lion replied, "I am willing to perform any service at any time. As your friend, I must protect your children. Go back, and comfort your dear family. I will take care of the men. That gang of villagers must be stopped from wreaking havoc in our forest. "

The great lion leaped into the lake and churned up the water as he charged toward the islet.

The men heard the splashing and looked to see what it was. When they saw the outline of the great beast and the light of the fire reflected in his eyes, they were terrified. "A lion!" they cried. "Run for your lives!" They all jumped into the water and swam as fast as they could in the opposite direction.

When the lion got to the foot of the tree, all the men were gone. The osprey, the turtle, and the hawk emerged from the shadows and thanked him for his successful rout of the men.

In a clear voice, the lion declared, "Our friendship is of great value to us all. We must be careful never to break these ties that bind us together."

Working together, they put out the men's fire, and each returned to his own home.

The female hawk gazed fondly upon her young and thought, "Ah! Through friends, my little ones are safe!" Filled with happiness and contentment, she said to her mate, "What a blessing to have such good friends! It is due to the help of our friends that our children are safe and sound. Each one stayed to do his part. In our helplessness, they took pity on us, and you, our children, and I have survived this terrifying night because of them. Truly, we live and prosper because we have and are good friends!"

These animals stayed together for the rest of their lives without breaking the bond of friendship. Eventually, they all passed away to fare according to their deserts.

Having concluded his story, the Buddha identified the birth: "At that time, the young married couple were the pair of hawks, Moggallāna was the great turtle, Rāhula was that turtle's son, Sāriputta was the osprey, and I was the lion."

190
What the Wise Despise
Bhisa Jātaka

It was while staying at Jetavana that the Buddha told this story about a discontented bhikkhu.

One day, while a young bhikkhu, who had come from a noble family in Sāvatthī, was walking for alms, he saw a beautiful woman and fell in love at first sight. Obsessed with desire, he neglected himself. Soon, like a deva nearing its end, the young bhikkhu began to exhibit signs of decline: his fingernails grew long, his robe became dirty, he forgot to eat, and he grew jaundiced and haggard.

The other bhikkhus noticed his condition, guessed the reason, and took him to see the Buddha.

"Is it true, Bhikkhu, that you are neglecting your practice?" the Buddha asked him.

"Yes, Venerable Sir, it is true," he admitted. "What is the reason?"

"I have fallen in love, Venerable Sir."

"After ordaining in this faith which leads to liberation, do not let yourself fail!" the Buddha admonished him. "Long ago, even when there was no Buddha in the world, wise men, having undertaken the religious life, were able to remain steadfast in their renunciation to the end. Not one of them

7

surrendered to even the slightest temptation!" Then the Buddha told this story of the past.

Long, long ago, when Brahmadatta was reigning in Bārānasi, the Bodhisatta was born as the son of a wealthy and influential brahmin and was named Mahā-Kañcana. When he was just a toddler, his parents had another son and named him Upa-Kañcana. Then, one after another, they had five more sons and finally, a daughter, whom they named Kañcanadevī.

When he was old enough, Mahā-Kañcana studied all the arts and sciences in Takkasilā. After he returned to Bārānasi, his parents were eager for him to marry and offered to find him a suitable match. "I am not interested in being the head of a family," Mahā-Kañcana told them. "I don't want a wife and children. Living at home seems like a prison to me. You have other sons. Let them get married and give you grandchildren. That life is not for me."

Although his parents begged him to change his mind, Mahā-Kañcana adamantly refused. When his friends tried to interest him in women, he told them that he had renounced the world.

Giving up on Mahā-Kañcana, the parents spoke of marriage to their other sons, but none of them was willing to wed. Kañcanadevī felt exactly the same. Eventually, with all their adult children still single, the parents died.

As the eldest son, Mahā-Kañcana performed the funeral rites for his parents. Distributing alms lavishly to wayfarers and beggars, he completely liquidated their estate. Then, Mahā-Kañcana, his six brothers, his sister, a servant, a maid, and a companion left Bārānasi to become ascetics in the Himavat. Finding a pleasant place near a lake covered with lotuses, they built a simple hermitage and began observing the religious life.

Every day, they all went into the jungle to gather fruit, berries, and roots. They went in separate ways, and, as soon as one of them found food, he called the others. Then, all together, amid laughter and chatter, they collected enough for the day. It was often as noisy as a market.

After a while, Mahā-Kañcana thought, "Look at us! We discarded our great family fortune worth eighty crores to take up the ascetic life, but we go greedily into the forest after wild fruit. Such frivolity is inappropriate. From now on, I will go alone to gather our food."

That evening, he called everyone together and announced, "Tomorrow, I want all of you to stay here and to continue your meditation. I will gather fruit for us all every day."

"No! Not so! That cannot be!" they shouted. One by one, they explained that they had followed him and had become hermits because of him. He was their teacher. It should be the younger ones who gathered food while he remained in the hermitage and continued meditating. After further discussion, it was agreed that Mahā-Kañcana, Kañcanadevī, and the maid would stay in the hermitage while the eight other men took turns gathering food.

After that, one of the men went each day by himself to gather food for all of them. When he had gathered enough, he returned, divided it into eleven portions, and arranged them on a flat stone. Then he ceremoniously rang the gong to summon the others. Each took his share back to his own leaf hut and ate alone. When no other food was in season, they ate only lotus stalks. Every day they practiced meditation diligently with the goal of achieving jhānic concentration.

Because of their outstanding virtue and great effort, Sakka's throne grew hot. As soon as the king of the devas realized the cause, he wondered whether the eleven were really ascetics and had overcome desire. He decided to test them by using his supernatural powers to make one portion of food disappear.

One day, when Mahā-Kañcana arrived after hearing the gong, he found no share for himself. "My share must have been forgotten," he said to himself, and he fasted that day.

The next day, when he found no share for himself, he thought, "I must have committed some fault, and my allotment has been held back by way of correction."

On the third day, when he found no share for himself, he believed that he was indeed being punished for some fault, and he resolved to make peace with the others. That evening, he sounded the gong, and everyone gathered in the center of the hermitage.

Near the hermitage, there was a deva residing in a huge tree, and that deva also heard the gong, appeared before the group, and stood to one side. Also, an enormous elephant, which had once been captured, but, proving to be untrainable, had escaped into the jungle, heard the gong, appeared before the group, and stood to one side. A monkey, which had been used by a snake charmer to play tricks on snakes but had escaped to the jungle, also heard the gong, appeared before the group, and stood to one side. The deva, the elephant, and the monkey greatly respected the ascetics and frequently visited the hermitage. Sakka was also there, but he was completely invisible.

"Who rang the gong?" they all asked. "I did," replied Mahā-Kañcana.

"Why, dear teacher?" they asked.

"Friends, who gathered food two days ago?" Mahā-Kañcana asked.

"I did, sir," replied one of them as he stood up. "When you divided the rations, did you set apart a share for me?" Mahā-Kañcana asked.

"Of course, I did, sir. I gave you the share of the eldest."

"Who gathered food yesterday?" Mahā-Kañcana asked. "I did, sir," replied another as he stood up.

"When you divided the rations, did you set apart a share for me?" Mahā-Kañcana asked.

"Of course, I did, sir. I gave you the share of the eldest."

"Who gathered food today?" Mahā-Kañcana asked. "I did, sir," replied a third as he stood up.

"When you divided the rations, did you set apart a share for me?" Mahā-Kañcana asked.

"Of course, I did, sir. I gave you the share of the eldest."

"Friends, for three days I have found no share of food for myself," Mahā-Kañcana explained. "The first day, I thought that someone had forgotten my share. The second day, I thought there must be some fault in me. Today, I decided that, if I was at fault, I would make my peace with you all. That's why I summoned you with the gong. The three of you have told me you put aside my portion of lotus roots, even though I could not find it. Now I must find out who took my portion each day. For those who have forsaken the world, theft is unbecoming, even if it is something as humble as a lotus stalk."

"What a wicked deed!" cried all the others. "Who could be so cruel?"

Upa-Kañcana immediately stood up and asked, "Master, may I declare myself innocent of this charge?"

"You may, Brother."

"May the one who stole your share of food have herds of horses and cattle and stores of silver and gold! May he be cursed with love for his devoted wife and children above all!" Upa-Kañcana declared.

As Upa-Kañcana made this declaration, the other ascetics covered their ears and cried, "No! No! Such a curse is too heavy to bear!"

"Brother, your oath is indeed heavy," Mahā-Kañcana agreed. "Obviously, it was not you who took my food. Please sit down."

The next brother stood up, paid his respects to Mahā-Kañcana, and declared, "May the one who stole your share of food have many sons, fine robes, and precious sandalwood! May his heart be filled with lust and craving!"

Each of the other men, in turn, stood to declare his innocence.

"May the one who stole your share of food have plenty of fame, land, sons, houses, and treasure that he values beyond understanding. May he remain ignorant of the passing of time."

"May the one who stole your share of food be a mighty warrior and a king on a great throne. May he rule the whole earth without ever being satisfied!"

"May the one who stole your share of food be a superstitious brahmin full of uncontrolled passion. May he be honored by kings and ever greedy for more."

"May the one who stole your share of food be a Vedic scholar, revered, praised, and worshiped by all for his holiness. May he incessantly crave more esteem."

"May the one who stole your share of food possess a rich village, with every luxury provided. May he die with his passions uncontrolled."

"May the one who stole your share of food be the village chief, intoxicated by music and dance, popular with all he meets, and favored by the king."

Then Kañcanadevī and the maid, in turn, each stood to declare her innocence.

"May the one who stole your share of food be the most beautiful of women! May the world's most powerful monarch love her best of all women and make her his chief queen."

"May the one who stole your share of food be proud of her station! May her food be sweet, and may she always have plenty!"

The tree deva, the elephant, and the monkey, in turn, each stood to declare his innocence.

"May the one who stole your share of food take care of the great Kajangal cloister, restore its ruins, and every day create a new window there."

"May the one who stole your share of food be caught and bound with six hundred chains, dragged and driven from the jungle to the city, and whipped and beaten all along the way."

"May the one who stole your share of food be put on a leash, with a garland on his neck and tin earrings in each ear. May he walk the highway in great fear and be forced to entertain loud crowds by playing with a snake!"

Firmly believing that all of his companions were innocent, Mahā-Kañcana feared that, perhaps, they suspected that he himself was lying, so he declared, "May one who swears the food was gone, if it was not, wallow in desire and ignorance. May worldly death come to him, at last, with his mind confused!"

After all these oaths had been solemnly sworn, Sakka made himself visible and said, "Each of you has sworn an oath to profess your innocence, to demonstrate your loathing of the act of theft as if it were spittle and phlegm spat on the ground. Now let me ask you why you so abhor lust and desire.

"Mahā-Kañcana, I will ask you first. Why do sages despise all the things that men in the world find so lovely and desirable? You disparage every single thing that others find worth seeking!"

"Desires are chains that bind, so we find misery in them and much to fear," Mahā-Kañcana answered without equivocation. "Desires seduce men to behave in vile, cruel, and dishonest ways. Those wicked acts carry men to hell after death. Because we ascetics know the misery that lust brings, we always curse desires. We never praise them."

This explanation so impressed Sakka that he declared, "Mahā-Kañcana, it was I who took your lotus stalks! It was a test for all of you. Now I truly know your purity and virtue. Mahā-Kañcana, here is your food!"

"Your Majesty!" Mahā-Kañcana replied, with a tone of reprimand in his voice. "We are not players providing entertainment for you. Nor are we your relatives or friends. Why, Sire, did you think that you could sport with us in this way?"

"Noble sage!" Sakka replied, attempting to placate the ascetic. "You are my teacher and my father. Please forgive me for taking this liberty with you. Please do not be offended. I know that you feel no anger toward me, because you are incapable of wrath."

"Your Majesty!" Mahā-Kañcana exclaimed joyfully. "Not one of us in angry with you! Nor is there anything to forgive! It is a blessed day when we are able to see the king of the devas coming to visit us! Let us all rejoice to see the food, once stolen, now restored to me!"

Sakka paid his respects to the company of ascetics and returned to Tāvatimsa. Mahā-Kañcana and his companions resumed their practice of meditation and, when they passed away, were reborn in the Brahma heavens.

Having concluded his story, the Buddha taught the Dhamma, and the discontented bhikkhu attained the first path. Then the Buddha identified the birth: "Sāriputta, Moggallāna, Punna, Mahā-Kassapa, Anuruddha, and Ānanda were the six younger brothers; Uppalavannā was Kañcanadevī; Khujjuttarā was the maid; Sātāgira was the deva; Citta the householder was the servant; Pārileyya was the elephant; Madhuvasettha was the monkey; Kāludāyi was Sakka; and I was the wise Mahā-Kañcana."

191

Until I Have Found a Way
Pañcuposatha Jātaka

It was while staying at Jetavana that the Buddha told this story about observing Uposatha.

On a full-moon day, the Buddha sat in the Hall of Truth surrounded by bhikkhus, bhikkhunīs, and five hundred white-robed lay followers.

"Are the lay disciples observing Uposatha?" he asked.

"Yes, Venerable Sir, we are," all five hundred answered.

"Well done! Long ago, the wise also observed Uposatha in order to subdue passion and to overcome craving." Then the Buddha told this story of the past.

Long, long ago, the Bodhisatta was born into a great brahmin family in Magadha.

When he grew up, he renounced the home life and became an ascetic. He went into the great forest that, at that time, separated the kingdom of Magadha from two adjoining kingdoms and built himself a simple hermitage. Not far from his hermitage, a wood pigeon lived with his mate in a bamboo grove, a snake lived in an ant-hill, a jackal lived in a thicket, and a bear lived in a den. These four animals frequently visited the sage to listen to his wise advice.

One day, the pigeon, with his mate behind him, left their nest and went looking for food. Suddenly, a hawk swooped down and grabbed the hen in his sharp talons.

Hearing her cry, the cock quickly turned around, but it was too late. He watched in horror as the hawk flew away with her limp body.

The pigeon had dearly loved his mate, and he was devastated that she was so brutally torn from him. His mourning was so great that he could not concentrate on anything. After a while, he thought "My mind is being tormented by terrible passion. I will not eat until I have found a way to subdue my passion!" He went immediately to the hermitage.

That same morning, the snake decided to hunt for food. As he emerged from his hole in the anthill, he saw a handsome, white, hump-backed bull. This bull, which belonged to the village headman and was the pride of the village, had just finished grazing. In an exuberant mood, the bull began pawing the ground around the anthill and playfully digging up and tossing the earth with his horns. Startled by the noise and thrashing movement, the snake tried to escape, but the bull happened to tread on the snake's tail. When the snake felt the sharp hoof, he became so angry that he reared up, spread his hood wide, and struck the bull with his venomous fangs. The bull fell dead in an instant, and the snake retreated back into his hole. When the villagers found the dead bull, they cried and honored him with garlands. Ceremoniously, they carried the beast away and buried him.

When everyone had gone, the snake emerged again from his hole. "Through blind anger, I have deprived that creature of life, and I have brought sorrow to the hearts of many," he thought. "I will not eat until I have found a way to subdue my anger!" He went immediately to the hermitage.

Some time before this, the jackal had gone hunting for food and had come across the carcass of a dead elephant. "Here's plenty of food!" he cried in delight. First, he tried to take a bite of the trunk, but it was like chewing on a tree. He tried the tusk, but that was like stone. He tried the stomach, but that was like a bamboo basket. He tried the tail, but that was like an iron rod. Finally, he tried the rear, and it was as soft as a lump of butter! It was so tender and so delicious that the jackal ate his way inside. Finding himself a little thirsty, the jackal drank some of the elephant's blood. Extremely satisfied, he spread the beast's organs to make a bed and lay down. "Here," he mused, "I have found food, drink, a bed, and a roof. Why should I think of going anywhere else?" Quite contented, he fell asleep. Without sunlight, he could not tell how many days he was there, but, when he was hungry, he ate, and, when he was thirsty, he drank.

In time, he had devoured all the flesh and had drunk all the blood. Chuckling to himself over his good fortune in having found such a remarkable feast, he crawled toward the hole by which he had entered. The sun and the wind, however, had dried out the carcass and had closed the rear tight. Search as he might, the jackal could find no exit. Completely trapped for many days, he was terrified that this enormous leather-covered skeleton would become his coffin.

Then, one day, there was an unusually heavy rain which softened the skin around the rear enough to allow a little light to shine through. Crawling toward the light, the jackal put his nose through the hole and pushed with all his might. After a great struggle, he managed to get his head out, but he was still trapped. "I have been tormented in here for too long!" he cried. "I must get out through this hole!"

He continued pushing and struggling all night, bruising every part of his body and scraping off all of his hair, but, by morning, the same day as the pigeon's mate was killed and the snake killed the bull, the jackal was finally able to free himself. He was no more than skin and bones and was as bare as a palm trunk. "I have brought all this trouble upon myself," he thought, "because of my greed! I will not eat until I have found a way to subdue my greed!" He went immediately to the hermitage.

That same morning, the bear emerged from his den to look for food. Feeling lazy, he decided that, rather than hunting for prey, he would find something in a village. He ambled to a nearby village on the border of the kingdom of Malla. Several villagers saw him and shouted "Help! A bear!" Suddenly, many villagers were chasing him with spears, staves, and pitchforks. The bear ran back toward the jungle and hid in a thicket, but the mob surrounded him. As they closed in, he made a break for it and was able to escape, but, as he ran for his life, the villagers threw stones and beat him with their weapons.

When he finally got back to his den, he was battered and bruised, and his broken head was streaming with blood. "I have brought all this trouble upon myself," he thought, "because of my laziness! I will not eat until I have found a way to subdue my laziness!" He went immediately to the hermitage.

That same morning, which happened to be a full-moon day, the ascetic had been thinking about his noble family and the honor his ancestors had enjoyed, and he was unable to achieve jhānic concentration. A Pacceka Buddha in the Himavat, as he surveyed the world, saw the ascetic and realized that he was no ordinary man. "This ascetic," declared the Pacceka Buddha, as he flew through the air toward the forest, "is destined to become a Buddha in the future. In this very birth, he can attain great wisdom, but I must help him."

While the ascetic was sitting in his hut, the Pacceka Buddha descended and sat on the ascetic's stone slab. When the ascetic emerged from his hut and saw someone else sitting on his own seat, he was greatly offended. He stomped toward the stone slab, snapped his fingers, and shouted, "You good-for-nothing! You shaven-headed hypocrite! Why are you sitting on my seat? You have no right to sit there!"

"Holy sage," the Pacceka Buddha replied, "Why are you conceited? I have attained the wisdom of a Pacceka Buddha. I can tell you that you will someday become a Buddha; you will be a Buddha named Siddhattha Gotama." Then the Pacceka Buddha explained to the ascetic the details of clan, family, and chief disciples. "Before that, however," he continued, "you must fulfill all the Perfections. Why are you so proud now? Your behavior is unworthy of you!"

The ascetic said nothing at all. He neither greeted nor paid his respects to the Pacceka Buddha. He neither apologized for his offensive behavior nor asked any questions.

"Sage," the Pacceka Buddha continued in a soft and gentle voice, "you must understand the limits of your piffling brahmin birth compared to my powers. See if you can rise up into the air as I do." Having challenged the ascetic, the Pacceka Buddha rose into the air, shook the dust from his feet onto the ascetic's coil of matted hair, and returned to the Himavat.

As soon as the Pacceka Buddha had left, the ascetic was overcome with grief. "That was a holy man!" he cried. "He was able to pass through the air like a fleck of cotton blown by the wind! He was a perfected Pacceka Buddha, but I didn't kiss his feet. I didn't ask him anything! All because of my stupid pride of birth! I didn't even ask him when I will become a Buddha!

"This pride of mine is going to lead me to hell if I don't do something about it! I will not eat until I have found a way to subdue my pride!"

The ascetic returned to his leaf-hut and sat down again to meditate. By examining the dangers of pride, he tried to focus his mind, but, unable to achieve very much concentration, he left his hut once more and went to sit on the stone slab.

As soon as he had sat down, the pigeon, the snake, the jackal, and the bear arrived. Each animal paid his respects and sat to one side.

"Friend pigeon, usually you come here later, after you have finished seeking food. Are you fasting today?" the ascetic asked.

"Yes, sir, I am," the pigeon replied.

"Why?"

"This morning, my mate and I were looking for food when a hawk swooped down and killed her. I feel her loss very deeply. Everything reminds me of her, and I cannot stop thinking about how much I loved her. I decided to spend the day fasting to control my passion. I must overcome passion so that it never comes back to oppress me."

"Friend snake, usually you come here later, after you have finished seeking food. Are you fasting today?" the ascetic asked.

"Yes, sir, I am," the snake replied.

"Why?"

"This morning, the headman's handsome white bull accidentally stepped on my tail, and, in a fit of anger, I bit him and killed him. I decided to spend the day fasting to control my anger. I must overcome anger so that it never comes back to oppress me."

"Friend jackal, usually you come here after you have eaten your fill of carrion, but now you look so lean. Are you fasting today?" the ascetic asked.

"Yes, sir, I am," the jackal replied.

"Why?"

"Some time ago, I found the carcass of an elephant. I was so greedy that I ate my way inside and stayed there. When the carcass dried, I became trapped, and it almost became my coffin. Fortunately, it rained and the hide around the rear softened enough to create an opening and I was able to escape. I decided to spend the day fasting to control my greed. I must overcome greed so that it never comes back to oppress me."

"Friend bear, usually you come here after you have finished seeking food. Are you fasting today?" the ascetic asked.

"Yes, sir, I am," the bear replied.

"Why?"

"This morning, feeling lazy, I decided that, rather than hunt for prey, I would go to a village to find food. The villagers spotted me and beat me until I was bloody, as you can see. I was lucky to escape alive! I decided to spend the day fasting to control my laziness. I must overcome laziness so that it never comes back to oppress me."

The animals then turned to the ascetic and said, "Sir, usually, at this hour, you are in the forest looking for fruit. Are you fasting today?"

"Yes, friends, I am," the ascetic replied.

"Why?"

"This morning, a Pacceka Buddha came and sat on this seat. Because of my pride of birth, I haughtily abused him. I never apologized to him. I neither bowed down to him nor kissed his feet. I didn't even ask a single question. I decided to spend the day fasting to control my pride. I must overcome pride so that it never comes back to oppress me."

The ascetic and the animals spent the day together, meditating and keeping the fast. Each tried in his own way to overcome his failing. Toward evening, the ascetic admonished the animals to be diligent and heedful at all times. Each animal returned to his own home, and the ascetic entered his hut.

For the rest of his life, the ascetic intensively practiced meditation on loving-kindness, and, when he passed away, he was reborn in the Brahma heavens. The animals, by following the admonitions of the wise ascetic, were also reborn in heaven.

Having concluded his story, the Buddha identified the birth: "At that time, Anuruddha was the pigeon, Sāriputta was the snake, Moggallāna was the jackal, Mahā-Kassapa was the bear, and I was the ascetic."

192
Every Creature from Its Cage Released
Mahā-Mora Jātaka

It was while staying at Jetavana that the Buddha told this story about a backsliding bhikkhu.[1]

When the bhikkhu was taken to see the Buddha, the Buddha asked him, "Is it true that you have relapsed?"

"Yes, Venerable Sir."

"What led you to do so?"

"I saw a woman dressed in a beautiful sari, and I was shaken."

"Is it any wonder that a woman should addle the wits of a man like you! Even a wise being, who, for seven hundred years had maintained his celibacy, on hearing a female's voice, backslid in a moment. If one who had made great attainments and achieved high honor could have come to disgrace, how much more the ordinary!" Then the Buddha told this story of the past.

Long, long ago, when Brahmadatta was reigning in Bārānasi, there was a peacock's egg with a shell as yellow as a kanikāra bud. When the shell broke, the Bodhisatta was born as a rare and magnificent golden peacock, with beautiful red lines under his wings.

---

1   The occasion for and the beginning of this story are identical to those of Tale 67.

In searching for a safe place to live, the peacock crossed three ranges of hills and settled on the plateau of a golden hill in Dandaka.

Every morning, he sat on the hill, watching the sun rise, and recited charms which he had composed. The first charm honored the sun:

"There he rises, the king all seeing, who makes all things bright with his golden light. You I worship, glorious being, who makes all things bright with your golden light. Through the coming day, keep me safe, I pray."

The second charm honored all the Buddhas who had passed away:

"Honor do I pay to all arahats, the righteous, fully enlightened. All honor to the wise, to wisdom, to freedom, and to all that freedom has made free. Through the coming day, keep me safe, I pray."

Only after uttering these charms to keep himself safe, did the peacock go to feed.

In the evening, the peacock returned to sit on the hilltop. As the sun went down, he meditated and again recited charms:

"There he sets, the king all seeing, who makes all things bright with his golden light. You I worship, glorious being, who makes all things bright with your golden light. Through the night, as through the day, keep me safe, I pray.

"Honor do I pay to all arahats, the righteous, fully enlightened. All honor to the wise, to wisdom, to freedom, and to all that freedom has made free. Through the night, as through the day, keep me safe, I pray."

One day, Queen Khemā, the wife of King Brahmadatta, had a dream in which she saw a golden peacock giving a religious discourse. She described her dream to the king and expressed her longing to hear the sermon of that golden peacock. The king asked his courtiers if there was such a thing as a golden peacock, but they did not know. They suggested that the brahmins would know. The brahmins told the king that golden peacocks did exist, but that they were extremely rare. When the king asked where such rare creatures could be found, the brahmins replied, "The hunters will certainly know." The king summoned all the hunters and asked them.

Only one hunter could answer. "Sire," he said, "on one of my forays in Dandaka, I once saw a golden peacock which lives there on a golden hill."

"Hunter," the king replied, "I command you to bring us that peacock. Do not kill it; you must bring it back here alive."

The hunter went across the ranges of hills to Dandaka. He repeatedly set snares in the peacock's feeding ground, but, even when the golden peacock stepped in a snare, the snare would not close. The hunter tried for seven years to catch the golden peacock, but he never succeeded. Eventually, he died on the Dandaka hill. Queen Khemā also died without having her wish fulfilled.

In his grief over the death of his queen, the king blamed the peacock for his loss and wanted revenge. He ordered that a golden plate be inscribed with this message: "In the Himavat, on the golden hill of Dandaka, there lives a golden peacock. One who eats the flesh of this bird will be immortal and will stay young forever." He placed this golden plate in a casket.

When the next king read the inscription, he became excited at the possibility of eternal youth and immortality. He sent one of his hunters to Dandaka with instructions not to return until he had captured the golden peacock. Like the first, this hunter not only failed to capture the peacock, but also died in the quest. The same thing occurred during the reigns of six successive kings.

The seventh king also sent a hunter to catch the golden peacock, but this hunter was cleverer than the others. He, too, was puzzled that the snare did not close when the golden peacock stepped into it. As he carefully observed the peacock, however, he realized that the bird was reciting a charm every morning before setting out in search of food and every evening before retiring. Convinced that this charm was protecting the golden peacock, the hunter caught a peahen in the marshes and trained her to utter a cry when he snapped his fingers.

Early one morning, the hunter went to the place where the golden peacock recited his charms. Before the peacock arrived, the hunter set up the snare, fixing its uprights carefully in the ground. He released the peahen in the area and hid himself. As soon as the golden peacock appeared, the hunter snapped his fingers, and the peahen uttered her cry.

Having lived all his life alone on the Dandaka hill, the golden peacock had never heard such a cry from a female. The beautiful note awakened desire in his breast. Leaving his charm unsaid, he strutted toward the peahen and unwittingly stepped in the snare.[2]

When the hunter saw him dangling at the end of the rope, he thought, "During the reigns of six kings, six hunters spent their whole lives trying to catch this king of peacocks. For seven years, I, too, failed. What great virtue this creature must possess to have survived so long! He was snared today only because he became enamored of this peahen and was unable to repeat his charm. I cannot hand over such a creature for a bribe. I don't want the king's honors. I will release this noble peacock."

As he started to emerge from his hiding place, he thought, "This bird is extraordinarily strong. If I go near him, he may think I am going to harm him. If he becomes frightened, he may struggle and hurt himself, even break a leg or a wing. I shouldn't go near him. I should stay here and cut the rope with an arrow." He strung his bow, fitted an arrow, and aimed at the rope.

---

2   From this point, this story differs from Tale 67.

At the same time, the peacock, hanging upside down in the snare, was thinking, "This hunter was able to trap me, at last, by making me sick with lust. I wonder what he intends to do with me. He will probably treat me very roughly. Where is he?" The peacock looked around, and saw the hunter with his bowstring pulled back, ready to shoot. "Oh!" he sighed. "He's going to kill me." He called out to the hunter, "I'm sure my capture will bring you wealth. Take me alive to the king. You're bound to get a sizable reward."

"This arrow isn't aimed at you," the hunter declared. "I'm going to cut the rope and set you free."

"What?" the peacock cried in surprise. "For seven years, you have pursued me. You've endured rain, hunger, and thirst in this forest trying to catch me. Now that I am trapped and helpless in your snare, why are you going to release me?"

When the man did not answer, the peacock declared, "My good man, by offering me my freedom, I can see that, today, you are giving up the taking of life! You are no longer a hunter!"

"Royal bird," the man asked, "when a person vows never to hurt another living thing, when other creatures have nothing to fear from him, what blessing will it bring?"

"If a man has vowed to harm no living creatures, and, if he abides by that vow, he will be praised by all in this present life, and, after death, he will be reborn in heaven."

"Some say, however," the hunter again asked, "that good deeds and generosity have no force and that the only happiness is in this life. I've earned my living as a hunter because hermits told me that there was no harm in it. Were they wrong?"

Even though the peacock was still dangling from the snare upside down, he continued teaching. "All can see the sun and the moon shining high in the sky. Are they of this world, or of another?"

"They are not part of our world," the hunter replied, "so they must belong to another world."

"Therefore," the peacock told him, "those who say that there is only this world and no other are either mistaken or lying. They are also wrong when they say that good and evil bear no fruit in other worlds."

"Noble peacock, please teach me how to live," the man requested earnestly. "Tell me what I must do, and show me how to follow the holy life, to save myself from falling into hell!"

"There are good men, good ascetics," the golden peacock replied, "men who have left the household life, who fast in the afternoon and wear simple yellow robes. They will answer your questions about this world and the other."

The answers which the golden peacock gave to this man, who, like a lotus bud waiting only for the touch of the sun's rays, had lived for a long time with his wisdom on the point of ripening, so filled him with the fear of hell that his craving and ignorance immediately vanished. In that moment, he gained complete understanding of the true nature of existence and became a Pacceka Buddha.

"As the serpent casts off his worn-out skin, as a tree sheds her withered leaves," he declared, "have I today renounced my hunter's life!" As he spoke these words, he cut the rope and released the golden peacock from the snare.

Then he asked the golden peacock another question. "I have been liberated from the bondage of all the defilements, but, in my house, there are many birds confined in cages. How can I set them free?"

"In becoming a Pacceka Buddha," the golden peacock told him, "you have gained the power to grant boons. If, with all your heart, you bestow a thing, even freedom, it will be received. The power of your boon is very great, and it may extend throughout Jambudīpa."

Pleased to hear this, the Pacceka Buddha declared, "May all those birds and animals which are fettered or confined in cages, hundreds of which there are in my former dwelling, be released from bondage! May they be free to fly away!"

As soon as he had uttered these powerful and heartfelt words, the doors of all the cages in his house burst open, and all the birds flew away, singing joyously. Not only that, but, throughout Jambudīpa, all tied and caged animals were set free. Not a single creature was left in bondage, not even a dog or a cat.

The Pacceka Buddha rubbed his forehead. Immediately, his old caste mark disappeared, and he took on the appearance of an ascetic of many years standing, fully endowed with the eight requisites. In gratitude, he paid homage to the noble peacock and reverentially circumambulated him. Then, rising up, he passed through the air to the cave on Mount Nandamūla, which is the residence of all Pacceka Buddhas. The peacock stepped out of the snare, quietly gathered food, and returned to his own cave.

Having concluded his story, the Buddha taught the Dhamma, and the backsliding bhikkhu attained arahatship. Then the Buddha identified the birth: "At that time, I was the golden peacock."

193
Military Strategy
Tacchasūkara Jātaka

It was while staying at Jetavana that the Buddha told this story about two elderly bhikkhus.

When King Mahā-Kosala gave his daughter, Kosaladevī, to King Bimbisāra, he allotted her a Kāsi village. After Prince Ajātasattu murdered his father, King Bimbisāra, King Pasenadi, who was Queen Kosaladevī's brother, took back that village. This led to a series of battles between King Ajātasattu and King Pasenadi. After the first battle, which ended in victory for King Ajātasattu, King Pasenadi asked his advisors for a strategy to capture his nephew.

His advisors mentioned that at Jetavana there were a number of bhikkhus who had been army officers before they ordained. The advisors suggested getting the opinion of some of those bhikkhus. The king was pleased with this idea, but, not wanting to ask the bhikkhus directly, he sent several spies to the monastery.

The spies stationed themselves outside the leaf hut of Venerable Dhanuggaha-Tissa and Venerable Mantidatta on the outskirts of the monastery. At the first light of day, Venerable Dhanuggaha-Tissa awoke, started a fire, and asked his companion if he was awake.

"Yes, I am wide awake. Is there something you wanted to talk about?"

"Yes. I was thinking about King Pasenadi. He is a fool. All he knows how to do is eat."

"What do you mean?"

"He allows himself to be beaten by King Ajātasattu, who is no better than a worm."

"What do you think he should do?"

"Well, Mantidatta, as you know, there are three kinds of strategy to use in a battle: the wagon strategy, the wheel strategy, and the lotus strategy. The king should use the wagon strategy to catch King Ajātasattu. He should hide some valiant men on the tops of hills on both sides, with the main force in front. Once King Ajātasattu is engaged in battle, with a shout, the men should close in on both sides, and he would be caught like a lobster in a lobsterpot."

As soon as the spies had heard all of this, they hurried back to tell the king. King Pasenadi immediately set out with a great army. He positioned his forces in the wagon plan, exactly as Venerable Dhanuggaha-Tissa had suggested, and easily captured King Ajātasattu. King Pasenadi held King Ajātasattu prisoner for several days, hoping to teach him a lesson. Then he released the rogue, warning him not to attack Kosala again. Because King Pasenadi was still fond of his nephew, however, in spite of the war, he gave his daughter, Princess Vajirā, to the younger king and sent him back to Magadha with great pomp.

Later, in the Hall of Truth, some bhikkhus were talking about how King Pasenadi had captured King Ajātasattu by following the strategy devised by Venerable Dhanuggaha-Tissa. When the Buddha heard what they were discussing, he said, "This is not the first time, Bhikkhus, that Venerable Dhanuggaha-Tissa has shown himself expert in strategy." At their request, the Buddha told this story of the past.

Long, long ago, in a village near the city gate of Bārānasi, there was a carpenter who often went into the jungle to cut wood. One day, he found a baby wild boar who had fallen into a pit. The carpenter rescued the young boar, took him home, and reared him as a pet. He called the boar Tacchasūkara (Carpenter-boar).

Tacchasūkara became the carpenter's assistant. He felled trees with his snout, fetched the carpenter tools in his mouth, and even held the tape when the carpenter needed to measure the length of a board.

When he was full grown, Tacchasūkara was a huge, strong, and healthy boar, and the carpenter loved him like his own son. The carpenter began to worry, however, that someone, not realizing that Tacchasūkara was tame, might harm him. Sadly, the carpenter decided to return the boar to the jungle.

One day, he loaded Tacchasūkara in a wagon and took him deep into the jungle, far from the village. Finding a site where he thought the boar would be safe and able to find food, the carpenter bade his friend a fond farewell and returned home.

Finding himself alone, Tacchasūkara did not feel at all safe. He immediately began hunting for other boars that he could live with. After searching all day, he finally found a large herd of boars. Running into their midst, he announced, "Greetings! How happy I am to join you, my relatives, and to live with you here where there is plenty of food and no enemies to fear!"

"Friend," one of the young boars replied, "you are certainly welcome to join our herd. We are pleased to have someone as cheerful as you seem to be. However, don't fool yourself! There certainly is one enemy lurking here. He slays even the strongest among us whenever he wants!"

"Who can this terrible foe be?" Tacchasūkara asked in surprise.

"It is a mighty beast with black and yellow stripes, teeth as sharp as swords, and claws which can tear your flesh like knives. When he comes, none of us has a chance against him."

"What are you saying? We have formidable tusks. We are tough and strong. Surely, we can overcome him if we work together. All we need is a good plan."

"That's a good idea!" the other boars agreed. "Rather than running away, let's all stand our ground together."

"Great!" Tacchasūkara shouted, delighted that his new companions were ready to fight the tiger. "Let's start planning! First, I need to know this beast's routine. Tell me, at what time does he usually come?"

"He always comes early in the morning. This morning, he came at dawn and killed one of our friends for breakfast. He's sure to come again tomorrow at the same time."

"All right," Tacchasūkara replied. "All of you should have your breakfast while it is still dark. Then, just before dawn, gather here, and I will tell you what we must do."

All the other boars went off in search of food, while Tacchasūkara scouted the area to determine how to arrange the herd to the best advantage to ensure their victory.

Very early the next morning, the entire herd assembled, and Tacchasūkara explained to them the rudiments of the wagon strategy and the wheel strategy. "In this case, however," he continued, "we must use what is called the lotus strategy." Then he proceeded to arrange them in this battle configuration. In the center, he placed the suckling babies. In a circle around these, he placed the sows, the mothers. The next circle was the old and wise barren

27

sows. These were surrounded by a circle of rambunctious boars who were still youngsters. The next circle was the adolescents who were just beginning to sprout tusks. The next circle was the full-grown tuskers. The final circle was the fierce old boars. In several places, outside these circles, he posted squads of ten or twenty strong boar warriors. In front of this "lotus formation," in the direction from which the tiger would approach, Tacchasūkara had the boars dig a small pit. In front of that, he had them dig another pit in the shape of a winnowing basket. Between the two pits was a narrow strip of land on which he himself would stand to face the tiger.

While the others were arranging themselves and digging the pits, Tacchasūkara went around with his stout, tusked lieutenants to supervise the preparations and to encourage them all.

When the sun rose, everything was ready.

At that time, the tiger emerged from the nearby hermitage of a false ascetic with whom he often stayed and strolled toward the thicket where the wild boars lived.

A boar who had been posted on lookout cried, "Our enemy is sighted, sir!"

"All right, everyone," Tacchasūkara said calmly. "Don't be afraid. Just watch the tiger, and, whatever he does, you do the same." They all looked up and saw the tiger standing on the top of the hill.

Standing at the farthest edge of the winnowing basket pit, the tiger stretched, shook himself, and urinated. In unison, all the boars stretched, shook themselves, and urinated. The tiger stared hard at the boars, surprised to see himself mimicked. The boars continued staring intently at the tiger. The tiger gave a great roar. Remaining in formation, the boars all grunted as loud as they could, which in chorus sounded like a great roar. This thoroughly disconcerted the tiger. "What's happened?" he wondered. "They've always run from me when I roared, but, now, they're standing in formation and facing me down. Some warrior must be training them. I think I had better not go near them today."

He turned around and slunk back to the hermitage. "What's this? Have you become a vegetarian?" the ascetic asked mockingly when he saw the tiger returning without a victim. "Have you taken up non-violence? Perhaps your fangs have forgotten how to bite? There's a herd of wild boars out there, and you come back an empty-handed beggar!"

"My teeth no longer bite, and my strength is gone," the tiger replied in a dejected tone. "Always before, those boars have scurried around, knocking each other over, trying to get away from me. Today they are standing shoulder to shoulder in sharp-tusked ranks. Somehow, they have found a leader who is teaching them discipline. They are a formidable army. If I were to charge in there, I'm sure I would be hurt. I'm afraid I have lost my taste for pork!"

"All alone the hawk hunts birds!" the ascetic cried, trying to encourage him. "By himself Sakka defeated the asuras. From a herd of beasts like that, a great tiger can take his pick whenever he wants!"

"You didn't see them!" the tiger protested. "No hawk, no tiger, and not even Sakka himself, can defeat a huge disciplined army which makes a united stand the way they do."

"Numbers are nothing!" the ascetic cried, egging him on. "Little fowl in great flocks and coveys fly together and fill the sky, but when the hawk swoops down, he takes any one he wants and flies away with ease. You're a tiger! You're a king! Don't you know your own strength? One roar and one powerful leap are all you need! When they see you charging, they will flee in all directions! I'm sure of it! Don't worry! Go and see for yourself! You'll see that I'm right!"

Persuaded by the sham ascetic's confidence in him, the tiger returned to the hill top. With his cruel, greedy eyes glinting, he bared his fangs and roared fiercely.

"The tiger's back, sir!

"Don't worry! Just stand your ground!" Tacchasūkara commanded, as he took his stand on the bridge between the two pits.

The tiger roared again. The boars again echoed his roar. Then, keeping his eye on the lone Tacchasūkara, the tiger ran at full speed downhill through the winnowing basket and made a great leap up toward his target. Tacchasūkara neatly disappeared into the other pit. Unable to reach the place where Tacchasūkara had been standing, the tiger tumbled back to the bottom of the pit. Tacchasūkara quickly scrambled out of his hiding place and dropped down on the stunned tiger. With his mighty tusks, Tacchasūkara slashed the tiger and gored his chest, piercing him to the heart. He dragged the carcass of the beast to the center of the pit and shouted to the herd, "Here! Take the villain! He's all yours!"

The first boars to reach the body each got a good mouthful, but those who arrived too late could only ask, "What does tiger meat taste like?"

Tacchasūkara approached his lieutenants, expecting them to be pleased that their enemy was dead. He was puzzled to find that they still looked worried. "Aren't you satisfied?" he asked.

"Sir," they replied, somewhat hesitantly, "you have managed the tiger very well, but there is another enemy. He's worse than ten tigers!"

"Who might that be?" asked Tacchasūkara.

"There's a crafty, phony ascetic, sir, who has always eaten the meat that the tiger took to the hermitage," they told him.

"All right!" Tacchasūkara replied. "Our work is not finished. Let's catch him, too!"

Tacchasūkara led a large group of boars, including tuskers, sows, and young ones, toward the hermitage. The ascetic was standing at the door of his hut, watching for the tiger to return. When he saw the troop of boars charging, he shuddered. "Good heavens! They must have killed the tiger, and now they are coming for me!" he cried, and ran away as fast as he could and climbed up a wild fig tree.

"There he is, sir!" the boars shouted to Tacchasūkara. "He has climbed that tree!"

"Which tree?" Tacchasūkara asked, as he looked around.

"That fig tree, sir."

"All right," Tacchasūkara called as he ran with them toward the tree. "We'll get him!"

He ordered the young boars to dig up the earth around the tree. He told the sows to carry mouthfuls of water from the nearby pond and to dump it around the tree. Soon, the tree was standing, with all its roots exposed, in the middle of a great muddy pool. Tacchasūkara sent all the others away and walked alone toward the tree. He knelt beneath it and, using his tusks as skillfully as an axe, cut through the roots. It wasn't long until the tree came down, but, before the false ascetic even touched the ground, the boars caught him and completely devoured his body.

The entire herd of boars gathered at that spot and raised an exuberant cry of jubilation.

A tree deva, who had been watching since the night before, smiled and declared, "How wonderful to see friends working together for a common cause. These wild boars, once completely vulnerable in the face of their enemies, joined together and defeated both that ferocious tiger and that phony ascetic!"

Tacchasūkara turned to his lieutenants and asked, "Is there any other enemy endangering the herd?"

"No, sir!" they replied. "Now, thanks to you, we are safe!"

The elders proposed making Tacchasūkara their king, and everyone agreed.

They placed Tacchasūkara on the roots of the fig tree and, using the rare conch shell of the false ascetic, sprinkled him with water in a coronation ceremony. They chose a young sow to be his consort.

This was the origin of seating a king in a chair made of fig wood and anointing him with lustral water from a conch shell with a clockwise spiral.

Having concluded his story, the Buddha identified the birth: "At that time, Devadatta was the false ascetic, Dhanuggaha-Tissa was Tacchasūkara, and I was the tree deva."

194
Moderation
Mahā-Vānija Jātaka

It was while staying at Jetavana that the Buddha told this story about traders.

Once, a group of traders visited Jetavana before setting out on a long journey. These men paid their respects to the Buddha, offered gifts, and took the refuges and precepts.

"Venerable Sir," they said, "if we return safely, we will come again to Jetavana and bow at your feet."

The next day, they left Sāvatthī with five hundred cartloads of merchandise. After a few days, they arrived at the edge of a dense jungle, where the road was poorly marked. Following the trail as best they could, they entered the jungle, but soon became hopelessly lost. As they wandered aimlessly through the jungle, they quickly used up all their water and ate all their provisions. Suddenly, they came upon a clearing, in the middle of which stood a huge banyan tree. Exhausted and afraid that they would all perish in the jungle, they unyoked their carts and sat down beneath the tree.

As they rested, sitting around the trunk of the magnificent tree, one of the traders noticed that the leaves were very glossy. He continued examining the parts of the tree and, after a few minutes, exclaimed, "My friends, look at this tree! Both the leaves and the branches seem to be moist. Doesn't it look as though water is actually running through the tree? Let's try cutting a branch. We might find something to drink. I'm certainly thirsty enough to try anything!"

Finding a saw in one of the wagons, they gave it to another of their group and sent him up the tree. He climbed onto a stout limb and sawed off a small branch on the eastern side of the tree. A stream of water gushed forth like a waterfall. All of the men drank their fill and rejoiced. Then they watered the oxen who were languishing in the coarse brush weeds around the tree. The fresh water was still flowing, so they all bathed and thoroughly refreshed themselves.

Curious to see what would happen, they sent the man up a second time with the saw, and asked him to cut off a branch on the southern side of the tree. Out came all sorts of delicious food. Everyone ate as much as he could, and still food remained. When the man used his saw to cut off a branch on the western side of the tree, out stepped a bevy of lovely women, who greeted the men, sang, and entertained them royally. Finally, they told the man to cut off a branch on the northern side of the tree, and they were showered with precious stones. The men all worked together to unload the merchandise they carried, and to fill the carts with the gems. Wealthier than they could have ever imagined, they retraced their steps through the jungle and returned safely to Sāvatthī.

After carefully unloading their treasure and placing it in their storerooms, the traders took garlands and incense to Jetavana. They made their offerings to the Buddha, paid their respects, and sat down on one side to listen to the Dhamma. The next day, they offered lunch to the Buddha and the bhikkhus and gave many gifts as well. As they made their donations, the traders declared, "Venerable Sir, we renounce all merit from these gifts. May it be granted to the deity of the great banyan tree in the jungle. That deity not only saved our lives, but also bestowed upon us all the treasure we brought back to Sāvatthī."

When the meal was finished, the Buddha asked the traders to tell him the details of their adventure, and they related all that had happened.

"You received this treasure because of your moderation," the Buddha replied. "You were wise not to be avaricious. Long ago, when this same thing happened, the men were overwhelmed by greed." At their request, the Buddha told this story of the past.

Long, long ago, a group of traders lost their way in the same jungle and rested under the same banyan tree. At that time, the tree was home to a mighty nāga king. Everything happened in exactly the same way, except that, after the ground was covered with precious gems, one of the traders exclaimed, "Why should we wait for these gems to come trickling out of this little branch? Let's cut down the tree at the root and dig out all the treasure!"

"My friend," replied the leader of the caravan, "What harm does this banyan do? This bounteous tree has granted us water, food, lovely women, and wealth beyond measure. Why would you cut it down? One that provides pleasant shade should not suffer for its hospitality!"

The other traders rose up and shouted down the leader, who was the only one to urge restraint. The leader walked away sadly and sat at a distance from the magnificent banyan tree. The others sharpened their axes and gathered around the massive trunk

The nāga king had been listening to all of this and shouted (though none of the men could hear him), "Those ingrates! I gave them water when they were thirsty, food when they were famished, maidens when they were lonely, and enough treasure to fill five hundred wagons. Now they have the audacity to cry, 'Let's cut down the tree at the root!' They are greedy beyond all endurance! Except for the leader, they must all die!"

The nāga king summoned his army. "Strike down those men!" he ordered. "Spare only the leader! Burn them to cinders!"

At the moment the traders lifted their axes, mighty nāga warriors attacked them and slew every one before a single axe could fall. Then the nāgas loaded the gems into the five hundred wagons and escorted the leader out of the jungle and back to his home. After they had secured all the treasure in his storeroom, they returned to the nāga realm.

Having concluded his story, the Buddha added, "The wise man sees his own good and never succumbs to the power of greed. Understanding the pain that comes from desire, he shakes off greed and aspires to live a contented, virtuous life. Thus, laymen, those traders were destroyed because of their greed." Then the Buddha taught the Dhamma, and all the traders attained the first path. Finally, the Buddha identified the birth: "At that time, Sāriputta was the king of the nāgas, and I was the caravan leader."

195
Candāla Champion
Mātanga Jātaka

It was while staying at Jetavana that the Buddha told this story about King Udena.

In a previous existence, Venerable Pindola had been a king in Kosambi and had been very fond of the royal park there. Remembering this, during the hot season, he often used his supernatural power to travel through the air from Jetavana to spend the hottest part of the day in the cool shade of that park.

One day, while Venerable Pindola was sitting under a magnificent sal tree in full flower and enjoying the bliss of his arahatship, King Udena entered the garden with his retinue. Since the king had been drinking steadily for the past week, he lay down in the arms of one of his women on the great royal stone and immediately fell asleep. When the women who were singing, playing instruments, and dancing realized that the king was asleep, they stopped and wandered around the garden. As they were picking fruit and gathering flowers, they came upon Venerable Pindola. They paid their respects and sat down to listen to his teaching.

The woman who was holding the king shifted her weight slightly and the king awoke. Not seeing the musicians, he cried, "Where have those good-for-nothing women gone without my permission?"

"They are over there, Sire," the woman said, pointing. "They have gathered around an ascetic and are listening to his teaching."

Enraged, the king stormed across the garden and confronted Venerable Pindola. "What do you think you are doing?" he shouted at the bhikkhu. "What right have you to sit here with the women of my court? I'll teach you!" He ordered that an entire basket of biting red ants be dumped on Venerable Pindola's body. Venerable Pindola, however, immediately rose into the air and admonished the king not to get angry and not to be so hasty. Then he returned to Jetavana and alighted at the entrance to the Buddha's Perfumed Chamber.

"Where have you come from?" asked the Tathāgata. Venerable Pindola told him what had happened, and the Buddha replied, "Pindola, this is not the first time that King Udena has tried to harm a religious man. Long ago, too, he did the same thing." At Venerable Pindola's request, the Buddha told this story of the past.

Long, long ago, when Brahmadatta was reigning in Bārānasi, the Bodhisatta was born outside the city as the son of a candāla and was named Mātanga. One day, as he was entering the city, the palanquin of Ditthamangalikā,[3] the daughter of a rich Bārānasi merchant, passed by. This young woman was on her way to the park, where she went every month with her friends. Mātanga stopped and stepped aside to get out of the way of the palanquin and the entourage. At that moment, however, Ditthamangalikā happened to peer out from behind her curtain. She saw Mātanga standing against the wall and asked one of her servants who he was. When she learned that he was a candāla, she became very upset. "Curses!" she cried. "The mere sight of an outcaste brings bad luck for the whole day! Our party is ruined!" She quickly rinsed her eyes with perfumed water to remove the ritual pollution and returned home.

Her friends were furious and turned on Mātanga. "You vile outcaste!" they shouted as the men beat him. "You have cheated us out of free food and liquor today!" They pelted him with stones and left him lying senseless on the ground.

When he regained consciousness, he thought, "I was just an innocent bystander, but Ditthamangalikā's friends beat me for no reason whatsoever. For that, I will marry her! I will not give up until she is given to me!" He found her father's house and lay down in front of the door, refusing to move. When anyone asked why he was lying there, he simply replied, "All I want is Ditthamangalikā."

3 Her name means "One who is superstitious about what is seen."

Mātanga lay there without moving, refusing to take any food. One day passed, then a second, a third, a fourth, a fifth, and a sixth. On the seventh day, Ditthamangalikā's family, afraid of being disgraced by having a candāla die on their doorstep, relented and gave Ditthamangalikā to him as his wife. "Stand up, Husband." Ditthamangalikā said quietly to him. "Let us go to your house."

"Madam," Mātanga replied, "I was severely beaten by your friends. I am weak from hunger and cannot walk. You must pick me up and carry me on your back!" Ditthamangalikā obediently lifted her husband and, in full sight of all the neighbors, carried him through the city gate to the candāla village.

Mātanga kept Ditthamangalikā in his house for a few days, without violating any caste rules. "Now that she has given up her pride of birth, I wish to show her the highest honor and to give her the best gifts," he declared. "The only way that I can do this is by renouncing the world." He summoned her and said, "Madam, unless I go to the forest to gather food, we will not be able to stay alive. Please wait patiently until I return. You must not worry!"

After instructing the members of his household to take care of Ditthamangalikā, Mātanga went into the forest and undertook the life of an ascetic. He practiced concentration meditation with such great energy and determination that, in only seven days, he had perfected the five extraordinary powers and the eight jhānas. "Now," he declared, "I will be able to protect Ditthamangalikā properly!" Using his newly acquired supernatural power, he returned to Bārānasi. He alighted at the gate of the candāla village and walked to Ditthamangalikā's house. As soon as she saw him, she began to weep. "Husband," she cried, "why did you desert me and become an ascetic?"

"Never mind, madam," he replied. "I intend to make you more glorious than before. In front of many people, will you be able to say one simple sentence?"

"I think so, Husband. What do you want me to say?"

"When anyone asks you about me, you must reply, 'My husband is not Mātanga. My husband is the great Mahā-Brahmā himself!' Can you do that?"

"Yes, sir, I can."

"Excellent! When they ask you where your husband has gone, you must reply, 'He has gone to the Brahma heavens.' If they ask when he will come back, you must say, 'In seven days, he will come, breaking through the disk of the full moon!' Can you do that?"

"Yes, sir, I can," she replied, and Mātanga went to the Himavat.

Ditthamangalikā went about her daily life in Bārānasi, and, whenever anyone asked, she loudly proclaimed, "My husband is not Mātanga. My husband is the great Mahā-Brahmā himself!" People believed her, and, soon, the story had spread throughout the city. In every quarter, people were telling each other, "Her husband is not staying with her because he is Mahā-Brahmā. Next week, at the full moon, he will return in all his glory!"

On the seventh night, when the full moon was high in the sky, Mātanga assumed the appearance of Mahā-Brahmā, and, with a great blaze of light which illuminated not only the city of Bārānasi, but also the entire kingdom of Kāsi, he broke through the moon. After circling the city three times, he began his descent. The multitude of worshipers shouted their adoration and offered garlands and incense as they followed him to the candāla village. The devotees of Brahmā reverently draped Ditthamangalikā's house with white cloth. In front of the house, they spread the ground with four kinds of perfume and erected a pavilion with a splendid throne in the center. At the door of the pavilion, they laid a layer of white sand as smooth as a mirror, scattered flowers, stretched awnings, and hung banners. They lit incense and a lamp with scented oil and invited Mātanga to sit on the throne.

When Ditthamangalikā entered, Mātanga understood that it was the proper time for her. He touched her navel with his thumb, and she immediately conceived. "Madam," he announced, "you are pregnant and will have a son. Both you and he will receive great honor and the highest tribute. The water that washes your feet will be used for the ceremonial sprinkling of kings throughout all of Jambudīpa. The water in which you bathe will become a magic elixir. Those who sprinkle it on their heads will be free from disease and will escape from bad luck. One who prostrates himself at your feet should offer you one thousand coins. One who kneels in respect should offer you one hundred coins. One who remains standing to greet you should offer you one coin. Madam, be diligent!" Then he stepped out of the pavilion. As the great crowd watched, he rose into the air and appeared to reenter the moon.

That great crowd remained standing outside the pavilion all night. The next morning, they placed Ditthamangalikā in a golden palanquin, and, crying loudly, "The wife of Mahā-Brahmā! Make way for the wife of Mahā-Brahmā!" they carried her into the city. As they made a procession around the whole city of Bārānasi, twelve leagues in extent, many worshiped her and offered coins according to Mātanga's instructions. That day, she received eighteen crores of coins.

In the city center, the people erected a great pavilion and decorated it with rich curtains. They invited Ditthamangalikā to stay there during her confinement, provided her with every comfort, and paid her great respect. After ten months, she gave birth to a son, whom the brahmins named Mandavya because he was born in the pavilion.

In front of the pavilion, the devotees had begun building a seven-story palace with seven magnificent entrance gates. All of the workers and the donors gained a great deal of merit in the construction, and the palace was completed about the time the prince was born. Mother and son moved into the palace, and Mandavya grew up there, amid great splendor. When he was seven years old, renowned teachers came and taught him the three Vedas. By the time he was sixteen, he was feeding sixteen thousand brahmins every day in the alms-hall at the fourth gateway.

One day, which happened to be a festival day, Mandavya, brilliantly dressed with golden slippers on his feet and a gold staff in his hand, was at the gateway giving directions to servants who were serving special rice porridge with fresh ghee, honey, and jaggery to the sixteen thousand brahmins. At that time, Mātanga was meditating in his hermitage in the Himavat. He directed his thoughts to Bārānasi and saw what was happening. "Ditthamangalikā's son is going in the wrong direction," he thought. "I must teach him how to give so that his gift will bring great fruit!" He passed through the air to Lake Anotatta, rinsed out his mouth, and assumed the guise of a poor wandering ascetic, with a ragged robe and an earthen bowl. Passing again through the air, he alighted at the alms-hall right in front of Mandavya.

"Where are you from?" the youth shouted. "Who are you, you wretched outcaste? You look more like a yakkha than an ascetic! How dare you show up here, in your vile, filthy rags, picked up from the garbage! You're not worthy to receive alms here!"

"This delicious food, sir," Mātanga replied gently, "is beautifully arranged and is being graciously offered. There is plenty here, and we take only what we need to live. Why not let a low caste man enjoy a bit, as well?"

"This food is prepared exclusively for brahmins," Mandavya retorted sharply, "given from my pious heart, that I may reap the blessing. It's not for the likes of you! Get out of here, you brute!"

Mātanga calmly replied, "Sow seed on high ground and on low, in good faith, and you will find those worthy to receive your gifts."

"Don't talk to me about worthy recipients!" Mandavya haughtily snarled. "I know where to sow my seeds of faith! For me, the noble brahmins, highborn and lofty, those who know the sacred scriptures, are a fertile field of merit."

Mātanga answered him, "Pride of birth, arrogance, drunkenness, greed, hatred, and ignorance! Those who harbor these wicked vices are a barren and infertile field for seeds of faith. Those in whom pride of birth, arrogance, drunkenness, greed, hatred, and ignorance find no place, they are a fertile field of merit!"

"This miserable beggar talks too much!" Mandavya shouted angrily. "Where are my servants? Gandakucchi, Upajjhāya, and Upajotiya!" he called. "Come here!"

The three servants came running and asked, "What is it, Master?"

"Who is this damned outcaste?" Mandavya asked. "Have you ever seen him before"

"No, sir!" they replied. "He must be a juggler, a gambler, or some other trouble-maker!"

"How did he get in?"

"We don't know, sir. He didn't come through the outer gates."

"Well, don't just stand there! Do something!"

"What shall we do, Master?"

"Seize the miserable outcaste! Beat him! Whip him until his back is raw! Torture him! Break his jaw! Kill him, if you feel like it! Just get rid of him!"

Before the men could touch him, Mātanga rose and stood poised in the air over their heads. "Reviling a sage," that champion of truth and right proclaimed, "is like swallowing a blazing ball of fire, biting hard iron, or leveling a mountain with your fingernails!"

While all the brahmins were gazing at him, Mātanga turned to the east and flew away. Making a determination that his footprints should be visible, he came down in a street near the eastern gate and begged for alms. Then he went to sit in a nearby hall to eat his meager fare.

All the devas of the city were outraged that Mandavya had dared to speak so rudely to the great sage. The chief of the devas grabbed Mandavya and twisted his neck so sharply that his head faced backward. "He must be punished for his wickedness!" the deva declared, but, out of respect for Mātanga, he did not kill the boy. Nevertheless, the youth's body was stiff, and his eyes rolled back in his head. Other devas grabbed the sixteen thousand brahmins and twisted their necks as well. They all appeared dead as they lay on the pavement with spittle dribbling from their mouths.

People informed Ditthamangalikā that something had happened to her son, and she hurried to the alms-hall. When she saw Mandavya, she was sure that he was dead and cried, "What has happened here? Who has done this to my son?"

Several bystanders tried to explain what had happened, but no one really knew.

"There was an ascetic here," said one.

"His robes were very dirty, like something picked up from the garbage," said another.

"He said something to your son," said a third. "He must have done this!" added another.

"No one else has the power to do such a thing!" Ditthamangalikā thought. "It must have been the wise Mātanga! He is steadfast and full of goodwill to all creatures, however. He would never make all these people suffer like this. I wonder what he did and where he has gone."

Aloud she asked, "In what direction did that ascetic go? In order to bring Mandavya back to life, we must make atonement for the offense."

"He rose into the air and went toward the eastern gate," several young men told her.

Ditthamangalikā took a solid gold pitcher and bowl and went with a company of maidservants to look for her husband. Near the eastern gate, she saw his footprints and followed them to the hall where he was sitting and eating his meal.

Ditthamangalikā walked into the hall, paid her respects to Mātanga, and stood in front of him. As soon as he saw her, he dropped the last bit of rice back into his earthen bowl. Ditthamangalikā poured water for him from the golden pitcher, and he washed his hands and rinsed out his mouth.

"I found my son stretched out on the floor," she said, "with his head twisted backwards and his eyes rolled back in his head. I'm afraid that he is dead! Who did such a cruel thing? "

"There are powerful devas all around who respect wise ascetics. Offended by your son's wicked and violent abuse, they must have decided to punish him."

"Devas!" she cried. "Please, wise sage, do not be angry with me! My brother, I love my son! I beg for your help and your protection."

"I neither have, nor have I ever had, thoughts of enmity," Mātanga assured her. "Your son has been badly educated. He is drunk with ignorant pride of birth and knows nothing of the true meaning of the scriptures."

"Yes, Brother," she replied. "Please forgive me for not teaching my son humility and tolerance. Though the wise are never fierce in rage, I know that he is prone to flashes of anger."

Mātanga was pacified by Ditthamangalikā's apology. "Let me give you an elixir," he offered compassionately, "which will restore your foolish son to you."

She held out the gold bowl, and he dropped into it the leftovers from his earthen bowl. "Place some of this rice in your son's mouth," he instructed her, "and he will be released by the devas and will return to normal. Mix the rest with water, and put it in the mouths of the afflicted brahmins, and they will also be restored." Then he arose and departed for the Himavat.

Ditthamangalikā placed the golden bowl on her head and returned to the palace, announcing as she walked, "I have the elixir of life! I have the elixir of life!"

When she reached the alms-hall, she knelt and put half of the rice in her son's mouth. Immediately, the devas fled, and Mandavya straightened his neck and got up. Brushing the dust from his robes, he asked, "Mother, what happened?"

"You know well enough that you have done wrong!" she replied. "Look at the miserable plight of the brahmins you feed!"

As Mandavya looked around, he was horrified and filled with remorse.

"Mandavya, my dear son," Ditthamangalikā admonished him, "you have been a fool! You must learn how to give so that your gift will bear fruit. Ignorant, greedy, hating, and conceited men like these are not fit for your generosity. Only those like the wise Mātanga are truly worthy. Gifts given to the wicked bear little fruit, but from offerings given to calm and holy men the reward is great. From now on, be generous to virtuous ascetics who, through their meditation, have perfected the eight jhānas. Offer your gifts to Pacceka Buddhas and to wise sages. Now, my son, let me give these servants the elixir and make them whole once more."

She poured water into the bowl, mixed it with the leftover rice, and placed a few drops in the mouth of each of the sixteen thousand brahmins. All of them got up and brushed the dust from their robes. Having been fed the leavings of a candāla, they regarded themselves as defiled. Knowing that they would be declared outcastes by other brahmins, they left Bārānasi in disgrace and went to the kingdom of Mejjha.

At that time, in Mejjha, there was a brahmin ascetic, named Jātimanta, living on the bank of the Vettavatī River. Jātimanta was obsessively proud of his brahmin birth. In order to humble him, Mātanga built a hermitage upstream from him and practiced his meditation there. One day, Mātanga intentionally dropped a toothstick he had used into the water. The toothstick floated downstream and got entangled in Jātimanta's matted hair while he was performing his ablutions. "Curse the brute who tossed this into the water!" he fumed. "I'll take care of whoever did it! Just let me lay my hands on him!" He walked upstream along the bank and found Mātanga.

"Did you throw a toothstick into the river?" Jātimanta asked Mātanga.

"Yes, I did," Mātanga replied calmly.

"What is your caste?"

"I am a candāla,"

"You vile outcaste!" Jātimanta shouted. "Damn you, you filthy brute! I forbid you to stay here another minute. Go downstream, where you belong! Make sure this never happens again!"

Mātanga calmly picked up his bowl and complied with the brahmin's demand. Even after setting up his residence downstream, however, all the toothsticks he threw into the river floated against the current and got entangled in Jātimanta's hair.

Jātimanta again stormed into Mātanga's hermitage. "Curse you!" he shouted. "If you stay here, in seven days, your head will split into seven pieces!"

Mātanga did not reply. "If I allow myself to feel any anger toward this man," he thought, "I will be violating my virtue. Nevertheless, I must find a way to break his pride."

On the seventh day, Mātanga used his supernatural power to prevent the sunrise. Throughout Jambudīpa people were inconvenienced by the lack of sun. Many devotees flocked to Jātimanta's hermitage and asked "Is it you, sir, who is preventing the sun from rising today?"

"No," Jātimanta answered, "I have nothing to do with it, but there is a candāla ascetic living downstream. I'm sure this is his doing."

The people proceeded downstream and asked Mātanga whether he was responsible for the sun's failure to rise.

"Yes, friends," Mātanga replied. "I have stopped the sun."

"Why did you do it?" they asked.

"That brahmin ascetic, who is your favorite, has reviled me. Although I am completely innocent, he despises me simply because of my caste. Only when he falls at my feet and begs forgiveness, will I release the sun."

They hurried back upstream and dragged Jātimanta, very much against his will, to Mātanga's hermitage and threw him down at Mātanga's feet. "Now, sir," they pleaded, "please release the sun."

"My friends," Mātanga replied, "If I released the sun immediately, this wretched man's head would split into seven pieces."

"Well, sir," they asked, "what are we to do?"

"Bring me a lump of clay," Mātanga told them. After they had brought it, he said, "Now put the lump of clay on this ascetic's head, carry him to the river, and lower him into the water."

The people did exactly as Mātanga had instructed. As they lowered Jātimanta into the water, the sun rose, the lump of clay split into seven pieces, and the ascetic, completely humbled, sank to the bottom.

"Now, where are those sixteen thousand brahmins who believed themselves defiled by eating my leftovers?" Mātanga wondered. "Let me humble them, too." He immediately perceived that they were staying with the king of Mejjha. Using his supernatural power, he transported himself to the capital and began walking for alms in the neighborhood where the brahmins were staying. The brahmins saw him and became worried. "If he stays here," they said to each other, "we will soon find ourselves without any support!"

Hoping to drive him away, they hurried to the king. "Sire," they complained, "a charlatan has just arrived in your capital. He is no more than a juggler, but he is posing as an ascetic and is begging in the streets. You must arrest him!"

"Of course!" replied the king, and he sent his men to seize Mātanga.

They found him sitting on a bench beside a well, quietly eating from his earthen bowl. One of the soldiers drew his sword and cut off the wise ascetic's head.

The devas instantly rose up and poured down a torrent of hot ashes, completely destroying Mejjha and all its inhabitants. Thus, it is said: "Because of the death of the glorious Mātanga, the entire kingdom of Mejjha was swept away by the devas!" Mātanga was reborn in the Brahma heavens.

Having concluded his story, the Buddha said, "Thus, this is not the first time that King Udena has abused a religious man." Then the Buddha identified the birth: "At that time, King Udena was Mandavya, and I was the wise Mātanga."

196
An Enduring Friendship
Citta-Sambhūta Jātaka

It was while staying at Jetavana that the Buddha told this story about two bhikkhus within Venerable Mahā-Kassapa's group, who were close and devoted friends.

The two bhikkhus walked for alms together, shared everything equally, and were never apart. One day, all the bhikkhus were praising their friendship. When the Buddha heard what they were discussing, he said, "Their friendship in one existence, Bhikkhus, is not surprising. Long ago, the wise maintained friendships unbroken through three or four lifetimes!" At their request, the Buddha told them this story of the past.

Long, long ago, when the monarch in Ujjeni, the capital of Avanti, was King Avanti, the Bodhisatta was born as a candāla and was named Citta. His mother's sister had a son of about the same age, who was called Sambhūta. The two cousins grew up together like brothers and worked as sweepers.

One day, the two lads went to sweep, one to the northern gate and the other to the eastern gate. That day, two young women, daughters of a merchant and of a brahmin, had planned to host a grand picnic in the park outside the city. They had ordered food, garlands, and perfumes and had invited friends, neighbors, and acquaintances. One of the women, along with her servants, left the city by the northern gate, and her friend, along with her servants, left the city by the eastern gate. Each saw one of the candālas working and asked, "Who is that?" Informed that it was a candāla, each woman became upset, regarding the sight of an outcaste as an evil omen. Both women quickly rinsed their eyes with perfumed water to remove the ritual pollution and returned home.

At each of the gates, the guests who had witnessed the incident were furious at being deprived of their entertainment and food. "You filthy outcaste!" they shouted. "You just cheated us out of free food and drink!" Some of the men began striking the sweepers, while the crowd continued shouting, "Why don't you stay out of the way? You have ruined our party!" The more the people shouted, the angrier they got, and the harder they beat the two sweepers. The boys were left, bloody and unconscious, just outside the gates. When they came to, they dragged themselves home and each recounted to the other what had happened. As they were commiserating, they wondered what to do. "All this pain and misery comes from our candāla birth," they moaned. Then one suggested, "Why should we continue to endure such discrimination and injustice? Let's disguise ourselves as brahmins and go to Takkasilā to study!" The other agreed that this was an excellent idea, and they left Avanti.

After arriving in Takkasilā, they began to study under a renowned teacher. Citta was extremely quick at mastering every subject, but Sambhūta was much slower and had difficulties with his lessons.

Once, a villager invited their teacher and the students for lunch. The night before they were to go, there was a heavy rain, and many roads flooded. The teacher summoned Citta and said, "My boy, given the condition of the roads, I cannot go to that villager's house. I want you to go in my place. Take the other students, and recite a blessing for the man. Eat what you want yourselves, and bring back a portion for me."

Citta obediently led all the students to the village. While the young students were washing their feet and rinsing their mouths, the villagers prepared rice porridge and set it on the table. "Let it cool," they warned, as the boys gathered around the table and sat down. Without thinking, Sambhūta took a lump of porridge, popped it in his mouth, and promptly burned his tongue. Feeling as if he were swallowing red-hot metal, he completely forgot his role and cried out to Citta in the candāla argot, "Hot as hell, ain't it!" Citta, likewise, forgot his disguise and replied in the same argot, "Spit it out! Spit it out!"

"What kind of language is that?" the other students wondered as they looked at the two and at each other.

After the meal, Citta recited a blessing, and they all returned to the master's house. The students gathered in small groups and began discussing what Citta and Sambhūta had said. When one of the students finally recognized it as the candāla dialect, he told the others, and they started reviling the two students. "Filthy outcastes!" they cried. "Pretending to be brahmins, you've tricked us all this time!" They surrounded the two cousins and beat them severely.

As they were being chased away from the master's residence, one of the students shouted, "You two are impure! Go off, and become ascetics!"

Following that suggestion, Citta and Sambhūta entered the forest and took up the ascetic life. After some time, they both died and were reborn as the fawns of a doe on the bank of the Neranjara. From birth, the two deer always went together. One day, after they had finished grazing, they were contentedly standing side by side under a tree. A hunter spotted them and threw a spear, which pierced and killed both of them.

Next, they were reborn as the young of an osprey on the bank of the Nerbudda River. At that time, too, they were very dear to each other. Even as adult birds, after feeding, they huddled close to one another, rubbing their heads and their beaks together. One day, a fowler noticed them and threw a net over them. Then he killed both of them with one blow.

After this, Sambhūta was reborn as the crown prince in Uttarapañcāla, capital of Kampilla, and, at his father's death, became king. Almost since birth, Sambhūta had been able to remember his candāla birth, and, at his coronation, he uttered two verses about it, which came to be regarded as his coronation hymn and were often repeated by his queen and other members of the court. Eventually, these verses were being sung by all the citizens of Uttarapañcāla.

The wise Citta was reborn in Kosambi as the son of the king's spiritual advisor, and he remembered all three earlier births, in their proper order. When Citta was sixteen, he left the home-life and became an ascetic in the Himavat, where he intensively practiced meditation and achieved jhāna. From his meditation, Citta realized that Sambhūta had become king. "While Sambhūta is still a young king," Citta thought, "I will never be able to instruct him, but when he gets older, I will visit him and persuade him to become an ascetic."

He waited for a full fifty years without going to Uttarapañcāla. By that time, the kingdom of Kampilla had become very prosperous, and King Sambhūta had sired many sons and daughters. Deciding that the time had come,

Citta used his supernatural power and traveled to the royal park. He seated himself like a golden image on the royal stone slab.

At that time, a young boy was gathering sticks in the park, and, while he worked, he sang King Sambhūta's coronation hymn. Citta called to him, and the boy put down his sticks and paid his respects to the ascetic. "Since early this morning you have been singing that same song," Citta said. "Don't you know any other song?"

"Oh, yes, sir. I know many others, but this is the king's favorite song so, while I am in the royal park, it's the only one I feel like singing."

"Is there a refrain to the king's verses?"

"I do not know, sir."

"Could you sing it if you heard one?" Citta asked.

"Yes, sir," the boy replied confidently. "I'm sure I could if I were taught."

"All right," Citta said, "I will teach you a refrain to sing after the king sings his two verses." After the boy had mastered the refrain, Citta instructed him, "Now, go and sing this to the king. He will be very pleased with you and will reward you for it!"

The lad hurried home, bathed, and dressed himself to go to the court. At the palace, he asked to be announced as a young man who wanted to sing a refrain to the king's hymn. The king immediately summoned him and asked him to sing his refrain.

"Sing your verses first, Sire," the boy said, "and I will sing my refrain in response.

The king sang:

> Every good deed bears fruit sooner or later.
> No deed is without result, and nothing is in vain.
> Behold Sambhūta, now great and mighty,
> Because his virtues have borne that fruit again.

> Every good deed bears fruit sooner or later.
> No deed is without result, and nothing is in vain.
> Who knows whether Citta is also great and mighty,
> Because his virtues, like mine, have borne that fruit again?

When the king had finished, the youth began singing:

> Every good deed bears fruit sooner or later.
> No deed is without result, and nothing is in vain.
> Come, Sire; you will find Citta near your city gate.
> His virtues, like your own, have borne their fruit again!

This refrain filled the king with joy, but raised many questions in his mind. "My boy," he asked, "how do you know about Citta? Did someone tell you? Are you yourself Citta?"

"I know nothing of Citta, Sire, but ..."

"How did you learn this song?"

"Sire, I learned this verse from an ascetic in your royal park. He told me that, if I sang this refrain to you, I would be rewarded."

"My boy!" exclaimed the king. "Your words are very sweet to my ear! I have been waiting my entire life to hear this refrain. What that ascetic said is very true! For your most excellent refrain, I grant you the income from an entire village and one thousand coins right away. Now I must hurry and find my brother Citta! I want to see him without delay!"

The king dismissed the boy and ordered that his chariot be prepared. "Oh, joy! Oh, rapture!" he shouted. "Beat the drums, and blow the conch! Today, in the royal park, I will meet my beloved Citta!"

He mounted his fine chariot and rode as swiftly as he could to the park. Dismounting at the gate, he walked to where Citta was sitting, paid obeisance, and sat down on one side. With a happy heart, the king exclaimed, "Many years ago, when I was crowned before a huge throng of people, remembering my brother, I sang a hymn. Now, as I greet this holy sage, I have found my brother, and my heart is full of joy!"

The king ordered that food be brought to Citta and that he be provided with every comfort. "My beloved brother," he cried, "my servants will fulfill your every wish! Let me show you how much I love you! I give you half my kingdom! Let us be kings together! Let us rule as brothers!"

Citta smiled at his friend's enthusiasm and calmly replied, "Your Majesty, sons, cattle, wealth, and power have no appeal to me. Seeing the miserable fruit of evil deeds and the benefits that good deeds bring, I would rather exercise stern self-control over myself. How long is this mortal life? At most, one hundred years—ten short decades—which rapidly succeed each other. When this natural limit is reached, what happens? A man withers as fast as a broken reed! Death will not pass me by, Sire. This is true, and I know it well. Therefore, what are pleasure, love, children, and wealth to me? From those fetters, I am free.

"The most wretched creatures on two feet are the candālas, lowly, servile, abused, and oppressed. You well remember that, long ago, you and I were born together as candālas in Avanti. You have forgotten that, after that, we were born as deer by the Neranjara and then as ospreys by the Nerbudda. Now we meet again as brahmin and khattiya. Our lives are short and inevitably end in death. There is no escape from the law of impermanence.

There is nowhere to hide to avoid change and death. Control your passions and your cravings, Sire. Avoid all unwholesome deeds, and practice virtue as much as you can. This, Sire, is what I urge you to do."

"Dear Brother," King Sambhūta replied, "what you say is very true. You are truly a holy man, and your words are full of wisdom. I must confess, however, that my desires are strong and difficult to overcome. I am filled with passions, and, because I am king, they are constantly catered to. Mired in this swamp of desires, I am like an elephant trapped in the mud, having sunk so deep that he cannot climb out. I cannot aspire to the sage's path that you have reached. Nevertheless, wise brother, as a loving father or mother would guide their dear son, please teach me how happiness may be won, tell me which way I ought to go."

"Your Majesty, since you cannot overcome your passions, which are common to all humankind," Citta admonished the king, "you must strive to rule wisely in spite of them. Do not demand unjust taxes of your people. Administer justice fairly, and treat all equally. Generously provide sages, brahmins, and ascetics with the requisites of food, clothing, medicine, and lodging. Give to the poor, and support the defenseless. This is the path to heaven.

"Here is another verse, Sire, which you should recall as you sit in your throne room, surrounded by your women and your courtiers:

> He had no roof to shelter him from the weather.
> Amid the dogs he lay.
> His mother nursed him while she swept,
> But he is king today!

"Now, Sire," Citta concluded, "I have given you my advice. Become an ascetic, or remain a king. Do as you see fit. Act according to your own abilities. I will follow my own path and reap the results of my own deeds!" Then he rose in the air, shook the dust from his feet onto the king's head, and returned to the Himavat.

As King Sambhūta watched him leave, he was profoundly moved. He immediately relinquished his throne in favor of his eldest son and followed his friend to the Himavat.

When Citta became aware that Sambhūta was coming, he went with his fellow ascetics to meet him. The sage warmly welcomed him, introduced him to the holy life, and taught him to meditate on the Four Brahma Vihāras. When they died, these two friends were born together in the Brahma heavens.

Having concluded his story, the Buddha said, "Thus, Bhikkhus, wise men of long ago continued to be firm and devoted friends through the course of those four existences." Then the Buddha identified the birth: "At that time, Ānanda was the wise Sambhūta, and I was the wise Citta."

197
The Gift of Eyes
Sivi Jātaka

It was while staying at Jetavana that the Buddha told this story about the incomparable alms given by King Pasenadi.

Inspired by Queen Mallikā, King Pasenadi wanted to surpass all other devotees and to offer alms of unparalleled splendor to the Buddha and the Sangha. He erected a splendid pavilion and furnished it with golden boats filled with fragrant incense and beautiful flowers. For seven days, he offered scrumptious lunches to the Buddha and the Sangha; all the while, khattiya maidens fanned the Buddha and the bhikkhus, and a royal elephant held a white umbrella over each of them. On the seventh day, the king offered all the requisites to the Buddha and to each bhikkhu. The king also presented the Buddha with a magnificent white umbrella and priceless furnishings, an elegant couch, a stand, and a matching footstool. This almsgiving, called Asadisadāna, was never equaled by anyone else, and each Buddha receives these gifts only once in his lifetime. When the Asadisadāna was completed, King Pasenadi waited expectantly, but the Buddha left without giving anumodana.

After having his own meal, King Pasenadi went to the monastery and asked the Buddha, "Venerable Sir, may I ask why you did not offer anumodana?"

"There were some in the court," the Buddha replied, "who were not pleased with your almsgiving.[4] It was in consideration of them that I did not offer anumodana. Misers do not go to heaven, and fools do not praise generosity. The wise, however, rejoice in giving and, by that alone, gain favorable rebirth."[5]

The king was greatly pleased with this response and offered the Buddha an outer robe worth one thousand coins. It was made of exquisite Siveyakke cloth from the kingdom of Sivi.

The next day, in the Hall of Truth, the bhikkhus were talking about the king's generosity and his incomparable gifts. When the Buddha heard what they were discussing, he said, "Bhikkhus, it is true that material things are acceptable gifts, but, long ago, a wise man, who gave such munificent gifts that his generosity resounded throughout Jambudīpa, was still dissatisfied and gave something which was much harder to give." Then he told this story of the past.

Long, long ago, when King Sivi was reigning in Aritthapura, the capital of the Sivi kingdom, the Bodhisatta was born as the king's son and named after his father. When he grew up, Prince Sivi studied all the arts and sciences in Takkasilā. After he returned to Aritthapura, he demonstrated his skill and knowledge to his father and was proclaimed crown prince. At his father's death, he inherited the throne and began ruling righteously, scrupulously observing the ten duties of a king. In particular, King Sivi devoted himself to unstinting generosity. He built six great alms-halls, one at each of the four gates, one in the city center, and one in front of his palace door. Each day, he gave alms worth six hundred thousand coins, and, on the four Uposatha days each month, he visited each of the alms-halls to supervise the distribution of alms.

One full-moon day, King Sivi rose early and, as he sat recollecting the gifts he had given, he thought, "Of all the things I own, there is nothing that I have not already given! Still, I am not satisfied! I want to give something more, something that is part of myself!"

He got up from his seat and declared, "Today, I will go to my alms-halls, and I vow that I will fulfill any request. If someone asks me to become his servant, I will take off my royal robes and do a slave's work. If someone asks for a part of my body, I will gladly give it. If someone asks for my heart,

---

4 The Buddha was referring to the king's minister, Kāla, who disapproved of the cost of the alms-giving. King Pasenadi immediately dismissed Kāla from his service and promoted Junha, another minister, who had enthusiastically overseen the alms-giving. (Dhammapada Commentary to Verse 177, Burlingame, Volume 3, p. 27)

5 Dhammapada 177

I will cut open my chest with a sword and, like pulling up a lotus from a calm lake, extract my own heart and give it to him! If someone asks for my flesh, I will cut flesh from my body and give it to him. If someone asks for my blood, I will slash my arm and let my blood flow either directly into his mouth or, if he prefers, into a bowl. If someone asks for my eyes, without a second thought, I will tear them out and give them to him."

He bathed himself with sixteen pitchers of perfumed water and put on his finest robes. After a meal of choice food, he mounted his richly caparisoned royal elephant and began a round of the alms-halls, determined to fulfill his vow. In Tāvatimsa, Sakka felt his throne becoming hot and immediately understood that the cause was King Sivi's declaration. "Will he be able to carry out his vow?" Sakka wondered. "I must test him." Assuming the appearance of a blind old brahmin, he descended from heaven and positioned himself in a prominent spot on a street in Aritthapura. When the king passed by on his way to the alms-hall, Sakka stretched out his hand and shouted, "Long live the king!"

"Are you asking for something, Brahmin?" King Sivi asked.

"Your Majesty!" Sakka replied. "Your generosity has been praised throughout Jambudīpa! Sire, I am blind, but you have two eyes. I have come a great distance to ask for one of your eyes. If you give me one, we will each have one eye with which to see!"

"Wonderful!" King Sivi exclaimed. "This is exactly what I was hoping for! This is my chance! Now I can fulfill my vow! Soon I will be able to give a gift that no one else has ever given!"

In his exuberance, King Sivi raised his hands to his face, ready to pluck out his eyes. "Here you are, sir!" he said to the brahmin. "Take my eyes."

Then he realized that hastily plucking out his eyes there in public was not proper. "Come with me to the palace," he said to the brahmin. "Let us consult my surgeon!"

The king summoned Sivaka, the royal surgeon. "Brahmin," the king said, "you asked for one eye, but I will give you both of my eyes! Your sight will be perfectly restored! Sivaka, please take out my eyes, and give them to this worthy brahmin!"

The royal advisors, the commander-in-chief, other courtiers, and all of the king's family immediately cried out, "No, Sire! Do not give away your precious eyes! Do not desert us! Give money, gold, pearls, thoroughbreds, even your great elephants! Give as much of the kingdom's wealth as you wish, but preserve yourself!"

Soon, the entire city of Aritthapura rang with the news that the king was going to give his eyes to an old wandering brahmin. Many people hurried to the palace hoping to dissuade the king.

"Who sent you?" they asked the brahmin. "Who suggested that you come to Sivi and to beg for an eye from our noble king?" The brahmin replied that Sakka had, indeed, encouraged him to approach King Sivi and to ask for his eye.

"Sire," he said, ignoring the people's murmurs, "it is now time. Please give me an eye. This is truly the greatest of gifts, so hard to part with!"

"Sivaka!" the king commanded. "Proceed with your work! Cut out my eyes, and give them to this brahmin!"

"No!" shouted the assembly. "Do not give away your eyes! Keep yourself safe for our sake!"

King Sivi raised his hand to silence the crowd. "Having already offered this gift," he declared, "I cannot renege on my word. If I did, I would be bound for hell! If never asked, one need not give; if asked for one thing, one should not give something else; but, having resolved to give, when this brahmin asks for my eye, I must comply or forever be a faithless liar!"

"Sire!" the courtiers shouted, trying once more to change his mind. "What do you hope to gain by giving away your eyes? What is it that you seek? Please tell us what your motive is for doing this."

"I do not seek for glory," the king replied. "Nor do I wish for power. It is not for rebirth in heaven that I give this gift. Generosity is the way of the righteous! Giving gifts brings joy to my heart, and giving is what I love!"

Turning to Sivaka, he said, "You are a friend and a comrade. Do as I ask. Use your skill to remove my eyes, and give them to this beggar."

"Sire, please reconsider!" Sivaka protested. "To give one's eyes is no minor matter."

"Sivaka," the king replied firmly, "I have already considered it thoroughly. Now proceed quickly. There is too much talk!"

As the king lay flat on his back, Sivaka thought, "As an accomplished surgeon, it is not proper for me to pierce the king with a lancet to extract his eyes. It must be done more subtly!" The surgeon put several herbs in his mortar and pounded them into a fine powder. He dipped a blue lotus in the powder and gently brushed the flower over the king's right eye. The eyeball rolled back, and the king experienced horrific pain.

"Reflect, Sire. It is not too late to stop this procedure!" Sivaka told the king.

"Go on, Friend. Please hurry!" the king commanded.

Again Sivaka dipped the flower in the powder and brushed it over the king's eye. The pain grew even more intense, and the eyeball protruded from its socket.

"Reflect, Sire! I can still restore it."

"Go on, Sivaka!" the king replied. "Be quick!"

The doctor dipped the lotus a third time in the powder and again brushed the king's eye. The pain was agonizing as the eyeball emerged completely from the socket and dangled by a nerve.

"Reflect, Sire! I can yet restore your eye."

Blood from the empty socket trickled down the king's face. His beautiful robe was stained red. Women and courtiers fell at the king's feet. "My Lord," they cried, "do not sacrifice your eyes! Please tell him to stop!"

"Be quick, Friend," the king repeated, as he patiently endured the excruciating pain.

"Very well, Sire," said Sivaka. With his left hand, the physician grasped the eyeball and, with the scalpel he held in his right hand, severed the nerve. Then he laid the eye on the king's palm.

"Brahmin, come here." called the king. "Dearer to me than this physical eye is the eye of omniscience! It is for omniscience that I have completed this action! Now you know my reason!" Holding the eye with both hands, he offered it to the brahmin. Sakka took it and placed it in the socket of his right eye. As he did so, he smiled as though he had just regained his sight.

When King Sivi, with his left eye, saw the brahmin's face, he exclaimed, "Ah, how excellent is my gift! Sivaka, give this brahmin my left eye!"

By the same process, Sivaka extracted the king's remaining eye, and Sakka placed it in the other socket. Leaving the blind king lying on the table, Sakka left the palace and returned to Tāvatimsa.

King Sivi remained in the palace a few days to recover from his surgery. The pain subsided, and scar tissue soon filled the sockets, which resembled a doll's eyes.

As soon as his wounds were healed, the king summoned his courtiers and announced, "A blind man is unfit to rule a great kingdom. I have decided to hand over the country to my ministers. I will retire to the royal park as an ascetic. You must arrange a guide rope in the park so that I can find my retiring place. I will need only one man to stay with me and to attend to my needs." The king summoned his charioteer and asked to be taken to the royal park, but the courtiers placed the king in a golden palanquin, carried him themselves to the park, and set him down beside the lake. During all of this, the king quietly reflected on his gift.

Again, Sakka's throne became hot. This time, he decided to restore King Sivi's eyes. Sakka descended immediately to the royal park and began walking back and forth near where the king was sitting.

When King Sivi heard the footsteps, he called out, "Who is there?"

"It is Sakka. I have come to visit you, royal sage, and to offer you a boon. I will grant whatever you wish."

"Your Majesty," King Sivi replied, "I have just renounced immeasurable wealth and power. Since I am blind, the only thing I wish for now is death."

"King Sivi," Sakka asked, "do you wish for death, because you actually want to die or only because you are blind?"

"It is because I am blind, My Lord."

"Your Majesty, no gift is everything in and of itself. When you gave your gift, there was a motive, however great or small, a practical consideration relating to this visible world. You were asked for one eye, but you gave both. The force of that offering, great and generous king, was so strong that, if you make an asseveration of truth about it now, your sight will be restored!"

"Sakka, if you wish to restore my sight," King Sivi replied, "just give me an eye as a consequence of my gift. Do not play this game!"

"Your Majesty, even though I am Sakka, I lack the power to give an eye to anyone. Yet, you may be assured, that, as the fruit of your incomparable gift, and for no other reason, your eye shall be restored to you! Make your asseveration of truth!"

King Sivi accepted Sakka's explanation and declared, "Whatever supplicant may come to me is welcome! Anyone who comes to beg from me is dear to my heart! If these solemn words of mine are true, let one eye appear!"

As he uttered those words, one eye grew back in the socket.

"A brahmin begged for one of my eyes, and to that blind mendicant I gave the pair. This act produced in me the greatest joy and happiness. If these solemn words of mine are true, let my second eye appear!"

As he uttered those words, the second eye grew back in the socket. These eyes, however, were neither natural nor divine. An eye given by Sakka cannot be called natural, but a divine eye cannot be produced in anything that is injured. These were the eyes of Absolute and Perfect Truth produced by the force of that asseveration.

As King Sivi's sight was being restored, Sakka used his supernatural power to assemble the entire court. Standing in the air above the crowd, Sakka proclaimed, "Oh, fostering king of Sivi, your noble words of truth have gained for you this incomparable pair of eyes! With these eyes, whichever way you cast your glance, you will be able to see one hundred yojanas! No rock or wall or mountain will block your perfect vision!" Sakka exhorted the king to be heedful and returned to Tāvatimsa.

King Sivi, surrounded by his retinue, returned in great majesty to the city and entered his splendid palace, Candaka, named after the eye in a peacock's tail.

The news that King Sivi's eyes had been restored spread across the kingdom and beyond. People thronged to the city to see him, to give him gifts, and to share his joy.

The king ordered that a great pavilion be erected at the palace gate and seated himself on the royal throne under a white umbrella. "People of Sivi," he declared, "you have witnessed that, because of giving, I received this wonderful pair of eyes, with which I can see clearly for one hundred yojanas, with no hindrance of rock, wall, or mountain! Understanding the efficacy of giving, therefore, you should never eat any food without giving some of it to others! Supreme generosity is the highest virtue! Self-sacrifice without regret will reap a great reward. When asked to give, even though what is asked is one's prized possession, who would say no? Practice generosity and kindness as much as you can, and you will be sure to be reborn in heaven!"

For the rest of his life, on every Uposatha day, King Sivi taught the law to a great gathering of people, who, faithfully following his teaching, gave alms generously and performed many other good deeds. When they passed away, they were all reborn in heaven.

Having concluded his story, the Buddha identified the birth: "At that time, Ānanda was Sivaka, Anuruddha was Sakka, my followers were the people of Sivi, and I was King Sivi."

198
The Teaching of the Golden Deer
Rohana-Miga Jātaka

It was while staying at Veluvana that the Buddha told this story about Venerable Ānanda.

When Devadatta released Nalagiri, the killer elephant, in Rājagaha, as the Buddha and the bhikkhus were on their almsrounds, Venerable Ānanda was willing to sacrifice his life to protect his teacher.

Later, bhikkhus were talking about Venerable Ānanda's devotion. When the Buddha heard what they were discussing, he said, "Bhikkhus, this is not the first time he has offered his life for my sake. He did the same long ago." Then he told this story of the past.

Long, long ago, when Brahmadatta was reigning in Bārānasi, the Bodhisatta was born as a handsome golden stag in the Himavat. His name was Rohana. Rohana had a younger brother, Citta, and a younger sister, Sutanā, who were as golden as he was. Rohana was leader of a herd of eighty thousand deer. He also took care of his aged parents, who were both blind.

One day, a hunter, who lived in a village in the Himavat, happened to see Rohana, and the sight made a great impression on him. When the hunter was on his deathbed, he described to his son the exact place where he had seen Rohana. "My boy," he said, "on that ridge, lives a magnificent golden deer. I saw him once with my own eyes. If the king should ever ask, you may tell him about it."

Some time after this, Queen Khemā, the king's consort, had a vivid dream in which she saw a golden stag seated on a golden throne from which he taught her the law in a voice as sweet as the sound of a golden bell. In her dream, the queen listened with rapt attention and delight to the stag's words, but, suddenly, without finishing his sermon, the beautiful deer stood up and walked away. "Catch that deer! Stop him!" the queen shouted as she awoke.

Her attendants burst out laughing. "Your Highness," they said, as she sat up in bed, "the palace is shut tight, with every door and window latched, and you are telling us to catch a deer!"

The queen realized that it was only a dream, but the strong impression of the deer remained with her. "Somewhere, there must be a golden deer," she said to herself. "If there were not, I would not have dreamed it. I must hear the teaching of that deer. If I tell the king that it was only a dream, he will not pay any attention. I must find a way to make him take me seriously." After breakfast, the queen returned to her bed and feigned illness. When the king entered her chamber, he immediately asked what was wrong.

"My Lord," she replied forlornly, "I have a craving."

"For what, my dear?"

"I must hear the discourse of a golden deer."

"My dear," replied the king, "that is ridiculous! There is no such creature as a golden deer."

"I'm sure there is!" she retorted firmly. "If I do not hear his sermon, I will die!" With a heart-wrenching moan, the queen turned her back on the king and lay perfectly still.

"All right, my dear," the king replied comfortingly, "I promise you that, if there is such a thing as a golden deer, it will be brought here, and you will hear his sermon."

The king summoned his advisors and asked whether any of them had ever seen or heard of a golden deer. None of them had ever seen one, but several advisors replied that they were sure that there were golden deer in the Himavat. They suggested consulting with hunters. The king summoned all the hunters and asked, "Have any of you seen or heard of a golden stag?"

One spoke up and repeated what he had heard from his father.

"My good man," the king said, "bring me that golden deer, and you will be richly rewarded! Go now, and catch it!" He gave the hunter enough money for expenses and dismissed him.

"I may not be able to bring the golden deer alive," the hunter thought, "but, at least, I will come back with the golden hide."

The hunter returned home, gave the king's money to his family, and set out for the mountains. He soon found the golden deer on the same ridge his father had described. Hiding in a thicket, the hunter carefully observed the deer's movements to ascertain where to set his snare.

The best place, he decided, was near the lake. He twisted leather thongs into a strong rope, formed a loop, which he attached to a pole, and set the trap at the spot where Rohana had stood to drink water.

The next day, after grazing, Rohana led the herd to the lake and took his usual position. Just as he started to drink, he placed one hoof into the snare and the loop tightened around his leg. Very mindfully, he considered, "If I give the signal of danger, all my herd will flee without drinking." He stood still, pretending to drink, giving no indication that he was caught. As soon as he saw that all eighty thousand deer had finished drinking and had stepped back from the water, he jerked at the noose to see whether it was possible to break it. The rope cut his skin. He jerked again, and it cut into his flesh. At the third jerk, the rope severed his tendon and touched the bone. Unable to break free, Rohana sounded a cry of danger. At once, the entire herd fled in terror.

As Citta was running with the others, he looked around for Rohana. Unable to see him, he realized that the danger must be to him. He immediately turned back toward the lake and saw his brother standing there, caught tight in the snare. Rohana saw him and cried, "Brother, don't come any nearer! It's dangerous! Go back! You must guide the herd to safety."

"No, Rohana!" Citta replied. "I will not desert you. My heart brought me back, and I will help you, even if it means my own life!"

"Citta!" Rohana protested. "Think of our parents! They are blind and helpless! You have to take care of them, or they will die! Go away! Don't linger here!"

"No, Rohana! My mind's made up," Citta insisted. "I will not leave you here alone."

Citta stood beside his brother and supported him on his right side, all the while trying to encourage him and to reassure him that he would be all right.

Sutanā was also fleeing with the herd, and, when she could not find her brothers, she, too, ran back to the lake.

"Little sister!" Rohana shouted to her. "Stop! Go back to the herd! I'm trapped in an unbreakable snare! It's dangerous for you here! Go and stay with the rest of the herd, where you will be safe!"

"No, Rohana!" Sutanā replied. "I will not desert you. My heart brought me back, and I will help you, even if it means my own life!"

"Sutanā!" Rohana protested. "Think of our parents! They are blind and helpless! Citta is here with me, so you have to take care of our parents, or they will die! Please go away! Don't linger here!"

"No, Rohana! My mind's made up," Sutanā insisted. "I will not leave you here alone." Sutanā stood at Rohana's left side, supporting and consoling him.

When the hunter heard the deer's cry and saw the herd fleeing, he was sure that he had indeed captured the leader. He grasped his spear and emerged from his blind.

As soon as Rohana saw the hunter, he cried, "Here comes the hunter! He has a spear! If you two stay here, he will kill all three of us! Flee! Quickly! Both of you!"

Citta saw the hunter but did not move a muscle. Sutanā, being young and timid, instinctively moved away a little in fear, but, almost immediately, she thought, "Where could I possibly go if I deserted my two brothers?" She stepped forward again to stand resolutely beside Rohana and watched the hunter approach.

The hunter looked at the three golden deer and wondered, "My snare could have caught only one deer. Why are the other two standing there? Are they his siblings?"

"Golden stag," the hunter called, "Those two deer with you are not trapped like you. Why are they standing there?"

Rohana answered, "They are my younger brother and sister. They won't leave me, even to save their own lives."

The hunter's heart softened when he heard that.

"Friend," Citta said to the hunter, "our brother is not an ordinary deer. He is the king of a great herd. He leads a virtuous life and cares for our parents, both of whom are feeble and blind. If you slay this righteous creature, you must also slay my sister and me, and, thus, you will be killing mother and father, as well. If you grant my brother a reprieve, you will bestow life on the five of us."

These moving words deeply affected the hunter. "Don't be afraid!" he said, lowering his spear. "I will release this noble deer. Your parents will be relieved when they find him safe."

"Why should I care about the king and his honors?" the hunter thought. "If I were to harm this majestic stag, I'm sure the earth would swallow me up and I'd go straight to hell!"

The hunter lowered the pole and cut the rope with his spear. Speaking softly, so as to reassure him, the hunter helped Rohana lie down on his side and eased his bloody hoof out of the noose. With hands more used to killing than healing, he realigned as best he could the ends of the damaged tendon, placed herbs inside, and closed the wound. Fetching some clear water from the lake, he gently rinsed the blood off the leg. Because of the power of the man's compassion and of Rohana's great virtue, the injured leg was, in an instant, perfectly healed. Golden hide completely covered the wound without leaving any trace of a scar. To show that his leg was as strong as before, Rohana leaped to his feet.

"Noble hunter!" Citta exclaimed. "May you and your family always be happy and blessed. My heart rejoices to see my brother free."

"Dear hunter," Rohana said, "I am very grateful that you have released me from this dreadful snare. I wonder why you set this trap. Did you act on your own, or did someone send you here to catch me?"

"Noble deer," the hunter replied, "I was, indeed, sent here by the king. His consort, Queen Khemā, wants to hear your discourse on righteousness."

"In that case, you have done a bold thing in setting me free! Please take me to the palace, and I will gladly speak to the queen."

"My Lord," the hunter replied in warning, "please reconsider your request. Kings are unreliable. Who knows what may happen. I don't trust the king's integrity. I advise you to stay here in the jungle, where you can roam where you want."

"You are very brave to say that and to allow me to go free," Rohana told him, "but you were promised a reward for catching me. You must receive what you have earned. Friend, rub my back with your hand."

The hunter did so, and his hand was covered with hairs of pure gold.

"What shall I do with these hairs, My Lord?" he asked Rohana.

"Take them, and show them to the king. Tell him that they are hairs from the golden stag which you captured. In my place, you can deliver my discourse which the queen wishes to hear. After the queen has heard you speak, her craving will be satisfied."

"Wonderful, royal stag!" the hunter exclaimed. "Please give me your discourse. Teach the law! I will listen and learn your words by heart!"

The hunter sat at one side, and Rohana proceeded to teach him the five precepts. He admonished him to be virtuous and mindful at all times. Then, for the king and the queen, he taught the ten duties of a king.

The hunter thanked Rohana and paid obeisance to him. Then he carefully wrapped the golden hairs in a fresh lotus leaf and placed them in his pack.

The three deer accompanied the man for a little way, before bidding him farewell and wishing him a safe return to Bārānasi. After he had left, they grazed and drank before returning to their parents. The old couple had heard that Rohana had been captured, so they were very anxious to learn how he had managed to escape from the hunter's snare.

Rohana gave his brother and sister all the credit, explaining that their faithfulness and wise words had softened the hunter's heart.

"May the hunter, his wife, and their children always be as happy together as we are now that Rohana is set free!" his father and mother exclaimed.

After his long journey, the hunter arrived in Bārānasi and presented himself at the palace. He paid his respects to the king and stood to one side.

"Well, hunter," the king said, "have you brought us the golden deer? Do you have anything to show for your efforts?"

"Sire," the hunter replied, "in the Himavat, on the ridge which my father had described to me, I quickly found the golden deer. I set my strong snare and easily trapped him. As I approached the snare, however, two other golden deer, quite free of any trap, stood by him. I was amazed by the sight and felt great pity. I realize that it is a wonder that I, a hunter who has killed innumerable animals in my many years of experience, should feel such compassion, but I truly felt that, if I had slain that deer, I would have fallen immediately into hell."

The king was utterly astonished. "Tell me about the deer! What did the stag look like?" he asked. "Who were the other two deer? Why did they stay with your captive? What made you feel such pity?" The king asked many questions, one after the other, without giving the hunter a chance to answer.

"Your Majesty!" the hunter finally interjected. "The three deer had hides of reddish gold. The two bucks had silvery horns, and the doe was very graceful. All three were extremely pleasing to behold, but the eldest, who was the king, was the most handsome stag I have ever seen. The other two were his younger brother and sister. They stood beside him to comfort him. It was the younger brother who begged me in the sweetest voice to spare his brother. He explained that his parents were old and blind and completely dependent upon them. He told me that, if I were to kill the three of them, I would also be killing the parents. It was because of that, Sire, that I could not bear to bring the golden deer to Bārānasi." Then he opened the lotus leaf and placed in the king's hand Rohana's golden hairs. "These hairs of pure gold are from the back of the royal deer. When he learned that your queen wished to hear a discourse, he asked me to deliver it in his place. He gave me his wonderful sermon, and I am prepared to repeat it to Her Royal Highness."

The king immediately prepared a golden throne, upon which he seated the hunter, summoned the queen, and requested that the hunter repeat the lesson that he had heard from the golden deer.

The hunter solemnly repeated the five precepts and admonished the king and queen to be virtuous and mindful at all times. He taught the ten duties of a king, and urged the royal couple to observe them scrupulously. "In this way, Sire" he concluded, "does one live righteously; this is how the devas have won their heavenly birth!"

Everyone in the court cried out in approval, and the queen's longing was fully satisfied.

"You are my great benefactor!" declared the king. "Be assured that I will rule with justice and show my people, by example, how to live!" The king was so pleased that he showered the hunter with great honor. He gave him a jeweled earring, one hundred gold coins, a lovely couch with cushions, a bull, and one hundred cows.

"Your Majesty," the hunter replied, "I gratefully accept these gifts for my family, but, as for me, I desire no house, no treasure, nor any cattle. Please allow me to become an ascetic!"

Receiving the king's consent, the hunter gave all of the king's gifts to his wife and went alone to the Himavat. He built himself a small hermitage and embraced the ascetic life. Through concentration meditation, he perfected the five extraordinary powers and the eight jhānas. When he passed away, he was reborn in the Brahma heavens.

Following Rohana's lesson, the king and queen continued to live virtuously and righteously and were also reborn in heaven. Throughout Kāsi, the teaching of the golden deer endured for one thousand years.

Having concluded his story, the Buddha identified the birth: "At that time, Channa was the hunter, Sāriputta was the king, a bhikkhunī was Queen Khemā, my father and mother were the golden stag's parents. Uppalavannā was Sutanā, Ānanda was Citta, the Sākyan clan were the eighty thousand deer, and I was the golden stag Rohana."

The Company We Keep
Sattigumba Jātaka

It was while staying at Maddakucchi, a deer park near Rājagaha, that the Buddha told this story about Devadatta.

Once, Devadatta rolled down a boulder, intending to kill the Buddha. Only a fragment of the stone struck the Buddha's foot, but that caused severe pain and a great deal of internal bleeding. Many bhikkhus gathered to see the Buddha, but, in order to get away from the crowd, he asked to be carried to Maddakucchi. From there, he was taken to Jīvaka's mango grove, where the great physician successfully treated the injury. Later, when the bhikkhus were discussing this event, one of them said, "Devadatta is terribly wicked, and so are all of his followers. The wicked keep company with the wicked, don't they?"

When the Buddha heard what they were talking about, he said, "This is not the first time that Devadatta has kept company with the wicked. It was the same long ago." Then he told this story of the past.

Long, long ago, when Pañcāla was reigning in Uttarapañcāla, the Bodhisatta was born as a parrot. He had one brother, who was younger, and their father was the king of the parrots. They lived in a grove of silk cotton trees on a high plateau in the heart of a deep forest. A little further up the mountain was a village of five hundred robbers. About the same distance down the mountain was a hermitage complex, where five hundred ascetics stayed.

Once, when the parrots were molting, the grove was struck by a whirlwind, which blew the two young parrots out of the nest. The younger fell among the weapons in the village, and the robbers named him Sattigumba. The elder fell in a flowerbed which grew on a sandy spot in the hermitage, and the ascetics named him Pupphaka.

Each of the parrots stayed in the place where he had fallen, so Sattigumba grew up surrounded by robbers, and Pupphaka grew up among sages.

One morning, King Pañcāla set out in his chariot to shoot game, accompanied by a host of soldiers. The king's hunt took him into that part of the forest. Taking his place in a blind set up in a dense grove, the king shouted, "Don't let a deer escape, or you'll answer for it!"

The beaters began beating the bushes, and a deer ran out of a thicket. The king drew his bow, but the animal leaped through a gap near the king and got away. The soldiers burst out laughing and teased the king for letting the deer escape.

Stung by their jesting, the king hollered, "All right! I'll catch that deer!" He jumped into his chariot and shouted, "Full speed!" The charioteer cracked his whip, and the horses galloped after the deer. The others joined the chase, but the king's chariot was too fast for them. Soon, the king and his driver found themselves alone, and the deer was nowhere to be seen.

At about noon, King Pañcāla decided to turn back. He noticed a pleasant glen with a shady pool and told the charioteer to stop. Alighting from his chariot, the king bathed and refreshed himself in the cool water. His charioteer brought a rug and spread it beneath the shade of a tree for the king to rest on. While the charioteer was massaging his feet, the king dozed off. After a few minutes, the charioteer himself stretched out and fell asleep. Unbeknownst to them, the spot the king had chosen was very near the robbers' village, but, since even the robbers had been enlisted to beat the bushes for the hunt, the village was empty, except for the parrot Sattigumba and a cook named Patikolamba.

As Sattigumba was flying over the glen, he saw the king and thought, "That fellow looks very rich! What a prize!" He immediately flew back to the village and shouted, "Patikolamba! Come quick! In the glen are a rich man and his driver. They're asleep, and no one's around to help them. Let's kill them and take their jewels and gold. We can pile branches on their bodies, and no one will be the wiser!"

The cook followed the parrot to the glen and immediately recognized the king. "Sattigumba," he cried, "are you mad? What are you saying? That is the king! How can you think of killing him and stealing his jewels? Kings are like blazing bonfires, dangerous to approach too near!"

"You talk like a coward, Patikolamba!" Sattigumba retorted sharply. "I'm not mad, but you are! You're shrinking from the calling that we live by!"

Their loud voices woke the king. He realized the danger he was in and roused his charioteer. "Quick!" he shouted. "Harness the horses! Take me away from that bloodthirsty parrot with murder on his mind!"

In a moment, the chariot was ready, and the horses were galloping away. "Stop them!" Sattigumba cried. "Don't let them get away with all that treasure. Take a javelin, a spear, or a bow! Don't let them get away! Kidnap! Murder! Mayhem! Demand a king's ransom!" He continued ranting and raving, but no one was listening, and King Pañcāla was soon out of sight.

In due course, the king happened to pass the hermitage. At that time, the ascetics were all in their huts, quietly meditating, and the only one stirring was the parrot Pupphaka. When Pupphaka saw the king, he went out to meet him. "Welcome, Sire!" he greeted the king courteously. "What happy chance has directed you to our humble abode? You must be hungry. We can offer some tender leaves and ripe fruit. To Your Majesty, that may not seem like much, but it is all we have. Please eat what you like, and enjoy some cool water from a spring on the hill."

The king was very pleased at this polite address. He thanked Pupphaka for his hospitality and said, "Not far from here, in a glen near a village, there was another parrot. He was very cruel and full of wicked words. He actually threatened to kill my charioteer and me and to rob us of our jewels. We fled as quickly as we could. What a delight it is to find this peaceful hermitage!"

"That parrot is my brother," Pupphaka explained. "We are, Your Majesty, sons of the same parents. We were born in the same tree, but we were separated while still young. Sattigumba grew up in the company of thieves, who live by trickery, cheating, stealing, and killing. That's all that he has learned. I grew up here among the ascetics, where there is self-control, sobriety, kindness, and hospitality. Those are the lessons I have learned.

"Those whom one respects, be they virtuous or vicious, will influence what one becomes. We are, in fact, shaped by our comrades and our friends. The wise man shuns bad company, for fear of its staining touch. Poison the arrow, and, before long, the quiver will be poisoned, too! Wrap a rotten fish in kusa grass, and soon the grass will smell the same! Keep company with fools, and find yourself a fool! In the same way, however, if you wrap a piece of sandalwood in a leaf, that leaf itself will soon smell sweet! Those who sit at wise men's feet will themselves grow wise. One should always avoid bad company and associate with the righteous!"

The king was pleased with this exposition. As the ascetics emerged from their huts, the king greeted them and invited them to take up their residence in his park. Repeating his request and prevailing upon them to accept his hospitality, he departed.

As soon as the king returned to the capital, he proclaimed immunity to all parrots. Some time later, the ascetics arrived in the capital and visited the king. He respectfully escorted them to the royal park, arranged their quarters, and cared for them as long as he lived. When he passed away to be reborn in heaven, his son became king and carried on the tradition of caring for the ascetics. This continued through seven generations of kings, who were all bounteous in alms. Pupphaka stayed in the forest until he, too, passed away to fare according to his deserts.

Having concluded his story, the Buddha identified the birth. "At that time, Devadatta was Sattigumba, his followers were the robbers, Ānanda was King Pañcāla, my followers were the ascetics, and I was Pupphaka."

200

One Night Apart
Bhallātiya Jātaka

It was while staying at Jetavana that the Buddha told this story about Queen Mallikā.

One day, there was a quarrel between King Pasenadi and Queen Mallikā. The king was so enraged with the queen that he completely ignored her existence.

The Buddha knew all about this quarrel and resolved to make peace between the two.

Early in the morning, he entered Sāvatthī for alms with a following of five hundred bhikkhus and stood at the palace gate. The king took the Buddha's bowl and led the entire party into the dining hall. The king had his servants bring the rice and cakes, but, as he started pouring the water of donation, the Buddha put his hand over the vessel and asked, "Sire, where is the queen?"

"What do you have to do with her, Venerable Sir?" the king asked in return.

"Her head is turned. She has become intoxicated with the honor she enjoys."

"Sire," the Buddha replied, "since you yourself bestowed this honor on her and elevated her to this rank, it is wrong for you to be so upset that she enjoys it. Rather than cast her aside, you must put up with the small offence that you feel she has committed against you."

The king hearkened to the words of the Teacher and sent for the queen. As soon as she came, she and the king together served the Buddha and the bhikkhus.

After the meal, the Buddha offered anumodana and said, "Long ago when you were both kinnaras, you couldn't bear to be parted." Then he told this story of the past.

Long, long ago, a king named Bhallātiya was reigning in Bārānasi. One day, King Bhallātiya felt a craving for charcoal grilled venison. Leaving his advisors to manage the affairs of the kingdom, he gathered his weapons and went hunting with a pack of well-trained pedigree hounds. At first, he stayed near the Gangā, but then he followed a tributary and went deep into the jungle. Every day, he killed deer and boar and dined on the roasted meat. After he had climbed to a considerable altitude, the jungle opened into a broad meadow, where the river was just a pleasant stream, full of fish and turtles. The sand at the water's edge was like silver, and the banks were lined with fruit trees in blossom. The flowers attracted a multitude of birds, butterflies, and bees, which were all flitting in and out of the shade.

As the king was walking along the riverbank, he saw two creatures, sitting by the water's edge and fondly embracing each other. After hugging each other tightly, they began to weep most sorrowfully. They then hugged each other and tried to dry their tears. Suddenly, they broke out weeping again and once more embraced tightly. The king silently watched the remarkable display of affection for a few minutes and wondered what they could possibly be crying about.

He signaled to his dogs to stay crouched in the underbrush, and he drew closer to the couple. So as not to frighten the creatures, he laid his weapons under a tree. When he was close enough to be heard, he softly asked, "Dear creatures, you are not like any animals I have ever seen. Who are you?"

"We are kinnaras," they said between sobs, "and we live here in these mountains. The peaks of Mallamgiri, Tikuta, and Pandaraka are our home."

"From the way you are embracing, I can tell that you are lovers, but you seem to be weeping from some great distress. Please tell me. What causes you such pain and sorrow?"

The kinnara replied, "One night, for the entire night, we were separated. Whenever we remember that night, we cannot help but weep. That night of great anguish should have been one of bliss, but it is lost forever."

"Why did you spend that night apart?" asked King Bhallātiya. "Obviously, it has cost you many tears."

"That day, we were in different parts of this meadow when a sudden storm arose," the kinnarī explained. "My lover, thinking that I had crossed the river, leaped across to find me. Actually, I was not far from him, gathering flowers. I wanted to make for us both, garlands of thyme blossoms, violets, narcissi, and other fragrant flowers. I was also making a bed of leaves and the petals of roses and other flowers so that we could sleep softly when night fell. I had already pounded some sandalwood to perfume our little love nest. I was just about to gather some lilies, fragrant with evening dew, when I noticed that the river had begun to swell with the rain in the mountains."

The kinnara continued, "Soon it was a fast-rushing spate, making it impossible for me to cross back to her. There we stood on either shore, gazing at each other. How we laughed and wept, calling over the river's roar. How we suffered that night! So near and yet so far! In the morning, the sun dried up the land, and the river fell. I crossed to the other side as soon as I could, and we embraced, both laughing and crying together.

"It's just three years shy of seven hundred years since we were separated that whole night long," the kinnarī said. "When two loving hearts are kept apart, one night can seem a lifetime."

"If that happened seven hundred years ago, how long is your lifespan?" asked the king.

"We live one thousand summers," the kinnara replied. "During that time, we are always strong and healthy, with neither illness nor physical pain. We have few sorrows and abundant delight. To the end, love's joys illumine our lives."

King Bhallātiya was touched by the responses of the kinnaras. "These creatures, less than human," he thought, "weep for seven hundred years over one night's separation! Here am I, lord of a great realm, leaving my magnificence and my duties to wander carelessly around in the jungle. I am making a great mistake!" Taking leave of the kinnaras, the king immediately returned to Bārānasi.

When his courtiers asked him if he had seen anything remarkable in the Himavat, he told them the whole story of the kinnaras. For the rest of his life, he gave up hunting, lived generously, and appreciated every fleeting day.

Having concluded his story, the Buddha said, "Take a lesson from the kinnaras, and never quarrel or bicker with your loved ones. Mend your ways so as to have no regrets when the end comes."

Queen Mallikā paid her respects to the Buddha and said, "Venerable Sir, I heard your words, so kind and good, with a tender and happy mind. Blessings on you! You have spoken well and freed me from all my sorrows."

From then on, King Pasenadi and Queen Mallikā lived together in harmony.

Then the Buddha identified the birth: "At that time, King Pasenadi was the kinnara, Queen Mallikā was the kinnarī, and I was King Bhallātiya."

201
The Nāga King's Quest
Campeyya Jātaka

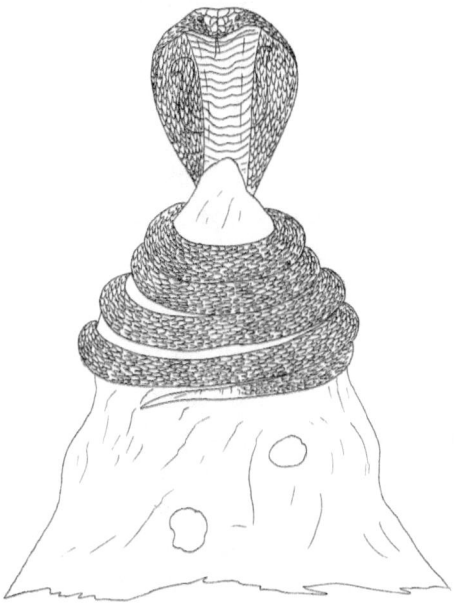

It was while staying at Jetavana that the Buddha told this story about observing Uposatha days.

"It is very good," the Buddha said to a group of lay followers, "that you are observing Uposatha. Long ago, even a nāga king renounced his glory in order to observe Uposatha." At their request, he told this story of the past.

Long, long ago, when King Anga was reigning in the kingdom of Anga and King Magadha was reigning in the kingdom of Magadha, there was a great river called the Campā flowing between the two kingdoms. The river was inhabited by nāgas, ruled by their own king, named Campeyya.

In the wars between the two human kingdoms, King Magadha sometimes conquered Anga, and King Anga sometimes conquered Magadha. One day, King Magadha, having lost a battle to King Anga, mounted his charger and fled, pursued by Anga's warriors.

When he came to the Campā, it was in full flood. The defeated king decided it was better to die by drowning than to perish at the hands of his enemies. He spurred his horse to leap into the swift-flowing stream, and they disappeared beneath the water's surface. At that moment, the nāga

79

king Campeyya was amusing himself with his court. When Campeyya saw King Magadha, he was impressed with his demeanor. He got up from his couch and rescued the drowning king. Reassuring King Magadha that there was nothing to fear, he placed him on his own seat. When King Magadha had recovered from the shock, King Campeyya asked why he had jumped into the river, and King Magadha explained everything.

"Don't worry, Sire!" replied King Campeyya. "I will make you master of both kingdoms!" He escorted King Magadha to his underwater palace and entertained him lavishly for an entire week. On the seventh day, he accompanied King Magadha to the riverbank and sent him back to his capital. With the assistance of the nāga king, in the next battle, King Magadha was able to defeat King Anga and to annex his kingdom.

King Magadha, now ruler of both countries, maintained a close friendship with King Campeyya. Every year, King Magadha built a jeweled pavilion on the bank of the Campā and offered valuable gifts to the nāga king, who emerged with a great retinue to receive the tribute. Citizens gathered on both sides of the river to behold the glory of the nāga king and his court.

At that time, the Bodhisatta was a peasant, who lived in a village near the river. Although he was extremely virtuous, his family was very poor. Every year, he joined the general public at the riverside and marveled at the opulence of the nāga king. He was so impressed by the splendor that he began to covet King Campeyya's greatness. When he died, the longing for the nāga king's glory was in his mind, and he was reborn as a nāga prince named Campeyya, with a body like a garland of jasmine, in that same palace.

Campeyya remembered his previous birth as a man and was filled with remorse. The young nāga prince languished around the palace and reflected, "As a result of my good deeds, I have merit laid up like corn in a granary, but, just because of my foolish fancy, I have been born in this horrible serpent's body. What do I care for life?"

A young female nāga named Sumanā fell in love with the prince. "Prince Campeyya is as handsome as Sakka!" she declared. "He was born to rule us, and I will be his queen!" Accompanied by a host of nāga musicians and dancers, Sumanā successfully seduced the prince and caused him to forget his suicidal thoughts. Overpowered by Sumanā's grace and beauty, he began enjoying the sensual pleasures so abundant in his magnificent palace. He was often found lounging pleasantly on his couch, dressed in luxurious robes, adorned with sparkling jewels, and surrounded by lovely maidens, of whom Sumanā was always his favorite.

When Campeyya became king, Sumanā became his queen, and he ruled wisely over his great kingdom.

After some time, however, his old dissatisfaction returned, and he again became listless and indifferent to worldly pleasures. He came to resent his carelessness and his idle lifestyle. "What do I care for this nāga kingdom?" he asked himself. "I should shake myself free of this place and observe the Uposatha." On each Uposatha day, he retired to his royal park, undertook the Uposatha precepts, and tried to meditate. Invariably, Queen Sumanā and the other female nāgas followed him, tempted him even there, and caused him to break his precepts.

"I must leave the palace entirely and go into the realm of men. There, I will be able to keep the precepts faithfully and to observe Uposatha as I should. Among men, I will learn the Truths and make an end of suffering."

After that, on every Uposatha day, he emerged from the river and lay down on an anthill beside the main road, not far from a village. There, he was able to observe Uposatha strictly. At dawn, he returned to his underwater palace.

Everyone who passed by noticed him on the anthill and, impressed by his demeanor, worshiped him with incense and flowers. The people who lived in that frontier village believed that this nāga king had supernatural powers to grant boons. They set up a pavilion and spread sand all around so that women who longed for a son could offer their prayers there. Every Uposatha day, the pavilion was filled with oil lamps, garlands, and perfume.

One day, as he was preparing to leave the palace, Queen Sumanā said to him, "My Lord, I know that, every Uposatha day, you go to the realm of men to keep the precepts. The human world is a perilous place, full of frightful happenings. If any danger should come to you, is there any way that I might be able to know about it?"

King Campeyya showed her a magical pond. "If anyone strikes or hurts me," he told her, "the water in this pond will become turbid. If a garula carries me off, the water will disappear entirely. If a snake-charmer seizes me, this water will become the color of blood." The queen was relieved to have these signs to inform her of his condition, and she bade Campeyya farewell with a lighter heart.

That day, King Campeyya made a firm determination. "Let anyone who desires my skin or any part of me," he declared, "take whatever he wants! Even if he wants to take me for a dancing snake, let him do so! I will not resist!" Thus, resolving to make an offering of his body, he lay down on the anthill. In the morning sun, his body shone like a coil of pure silver.

A young brahmin, returning home from Takkasilā, where he had studied with a famous teacher, happened to pass the anthill where Campeyya was fasting. This youth had learned a powerful charm with which he could subdue any living thing.

When the brahmin saw the majestic nāga king, gleaming like silver on the anthill, he was overjoyed. "What a magnificent snake!" he declared. "By making him dance in all the towns and villages I pass through on my way home, I will easily make a fortune!"

He began reciting his charm and approached the anthill. Campeyya immediately felt that his ears were being pierced by burning needles and that his head was being struck by a mighty sword.

"What is happening?" he wondered. He opened his eyes and saw the brahmin youth drawing near. "My poison is so powerful that with only my breath I could shatter his body, but, by harming him, I would be breaking the precepts and destroying my virtue. I must not look at him!" He closed his eyes and lay quietly, enduring the pain.

While the brahmin continued reciting his charm, he was also chewing some herbs. He stood beside the anthill and spat at Campeyya. Wherever the spittle, mixed with the juice of the herbs, touched the nāga's body, painful welts arose. While reciting the charm to render Campeyya harmless, the brahmin grabbed the great nāga by the tail and stretched him out full length on the ground. Using his staff like a rolling pin, he pressed the snake's body from head to tail. Then, with all his strength, he crushed Campeyya's head. He pried open Campeyya's mouth and spat some of the herbal juice down his throat, which caused the nāga's mouth to fill with blood. Campeyya's silvery scales were smeared with blood, and he was in unbearable pain. Despite all of this torment, the nāga king did not open his eyes. He patiently endured that torture, determined not to violate his virtue.

Satisfied that the serpent was sufficiently weakened, the brahmin quickly fashioned a wicker basket, into which he forced the nāga's battered coils.

He carried Campeyya to a nearby village and made him perform in the middle of a large crowd. The nāga king made his body appear first black and then blue; sometimes gigantic and sometimes small. Whatever the brahmin commanded, Campeyya did. As he danced to the brahmin's music, he spread his hood wide so that it appeared to be one hundred or one thousand hoods, both thrilling and frightening the audience.

The people were so impressed with the nāga's performance that they showered him with coins. In just that first day, the brahmin collected one hundred coins. He repeated his snake-charming act in every village and collected the same amount every day. At first, he had intended to release the nāga, once he had earned one thousand coins, but, having made that incredible fortune in only ten days, he thought, "I have become rich from performing in these insignificant villages. Imagine how much more I will make in the towns on my way! Once I get to Bārānasi, I will get even more from the king and all the courtiers!" Having quickly gained a reputation as a snake charmer, he hired an attendant and bought a carriage for himself and a cart to transport his props and costumes and Campeyya's basket. From then on, the brahmin traveled in grand style from town to town, forcing the hapless nāga to perform in each and making more money than he'd ever dreamed of.

At first, the brahmin had killed frogs for Campeyya's meal, but the nāga had refused to eat anything that had been killed for his sake. Then the brahmin offered him parched corn with honey, but Campeyya refused even this, thinking, "If I agree to take food from this brahmin, he will certainly never let me go, and I will be a prisoner in this basket until I die of old age."

After one month of traveling and forcing Campeyya perform every day, the brahmin reached the gates of Bārānasi. He figured that, once he had finished his performance in King Uggasena's court, he would let the nāga go.

The brahmin's reputation had preceded him. King Uggasena actually sent for him and commanded a grand public exhibition, which the snake charmer promised for the next day. The king immediately made a proclamation, accompanied by a drum, inviting everyone in the city to the palace.

The next morning, the courtyard of the palace was gaily decorated, and thousands of people had gathered. When the brahmin entered, everyone cheered wildly in anticipation. He placed Campeyya's new jeweled basket in the center and sat down in the chair reserved for him. The king descended from his chamber and sat on his throne at the front of the stage. The brahmin opened the basket and forced the nāga to dance. Everyone watching was immediately captivated. They all waved scarves and showered the noble Campeyya with gold coins and jewels.

Meanwhile, back in the nāga palace, Sumanā had become concerned. "It's been a month since my dear husband left," she sighed. "I know he can take care of himself, but he has never been away this long. I wonder why he is lingering in the realm of men? I am afraid something dreadful has happened."

She went to check the pond and discovered that the water was as red as blood, which meant that Campeyya had been caught by a snake-charmer. She hurried as fast as she could to the anthill where he always observed Uposatha. She could clearly make out where he had been caught and where he had been tortured. She wept as she imagined the agony he must have suffered. From local villagers, she learned the details of how the brahmin had forced her husband to perform. She figured that the brahmin would have taken his prize to Bārānasi, so she, too, headed in that direction. At each village she passed through, she learned that he had, indeed, appeared there and that the brahmin had earned a considerable sum from Campeyya's performance.

Sumanā arrived at the king's palace just as Campeyya had completed his first dance. When he looked up and saw her hovering above the courtyard, he felt ashamed, crept back into his basket, and lay there.

"What is the matter?" King Uggasena shouted. "Why has your serpent stopped dancing?" Before the brahmin could offer an excuse, the king glanced up and saw Sumanā, blazing like lightning. "Who are you?" he asked. "Are you a deva? You are certainly not human!"

"Your Majesty," Sumanā replied, "You are right. I am not a human being, but neither am I a deva. I am a nāga queen, and I have a reason for being here!"

"You look angry, but in your eyes I see tears!" said the king. "Tell me what is wrong! Why have you come?"

"This great serpent, Your Majesty," Sumanā explained, "is, in fact a noble nāga king. He was captured and cruelly tortured by this brahmin purely for profit. I demand an end to his exploitation. Sire, please free my lord!"

"What you say is very strange." replied the king. "How could such a puny man capture such a mighty creature?"

"This nāga, King Campeyya, possesses a power which could reduce Bārānasi to cinders," Sumanā told the king, "but he is self-restrained and loves virtue. At all times, he tries to curb his wrath with righteousness. Every full-moon day, he practices austerities and meditates on an anthill near a village on the bank of the Campā. It was at this time last month that this brahmin found him. Because he had taken the vows for the Uposatha day, he refused to become angry or to resist this wicked snake charmer. Please free my husband for my sake, Sire! In his palace, sixteen thousand bejeweled women look to him as their refuge and their king. Even if you must purchase his freedom, Your Majesty, please release him, and gain the merit for rendering justice!"

"All right, I accept your plea," the king declared. "It gives me great joy to release this serpent. Brahmin, let him go! For his freedom, I offer you gold, jewelry, a herd of cattle, a village, and lovely wives. I claim the merit for myself!"

"I want no gifts, Your Majesty!" the brahmin replied. "Let me release him on my own and claim the merit for myself!"

The brahmin took Campeyya from the basket and placed him on the ground. The nāga king crawled into a bed of flowers and soon emerged in the form of a handsome young man in elegant robes and stood with quiet dignity before the king. Sumanā descended and stood beside him in the form of a beautiful young lady. The two of them appeared to have just emerged from the earth. Each pressed his palms together to pay his respects to King

Uggasena. "Your Majesty, great king of Kāsi," King Campeyya said, "we honor you before we take our leave to return to our own palace."

"Wait! Do not leave just yet!" ordered the king. "Tell me! Are you really the king of sixteen thousand women? Do you really have a palace? Where is your kingdom? How can I believe these things?"

"Your Majesty, I am what my queen has told you! My kingdom lies beneath the Campā. The wind may move the mountains, the sun and the moon may fall from the sky, and rivers may flow upstream, but I will never tell a lie. The sky may split, the seas dry up, and Mount Sineru topple, but I will never tell a lie!"

"I am not convinced," King Uggasena replied bluntly. "It's up to me whether or not to believe you. You have given me no proof except your word. What's more, you have not even thanked me for releasing you. You really ought to express your gratitude before you leave."

"Your Majesty," King Campeyya said with a deep bow of respect, "it is with my whole heart that I offer to you my deepest thanks. One who fails to show gratitude should never enjoy happiness. Instead, he should die in prison and be reborn to burn in hell! You have showed as much kindness to us nāgas as a mother would show to her only beloved son. In return for your kindness, we nāgas wish to serve you in return."

"That is spoken like a true monarch!" declared King Uggasena. "Now I believe everything you say! Avoid anger and hatred as we flee from fire in the heat of summer! May you always be safe from garulas!"

King Uggasena expressed his keen desire to visit the nāga realm, and King Campeyya invited him to accompany them on his return. King Uggasena immediately ordered his men to prepare the elephants and to hitch the Cambodian mules to the royal chariots.

When they arrived at the Campā, King Campeyya used his great power to make everything in the nāga realm visible, and King Uggasena was dazzled and awed by its magnificence. The path leading to the palace was sprinkled with golden sand. The ramparts were decorated with delicate flowers of coral, and the towers were covered with gold. Majestic trees provided shade. Inside the palace, the air was scented with one thousand perfumes. Lovely nāga maidens danced gracefully to the music of celestial harps. King Campeyya seated his royal guest on a golden throne and summoned a bevy of beautiful nāga maidens to serve him delicious food from golden dishes. For seven days, King Uggasena and his retinue enjoyed the very finest of nāga hospitality.

"Mighty nāga king, why did you forsake all this magnificence," King Uggasena asked, "to lie on an anthill, observing Uposatha in the vulgar realm of men?"

"Sire, I do not observe Uposatha," King Campeyya replied, "to seek for sons or wealth. I undertake the precepts to control myself and to overcome craving, if I can, so that I may be reborn in the realm of men!"

"But, Sire," King Uggasena protested, still greatly puzzled, "having seen what I have seen, I cannot believe that anything that we have in our human realm surpasses what you have here. Why do you want to be reborn a man?"

"Living the holy life in full, and practicing complete self-control are possible only in the realm of men. If I am born a man, my goal will be to seek an end to birth and death!"

King Uggasena was greatly impressed with the nāga king's wisdom. "It behooves me to pay my respects to one as noble and as wise as you, my friend. Having seen the example you are setting, I resolve to live uprightly from this day on."

"Your Majesty!" King Campeyya admonished him. "For the rest of your days, live virtuously, rule with righteousness, and respect the wise!"

As King Uggasena was preparing to leave, King Campeyya waved his hand over his wealth and announced, "Sire, take anything you want. This treasure means nothing to me! Cover your walls with silver! Fill your palace with nāga gold! Take wagonloads of pearls and coral! Let nāga treasure increase the wealth of Bārānasi beyond description! Beautify and enrich your city! Then rule it wisely, and rule it well!"

King Uggasena accepted the offer, and thanked King Campeyya for his generosity. The nāgas loaded everything that he had selected into several hundred carts and transported the treasure to Bārānasi. King Uggasena himself returned to his capital with great pomp in a splendid procession. It has been said that, from that day on, all Jambudīpa was covered with nāga gold.

Having concluded his story, the Buddha identified the birth: "At that time, Devadatta was the snake-charming brahmin, Rāhula's mother was Sumanā, Sāriputta was King Uggasena, and I was Campeyya, the nāga king.

202
The Prince of the Iron House
Ayoghara Jātaka

Buddha told this story about the Great Renunciation. "Bhikkhus," the Buddha said, "this is not the first time that the Tathāgata has renounced the world. He did the same long ago." Then he told this story of the past.

Long, long ago, when Brahmadatta was reigning in Bārānasi, his chief queen had, in a previous life, been the second wife of a man whose first wife was barren. When the second wife had given birth to a son, the barren wife had become implacably jealous. As the barren wife was dying, she had made a terrible wish to be reborn so that she would be able to devour her rival's children. Getting her wish, she had been born as a yakkhinī, and she remembered her grudge.

Shortly after the queen gave birth to her first son, the yakkhinī found her way into the palace and grabbed the baby from the queen's arms. The queen tried to shout, "A yakkhinī has snatched my son!" but, before she could get the words out of her mouth, the yakkhinī gobbled the baby up like a tender green onion and fled. The entire court was horrified, and the king had no idea how to protect the queen against a yakkhinī.

The next time the queen gave birth, the king posted soldiers around her chamber, but the yakkhinī, having disguised herself as a well-wisher, easily gained entry. As she drew near the bed, she transformed back into her real form, grabbed up the newborn boy, devoured him, and escaped once again.

When the queen became pregnant for the third time, the king asked his advisors how to protect the baby after birth. One advisor said that yakkhas were afraid of palms and suggested that the queen be surrounded by palm fronds. Another said yakkhas could not enter a building made of iron.

The king liked the latter idea and summoned the blacksmiths. He ordered them to build a house in a pleasant spot in the center of the city. It was to be a beautiful and comfortable dwelling with pillars and many rooms, but it was to be made entirely of iron. When the blacksmiths had completed their work, the king had the iron house fully furnished and illuminated with thousands of oil lamps.

As the time for the queen's delivery drew near, the king escorted her and her nurses to the iron house, made sure she was comfortable, and closed it up. Around the house, he posted a heavy guard. When the baby, who was, in fact, the Bodhisatta, was born, he had all the auspicious marks and was named Ayoghara, Iron House. No one knew it, but the yakkhinī had died while fetching water for Vessavana,[6] and the threat to the prince was gone.

As a boy, Prince Ayoghara was confined to the iron house. He was never allowed to wander outside its rooms and was even tutored in all the arts and sciences inside.

One day, the king asked his courtiers how old his son was, and they replied that he had just turned sixteen. "Wonderful!" replied the king. "He is strong, well-educated, and ready to become a hero! He is certainly capable of defending himself now against even one thousand yakkhinīs! In fact, my friends, he is old enough to rule the kingdom. Let him become king in my place!"

The king ordered the city be completely cleaned and decorated for the coronation ceremony and festival. The state elephant was magnificently caparisoned and stationed outside the palace. The prince was taken out of the iron house and escorted to the palace. Courtiers dressed him in the finest ceremonial robes, and the king assisted him in mounting the magnificent elephant. The courtiers said to him, "Your Highness, make a circuit around the city, and meet your loyal subjects. Take a look at your inheritance, and return to salute your father, the king of Kāsi. Today, you will receive the white umbrella, and you will become our king!"

---

6 It was the duty of yakkhinīs to fetch water from Lake Anotatta for Vessavana's use. Each yakkhinī served her turn, perhaps as long as four or five months. Sometimes she died from exhaustion before the end of her term.

In a great procession, Prince Ayoghara made his ceremonial circuit around the city. For the first time in his life, he saw the streets, houses, shops, and markets that made up the bustling city of Bārānasi. He passed by many beautiful parks, lakes, and gardens. As he rode along, greeted by the rejoicing throngs, he pondered, "For sixteen years, my father kept me locked away in that iron prison. Not even once did he let me see this beautiful city. I wonder why I was treated like that."

He called one of his attendants and asked, "Sir, what fault do I have that caused my father to keep me in prison for sixteen years?"

"My Lord," the attendant answered, "there has never been any fault in you. A yakkhinī devoured your two elder brothers as soon as they were born. It was for your own protection that your father placed you in that iron house. That iron house saved your life!"

The prince continued reflecting. "For ten long months, I was confined in the watery dungeon of my mother's womb. Then, for sixteen years, I was confined in that depressing iron house, with no chance even to peep outside. Although I have escaped destruction at the hands of the yakkhinī, I am certainly still subject to old age and death. What do I care for royalty? Why should I want the throne? If I become king, the palace would be but another prison from which I could never escape. This very day, I must renounce all of this and ask my father's permission to leave."

The procession returned to the palace, and the prince dismounted from the elephant. He entered the palace and saluted his father. The king gazed at his handsome son with great pride and affection. "Take my son," he ordered his ministers, "place him on a pile of jewels, sprinkle him with water from three conch shells, and raise the white umbrella of kingship over him. Let us pay our respects to our new king!"

As the ministers approached, Prince Ayoghara held up his hand and said, "Father, I want nothing to do with royalty. I do not wish to be king. I beg your permission to leave Bārānasi and to become an ascetic in the Himavat."

This abrupt request shocked the king. "What are you saying?" he asked. "Why would you leave your kingdom, my son? Why do you want to become an ascetic?"

"Your Majesty," replied the prince, "for ten months, I was a prisoner in my mother's womb. For sixteen years, I was a prisoner in your iron house. These were to me the same as Ussada hell. I may be safe from the yakkhinī now, but I am still liable to old age and death. I see the palace as another prison and another hell. I am weary of existence. That is why I want to become an ascetic.

"Sire, your mighty army, your elephants, and your horses are of no avail against the coming of death. You may escape from other enemies, yet the enemy of aging and death will triumph over even the greatest military force. That is why I want to become an ascetic.

"Mountains crumble, oceans dry up, and even stars grow cold. In time everything ends in nothing. That is why I want to become an ascetic.

"The elements of life constantly decay and dissolve. Young, old, or middle-aged—all men and women fall like ripe fruit from a shaken tree. That is why I want to become an ascetic.

"One's prime of life is over in a moment. When life flies by so quickly, joy and love are mere flashes in a pan. They come and go quickly, and no one can trust them. That is why I want to become an ascetic.

"Even a criminal may find a way to halt punishment by the king, but no one can halt the hand of death. Rich, poor, powerful, or weak—death shows neither pity nor respect, treating all the same. The juggler and magician use sleight of hand to fool our eyes, but no trick can deceive death. That is why I want to become an ascetic.

"The great physicians of old, Bhoga, Vetarani, and Dhammantari, could treat diseases and even cure the venomous serpent's bite. Where are they now? Unable to cure the bite of death, they, too, are dead. That is why I want to become an ascetic.

"There are some who are well-versed in spells and can make themselves invisible. Yet even they are not invisible to the eyes of death. That is why I want to become an ascetic.

"Only one who walks in righteousness is safe. The holy life well lived has the power to protect and bless. The righteous man is happy in this world and the next. The unrighteous man is miserable in both. That is why I want to become an ascetic.

"Therefore, Sire, please keep your kingdom for yourself. I want no part of it. Even as I talk with you, old age and death draw closer."

Then, as a young lion might break out of his golden cage, the prince departed.

"I do not want the kingdom any more either!" shouted the king as he followed his son. As soon as the king had gone, the queen, the courtiers, the brahmins, the artisans, the householders, and everyone else in the city also left to become ascetics in the Himavat.

Sakka sent Vissakamma to build a hermitage for Prince Ayoghara. To accommodate the entire population of Bārānasi, the hermitage was twelve yojanas long and seven yojanas wide and was furnished with everything necessary for the ascetic life. For the rest of his days, Ayoghara instructed the others in the law and in meditation on the Four Brahma Vihāras. Everyone in the hermitage was spared rebirth in hell, and some were even reborn in the Brahma heavens.

Having concluded his story, the Buddha identified the birth: "At that time, my parents were King Brahmadatta and his queen, my followers were the citizens of Bārānasi, and I was the wise Ayoghara."

203

The Fifth Precept
Kumbha Jātaka

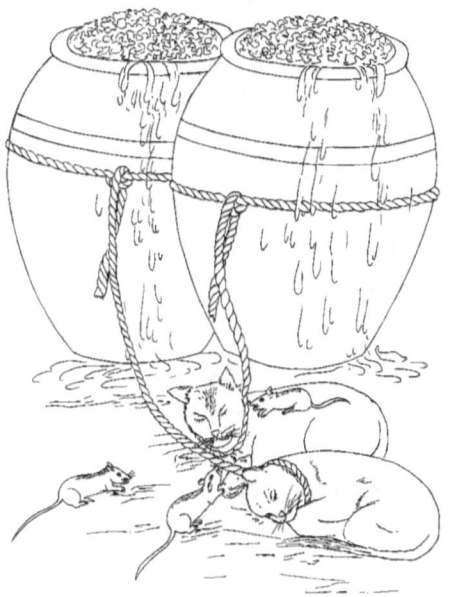

It was while staying at Jetavana that the Buddha told this story about Visākhā and her five hundred friends, who were strong drinkers.

One day, Visākhā was invited by five hundred women she knew to join in celebrating a festival in the city.

"This is a drinking festival," Visākhā replied. "I do not drink."

"All right," the women said, "go ahead and make an offering to the Buddha. We will enjoy the festival."

The next morning, Visākhā served the Buddha and the order of bhikkhus at her house and made a great offering of the four requisites.

That afternoon, she proceeded to Jetavana to offer incense and beautiful flowers to the Buddha and to hear the teaching. Although the other women were already quite drunk, they accompanied her. Even at the gate of the monastery itself, they continued drinking. When Visākhā entered the hall, she bowed reverently to the Buddha and sat respectfully on one side. Her five hundred companions, however, were oblivious to propriety. They seemed, in fact, not to notice where they were. Even in front of the Buddha, some of them danced, some sang, some stumbled around drunkenly, and some bickered.

In order to get their attention, the Buddha emitted a dark blue radiance from his eyebrows, and everything suddenly became dark. The women were terrified with the fear of death and instantly became sober. The Buddha then disappeared from his seat and stood on top of Mount Sineru. From the curl of white hair between his eyebrows he emitted a ray of light as bright as if one thousand moons and suns were rising. "Why are you laughing and enjoying yourselves," he demanded, "you, who are always burning and surrounded by darkness? Why don't you seek the light?"

The Buddha's words touched their now-receptive minds, and all five hundred women attained the first path.

The Buddha returned and sat down in his chamber. Visākhā bowed to him once more and asked, "Venerable Sir, what is the origin of this custom of drinking alcohol which destroys a person's modesty and sense of shame?" In answer to Visākhā's question, the Buddha told this story of the past.

Long, long ago, when Brahmadatta was reigning in Bārānasi, a hunter named Sura went to the Himavat from his hometown in Kāsi to look for game.

In that remote forest, there was a unique tree whose trunk grew to the height of a man with his arms held up over his head. At that point, three branches spread out, forming a hollow about the size of a big water barrel. Whenever it rained, the hollow filled up with water. Around the tree, grew a bitter plum tree, a sour plum tree, and a pepper vine. Some of the ripe fruit from the plum trees and the seeds from the pepper vine fell directly into that hollow. Nearby, there was a patch of wild rice. Parrots plucked the heads of the rice and sat on the tree to eat. Some of the grains fell into the water. Under the heat of the sun, the fruit, the seeds, and the grain fermented, and the liquid in the hollow became blood red.

In the hot season, flocks of thirsty birds went there to drink. Swiftly becoming intoxicated, they wildly spiraled upwards, only to fall drunkenly at the foot of the tree. After sleeping for a short time, they woke up and flew away, chirping merrily. A similar thing happened to monkeys and other tree-climbing animals.

The hunter observed all this and wondered, "What is in the hollow of that tree? It can't be poison. If it were, the birds and animals would die." He drank some of the liquid and became intoxicated the same as they had. As he drank, he felt a strong desire to eat meat. He kindled a small fire, wrung the necks of some of the partridges, squirrels, and other creatures lying unconscious at the foot of the tree, and roasted them over the coals. He drunkenly waved one hand as he stuffed his mouth with the other.

While he was drinking and eating, he remembered an ascetic named Varuna who lived nearby. Wishing to share his discovery with the ascetic,

Sura filled a bamboo tube with the liquor, wrapped up some of the roast meat, and set out for the ascetic's leaf hut. As soon as he arrived, he offered the ascetic some of the beverage, and both of them ate and drank with gusto.

The hunter and the ascetic realized that this drink could be the way to make their fortune. They poured it into large bamboo tubes, which they balanced on poles slung across their shoulders, and carried it to a border outpost of a nearby kingdom. From there, they sent a message to the king that drink-makers had arrived. When they were summoned, they took the alcohol to the capital and offered it to the king. The king took two or three drinks and became intoxicated. After a few days, he had consumed all that the two men had carried and asked if there was any more.

"Yes, Sire," they answered.

"Where?" asked the king.

"In the Himavat."

"Go and fetch it," ordered the king.

Sura and Varuna went back to the forest, but they soon realized how much trouble it was to return to the mountains every time they ran out. They took note of all the ingredients and gathered everything needed so that they were able to brew the alcohol in the city. The citizens began drinking liquor, forgot about their work, and became poor. The city soon looked like a ghost town.

At that point, the two drink-makers left and took their business to Bārānasi, where they sent a message to the king. There, too, the king summoned them and offered them support. As the habit of drinking spread, ordinary business deteriorated, and Bārānasi declined in the same way. Sura and Varuna next went to Sāketā, and, after abandoning Sāketā, proceeded to Sāvatthī.

At that time, the king of Sāvatthī was named Sabbamitta. He welcomed the two merchants and asked them what they wanted. They asked for large quantities of the main ingredients and five hundred huge jars. After everything had been combined, they put the mixture in the jars and tied a cat to each jar to guard against rats.

As the liquor fermented, it began to overflow. The cats happily lapped up the potent drink that ran down the sides, became thoroughly intoxicated, and lay down to sleep. Rats came and nibbled on their ears, noses, and tails.

The king's men were shocked and reported to the king that the cats tied to the jars had died from drinking the escaping liquid.

"Surely these men must be making poison!" the king concluded, and he immediately ordered them both beheaded. As Sura and Varuna were being executed, their last words were, "Sire, this is liquor! It is delicious!"

After putting the drink merchants to death, the king ordered that the jars be broken. By then, however, the effects of the alcohol had worn off, and the cats were playing merrily. The guards reported this to the king.

"If it had been poison," the king said, "the cats would have died. It may be delicious after all. Let us try it."

He ordered that the city be decorated and that a pavilion be set up in the courtyard. He took his seat on a royal throne under a white umbrella and, surrounded by his ministers, prepared to drink.

At that moment, as Sakka was surveying the world, he wondered, "Who is dutifully taking care of his parents? Who is conducting himself well in thought, word, and deed?"

When he saw the king seated in his royal pavilion, ready to drink the brew, he thought, "If King Sabbamitta drinks that liquor, the whole world will perish. I will make sure that he does not drink it."

Sakka instantly disguised himself as a brahmin and, carrying a jar full of liquor in the palm of his hand, appeared standing in the air in front of the king. "Buy this jar! Buy this jar!" he cried.

King Sabbamitta saw him and asked, "Where do you come from, Brahmin? Who are you? What is in that jar you have?"

"Listen!" Sakka replied. "This jar does not contain butter, oil, molasses, or honey. Listen to the innumerable vices that this jar holds.

"Whoever drinks this, poor silly fool, will lose control of himself until he stumbles on smooth ground and falls into a ditch or a cesspool. Under its influence, he will eat things he'd never touch in his right mind. Please buy it. It is for sale, this worst of jars!

"The contents of this jar will distract a man's wits until he behaves like a brute, giving his enemy the fun of laughing at him. It will enable him to sing and dance stupidly in front of an assembly. Please buy this wonderful liquor for the obscene gaiety it brings.

"Even the most bashful loses all modesty by drinking from this jar. The shyest man can forget the trouble of being dressed and can shamelessly run naked around the town. When he's tired, he'll happily rest anywhere, oblivious to danger or decency. Such is the nature of this drink. Please buy it. It is for sale, this worst of jars!

"When one drinks from this, he loses control of his body, tottering as if he cannot stand, trembling, jerking, and shaking like a wooden puppet worked by another's hand. Buy my jar. It's full of wine.

"The man who drinks from this is prey to every danger because he leaves his senses. Burning to death in bed, becoming the victim of jackals, drowning in a puddle, being reduced to bondage or penury—there is no misfortune that drinking this may not lead to.

"Imbibing this, men may lie senseless on the road, soiled with their own vomit, and licked by dogs. A woman may become so intoxicated that she will tie her beloved parents to a tree, revile her husband, and, in her blindness, even abuse or abandon her only child. Such is the merchandise contained in this jar.

"When a man drinks from this jar, he can believe that all the world is his and that he owes respect to no one. Buy this jar. It is filled to the brim with the strongest drink.

"Addicted to this drink, whole families of the highest class will squander their wealth and ruin their names. Buy this jar, Sire. It is for sale.

"In this jar is a liquid which makes tongue and feet lose control. It creates unreasoning laughter and weeping. It dulls the eye and impairs the mind. It makes a man contemptible.

"Drinking this will create strife. Friends will quarrel and come to blows. Even the old devas were susceptible and lost their heaven because of drink. Buy this jar, and taste the wine.

"Because of this beverage, falsehoods are spoken with pleasure, and forbidden actions are performed with joy. False courage will lead to danger, and friends will be betrayed. The man who drinks will dare any deed, unaware that he is dooming himself to hell. Try this drink, Sire. Buy my jar.

"The one who drinks this brew will sin in thought, word, and deed. He will see good as evil and evil as good. Even the most modest person will act indecently when drunk. The wisest man will babble foolishly. Buy this lovely liquid, and become addicted. You will grow accustomed to evil behavior, to lies, to abuse, to filth, and to disgrace.

"When thoroughly drunk, men are like oxen struck to the ground, collapsing, and lying in a heap. No human power can compete with the poisonous power of liquor. Buy my jar.

"In short, drinking this will destroy every virtue. It will banish shame, erode good conduct, and kill good reputation. It will defile and cloud the mind. If you can allow yourself to drink this intoxicating liquor, Sire, buy my jar."

When the king heard this, he realized the misery that would be caused by drinking alcohol. Overjoyed at being spared the danger, he wished to express his gratitude. "Brahmin!" he cried, "you have outdone even my mother and father in caring for me. In gratitude for your excellent words, let me give you five choice villages, one hundred serving women, seven hundred cows, and ten chariots with pure-bred horses. You have been a great teacher."

"As king of the devas," Sakka replied, revealing his identity, "I have no need of anything. You may keep your villages, servants, and cattle. Enjoy your delicious food, and be contented with sweet cakes. Take delight in the truths I've preached to you. In this way, you will be blameless in this world, and you will attain a glorious heavenly rebirth in the next."

With these words, Sakka returned to his own abode.

King Sabbamitta vowed to abstain from alcohol and ordered that the jars be smashed. From that day on, he kept the precepts and generously gave alms. He lived a good life and was, indeed, reborn in heaven.

Later, however, the habit of drinking alcohol spread across Jambudīpa, and many people were affected.

Having concluded his story, the Buddha identified the birth: "At that time, Ānanda was the king, and I was Sakka."

204
The Noble Six-Tusked Elephant
Chaddanta Jātaka

It was while staying at Jetavana that the Buddha told this story about a bhikkhunī.

One day, a young bhikkhunī, who had come from a good family of Sāvat-thī, went with some other bhikkhunīs to hear the Buddha teach. Impressed by his grace and beauty, she wondered whether she had been connected to the Buddha in a previous life. In a flash, she recollected that, in a previous life, the Bodhisatta had been the great white elephant Chaddanta and that she had been his wife. Remembering that, she felt great joy, and she laughed aloud. Then she realized that few wives are well-disposed to their husbands, and she wondered what kind of wife she had been. As the memory came back to her more clearly, she recalled that she had harbored a grudge against him and that, in another life, she had sent a hunter to kill him. Recalling that, she was overcome by sorrow, and she burst into tears.

The Buddha saw this and smiled. When the assembled bhikkhus asked him why he had smiled, he replied, "Bhikkhus, this young sister wept when she recalled an offense that she had committed against me." At their request, he told this story of the past.

Long, long ago, a herd of eight thousand royal elephants lived in a golden cave on the west side of Lake Chaddanta in the Himavat. At that time, the Bodhisatta was born as the son of the king of the elephants and was named Chaddanta. He was pure white, and, when he was full grown, he was magnificent, with a trunk like a silver rope and six beautiful tusks which emitted rays of six colors. When his father died, Chaddanta became king, and his two chief queens were named Mahā-Subhaddā and Culla-Subhaddā.

During the rainy season, all the elephants stayed in the golden cave, but in the hot season, Chaddanta enjoyed standing with his queens at the foot of a great banyan tree that grew at the north-east corner of the lake, where a cooling breeze blew off the water.

One day, while King Chaddanta was near the banyan tree, one of his followers told him that the trees in the great sal grove were in flower, and he went there with both queens. While they were grazing, Chaddanta happened to bump a sal tree with his massive forehead. This caused the branches of the great tree to shake, and Culla-Subhaddā, who was standing downwind, was showered with dry twigs and dead leaves which were covered with red ants. Mahā-Subhaddā, who was standing upwind, was showered with flowers, pollen, and green leaves. When Culla-Subhaddā saw Mahā-Subhaddā covered with golden pollen, she thought, "Obviously, he prefers her. He showers her with flowers and pollen, and lets dry twigs, dead leaves, and red ants fall on me!" This feeling developed into a grudge which she bore against Chaddanta. "I'll get even with him!" she swore silently to herself.

On another day, the herd of elephants went into the lake to bathe. First, two young elephants rubbed Chaddanta with roots. Then they bathed the two queens. Finally, the rest of the herd bathed themselves, played in the water, and gathered lotuses and water lilies to adorn Chaddanta and the queens.

One elephant plucked an unusual lotus stalk with seven perfect blossoms and offered it to Chaddanta, who sprinkled his forehead with it and presented it to Mahā-Subhaddā. This caused Culla-Subhaddā's resentment to increase.

Also living in this part of the Himavat was a group of five hundred Pacceka Buddhas whom Chaddanta often visited to pay his respects. One day, Chaddanta offered them a meal of lotus stalks sprinkled with nectar. At the same time, Culla-Subhaddā gave them some ripe fruit she had collected. As she made her offering to the Pacceka Buddhas, she made a fervent wish to be reborn as the daughter of a king so that she could marry the king of Kāsi. "When I become chief queen," she thought, "I will ask the king to send a hunter with a poisoned arrow to slay this elephant. Then I will have my sweet revenge!"

After making that cruel aspiration, Culla-Subhaddā stopped eating and pined herself to death. She was, indeed, reborn as the daughter of the king of Madda and was named Subhaddā. When she was of age, she married the king of Kāsi and became his chief queen. Recalling her former existence, she realized that, since all her wishes had been fulfilled, she was in a position to carry out her revenge. She rubbed her body with oil, put on a soiled robe, and lay in bed, pretending to be sick.

The king asked where she was and, hearing that she was ailing, entered her bedchamber. He sat on her bed, stroked her back, and asked, "My peerless queen, why are you so pale? Why are you fading?"

"My dear lord, I had a dream, because of which I have developed an intense desire, but I know that it is unattainable, so I will just waste away."

"My dear," replied the king, "anything that we can grant will be yours. Please tell us what it is that you desire so strongly. I'm sure we can get it for you."

"Sire, what I desire is not an easy thing to obtain. I will tell you, but it is better that I not tell you right away. Please summon all the hunters, and I will explain what it is in their presence."

"No easier said than done, my dear!" replied the king, delighted that this request was so easy. He immediately gathered all the hunters in Kāsi.

When the hunters were assembled in the courtyard, the king stood at an open window and called the queen. "Come, my dear! Here are our brave hunters, gathered according to your wish. They are skilled in tracking, fierce in fighting, and all are pledged to me."

The queen looked out the window and shouted, "Hunters! In my dream, I saw a great white elephant with six radiant tusks. So intense was my dream that now I must have those tusks. If any one of you can bring me those beautiful tusks, I will live! If not, I will die. Nothing else can save my life!"

In the courtyard, there was a murmur of voices. None of the hunters had ever seen or even heard of a six-tusked elephant. Through a spokesman, they asked the queen whether her dream had also revealed to her where such an elephant was to be found.

Queen Subhaddā surveyed all the hunters and, recollecting her previous birth, spied one who had also been an enemy of Chaddanta in the past. He was a strong and cruel hulking giant of a man named Sonuttara. His face was disfigured with scars, and his teeth were yellow. "This man will be able to do what I want," thought the queen. She pointed Sonuttara out to the king and asked permission to talk directly with him. The king agreed and asked Sonuttara to come inside the palace. The queen took him to a room on the highest floor of the palace, threw open a window to the north, and said,

"Due north, beyond those seven mountain ranges, you will find a golden cliff. In the cliff is a vast golden cave. Below the cliff, near a beautiful lake, is a huge banyan tree. In that area, there is a herd of eight thousand royal elephants. They are fierce and formidable. If these elephants see a man, they will charge and destroy him."

When Sonuttara heard this, he was frightened. He suggested that the queen might be satisfied with gold or pearls or turquoise rather than ivory.

"This has nothing to do with wanting ivory!" retorted the queen. "Don't mistake my motives! This is about spite! I have been injured, and I want revenge! Bring me the tusks of the leader of that herd, and you will have five choice villages as a reward!

"Friend hunter," she continued, "in my previous life, I was one of the chief queens of that royal elephant. When I made an offering to some Pacceka Buddhas, I wished for the power to kill that six-tusked elephant and to obtain his tusks. This is not a dream that I had; it is a reality that will be fulfilled. I can guarantee that you will succeed. Go, and have no fear!"

"So be it, Your Highness," replied Sonuttara, greatly heartened by the queen's explanation. "Tell me exactly how to find this beast you hate so much and how to capture him, and I will do it!"

"The king of the elephants takes a bath every day," she began, recalling details of her previous life, "at a spot in the lake near the banyan tree. After grazing near the banyan tree, he and his beloved mate will go there to bathe. Whenever possible, that royal elephant also pays his respects to yellow-robed ascetics and Pacceka Buddhas."

"Your Highness," Sonuttara replied, "I understand perfectly. I will kill that elephant, and I will bring you his tusks."

Delighted with Sonuttara's determination, the queen gave him one thousand coins and said, "Go home, and prepare yourself for your journey. I will supply you with all the tools you will need. Be ready to set out for the golden cliff in seven days."

The queen immediately set to work. She summoned smiths and ordered them to make special iron tools for Sonuttara. She told them to make an axe, a spade, an auger, a hammer, a bamboo cutter, a sickle, a staff tipped with adamantine, a peg, and a three-pronged grappling hook. She gave them the exact specifications for each tool and told them to have them all finished within six days. She summoned leather workers and ordered them to make a sack, about the size of a large water pot, a parachute, and an assortment of ropes and straps. She told them also to have everything ready in six days.

The smiths and leather workers finished their tasks in good time and delivered everything to the palace. The queen had all the tools packed in the leather sack and gathered all the provisions Sonuttara would need for the journey.

On the seventh day, Sonuttara returned to the palace and stood respectfully in the presence of the queen. She indicated the sack to him and said, "Friend, this sack contains all the tools you will need for your journey." With his stout arm, Sonuttara picked up the sack as if it were a mere trifle, and placed it on his hip. The queen gave all the provisions to the hunter's attendants to carry.

Sonuttara bowed to the king and the queen and set out in a chariot, followed by his attendants. When he reached the border of Kāsi, he sent the servants back and proceeded with several local men as guides. When he reached the jungle, he sent those men back and proceeded on alone. He had to cut his way through tracts of tall grass and reeds with the sickle. When he came to thickets of thorn, cane, and bamboo, he used the bamboo cutter. If a thicket was too dense for him to cut his way through, he made a bamboo ladder and climbed to the top. With great ingenuity, he laid down pieces of split bamboo and crawled along, pulling the pieces from behind and replacing them in front, until he reached the other side. Sometimes, the jungle was so thick that even a snake could not penetrate it. In that case, he felled trees with an axe. On the largest trees, he had to use the auger first. To keep from sinking in marshes of mud and quicksand, he used planks in the same way he had used split bamboo to cross the thickets. He fashioned a rude canoe and paddled through flooded swamps.

When Sonuttara reached the first great mountain, he attached a rope to the grappling hook and flung it as high as he could. When it was secure, he climbed up. He used the iron staff tipped with adamantine to drill a hole in the mountainside and hammered the peg into the hole. Then he stood on the peg and threw the grappling hook again. He repeated the process until he scaled the peak.

He descended in much the same way, sitting in the sack and lowering himself down, uncoiling the rope like a spider letting out its thread. Finally, he let his leather parachute catch the wind and floated down gently like a bird.

Having crossed so many kinds of terrain, including six mountain ranges, he climbed, at last, to the top of the golden cliff. In the distance, he could see the great banyan tree. Beneath it, he glimpsed the pure white six-tusked elephant with his queen, surrounded by his huge herd of royal elephants, ready for a fight. Before him lay the beautiful Lake Chaddanta, and, near the banyan tree, he could see the pleasant bathing pool.

From this vantage point, he watched the elephants for some time to familiarize himself with their habits and movements.

Descending to the jungle, he cut four trees to make sturdy posts and one more to make planks. When the elephants went to bathe, he took out his spade and started digging a square pit, big enough for him to hide inside, in the exact spot near the banyan tree where the king elephant always stood. He carefully sprinkled the earth he dug out on the water so that there was no pile to be seen. In each corner of the pit, he placed a stone as the base for a post. He used ropes to secure the posts and spread planks to form a roof. At one side, he left an entrance for himself. He also made a small hole the size of an arrow. Finally, he hid the planks beneath a layer of earth and leaves. He worked on the pit all night. At daybreak, when everything was ready, he put on the yellow robe of an ascetic, took his bow and one poisoned arrow, and descended into the pit.

As the great white elephant passed overhead, Sonuttara shot his poisoned arrow, and Chaddanta cried out in pain. The herd panicked and fled, crushing trees and trampling grass in their flight. Maddened with pain, Chaddanta looked around, ready to trample his attacker, but, when he spotted the yellow robe, he immediately controlled his anger and knelt in respect. At the same time, he realized that the man he saw had shot the arrow, and he declared, "One who is stained by evil, a stranger to truth and righteousness, has no right to wear the yellow robe. Only one who has renounced evil and upholds truth and righteousness should dare to don that robe. Why did you wound me?" he asked Sonuttara. "Did you act on your own, or has someone else set you at this evil task?"

"Subhaddā, queen of Kāsi, has sent me here to obtain your six radiant tusks to satisfy her longing."

Chaddanta immediately recognized the handiwork of his former wife Culla-Subhaddā. "The queen is not really interested in my tusks," he told Sonuttara. "She sent you here because she wants to kill me! I have a great store of ivory I could give you, but that wretched female wants my life instead. Go ahead! Saw off my tusks! Tell the shrew to be of good cheer, and let her know that the one she hates is dead." In spite of the excruciating pain, Chaddanta lay on his side, to make it easier for Sonuttara to cut off the tusks.

Sonuttara climbed out of the pit and picked up his saw. He approached the elephant, but Chaddanta was more like a mountain than an animal, and the hunter, even though he was a large man, could not reach the tusks from the ground. He climbed up the silver trunk and stood on Chaddanta's forehead. Unable to get at the tusks from there, he jumped down into the elephant's mouth, kicking him in the jaw and cutting into the flesh with his jagged saw. Chaddanta's mouth filled with blood. Sonuttara kept shifting from place to place, sawing here and there, trying to find the right angle to cut, but not succeeding. The pain he caused Chaddanta was a torment, but the great elephant endured it patiently.

Finally, he cried out to the hunter, "Sir, can't you just cut off the tusks?"

"No!" Sonuttara replied simply.

"All right," Chaddanta said with a feeble voice. "I am too weak now to raise my trunk, but if you will lift it up for me and let it seize the handle of the saw, I will do it for you." With the man's assistance, Chaddanta held the saw with his trunk and moved it back and forth until the tusks were severed.

When all six magnificent tusks were lying on the ground, Chaddanta said, "Don't misunderstand me, Friend. I am not giving you these tusks of mine because I do not value them, nor am I giving because I want to become Sakka, Māra, or Brahmā. To me, the tusks of omniscience are one hundred thousand times dearer than these ivory ones. May this meritorious act enable me to attain omniscience!"

Although Chaddanta's strength was rapidly fading and his voice was almost inaudible, he asked softly, "How long did it take you to reach here?"

"Seven years, seven months, and seven days," Sonuttara replied.

"By the power of these tusks," Chaddanta told him, "you will reach Bārānasi in seven days. Go quickly, and you will be safe. Farewell."

Sonuttara hurried away, and, even before Mahā-Subhaddā and the rest of the herd returned, Chaddanta died. When they found his body, all eight thousand royal elephants wept bitterly. Sorrowfully, they formed a solemn procession to the abode of the Pacceka Buddhas and announced, "Venerable Sirs, the noble elephant who took such joy in providing you with the requisites has been killed by a poisoned arrow, and his beautiful tusks have been cut off. Please come and see his body before we cremate it." The five hundred Pacceka Buddhas arrived just as two young elephants were lifting up Chaddanta's body. They adroitly manipulated it so that it appeared that their king was paying a final homage to the Pacceka Buddhas. Then they placed their king's body on the funeral pyre, and the Pacceka Buddhas chanted all night while it burned. When the flames were, at last, extinguished, the herd bathed and solemnly returned with Mahā-Subhadda at their head to their home in the golden cave.

Just as Chaddanta had told him he would, Sonuttara returned to Bārānasi in only seven days. When he was ushered into the queen's presence, he said, "Here are his tusks, Your Highness. The beast against whom you held a grudge is dead."

"Are you sure that he is dead?" the queen asked.

"Yes, Your Highness," Sonuttara assured her. "I killed him myself with a poisoned arrow."

She accepted those incomparable tusks, which were still emitting six-colored rays of light, and placed them on her lap. As she gazed at them, she recollected the one who, in a former existence, had been her husband and thought, "At my instigation, this cruel hunter has brought these tusks which have been cut from the auspicious elephant that he slaughtered with a poisoned arrow!" Suddenly, she was filled with a sorrow so great that she could not endure it. Her mind was completely overcome with grief. The poor fool's heart broke, and, right there, she died.

Having concluded his story, the Buddha taught the Dhamma, a multitude attained the first path, and, not long afterward, that bhikkhunī became an arahat. Then the Buddha identified the birth: "At that time, this bhikkhunī was Queen Subhaddā, Devadatta was the cruel hunter, and I was the noble Chaddanta."

205
It's All the King's Fault
Gandatindu Jātaka

It was while staying at Jetavana that the Buddha told this story about the king of Kosala.

One day, when King Pasenadi was visiting Jetavana, the Buddha counseled him. "Sire," he said, "a king should rule his kingdom with righteousness. If the king is immoral, the court officials are immoral, and the people suffer. A wicked person may accept bribes, but no bribe can postpone death. No one can escape death, and, as for rebirth, one has no support other than his own virtuous actions. Even when there was no Buddha Sāsana in the world, a king who followed wise advice governed righteously, and was reborn in heaven." Then he told this story of the past.

Long, long ago, when Pañcāla was reigning in Kampilla, the entire kingdom of Uttarapañcāla was in a terrible condition. The king was an unjust monarch with evil habits. The king's ministers were also corrupt, and the people were unbearably oppressed by excessive taxation. Afraid that, if their property were well-kept, they would be more heavily taxed, citizens allowed their houses to fall into disrepair. In what had been prosperous villages, only ramshackle huts remained.

At festival time each year, King Pañcāla made lavish offerings to the deva of a particular tinduka tree just outside the city. That deva, being well aware of the situation in the country, pitied the people and wished to help them. "This king is terrible!" he thought. "His kingdom is deteriorating rapidly, and only I can correct him. Because he honors me with generous offerings, I owe it to him to advise him well."

That night, the deva stood in the air at the head of the king's bed and emitted a beautiful aura. The king was startled by the bright light and asked who was there.

"Sire, I am the deva of the tinduka tree. I have come to give you some counsel."

"What advice do you have for me?" asked the king.

"Sire, because of your negligence, the kingdom is rapidly going to ruin. If you continue acting in the way you are now, you will soon have nothing to give your sons. If you lose your domain, you will lose your reputation, as well. The whole world will scorn you. Furthermore, not only do careless kings lose their kingdoms, but, after they die, they are reborn in hell. Diligence leads to heaven, but laziness leads to hell. If you accept the truth, you may change your fortune. You must change your ways and preserve your realm."

The deva disappeared, but the king was deeply shaken. He certainly believed what the deva had said regarding heaven and hell, but he wondered whether the situation in his kingdom was really as bad as all that. He decided to find out for himself. The next morning, he gave his ministers authority over the kingdom, and, disguised as an ordinary traveler, he left the capital with only one brahmin advisor.

Not far from the city, they came to a village where almost all the houses looked empty, with brambles piled all around them. They saw one old man carrying bundles of brambles. As soon as his wife and children were safely out of the house, he locked the door and spread the brambles in front of the house. Then the whole family hurried away to the forest. The king and his advisor sat down to see what would happen. A little later, soldiers arrived and patrolled the streets, and court officials wandered from house to house. In the evening, as soon as the soldiers and officials had left, the citizens returned from the forest. As the old man approached his door, he stepped on a sharp thorn, which punctured his foot. He sat on the doorstep, and, as he pulled out the thorn, he loudly cursed the king. "Just as I am suffering from this thorn," he cried, "let the king be struck by an arrow and cry from pain."

The brahmin walked over to where the man was sitting and said, "My good man, you are old, and your eyes are weak. What does your being injured by a thorn have to do with the king?"

The old man answered angrily, "It's because of the king that I am racked with pain. Every day, the king's tax collectors harass us. The only way we can avoid them is to hide in the forest all day. Because we are also beset by thieves, we have to protect our homes by scattering these thorns all around."

"What the old man says is true," the king said to the brahmin. "It really is my fault. I must go back and rule justly."

The deva was pleased to hear this, but he wanted the king to learn more, so he caused the brahmin to protest. "Sire," said the brahmin, "don't be hasty. Let's investigate the situation further."

The king agreed, and they went on to another village. At one house, they saw a poor old woman who was telling her two grown daughters that it was too dangerous for them to go to the forest and that she would gather firewood herself. The king watched her climb a tree to get some dead branches, but, unfortunately, she slipped and fell out of the tree. Lying on the ground in great pain, she loudly cursed the king, "Oh, when will this king die? As long as he lives, my daughters will remain unmarried!"

The brahmin went up to her and said, "My good woman, you are being unfair! Surely, you can't expect the king to find a husband for every single young woman in the kingdom."

The poor woman indignantly replied, "My words are true and fair. We ordinary folk are defenseless, harassed by thieves and oppressed by tax collectors. In times like this, marriage is out of the question for poor young women. With no husbands to protect them, they're unhappy, and we are all miserable!"

Hearing this, the king thought, "She has a very good point."

Next, they came upon a farmer plowing his field. As he was turning around at the edge of his field, the plowshare struck his ox's leg. As he examined the ox's bloody leg, the farmer cried, "May the king be felled by his enemy's spear just as my poor ox was wounded by this plowshare."

The brahmin went up to him and said, "You have no reason to be angry with the king. You were the one plowing, so it is your fault."

"I'm angry with the king with good cause," replied the farmer heatedly. "We common folk are defenseless. At night, we're attacked by thieves, and, during the day, we're hounded by tax collectors. Today, the king's men even confiscated my lunch packet, so my cook is preparing a second lunch for me. It's late, and she hasn't brought it yet. I'm so weak with hunger that I slipped, and my ox was injured."

"He's right!" the king said.

Early the next morning, they came to another village where they saw a farmer milking a cow. Suddenly, the vicious cow kicked the farmer, knocking him over, upsetting his stool, tipping over the pail, and spilling the milk. "May the king fall in battle!" the man swore loudly. "May he be cut down by a sword, just as I have been felled by the kick of this cursed cow!"

The brahmin went up to the farmer and said, "My good man, cows often kick while being milked. What does that have to do with the king? Why do you abuse him?"

"The king is clearly to blame," the farmer insisted, "for defenseless folk are cruelly oppressed in his realm. Some of our dairy cows have been confiscated. Others we have had to sell to get money to pay taxes. Now, here I am trying to milk a wild cow that isn't used to being milked! Our daily life is in disarray, and it is all the fault of the king!"

"He speaks the truth," the king said to the brahmin, as they turned onto a path leading to the highway back to Kampilla.

On their way back to the capital, as they were passing through another small village, they heard the mournful bawl of a cow. Following the sound, they came upon the creature, lowing inconsolably. There was plenty of grass and water for her, but she wasn't grazing. Upset by her suffering, some village boys cried, "Let the king be childless! Let him weep and moan just like this poor cow, mourning her dead calf!"

The brahmin went up to them and said, "Boys, when a beast strays from the herd and lows to express its distress, what does that have to do with the palace? Why do you curse the king?"

"The king's sin in this case is very clear, Brahmin," the boys answered sharply. "We are always being oppressed by the king's tax collectors who take whatever they wish with impunity. Some of the king's men just killed this poor cow's dappled calf and stripped off its skin to make a sword-sheath. Why should a healthy newborn calf be killed, just for a sheath for a knife?"

"We were wrong," the king said. "You speak the truth."

A little later, they came to a dried-up pond where crows were killing frogs with their sharp beaks and devouring them. The deva caused the king and his advisor to understand the speech of the frogs. "Let the king and his whole family be killed in a fight and eaten," one big frog cried, "just as we poor frogs are being consumed by vicious crows!"

"Frog," the brahmin called out, "a king cannot be expected to guard every creature in his kingdom. It's certainly not the king's fault that crows eat living things like you when they get the chance."

"You are much too flattering to the king," the frog replied. "If the ruler were righteous, his realm would be peaceful, happy, and prosperous. Crows would enjoy the offerings left at local shrines, and they would have no need to kill us poor frogs."

The brahmin and the king shook their heads sadly and said to each other, "All creatures, down to the very frogs, curse us!"

Shaken by this revelation, the king and his adviser made their way quickly back to Kampilla. The king resolved to give up his bad habits and to rule righteously. He exhorted everyone in his court to stop their corrupt practices and to live virtuously. From then on, following the advice of the deva of the tinduka tree, the king and all the courtiers devoted themselves to generosity and other meritorious deeds.

Having concluded his story, the Buddha said once more to King Pasenadi, "Sire, a king should abandon evil and rule his kingdom with righteousness." Then the Buddha identified the birth: "At that time, I was the deva of the tinduka tree."

206

The Taming of the Beauty
Kusa Jātaka

It was while staying at Jetavana that the Buddha told this story about a discontented bhikkhu.

One day, while this bhikkhu was walking on his almsrounds in Sāvatthī, he encountered a beautiful woman and became infatuated. Overwhelmed by passion, he neglected himself. He began wearing dirty robes and letting his nails and hair grow. He pined away and became sallow until his veins stood out. He appeared jaundiced, weak, and ill. In the same way that a deva who is approaching the end of his heavenly existence exhibits five clear signs, so does a bhikkhu who is in danger of giving up his practice. The deva's heavenly garland withers; the bhikkhu's faith fades. The deva's robe becomes soiled; the bhikkhu's morality is stained. The deva's body loses its beauty; the bhikkhu's discontent mars his features. The deva's body is soaked with perspiration; the bhikkhu becomes mired in corruption. The deva no longer takes pleasure in his heavenly abode; the bhikkhu no longer delights in solitude. When all of these unhappy signs became evident in that bhikkhu, his friends took him to the Buddha.

When he confessed to the Buddha that he was discontented, the Buddha said, "Bhikkhu, do not be a slave of passion. This is a wicked woman.

Conquer your passion for her, and take pleasure again in the Dhamma and the Discipline. In the past, because a man fell in love with a woman, he abandoned his spiritual quest and spent his life mired in the world." Then he told this story of the past.

Long, long ago, when Okkāka was reigning in Kusāvatī,[7] the capital of the Malla kingdom, his queen consort was Sīlavatī. The king ruled righteously, but he had no children. The citizens were worried that, without an heir, the kingdom was in danger. When they gathered and complained to the king, he opened his palace window and said, "No one in the kingdom is behaving wickedly. I am ruling well. Why are you reproaching me for wrongdoing?"

"Sire," the spokesmen replied, "no one is behaving wickedly, but we are concerned that, without an heir to inherit the throne, a stranger might come and seize the kingdom. We urge you to do everything in your power to produce a son who can rule your kingdom after you."

"What should I do?" asked the king.

"Sire," the spokesman replied, "first, send some of the dancing women of the palace into the street every day for a week. Declare that their performance is a religious act, sanctioned by piety. If any of them conceives and delivers a son, he can be appointed crown prince."

The king accepted the suggestion and chose several of the most beautiful and seductive dancing women, but none of them conceived.

The committee of citizens next suggested sending some women of good standing from the court into the street, and the king agreed, but none of these women conceived.

The committee of citizens suggested sending some women of the highest rank from the harem, and the king agreed, but none of these women conceived.

"Alas!" the king despaired. "It seems that I will never have a son!" The citizenry again began clamoring in front of the palace, demanding that the king do something to produce an heir to the throne.

"Please!" the king pleaded. "I have sent innumerable women from the palace into the streets, but not one of them has conceived. What more can I do?"

"Sire," the spokesman replied, "surely, none of those women had enough merit to conceive a son. There is, however, one virtuous lady in the palace. You must now send the queen consort, Sīlavatī, into the streets. She will surely have a son!"

Seeing no alternative, the king agreed to this demand. For seven days, he had it proclaimed by beat of a drum that, on a certain auspicious day, Queen

---

7   Kusinārā, the city where the Buddha entered Parinibbāna.

Sīlavatī would descend to the street for a religious ceremony to produce an heir. All men who wished to participate were to gather in front of the palace.

On the appointed day, a large crowd of men, freshly bathed and handsomely dressed, had assembled, waiting for the queen. Each man was eager to make love to the queen in performance of his duty to the king.

As the beautiful queen, wearing a gorgeous gown of silk, was carried on an elegant couch down the steps of the palace, Sakka's marble throne showed signs of heat. Sakka immediately realized that this was because of the great virtue of the queen who was desirous of a son. "I will grant her wish!" Sakka declared. "Who is worthy to be her son?" he wondered. "Of course, it must be the Bodhisatta, who is nearing the end of his existence in Tāvatimsa!" Although the Bodhisatta was expecting to be reborn in a higher heaven, Sakka prevailed upon him, for the welfare of the world, to go instead to the realm of men, to be conceived by Queen Sīlavatī, and to become heir to King Okkāka's throne.

So that no man could take advantage of the virtuous queen, Sakka, disguised as an elderly brahmin, appeared in the midst of that crowd of stalwart men. When all the others saw him, they began to laugh. They mocked his advanced age and cheap clothes and asked why he had bothered to come.

"Why pick on me?" Sakka retorted. "I may look like an old man, but my passion and my virility are still healthy and strong. You will see that I am more worthy than any of you!" Using his supernatural power, Sakka advanced to the front of the crowd, and, at the instant that the queen's couch touched the ground, he took her hand and led her away.

"Look at that old brahmin!" cried some of the men. "What is he doing? Where is he taking the queen?" shouted others. "Shame on him! Why doesn't he act his age?" cried many more. They were all outraged to have been denied their pleasure, but they had to admit that the queen was gone. Watching from the window of the palace, the king had also seen the old brahmin lead the queen away and was highly displeased.

Escaping swiftly with the queen through the city gate, Sakka caused a house to appear. Its door was open, and the queen could see a pile of sticks inside. "Is this your house?" she asked scornfully, still believing that he was an old and poor brahmin.

"Yes, Lady," Sakka answered softly. "I used to stay here alone, but now there are two of us! Please rest for a while on this bed of sticks, and I will fetch some rice for a meal. He gently touched her with his hand, which sent a divine thrill through her body, and she lost consciousness. Sakka instantly conveyed her to Tāvatimsa and laid her gently on a divine couch in his magnificent palace. On the seventh day, she awoke and, beholding the splendor around her, realized that her captor was not an old brahmin at all, but Sakka himself.

When she opened her eyes, Sakka was sitting at the foot of a glorious coral tree, surrounded by heavenly musicians. Rising from her couch, Queen Sīlavatī approached, saluted him, and sat respectfully on one side. "Sīlavatī," Sakka said, "I offer you a boon. Choose what you most desire!"

"Sire," she replied without hesitation, "grant me a son."

"Of course, Madam," Sakka said, "but not just one; I will give you two sons. One of them will be ugly but wise, and the other will be handsome but dull. Which one do you wish to have first?"

"Please let me have the wise one first, Your Majesty," she requested.

"Granted," said Sakka. He gave her a sprig of kusa grass, a heavenly robe, sandalwood, a flower from the coral tree, and a lute called Kokanada.

"Your Highness," Sakka said, "it is time for you to return to the palace." He transported her to the king's bedchamber, laid her beside the sleeping king, and gently touched her with his finger. With that touch, the Bodhisatta was conceived in her womb.

Queen Sīlavatī immediately knew that she was pregnant. When the king woke, he was surprised to see her and asked her how she had returned.

"Sakka brought me back, Sire."

"With my own eyes I saw an old brahmin take you away. Why are you trying to deceive me with this talk of Sakka?"

"Believe me, Sire," she insisted. "That brahmin was Sakka, and he took me to Tāvatimsa."

"My dear," retorted the king, "how can I believe such an incredible story?"

Queen Sīlavatī showed him the kusa grass and said, "This was a gift from Sakka."

"My dear," said the king, "kusa grass grows everywhere in Jambudīpa."

"Well, look at this!" she said, throwing off the covers. "This robe was also a gift from Sakka."

The king was dazzled. "My dear!" he exclaimed. "Surely only Sakka could have given you such an exquisite robe. Please forgive me!" After a pause, he said, "But the question remains. Are you expecting a child?"

"Yes, Your Majesty," she announced, "I am pregnant, at last, and it will be a son!"

The king was so happy at hearing this that words failed him. He quickly busied himself making sure that the queen was comfortable. He called the servants and ordered that everything be done to care for his expectant queen and her unborn son.

After ten lunar months Queen Sīlavatī delivered a son. The king and queen named him Kusa after the grass which she had received from Sakka. As Sakka had predicted, the boy was extremely ugly. While Prince Kusa was still a toddler, the queen gave birth to a second son. This boy was very handsome, and they named him Jayampati.

After having waited so long for an heir, the king made every effort to ensure that the boys were well brought up and properly trained. Of course, Prince Kusa, though he remained ugly, was so clever that he needed no teacher at all. He had an innate ability to master every subject and every skill effortlessly. Jayampati, on the other hand, though he seemed to become more handsome every day, was unable to learn anything or to master any skill, even under the very best teachers.

One day, when Kusa was sixteen years old, King Okkāka announced to the queen, "My dear, we are getting old. I would like to retire and to present the royal umbrella to your elder son. As soon as he is married, we can hold a grand festival to celebrate his coronation. Please ask your son whether there is any princess he favors. Let us begin the search for a suitable bride for him and bring her to Kusāvatī to be his queen."

Queen Sīlavatī readily agreed and sent a trusted maid to discuss the issue with the prince. When Prince Kusa learned of the king's intention, he thought, "I am ugly. No beautiful princess is going to want to be my bride. Anyone my parents might bring will take one look at me and run away! That would be mortifying for the whole family and would bring shame on the kingdom. Since I can never marry, I should not be king! After all, what is the household life to me? I will dutifully look after my parents as long as they live, and, at their death, I will renounce the world and become an ascetic!" Aloud he said to the maid, "Please tell my parents that I do not wish to marry. I have no need of a kingdom nor of any festivities. When my parents pass away, I will leave Kusāvatī and take up an ascetic life."

The maid repeated this message to the king and the queen, but they were terribly disappointed and refused to accept his decision. After a few days, the king asked his son to reconsider, but the prince refused. Three times, the king begged him to allow them to choose a bride for him and to accept the crown, and, three times, Prince Kusa refused. The fourth time the king asked, the prince thought, "It is hardly proper for me so adamantly to oppose my parent's wishes. Let me see if I can find a way to arrange it so that I am not so strongly refusing to obey them." He summoned the royal goldsmith, gave him a large quantity of gold, and commissioned him to make a golden image of a beautiful woman.

As soon as the goldsmith left, Prince Kusa took the same amount of gold and fashioned a statue himself. This statue was not only perfectly lifelike, but the young woman it depicted was supremely beautiful. He dressed the image in fine linen and placed in his own chamber.

When the goldsmith proudly brought his handiwork, Prince Kusa criticized it, and told the man to fetch the statue from his royal chamber. The goldsmith went to the room and opened the door. As soon as he saw the statue, he closed the door in embarrassment, thinking he had intruded upon a deva, who was waiting to take her pleasure with the prince.

"Your Highness," the goldsmith whispered to the prince, "there is a beautiful deva waiting for you in your chamber. I didn't dare to go inside."

"Friend," the prince said laughingly, "that is just a statue. Go back to my room, and bring it to me."

Having assured himself that his own statue was perfect, the prince ordered the goldsmith to put the inferior image in a storeroom. He had servants dress the beautiful statue in a silk sari and place it in a carriage. Then he sent it to the queen with a message: "Dear Mother, this is an image of the woman who will be my bride. When you find her, I will marry her." He was sure that his parents would never find a woman as beautiful as the statue, and he was pleased that he would no longer have to reject their proposal.

The queen summoned some advisors and told them, "My elder son, who will become king, was a gift from Sakka and has great merit. He must have a queen worthy of him!" Showing them the golden statue, she said, "This is an image of the woman who will be his bride. She is surely a princess. Take this golden statue to all the kingdoms of Jambudīpa. When you discover the woman it depicts, present the statue to her father and say, 'King Okkāka wishes your daughter to marry his elder son and to become the queen of Malla.' As soon as you return with the news, the king and I will go ourselves to arrange the nuptials."

The advisors placed the golden image in a closed carriage and left Kusāvatī with a large entourage. In each royal city they visited, they dressed the image in an exquisite silk sari, draped it with garlands, placed it in on a golden stand beside the path to the tank. The advisors stood unobtrusively nearby so that they could hear what people said as they passed by.

The statue was so striking that everyone noticed it, but no one dreamed that it was not a real woman. Some addressed her in a friendly manner, and others whispered so that she would not hear. "Look at that young woman. She looks like a deva!" "Why is she waiting there?" "I wonder where she's from." "It's a pity we have no one to compare with her in our city!" When the advisors heard such remarks, they knew that there was no likely candidate there. As soon as it was dark, they put the image back in the closed carriage and moved to the next capital.

In their wanderings, they reached Sāgala, the capital of Madda. They set up the golden statue as they had done before and stood aside to watch and to listen.

The king of Madda had eight extraordinarily lovely daughters, of which the eldest and by far the most beautiful was Princess Pabhāvatī. Princess Pabhāvatī was so beautiful that her body gave off a captivating radiance. The princess had a hunchbacked nurse, who was her special attendant. That evening, the nurse went with eight maids carrying water pots to fetch water for the princess' shampoo and bath. On her way to the tank, the nurse caught sight of the golden image and, thinking that it was Pabhāvatī, exclaimed, "Look at that ill-behaved girl, sending us to fetch water and then hurrying ahead of us to the tank!" Rushing over to the image, she cried, "Look at you, going out on your own! Your father would be furious!" She reached out and slapped the statue on the cheek, tearing a hole in the soft gold. Shocked to discover that it was only a statue, she started laughing. "Look at what I did!" she shouted to the maids. "I thought that this was my naughty daughter, so I slapped her. But it's only a statue, and now I can see that it is not nearly so beautiful! I've broken it, and I even hurt my hand doing so!"

The advisors quickly confronted the nurse, and one of them asked, "Madam, are you claiming that your daughter is more beautiful than this image?"

"Yes, I am, young man! When I first saw this statue, I thought it was my daughter. Of course, by 'my daughter,' I mean the eldest daughter of our king. She is the most beautiful woman in Jambudīpa, and this statue, even though it's pure gold, doesn't hold a candle to her!"

The advisors were delighted that their long journey seemed to be ending successfully. They replaced the statue in the covered carriage, took it to the palace, and asked to see the king. After greeting him, they said, "Your Majesty, King Okkāka wishes your daughter, Princess Pabhāvatī, to marry his elder son and to become the queen of Malla. We are prepared to offer this golden statue as a present from the king."

The king felt that an alliance with the king of Malla would be highly advantageous and was happy to accept their proposal. The advisors announced that they had to return to Kusāvatī, but they promised that their king and queen would come to arrange the nuptials. After offering them generous hospitality, the king let them go.

King Okkāka and Queen Sīlavatī were overjoyed and set out immediately with a great retinue for Sāgala. When they arrived, they were met with great honor and lavishly entertained. Queen Sīlavatī was anxious about her son's future and asked to see her daughter-in-law. Pabhāvatī, magnificently attired, came and greeted her mother-in-law. As soon as the queen saw the princess, she thought, "What a strikingly beautiful young woman! If she sees my ugly son, she will surely run away. I must find a way to keep her, despite his ugliness." Aloud, she said, "Sire, my daughter-in-law is quite worthy of my son. We are pleased, but in our royal family, there is a tradition. If your daughter is willing to abide by this tradition, we will take her to Kusāvatī."

"And what might this tradition be?" the king inquired.

"In our family," the queen said, "a man and his wife, in this case, the king and the queen, are not permitted to see each other's faces until the woman has conceived. This tradition must be strictly kept. Of course, one hopes that this will not last long."

"My dear Pabhāvatī, can you accept this condition?" the king asked his daughter.

"Yes, Father, I can," she replied.

Both families were extremely pleased. King Okkāka and Queen Sīlavatī gave many rich presents to Pabhāvatī's parents and escorted her to Kusāvatī, which was gloriously decorated for the coronation and the royal wedding. To commemorate the occasion, all prisoners throughout the kingdom were released. At the end of the festivities, Kusa was declared king, and Pabhāvatī became his queen consort.

Forced to follow the queen mother's scheme, Kusa and Pabhāvatī were not allowed to see each other. Each evening, after Queen Pabhāvatī had climbed into bed, the lights were put out, and King Kusa entered the chamber. They were together at night, but, before dawn, he had to leave. After a few days, Kusa told his mother that he wanted to see Pabhāvatī, but she refused, reminding him that the queen had not yet conceived. Again and again, he begged, and finally, due to a mother's tenderness, she relented. "Tomorrow, disguise yourself as a mahout, and wait in the elephant stables." she said. "I will take Pabhāvatī there, and you can surreptitiously gaze upon her to your heart's content. You must be very careful, however, not to let her know who you are!" Very excited, Kusa readily agreed.

The next day, as she had promised, Sīlavatī suggested that Pabhāvatī accompany her to inspect the royal elephants. As the queen mother led Pabhāvatī through the stables, she pointed to each tusker and gave his name. After they had passed the spot where Kusa was sitting in the straw, he tossed a piece of dried elephant dung, which struck Pabhāvatī on the back. Instantly, she turned, showing her full face, absolutely radiant, in spite of her anger. She realized who had thrown the filth at her and scowled furiously. "I'll get the king to cut off your hand!" she cried. Sīlavatī tried to placate her daughter-in-law by rubbing her back, and the two women quickly left the stables.

Thoroughly captivated by Pabhāvatī's beauty, Kusa wanted to see her again, so he told his mother that he would wait in the horse stable. When his mother led the queen into the stable, Kusa pulled the same trick with a piece of dried manure, and Pabhāvatī reacted in the same way. Sīlavatī again tried to calm her, and they hurried away.

The next day, Pabhāvatī told her mother-in-law that she longed to see Kusa, but Sīlavatī refused, reminding her that she had not yet conceived. Pabhāvatī begged again and again, and, finally, Sīlavatī said, "All right, tomorrow, there will be a royal procession through the city. You may stand at your open window. You will see the king sitting on his royal elephant."

Sīlavatī summoned her two sons and arranged that the handsome Prince Jayampati, dressed in elegant robes, would sit in the royal seat atop the elephant, and that King Kusa, disguised as a mahout, would sit behind him. As the procession passed the palace, she said to Pabhāvatī, "Behold the glory of your lord!"

Gazing at Jayampati, Pabhāvatī murmured, "Ah, yes, indeed! I have a husband not unworthy of me!" At the same time, King Kusa was gazing intently at his elegant queen. Transported by her radiant face, he exuberantly gestured at her. After the procession had passed, the queen mother asked Pabhāvatī whether she had indeed seen her husband. "Yes, Madam, I did, but that ugly and uncouth mahout we saw in the stables was sitting behind him. It seemed that the mahout was waving at me. Why is such an inauspicious creature allowed to sit so close to the king?"

"It is desirable, my dear, to have a guard behind the king," the queen mother explained.

"That mahout is too bold!" Pabhāvatī thought. "He doesn't act like a servant at all! I wonder whether he is actually King Kusa? He is certainly hideous, and, if, indeed, he is the king, that is why they won't let me see him!"

To confirm her suspicion, she sent her nurse to follow the procession and to find out whether the real king was sitting in front or behind.

"My dear," asked the nurse, "how can I tell?"

"The one who gets down from the elephant first is surely the king," Pabhāvatī told her.

The nurse hurried out and saw Kusa get off first, followed by Jayampati.

As he was climbing down, King Kusa noticed that the hunchbacked old woman was watching closely and guessed why she was there. He summoned her and strictly ordered her not to reveal his secret. When the nurse returned to her mistress' chamber, she reported, "My dear, the handsome man who sat in front got down first." Pabhāvatī believed her and was reassured.

Days passed, and the royal couple were still separated during the daylight hours. Kusa once more begged his mother to arrange for him to see Pabhāvatī. Unable to refuse, Sīlavatī agreed on the royal garden. The next day, Kusa concealed himself behind a particularly large lotus flower and waited. In the evening, Sīlavatī led Pabhāvatī on a tour of the garden, pointing out various trees and flowers. When they reached the lotus pond, where lotuses of the five colors were blooming, the water looked so enticing that Pabhāvatī took a notion to bathe, and she stepped with her attendants into the water. She noticed the magnificent lotus and stretched out her hand to pick it. At that instant, Kusa pushed the flower aside, and grasped Pabhāvatī's hand. When she saw his face, she screamed, "Help! A monster has caught me!"

The king shouted "I am King Kusa!" and she fainted. As she fell, Kusa released her hand and ran away. On recovering consciousness, she reflected, "That was King Kusa who grabbed my hand. I heard him shout. He was the same one who threw dung at me in the elephant stable and manure in the horse stable. He was sitting behind that handsome man in the procession and made fun of me! He must have met my nurse and told her not to tell me the truth. He is ugly and repulsive! I will not be stuck with such a hideous and obnoxious husband! I won't stay here another instant. I'll try to find a way to marry someone else!"

She ordered the advisors who had come with her from Sāgala to prepare her chariot. "I will leave today!" she told them. "I must get away from here!"

When they informed King Kusa of this, he thought, "Let her go! If I tried to keep her here, her heart would break. I will find a way to bring her back!"

Pabhāvatī returned to her father's palace in Sāgala, and Kusa was left to spend lonely nights in Kusāvatī.[8]

---

8   This situation was the result of actions the two of them had taken in a previous existence. Long before, in a suburb of Bārānasi, one family had two sons, and another family
had a daughter. The girl married the elder brother, but the younger brother remained single
and, after their parents died, continued living with his brother and his sister-in-law. One
day, the wife baked some delicious cakes. The younger brother was in the forest, so a cake
was put aside for him. When a Pacceka Buddha came to the door for alms, the wife placed
her brother-in-law's cake in his almsbowl. Just then, the younger brother returned and asked
for his cake. "Brother, don't be angry," she said. "I have given your cake to that Pacceka
Buddha. I'll bake you another one!" His temper flared, and he shouted, "After eating your
own cakes, you give mine away!" Hurrying after the Pacceka Buddha, he took the cake out
of his bowl. Mortified, the wife invited the Pacceka Buddha to her mother's house and filled
his bowl with fresh ghee. As the ghee in the bowl glowed in the sunlight, she made the
aspiration, "Wherever I am born, may my body be as radiant as this, may I be incomparably
beautiful, and may I never have to live with this rude fellow again!" The young brother-in-
law realized the severity of what he had done and dropped the cake back into the Pacceka

Kusa was so overcome with grief at Pabhāvatī's leaving him that his attendants could not look him in the eye. Without her radiant beauty, his palace seemed a desolate prison. All day, he languished in his chamber, moaning, "By this time she has reached the border; by now she is back in Sāgala." Unable to endure the separation, he went to his mother and declared, "Dear Mother, I am going to bring Pabhāvatī back. Until I come back, you are to rule in my place."

The next morning, his mother prepared delicious food for his journey and placed it in a golden bowl. As she gave him the bowl, she warned him that women could be devious, so he had to be careful. Kusa paid his respects to his mother and solemnly said, "If I'm still alive, I will see you again!" After arming himself with the five weapons, he put the Kokanada lute from Sakka in a bag with one thousand coins and set out.

Being strong and vigorous, Kusa traveled fifty yojanas by noon, stopped for lunch, traveled another fifty yojanas, and reached the gate of Sāgala by nightfall. Exhausted after his hard journey, he bathed and refreshed himself before entering the city. As soon as he stepped through the city gate, by the power of his virtue, Pabhāvatī was disturbed. Unable to stay on her couch, she got up and lay on the floor.

As he was wandering the streets, a local woman noticed him and invited him to rest in her house. She washed his feet and offered him a bed to rest on while she fixed a meal for him. Pleased with her kind hospitality, he gave her the one thousand coins. Leaving his weapons and the bag at her house, he went to the elephant stables with his lute.

"If you let me stay here," Kusa proposed to the mahouts, "I will play music for you." They readily agreed and gave him a corner in which to sleep. After a good rest, he sat up and began playing the lute and singing. The music from the divine lute filled the city, and everyone could hear it. As soon as Pabhāvatī heard it, she thought, "That music can come from no lute but his! King Kusa has come to Sāgala to find me!"

The king was enraptured by the music and thought, "I must have that musician for my minstrel! Tomorrow, I will send for him!"

Kusa, however, felt that he had chosen the wrong place. "If I stay here," he thought, "I will never get even a glimpse of Pabhāvatī!" At daybreak, he had breakfast in an eating house, sought out the workshop of the royal potter, and became his apprentice. One day, he carried a large basket of clay to the workshop and was given permission to make his own pots. Kusa was so

---

Buddha's bowl. As he did so, he made the aspiration, "In the future, even though this woman lives one hundred yojanas away, may I have the power to carry her off as my bride." Thus, in this life, she would have nothing to do with him. Because he had angrily taken the cake, he was born ugly.

naturally skillful that, as he sat at the potter's wheel, he quickly threw all sorts of pots, both large and small. He fashioned one exquisite pot especially for Pabhāvatī, decorating it with intricate figures which only she would recognize. By the time he had finished, the shop was full of pots. After they had all been glazed and fired, the potter took some of them, including the special pot, to the palace.

The king took one look at the pots and asked who had thrown them.

"I did, Sire," the potter replied.

"Don't try to fool me!" exclaimed the king. "I have seen your work, and I am quite sure that you did not make these pots. Who did?"

"Actually, Sire, my apprentice made them," the potter admitted.

"Your apprentice?" snapped the king. "You should call him your master! Learn your trade from him, and, from now on, let him make all the pottery for my daughters." He handed the potter a sack of money and said, "Give your pots to my daughters, and give that skillful man these one thousand coins."

At the apartments of the princesses, the potter presented the pots and said, "Your Highnesses, these were made for your pleasure."

When he handed Pabhāvatī the special pot, she recognized her own likeness and that of her hunchbacked nurse and knew at once who had made it. She angrily returned it to the potter and cried, "I don't want that! Take it away, and give it to someone else!"

Her sisters laughed and teased her. "You must think that King Kusa made that!" they said. "The potter made it, silly! It's beautiful! You should keep it!" Pabhāvatī did not tell them that she knew that Kusa was there and that he really had made it.

While Kusa was waiting for the potter to return, he realized that, again, he was in the wrong place to be able to see Pabhāvatī. The potter gave Kusa the money and told him that the king was extremely pleased with his work and had ordered that he make all the pots for the princesses, but Kusa apologized and told the potter to keep the money.

He left and became the apprentice to the royal basket maker. After quickly mastering this new craft, Kusa wove a number of baskets for the princesses. Then he fashioned a gorgeous palm-leaf fan for Pabhāvatī on which he depicted Pabhāvatī herself as queen standing under the white umbrella in the banquet hall of his palace.

The basket maker took Kusa's baskets and the fan to the palace, and the king reacted in the same way as he had with the potter. He gave the basket maker a sack of money and said, "Give your baskets to my daughters, and give that skillful man these one thousand coins. From now on, let him make all the baskets for my daughters."

As soon as Pabhāvatī saw the fan, she threw it down and cried, "I don't want that! Take it away, and give it to someone else!" Of course, her sisters did not recognize the figure and teased her in the same way as before. Again, Pabhāvatī kept secret what she knew.

Again, Kusa felt that he was in the wrong place. He told the basket maker to keep the money and left.

Next, he became the apprentice of the royal gardener. After quickly learning the art of making garlands, Kusa made all sorts of floral arrangements for the princesses. Then he made a magnificent garland for Pabhāvatī, intricately depicting images of both himself and Pabhāvatī.

The gardener took them all to the palace, and the king reacted in the same way as he had with the potter and the basket maker. He gave the gardener a sack of money and said, "Give your garlands to my daughters, and give that skillful man these one thousand coins. From now on, let him make all the garlands for my daughters."

As soon as Pabhāvatī saw the beautiful garland, she threw it down and cried, "I don't want that! Take it away, and give it to someone else!" Of course, her sisters did not recognize the figures and teased her in the same way as before. Again, Pabhāvatī kept secret what she knew.

Again, Kusa felt he was in the wrong place. He told the gardener to keep the money and left.

Next he became the apprentice of the royal chef. One day, as the chef was leaving the kitchen to take the food he had prepared to the king, he gave Kusa a bone with only a scrap of meat attached and told him to cook it. Kusa quickly began simmering the bone in a special blend of herbs and spices, and the savory aroma pervaded the entire city. The king's mouth began watering, and he asked the chef whether he was preparing more meat in the kitchen.

"No, Sire, but I gave my apprentice a bone to cook. That must be what you smell."

The king ordered that that dish be brought to his table. Just a small spoonful of the broth on the tip of the king's tongue awakened every taste bud! The delicate flavor so thrilled the king that he gave the chef one thousand coins for the apprentice and said, "From now on, I want your apprentice to prepare all the food for me and for my daughters! You may deliver the dishes to my table, but let your apprentice take the dishes to the princesses."

When Kusa heard this, he rejoiced. "At last," he thought, "I will be able to see Pabhāvatī." He told the chef to keep the money from the king.

After giving the king's portion to the chef, Kusa loaded the dishes for the princesses on the trays of a carrying-pole and set off for the princesses' apartments. Pabhāvatī saw him climbing with his burden and thought,

"Look at that! He is working like a servant! Such labor is totally unsuitable for a king! I can't stand the sight of him! How can I drive him away? I hate the thought of even speaking to him, but, if I keep quiet, he'll stay here and keep looking at me."

She left her door ajar and said in a loud voice, "Kusa, it is not right for you to do this menial work! Go back to Kusāvatī, and act like a king! I hate seeing your ugly face! Go away!"

Kusa paid no attention to her words. All he thought was, "Ah! I have succeeded in making her speak to me! I have heard her beautiful voice!" Standing outside her door, he put down his carrying-pole and said, "Fair Pabhāvatī! I must be mad! Here I am wandering all alone, just to win your love! Having been bewitched by the spell of your beauty, I no longer delight in my native land! I have forsaken Malla for Madda to have you within my sight!"

"No matter how much I insult him and revile him," Pabhāvatī thought, "he tries to win me back! No matter how hard I try to wound him, he tries to gain my love! What if he announces, 'I am King Kusa!' and takes my hand? Who could stop him? I hope no one has already heard him!" She quickly shut her door and locked it. Kusa picked up his carrying-pole and took all the food to the apartments of the other princesses. Pabhāvatī sent her nurse to get her share, but, when she realized that Kusa had cooked it, she said, "You eat it. I will not eat what he has made. You can give me your food instead. Now, for heaven's sake, don't tell anyone that King Kusa is here!"

A little later, Kusa shouldered his carrying-pole again and went to the princesses' apartments to retrieve the dishes. He was devastated that Pabhāvatī's door was tightly closed so that he could not see her. He wanted to find out whether she had any spark of affection for him, so, as he passed her door, he purposely stumbled, dropping all the dishes with a great clatter. He groaned loudly and fell in front of her door.

Hearing the commotion and his groans, Pabhāvatī opened her door. When she saw him lying there beneath his pole and surrounded by broken dishes and scraps of food, she thought, "Here is the greatest monarch in all of Jambudīpa, enduring pain every day for the sake of my love! He is not accustomed to this manual labor. He must have fallen under the heavy load. Poor thing! Is he breathing? Is he still alive?" Suddenly concerned, she bent over him to check. With one eye half open, he filled his mouth with saliva and spat in her face.

"Wretch!" she cried, straightening up and retreating into her room. "You are the vilest creature on the face of the earth! Go ahead and woo me, King, but your love will be unreturned!"

Because Kusa was madly in love with Pabhāvatī, her abuse rolled off him like water from a lotus leaf. With no resentment whatsoever, he declared, "If a man can possess the one he cherishes, it matters not whether he is loved or unloved."

"You might as well try to dig through rock with a piece of brittle wood or to catch the wind in a net," she retorted, "as to court an unwilling woman!"

"Dear lady," the king replied softly, "from your beautiful countenance, one would think that you are kind and gentle. Are you really as hard-hearted as stone? Consider how far I have come to win your love. How is it that I have received no word of welcome? When you frown at me with your sullen look, I am but a lowly cook's assistant, but, if you were to smile at me, I would once more become the king of Kusāvatī, and you would be my queen!"

"This man is unbearably stubborn and tenacious!" Pabhāvatī thought. "How can I get rid of him? I need to make up a story that will drive him away." Aloud she said, "Kusa, please listen to me. Everyone knows that the predictions of fortune tellers are true. At the time of your proposal, I consulted the famous soothsayers in Madda, and they said, 'If you marry King Kusa, you will be cut into seven pieces!' Therefore, I beg you to leave me alone!"

"Dear lady," Kusa retorted, "I, too, consulted fortune tellers in my own kingdom, and they all predicted that, for the fair Pabhāvatī, there could be no other husband than the lion-voiced Kusa! Being skilled myself in reading omens, I completely agree! Therefore, your resistance is in vain!"

Slamming the door and locking herself in her chamber, she moaned, "He is shameless! Let him stay or run away! I don't care! I will have no more to do with him!" From then on, she was careful not to let him catch even a glimpse of her.

He continued working in the kitchen, but his work became drudgery. Every day, after an early breakfast, he cut firewood, washed dishes, and fetched buckets of water with his carrying-pole. He still prepared various dishes and delivered them to the princesses, but they treated him like the cook's assistant that they assumed he was. Hoping to catch sight of Pabhāvatī as he passed her door every day, he endured constant indignities.

One day, as the hunchback nurse was passing by the kitchen door, he called to her, but, afraid of incurring her mistress' wrath, she pretended not to have heard him and hurried away. Kusa ran after her, calling frantically. Finally, she turned and snapped, "Stop bothering me! I don't know you, and I won't listen to anything you have to say!"

"Both you and your lady are very obstinate," Kusa replied. "Here I am so close, but I do not even get a report of her health."

"Well," she replied slyly, "what is it worth to you?"

"Madam!" Kusa exclaimed with a smile. "If I give you a present, can you soften Pabhāvatī and let me see her?"

"I could do that, Sire."

"If you can, indeed, soften her, I will straighten your back and present you with a lovely golden necklace, as well. In fact, if you could induce the slender-limbed Pabhāvatī to lay a loving hand on me, to laugh with joy at the sight of me, simply to smile at me, to speak a word to me, or even just to look at me, I would gladly give you that golden necklace!"

The old nurse smiled at Kusa and said, "Go on your way, Sire. In a very few days, I will deliver Pabhāvatī to you. You will see what I can do!"

The old nurse thought for a while and devised a plan, which she was sure would work. One day, after thoroughly cleaning Pabhāvatī's chamber, she placed a chair for herself outside the door. Beside the chair, she placed a stool, covered with a spread, for the princess. Seating herself there, she called, "Come, my dear, let me brush your hair and check your head for nits. Sit here, and put your head in my lap!" The nurse brushed the princess' hair, scratched a bit, and softly exclaimed, "Oh, look at the lice!" She took nits from her own head, put them in the princess' hair, and picked them out. Continuing this ruse and brushing gently, to a slow and lilting melody, she sang, "There is one who is very wise. His wealth is also great. His love is true and never dies. When he asks for just a smile, why does My Lady hesitate? For just a glimpse he labors on as a lowly kitchen cook!"

At this, Pabhāvatī jumped up and began screaming furiously at the nurse. Ready for the attack, the nurse grabbed the princess by the neck, shoved her inside her room, slammed the door, and held it shut.

Pabhāvatī continued cursing through the door. "You detestable hunch-backed slave!" she shouted. "You deserve to have your tongue cut out for daring to speak to me like that!"

The old woman held the door shut and retorted "Pabhāvatī, you are a worthless, spoiled child! Granted, you are beautiful, but what good are your good looks going to do anybody? Do you plan to spend the rest of your life in your father's palace? You can never marry anyone else, you foolish woman! Think about King Kusa! Don't look at his face or his figure! Admire him for his glory, his wealth, his power, and his kingdom! Admire him for his voice, which is both sweet and as deep as a lion's! Admire him for his many skills and his courage! Admire him for his wisdom and his virtue! It doesn't matter what he looks like. You should respect him and please him because he is a good man, who loves you dearly!"

Pabhāvatī refused to listen. "You crooked-backed witch!" she shouted. "Keep your voice down! I don't want everyone to hear about this! When I catch you, I'll teach you a lesson!"

"I have been very good to you, mistress," the nurse replied. "I haven't yet told your father that King Kusa is here, but maybe that's what I should do today!"

"No, please!" Pabhāvatī whispered, suddenly intimidated. "Don't tell the king that Kusa is here," she pleaded. In many sweet words, she began trying to appease her nurse. The nurse, having successfully pacified the princess, slowly opened the door.

Meanwhile, Kusa was losing hope of ever seeing Pabhāvatī. He realized that he had been in Sāgala for seven months, working like a slave under extremely uncomfortable living conditions with nothing to show for it. He was disappointed and frustrated. "No matter what I do," he lamented, "I can't get a glimpse of her, nor can I even hear her voice. What do I need her for, anyway? She's a cruel and selfish woman, and she's never going to change. The devas must be laughing at me! I might as well go home to my parents!"

Sakka heard these complaints and resolved to help him find a way to see the arrogant princess and even to win her back.

Recalling Pabhāvatī's claim that the fortune tellers had mentioned her being cut into seven pieces, Sakka had an idea. To each of seven powerful kings of Jambudīpa, he wrote a personal message, seemingly from the king of Madda: "My daughter, Pabhāvatī, has separated from King Kusa of Malla and has returned to Sāgala. I would be honored to have you come to Sāgala to accept this most beautiful young woman as your queen."

All seven kings with their great retinues arrived in Sāgala on the same day. When they learned that each had been sent the same letter, they became furious with King Madda. "This is an outrage!" they cried. "He's mocking us! Does he think one woman can marry seven different kings? All right, let's show him! We'll demand that he give Pabhāvatī to all of us, or we'll fight him and destroy Sāgala!"

Their threats greatly alarmed King Madda, who, of course, knew nothing about the original letters. When he conferred with his advisors, they replied, "If you refuse to give Pabhāvatī to these seven powerful kings, they will certainly attack the city and destroy us. Then they will seize your kingdom and divide it among themselves. While our fortifications are still intact, it would be better to send Pabhāvatī to them and to satisfy their demand."

"Sirs," the king countered. "I cannot give my daughter to all seven kings! That is most unseemly for a princess such as she! Nor can I give her to any one of them. If I did that, the other six would join together and attack me.

What a stupid, frivolous girl she is! She cast off the greatest king in all of Jambudīpa. She should have been satisfied with King Kusa! All right, let her get the reward she deserves for returning home. I'll have her carved into seven pieces, and I'll send one piece to each of the seven kings. That is the only solution that will spare us from war. I cannot allow the country to be destroyed because of a vain and selfish girl! That is my answer to the kings. Let it be proclaimed!"

The story spread like wildfire, and the nurse hurried to inform Pabhāvatī. "Mistress!" she cried. "There are seven kings camped outside the gate, and they are demanding that you be given to them. Your father has decreed that you be cut into seven pieces and that one piece be given to each king. You are doomed!"

Pabhāvatī was terrified and began shaking. Turning as white as a ghost, she went with her sisters to see her mother. When the queen confirmed that she had also heard the same news that the nurse had reported, Pabhāvatī began weeping. Catching sight of her ashen face in the mirror, she wailed, "Mother dear, can it be true that this delicately powdered face of mine will soon be carelessly thrown into the mud of the charnel ground? Will my long black hair, fragrant with sandalwood, be scattered by vultures as they fight for my flesh? Will my slender alabaster arms be cut off and cast away for savage wolves to pick up? Can it be true that my elegant body will be cut into seven pieces and despoiled by dogs and jackals? Promise me, Mother, that, when the scavengers have finished, you will salvage some of my bones and burn them quietly. In my ashes, plant a kanikāra tree, which will bloom as winter ends. At that time, point to the yellow flowers, and say, "Such was my beautiful child, Pabhāvatī!"

Unable to comfort the distraught Pabhāvatī, the queen left her with her sisters and hurried to confront the king in his chamber. "Husband! Sire!" she cried. "Is the monstrous story true? Can it be that you are really planning to execute your beautiful daughter? What is this about rival suitors and seven pieces? Surely this is all nonsense!"

"My dear," the king replied, "your daughter repudiated the greatest king of all Jambudīpa. As far as she is concerned, she has no husband. Now seven kings with their armies have come to ask for her hand. They are demanding that I give her to them. If I don't, they will attack and destroy Sāgala and all of us. Rather than have her live in disgrace as the concubine of seven kings, I have decided to give one piece of her body to each. This is the fate she deserves for returning home before the dust of her going had even settled. I have already called the executioner, and he is preparing to chop her body into seven equal portions. Let her prepare herself! As long as she is alive, she is a danger to us all!"

The queen hurried back to her daughter and lamented, "Pabhāvatī! My beautiful Pabhāvatī! Your father is indeed serious! Your pride has been your undoing! You should have stayed with King Kusa! That great king could have given you everything—comfort, luxury, prestige, and security. Life in his golden kingdom would have been as good as heaven, but you abandoned that for the realm of Yama! When you turned your back on Kusa and his royal court, you brought your own doom. Darling, why did you leave Kusa? If only King Kusa were here now!" she cried, more to the devas than to Pabhāvatī. "He would put those seven rowdy kings to flight and free my dear girl from her unspeakable fate. Kusa, wise, noble, and strong! He alone could save our realm and free us from our woe!"

With a shock, Pabhāvatī clearly realized the situation she was in and what she could do to help herself. "My mother is right!" she thought. "Kusa is all of those things! He can help me! Actually, my mother does not know how great Kusa really is! Furthermore, she has no idea that he is here and that he has been here for seven months, faithfully and humbly slaving away as a cook for the sake of my love!" Aloud, she said, "You're right, Mother! That almighty conqueror, the wise and noble Kusa, will, indeed, defeat our enemies, and he will do it because of his love for me!"

"Are you mad, my daughter?" the queen asked. "Has the fear of death unhinged you? Why are you babbling like a child? How can Kusa save us? He is not here! If he were, we certainly would have known about it."

"Mother, let me show you!" Pabhāvatī exclaimed, as she took her mother to the window.

In the courtyard below, Kusa was squatting at the well and scrubbing pots and pans. No one could hear, but he was saying to himself, "Soon, my kitchen work will be over! Today, my fondest dream will come true! Pabhāvatī is terrified of meeting a violent death, and I alone can save her!"

Pabhāvatī pointed and asked her mother, "Do you see that cook's assistant scouring those heavy pots?"

"What?" the queen cried. "Are you my daughter? How dare you take a slave for a lover after having rejected a king? You're a disgrace to us all!"

"Mother!" Pabhāvatī pleaded. "I would never disgrace my royal birth! That cook's assistant is not a slave! That is King Kusa, the heir to King Okkāka, and he has been here for seven months! Though he is meant to feed twenty thousand ascetics in his royal alms-halls, he has happily prepared dishes every day for the one he loves. In his own kingdom, he owns twenty thousand elephants, twenty thousand thoroughbred horses, and twenty thousand chariots. He pastures twenty thousand handsome bulls and milks twenty thousand rich cattle. The one you see at the well is no slave! In truth, he is the greatest king in all Jambudīpa, King Kusa of Malla, and he is my husband!"

"My dear child," the queen replied, "I have never known you to tell a lie, so I must indeed believe you. Now I must inform the king. If that is truly King Kusa, it changes everything!"

Even after hearing it from both his wife and his daughter, the king did not believe that King Kusa had been working in the palace for seven months. He sent for the hunchbacked nurse and asked her. When she told him exactly the same story, he had to accept that it was true.

He turned to Pabhāvatī and growled, "I'm ashamed of you, Pabhāvatī! When this mighty king followed you here, how could you have let him work so hard? How could you have kept this from us for seven months? Have you no shame? He is a king, and he is your husband!"

The king hurried to the courtyard to apologize to Kusa. "Your Majesty," he called to Kusa, "we failed to recognize you in this disguise. If we offended you in any way, please forgive us. We beg you to excuse our rudeness and our faults."

"Your Majesty," Kusa replied, not wanting to blame the king in any way or to hurt his feelings, "the fault is all mine. I realize that it was wrong of me to play the servant's role. I did not come as a king, however, and I wanted only to win your daughter by my own merits. I myself chose to remain in disguise. There's nothing to forgive."

Bolstered by Kusa's generous and kindly words, the king fetched Pabhāvatī. "Go, you foolish girl, and beg the pardon of King Kusa. You have acted abominably toward him! If you can appease him, perhaps he will be willing to save your life!"

Standing at the well, in his cook's apron, stained with blood and grease, Kusa thought, "Today, I will tame this willful woman, break her pride, and see her prostrate herself at my feet!" He quickly poured all the water he had drawn onto the unpaved earth around the well. He trampled the ground with his bare feet creating a mass of mud as big as a threshing-floor. Unhesitatingly, Pabhāvatī walked through the mud to where he stood, knelt, and grasped his ankles. Unconcerned that her robe, her hands, and her face were covered with mud, she cried, "Sire, I stoop to kiss your feet! Please forgive me for my faults! Be not angry with your foolish wife! I promise that, if you allow me, I will never again offend you in any way. Please save me from the fate of being cut into seven pieces and given to the seven mighty kings encamped outside our city gate."

"At last, she is mine!" Kusa silently rejoiced. "Now I must comfort her and ease her mind." He gently raised her from the ground and said: "Dear Pabhāvatī, I feel no anger toward you. I, too, promise never to offend you in any way. I will bear any burden for your sake. I will save you from the seven kings and reclaim you as my queen! Go now. After a refreshing bath, put on your formal robes, and wait in the palace." To the entire court, with his voice as deep as a lion's, he shouted, "As long as I am alive, no one but me shall have the fair Pabhāvatī! Let everyone hear of my coming! I am ready to fight! Prepare my chariot and my thoroughbreds!"

The king of Madda ordered his ministers to serve as a guard of honor to Kusa. They arranged his bath, and barbers trimmed his beard and oiled his hair. When he was dressed in all his splendor, surrounded by his attendants, he ascended to the palace. Looking around, he clapped his hands, and the whole earth trembled. "Such is my power!" he declared.

Regarding the chariot as inadequate, King Madda insisted that King Kusa mount the richly caparisoned royal elephant, which in many previous battles had proven itself to be invincible. Kusa agreed and summoned Pabhāvatī. He seated himself on the back of the elephant as a white umbrella was held over him and arranged a space for his queen. With Pabhāvatī seated behind him, he rode out of the city by the eastern gate at the head of a full army of elephant troops, cavalry, charioteers, and infantry.

At the sight of the combined forces of the seven kings, he roared three times again with his lion-like voice, "I am King Kusa![9] Let those who value their lives surrender! How dare you come to court my wife while I am still among the living! She is riding here behind me! If you wish to live, surrender now!" This battle cry was enough to defeat the besieging kings.

Many warriors, who had considered themselves brave, fled in fear. The kings, no longer the least bit interested in fighting for Pabhāvatī and afraid for their lives, were easily captured and bound.

Kusa led his prisoners to the king and said, "Behold, Sire! Here are your foes. They are at your mercy. Slay them or free them, as you choose."

"My son," the king replied, "these are your prisoners, not mine! Their fate depends on you, our sovereign lord!"

"It would be a shame to slay these excellent men," Kusa observed. "Although they laid siege to this city, making war was not their intention. They came in good faith. They are sovereign kings. Of what use would be their

---

9 Four great sounds that were heard throughout Jambudipa were made by Mahā-Kanha (Tale 181), Ālavaka (q.v. in The Glossary of Personal Names in the Appendix), Kusa, and Punnaka (Tale 215).

death? Let us not waste their blood. It would be better to bring their mission to a profitable conclusion."

Turning to face the king of Madda, he said, "My dear Father-in-law, in addition to my queen, you have seven fair daughters. Why not give them to these seven kings and let them also be your sons-in-law?"

That suggestion was accepted without hesitation; the king ordered that his seven daughters be formally dressed and presented in marriage, one to each king. The seven warrior kings praised King Kusa for his wise resolution of the conflict, expressed their immense gratitude for the boons they were receiving, and pledged their loyalty to him for as long as they lived. In one swift stroke, King Kusa had managed to unite by marriage nine great kingdoms of Jambudīpa under his sovereignty.

Delighted with Kusa's mighty and bloodless triumph, Sakka descended to the battlefield and presented the wise conqueror with the renowned Verocanamani, a remarkable octagonal jewel of extraordinary brilliance.

King Kusa and Queen Pabhāvatī, at last united in perfect harmony, carried Sakka's precious gift as they traveled back to Kusāvatī. They were welcomed by his parents and the entire population of the kingdom. King Kusa and Queen Pabhāvatī lived together in peace and prosperity for the rest of their lives.

Having concluded his story, the Buddha taught the Dhamma, and the discontented bhikkhu attained the first path. Then the Buddha identified the birth: "At that time, my parents were Kusa's mother and father, my followers were members of the royal household, Ānanda was Prince Jayampati, Khujjuttarā was the nurse, Rāhula's mother was Queen Pabhāvatī, and I was King Kusa."

207
The Man-Eater of Jambudīpa
Mahā-Sutasoma Jātaka

It was while staying at Jetavana that the Buddha told this story about Venerable Angulimāla.

One of the advisors of the King Pasenadi had a son named Ahimsaka. He was an intelligent youth, and, when he was old enough, he was sent to Takkasilā for his education. He proved to be an exceptional student; so much so that his fellow students were jealous of him and spread a rumor that he was having an affair with the teacher's wife. The teacher believed the gossip and was enraged. Wanting to have his star pupil killed, he devised a wicked plan. Rather than accepting money, the teacher told Ahimsaka that the fee for his studies was one thousand fingers, one from each victim that he killed. Bound to his teacher by a pledge of honor, the poor young man could see no alternative but to comply.

Ahimsaka returned to Sāvatthī and began his bloody quest. He became a brutal and merciless killer, attacking anyone he could find on the highways around the capital. Utterly fearless, he was known to attack groups of ten, twenty, and thirty, sparing no one. Villages became deserted, and people were terrified to travel. At first, Ahimsaka hung the fingers on a tree, but crows ate them. In order to keep count of his victims, he started to wear a garland (māla) of fingers (anguli) around his neck, and he became known as Angulimāla.

Terrorized, the people finally rose up and appealed to the king for help. They demanded that the king catch Angulimāla and stop his killing spree. To comply with their demand, the king mobilized a force of five hundred soldiers to capture the outlaw.

When Angulimāla's mother heard that the king himself intended to catch the murderer, suspecting him to be her own son, she set out to warn him. It so happened that, by this time, Angulimāla had collected 999 fingers. He needed only one more to reach his goal. When he saw his mother, he decided to kill her as his final victim.

That morning, when the Buddha surveyed the world, he saw the mass murderer, and he knew that he would attempt to kill his own mother. Knowing that Angulimāla was ripe for insight but would fall into hell if he committed matricide, the Buddha set out to save him.

When Angulimāla saw the Buddha walking alone, he thought it would be very easy to kill him, so he abandoned the idea of killing his mother and ran after the Buddha instead. With his supernatural power, the Buddha prevented Angulimāla from catching him, no matter how fast the bandit ran. Frustrated, Angulimāla shouted, "Stop, Bhikkhu! Stop!"

"I have stopped, Angulimāla," the Buddha calmly replied. "Now, you must stop."

Puzzled by this, but knowing that bhikkhus told the truth, Angulimāla asked, "What do you mean?"

"I have completely stopped all violence toward living beings," the Buddha replied. "You go on killing. I have stopped, Angulimāla. You have not stopped."

"At long last, a sage has come to the great forest for my sake!" Angulimāla declared. "Having heard your admonition, from now on, I will abandon evil!" He hurled his sword and other weapons over a cliff, paid homage at the Buddha's feet, and asked for ordination.

"Come, Bhikkhu!" the Buddha declared, and Angulimāla was instantly provided with all the requisites.

With the newly-ordained Venerable Angulimāla as his attendant, the Buddha returned to Jetavana.

On his way to the forest in search of the mass murderer, King Pasenadi, with the brigade of soldiers, stopped at Jetavana to pay his respects to the Buddha. After the king had bowed down to the Buddha and sat at one side, the Buddha asked him, "What is it, Sire? Why have you set out with such a large force? Have you been attacked by one of the neighboring kingdoms?"

"No, Venerable Sir, no hostile king has attacked Kosala. There is a bandit called Angulimāla who is terrorizing Sāvatthī. He has killed hundreds of travelers, showing no mercy to anyone. I am going with these troops to capture him and to stop his killing spree."

"Sire, suppose you were to see Angulimāla with his hair and beard shaved off, wearing the yellow robe, having gone forth from the homelife into homelessness, refraining from killing living beings, restraining the senses, and virtuous. What would you do to him?"

"We would bow down to him, Lord. We would offer him requisites. We doubt, however, that there could be such virtue and restraint in such an unruly and evil character."

With his right arm, the Buddha pointed to a bhikkhu sitting near him and said, "That, Sire, is Angulimāla." King Pasenadi was terrified, and his hair stood on end. The Buddha sensed the king's fear and said, "Don't be afraid, Sire. He poses no danger to you."

The king went over to Venerable Angulimāla and asked, "Venerable Sir, are you really Angulimāla?"

"Yes, Your Majesty."

"Venerable Sir," King Pasenadi said, "please allow me to offer you the requisites for your livelihood."

Since Venerable Angulimāla had undertaken the dhutanga vows, including the wearing of robes made of cast-off cloth, he replied, "Enough, Sire. My triple robe is complete."

King Pasenadi bowed again to the Buddha and said, "It is wonderful, Venerable Sir, it is marvelous how the Blessed One tames the untamed, brings peace to the unpeaceful, and leads to Nibbāna those who have not attained Nibbāna. Venerable Sir, we ourselves could not tame him with force and weapons, yet the Blessed One has tamed him without force or weapons. And now, Venerable Sir, we depart. We are busy and have much to do."

For some time, even though Venerable Angulimāla was a fully-ordained bhikkhu, many people still thought of him as the vicious murderer and refused to offer alms. Later, however, by making an asseveration of truth, Venerable Angulimāla saved the life of a woman and her baby during a difficult and dangerous delivery. When this became well known, devotees began paying him a great deal of respect, and he easily obtained alms. Venerable Angulimāla cultivated solitude for intensive meditation, and, in no long time, he achieved arahatship.

One day, in the Hall of Truth, bhikkhus were talking about Venerable Angulimāla. "It was a miracle, Friends," one said, "that the Buddha peacefully reformed and humbled the cruel and bloodstained murderer that Angulimāla was before. Truly, Buddhas do mighty works!" When the Buddha heard what they were discussing, he said, "There is no marvel, Bhikkhus, in my converting him now that I am enlightened. I also tamed him when I had only limited knowledge." Then the Buddha told this story of the past.

Long, long ago, when Brahmadatta was reigning in Bārānasi, the Bodhisatta was born as the son of King Koravya in Indapatta, the capital of the Kuru kingdom. Because he was fond of soma juice,[10] he was called Prince Sutasoma. When he was old enough, his father sent him to Takkasilā for his education. At the same time, King Brahmadatta sent his son, Prince Brahmadatta, there for his studies too, and the two princes traveled on the same road. Along the way, the two princes happened to stop to rest on the same bench in a hall near the gate of a city. After friendly greetings, they introduced themselves. Learning that they were both sons of great kings and that they were going to Takkasilā to study with the same teacher, they struck up a friendship and continued traveling together. When they reached Takkasilā, they went to their teacher's house and asked to be taken under his tutelage. At that time, there were one hundred other princes from Jambudīpa already studying with that teacher.

Sutasoma, being the brightest student, soon gained proficiency in every subject. Because Prince Brahmadatta was his close friend, Sutasoma acted as his private tutor, so that Brahmadatta also made exceptional progress while the others learned satisfactorily on their own. Eventually, they all completed their studies and left Takkasilā to return to their own kingdoms.

As they parted company, Sutasoma urged them all to keep the precepts, particularly to abstain from taking any life, and to observe Uposatha days. He especially urged Brahmadatta to maintain his virtue, because, being adept at seeing the future by reading various signs, he knew that his friend would face great danger after he became king of Kāsi. They all thanked Sutasoma for his care in teaching them. After they returned home, all the princes informed Sutasoma by letter that they were following his advice. Sutasoma corresponded with them and always encouraged them to be diligent.

All his life, Prince Brahmadatta had eaten meat at every meal, and he continued this custom after becoming king. For full-moon days, when no animals were slaughtered, the royal cook always procured the king's meat in advance and put it aside. Once, when the man was careless, palace dogs sneaked into the kitchen, got hold of the meat, and ate it all. The frightened cook searched all over the city but was unable to find any meat. "If I

10 A drink made from the soma plant. In ancient India, it was considered sacred and was praised for its energizing and, perhaps, psychedelic qualities.

don't serve the king meat for his dinner, he will kill me!" fretted the cook. "What can I do?"

In desperation, in the middle of the night, the cook went stealthily to the charnel ground outside the city walls. There he found the exposed corpse of a man who had just died and sliced off a piece of flesh from the thigh with his cleaver. Then he hurried back to the palace without letting anyone see him. The next day, he chopped the flesh into small pieces so that it could not be recognized, roasted it thoroughly, and served it to the king as though it were ordinary meat.

In a previous birth, King Brahmadatta had been a yakkha who had devoured vast quantities of human flesh. As soon as a tiny piece of this meat touched his tongue, the king felt a thrill throughout his body. Though he did not realize what it was, that first taste of human flesh immediately reawakened his past addiction.

"How can I get the cook to tell me what kind of meat this is?" wondered the king. Without swallowing that mouthful, he spat the meat onto the floor.

When the cook saw that, he said, "Sire, there is nothing wrong with that meat. You can safely eat it."

Without answering the cook, Brahmadatta ordered all the other servants to leave the room. When they were alone, the king said to the cook, "Of course, it is not spoiled, but please tell me what kind of meat it is."

"It is what Your Majesty has enjoyed everyday," the cook answered evasively,

"You have never served me meat with a flavor like this before!" Brahmadatta protested.

"Well, perhaps it was especially well-seasoned today, Sire," the cook replied.

"Are you sure it is just the recipe that is different? Tell me what this meat is, or you will pay with your life!" he demanded.

The cook realized that he could no longer conceal the truth. Begging for mercy, he confessed what he had done.

"Never mention a word of this to anyone," the king whispered. "From now on, you can cook as usual for everyone else, but you must prepare human flesh like this for me every day!"

"Sire," the cook protested, "that will be very difficult!"

"Not at all," the king assured him. "There is nothing to worry about. It will be very easy!"

"Where can I get human flesh every day?" the cook asked, trembling.

"Aren't there a lot of men in prison?" the king asked with a chuckle.

Every day, the cook butchered one prisoner and served his flesh to the depraved king, but no one knew what was going on. When, at last, the prison was empty, the cook asked the king what he should do. The king suggested dropping a bag of money each day on the street and arresting the person who picked it up. At first, this ploy was successful, but eventually the citizens realized that even petty thieves were disappearing, and everyone became so honest that not a single person would touch anything that did not belong to him. People crossed to the other side of the street for fear of being seen anywhere near a dropped jewel or a bag of gold.

The king then ordered the cook to conceal himself in dark alleys and, every night, to kill some solitary pedestrian for butchering.

Every morning, a cry of lamentation was heard somewhere in the city when a mutilated body was found. One day, it was, "I have lost my father!" Another day, "Someone has killed my mother!" A third day, "Our elder brother has been murdered!"

"Some lion or yakkha is attacking one person every night!" cried a panic-stricken citizen.

"Look!" cried another. "This wound was made by a knife, not an animal!"

"It must be a person who craves their flesh!" cried a third, horrified.

"There is a cannibal on the loose in our city!" shouted others.

A great, angry crowd rushed to the palace and demanded that the king do something about this abomination.

"My friends, what is the problem?" the king asked.

"Sire," everyone cried, "there is a man-eating killer running wild in the city. He is stalking the streets at night. You must stop him!"

"What can I do?" asked the king. "I don't know who it is, or where he is going to strike next. Do you want me, your king, to patrol the city every night?"

The people were disgusted by the king's indifference and appealed to the commander-in-chief, General Kālahatthi, to capture the serial killer.

Kālahatthi took their complaint very seriously. "Give me seven days," he told the citizens. "I will arrest this killer and bring him to justice." He immediately ordered his soldiers to patrol all the city streets at night and to capture the man-eating murderer without fail.

That night, the cook attacked a woman who was hurrying home at dusk. He quickly carved her body into pieces and began stuffing them into his basket. He was so busy that he did not see the soldiers approaching. They seized him and beat him severely. They tied his hands behind his back and shouted "We've caught the man-eater!" People rushed out of their houses and would have beaten the terrified cook to death, had the soldiers not prevented it. Hanging the basket of flesh around the cook's neck, the soldiers dragged him before the commander-in-chief.

General Kālahatthi studied the bruised and bloody man the soldiers had brought in, and he could hardly believe that he was himself eating his victims. "You have been caught red-handed," he said to the cook, "so we know for sure that you killed this woman. Your basket is full of pieces of meat which seem to be for cooking. Tell me, have you been killing these men and women and eating them yourself, or is someone paying you to do it?"

"I didn't slay this woman for myself," the cook maintained. "Nor did I kill her for money. I have committed one murder every night at the command of our sovereign. It is he who is eating human flesh! I am merely his cook!"

"What are you saying?" General Kālahatthi cried, aghast. "Do you expect us to believe that His Majesty has an unnatural greed and that he has been forcing you to carry out these hideous acts? We'll talk to the king and find out the truth, but we can't do anything until tomorrow morning."

"Certainly, General!" agreed the cook. "Take me before the king as soon as possible tomorrow morning. I will accuse King Brahmadatta to his face. You'll see that I am telling the truth!"

The commander-in-chief put the cook in a cell and had him closely guarded all night. By dawn, the whole city was in an uproar; everyone had heard about the cook's capture. There were rumors that he had confessed and that the king was somehow involved. People were storming the palace to learn the truth. The commander-in-chief stationed soldiers around the city to control the crowds. Then he hung the basket of foul-smelling flesh once more around the cook's neck and marched him, under heavy guard, to the palace.

King Brahmadatta had breakfasted the day before, but had gone without his supper. He had sat up the whole night, expecting his cook to come at any moment. "No cook today, either!" he muttered. "I wonder what the commotion is."

At that moment, General Kālahatthi burst through the door and led the cook into the king's chamber. "Sire!" he said coldly, "This man, your cook, says that he was sent into the streets to kill innocent men and women, your loyal subjects, to furnish you with human meat. Please, Your Majesty, assure us that this is not true!"

"It is true," the king replied, without offering any excuse. "It was, indeed, done at my request. The cook is not to blame."

The commander-in-chief was absolutely dumbfounded. Thoughts raced through his mind. "Our king is a brute! He does not deny anything! That explains why the prison is empty. He must have been eating human meat for a long time! I must stop him from this barbarism!"

"Sire," he said aloud, "now that this has come out into the open, you must desist immediately. You must never again eat human flesh!"

"Kālahatthi," the king replied very matter-of-factly, "I can't stop! No matter what you say, I can't give it up! I can't stop myself!"

"Sire," pleaded the commander-in-chief, "if you don't stop, you will destroy both yourself and your realm."

"General," replied the king, "I can't help it. Even if I lose my kingdom, I cannot possibly control my craving!"

"Sire, let me tell you a story," said General Kālahatthi. "Once upon a time, there were six great monster fish in the ocean. Ānanda, Timinanda, and Ajjhoroha were each five hundred yojanas long, while Timigalo, Timirapingalo, and Mahātimirapingalo were each one thousand yojanas long. All six of them thrived on eel grass.

"Ānanda lived at one side of the ocean, and many fish came to see him. One day, the ordinary fish thought, 'In the animal kingdom, bipeds and quadrupeds have their kings, but we fish have no king. Why shouldn't we also have a monarch?' All the fish discussed the matter, and agreed to declare Ānanda their king. After that, all the fish in the ocean paid their respects to Ānanda both morning and evening.

"One day, while Ānanda was eating in a clump of eel grass, he accidentally bit a small fish. The taste thrilled him. 'All my life,' he thought, 'I've never eaten anything this delicious!' He wondered what it was. He spat it out and discovered that he had been eating another fish. 'I must have more!' he silently resolved. 'When the fish come to pay their respects, I will devour one or two of them as they are leaving. If I am careful, no one will ever know. If they find out what I am doing, they'll stop coming, and I won't get any more!'

"The fish continued to pay their respects to Ānanda, and each time, as they were leaving, the great fish grabbed the last one or two in the line and devoured them.

"In time, the fish noticed that their numbers were diminishing and wondered why. Among them, there was one wise older fish who thought about the problem and suspected Ānanda, reasoning that the king certainly had the best opportunity. In the evening, when the fish visited the king, that wise fish hid in the lobe of Ānanda's ear. His suspicion was confirmed when he saw Ānanda snap up the last two fish as they were turning to go. He gasped as he saw the king ravenously eat his two comrades with great relish. The wise fish calmed himself, however, waiting until Ānanda was asleep before sneaking away to report on what he had seen.

"When the other fish heard the news, they were disgusted and became terrified of the king. Not only did they stop visiting him to pay their respects, they completely abandoned that part of the ocean and fled to a safer place.

"Ānanda was surprised that his subjects did not call on him anymore. He went looking for them, but, of course, he found no one at all. He wondered where they had gone. Having become addicted to the taste of fish, he was no longer satisfied with eel grass. Scorning anything but the flesh of fish, he grew progressively weaker from hunger. One day, as he was searching again for the other fish, he discovered a mountain rising from the bottom of the ocean. 'Perhaps some fish are hiding inside a cave in this mountain,' he thought hopefully. 'I will encircle the mountain and watch for them. They will have to come out eventually.' He wrapped his long and supple body around the mountain. Suddenly, he saw, right in front of his face, the tail of a great fish. 'This large fish must live near this mountain, and now he is mocking me!' He lunged forward and, with his enormous mouth and razor sharp teeth, bit off the tail, intending to eat it. Of course, it was his own tail, and the pain he caused himself was excruciating.

"The scent of Ānanda's blood attracted millions of fish from all over the ocean. Beginning at the stump of his tail, they devoured the great fish all the way to the tip of his nose. Of Ānanda's huge carcass, there was nothing left but an enormous skeleton.

"Your Majesty," Kālahatthi concluded, "King Ānanda's demise was the natural and inevitable end of becoming a slave to a cannibalistic appetite. He lost all that he treasured and destroyed himself as well. Please take heed of what I am saying, Sire! Stop eating human flesh, or you will share that fish's horrible fate!"

"Kālahatthi," King Brahmadatta retorted, "you are not the only one who knows such stories. Let me give you another example!

"Once upon a time, there was a gentleman named Sujāta here in Bārānasi. He supported five hundred ascetics, who had come down from the Himavat and were staying in a nearby park. Although he prepared alms for them every day, they sometimes walked for alms in the countryside and brought back pieces of jambu.

"One day, Sujāta remarked, 'This is the third or fourth day that the sages have not come to receive my alms. I wonder why.' Taking his little boy's hand, he went to the park and found them finishing their lunch. Sujāta paid his respects and asked them, 'Holy sirs, what are you eating?'

"'Jambu, sir,' they replied.

"Sujāta's son asked for some of the fruit, and the leader of the ascetics gave him a small piece. He ate it and was so charmed with the delicate flavor that he kept on begging for more.

"Sujāta wanted to listen to the ascetics' teaching, so he scolded his son. 'Stop crying!' he said. 'You can have more jambu when we get back home.'

"After the ascetics had finished teaching, Sujāta and his son returned home. The boy immediately asked for some jambu, but, of course, Sujāta had none to give him. The poor boy had been deceived by his father's little lie, so he kept up an incessant cry of 'Give me jambu!'

"When the ascetics left to return to the Himavat, they were not able to see the boy again, but they sent him a present of jambu, preserved in sugar. As soon as this luscious fruit touched the tip of the boy's tongue, he was inexorably addicted to its delicate flavor. Thenceforth, he was unable to eat any other food. When it was gone, he demanded more, but, since there was none to be had, he ate nothing, and, after seven days, he died.

"Like Sujāta's son, I have enjoyed the most delicious of all flavors. Nothing else can quench my appetite. If I am deprived of human flesh, I have no desire to live."

"Oh, dear!" Kālahatthi thought. "The king's diabolical appetite seems truly insatiable, but I must not give up!"

"Sire," he said aloud, "Even if you say you have no desire to live, think of your family, who love you and will grieve when you are gone. Think of your loyal subjects who have admired you since you were a child! You must desist from this abomination!"

"Kālahatthi," the king replied. "It is impossible! I love my family and my subjects, but I love the taste of human flesh far more!"

"Here is another story," the commander-in-chief began.

"Once upon a time, in this very city of Bārānasi, there was a brahmin family which kept the five moral precepts. They had one dear son, the delight of his parents, a wise child, well-educated and good. This boy spent his time with a group of boys his own age. The other members of the group ate fish and meat and drank alcohol, but this boy maintained a vegetarian diet and abstained from liquor.

"Eventually, his friends began complaining, 'Because this fellow doesn't drink, he doesn't pay his fair share when we go out. We should get him to drink somehow!'

"The next time they got together, one of them said, 'Friends, let's have a party!' and the others all agreed.

"'You go ahead without me,' the boy said. 'All of you drink, but I don't.'

"'That's not a problem!' they all cried. 'We'll make sure that there is some milk for you to drink. Don't miss out on the fun!'

"'All right,' he said, 'in that case, I will join you.'

"Before the party, the rogues went to the garden and fashioned some leaf cups. They filled each cup with hard liquor and sealed it tight. Then they hid the cups among some lotus leaves. That evening, they were all enjoying themselves at the party. The friends were drinking heavily, and the boy was drinking his milk. Suddenly, the leader of the group shouted, 'Bring us some lotus nectar!' One of the rogues fetched the leaf cups and passed them around. Another one cut a hole in the leaf and began drinking. Others followed his example. Holding up his cup, which he had not yet opened, the boy asked what it was. 'It is lotus nectar,' the leader replied. 'It is very sweet, and it is completely harmless!' Believing him, the boy cut a hole in his own cup and drank. The new taste sent a thrill through his entire body. He emptied the cup in one swallow and asked for more. After he had drunk quite a bit, his erstwhile friends offered him some broiled meat, which he ate without thinking. When he was thoroughly drunk, they told him, 'Friend, this is not lotus nectar. It is whiskey!'

"'Really? Is that so?' he replied, slurring his words almost incomprehensibly. 'I never knew such a sweet taste! Bring more! I want more!' They gave him much more, no longer disguising it in leaf cups. He drank everything they poured, without even pausing for breath. He kept asking for more, but, finally, they told him that the liquor was all gone.

"'Don't you dare hold out on me!' he cried. 'Fetch me more! You can take my ring to pay for it!' He gave them his signet ring set with precious gems and told them to bring as much as it would buy. After drinking with them all night, his eyes were bloodshot, his whole body was trembling, and he was babbling incoherently. His companions helped him stagger home and put him in bed, where he slept the whole of the next day.

"When his father found out that he had been drinking, he was furious. 'Son,' his father shouted, 'how could you have done such a stupid thing? No one in our family has ever drunk before! Never do it again.'

"'Dear Father, what is my offence?' asked the boy.

"'You drank liquor!' his father replied.

"'I had never tasted anything so sweet, so delicious!' the boy replied innocently.

"When he heard this, the father thought, 'If he becomes an alcoholic, our family will be destroyed, and our prosperity will disappear.' Aloud he said, 'Dear boy, abstain from alcohol. If you don't stop drinking, I will throw you out of this house and have you exiled from the kingdom!'

"'Threaten me as you will, Father,' the boy replied, 'I will not give up drinking. You are asking me to give up what I love most. To get it, I will go wherever I have to go and do whatever I have to do. If you want me to leave, I will leave, never to live with you again. I guess you don't love me anymore. If you did, you would never ask me to give up the only thing that makes me happy!'

145

"'Well, my boy,' the father said sadly, 'if you are willing to give us up, we give up on you! We will find some other son to inherit our wealth. If you prefer your drink to your family and your home, begone! Go where we will no longer hear your cursed name!'

"The unhappy father applied to the court, disinherited his son, and drove him out of the house. The young man was soon destitute. Wearing rags and begging for food, he slept in the street. Reduced to that wretched state, he spent any money he could find on liquor. One day, he was found leaning against a wall, dead.

"Sire," Kālahatthi begged, "if you refuse to heed my warning, like that alcoholic youth, you will be banished from the kingdom!"

"Kālahatthi," the king insisted, "I cannot control my craving for human flesh. Let me illustrate my point. That same Sujāta, that I told you about a few minutes ago, once glimpsed the celestial nymphs who accompanied Sakka when he paid his respects to the five hundred ascetics. Sujāta was so bewitched by the incomparable beauty of those apsaras that he rejected earthly women as female ghouls. Crying deliriously, 'Bring me an apsara! I must have an apsara!' he could neither eat nor drink and died of starvation. His obsession was like my addiction," Brahmadatta concluded. "Having tasted the rarest and the most delectable of viands, if deprived of human flesh, I will die of starvation."

"This king styles himself to be a great epicure," General Kālahatthi thought, "but I must make him see reality!"

Aloud he said, "Once upon a time, Sire, ninety thousand golden geese lived in the Golden Cave on Mount Cittakuta. During the rainy season, they could not leave the shelter of the cave because they could not fly well if they got their wings too wet. If they tried, they would fall into the sea and perish. As the rainy season was approaching, they gathered wild paddy from the nearby lake and stored enough in the cave to last them for the four months of the rains. Each year, as soon as all ninety thousand geese had entered the cave, an Unnanābhi spider, as big as a chariot wheel, began spinning a web at the cave entrance. Each thread was as thick as the strap of a cow's halter. Every month, the spider spun a new web.

"The geese had learned that, although the webs were strong, it was not difficult for a strong goose to break through a single web. It took a special strength, however, to break though multiple webs. To ensure that they could escape at the end of the rainy season, the geese always gave one young goose a double portion of food, making him strong enough to break through a number of webs. When the sky cleared, this young goose flew at the head of the flock, crashing through the four webs and allowing all the other geese to escape behind him.

"One year, the rainy season was prolonged to five months, and the rations the golden geese had stored were completely depleted. The geese discussed what they should do, and they decided that, in order for any of them to survive, they would have to eat their eggs. When there were no more eggs, they ate the goslings. When there were no more goslings, they ate the oldest members of the flock.

"By the end of five months, when the rain had finally tapered off, the spider had finished five webs. Because they had eaten the flesh of their kin, the golden geese were feeble and degenerate. Even the young goose who had received an extra portion of food every day, was not as strong as in previous years. When it was time to leave, the young goose managed to break through four of the webs, but he could not break the fifth, and he became stuck there. The spider immediately cut off his head and drank his blood. The other geese were so weak that they could not even break through the one final web, and they, too, got entangled. The Unnanābhi spider sucked the blood of each and every one, and that species of golden geese became extinct.

"Sire," the commander-in-chief concluded, "magnificent golden geese completely died out after eating the flesh of their own kind. You, too, run the same risk! You must stop!"

King Brahmadatta started to give another counter example, but the citizens in the courtyard, who had heard everything, began shouting. Several voices called out, "General Kālahatthi, what are you going to do?" "Is he a king or a wicked, man-eating yakkha?" "If he does not promise to stop, expel him from the kingdom!" "Don't let him give any more excuses!" "Is he always going to be a murderer?" "If the king keeps killing, let's kill him!"

General Kālahatthi summoned the king's family and all the members of the court, who soon appeared in their finest formal wear. The commander-in-chief pointed to the queen, the handsome princes, the lovely princesses, and all the king's attendants and said, "Your Majesty, here is your beloved family. Here are your advisors and all your attendants. This is all you have ever dreamed of having. You are the great king of Kāsi. To maintain this magnificent status, you must give up this craving for human flesh. This is your last chance."

The king waved his hand over the entire assembly and said, "None of this is dearer to me than human flesh!"

"In that case, you must go!" General Kālahatthi declared, "Leave the city, and leave the kingdom! You are no longer our king! We do not even recognize you as a citizen of Kāsi! Depart!"

"Kālahatthi," Brahmadatta said, "I willingly relinquish my kingdom. I am ready to leave, but please grant me just one favor. Let me have my sword and my cook."

"Very well," the commander-in-chief agreed. "You may take your sword, your cook, a cooking pot, and a basket. Soldiers will escort you to the border of Kāsi to make sure that you actually leave the kingdom."

From that day, Brahmadatta became known as Porisāda, the Cannibal. He lived in the jungle at the foot of a banyan tree. Every day, he hid by the roadside waiting for travelers. After he had killed his victim, he took the body to the cook, who butchered it, cooked it, and served it to him, as though he were still a king.

After some time, he gained such notoriety that all he had to do was shout, "I am Porisāda!" and even strong men fainted and fell senseless to the ground. He could pick up any one he fancied, by the head or by the heels, and carry him back to the cook.

One day, the inevitable happened. Porisāda did not find anyone on the road, and he returned empty-handed to the banyan tree.

"What's the matter, Sire?" the cook asked.

"Nothing," replied Porisāda. "Just put the pot on the fire!"

"But where is the meat, Sire?"

"Oh! I will find something," he replied.

The cook began quaking. "I am a dead man!" he thought. He built a fire and set a pot of water on the stones, but, the whole time, his hands were trembling. Porisāda approached him from behind and killed him with one stroke of his sword. He cut the body into pieces and threw them into the pot. From then on, Porisāda was entirely alone and had to cook his meat himself.

Throughout Jambudīpa, people were talking about the cannibal lurking in that great stretch of jungle, who was killing travelers and eating their flesh.

At that time, a wealthy brahmin trader was traveling across Jambudīpa on that road, from the east to the west, with a caravan of five hundred wagons loaded with goods. He had heard stories about Porisāda, so, before he entered the jungle, he stopped in a village and hired a troop of able-bodied men as bodyguards. He paid them one thousand coins apiece to escort him safely to the other side of the jungle. He let the wagons go ahead, and, dressed in fine silks and surrounded by his bodyguards, he sat in an elegant rig, drawn by matching white oxen, at the very rear of the caravan.

As the wagons approached, Porisāda was watching from a tall tree. He was not at all interested in the skinny drovers, but, as soon as he saw the plump brahmin, his mouth began to water. When the brahmin was directly beneath the tree, Porisāda jumped down and shouted, "I am Porisāda!" His sword was flashing so fiercely that the guards fell to the ground for fear of being decapitated. Porisāda quickly seized the brahmin by his feet and slung him over his shoulder, head downwards. The dazed brahmin was carried off, his head striking against Porisāda's heels.

The guards picked themselves up and shouted, "After him! We are each being paid one thousand coins to protect that brahmin. We can't let him be taken like this! Come on!"

They ran in pursuit of Porisāda, who was slowed by his hefty burden. At one point, he glanced back and saw that the fastest guard was right behind him. Porisāda quickly leaped over a low bush. When he landed, an acacia splinter pierced his foot, and he cried out in pain. Hardly able to run, he limped on as fast as he could, leaving a trail of blood.

As soon as the guard saw the blood, he shouted, "Come on, men! He's wounded! Don't give up! We'll get him now!" The rest of the men could see how exhausted Porisāda was, so they redoubled their efforts. Realizing how close they were, Porisāda dropped the brahmin and worried about his own safety. When the guards reached the brahmin, they helped him to his feet and comforted him. Their master safely rescued, they no longer cared what happened to the monster and returned to the caravan.

Porisāda was relieved to see the men turn back, but he was still in great pain. He kept hobbling along with great difficulty until he reached the banyan tree. He lay down among the great tree's aerial roots and prayed to the deva of the tree. "My Lady, deva of this tree," he moaned, "if you can heal my wound within seven days, I swear that I will bathe the trunk of your tree with blood from the throats of the one hundred one kings of Jambudīpa. I will drape their viscera all around this tree like a garland, and I will offer you a sacrifice of the five kinds of sweet flesh!"

For several days, Porisāda lay at the foot of the banyan tree and slept. His injury, though painful, was not infected and healed naturally. When he awoke without any pain, he was overjoyed and extremely grateful to the tree deva. Not having eaten since his encounter with the brahmin, he was ravenous. He easily killed several travelers, ate them, and recovered his full strength. "Now," he declared, "I must fulfill my vow to this deva for curing my wound."

Porisāda picked up his sword and set out on his quest to capture the one hundred one kings of Jambudīpa, who had been his fellow students in Takkasilā years before. As Porisāda was leaving the jungle, a yakkha saw him and recognized him as a companion in a previous existence. "Hello, Friend, do you remember me?" the yakkha called.

"No, I can't say that I do." Porisāda answered. "Should I?"

"In a previous life," the yakkha explained, "you were a yakkha like me. Oh, the men we killed and ate together! You were such a fierce fellow!"

"Of course!" Porisāda shouted. "Now I remember! It's good to see you again!" He embraced the yakkha warmly. They sat down together and discussed their adventures since the time they had last been together. After explaining his current quest, Porisāda added, "Fulfilling my vow would be much easier with your help! Can you join me?"

"I wish I could," the yakkha replied, "but I have to take care of some business of my own. However, there's something I can do for you. Let me teach you a spell that will give you superhuman strength and incomparable speed!"

Porisāda enthusiastically accepted his old friend's offer and memorized the spell. When he took off again, he was as fast as the wind. He suddenly appeared in the palace of a neighboring kingdom, shouted his name, grabbed the king by the feet, and was gone before anyone realized what was happening. With the captive king slung over his shoulder and allowing his victim's head to bump his heels as he ran, Porisāda returned to the banyan tree. Before the king had recovered from his shock, Porisāda drilled holes in the palms of his hands and passed a leather thong through the holes. He tied the thong to the tree and let the king hang with his toes barely touching the ground. In only seven days, Porisāda was able to criss-cross Jambudīpa, capture one hundred kings, and hoist them up in the same way. The one hundred kings were suspended from the tree, twisting slowly in the wind like withered flowers.

Porisāda realized that he was one king short of fulfilling his vow, but he still had a spark of humanity left in him. "Sutasoma was my best friend and my tutor," he sighed. "If I captured him, Jambudīpa would be entirely desolate!" Hoping that the deva would not notice that his offering was incomplete, he kindled a fire and sharpened a stake.

The deva watched with dismay. "He is preparing to offer a bloody sacrifice to me, but I had nothing to do with healing his wound! There is going to be a great slaughter here. What can I do? I can't stop him by myself! I need to find help." She first went to the Four Great Kings, but they said that they could do nothing. She hurried to Sakka, told him the whole story, and appealed to him to intervene.

"I myself cannot stop Porisāda," Sakka replied, "but I can tell you who can!"

"Who, Great Lord?" the deva begged, "Who can prevent this massacre?"

"In the realms of devas and men," Sakka told her, "there is no one but King Sutasoma who can tame Porisāda and cure him of his craving for human flesh. If you want to save those one hundred kings, you must demand that Porisāda fetch Sutasoma before offering any sacrifice to you."

"Thank you, Sire! I will do that!" said the deva.

Instantly, she disguised herself as an ascetic and began walking near the banyan tree. When Porisāda heard the footsteps, he wondered whether one of the kings had managed to escape. When he saw that it was an ascetic, an idea came to him. "That ascetic is probably a khattiya!" he reasoned. "If I capture him, I can say that I am sacrificing one hundred one warriors and fulfilling my promise!"

He grabbed his sword, jumped to his feet, and raced after the ascetic. Porisāda chased the ascetic for three yojanas, but he could not overtake him. Streams of sweat poured from his body. "What's going on?" he wondered. "For seven days, I used my friend's spell, and I could easily have caught a charging elephant or a horse galloping at full speed, but now, even though I'm running as fast as I can, I can't touch this ascetic, who is walking at a normal pace. Wait! These ascetics usually do what they're asked. If I can get him to stand still, I'll have him!" Aloud he shouted, "Stand, Holy Sage!"

"I am standing!" the ascetic replied. "You, too, should stand!"

"What do you mean?" Porisāda retorted. "An ascetic, even to save his life, should never tell a lie. How can you say, 'I am standing!' when I am running at full speed and still cannot catch you? Perhaps, you'll also say that my sword is a harmless stick fixed with a heron's feather!"

"I stand steadfast in righteousness," the ascetic replied. "Is there righteousness in trying to pass off one hundred when one hundred one were promised? Is there righteousness in the deceit of replacing a king with an ascetic? Will the robber who has stayed here a short time doom himself to the suffering of hell with his deceit?"

The deva abandoned her disguise and stood in her own glorious form, blazing like the sun in the sky. Porisāda was overwhelmed and asked who she was. She answered truthfully, and Porisāda was delighted to see his patroness. "Be strong!" she admonished him. "Bring me the great king, Sutasoma. Fulfill your vow and, with your sacrifice, win yourself a place in heaven!"

"Do not worry about Sutasoma. I will bring him!" Porisāda assured her. "Please return to your own abode, and be at peace!"

As the deva reentered her tree, the sun set, and the moon rose. Porisāda, who was well-versed in astrology, ascertained that the next day would be the Phussa conjunction of the planets, which was universally associated with the washing of the royal head. This meant that Sutasoma would be going to the tank in the royal park to bathe, which would provide an excellent opportunity for his capture. As Porisāda was considering his plan, however, he realized that Sutasoma would have heard about the other kidnappings and would certainly have posted a strong guard all around. "If I want to catch him, I should go to Migacira tonight before the soldiers get there."

Porisāda hurried to Indapatta, made his way to the park, entered the tank, and hid under a lotus leaf. In a previous life, at the time of Kassapa Buddha, the man-eater had initiated a distribution of milk by ticket and, when a fire room had been built, provided the bhikkhus with an axe, firewood, and the fire itself. His generosity had been well known at the time, and the merit of that offering still remained with him. Because of that merit, the fish and turtles, in deference to him, moved away to the edges of the tank.

Early the next morning, guards were stationed around the park for three yojanas in every direction. King Sutasoma mounted his richly caparisoned elephant and, with an army escort, left the city for the park. As the king was passing through the eastern gate, a brahmin, standing on a small rise some distance from the gate, raised his hand in salutation and cried, "Victory to Your Majesty!"

King Sutasoma, having excellent eyesight, clearly saw the brahmin and directed his elephant toward that spot. "Where are you from, brahmin?" he asked. "Who are you, and why have you come here? Whatever it is, I will grant your wish on this auspicious day!"

"My name is Nanda," the brahmin answered. "I have traveled one hundred twenty yojanas from Takkasilā to bring Your Majesty four profound truths. They were taught to me by Kassapa Buddha, and they are worth one hundred coins each. Hearing of Your Majesty's greatness, I resolved to come and to teach them to you. Let us go to your palace, where you can listen carefully while I recite them."

Sutasoma was delighted. "Master," he said, "you have done well to come to me. Unfortunately, I cannot turn back now. Today is the Phussa conjunction, and I must perform the ceremonial washing of my hair. After bathing, I will return and listen to your truths with the greatest of pleasure. Please do not be dissatisfied with me or reproach me for that which I cannot help!"

To his attendants, the king said, "Escort this brahmin to the home of one of my advisors, and offer him all hospitality."

The king continued to the park and entered by the gate in the formidable wall, which was eighteen hatthas high and guarded by elephants, horses, chariots, archers, and foot soldiers.

When Porisāda saw the king, he thought, "Fully dressed, Sutasoma must be awfully heavy. I'll wait until he takes off his robes. Then I'll seize him!"

The king approached the tank, and attendants removed his robes of state. As he stood on the steps, clad in only a light dhoti, the attendants bathed him, shaved his beard, and shampooed his hair. As they were placing the garland of scented flowers around his neck, Porisāda leaped up, whirling his razor-sharp sword over his head, and shouted, "I am Porisāda!" He seized Sutasoma and placed him on his shoulder, not head downward as he had handled the other kings, but upright, out of respect for his tutor. Rather than running toward the gate, he leaped over the high wall and landed on the back of one of the elephants. As he jumped from there, he toppled a horse, smashed a chariot, knocked over several archers, and trampled a good number of foot soldiers. He was like a powerful whirling top as he sped away for three yojanas, carrying Sutasoma as if he were a feather.

Porisāda looked back and saw that no one was pursing him, so he slowed his pace. Feeling the drops of water which fell from Sutasoma's wet hair, Porisāda asked, "Why are you crying, Your Majesty? Are you afraid of death? Are you crying for your family, yourself, or your gold?"

"I am not weeping at all," Sutasoma replied, "not for myself, my wife, my child, my realm, nor my gold. I should be crying, however, for a promise unfulfilled. This morning I made a promise to a brahmin that I would return and hear his teaching. I want to save my honor by keeping my word. Let me fulfill that promise, and I will return to you."

"Do you expect me to believe," Porisāda scoffed, "that, if I let you return to your palace, where you are safe and comfortable, you will come back here? No one saved from the jaws of death would ever willingly return to face certain destruction!"

"My friend, you are utterly wrong!" Sutasoma declared. "An innocent man would prefer death to a life clouded by doubt and suspicion. Telling a lie, even to save his life, would doom a man to hell. It's more likely for the wind to turn the mountains around or to knock the sun and moon from the sky or for rivers to flow upstream than for me to tell a lie."

Seeing that Porisāda still did not believe him, Sutasoma asked to be placed on the ground so that he could swear upon his honor. Porisāda saw no harm in that and set his captive down. Sutasoma reached out and said, "As I touch your sword, I pledge my solemn vow. I will go to Indapatta and keep my word. As soon as I have paid my debt and my honor is restored, I will return for you to do with me as you will."

"All right! Go and keep your promise to the brahmin. When you have finished, come back to me. I will be waiting at the great banyan tree, but I don't really believe that you will come back."

"Don't worry, my friend," Sutasoma said. "I only need to hear four truths, each worth one hundred coins. After I have heard them and given the brahmin his fee, I will definitely return, no later than daybreak tomorrow."

"My honor is at stake, too." Porisāda added. "I promised the deva all one hundred one kings. If you don't come back, I won't be able to fulfill my vow! The deva has explicitly declared that you are essential. Don't make me lose face!"

"My man-eating friend, you've known me since we were both boys together. You know that I have never, even in jest, told a lie. Now that I am the anointed king of a great kingdom, why should I lie? Please have faith in me! I will be part of your offering."

"All right! I believe you!" Porisāda said, "You've sworn on the honor of khattiya. See that you act honorably!"

As Sutasoma left, Porisāda thought, "This Sutasoma swore on khattiya honor, so, if he breaks his word, he's not worthy of his title. If worse comes to worse, I can offer my own khattiya blood, drawn from my right arm, to the deva. Let's see how good his word really is!"

When Porisāda captured Sutasoma, the soldiers, having great confidence in their king, thought, "King Sutasoma is wise and a most eloquent teacher. If he gets a chance to talk, he will, no doubt, reform that man-eater and return safely to us. Nevertheless, we cannot go back and tell the people that we let a cannibal capture him. They would be furious. Better we wait here until he returns." They set up camp outside the city walls.

When his men saw King Sutasoma returning, like the moon freed from the jaws of Rāhu, they rejoiced and went out to meet him. "Sire, were you disgusted by the man-eater?" they asked.

"Not at all!" the king replied. "Porisāda did something very difficult, more difficult than anything my parents ever did. Although he is a fierce and violent creature, after listening to my talk, he allowed me to return here."

His attendants dressed him in his royal robes, mounted him on an elephant, and escorted him into the city. The citizens rejoiced when they saw him, but, because of his zeal for the law, Sutasoma went directly to the palace and summoned Nanda. When the brahmin arrived, the king ordered his attendants to bathe the man, to trim his hair and beard, and to dress him in the finest clothes. Nanda was given the king's own meal while the king himself took a bath.

Sutasoma placed the brahmin on an elegant throne, while he and the rest of the court sat on low seats. "Master," Sutasoma said, "we would like to hear the four truths which you have brought to us."

The brahmin washed his hands, reached into his bag, and took out a beautiful book. "Sire," he began, "these four truths, each worth one hundred coins, were taught to me by Kassapa Buddha. They are conducive to the elimination of lust and to the attainment of Nibbāna:

"Keep company, Sire, with those who have stilled their minds; avoid the wicked and the foolish, that you, too, may gain that greatest peace.

"Let your friends be only from the good and wise; from them learn the truth, that you may grow in virtue.

"Just as the elegant royal chariot deteriorates, our bodies decline with age, but the truth proclaimed by the wise never fades.

"The sky is high, and the earth is wide, but greater than these is the reach of truth, ever to be cherished."

When the brahmin had finished, Sutasoma declared, "My journey here has certainly not been without its reward!" He was, in fact, overwhelmed by the significance of the truths he had just heard. "These truths are not the words of a disciple or a poet," he reflected. "They were spoken by the Omniscient One himself! They are priceless! Even the entire world, filled to the Brahma heavens with the seven precious things, would not be adequate compensation for these truths! For teaching them to me, I should give this Brahmin, at least, the sovereignty over this city of Indapatta. His gift is worth a kingship!"

As Sutasoma was contemplating how he should reward Nanda for his incomparable lesson, he studied the brahmin's face. Being an accomplished interpreter of physiognomy, he found no indication that Nanda was fit to be a king, a commander-in-chief, or even a village leader. He did, however, see signs of wealth, and he instructed his treasurer to fill four purses with one thousand coins each.

"Did I hear you correctly, Master," Sutasoma asked the brahmin, "that you believe these truths are worth one hundred coins each?"

"That is correct, Your Majesty," Nanda replied.

"Does that mean that other kings have paid you four hundred coins when you have recited these truths to them?"

"That is correct, Your Majesty," Nanda agreed.

"Master, you are ignorant of the incomparable value of what you possess," Sutasoma told him. "From now on, Nanda, let these truths be valued at one thousand coins each! That is what they are worth to me! Take these four thousand coins when you go." Sutasoma gave him the four purses and a small vehicle, as well. "Convey this brahmin safely to his home!" he ordered his attendants, and he dismissed him.

Throughout the palace, there were loud cries of "Bravo! The king has properly honored the brahmin's truths! Bravo for our king!"

The king's parents, however, being greedy by nature, were furious. When Sutasoma went to their apartment to pay his respects, instead of congratulating him, his father berated the king.

"My son," he shouted, "how could you have paid four thousand coins after hearing a few sentences that were valued at only one hundred each? You probably could have had them for less if you had bargained! No one but a fool pays more than he has to for anything!"

"Do not castigate me, Father, just for the sake of money!" Sutasoma replied. "It's not wealth that I care about. It's learning! Through friendship with sages, I yearn to increase my knowledge. As fire craves ever more fuel and as the ocean craves ever more water, so the wise crave knowledge. I will always long to hear the profound words of the wise! Even if my humblest servant were to speak truths that I had never heard, I would grant him the highest honor and still ask for more.

"Dear Father," Sutasoma continued, "this morning, before I was captured by the man-eater, I had promised that brahmin that I would listen to this teaching after my bath. Because I had made that vow, Porisāda allowed me to return. Now I must go back to the jungle as his captive. Please accept the sovereignty of Kuru, Father. Become king again in my place! This realm is yours once more, with all its wealth and pomp of state. Please do not blame me for anything, Father. Think nothing ill of me, for I must return to die at Porisāda's hand!"

"My dear Sutasoma, what are you saying?" his father asked in disbelief. "There's no need for you to go back! I will ride at the front of an army and seize the man-eater! What else is an army for, if not to protect our king and to slay his foe?"

"You don't understand," Sutasoma began in explanation.

His mother, with tears in her eyes, joined her husband in begging him to stay. "Don't go, my son!" she cried. "You must not go!"

The news spread like wildfire, and, soon, the entire court was imploring him not to return to the cannibal. "Don't leave us helpless, Sire!" they shouted. "Stay and protect your people!" The whole city was in an uproar.

"Porisāda accomplished a tremendous feat," Sutasoma explained to the crowd. "Even though I was surrounded by all my attendants and all my armies, he captured me, and I was helpless. He allowed me to come back to the palace only after I had sworn on khattiya honor that I would return after I had heard the four truths. Remembering our friendship in our youth and acknowledging his noble act in allowing me to return, how could I violate the solemn oath I swore? In order to be worthy of the title of king,

I must now uphold my vow and return to be his prisoner, even though it means my death."

To comfort his parents, he said, "Dear Father and Mother, please understand that I have acted virtuously and that controlling my sense desires is no difficult matter for me. There is no need for you to worry about me!" He bade farewell to his parents, admonished the people to be diligent, and departed.

In the jungle, Porisāda was sitting under his banyan tree. Having rekindled his fire, he was sharpening another spit. "If my friend Sutasoma wishes to return," he thought, "let him return. If not, I will go ahead and roast these one hundred kings as an offering to the deva. She'll just have to accept it." The man-eater looked up from his work and saw Sutasoma walking toward the tree. "My friend," he called out, with a big smile, "have you done what you wanted to do?"

"Yes, Friend," Sutasoma replied. "I heard the truths that Kassapa Buddha taught to the brahmin Nanda, and I paid due honor to the brahmin for reciting them. Now I have returned as I promised I would. You may kill me as a sacrifice to the deva or to satisfy your own addiction to human flesh."

"This king is fearless!" Porisāda thought. "His speech shows that he has overcome all fear of death. I wonder how he got this power. Of course! It must be from the four truths from Kassapa Buddha that he just heard. I must get him to repeat these truths to me so that I, too, will be free from the fear of death!" Aloud he said, "The fire is not ready yet. By waiting until the coals are really hot, we will in no way compromise the sacrifice. Why don't you teach me those four truths you just heard, which you said were worth one hundred coins each?"

"This man-eater is extremely wicked," Sutasoma thought. "Now is my chance to make him feel ashamed and to make him change." Aloud he said, "Porisāda, you are an evil creature. Because of your carnal appetite you have committed unspeakable crimes. Those truths, whose true value I have declared to be one thousand coins each, proclaim what is righteous. What do you have to do with righteousness? Your hands are smeared with blood. To one as violent as you, what benefit could there possibly be in sacred truths?"

Because of Sutasoma's overwhelming loving-kindness, Porisāda did not get angry, but he tried to justify himself. "Friend Sutasoma, am I the only one who is unrighteous?" he asked. "There's no great difference between one who kills and eats an animal and one who kills and eats a man. Both are guilty and, after death, are treated just the same. Why am I the only one who is blamed for being wicked?"

"Porisāda, you know as well as I," Sutasoma replied, "that, according to khattiya law, there are things which can be eaten and things which cannot. You are wicked because you insist on eating forbidden meat!"

"Sutasoma," Porisāda countered, "you speak of khattiya law, but surely you violated the warrior's code[11] by coming back to certain death after you had been freed and returned to the comfort of your palace."

"Friend," Sutasoma replied, "a king must be well-versed in khattiya law. I may know it well, but I do not govern myself according to it alone. Those who follow the khattiya tradition, without regard for truth and virtue, doom themselves to hell. Having made a solemn vow to you, I returned, true to my word. Now, go ahead, and make your sacrifice!"

"What blessing do you see in truth?" Porisāda asked. "You have a grand palace, a rich kingdom, elephants, horses, cattle, and a huge household. Why do you keep your word and lose all that?"

"Of all the sweet things in this world, none is sweeter than the joy of truth!" Sutasoma replied, with a face as radiant as the full moon. "Those wise sages who abide in the truth are able to escape from birth and death and win the further shore!"

"Sutasoma, you are very skillful with words, and your voice is as sweet as honey," Porisāda declared with honest admiration for his former tutor. "How is it that you can stand there, watching me fan this fire and sharpen this spit, which you know is intended for you, and not fear death? How is it that you can turn your back on worldly pleasures without hesitation and face death without a qualm? Does this fearlessness come from the four truths of Kassapa Buddha?"

"I have done innumerable virtuous deeds," Sutasoma replied, "and my generosity is well known. I have confidence in the path that I have laid to the next world. Why should I have any fear of death? With no regrets, I'll make my way to heaven. Carry out your sacrifice, and devour your prey!

"I have taken care of my parents, been loyal to my friends and relatives, and ruled with righteousness and justice. I have confidence in the path that I have laid to the next world. Why should I have any fear of death? With no regrets, I'll make my way to heaven. Carry out your sacrifice, and devour your prey!"

When Porisāda heard this resounding declaration, he realized the extent of the wickedness of his intention. "Sutasoma is truly a virtuous and wise man," he thought. "In all of Jambudīpa, there is no other sage like this!

---

11 Porisāda is interpreting the khattiya code to say that performing one's duty, which for a king would include self-preservation, is more important than honesty. It could be interpreted further to claim that, in performing his duty, a khattiya is allowed to commit even evil acts.

Above all else, he treasures truth and virtue, and he is not in the slightest afraid of death! Those truths that he received must be of unrivaled excellence and incomparable worth! If I were to kill him, I would be condemning myself to hell!"

Aloud he said, "My friend, you are not the sort of man that I should eat! Only a fool would knowingly drink a cup of poison or blithely pick up a venomous snake! If I were to dare to eat a virtuous man who cannot tell a lie, my head would split into seven pieces! The earth would open and swallow me, and I would fall straight down to hell!" After a slight pause, Porisāda humbly continued, "Sire, when men hear the truth, they may learn to distinguish good from evil. If I could hear those truths, perhaps my heart, too, would be filled with joy and an appreciation for the truth."

"At last, Porisāda is ready to hear the verses," Sutasoma thought. "It is the right time to reveal them to him!" Aloud he said, "Listen carefully, and I will recite the truths exactly as I heard them from the brahmin Nanda."

Sutasoma delivered the four truths so beautifully that the devas in the six sensuous heavens[12] all gave one great cry of appreciation.

These truths, which had first been proclaimed by Kassapa Buddha, were so eloquently recited by the wise Sutasoma, that Porisāda was overwhelmed. His body was filled with the five kinds of joy, and his mind began opening to the truth. Porisāda wondered, since he had no gold, how he might compensate Sutasoma for teaching him these incomparable truths. He thought for a moment and said, "These truths, so rich with meaning and so clearly expressed, make my heart rejoice! In return, I have nothing to offer you, but let me grant you four boons, one for each truth!"

"What boon could you offer me?" Sutasoma scoffed. "You do not understand your own mortality! You cannot distinguish good from evil! You can't tell heaven from hell! As a slave to your own carnal appetite, how can a miserable wretch like you offer me a boon? Furthermore, how can I trust that you will grant what I ask? If you don't like what I ask for, you'll just renege on your promise, and what wise man would risk arguing with you?"

"Sire," Porisāda insisted, "you must believe me. No one should promise a boon and renege on his offer. I vow to respect my promise. I, too, have my honor! Fearlessly choose your boons, Sire. If it is in my power, I will grant whatever you ask, even if it costs me my very life!"

"He has spoken bravely!" Sutasoma thought. "Now Porisāda is ready to be taught. I will accept his generous offer and bring an end to his depravity, but I must proceed carefully so as not to devastate him all at once."

---

12   See Planes 611, in The Thirty-one Planes of Existence in the Appendix.

Aloud he said, "My friend, I believe you, and I will accept your offer. My first boon is that you may live safe and sound for one hundred years!"

Porisāda was deeply moved, hardly believing his ears. "Even though I have taken this man away from his kingdom and threatened his life, he now wishes long life for me, a notorious man-eater!" Aloud he said, with a hearty laugh, "Sutasoma, I gladly grant you this first boon!"

"My second boon," Sutasoma continued, "is that you refrain from eating these one hundred kings that you have captured."

Porisāda was slightly taken aback that Sutasoma would ask him to give up so much, but, calculating that he would still be able to go through with his sacrifice and confident that he would find other food, he said, "Sutasoma, I gladly grant you this second boon!"

Those kings, with their hands tied above their heads and hanging from the tree, had been watching Porisāda build his fire, and were sure that they would be killed. When Sutasoma arrived, they began to feel some hope. Unable to hear clearly what was being said, they encouraged each other: "Don't worry! Somehow Sutasoma will save us!"

"My third boon," Sutasoma continued, "is that you release these one hundred kings and restore them all to their own kingdoms."

Earlier, Porisāda would have been stunned by the magnitude of this boon, but he had come to realize that his vow to Sutasoma was more important than a bloody offering to the deva, so he could say, "Sutasoma, I gladly grant you this third boon!"

"Porisāda, no, let me change that and say, King Brahmadatta!" Sutasoma continued, "Your kingdom is distracted, and your people are dismayed. They are afraid of you and hide from your sight. Still, you are their rightful king. That kingdom could be yours again. My fourth boon is that you abstain from eating human flesh."

Porisāda clapped his hands and laughed. "Friend, you don't know what you are asking!" he declared. "How could I possibly grant you this boon? I cannot overcome my craving for this flesh. That is why I am here in the jungle! My friend, for your fourth boon, you must choose something else."

"Sire! You promised to grant whatever I asked for, even if it cost you your life!" King Sutasoma reminded him. "Wise men never allow duplicity in their speech. Good men are always true to their promises. You told me to choose boons fearlessly, but now you're telling me to choose a different boon. What you said then and what you're saying now do not agree!"

"For the sake of my addiction to human flesh, I have committed evil deeds of every sort," Porisāda cried, weeping pitifully. "For this pleasure, I have already suffered unspeakable disgrace and shame. Having done all this without a qualm or regret, why should I now care if I do not grant you this boon?"

"Friend!" Sutasoma replied. "One who would give up wealth to save a limb would sacrifice a limb to save his life. A wise man, however, would gladly give up wealth, limbs, and life itself to preserve what's right. You boldly declared that you have honor, too. You, too, must keep your word and do that which is right!"

Porisāda began shaking with fear. "Sire," he cried, "what am I to do? I know that I must not deny your request, but I know that I cannot abstain from human flesh! My addiction, my craving, my passion is too strong! I love human flesh! I live for it. I cannot give it up! Please, Sire, choose something else!"

"You say that you cannot abstain from eating human flesh," Sutasoma continued, "because you love the taste. A king should never commit evil deeds for pleasure. One who sacrifices his life for the sake of pleasure is a fool! Whoever insists on his own pleasure, even to the point of doing evil and sacrificing his life, drinks from a poisoned cup and dooms himself to woe and suffering in the next world. Whoever forgoes pleasure to maintain virtue, drinks from a nourishing cup and awakens to bliss in the next world. Uphold righteousness, and, by your merit, you will attain happiness in this life and in the next, as well."

"Sutasoma, I gave up everything for the sake of this pleasure," Porisāda pleaded. "For this, I came to live in this jungle. How can I give you the boon you are asking?"

"One who teaches the truth to another not only removes the hearer's doubts and perplexities, but he becomes a refuge to his friend, a place of safety, and a rock. When you were young, my friend, I was your private tutor, and I taught you well. Now I have given you four profound truths of a Buddha, worth one thousand coins each. You should respect me and obey my words. It is not right for you to go against the words of so excellent a teacher."

"It's true that Sutasoma was my teacher," Porisāda reflected. "It's also true that I freely gave him the choice of a boon. What else can I do? I cannot refuse him." With tears streaming down his face, the man-eater fell at King Sutasoma's feet, crying: "This food is so delectable! It is ambrosia to my tongue! It is the sole reason that I have stayed on alone in this jungle for so long! But, since you are my teacher and my friend, Sutasoma, I grant you this fourth boon!"

"Bravo! Congratulations, Friend!" Sutasoma exclaimed. "By this determination, you are establishing yourself on the path of righteousness. I have accepted the boons you offered me. Now let me ask one more thing. Please undertake the five precepts. To one who is firmly grounded in this moral practice, even death can be a blessing."

"Very good, Master," Porisāda answered, "please give me the five moral precepts."

Sutasoma recited the five precepts, and Porisāda repeated them sincerely. At that moment, all the devas who dwell on earth gathered around and proclaimed, "There is no one else in all the planes of existence who could have accomplished this feat! Sutasoma has wrought a miracle!" They applauded until the jungle echoed with their cries. When the one hundred kings, still suspended from the banyan tree, heard the applause and the cheering, they joined in the rejoicing. The Four Great Kings added their great voices, and it became a universal roar of approval, which reached the Brahma heavens.

"Now, Friend," Sutasoma said, "release the kings!"

Porisāda took a step toward the banyan tree, but, suddenly, he thought, "To these one hundred kings, I am a hated enemy! As soon as they are released, they will cry, 'Seize him! He is our foe!' and they will attack me. Nevertheless, I cannot violate the precepts which I have accepted from Sutasoma. He must help me so that I will be safe." Aloud he said, "Teacher, let us go together and release the kings. I have done what you asked, now please do what I ask of you."

"Of course, my friend. Let us do it together. I will protect you."

Sutasoma stood with Porisāda in front of the tree and said, "Friends, you have suffered greatly because of this cannibal. He has indeed grievously wronged you. However, please promise that you will not so much as lay a finger on him after you have been released."

The kings replied, "While we have been strung up on this banyan tree, we have wept copious tears. We do not deny that we loathe this man-eater who has wronged us beyond measure. Despite that, for you, Sutasoma, we all make a solemn vow never to harm him, if only we may live!"

Sutasoma asked them to regard Porisāda as their father, and they agreed to that, as well.

"You are safe, Porisāda," Sutasoma told him. "Now release the kings." Porisāda took his sword and cut the thong that held one of the kings. That poor man, however, was so exhausted after not eating for a week that he crumpled in a heap on the ground.

"Friend," Sutasoma cried, "please be careful! Do not cut them down like that! That is too cruel!" He walked up to a second king and grasped him firmly around the waist. "Now cut the thong!" he said. Porisāda did so, and Sutasoma gently let him down and tenderly laid him on the ground as if he were his own son.

When all one hundred warriors were cut loose, Sutasoma bathed their wounds and gently teased the cords from their hands as a mother would take the string from a child's pierced ear. He washed off the clotted blood and applied ointment to the wounds. After he had done this to all one hundred kings, he performed an asseveration of truth, and their wounds were instantly healed.

Porisāda prepared some herbal broth and gave it to them as the sun set. The next day, the kings were given rice water at dawn, at noon, and in the evening. On the third day, they were able to accept gruel with boiled rice.

King Sutasoma asked the kings whether they felt strong enough to travel, and they all assured him that they did. "Come," he said to Porisāda, "let us go to Bārānasi!"

Porisāda fell, weeping at the king's feet. "Go ahead, my friend!" he cried, "Accompany these kings back to their own kingdoms. I will stay here and live on roots and wild berries."

"No, dear friend!" Sutasoma replied. "Your life here is finished. You have a delightful kingdom! Go back, and reign in Bārānasi!"

"Dear Sutasoma, it is inconceivable for me to go back!" Porisāda protested. "To all the citizens of Kāsi, I am an enemy. They hate me! If they see me, they will all cry, 'This monster ate my mother!' 'He killed my father!' 'Execute the criminal!' They will pelt me with stones and kill me or, at least, drive me away. Having been established by you in the moral precepts, I cannot fight back, even in self-defense, lest I kill someone. No, my friend, I cannot go back! You must go! I will stay here alone! Abstaining from human flesh, I wonder how long I will survive. It doesn't matter! My greatest sorrow is that I will never see you again!" Porisāda continued weeping.

Sutasoma stroked his friend's back and said gently, "My friend, I have just tamed the cruel and wicked wretch that you were. I will reestablish you in Bārānasi! If I fail in that, I will divide my own kingdom and give half of it to you!"

"But Sire," Porisāda objected, "I have enemies in your kingdom, too!"

"Friend, in Bārānasi, stands the most magnificent palace in Jambudīpa! The food there is the most delicious of all! When you lived there, you were surrounded by noble ladies, magnificently attired, who anticipated your every wish! You used to recline on an elegant couch, piled high with silken pillows and covered with a soft woolen coverlet. You were often entertained until late at night by the rhythm of drums, enchanting music, and charming songs. Your pleasure garden was filled with fragrant flowers and rare trees. Bārānasi holds abundant beautiful sights, entrancing sounds, and tempting smells on every corner! All this can be yours again! Why abandon it to stay here alone in this dismal jungle? I will reestablish you there before returning to my own kingdom. Let us go together! I promise you that all will be well!"

Sutasoma's eloquent description of Bārānasi reawakened Porisāda's love for his kingdom and his desire to live there once again. He was sure that he could depend on his old friend not only to protect him but also to reestablish him as king as skillfully as he had established him in virtue.

"Friend Sutasoma," he cried, "When heavy rain falls on dry ground, the water disappears. In the same way, friendship with the wicked can quickly fade. When heavy rain falls on a river, the water stays and swells the current. In the same way, friendship with the good can be trusted to endure. I now understand that nothing is better than fellowship with a virtuous friend! Nothing can be worse than associating with the wicked! Friendship with the bad leads to decay and misery. It was that coarse and wicked cook, who first tricked me into eating human flesh. Because of that, I committed unspeakably evil deeds which would have carried me to hell! Friendship with the good leads to growth and happiness. By associating with you, Sutasoma, I will refrain from evil and will do many good deeds, which, I hope, will someday carry me to heaven."

Sutasoma led Porisāda and the one hundred kings out of the jungle. From a frontier village, they sent a messenger to Indapatta, and Sutasoma's father dispatched an army to escort them all to Bārānasi. As they traveled through the countryside, people brought Sutasoma food and presents and followed in his train. By the time he reached Bārānasi, he was accompanied by a large crowd.

General Kālahatthi was still commander-in-chief, and Porisāda's son had become king. Townspeople rushed to the palace. "We have heard that King Sutasoma has tamed and reformed Porisāda and has brought him back to Bārānasi. We will not allow him to enter the city!" they cried. The king quickly closed the city gates and stationed guards to keep Porisāda out.

Sutasoma left Porisāda with the one hundred kings some distance away and approached the gate with some of his advisors. "I am King Sutasoma of Indapatta!" he shouted. "Open the gate!"

The king permitted Sutasoma to enter the city, and soldiers escorted him to the palace. The king and the commander-in-chief greeted Sutasoma, led him inside, and seated him on the throne. Sutasoma summoned the former queen consort and the royal advisors. Turning to Kālahatthi, he asked, "General, why won't you allow King Brahmadatta to enter the city?"

"He is a monster! While he was king, he wickedly killed and devoured many of his subjects. He blatantly broke khattiya law, and we cannot allow him to return."

"I can assure you all," Sutasoma replied, "that Brahmadatta will no longer act in that way. I have tamed him, and you never need fear him again."

Turning to Kālahatthi again, he said, "General Kālahatthi, you owe your position and your power to Brahmadatta. You were his close friend. You should now act in his interest."

Turning to the young king, he said, "Sire, children should respect and care for their parents. One who cherishes his father and mother will go to heaven. One who denies and abuses them will go to hell. You, too, should now act in his interest."

Turning to the former queen, he said, "Your Highness, Brahmadatta raised you to your exalted position and blessed you with sons and daughters. You, too, should now act in his interest."

To the entire court, he said, "I have completely reformed Brahmadatta, and I have established him in the five precepts. Not even to save his own life, will he harm anyone. Let me now expound to all of you that moral law.

"A king must never harm innocent subjects anywhere in his realm. No friend should ever take advantage of another friend by treachery. A woman must not stand in fear of her husband. Children must protect their aged parents.

"A council hall does not deserve the name if those who gather there are not wise. The wise are those who have abandoned greed, hatred, and delusion. They never fail to teach the truth to others, far and wide. A sage who, surrounded by fools, remains silent will never be recognized as wise, but, if he speaks even a single word of truth, all will know his worth. Respect the sages who teach virtue and glorify the truth. The emblem of a saint is noble speech. The flag he flies is everlasting truth."

Everyone was delighted with this exposition of moral law. The king and the commander-in-chief, in consultation with the advisors, agreed to allow Brahmadatta to enter the city.

A proclamation, accompanied by a drum, was made throughout the city: "Citizens, do not be afraid! King Sutasoma of Kuru assures us that Brahmadatta has been tamed and established in righteousness! We are allowing him to reenter the city. You have nothing to fear!"

King Sutasoma led a great multitude to greet Brahmadatta. After his hair and beard had been trimmed and he had been bathed and dressed in fine robes, his son, the commander-in chief, and the advisors placed him on a heap of precious stones, sprinkled him with lustral water, and led him into the city.

Once again recognized as King Brahmadatta, the former Porisāda honored the one hundred kings. He paid the greatest respect to King Sutasoma, his friend and teacher. All Jambudīpa rejoiced that Sutasoma, lord of men, had converted the man-eater and had re-established him on the throne.

Impatient to have him back, the citizens of Indapatta sent a message urging their king to return. King Sutasoma, however, stayed in Bārānasi for one month. When it was time to leave, he bade fond farewell to King Brahmadatta. "Be zealous in virtue, Friend," he encouraged the king. "Have alms-halls erected at the city gates and at your palace door. Be generous and righteous. Observe the ten duties of a king. Be vigilant against all evil desires and evil deeds."

King Sutasoma left Bārānasi with the one hundred kings. He went a short way with them, then sent each, with an escort, to his respective capital. Before parting, they embraced Sutasoma and expressed their great gratitude to him for saving their lives.

Indapatta was decorated like Tāvatimsa. King Sutasoma entered the city in a great procession. After paying his respects to his parents and expressing his pleasure at seeing them again, he ascended the palace tower and sat on the throne.

Shortly after returning, King Sutasoma reflected, "The deva of the banyan tree was very helpful to me. I should see that she receives a suitable offering." He sent a team of workers to level the ground under the banyan tree, from the farthest limit of its branches, and to enclose the area with a beautiful balustrade. At the four cardinal points, the men erected magnificent carved gates with graceful arches. Near the tree, the king had a vast lake constructed and established a village beside it. Because the village was settled on the spot where the man-eater was converted, it was called Kammasadamma. The king sent many families to live there, and, eventually, Kammasadamma grew into a prosperous city with eighty thousand shops. All the inhabitants paid great respect to the deva of that noble tree.

For the rest of his life, King Sutasoma ruled wisely and with justice. The one hundred one other kings all followed his advice. They ruled righteously, performed good deeds, gave generous alms, and observed the moral law. When they passed away, all were reborn in heaven.

Having concluded his story, the Buddha identified the birth: "At that time, Angulimāla was Porisāda, Sāriputta was Kālahatthi, Ānanda was Nanda, Mahā-Kassapa was the deva of the banyan tree, Anuruddha was Sakka, my followers were the other kings, my parents were Sutasoma's father and mother, and I was King Sutasoma."

208
Prince Temiya
Mūgapakkha Jātaka

It was while staying at Jetavana that the Buddha told this story about the Great Renunciation.

One day, in the Hall of Truth, the bhikkhus were talking about the Blessed One's Great Renunciation. When the Buddha heard what they were discussing, he said, "No, Bhikkhus, my renunciation after fully realizing the Ten Perfections was not so remarkable. Long ago also, when my wisdom was still immature, while I was still striving to attain the perfections, I left my kingdom and renounced the world." At their request, he told this story of the past.

Long, long ago, in Bārānasi, the king of Kāsi had sixteen thousand wives, but not one had given birth to a son or a daughter. The entire kingdom was upset at the lack of an heir. The citizens urged the king to pray for a son. The king in turn urged his wives to pray. Even though the women ardently worshiped the moon and other deities, none became pregnant.

Then the king approached his chief queen, Candādevī, daughter of the king of Madda, who was devoted to good deeds. He earnestly encouraged her to pray for a son to succeed to the throne.

On the full-moon day, Queen Candādevī observed Uposatha. As she was reclining on her couch, she reflected on her virtuous life and proclaimed, "If I have never broken the precepts, by the truth of my vow, may a son be born to me."

This asseveration of truth and the power of her piety caused the seat of Sakka, king of the devas, to become hot. Sakka quickly ascertained the cause and declared, "Queen Candādevī is asking for a son. I will give her one!"

At that time, the Bodhisatta, after having reigned for only twenty years in Bārānasi and having suffered for eighty thousand years in Ussada hell, was living in Tāvatimsa. His time there was expiring, and he was hoping to be reborn in the higher heavens. Sakka approached him, however, and said, "Friend, if you are born in the realm of men, you will be able to attain the Ten Perfections, which will be of great benefit to mankind. At this moment, Candādevī, the chief queen of Kāsi, is praying for a son. Please agree to be born to her."

The Bodhisatta reluctantly consented. At the same time, five hundred other devas descended to be reborn to the wives of the king's ministers.

The queen felt as if her womb were full of diamonds. She immediately announced her pregnancy to the king, who ordered that everything possible be done for the well-being of the unborn child. After a full term, she gave birth to a beautiful son who had all the auspicious characteristics of a great person.

As soon as the king heard that his son had been born, joy arose in his heart, and he felt great paternal affection. He called together all his ministers and asked whether they could share his happiness. "Sire," they cried in one voice, "the entire kingdom has been uneasy, but, now that the kingdom has a successor, we rejoice with Your Majesty! We are overjoyed."

The king arranged for sixty-four nurses to care for the heir apparent. After paying honor to his son, he offered the queen a boon, which she gratefully accepted, asking that she be permitted to redeem it at some future time.

The king then called his commander-in-chief and announced, "My son needs a retinue. Find out how many babies have been born to noble families today." The general reported to the king that the wives of five hundred ministers had also delivered sons. To each of them the king sent princely garments and ordered five hundred nurses to care for them.

On the day of the prince's naming, the king invited brahmins to examine the baby's horoscope and asked whether there was any danger threatening him. The brahmins replied that the child showed every sign of good fortune. They were unanimously of the opinion that the prince would rule not just one continent but the entire world. Overjoyed to hear this, the king handsomely rewarded all the brahmins. The prince was named Temiya, because it had rained all over the kingdom of Kāsi on the day of his birth, and he had been born wet.

When Prince Temiya was one month old, attendants dressed him and brought him to the king. The king hugged him, cradled him on his lap, and played with him.

At that time, four robbers were brought before the king. With the baby still in his arms, the king sentenced the thieves. The first thief was to be given one thousand strokes with a whip barbed with thorns; the second was condemned to prison in chains; the third was to be executed with a spear; and the fourth, impaled.

When the baby heard his father's harsh words, he was terrified. "My father," he thought, "because he is the king, is committing cruel deeds, for which he will suffer the consequences! These are the sorts of grievous acts which condemn men to hell!"

A little later, the nurse took the baby from his father and laid him on a sumptuous bed under a royal white umbrella. After a short nap, the infant awoke. When he opened his eyes, the first thing he saw was the white umbrella, and his fear increased. As he lay there, the prince pondered, "How did I come to this palace?" At first, he recalled that he had come from the realm of the devas. Then he remembered that, prior to that, he had endured horrible tortures for ages in hell. At last, he recalled that, before being reborn in hell, he had been a king in that very city. "I was king here for only twenty short years," he recalled, "but, for that, I suffered for eighty thousand years in hell. Now here I am again, reborn in this wicked house! I just saw my own father utter cruel speech and pass the kind of sentences that lead to perdition. If I become king, I will again be reborn in hell and suffer great pain there!" This realization so alarmed him that his lovely golden body became pale and faded like a crushed lotus petal. He thought as hard as he could about how he might escape that house of criminals.

At that moment the deva of the royal umbrella, who in a previous birth had been his mother, spoke to him. "Darling Temiya, fear not. If you wish to escape, there is a way. Pretend to be a cripple. Even though your hearing is acute, pretend to be deaf. Pretending to be mute, utter no sounds. Show no sign of intelligence! If you can make everyone think you are a fool, you will never become king. If you can endure the contempt of others, you will escape the fate you fear."

"Dear Mother, thank you for helping me," the prince whispered. "Your advice is very good, and I will follow it." From that moment on, the baby did exactly as the deva had suggested, and he stopped responding to anything that happened around him.

The prince's sudden passivity greatly alarmed the king. He tried in many ways to rouse the baby, but to no avail. He had the five hundred young nobles brought to live in the palace, hoping that their presence would stimulate the infant. When the other babies became hungry, they immediately began crying for milk, but Temiya never uttered a sound. "Better to die of hunger and thirst," he reflected, "than to reign and go to hell." The nurses could not understand what was wrong and reported everything to the queen. The queen spoke to her husband, and the king called in the brahmins to look for omens.

"Sire," they replied, "you must not feed the prince until he cries. When he becomes truly hungry, he will cry and then nurse." The wet nurses tried to follow this suggestion, but the baby never cried. So strong was his resolve that, although he was parched and tortured by thirst, his fear of hell's torment kept him from uttering even the tiniest noise. Afraid that the baby would die, his mother or one of the nurses invariably yielded and gave him milk, even though he hadn't cried. During his first year, they repeatedly tried to force him to cry for milk, but he never did.

The prince's nurses were thoroughly puzzled by the baby's silence, his lack of response to stimuli, and his apparent inability to squirm or crawl. His hands and feet were normal. His eyes and ears seemed normal. He was perfectly formed without any visible handicap. For the first month, they recalled, he had been an active, ordinary baby. He had not suffered any illness or fever to account for this drastic change. They reasoned that his passivity had to spring from another cause, and they resolved to find it.

They gathered the five hundred little boys around the prince and had servants bring in delectable sweets. The others scrambled for the cakes and devoured them eagerly. The prince did not even look at them. Sitting perfectly still, he steeled his resolve and warned himself, "Temiya, eat those treats, and you will go to hell!"

The nurses tried the same experiment with the sweetest fruit of the season, but the result was exactly the same. The other boys squabbled over the fruit and gobbled it up, but the prince never moved.

Servants presented the boys with an amazing assortment of marvelous toys, including model chariots, horses, and elephants. The ministers' sons excitedly grabbed the toys and began playing with them. The prince seemed not even to notice.

When he was four years old, servants prepared special dishes which they knew were most popular with boys his age. The other children were delighted to receive such wonderful food. The prince, pretending that he was unaware of how good the food smelled, watched the feast and thought to himself, "Temiya, innumerable were the past births when you got no food at all." His silence and lack of response pained his mother's heart. Finally, unwilling to allow her son to starve, she fed him with her own hand.

When he was five years old, the servants decided to test the prince with fire. They built a large house with many doors and covered it with palm fronds. They set the prince and the other boys in the middle of the house and set fire to it. Shrieking in fear, the five hundred boys fled in every direction. The prince, without moving so much as an eyelid, watched the flames and thought, "Better to burn here than to burn again in the fires of hell." The servants watched as the flames got closer and closer to where he was. Finally, realizing that the prince was, indeed, not going to move, they rescued him.

When he was six years old, servants assembled all the boys, with the prince in the center, in the courtyard of the palace. Suddenly, the gates flew open, and an elephant, trumpeting fiercely and striking the ground with its trunk, charged into the courtyard. The five hundred boys scattered in a panic. The prince, thinking only how much fiercer the guardians of hell were, remained motionless. The well-trained elephant ran straight toward the prince, picked him up with its trunk, and made as if to dash him against a tree. The prince did not respond in any way. At a signal from the hidden mahout, the elephant set the prince down gently on the ground and was led away.

When the prince was seven, servants released snakes, whose fangs had been extracted, into the area where the boys were playing. As the serpents slithered toward the children, the ministers' sons ran shrieking in terror. The prince pretended not to be aware of the danger. He thought, "It is better to die by the bite of one of these serpents than to return to hell!" The largest cobra coiled itself around Temiya's body and spread its hood, but the prince remained motionless. Unsuccessful once more, the attendants caught and removed all the snakes.

Having repeatedly failed to tempt the prince with food or to frighten him in any way, the servants decided to try to amuse him. They decorated the palace for a party and invited a mime troupe to present their best performance. The other boys laughed, applauded, and shouted, "Bravo!" The prince, reminding himself that in hell there was never an instant's laughter, remained stone-faced.

At another time, they sent an actor into the courtyard where the boys were playing. Brandishing his sword, he charged wildly into the group. The man shouted, "Where is that devilish son of Kāsi's king? I will cut off his head!" The other boys shrieked in terror and ran away, but the prince recalled the horrors of hell and sat motionless, as though he were unconscious. The man stood over the prince and pressed his sword against the boy's neck, but the prince showed not the least bit of fear. At last, the man gave up.

When Temiya was ten years old, the servants decided to find out whether or not he was really deaf. They hung a curtain round his bed and surrounded it with conch-blowers. At a signal, they all gave a mighty blast of their conches, which created a noise loud enough to wake the dead. The boy gave no sign of surprise. The servants tried the same experiment with drums, but they were unable to break the prince's resolve.

One night, in order to test his sight, attendants simultaneously lit hundreds of lamps around his bed, creating a blinding blaze of light, but the prince did not move a muscle in surprise.

Certain that the prince would be sensitive to physical pain, the servants smeared his entire body with molasses, laid him in the open, and allowed fierce red ants to swarm all over him, biting his tender skin. Although the prince felt that he was being pierced with thousands of needles, he recalled how much worse the torments of hell were. He did not permit himself to show the slightest reaction. Finally, his attendants were forced to give up.

When the prince was fourteen, servants devised another test which they hoped would bring the prince out of his passive state. No one bathed him or rinsed his mouth or changed his clothes, and he was reduced to a filthy, stinking mess. The poor child looked like a prisoner in a dungeon, covered with dirt and crawling with lice. Then his attendants reviled him, saying, "Temiya, you are grown up now. Aren't you ashamed? Why are you lying there? Get up and clean yourself." The prince, remembering the torments of hell, lay quietly and endured his squalor and stench, until, at last, they relented and cleaned him up.

At another time, the servants placed pans of glowing hot charcoal all around and under his bed. Blisters and welts broke out all over his body, but the boy did not move. Although he felt considerable pain as the blisters swelled and broke, he reflected, "The fire of Avīci Hell flares up one hundred yojanas. This heat is much easier to bear than that." At last, his parents relented, ordered the fires removed, and soothed his burns with ointment.

"Dear Temiya," the king and queen tearfully implored him, "you were born to us only after many prayers. We waited many years for you. Please do not destroy us now. You are not disabled by any birth defect. Please behave normally, and give us hope!" The prince heard their heartbreaking pleas, but he lay still as if he had not heard anything at all. Unable to provoke even the slightest response from the boy, his parents went away disconsolate. Later, they approached him individually and pleaded with him to show some sign that he could hear or see or feel, but he never relented. His resolve to escape the torments of hell was unshakable.

When he turned sixteen, his parents hoped that he would respond to sensuous pleasures. They summoned beautiful, talented women and promised that whoever managed to make the prince laugh or succeeded in seducing him would become his wife.

Attendants bathed the prince in perfumed water, dressed him in royal garments, and laid him on a couch. The women gathered around him, singing and dancing seductively. The prince watched them without giving any indication that he was aware of their presence. He fully understood what the women were trying to do but was adamant in his resolve not to succumb to their charms. Afraid that they might touch his body, the prince held his breath. The women had been baffled when the prince had ignored them, but when he stopped breathing, they became alarmed. Calling his parents, they said that he was stiff and unresponsive as if he were a goblin instead of a boy.

Thus, for sixteen years the king and queen had tried in vain to elicit some response from their son. They had subjected the prince to sixteen great tests and innumerable smaller ones, all to no avail. The king summoned the brahmins who had seen auspicious omens at the prince's birth and had unanimously predicted his good fortune. He demanded an explanation. How could they have said that the crown prince faced nothing but good luck in his life, when, in reality, he was an unresponsive, handicapped, helpless deaf-mute?

"Your Majesty," a spokesman for the brahmins replied, "sixteen years ago, we knew the truth, but we were afraid to grieve you by telling you that your beloved son, born after so many royal prayers, would be like this."

"What must be done now?" the king asked.

"Sire, if this prince remains here, there is a threefold danger: harm may come to you, to your kingdom, or to your queen. The best thing for you to do is to have some ill-omened horses harnessed to an unlucky chariot. You must have the prince placed in the chariot, driven out of the city by the western gate, and buried in the charnel-ground!"

Alarmed by the peril he was in, the king immediately accepted their advice.

When Queen Candādevī heard the news, she rushed to the king and asked to claim the boon which the king had given her when the crown prince was born. The king immediately agreed and asked her what she wanted.

"Give the kingdom to my son," she replied.

"My dear, I cannot do that," protested the king. Your son is completely ill-fated. His presence is a great danger to us all."

"Sire, if you will not give him the kingdom for life, then give it to him for seven years."

"I cannot, my queen."

The queen continued begging, reducing the length of time to six years, to five years, to four, to three, to two, and finally to only one year.

Each time the king repeated, "I cannot, my queen."

"Then give it to him for seven months," she pleaded.

"My queen, I cannot," insisted the king.

Again, the queen continued begging, this time reducing the time to six months, to five, to four, to three, to two months, to one month, and even to half a month.

Each time the king repeated, "I cannot, my queen."

"Then give it to him for seven days."

"That much I can do," the king conceded. "You have your boon."

The queen had her son carefully groomed and richly dressed. Attired in royal robes and jewelry, he was placed on a royal elephant and led triumphantly clockwise round the brightly decorated city with a white umbrella held over his head. The procession was led by a drummer, and a crier proclaimed, "This is the reign of Prince Temiya!"

When the procession was finished, he was taken down from the elephant and laid on his royal bed. His mother implored him, "My darling Temiya, because of you, I have wept day and night. For sixteen years, I have had no sleep. My heart is pierced with sorrow. I know that you are not really crippled or deaf and dumb. I plead with you. Do not make me utterly desolate." In this way, for five days she implored her son to show some sign of recognition.

On the sixth day, the king called his charioteer Sunanda and said, "Early tomorrow morning, hitch some ill-omened horses to an unlucky chariot, and put the prince in it. Take him out of the city by the western gate. Go to the charnel ground, and dig a hole there. Throw the boy into the hole. Kill him by breaking his skull with your spade. Scatter dirt over his body, and fill up the hole. Heap the earth over his unmarked grave. Then, after bathing yourself, come back, and report to me."

All that night, the queen tearfully implored her son to give her some sign. "My child, the king of Kāsi has given orders that you are to be buried in the charnel-ground. Tomorrow, you will certainly die, my dear boy."

When he heard this, he thought to himself, "Oh, Temiya, your sixteen years of effort are almost over!" He was happy, but his mother's heart was almost broken. Although he knew how she suffered, he didn't dare to speak to her for fear that he might not attain his goal.

Early the next morning, Sunanda, the charioteer, prepared the ill-fated chariot. Entering the royal chamber, he spoke to the queen, "Your Majesty, do not be angry with me. It is the king's command." While the queen was still embracing her son, Sunanda pushed her away, lifted the prince as easily as a bundle of flowers and carried him out of the palace.

Left alone in the chamber, the queen beat her breast and bewailed her son's fate. The prince wanted to call out to her, but, again, he dared not. "If I speak now," he said to himself, "all my efforts will have been for naught. If I remain firm, I will save myself and my parents."

The charioteer placed the prince in the chariot and announced, "Now I will drive this chariot to the western gate." Unwittingly, he directed the horses to the eastern gate. When the wheel struck the gatepost, the prince heard the sound and knew that he had accomplished his goal. He became glad at heart.

Leaving the city, they entered the forest, but the devas made it appear to be the charnel ground. Believing that he had arrived at the proper place, Sunanda stopped the chariot. First, he removed the prince's jewelry and tied it in a bundle. Then he picked up his spade and began to dig a hole.

"Now I must exert myself," thought the prince. "For sixteen years, I have not moved my hands or feet. Do I still have control over them or not?" He sat up, rubbed his hands together, massaged his legs, and determined to get out of the chariot.

As his foot came down to step out of the chariot, the earth rose up to meet it. He stood up and walked back and forth several times. With each step his strength increased, until he felt that he could walk one hundred yojanas.

"If the charioteer struggles with me," he wondered, "do I have the strength to deal with him?" To test himself, he took hold of the rear of the chariot and lifted it up as if it were a child's wagon. Satisfied that he was sufficiently strong, he then realized that he needed to clothe himself properly.

At that instant, Sakka's throne became hot, and he understood, "Prince Temiya has attained his desire! Now he wants to be appropriately dressed. Ordinary garments will not do!" He immediately called Vissakamma, his assistant, and instructed him to take heavenly garments and the finest jewels for the prince.

Vissakamma dressed Temiya in ten thousand pieces of heavenly silk and magnificent jewelry so that he looked like Sakka himself. The prince stepped to the edge of the hole and spoke to the charioteer. "My good man," he asked, "why are you working so hard to dig this pit? Pray, what is it intended for?"

Without looking up, Sunanda replied, "Our king has found that his only son is a crippled idiot. I was ordered to dig this hole to bury him in."

Temiya answered him in a clear, firm voice. "I am neither deaf nor dumb, my friend. Listen to me! I am not crippled. I'm not even lame. Take a look at me. If you were to bury me in these woods, you would certainly be guilty of a great crime!"

Startled, the charioteer said, "What? The crown prince was in pitiful shape when I brought him here!" Stopping his digging, he looked up. When he saw the prince's handsome figure, he couldn't believe his eyes. "Are you a deva? Are you Sakka, lord of all? How should I address you?"

"No," Temiya answered, "I am not Sakka. I am the son of your king, the king of Kāsi. I am the one you planned to bury in that hole. Think carefully about gratitude! After sitting and resting beneath a tree, enjoying its shade and shelter, I would never harm even a small twig of that tree. Only one who is very wicked harms his friends. Your king is like that sheltering tree, and I am a branch. You, my good man, are the weary traveler resting in its shade, so, how could you ever harm me?"

Sunanda could not recognize in this magnificent creature before him any resemblance to the pathetic youth he had brought in the chariot.

Then Temiya made the woods resound with his beautiful voice as he praised friendship. "He who is faithful to his friends may wander far and wide, but he will always find welcome, and his wants will always be supplied. Because he is faithful to his friends, he will be honored. He will be respected by warriors and unharmed by enemies. The man who is faithful to his friends is the best of kin. The one who is faithful to his friends will always be rewarded for his labor and will prosper. When in danger, he will find succor. Like the banyan tree, which defies the wind, strengthened by its branches which have rooted all around, the faithful man will weather even the rage of the fiercest foes." As he described the benefits of friendship, the devas applauded.

Sunanda was not yet convinced, so Temiya stepped closer. When the charioteer realized that it was, indeed, the prince, he immediately fell at the royal feet and pressed his palms together in respect.

"Come, Your Highness," he cried, "let me take you back to the palace where you will be welcomed. You can sit on the throne and reign as king. You needn't remain here in the forest."

"I don't want the throne or wealth," the prince replied. "Being king entails too many harsh decisions and cruel acts for me."

"Come, Your Highness," Sunanda repeated, unable to grasp the prince's meaning. "The cup of welcome will be prepared for you. Your parents will be so happy to see you that, I am sure, they will give me great gifts as well. The entire kingdom will be grateful to me for taking you back, and I will be generously rewarded."

"Have you forgotten that my parents abandoned me? Since my father condemned me to death and my mother gave me up, I no longer have a home. Forsaken as I am, I will undertake the ascetic's vow here in this forest."

As the prince said this, his mind filled with delight, and he uttered a hymn of triumph: "Even those who never hurry, if their desire is strong enough, can win sweet victory! Charioteer, today I have achieved great holiness. My effort has been crowned with success. I fear nothing!"

"Your Highness," the puzzled charioteer said, "I don't understand. You speak so clearly, and your voice is very pleasant to hear. Why were you silent for so long? Why did you never speak to your parents?"

"When I was born, I was a normal child. Then, one day, my father held me and played with me on his lap. While he held me, he passed sentence on four criminals. He sentenced two of them to harsh punishment, and the other two to be executed. This upset me terribly. I remembered that, once, long ago, I had also been a king. Because I also committed cruel acts like that, which are, after all, part of being a ruler, I suffered in hell. Although I reigned for only twenty years, I spent eighty thousand years of torment in hell. Recalling that indescribable suffering, I resolved never again to become king. That is why I never spoke, even though my loving parents were near. In order to avoid the throne, I pretended that I could not see, hear, or speak. Even though I had to wallow in filth, I played the idiot and cripple. When I had to suffer immense physical pain, I remembered that the tortures of hell were so much greater. Human life is short, but the lifespan in hell is very long. Knowing this, I will never let anger arise. I will never mete out justice, which is really just another name for vengeance."

This story touched Sunanda deeply. He was impressed that the prince could discard his throne as if it were carrion. As he listened, the desire arose in him, as well, to become an ascetic, and he declared his resolve to the prince.

Temiya knew, however, that, if the charioteer did not return, the horses, the chariot, and the ornaments, for which he, the prince, was responsible, would be lost. His parents would never know the truth and would not come to see him, which would be a great loss for them. He reasoned that people might also believe that he had always been a yakkha and had devoured the horses and the charioteer.

"No," he said to Sunanda, "you are not yet a free man. First, you must return the chariot, report everything that has happened here to the king and queen, and, as they say, pay your debts. Then you can follow me in the ascetic's life."

The charioteer fretted to himself, "What if he leaves while I am returning to the city? If his parents don't find him here, they will punish me! I must get his promise to wait here until I return with them."

"Since I am obeying your command, Prince Temiya, please stay here until I've fetched the king. He will be overjoyed when he sees your face!"

"I promise to wait here," the prince assured him. "Please tell my parents how much I wish to see them. Hurry back!"

The queen, standing at her window, anxiously awaiting news of her son, was the first to see the charioteer return. "He comes back alone!" she cried. "My child is dead! His body lies in the charnel ground, under a heap of earth!"

Confronting the man, she wept, saying: "My worst enemy may now rejoice; my son's murderer has come back. Tell me! Did my poor crippled child utter a cry as he struggled helplessly? Did he resist, even feebly?"

"Your Majesty," Sunanda replied, "if you will promise to pardon me for all that I say, I will tell you exactly what happened."

"Of course, I will pardon you," the queen assured him. "Please give me all the details. I must know."

"Your Majesty, your son is no invalid. He is not deaf, and his speech is clear. At home, he played a role for you, because he dreaded inheriting the throne. He remembered an old birth when he was a king; when he died from that life he found himself in perdition. Twenty years of luxury were followed by eighty thousand years in hell for his actions while he reigned. That bitter taste of royalty terrified him so much that he pretended to be deaf and dumb whenever you were nearby. Your child is perfectly sound; he's straight and strong, and his wits are clear. Now he seeks liberation in the forest as an ascetic. If you wish to see your noble son, come with me at once. I will take you to Prince Temiya, perfectly well, strong, calm, and free."

Alone in the forest, Temiya was eager to take the ascetic vow. Knowing this, Sakka summoned Vissakamma, and said, "Prince Temiya wishes to take the ascetic vow. Go and make a hut of leaves for him, and see to all his needs." Vissakamma swiftly built a hermitage with separate cells for meditation and for sleeping in a lovely grove of trees. He dug a tank for water and made fruit trees grow nearby.

When Temiya saw the hermitage, he knew that it was Sakka's gift. Entering the hut, he put on his rough ascetic's garments, tied up his matted hair, and picked up a staff. Walking to and fro in the grove, he kept repeating, "What bliss! What bliss!" and delighted in his renunciation. He returned to the hut, sat on a ragged mat, and meditated joyously.

In the evening, he went out to gather some leaves from one of the trees in the grove. He soaked the leaves in water and ate them as if they were regal fare. Then he resumed his meditation.

Meanwhile, as soon as the king heard Sunanda's report, he ordered his general to prepare for the journey to meet Prince Temiya. The king took the entire court, along with his whole army, to the place where Temiya was staying in tranquil meditation.

When the king arrived at the hermitage, the prince greeted him warmly and inquired about his parents' health. Then he asked whether the king was careful to abstain from drinking alcohol and to practice generosity. The king assured his son that he never drank and that he gave alms regularly. After more polite talk and inquiries about the welfare of the kingdom, the prince asked his father to sit on a couch, but the king, out of respect for his son, refused. He also refused to sit on a bed of leaves prepared for him but contented himself with sitting on the bare ground.

Temiya apologized that the only food he had was the leaves he had soaked, but he offered to share them with the king. "Oh, no," the king protested, "no leaves for me! I dine on the finest hill rice prepared with tender meat!"

At that moment, Queen Candādevī arrived, accompanied by her royal attendants. Her eyes were filled with tears as she embraced the feet of her beloved son and sat at one side.

"My Lady, look at the food your son is eating," the king said as he put some leaves in her hand and in those of her attendants.

"My Lord," the women cried in amazement, "do you really eat such food? How can you endure such hardship?"

"Yes, my son," the king said, "please tell us how you can live on such coarse food and still have a clear complexion and such good color?"

Answering his father, the prince said, "Sleeping on this bed of leaves is pleasant enough. There are no fierce guards near my simple bed. Neither regretting the past nor fearing the future, I meet the present as it comes. That's how I keep my health."

The king was extremely impressed by the prince's manner and speech. He thought to himself, "I will crown him king right here and take him back with me. I am ready to step down. He can have the kingdom!"

To Temiya he said, "Come, my son. You are my heir! My elephants, chariots, cavalry, infantry, and all my pleasant palaces, I offer to you. I am ready to step down and to give you the kingdom. Why linger in these woods? There is nothing for you here in this rude hermitage. Come back to Bārānasi, and rule over us. You will be obeyed in everything. Enjoy your kingdom and your youth to the fullest!"

With a clear voice, the prince answered, "No, Father. Let me leave the world with all its conceit. Wise men say that an ascetic life suits the young. All I want is to live as an ascetic; I have no need of a throne. I have seen the boy, crying for his mother and father. In no time at all, he himself fathers a son. Then he himself grows old and dies. The lovely young daughter soon ages and is cut down like green bamboo by death. I will not put my trust in mortal life and be cheated. Life is short. We are like fish in ponds that dry up. Our lives are blighted by old age before we are struck down, deprived of happiness, success, wealth, and title. Why talk of crown or throne? The lady sits at her loom, weaving, and, each day, her task grows less and less. In the same way, our lives waste away to nothing. Just as the river speeds onward to the sea, our lives rush onward toward death. Just as the river sweeps away trees from its banks, so are we swept and carried away to ruin by aging and death."

As the king listened to his son's speech, he felt himself also becoming disgusted by the secular life. In his enthusiasm, he exclaimed, "I will not go back to the city, I will become an ascetic here. Return to the palace, and accept the white umbrella. Become king instead of me. Rule happily!"

"Father," Temiya insisted, "I have seen through wealth, power, sport, and royal prestige. I have seen them for what they really are. Empty! What is wife or child to me? I am free from those traps. I know that death follows us like a murderer, intent on killing. What can power mean to one who sees the shadow of death? I am set free from all chains. Return to the capital with your crown. I do not want to be king!"

Upon hearing Temiya's ringing words, the king, the queen, and all the ladies of the court determined to adopt the ascetic life. The king issued a proclamation that all who chose to become ascetics with his son were free to do so. He ordered that the doors of his treasuries be thrown open. He had an inscription posted on a pillar declaring that anyone who wanted to, might take freely from his treasures. Citizens left their houses with the doors open and flocked round the king. The king, the queen, and the multitude took their ascetic vows together at Temiya's feet.

Vissakamma's hermitage extended three yojanas in length. Temiya assigned the huts in the center to the women so that they would be protected. The outer huts he gave to the men. Everyone gathered in the morning to eat the fruits of the trees which Vissakamma had planted. Temiya, knowing the minds of all and aware of the susceptibility of each of them to thoughts of lust, hatred, or greed, was able to offer teaching suitable to each person. Under his instruction, all of them made rapid progress in their meditation.

When a rival king heard the rumor that the king of Kāsi had become an ascetic, he decided to seize Bārānasi and to make it his own capital. When he entered the city, he found it lavishly decorated, just as it had been when the king left. Going to the palace, he saw heaps of precious stones lying about. Afraid that some sort of danger lurked in all this wealth, he asked some drunken revelers which direction the king had taken when he left. Accordingly, he left the city through the eastern gate and followed the river.

Aware, because of his extraordinary power, that the rival king was coming, Temiya welcomed him and taught him, as well.

This king and his entire army also took ascetic vows. Exactly the same thing happened with another king. Thus, three kingdoms were abandoned. State elephants and horses were freed to roam wild in the woods. Chariots crumbled and decayed. The money from the royal treasuries, having become worthless, was scattered everywhere.

All these ascetics achieved profound levels of concentration and, at the end of their lives, were reborn in the Brahma heavens.

Even the animals of the forest, their minds having been calmed by the presence of all those sages, were eventually reborn in various heavens.

Having concluded his story, the Buddha added, "Not only now, but also formerly, I left a kingdom and became an ascetic." Then the Buddha identified the birth: "At that time, Uppalavannā was the deva in the umbrella, Sāriputta was the charioteer, my parents were the king of Kāsi and his queen Candādevī, my followers were the members of the court, and I was the wise Temiya."

209
Mahā-Janaka
Mahā-Janaka Jātaka

It was while staying at Jetavana that the Buddha told this story about the Great Renunciation.

One day, in the Hall of Truth, bhikkhus were talking about the Buddha's Great Renunciation. When the Buddha learned what they were discussing, he said, "This is not the first time that the Tathāgata made a great renunciation." At their request, he told this story of the past.

Long, long ago, there was a king named Mahā-Janaka reigning in Mithilā, the capital of Videha. He had two sons: Arittha-Janaka, the elder, who was the crown prince, and Pola-Janaka, the younger, who was the commander-in-chief. When King Mahā-Janaka died, Arittha-Janaka became king, and he promoted his younger brother to crown prince.

Almost immediately, someone in the palace started a rumor that Pola-Janaka was scheming to kill his brother and to usurp the throne. King Arittha-Janaka heard this rumor so often that he finally arrested his brother. In spite of Pola-Janaka's pleas of innocence, the king had him bound in chains and imprisoned near the palace.

Prince Pola-Janaka declared, "I swear that I have neither ill-will nor any wrong intentions toward my brother. If this is true, let these chains fall from my hands and the door swing open!" As soon as he had made this asseveration of truth, his chains fell, and the door flew open.

The prince immediately fled to the frontier. Villagers there recognized him and, believing in his innocence, helped him hide so that his brother could not re-arrest him.

In time, Prince Pola-Janaka gained the trust and support of all the villages along the border. "When I left Mithilā," he proclaimed, "I was not my brother's enemy, but now I surely am!" With a large force, he set out for Mithilā. As he approached the capital, his army grew steadily larger. He camped outside the city gate, and many from inside the city came out to join his force. He sent a message to his brother, "When I was living in Mithilā, I was not your enemy, but I am now! Cede your kingdom, or fight to defend it!"

As the king went off to fight, he said to the queen, "Lady, war is unpredictable. If I die, please take care of the child in your womb." Not long afterwards, Pola-Janaka's soldiers killed the king and defeated his army.

As soon as the queen learned that her husband was dead, she put her gold, jewels, and other valuables in a basket, spread a napkin over them, and covered everything with a layer of uncooked rice. Dressing herself in some soiled and tattered clothes and smearing her face and hair with dirt, she placed the basket on her head and left the palace by the servants' entrance. No one recognized her that morning as she made her way to the northern gate of the city. Once outside the city walls, she did not know which way to go, for she had never traveled before. She had heard of Campā, and she knew that it was the name of a city, so she asked passers-by whether they were going that way.

Since the child in the queen's womb was the Bodhisatta, Sakka's throne became hot. Realizing that the Bodhisatta was in danger, the king of the devas descended to earth. He created a covered carriage with a bed in it and disguised himself as an old driver. As he passed the queen, he asked loudly if anyone wanted to go to Campā.

"That is where I want to go, Father," said the queen.

"Then climb into this carriage, lady, and take your seat," Sakka told her.

"Father," she protested, "I am expecting a baby soon, so I dare not climb up. I will follow behind the carriage. Please, just let me put my basket inside because it is heavy."

"What are you saying, Mother?" asked Sakka. "There is no carriage like mine!" Using his supernatural power, Sakka caused the earth where the queen was standing to rise to the level of the carriage the moment the queen started to climb into it. "Just step in!" he said. She did so, and, finding the bed, she lay down and immediately fell asleep.

At midday, Sakka stopped the carriage at a river. "Mother," he called gently, "please get down and bathe in the river. At the head of the bed you'll find some fresh clothes to change into." As she was getting back into the carriage, he said, "Beside the bed is a rice cake for you to eat." After she had eaten, she lay down again.

In the evening, she could see a watchtower in the wall of what appeared to be a great city. "What city is that, Father?" she asked.

"That is Campā, Mother." Sakka replied

"How can that be, Father?" she asked. "Isn't it sixty yojanas from Mithilā to Campā?"

"Yes, it is, Mother," he replied, "but I know a shortcut."

He stopped the carriage at the southern gate and said, "Mother, my village lies further on, but you can enter the city here." When she was safely out of the carriage, he drove away. As soon as he was out of sight, he returned to Tāvatimsa.

The queen entered a public resthouse beside the gate and sat down. At that moment, a brahmin with his five hundred students passed by on their way to bathe. As soon as he saw her sitting there, looking so regal and so beautiful, by the power of the Bodhisatta in her womb, he felt an immediate affection for her as for a youngest sister. Leaving his students outside, he went alone into the resthouse and asked her, "Sister, where do you come from?"

"I am the chief queen of King Arittha-Janaka in Mithilā," she said.

"Why have you come here?" he asked.

"My husband, the king, was killed by his brother, Pola-Janaka. I fled in fear to save the life of my unborn child."

"Do you have any relatives in this city?"

"None, Brother."

"Do not worry. I am a well-known teacher here. I will watch over you as if we were siblings of the same mother. Now, in a loud voice, shout 'Brother!' clasp my feet, and cry as if we have been reunited after a long separation."

She did so, and he lifted her up. As the two of them were embracing, the students rushed up to see what was happening. He explained that she was his youngest sister, who was born after he had left home.

"Oh, Teacher!" the students cried. "It is wonderful that you have found her after all this time!"

He ordered some of his students to arrange for a grand covered carriage. As soon as it arrived, he placed her in it and sent her to his own house. He instructed the driver to tell his wife that this was his sister and that his wife was to make her feel at home.

The brahmin's wife treated the queen with great respect, giving her a hot bath and preparing a bed for her. When the brahmin returned home, he told the servants to call his sister so that she could eat with him.

Shortly after her arrival, the queen gave birth to a healthy son, whom she named Mahā-Janaka after his grandfather. As the child was growing up, he played with the children in the neighborhood. One day, his playmates were talking about their parents. Some of them boasted about their own birth, and teased him that he did not have a father. Being a sturdy lad, he hit them in retaliation, and made them cry. When their parents asked who had hit them, they answered, "The widow's son."

The little prince went home and said, "Mother, my playmates always call me the widow's son. Who is my father?"

The queen did not yet want to reveal that he was a prince, so she replied, "The brahmin is your father."

The next day, when his playmates again teased him, he shouted, "The brahmin is my father!"

"How can he be your father?" they retorted. "He's your mother's brother!"

The prince had not yet been weaned, so, that evening, while he was nursing, he took his mother's breast in his teeth and said, "Tell me the truth! Who is my father? If you don't tell me, I will bite your nipple."

Realizing that she could no longer deceive him, she said, "My child, you are the only son of King Arittha-Janaka of Mithilā. Before you were born, your father was killed by your uncle, Pola-Janaka. I fled to this city to save you. To protect us, the good brahmin has treated me as his sister and taken care of us as if we were his own family."

After that, Mahā-Janaka did not get angry when his playmates called him the widow's son, but he never told anyone the truth. He grew into a handsome young man, mastering every subject and exhibiting skill in all the arts.

When he reached sixteen, he asked his mother if she had any money for him. "If you don't," he said, "I will go into trade to make money, and I will regain my father's kingdom."

"Dear son, I did not come here empty-handed," she told him. "I have a great store of pearls, rubies, and diamonds. Take it all. It is enough to win the throne. You don't need to go into trade."

"No, Mother," he replied, "I will only take half of what you have. I will use that to travel to Suvannabhūmi. I'll make my fortune and return to seize the kingdom."

His mother begged him not to do such a foolish thing. She warned him that there were great dangers at sea and that his chances of making a profit were very slim. Despite her pleas, he was determined to try his luck. He joined with six other traders and invested half of her wealth. The group loaded a ship with expensive goods, wagons, and oxen and left for Suvannabhūmi.

The vessel sailed for seven hundred yojanas, but, after a week, it hit rough water and sprang a leak. Planks gave way, the water rose, and the ship began to sink. The crew and the merchants cried and invoked their various deities, but Mahā-Janaka neither wept nor prayed. Knowing that the ship was doomed, he smeared his body and clothing with ghee, ate as many rations as he could manage, and climbed to the top of the main mast.

As the ship sank beneath the surface, the mast remained upright, but the men and animals on the deck became food for the sharks and turtles. The water around the submerged vessel turned blood red as it was churned up by their frenzy.

From the top of the mast, Prince Mahā-Janaka threw himself with all his strength in the direction of Mithilā. He landed in the emerald sea, safely beyond the ravenous predators.

On the day that Prince Mahā-Janaka had embarked for Suvannabhūmi, King Pola-Janaka had fallen seriously ill and was unable to leave his bed. As the ship sank, the king died.

For seven days, Mahā-Janaka swam steadily without changing his pace. When he saw the full moon rise, he rinsed his mouth with salt water and began observing Uposatha.

In that sea, a female deva named Manimekhalā had been appointed guardian by the Four Great Kings. In charging her with her duty, they had told her, "Beings who are virtuous, who respect their parents, and who observe Uposatha do not deserve to perish in the sea. If any virtuous people become shipwrecked, you must save them."

For the seven days that Mahā-Janaka had been swimming, Manimekhalā had been absorbed in her divine happiness and had neglected to look about. At last, recollecting her responsibility, she surveyed the water and saw Mahā-Janaka struggling. When she noticed that he was observing Uposatha, she thought, "If Prince Mahā-Janaka had perished because I was remiss, I would have lost my place in the divine assembly! Now I must save him, but, first, let me test him!"

Assuming a beautiful form, she stood in the air not far from where he was swimming and asked, "Young man, why are you striving manfully in mid-ocean? Are you all alone? Where are your friends?"

Mahā-Janaka thought, "I have been swimming for seven days. All this time, I have not seen another living being. This must be a deva who is speaking to me now!" Aloud he said, "As long as I am alive, I see it as my duty to strive with all my strength."

"Well, it seems obvious to me that here in the deep sea your striving is useless," Manimekhalā replied. "There's nothing you can do, and you are going to drown!"

"Why do you say that?" Mahā-Janaka retorted. "If I struggle as hard as I can, I cannot be blamed even if I die. He who does as much as he can should not feel ashamed if he fails."

"Why exhaust yourself for nothing?" the deva taunted him. "Since you are going to die anyway, you might as well relax!"

"The man who thinks that there is no chance to win and, thus, gives up without a fight is the one who should be blamed when he loses!" Mahā-Janaka declared. "Only the future will show whether our plans will succeed or fail. Don't you see, friend deva? My struggling has kept me alive this far, whereas all my companions on the same ship drowned. The ship sank, but I saved myself. Now here I am, and you are standing by my side. As long as I am alive, I will struggle as hard as I can to get through these ocean waves and to reach the shore. As long as my strength holds out, I will strive until I can strive no more."

"You are truly brave," Manimekhalā shouted, "to continue fighting on in this fierce, unbounded sea, struggling to do your duty like a man, never wavering, never shrinking from your task! Tell me where you wish to go. There will be no more obstacles to hamper you!"

"My destination is Mithilā!" Mahā-Janaka loudly proclaimed.

Manimekhalā lifted him gently from the water as if he were her own child and sped toward Mithilā. As they flew through the air, the prince, his body wet with salt spray, was lulled by the heavenly contact, and he slept soundly.

Manimekhalā carried the prince to the royal park and laid him on his right side on the ceremonial stone in the mango grove. Leaving him in the care of the devas of the park, she returned to the sea.

King Pola-Janaka, having left no son, was survived by only one daughter, a wise and learned princess named Sīvalī. On his deathbed, ministers had asked the king who should succeed him, and he had replied, "Give the kingdom to the man who can please my daughter Sīvalī, who can determine the head of the square bed, who can string my bow, and who can find the sixteen great treasures."

The ministers had asked what he meant by the sixteen great treasures, and he had replied, "The rising sun and the setting sun; outside, inside, and neither outside nor inside; the mounting, the dismounting, the four sal pillars, and a yojana around; the ends of the teeth, the end of the tail, kebuka, and the ends of the trees. There the sixteen great treasures can be found."

Seven days after King Pola-Janaka's funeral, the ministers met to discuss the succession. "The king's first stipulation was that the kingdom should go to one who pleased his daughter," they recalled. "Who might that be?"

They all agreed that the commander-in-chief had always been a favorite of the king. They decided to let him try.

The commander-in-chief went to door of the princess' apartment and announced his presence.

She knew very well why he had come, so she tested him to see if he had the wisdom necessary to rule. "Come here," she called.

Eager to please her, he raced up the stairs and stopped in front of her.

"Run back down the stairs!" she commanded him.

He turned around and ran down the stairs as fast as he could.

As soon as he was at the bottom, she called, "Come here!" and the commander-in-chief ran up the stairs again.

Perceiving his lack of wisdom, she commanded, "Massage my feet!"

He immediately knelt and put his hands on her feet.

The princess kicked him in the chest, knocking him flat on his back. Then she ordered her attendants to beat him and to throw him out.

When the ministers saw him, they asked about his meeting with the princess.

"Don't ask!" he replied. "She's not human!"

The ministers successively sent the treasurer, the cashier, the keeper of the umbrella, and the sword bearer, but the princess embarrassed them all in the same way.

The ministers met again. "The king's second stipulation was that the kingdom should go to one who could determine the head of the square bed," they recalled. The ministers showed the square bed to innumerable suitors, but no one could figure out which side was the head.

The ministers met again. "The king's third stipulation was that the kingdom should go to one who could string his bow," they recalled. The ministers had the bow brought out, but, since it took one thousand men to string the mighty weapon, no one could do anything with it.

The ministers met again. "The king's fourth stipulation was that the kingdom should go to one who could find the sixteen great treasures," they recalled. The ministers recited the clues which the king had taught them, but no one could understand any part of the meaning.

"The kingdom cannot last without a king!" cried the populace. "We need a king!"

The ministers met again to discuss the problem. The chief advisor suggested that the royal chariot could choose the new king by means of divination. He explained that, if the chariot, bearing the five symbols of royalty, were sent through the streets, it would stop in front of the man who was suitable to become king.

The ministers all agreed that this was a good suggestion. The city was beautifully decorated, and a proclamation was made. The royal chariot was hitched to four superb horses and the royal symbols were placed inside it. After a ceremony asking the heavens to give them a ruler, the chariot was sent out. The horses circled the palace and turned onto the main road, with the ministers and a large group of citizens silently following behind.

The commander-in-chief and other officials thought the chariot was coming for one of them. They each stepped forward, but the chief advisor stopped them. "Don't interfere!" he warned. "Let the chariot stop where it will, even if it has to go one hundred yojanas." Of course, the chariot passed them all by. The horses continued all around the city and exited by the eastern gate, heading toward the royal park. The horses pulled the chariot into the park, slowed to a walk, and sedately circled the great ceremonial stone. They stopped there as if waiting for the king to mount the chariot.

The chief advisor saw Mahā-Janaka and said to the ministers, "Sirs, someone is lying on the stone, so we must determine whether he is worthy of the white umbrella. If he is an ordinary man, when he wakes up, he will jump up in alarm. If he has merit, he will not look at us. Have the musicians begin playing!"

The royal musicians began beating their drums and blowing their horns, which created a terrific din. Mahā-Janaka awoke and looked round. When he saw the huge throng of people, he realized that the white umbrella had come to him, so he turned and lay on his left side.

The chief advisor examined Mahā-Janaka's feet and exclaimed, "This man has the marks of one who will not rule only one continent but all four! Sound the instruments again!"

The musicians began again, even more loudly than before. Mahā-Janaka uncovered his face, turned onto his right side, and looked at the crowd. The chief advisor paid his respects and said, "Rise, Your Majesty! The kingdom belongs to you."

"Where is the king?" the prince asked.

"He is dead."

"Didn't he leave a son or brother?"

"No, Your Majesty."

"All right," he said as he roused himself and sat cross-legged on the stone slab. "I will accept the kingdom."

The ministers brought out lustral water and anointed him on the stone. The new king mounted the chariot and accepted the symbols of royalty. The chariot carried him into the city. He entered the palace and began discussing arrangements with the ministers.

The princess, wishing to test Mahā-Janaka, instructed a servant, "Tell the king that I wish to see him, and tell him to come immediately."

Ignoring the princess' summons, King Mahā-Janaka continued explaining to the ministers how he wanted his court to be organized.

The servant returned and told the princess that the king had paid no attention to her message. The princess realized that Mahā-Janaka was indeed a man of lofty nature. To be sure, she sent a second and a third messenger, each with the same result.

When the king had concluded his conference with the ministers, he proceeded to the throne room at his stately pace and began climbing the stairs of the dais. The princess could not resist his majestic bearing and stepped forward to give him her hand. Gently leaning on her hand, he ascended the dais and seated himself on the throne beneath the white umbrella. "Did the king leave any instructions when he died?" he asked the ministers.

"Yes, he did," they replied. "He said that the kingdom should go to the one who could please Princess Sīvalī."

The king replied, "You saw that Princess Sīvalī gave me her hand to lean on. I have succeeded in pleasing her. What else did he say?"

"He said that the kingdom should go to the one who could determine the head of the square bed," they replied.

When they showed him the square bed, he said, "All four sides look the same, so this is rather difficult to determine, but it can be done." He took a golden needle from his turban and handed it to the princess. "My dear," he said, "please put this in its proper place." She carefully laid the needle on one side of the bed.

The king pointed at the spot where the golden needle lay and said, "That is the head of the square bed!" The ministers were extremely satisfied. "What else did he say?" Mahā-Janaka asked.

"He said that the kingdom should go to the one who could string his bow which requires the strength of one thousand men," the ministers replied.

He asked them to bring him the bow, and, while still sitting on the bed, he strung it as easily as if it had been a carding bow.

"What else did he say?" Mahā-Janaka asked.

"He said that the kingdom should go to the one who could find the sixteen great treasures," the ministers replied.

"What are the clues?" he asked.

The ministers recited the list, "The rising sun and the setting sun; outside, inside, and neither outside nor inside; the mounting, the dismounting, the four sal pillars, and a yojana around; the ends of the teeth, the end of the tail, kebuka, and the ends of the trees. There the sixteen great treasures can be found."

As Mahā-Janaka listened to these clues, the meaning became as clear to him as the moon in the sky. "There is not time today," he said. "We will reveal the treasures tomorrow."

The next day, the king assembled the ministers and asked them, "Did your king feed Pacceka Buddhas?"

"Yes, he did," they replied.

"When the Pacceka Buddhas came, where did he greet them?"

When they showed him the place, he explained, "When the king spoke of the rising sun, he did not mean the sun in the sky. Pacceka Buddhas are sometimes compared to the sun. Let us dig here." Workers dug at the spot where the king had greeted Pacceka Buddhas and discovered a pot of gold.

"Where did the king stand when he bade farewell to the Pacceka Buddhas?" King Mahā-Janaka asked.

They showed him the place, and he ordered the workers to dig there. They found a second pot of gold.

The entire court was thrilled by King Mahā-Janaka's wisdom and applauded. They recalled how others had wandered about, watching the rising sun and digging here and there, without finding anything.

"Outside and inside," King Mahā-Janaka explained, "must refer to the palace. Let us dig just outside the palace gate." He ordered workers to do so, and they discovered a third pot of gold. He had them dig just inside the palace gate, and they discovered a fourth. They discovered a fifth directly below the threshold of the gate itself, neither outside nor inside.

"Now," King Mahā-Janaka continued, "show me where the king mounted his royal elephant." When the ministers showed him that place in the courtyard, he said, "This must be what the king referred to as 'the mounting.'" He ordered workers to dig there, and they discovered a sixth pot of gold. They discovered a seventh pot of gold at the place where the king dismounted from the royal elephant.

"In the palace," King Mahā-Janaka continued, "is a couch where the king reclines when courtiers come to pay their respects. What kind of wood is that couch made of?" he asked.

"Your Majesty," the ministers replied, "it is made of the finest sal wood."

"That's what I thought," King Mahā-Janaka replied. "Please show it to me."

He ordered workers to move the couch and to remove the stones on which the four legs had rested. Under each stone, they found a pot of gold. "These are the four sal pillars," explained the king. Everyone applauded this further display of wisdom.

"The next clue is "a yojana around," King Mahā-Janaka continued. "Now a yojana is as far as one yoke of oxen can travel, so the yoke itself is sometimes called a yojana. Let us now replace the royal couch to its original position." The workers did so. "Now," Mahā-Janaka continued, "please dig around the couch at a distance equal to the length of the yoke of the ox-cart." The workers did so, and discovered a twelfth pot of gold.

"The ends of the teeth" the king continued," must refer to the spot below the tips of the tusks of the royal elephant when he is standing in his stable." The workers dug there and discovered a thirteenth pot of gold. "The end of the tail must refer to the spot below the tail of the royal stallion when he is standing in his stall." The workers discovered a fourteenth pot of gold there.

"Kebuka' is a very old word for water," explained the king. "Let us drain the royal lake." When that was done, workers found a fifteenth pot of gold. "The ends of the trees," the king concluded, "must refer to the edge of the circle of shade of the great sal trees in the royal park at noon." The workers dug there and discovered the sixteenth pot of gold.

Everyone in the court shouted their approval and applauded wildly.

"Did the king say anything else?" Mahā-Janaka asked.

"No, Your Majesty," the ministers replied, "he did not."

"These sixteen pots of gold," declared King Mahā-Janaka, "are to be used to erect five alms-halls, one at each of the city gates and one in the city center." When the buildings were finished, the king personally distributed alms there every day.

King Mahā-Janaka was eager to see his mother again, so he invited her and the brahmin to move from Campā to Mithilā. When they came, the king paid them great honor and provided them with a fine house.

The news of King Mahā-Janaka's wisdom and triumphs spread throughout the kingdom, and people thronged to Mithilā for the coronation festival. The city was gaily decorated and every household prepared gifts to offer to the king. The city was filled with musicians, singers, dancers, jugglers, and magicians. In the palace, King Mahā-Janaka sat on a magnificent throne on a splendid dais under the white umbrella. On one side, sat the ministers and advisors, and, on the other side, sat the wealthy citizens of Mithilā. As he was sitting there, King Mahā-Janaka recollected his ordeal in the ocean. "If I had not shown courage and determination in the great ocean, I never would have attained this glory!" he thought. "Certainly, in every situation, striving is the right thing to do!" This thought filled his mind with joy.

King Mahā-Janaka ruled Videha with wisdom and righteousness, scrupulously observing the ten duties of a king. He delighted in serving Pacceka Buddhas whenever they visited the city. In time, Queen Sīvalī gave birth to a healthy son who had all the auspicious omens, and they named him Dīghavu. When Prince Dīghavu grew up, he was designated crown prince.

One day, the royal gardener brought a large basket of fresh fruit and another of fresh flowers to the palace. The king was extremely pleased. He rewarded the gardener and told him to prepare the park for a royal visit.

As soon as the park was ready, the king mounted the royal elephant and rode out, followed by his retinue. At the entrance to the park, there were two magnificent mango trees, one without fruit and the other laden with sweet yellow mangoes. Since the king had not yet eaten any of the fruit, no one else dared to touch it. As the elephant passed by the tree, the king reached out, picked a particularly succulent, ripe mango, and bit into it. The moment he tasted the tender flesh of the mango, he was thrilled by the divine flavor. "When I return, I will have some more," he thought as he continued into the garden.

Later, as he was leaving the park, he saw that the barren tree was still as beautiful as a mountain of emeralds. The other tree, however, was in a dreadful state. Its branches had not only been stripped bare of fruit and leaves but had been severely bent and broken. As soon as the populace had seen the king take fruit from the tree, they had descended en masse to gather fruit for themselves.

The king was greatly moved by this contrast. "The tree without any mangoes has been able to maintain its leaves and its beautiful shape, but the tree laden with mangoes has been almost destroyed. The barren tree is much more fortunate than the fruitful one. The man who owns property has constant worries and fears, but the man who owns nothing is free of anxiety. We might say that the life of a king is like the fruitful tree and that the life of an ascetic is like the barren tree. I do not want to be like the fruitful tree; I want to become like the barren one! I will renounce the world and become an ascetic!"

When King Mahā-Janaka returned to the palace, he summoned the commander-in-chief. "General," the king announced, "today, I am turning the affairs of the kingdom over to you and the chief judge. The two of you are to govern the kingdom. I will live as an ascetic on the top floor of the palace.

I will need only one servant to bring me food, water, and other requisites. No one else is to see my face."

The courtiers were sad not to be able to see the king. They wondered why he was no longer interested in ruling the kingdom. They could not understand why he no longer took pleasure in music and dance. One day, they asked the servant about the king's well-being.

"The king does not talk to me any more," the servant replied, "but I have seen him deep in meditation. He looks detached and peaceful. He never asks me for anything. The other day, though, I overheard him talking. He was saying, 'Who will guide me to the place where the Pacceka Buddhas stay? They have left behind all desires and, in a stormy world, they alone roam at peace. Where can I find those wise beings who, freed from all ties, are clear-eyed and sorrowless? Where do they reside?' Of course," the servant continued, "no one knows where the Pacceka Buddhas are. They come and go as they please."

At this time, the life span for human beings was ten thousand years. Mahā-Janaka had been king for almost seven thousand years, so he still had three thousand years of his life remaining. He had been living like an ascetic on the top floor of the palace for only four months, but he was not contented. Ever since he had seen the two mango trees and had resolved to become an ascetic, the palace seemed like a prison, like hell. Often, he sat in his room and moaned, "When will I be able to leave Mithilā? Even though this city is spacious and beautiful, well-designed, prosperous, and lively, I long for the Himavat! I want to wander through the forest in solitude, subsisting on fruit and turning my mind to meditation!" At last, he felt that the time had come, and he decided to leave the capital and to become a true ascetic.

After secretly instructing his servant to procure yellow robes and an earthen pot from the market, he sent for a barber to cut his hair and beard. He donned the yellow robes and, feeling very much like an ascetic, resolved to leave the next morning.

Early that same morning, Queen Sīvalī told the most beautiful concubines to dress with special care and led them to visit the king. As she was ascending the staircase, she met the king as he was coming down, but, mistaking him for a Pacceka Buddha, she made a respectful salutation and stood to one side. When she reached the top floor and saw the king's freshly-shorn locks lying on the floor, she realized whom she had seen on the stairs.

"Come, friends!" she shouted to the other women as she hurried back down the staircase. "We must beg the king to come back!" Catching up with the king in the courtyard, the queen and her attendants loosened their hair, beat their breasts, and began wailing plaintively, "Why are you leaving us,

Your Majesty? Please do not abandon us!" In this way, they followed him through the gate of the palace.

Their cries disturbed the whole city, and many people joined them. "Please stay, Your Majesty!" they shouted. "How will we ever find such a just and good ruler again?"

King Mahā-Janaka continued walking as if he were alone.

Queen Sīvalī sent a message to the commander-in-chief, instructing him to set fire to several derelict houses near the city gate and to ignite brush fires throughout the city. As soon as she could see the smoke, she fell at the king's feet and cried, "Your Majesty, Mithilā is in flames! You must return and save your city!"

"What are you saying, Queen?" the king replied. "I no longer have a city. We, who own nothing of our own, live without a care. Mithilā's palaces may burn, but nothing of mine is consumed by those flames." He continued walking and left the city by the northern gate.

Queen Sīvalī sent another message instructing the commander-in-chief to create the illusion of a disturbance in the northern villages. Very soon, armed men were running here and there. Villagers ran past the king shouting, "Help! Brigands are destroying our houses!" Others hurried past bearing stretchers on which lay men and women daubed with red lac, simulating blood.

The queen again fell at the king's feet and cried, "Your Majesty, bandits are wreaking havoc throughout the land! Please do not desert the kingdom in our time of need!"

The king knew that no bandits would dare rise up while he was still king and that this was Sīvalī's doing. Calmly, he replied, "Those of us who have nothing live without a care. Truly, the kingdom may be despoiled, but nothing of mine can be harmed." He continued walking away from the city, but many people followed, crying for him to return.

"If these people do not return to the city of their own accord," he thought, "I must make them go back." Standing on a rise in the road, he turned to the ministers who had followed him and asked, "Whose kingdom is this?"

"It is yours, Sire," they replied.

"In that case," declared the king, drawing a line with his staff across the road, "I order you to punish anyone who steps over this line!" He turned and walked on.

Not daring to disobey his command, the crowd stood as if frozen and cried, "Your Majesty! Please come back!" Even the queen herself dared not cross the line, but she was so overcome with emotion that she swooned and fell across the line. Suddenly someone shouted, "Look! The queen has crossed the line! We can, too!" Everyone surged across and followed the king.

Mahā-Janaka walked in the direction of the Himavat. For sixty yojanas, he was followed by the queen, her attendants, the army, the royal horses and elephants, and innumerable citizens of Videha.

At that time, an ascetic named Nārada, who was meditating in a cave in the Himavat, arose from seven days of ecstatic bliss and surveyed all of Jambudīpa to see if there was anyone else seeking that bliss. He immediately perceived Mahā-Janaka and realized that, having made his great renunciation, the king was unable to turn back the multitude of followers. "These people, including the queen, are an obstacle to him." Nārada thought. "I must give him an exhortation to strengthen him in his purpose."

With his supernatural power, he stood in the air in front of the king and asked, "Ascetic, what is all this noise? It sounds like a festival! Why is this great crowd gathered around you?"

Mahā-Janaka replied: "I have cut all bonds. With a happy heart, I've left the world, but these folks are begging me to return."

"Don't suppose that you have already reached your goal," Nārada admonished him. "There are still many hindrances yet to overcome."

"Nothing can sway me from my determination!" Mahā-Janaka exclaimed. "What could possibly interfere with my progress as I press onwards to my goal?"

"Drowsiness, laziness, daydreaming, temptation, and discontent—these are some of the foes you must conquer before claiming victory!"

"Thank you, Sage!" Mahā-Janaka shouted. "You have given me some wise words of warning, and I thank you with all my heart! Please tell me who you are."

"I am known as Nārada. My last advice to you is to keep company with other sages and to meditate on the Four Brahma Vihāras. Face any shortcoming or lack with patience and serenity. Neither pride nor self-abasement suits a sage. Let virtue, knowledge, and the law guard you on your way." He bade Mahā-Janaka farewell and returned to his cave.

Another ascetic, who was named Migajina, had also just arisen from an ecstatic trance. When he saw Mahā-Janaka, he also decided to offer him advice. He stood in the air in front of Mahā-Janaka and said, "I see that you have forsaken a kingdom. Have your subjects, your advisors, your family, or your friends wounded your heart and caused you to seek refuge here?"

"I have done no wrong to anyone," Mahā-Janaka replied, "and none has done me any wrong. I saw suffering all around; I saw beings helplessly caught up in the world. I took this as a warning and began my ascetic's life."

"Surely, no one would choose the ascetic's life without a teacher to guide him," Migajina said. "Who encouraged you to leave your life of ease?"

"No one urged me to become an ascetic," Mahā-Janaka replied. "Let me tell you what happened. As I was leaving my royal park one day, surrounded by courtiers and companions, I saw a mango tree, despoiled and broken by the throngs that sought its fruit. Nearby was another mango tree still in all its glory for the simple reason that it was barren. The fruitful tree was forlorn, with leaves stripped and branches bare, while the unproductive tree was still green and strong, untouched by the multitude. I realized that we kings are like that fruitful tree, with many a foe to rob us of our fruits. The elephant is slain for ivory, the panther for his skin. In the end, all will be separated from their pride, their wealth, and their joy. It is better to leave it all now and to seek wisdom through solitude. Those two trees were my teachers, and from them I learned to see the better way."

Migajina, having heard the king, exhorted him to be steadfast and returned to his own abode.

When he was gone, Queen Sīvalī fell at the king's feet, and said: "Sire, your subjects are bereft at your leaving. Please comfort them. Before you go, crown your son to rule in your place. Then, if you must, leave the world and wander on alone!"

"Lady," Mahā-Janaka replied, "I have already left behind subjects, home, family, and kingdom. Those are no more to me."

"My Lord," the queen cried out in desperation, "if you become an ascetic, what shall I do?"

"Do as you please, but, if you teach my son to rule while sinning in thought, word, and deed, you will meet an evil end. A beggar's portion, received as alms, say the wise, is all we need!"

As Mahā-Janaka counseled the queen, the sun set. The courtiers and the citizens resigned themselves to the loss of the king and turned back. The queen, firm in her resolve to follow the king and to persuade him to give up his quest, stayed on. She ordered that part of the army and a few ministers follow her, as well. Mahā-Janaka withdrew to the root of a tree to pass the night, and the queen encamped in a suitable place. Early the next morning, after performing his ablutions, Mahā-Janaka went on his way; the queen stayed close to him, and the army and ministers followed.

That morning, in the city of Thuna, a man had bought a large piece of meat from the market, put it on a skewer, and grilled it over some coals. When it was nicely cooked, he had placed it on a board to cool and had gone on with his work. While his back was turned, a stray dog had grabbed the meat and run off with it in his mouth. The man had given chase as far as the southern gate of the city but, finally, out of breath, had given up.

At that moment, it so happened that Mahā-Janaka and the queen were approaching the gate from different directions. The dog saw them, and, fearful of being cornered, dropped the meat and ran away. Mahā-Janaka saw the meat and waited to see whether anyone claimed it. When he was sure that it had been truly abandoned, he picked it up, wiped it off, and put it in his earthen bowl. Finding a pleasant spot beside a small spring, he sat down and began to eat.

When the queen saw this, she thought, "If he were worthy to rule the kingdom, he would never eat the filthy leavings of a dog. He is not really my husband at all!" Aloud she asked, "Sire, how can you eat such a disgusting piece of garbage?"

"It is your own blindness," Mahā-Janaka replied, "that prevents you from seeing the special value of this piece of alms."

"Even if he is dying of starvation," she retorted, "a noble person would be loath to eat such a revolting mess as that! Have you no shame, Sire?"

"The leavings of neither a householder nor a dog," Mahā-Janaka replied, "are forbidden food. If obtained by lawful means, all food is pure." Calmly, he continued eating, savoring the meat as if it were ambrosia. Then he rinsed his mouth with water.

Sivali was still following him when he returned to the city gate. Some children were playing there, and one girl was shaking some sand in a small winnowing basket. On one wrist, she had a one bangle, and, on the other wrist, she had two, which jangled against each other. Mahā-Janaka noticed this and thought, "Sīvali keeps following me. A wife is a curse to an ascetic. People will blame me, saying that, even though I have left the world, I cannot leave my wife. This girl will be able to tell Sīvali why she should turn back and leave me alone." Standing beside the girl, he asked, "Child, why is one of your wrists so musical while your other wrist is quiet?"

The girl replied: "Ascetic, on this arm, there are two bangles, which jangle when they strike each other. On the other arm, the single bangle is silent because it is alone. The pair are noisy, but the one is quiet. It is peaceful on its own. Only one who is alone is happy."

"Listen to what this young girl says!" Mahā-Janaka said to Sīvali. "Her words are true. Your accompanying me is a cause for shame, and, for it, I will suffer all the blame. Here are two paths. You go by one, and I will take the other. Do not refer to me as your husband any longer. You are no longer my wife. Goodbye."

The queen told him to take the better path to the right, and she went off to the left. After a short time, however, she was so overcome with grief that she turned back and hurried to catch up with him. As he entered the city of Thuna, she was again following him.

On his almsrounds in the city, Mahā-Janaka arrived at the house of a fletcher, who was busy working. Mahā-Janaka stood at one side while the fletcher heated an arrow in a pan of coals, wetted it with some sour rice-gruel, and, closing one eye, held it to the other eye to see whether it was perfectly straight. "Perhaps this man," Mahā-Janaka reflected, "can teach Sīvalī a lesson."

"Sir," Mahā-Janaka said, "why do you close one eye and gaze intently with the other? Does that improve your sight?"

The fletcher replied, "The wide horizon, which both eyes give, distracts me. By using only one eye, I get a single line, my aim is fixed, and my vision is true."

Mahā-Janaka silently continued on his rounds. Having collected enough food, he found a pleasant spot outside the city and sat to take his meal. When he finished, he said to Sīvalī, "The fletcher's words were the same as those of the girl. If you continue to follow me, I will be overwhelmed with shame. If I were to yield to your request, I would be sorely blamed. Here again are two paths. You take one, and I will take the other. Do not refer to me as your husband any longer. You are no more my wife. Goodbye."

Despite Mahā-Janaka's exhortations, Sīvalī stubbornly continued to follow him.

As they approached a deep forest, Mahā-Janaka plucked a stalk of munja grass from beside the road. "Sīvalī," he said, holding up the stalk of grass, "just as this stalk cannot be reconnected to its root, so our lives can never be rejoined."

Hearing this and seeing the broken grass, Sīvalī, at last, understood that her relationship with Mahā-Janaka had indeed come to an end. Unable to control her grief, she fell senseless on the road. Mahā-Janaka quickly plunged into the forest, carefully obliterating his footsteps as he went. The ministers hurried to the prostrate queen, sprinkled her with water, and rubbed her hands and feet. When she regained consciousness, she asked weakly, "Where is the king?"

"Your Highness, we have no idea!" they replied. "We last saw him talking with you."

She ordered them to search for the king, but no one could find a trace of him.

Sadly, the queen turned back. As she returned to the capital, she erected five cetiyas—one at the place where she had last seen Mahā-Janaka, a second at the place where he had talked with the fletcher, a third at the place where he had talked with the girl, a fourth at the place where he had eaten the meat, and a fifth at the place where he had met Nārada and Migajina. At each cetiya, she paid her respects with flowers and incense.

When she reached Mithilā, she summoned her son and performed his coronation in the mango grove of the royal park. Then she had the new king mount the royal elephant and, surrounded by the army, return to the city. She herself stayed in the park and became an ascetic. She practiced meditation, achieved jhāna, and was reborn in the Brahma heavens.

Mahā-Janaka entered the Himavat and, within seven days, perfected the five extraordinary powers and the eight jhānas, never again to return to the habitation of men.

Having concluded his story, the Buddha added, "This is not the first time that the Tathāgata made a great renunciation." Then he identified the birth: "At that time, Uppalavannā was Manimekhalā, Sāriputta was Nārada, Moggallāna was Migajina, Khemā was the girl, Ānanda was the fletcher, Rāhula's mother was Queen Sīvalī, Rāhula was Prince Dīghavu, my parents were King Arittha-Janaka and the queen, and I was King Mahā-Janaka, who became an ascetic."

210

Golden Sāma

Suvanna-Sāma Jātaka

It was while staying at Jetavana that the Buddha told this story about a bhikkhu who was supporting his parents.

In Sāvatthī, there was a well-to-do merchant whose wealth amounted to more than eighteen crores. This merchant had only one son whom he loved very much.

One day, when the lad stepped onto the balcony of the house and looked down on the street, he saw a great crowd of people carrying incense and garlands on their way to Jetavana and decided to join them in hearing the Dhamma. When he arrived at the monastery, he distributed robes and medicine to the bhikkhus, honored the Buddha with flowers and incense, and sat down respectfully at one side.

He listened carefully to the Buddha's teaching and came to understand the evil results of sensual desire and the blessings that follow from living the holy life. After the rest of the assembly had departed, he asked the Buddha for ordination but was told that he needed his parents' permission.

The young man returned home and asked his parents, but they refused because he was their only child. He was so determined to become a bhikkhu, however, that he vowed he would not eat until they allowed him to ordain. After he had fasted for one week, his parents relented.

The young man was ordained and practiced very diligently under his teacher, thoroughly mastering the Buddha's Dhamma.

After five years at Jetavana, he thought, "There are too many distractions in this monastery. If I continue to stay here, I can make no attainments. I must find a place more conducive to achieving insight." He asked his preceptor for instruction in meditation and left to practice by himself in the forest near a remote frontier village.

He stayed there for twelve years, meditating earnestly and striving to achieve insight, but he made no attainments whatsoever.

One day, a wandering bhikkhu happened to visit the forest hermitage where that bhikkhu was staying. The resident bhikkhu performed the duties of hospitality and asked where his guest had come from. Learning that his guest had just come from Jetavana, he asked after the health of the Buddha and the great disciples. Then, without revealing his own identity, he asked for news of his parents, referring to them by name and describing them as "that well-to-do merchant family in Sāvatthī."

"Oh, friend, don't ask for news of that family."

"Why not, sir? What has happened?"

"I've heard that there was one son in that family, but he left to become a bhikkhu. After he left, the family went to ruin. Tenants cheated them, and dealers refused to pay for their goods. By himself, the old man was not able to demand payment, so their income disappeared. Business associates took advantage of the aging couple, and dishonest servants stole from them. Several years ago, they had to sell their house. When that money was gone, they were reduced to begging for food, dressed in rags. It's a pitiful story, sir!"

When he heard this, the bhikkhu began to weep silently.

"Friend," the visiting bhikkhu asked, "what is it? What is the matter?"

"Sir," the resident bhikkhu replied, "that old couple are my father and mother. I am that son who abandoned them."

"Then it is true, my friend," the guest said sadly. "It is because of you that the poor old couple are so miserable. Since they are your parents, shouldn't you go back and take care of them?"

For the rest of the day, the resident bhikkhu reflected on his situation. "For twelve years," he thought, "I have persevered in my meditation, but I have achieved nothing, neither path nor fruit. I must be unfit to be a bhikkhu. I should go back to the household life, support my parents, practice generosity, and win for myself a place in heaven."

The next morning, he gave his forest hermitage to the visiting bhikkhu and left to return to Sāvatthī. Close to the city, he arrived at a fork in the road just behind Jetavana. One road led to Jetavana; the other road led to the city. He stood at the fork and wondered, "Which should I do first? Should I visit the Buddha or go and see my parents? In the past, I spent a lot of time with my parents, and I will be living with them again soon. From now on, however, I will only rarely have an opportunity to see the Buddha. Today, I will visit the Perfectly Enlightened One and hear the Dhamma. After all these years, tomorrow morning is soon enough to see my parents."

He took the road leading to Jetavana and arrived at the monastery in the evening.

That morning, as the Buddha had surveyed the world with his perfect vision, he had seen the bhikkhu's potential. In the evening, knowing that the bhikkhu was in the assembly, the Buddha taught the Matuposaka Sutta,[13] praising the virtues of one's parents. As the bhikkhu listened, he thought, "I had decided to support my parents as a layman, but the Buddha has said that a son can also be helpful to his parents as a bhikkhu. I have spent twelve years in the forest, never seeing the Buddha, and I failed to reach the goal of the ascetic life. Now I can see my way clear to staying in Sāvatthī as a bhikkhu and supporting my parents as well. I will not disrobe!"

Having made that important decision, he accepted his ticket for gruel for the next day's meal, but, after twelve years in the forest, he couldn't help feeling that accepting food in this way was an unpardonable offense.

The next morning, as he was going into Sāvatthī, he wondered once more, "Should I first accept the gruel, or should I go directly to see my parents?"

Not wanting to meet his parents empty-handed, he decided to get the gruel first. After he had accepted the alms, he walked toward his old house and saw his parents sitting on the ground, leaning against the wall on the opposite side of the road. They were quietly drinking the broth they had gotten on their own begging rounds. Seeing them in this condition, he was so overcome with emotion that he could only stand there silently as his eyes filled with tears.

When his mother saw him, she said respectfully, "Venerable Sir, we have nothing fit to offer you. Please pass on."

The sound of her voice was almost more than he could bear, and, unable to move, he just stood there as she repeated her words a second and a third time.

At last, his father said, "Wife, can that be our son? Go and see." His mother stood up and walked toward him. As soon as she recognized her son, she fell

---

13 Samyutta Nikāya, Sagāthā Vagga, Brāhmana Samyutta, 7, 19.

at his feet and began sobbing. Her husband joined her, and the two of them lay prostrate before the bhikkhu, crying loudly.

"My dear parents," the bhikkhu said, also weeping. "Please don't despair. Take this gruel. I will support you." After they had eaten the gruel, he went on almsrounds for solid food, which he also gave to them. Then he sought alms for himself.

He managed to find a suitable place for himself to stay nearby and continued to care for his parents in this manner. Every day, he gave them all the alms he received, even those from the fortnightly distribution. Afterward, he would go on a second almsrounds for his own food. Whatever provisions he received for the rainy season, he gave to his mother and father. For himself, he kept only worn-out garments, which he dyed behind closed doors.

It seldom happened that he collected enough food for all three. Occasionally, he received nothing at all. As he watched over his parents, he grew pale and thin. The other bhikkhus began to comment, "Your complexion used to be bright, but recently you've become awfully pale. Are you ill?" they asked.

"No," he replied, "I'm not suffering from any illness, but I have a great burden." Then he explained his situation.

"Friend," they admonished him, "the Buddha does not allow us to waste the offerings of the faithful. You are committing an offence by giving the alms you receive to laypeople."

He had not thought about it in that way before and began to feel ashamed.

His friends felt duty-bound to disclose his offense and reported the matter to the Buddha.

Although the Buddha already knew all about it, he sent for the bhikkhu and asked him, "Is it true, Bhikkhu, that you are using the alms you receive to support laypeople?"

The bhikkhu confessed that it was true.

"Who are these laypeople you are supporting?"

"Venerable Sir, they are my parents."

"Well done! Well done! Well done!" the Buddha proclaimed. "You are taking the path on which I also journeyed long ago. I, too, supported my parents by going on almsrounds."

When the bhikkhu heard this, he was greatly relieved and encouraged, but the other bhikkhus were surprised. At their request, the Buddha told this story of the past.

Long, long ago, not far from Bārānasi, there were two villages of hunters, each of about five hundred families, one on each side of the river. The two village chiefs had been good friends from childhood. They had made an agreement that, if one of them had a daughter and the other a son, they would see the two married.

It so happened that a son was born to the chief of the village on the near side of the river. He was named Dukūlaka because, immediately after birth, he was wrapped in fine cloth. At about the same time, a daughter was born to the chief of the village on the opposite side. She was named Pārikā because she was born on the far side of the river. Both children were fair and hand-some. Even though they grew up in hunting villages, neither child would have anything to do with the hunting, nor would either one ever harm any living creature.

When the two children became sixteen, their parents began talking to them about their betrothal. Each family praised the virtues of the other and urged the young people to begin preparing for the marriage. Dukūlaka and Pārikā, however, had recently descended from the Brahma heavens, and neither was the least bit interested in marriage. "Do not mention marriage to me ever again!" shouted Dukūlaka. This upset his parents very much. Not taking his rejection seriously, they persisted, repeating the proposal three times. Dukūlaka remained steadfast and finally shouted, "Don't you under-stand? I do not want to get married! I don't want a household life!" Pārikā, likewise, rejected her parents' proposal and responded by putting her hands over her ears and running from them.

Although both Dukūlaka and Pārikā were distraught by their parents' nag-ging, neither knew that the other was also refusing. Secretly, each sent the same message to the other. "If you wish to marry, please find yourself another partner. I have no interest in marriage—not with you, nor with anyone else!"

Both families remained deaf to the youths' protestations and made all the arrangements for the wedding ceremony, insisting that the young people go through with it. Dukūlaka and Pārikā allowed the ceremony to be performed, but they lived together in name only, never so much as even touching one another with desire. They continued to lead exemplary lives, practicing all forms of generosity, compassion, and loving-kindness.

Their refusal to follow their traditional occupation exasperated their par-ents. Dukūlaka's parents complained openly to the newlyweds, "Don't you realize that you are causing shame to yourselves and to us? You were born into families of hunters, but you don't hunt and you don't fish as we do. In fact, we have never seen you kill anything, not even an insect! You don't even want to live together as husband and wife. You don't want children. What will become of you?"

"My dear parents," Dukūlaka replied gently, "if you will give us your permission, we will become ascetics this very day."

"If that is what you really want to do," his parents answered wearily, "go ahead. We have done as much as we can for you." Dukūlaka and Pārikā immediately prepared for the journey, bade their parents farewell, and set out to follow the Gangā to the region of the Himavat. When they reached the point where the Migasammatā River enters the Gangā, they turned and followed that river into the mountains.

At that moment, in Tāvatimsa, Sakka's throne grew hot. "Vissakamma," he called, "two great beings have just entered the Himavat. You must build a hermitage for them near the Migasammatā River. Make separate dwellings for the two, and stock them with all the necessities for ascetics."

Choosing an ideal spot, Vissakamma quickly constructed a hermitage, laid out a footpath, and drove away all the noisy animals.

Dukūlaka and Pārikā saw the footpath and followed it to the hermitage. "This is a gift from Sakka!" Dukūlaka exclaimed. He took off his outer garment, put on a robe of red bark, threw a black antelope hide over his shoulder, and twisted his hair into a knot. Pārikā, likewise, donned the garments which Vissakamma had left for her. The couple retired to their respective huts, and, radiating loving-kindness toward all creatures, began their simple life as ascetics. Through the influence of their benevolence, all the birds and animals in that part of the forest stopped behaving violently and none harmed another.

Every morning, Pārikā fetched water and swept the hermitage. Then they went together to collect fruit, nuts, roots, and berries for their meal. The rest of the day, they spent meditating in their respective huts. Sakka kept watch over them, making sure that they lacked nothing.

One day, Sakka foresaw that both of these ascetics were going to lose their sight. He appeared before Dukūlaka and announced, "Sir, a great danger threatens you. You and Pārikā must have a son who can take care of you. You must follow the way of the world."

"Sakka," the ascetic exclaimed, "how can you suggest such a thing to me? Even when we lived in the village, we were disgusted by carnal desires. Now that we have become ascetics, it is unthinkable for us to engage in such behavior."

"All right," Sakka conceded, "but, nevertheless, you must have a son. At the appropriate time, simply touch Pārikā's navel with your fingers." Dukūlaka agreed to do that much, and he explained the matter to Pārikā. When Pārikā told him that the time had come, he brushed her navel with his fingers.

At that moment, the Bodhisatta descended from the heavenly realm and was conceived in Pārikā's womb. Ten months later, with the help of kinnaris from the mountains, Pārikā delivered a son with a golden hue, whom they named Suvanna-Sāma. They gently washed the baby and prepared a space for him in Pārikā's hut. Whenever the two of them went out to collect fruit, kinnaras came to watch the baby.

Sāma grew to be a wonderful child, and Dukūlaka and Pārikā cherished him dearly. In time, he was old enough to stay by himself, and the kinnaras no longer came. He took care of the house while his parents gathered the food. He often worried that some danger would befall them while they were in the forest. Each day, until they returned with their baskets, he watched the path, afraid that they had had an accident.

One evening, as Dukūlaka and Pārikā were returning home with the flowers, fruit, and roots they had collected, a sudden storm arose. They took shelter under a tree and waited for the storm to subside. Unfortunately, under that tree, there was an anthill, which was the abode of a fierce cobra. As Dukūlaka and Pārikā were standing there, the rain dripped from their bodies. It carried the smell of their perspiration, which infuriated the snake. In a rage, the serpent rose up with hood spread and sprayed them with blinding poison.

"Pārikā!" cried Dukūlaka, "What happened? Everything has gone black! I can't see anything!"

"Dukūlaka!" Pārikā cried, "I'm blind, too. I can't see. What happened?"

"We're doomed!" they cried together, as they dropped to the ground and began groping about to find the path. "What sin did we ever commit to cause such a disaster?"

In a previous life, Dukūlaka had been a famous doctor with many wealthy patients. After he had treated a man for an eye disease, the man had refused to pay. "What can we do about it?" he asked his wife, who was the Pārikā of this birth.

"Never mind about his money," she replied. "Let's teach him a lesson he'll never forget. Make some salve, and tell him to apply it to his eye. As soon as he does, he'll go blind in that eye. That'll show the old skinflint!" The doctor did exactly as his wife had suggested, and the patient did indeed lose his sight in the treated eye. Because the couple had committed that wickedness in their previous lives, both of them suffered blindness in this life.

Waiting alone in the hermitage, Sāma was becoming more and more anxious. He had never known his parents to be so late in returning. At last, he decided to go in search of them. As he walked along the familiar paths, he looked for them on both sides and called out their names.

As soon as she heard him coming, Pārikā shouted, "Sāma, stop! Don't come any further!

"Be careful, Son! There's something dangerous here, and we don't know what it is! Don't come any closer!"

Sāma could see them crawling along the path, but he could not understand what the problem was. He looked around and found a long stick, which he extended toward them. They grabbed hold of it, struggled to their feet, and, still holding the stick, joined him.

"You're blind!" he cried when he understood their condition. "What happened?"

"We're not sure," Pārikā replied. "When it started raining, we took shelter under a tree."

"It seems there was an anthill there," Dukūlaka added, "and that made us blind."

"Oh, my dear parents," Sāma cried, embracing them, "there must have been a cobra living there. You probably made him angry, and he sprayed venom in your faces."

The three of them sat down in the middle of the path. Sāma sobbed as he embraced his parents and tried to comfort them. After a few minutes, his sobs were mixed with laughter. "Son," Pārikā asked, "are you laughing or crying? What's going on?"

"I am crying," Sāma replied, "because you have lost your sight while you are still young, but I am laughing because now I will be able to take care of you! My dear parents, don't worry about anything. I will look after you. At last, I will be able to repay you for all the care you have given me since I was born."

Sāma took his parents by the hand and led them slowly back to the hermitage. He put them to bed and made sure they were comfortable. While they were resting, he tied guide ropes in all directions so that the couple could easily go from their sleeping rooms to the sitting room and to all the other rooms. He also tied ropes around the garden and from the hermitage as far as the path.

Sāma kept his promise to take care of his parents. Every morning, he swept their apartments, carried water from the river, prepared their food, and set out the neem sticks for cleaning their teeth. Only after they had finished, did he take his own meal. When he was sure that his parents were comfortable, he paid his respects and, surrounded by a herd of tame deer, went into the forest to collect food. Very often, kinnaras joined him and helped him gather delicious fruit, nuts, berries, and roots. In the evening, he returned with the most delectable food the forest had to offer. Before retiring, he again carried water from the river, built a fire, and prepared a steam bath for his parents. In spite of their blindness, Pārikā and Dukūlaka were very comfortable, and Sāma was very happy taking care of them.

The king in Bārānasi at that time was named Piliyakkha. One day, King Piliyakkha developed a sudden craving for fresh venison and decided to go hunting in the Himavat. Intending to be gone for some time, he entrusted the kingdom to his mother, took his best weapons, and left.

Near the Migasammatā River he found the hoofprints of many deer and decided that it would be a good place to hunt. He built a blind with boughs and branches, fitted a poisoned arrow into his bow, and sat quietly waiting for the deer to return from drinking at the river.

Sāma had just come back from the forest with his basket full of food. He greeted his parents and announced, "I am going to the river to bathe and to fetch some water. I will be back shortly." As he stepped out of the hermitage, he was surrounded by his tame deer. Choosing two from the herd, he gently embraced their necks, put the jars on their backs, and allowed them to accompany him to the river.

The king heard footsteps and turned to look. He was amazed to see this young man with his handsome golden hue walking beside the prancing deer. "In all my wandering in this region," he said to himself, "I have never encountered any other human being. Could this be a deva or perhaps a nāga? I could ask him, but, if he is a deva, he will fly up to heaven, and, if he is a nāga, he will sink into the earth. If I go back to Bārānasi and tell anyone about this marvelous creature, I'll be asked what it was. If I say I don't know, my ministers will make fun of me."

From his blind, the king continued quietly watching while Sāma stepped into the water to fill the water jars. The deer stood calmly at the river's edge, drinking.

"If I aim carefully," the king thought, "I can wound the creature. Then I will talk to it and find out what it is." At the very instant the king let fly his arrow, Sāma shifted his weight to place one of the water jars on his shoulder, and the arrow pierced his right side, exiting cleanly from the left.

The deer immediately fled in terror, but Sāma, in spite of the excruciating pain, continued to balance the water jar as best he could, even as the blood flowed from his wounds. Mindfully, he stepped out of the water and set the jar on the riverbank. Then he scooped some sand into a pile for a pillow and lay down on his side, with his head in the direction of his parents' hut. He looked like a golden image on the silvery sand.

"I have no enemies in the Himavat," he said softly. "I have no ill-will toward anyone." As he spoke, blood began oozing from his mouth. He moved his head slightly to look around, but, not seeing anyone, he asked, "Who has wounded me from ambush while I filled my water jars? Was it a brahmin, a warrior, or a hunter? Who can my unknown enemy be? My flesh cannot be eaten. My skin cannot be tanned. Why did you shoot me?" Almost breathless, he asked again, "Who are you? What is your name? Please answer me honestly."

The king trembled as he heard these words. "Although I shot this youth with a poisoned arrow," he whispered to himself, "he neither curses me nor blames me. In spite of his pain, he speaks gently. I must answer him."

"I am Piliyakkha, king of Kāsi," he said aloud, drawing near to where Sāma lay. "I came here to hunt deer. I'm a skillful archer with a steady hand. I am able to strike even a nāga who comes within my view. Now tell me who you are? Who is your father?"

Sāma thought, "This king would believe anything I said. I could tell him I was a deva, a kinnara, a warrior, or a nāga, but one must always speak the truth." Aloud, but with a voice growing ever weaker, he said, "While I lived, they called me Sāma, the son of a hunter who became an ascetic. Now I lie here, pierced by your poisoned shaft, as helpless as a wounded deer, victim of your deadly skill, bathed in my own blood. Weak and faint, I ask again, why did you shoot me? My flesh cannot be eaten; my skin is unsuited for leather. What did you hope to gain by killing me?"

When the king heard this question again, he was too ashamed to tell the truth. "It was an accident," he lied. "I was aiming at a deer, but when the animal saw you, it fled in fright. I didn't mean to hurt you at all."

"What are you saying?" Sāma asked, trying to laugh. "There isn't a single deer in the Himavat that would run away from me! Since I was a toddler, no animal has ever fled in fear of me. Even the yakkhas are my friends! It is impossible that this deer you were trying to shoot took flight because it was afraid of me!"

"How wicked can I be?" the king groaned to himself. "Not only did I injure this innocent youth, I have also maliciously lied about it!"

"Sāma," he cried aloud, "you did not startle any deer. I was not aiming at a deer. My arrow was aimed at you. Greed overcame me. I wanted you as a prize, but I meant only to wound you so that you would not run away. But, surely, you don't stay alone in this forest. Where are you from? Where is your family? For whom were you fetching water?"

Sāma began weeping, and more blood flowed from his mouth as he answered. "Sire," he said, weakly, "my parents live in a hermitage not far from here. They are both blind. I came to fetch water for them. There is no water in the hermitage, and they have only a week's supply of food left. Without me, they will die. I don't care about my own death. Death is the common fate of all, but it grieves me to think what will happen to my mother and father! They will be worrying about me all night long. They will sit on the porch listening for my footsteps. In the morning, they will wander aimlessly, crying for their missing son, and then they, too, will die, abandoned in the forest. I know that I am dying, and I will never see their dear faces again!"

When the king heard this, he also began weeping. "This young man has dedicated himself to caring for his parents," he said to himself. "Even now, despite his pain, he thinks only of them. I have sinned against this innocent youth. How can I comfort him?"

"Sāma," the king cried aloud, "do not despair! I will take care of your parents. I will serve them as you have done. If necessary, I will stay here in the forest. When I am in hell, what good will my kingdom be to me? I promise that I will devote myself to your parents and that they will want for nothing. This is the least I can do to make up for my great sin. Tell me where they are. I vow to be like a household slave to them."

"Your Majesty is very kind," Sāma whispered, his voice almost gone. "If you will care for my parents, I can die in peace. About two hundred bow-lengths from here, there is a path through the trees that leads to their hermitage. Go now, and attend to them if it pleases you." Sāma feebly pressed his palms together and whispered with his last breath, "Honor to you, Sire. Look after my poor blind parents, I beg you. Please convey my love to them."

At that instant, the poison reached Sāma's heart. He closed his eyes and lost consciousness.

"Sāma!" the king cried, weeping uncontrollably. "No! No! No! Just a moment ago, you were talking with me, and now your body is lifeless and rigid. What have I done? How could I have killed this righteous youth?" he beat his breast and wailed loudly. "Sāma, dear boy, you never harmed anyone or anything, but now you are dead. Now I understand that truly everyone must die. I, too, must one day die, but for me, hell awaits. I'm sorry, Sāma! Forgive me!" The king remained kneeling beside the body of Sāma and wept even more loudly.

Suddenly, the king became aware of a bright light. He raised his head and gazed toward the middle of the river. There he saw a very bright light hovering in the air. Peering more closely, he could see that it was a deva.

"Who are you?" he asked. "Why have you come here?"

Drawing closer to the riverbank, the deva answered, "My name is Bahu-sodarī. Seven lives ago, I was this boy's mother. Since then, I have continued to regard him with a mother's affection. Just now, although I was absorbed in divine bliss, I suddenly realized that something had happened to Sāma. What is it? How is my son?" she asked. "No!" she cried as she looked beyond the king. "You needn't answer. I can see that he is dead and that you have killed him. You have done a wicked deed! This boy was innocent. His parents did nothing wrong, yet, with one arrow, you have slain all three. Only by caring for his blind parents can you assuage your guilt and find blessedness."

"Yes," the king replied between sobs. "I have vowed to do that. To you, I renew that pledge, and by so doing, may I escape the clutches of the king of hell." As quickly as she had come, the deva disappeared.

"What is a kingdom to me?" the king repeated. "Sāma, I promise that I will devote myself to your beloved parents." The king gathered flowers and placed then on Sāma's body. After he had respectfully sprinkled the body with water and circumambulated it three times, he picked up the water jar which Sāma had filled and, with a heavy heart, took the path to the hermitage.

As he approached the hermitage, Dukūlaka called out, "Whose footsteps do I hear? Those are not Sāma's light steps! Who are you, Sir?"

The king stopped and considered, "If I say right away that I have killed their son, they will be angry. If they were to reproach me, my anger might flare up and cause me to do something outrageous, and I might commit yet another sin. Let me just identify myself first."

Setting down the jar, the king stood in the doorway and declared, "I am Piliyakkha, king of Kāsi. I came here to hunt deer. I'm a skillful archer with a steady hand. I am able to strike even a nāga who comes within my view."

"Welcome, Sire!" Dukūlaka answered. "We are extremely honored to greet you! How fortunate we are that you came by here! Your Majesty is mighty and glorious, but I beg you to take some of our fruit, leaves, and roots. Although they are nothing special, please take the best, Sire, and eat. If you are thirsty, please help yourself to some cool water."

"Oh, dear," the king thought, "since this man greets me so warmly, I do not dare come right out and say, 'I have just killed your son!' What shall I do?"

"Pray, tell me," the king said aloud, "I can see that you are blind. Can one like you roam the woods alone? Your hermitage is well-kept, and your pantry well-stocked. Surely you did not collect this fruit yourself. Who brought it to you? The one who gathered such a variety must have good eyes!"

"You are right, Your Majesty. We have a son. Sāma is his name. He is still young and not very tall, but he is a handsome boy with long black hair. One could not ask for a more devoted child. He takes care of everything for us. It was he who brought the fruit just before going off to fill our water jars. He will be back shortly. Please sit down so that you may meet him when he returns."

"Of course, Sāma, your devoted son," the king repeated. "Oh, sir, Sāma, your son," he stammered. "The handsome boy—I shot him with my arrow! He lies yonder, drenched in blood."

When Pārikā heard this, she burst from her own hut, groping along the guide rope. "What did I hear?" she cried. "Dukūlaka, who is this man who says that Sāma has been killed? It can't be true. Why is he trying to break my heart?"

"Pārikā, my dear. Please be calm. The king of Kāsi is here. It seems there has been an accident and that he shot our beloved Sāma, but we must control ourselves. We must not blame him."

"How can I control my feelings about the man who did such a thing?" Pārikā said with emotion. "Suvanna-Sāma was our darling son, radiant like the sun in heaven. We raised him from a baby, and he was our sole support. How can we survive without his care?"

"Yes, my dear," Dukūlaka answered, still trying to calm her, "Sāma was a darling boy. He was, indeed, our sole support, but the wise must abstain from all anger and hatred toward those who do them wrong."

Unable to control her grief, Pārikā collapsed in tears. "Sāma, my son! Sāma, my darling!" she kept repeating as she wept. Even Dukūlaka could not hold back the tears as he realized that they were indeed alone and that he would never more hear Sāma's cheerful voice as he returned from the forest.

"Please, kind sir and gentle madam," the king said, as softly as he could, "I beg of you to weep no more, neither for Sāma nor for yourselves. I promise that I will take care of both of you. I will be like your son, and you will want for nothing. I will stay here and care for you. I will be your slave. I am very skillful with the bow. I can hunt. Every day, I will gather roots, leaves, and fruit. I will provide all the food you need."

"No, Sire," Dukūlaka protested. "That would not be right. You are our king, and we pay homage to your feet."

"Sire," Pārikā added, "it would, indeed, be indecorous and improper for you to stay here with us."

"This is astonishing!" the king said to himself. "I have killed their son. I have committed an unpardonable sin against this blind couple, but they have not uttered one harsh word against me. After what I have done, they still treat me kindly."

"Good couple," he said aloud, "your respect is most admirable, but I must atone for what I have done. You must allow me to become your devoted son. From now on, you will be father and mother to me! This is more important than even a kingdom."

"No, Sire," Dukūlaka repeated. "You are still our king. We have no need of your service."

The couple respectfully pressed their palms together and raised them to the king. "All we ask of you, Sire," Pārikā said, "is that you take the end of this staff and lead us to where our darling Sāma lies. We want to touch his face. We will be contented just to be near him, and, seated by his side, we will patiently await our own end."

This was more than the king could bear. If, indeed, as the deva had said, all three died because of his arrow, he would certainly fall into hell.

"Ah, but the place where Sāma lies is extremely dangerous. There are fierce beasts about, and the sun has already set. You had better stay here till morning. Let us not tempt the dangers of the forest at night."

"We have no fear of beasts of prey," Dukūlaka replied calmly. "They can do us no harm."

"We want only to bid farewell to our darling boy," Pārikā pleaded.

"Of course," he conceded. "Come! I will take you to him." He took the end of the staff they extended toward him and gently led them to the river. As his own hand trembled in grief, he guided their hands to touch Sāma's body. The old couple immediately fell to the ground and wept. Dukūlaka clasped the boy's head to his bosom, and Pārikā caressed his feet.

"Sāma," they cried, "are you asleep? Are you angry? Have you forgotten your parents? Who will care for us now, helpless, blind, and old? Dear Sāma, you were our only comfort, and now you are gone!"

Suddenly, Pārikā released Sāma's feet and struck her breast with her hand. "Enough of grief for my son," she cried. "Grief is useless. Surely, he is only unconscious because of the strong poison."

"From the moment Sāma was born," she proclaimed in a clear voice, "he was a virtuous boy! If this be true, may this poison in his blood lose its power and become harmless. Our son Sāma always spoke the truth, and he cared for his parents night and day. If this be true, may this poison in his veins be neutralized. Whatever merit his father and I have gained, may it overcome the strength of this poison, and may our darling son not die!"

Sāma, who, a moment before, had lain lifeless, stirred and turned onto his side.

Dukūlaka solemnly repeated the asseveration for himself, and, while he was still speaking, Sāma rolled over on his other side.

The deva, Bahusodarī, appeared and proclaimed, "For many years have I lived alone on Mount Gandhamadana in the depth of the forest. Not one of earth's inhabitants is dearer to my heart than Sāma. By this truth, may all the poison in Sāma's body lose its power and disappear."

As soon as the deva had finished pronouncing her solemn asseveration, dawn broke. Sāma opened his eyes and sat up. His golden hue returned, and he looked as fair and as vigorous as before. At the same moment, his parents' sight was fully restored.

Dukūlaka and Pārikā wept with joy to behold their beloved son.

"My dear parents," Sāma said as he embraced them both, "here is your Sāma, safe and well. Once more, you can see me with your own eyes. Rejoice, and weep no more!" Standing up and turning toward the king, he continued, "Sire, you are welcome here. As our honored guest, we offer you the choicest fruit and fresh water from the mountain steam."

"I don't understand! This is amazing!" the king stammered. "I can't believe it! Only a short while ago, I saw you dead, but now you are alive and well!"

"Your poison rendered me unconscious," Sāma explained. "It was so strong that you thought I was dead. You must know that those who righteously care for their parents in infirmity are watched over by the devas. To reward their piety, the devas will come to heal their sicknesses. Those who dutifully care for their aged parents are praised by the devas and will be blessed with rebirth in heaven."

"Sāma!" the king cried out, pressing his palms together and raising them in respect to the boy. "You are truly blessed by the devas. Your virtue is unsurpassed. Please help me! Protect me from my great sin!"

"Your Excellency," Sāma replied, "to enjoy divine happiness here and to reach the realm of the devas in the next life, you must rule righteously, observing the ten duties of a king.

"First, you must honor and respect your father and mother. Second, you must respect and care for your wife and children. Third, you must be honorable toward your friends and nobles. Fourth, you must treat your ministers and your army with fairness. Fifth, you must protect all the towns and villages and treat the citizens fairly. Sixth, you must rule the kingdom wisely and maintain its borders. Seventh, you must support religious ascetics. Eighth, you must show compassion to all birds and beasts. Ninth, you must practice the law in all matters. Tenth, you must always act according to the law.

"By observing these ten duties of a king, you will find happiness in this life and bliss in heaven in the future. The highest of the devas won their heavenly bliss by performing their duty." Sāma concluded his teaching by establishing the king in the five precepts, which the king gratefully accepted with bowed head.

Before returning to Bārānasi, the king paid his respects to Sāma and his parents. For the remainder of his reign, he ruled righteously, carefully following Sāma's wise advice, generously giving many gifts, and performing other virtuous acts. When he passed away, he was reborn in heaven.

Sāma and his parents continued living in the forest and practicing meditation. They perfected the five extraordinary powers and the eight jhānas, and, when they died, they were reborn in the Brahma heavens.

Having concluded his story, the Buddha added, "Bhikkhus, it is an ancient tradition among the wise to support their parents." Then he taught the Dhamma, and the bhikkhu attained the first path. Finally, the Buddha identified the birth: "At that time, Ānanda was the king, Uppalavannā was the deva, Anuruddha was Sakka, Mahā-Kassapa was Dukūlaka, Bhaddaka-pilani was Pārikā, and I was Suvanna-Sāma."

211
King Nimi's Grand Tour
Nimi Jātaka

It was while staying in Makhādeva's mango grove near Mithilā that the Buddha told this story about a smile.

One evening, the Buddha, accompanied by a large group of bhikkhus, was walking up and down in that grove. He noticed a pleasant spot and allowed a smile to be seen on his face. When Venerable Ānanda asked the Buddha why he smiled, the Buddha replied, "Long ago, Ānanda, I practiced deep meditation in this spot." Then he sat down on a prepared seat and, at Venerable Ānanda's request, told this story of the past.

Long, long ago, the king in Mithilā, the capital of Videha, was named Makhādeva.[14] As a young man, Makhādeva had spent eighty-four thousand years in pleasure. He had served another eighty-four thousand years as crown prince. He was still healthy and vigorous when he became king. Nevertheless, he ordered the royal barber to inform him as soon as he saw a gray hair on his head. Eighty-four thousand years later, the barber noticed a couple of white hairs and dutifully informed the king. "Pull them out with tweezers,

---

14 This incident is also related separately as Jātaka 9, Makhādeva Jātaka, not included in this anthology

and lay them on my hand!" commanded the king. On seeing them, he was as shaken as if he had seen death standing in front of him. "These gray hairs have a deep meaning for me," he said solemnly. "The time has come for me to leave the world."

The king rewarded the barber by giving him a village and sent for his eldest son. "My son," he announced, "the entire burden of state is now on your shoulders. I am going to renounce the world."

"Why, Father? Why?" asked the crown prince.

"Gray hairs have appeared on my head. These messengers announce the relentless passage of time. I am getting old, and it is time for me to renounce worldly life."

After giving his son a great deal of excellent advice about ruling wisely, he arranged the coronation ceremony and left Mithilā. For another eighty-four thousand years, Makhādeva lived as an ascetic in a mango grove near the city, practicing meditation and cultivating the jhānas. After he died, he was reborn in the Brahma heavens.

In the same way, the new king renounced the world as soon as gray hairs were found on his head. After many years of meditating as an ascetic, he, too, was reborn in the Brahma heavens. His son, also, did the same. Thus, one king after another renounced the world and became an ascetic in that same mango grove.

Makhādeva, the first of the line, looked down from the Brahma heavens to ascertain his family's fortune and was gladdened to see that eighty-four thousand kings, less two, had renounced the world. "Will the noble tradition continue or not?" he wondered.

Looking into the future, he saw that it would not. Thus, he resolved that he would be the last to carry out the tradition he himself had established. Leaving heaven, he was conceived in the womb of the king's consort in Mithilā.

On his name-day, the soothsayers, looking at his marks, said, "Your Majesty, this prince has been born to complete your family tradition. He will be the last in this great family of ascetics."

Hearing this, the king proclaimed, "Since this boy has been born to round off my family like the hoop of a chariot-wheel, let him be named Nimi!"

All his life, Prince Nimi was devoted to giving, to virtue, and to observing every Uposatha day. When the king, his father, was shown a gray hair from his head, he, like generations of kings before him, presented a village to his barber, gave the kingdom to his son, became an ascetic in the mango grove, and was reborn in the Brahma heavens.

King Nimi, in his devotion to almsgiving, built five almshalls, one at each gate, and another in the middle of the city. From these halls, he distributed great gifts. He urged the citizens to be mindful and virtuous, instilling in them the fear of death. By both example and exhortation, he encouraged his subjects in almsgiving and good deeds, showing them the road to heaven. Throughout the kingdom, the people praised King Nimi and gave him credit for their virtue. Everyone followed his wise teaching, and, when they died, so many were reborn in the heavens that the hells were virtually empty.

In Tāvatimsa, the devas, who had been citizens of Nimi's kingdom, often assembled in the great hall to pay tribute to their teacher and to praise his virtues. "Hail to King Nimi!" they cried. "It is by following his example and by heeding his wise teaching that we have reached this divine enjoyment."

On a full-moon day, as King Nimi was observing Uposatha, he pondered which was more fruitful—almsgiving or the ascetic life. As soon as the question crossed the king's mind, Sakka's throne became hot. Sakka understood King Nimi's question and resolved to answer it himself. He immediately descended to Mithilā and illuminated the palace with a blaze of light.

Finding the king in his royal chamber, he announced, "I am Sakka, and I have come to resolve your doubt. Both almsgiving and the ascetic life are praise-worthy, are followed by great men, and may lead to rebirth in heaven. Consider, however, those great and generous kings—Dudīpa, Sāgara, Sela, Mucalinda, Bhagīrasa, Usindara, Atthaka, Assaka, and Pathujjana. Despite their remarkable generosity and their sacrifice, they were unable to escape from the peta realm.

"The holy life, on the other hand, brings perfect purity. Those great ascetics—Yāmahanu, Somayāga, Manojava, Samudda, Māgha, Bharata, Kalikara, Kassapa, Angīrasa, Akitti, Kisavaccha—all passed beyond and were reborn in the Brahma heavens.

"So far, I have spoken only of the distant past. Let me tell you now what I myself know from personal experience. Long ago, in the far north, where the Sida River is deep and surrounded by steep mountains, there was a hermitage with ten thousand ascetics. At that time, I was living there, and I, too, kept the vows of the holy life, but I tended to the others. Without regard to caste, I took care of all their needs. Every man, no matter which caste, is bound by his own actions so, without righteousness, he may fall into hell. If purified by good conduct, like those ten thousand ascetics, however, he is destined for heaven. Having experienced this, I know it to be true.

"Therefore, Your Majesty, although both almsgiving and the ascetic life bear fruit, and men are wise to follow both, there is no doubt that the holy life is more fruitful by far." Having clearly answered King Nimi's question, Sakka returned to his heaven.

As soon as Sakka reappeared in Tāvatimsa, his divine companions asked him where he had been. When the devas who had been citizens of Nimi's kingdom heard Sakka extol the wonderful qualities of King Nimi, they longed to see him again. "Please, Sire," they begged, "send for King Nimi! Bring him here so that we may once again see our teacher!"

Graciously agreeing to their request, Sakka sent Mātali with the divine chariot to fetch the king.

The few minutes that Sakka spent speaking with the devas and giving the order to Mātali were the same as one month in the human realm. Thus, it was another full-moon day. King Nimi was again observing Uposatha. He had opened his eastern window and was sitting on the upper floor of his palace. Surrounded by courtiers, he was reflecting on virtue. Those not keeping the precepts had eaten their evening meal and were sitting in their doorways speaking quietly. Just as the moon's perfect disk rose in the east, Mātali's chariot, drawn by a team of one thousand magnificent horses and shining as brightly as the moon itself, also appeared.

"Look," someone shouted, "there are two moons tonight!"

A few seconds later, another exclaimed, "That's not a moon! It's a heavenly chariot!" For a brief moment, the people wondered why a heavenly chariot was flying to Mithilā, but they quickly realized that Sakka must have sent his chariot to fetch their own righteous king. As they watched the chariot speeding directly toward the palace, everyone cried out in delight. "Doesn't it make you shiver with joy that the very devas want to see our king!"

Mātali turned the chariot and brought it to rest just outside the windowsill and invited the king to enter. "Come, noble king, mount this car. The devas of Tāvatimsa are waiting for you in Sudhamma Hall."

Addressing the members of his household and the citizens assembled in the courtyard below, King Nimi announced, "In a short time, I will return. While I am away, be heedful, do good, and give alms." Then, eager to see the dwelling place of the devas, he stepped into the chariot.

As they drove away, Mātali asked which route to Tāvatimsa the king preferred, by way of the heavens or by way of the hells.

"I have never seen either of these places before," the king replied. "I would like to see both!"

"It isn't possible to see both at once. Which do you want to see first?" Mātali asked again.

King Nimi was sure that he was destined for heaven, so he asked Mātali to take him to hell, that he might have a chance to see the abode of the evil-doers.

Mātali urged the horses on, and, in an instant, they arrived at a great flaming river from which arose the stench of corrosive brine. King Nimi watched with terror as naked beings were cast repeatedly into the burning water.

He asked Mātali what wicked deeds these creatures had committed.

"This is the Vetarani River," Mātali answered. "It is reserved for those who are strong but use their strength to harm the weak and to oppress the vulnerable."

Mātali caused the Vetarani River to disappear and drove onwards to a place where King Nimi saw fierce dogs and huge birds tearing at the flesh of beings who were helpless to resist.

"What have these creatures done to deserve such torture?"

"These black hounds and speckled vultures prey upon those who, as misers, brahmins, and ascetics, cheated and hurt others by word or deed."

As they drove through the various levels of hell, King Nimi saw innumerable beings suffering excruciating torture. In each place, he asked Mātali what those beings had done, and Mātali explained how evil ripened and bore fruit.

Beings lay prostrate with their bodies all ablaze; they had tortured innocent beings.

Beings with charred bodies were struggling in a pit of fiery coals; they had borne false witness, had bribed others to lie for them, or had refused to pay a debt.

Beings were being cast headfirst into a flaming iron cauldron; they had intentionally harmed virtuous ascetics.

Beings were being wrung by the neck and cast into a cauldron of boiling water; they had caught birds and killed them by wringing their necks.

Beings, scorched by unbearable heat, were stooping to drink in a shallow river, but just before their lips touched the water, it turned to chaff; they had been merchants who had cheated the poor by mixing chaff with good grain.

Beings were being pierced and stabbed with hundreds of spears; they had stolen others' property, such as gold, silver, or cattle.

Beings were being cut to pieces; they had been fishermen, hunters, and butchers, who had slaughtered animals.

Starving beings were drinking from a foul lake full of excrement; they had betrayed and hurt their trusting friends.

Beings, scorched by unbearable heat, were drinking from a vile lake of putrefying blood; they had killed their own mothers or fathers.

Beings whose tongues were pierced by hooks, each with one hundred sharp barbs, were dribbling and flopping in pain like fish on the shore; they had been greedy merchants who had cheated their customers by lying and deceiving them, like those who catch fish with baited hooks.

Beings, buried waist deep in mud, whose bodies were smeared with blood and blazing, were stretching out their arms and wailing; they had been women who, leading lustful, unclean lives, had been unfaithful to their husbands.

In the hell called Naraka, beings were being cast headlong into an abyss filled with blazing coals; they had been men who had seduced others' wives.

At last, they arrived at a gruesome place where beings were thrashing about and writhing in agony. Mātali explained that this was the hell of false teachers, who had led others astray by teaching that there is no evil in bad action and no merit in good action.

Meanwhile in Tāvatimsa, all the devas were sitting in the glorious Sudhamma Hall, waiting for King Nimi's arrival. Even Sakka began to complain that it was taking Mātali a long time to return, but then he realized what was happening. He called a young deva and commanded, "Go quickly, and tell Mātali to bring the king directly here. He is using up King Nimi's mortal life and must not go touring through any more hells."

When Mātali received the message, he instantly made all the other dreadful hells in the four quarters appear to King Nimi in a flash. "Now, mighty monarch, you have seen where all the wicked go," Mātali said, as he turned the horses and urged them on. "Let us hurry to Tāvatimsa."

A few moments later, the king beheld a magnificent palace with pinnacles of jewels and gold. The palace was surrounded by a park with majestic trees. At one side, was a lovely lake covered with lilies. In a gabled chamber at the front, a beautiful deva was seated upon a couch. Attended by one thousand nymphs, the deva was looking out through an open window. "Who is that?" King Nimi gasped with delight.

"The deva who dwells in that mansion," Mātali told him, "was named Birani in her previous life. She was the slave of a brahmin. Once, she welcomed a guest and cared for him as a mother cares for her son. For that deed, she now inhabits this glorious mansion."

Next, the king was dazzled by seven golden mansions, in the midst of which stood a richly dressed and mighty deva. Mātali explained that this deva had been a layman named Sotadinna who had generously given alms. He had built seven hermitages for seven ascetics and had supplied all their needs. He had also faithfully observed all the Uposatha days

Next, they passed a palace made of crystal, twenty-five yojanas high. Its many stories were supported by hundreds of columns made of the seven precious things. The windows were covered by delicate lattices, and little bells tinkled from the eaves. The roof was adorned with hundreds of pinnacles, and, from the highest, a magnificent banner of gold and silver fluttered in the wind. At one side of the palace, was a spacious park with a lovely lake, covered with lilies and surrounded by majestic trees and bright flowers. The entire palace and its grounds were filled with beautiful female devas singing and playing heavenly musical instruments. Mātali explained that these devas had been laywomen who, living mindfully and practicing generosity, had faithfully observed the Uposatha days.

The chariot passed five other palaces—two made of crystal, two of jewels, and one of gold. All of them were surrounded by lovely gardens and filled with beautiful women. Mātali explained that the devas who lived in the mansions had been laymen who, delighting in generosity, had donated parks and wells to the community, had provided ascetics with all the requisites, and had faithfully observed all the Uposatha days.

While Mātali was explaining these eight heavenly mansions to King Nimi, Sakka was once more concerned that the charioteer was taking too long to return. He sent another messenger to speed Mātali along. On hearing this second message, Mātali revealed all the other mansions of heaven in a flash. King Nimi was overwhelmed and filled with joy to see such glory. "Good ripens and bears fruit," Mātali reminded him. "Morality, generosity, wisdom, and faith have led to these mansions. Now, Your Majesty, we must hasten to appear before Sakka."

As they sped toward Tāvatimsa, they saw the seven hills—Sudassana, Karavika, Isadhara, Yugandhāra, Nemindhara, Vinataka, and Assakanna—which surrounded Mount Sineru.

They passed the heaven of the Four Great Kings and arrived at the great Cittakuta Gate. Mātali pointed out the life-like statues of Sakka, which stood at the entrance to Tāvatimsa like guardian tigers.

As soon as they had passed through the gate, King Nimi was showered with heavenly flowers and perfume by the devas who had gathered there to greet him. They presented him with splendid gifts and accompanied the chariot to the incomparable Sudhamma Hall. King Nimi dismounted from the chariot and, stepping between the finely wrought, eight-sided columns made of rare and precious gems, entered the hall, where he was given the seat of honor beside Sakka himself.

Sakka offered Nimi various celestial pleasures, but the king declined, declaring that he would wait until he had truly gained them for himself by his own deeds, knowing that that would lead to happiness without remorse. When the devas asked King Nimi about his journey to Tāvatimsa, he praised Mātali at great length for his thorough tour of the realms of hell and heaven and his illuminating explanation of the cause for each destination. All the devas were delighted with the conversation, and they urged King Nimi to stay with them, but, after seven human days, he expressed his wish to return. Bidding farewell to Sakka, he once again mounted the heavenly chariot.

Taking no detour, Mātali drove directly eastward to Mithilā. As soon as the chariot appeared over the city, the citizens raised a great cry of joy to see their king returning. Mātali circled the city clockwise and deposited the king at the same window from which he had departed. When Mātali was sure that the king was safely back inside the palace, he bade farewell and urged the horses to take him quickly back to Tāvatimsa.

Everyone wanted to know what Tāvatimsa was like, and the king more than satisfied their curiosity with his descriptions of the various hells and heavens. He told of the splendor of the Sudhamma Hall and the extreme happiness of Sakka and the other devas. He concluded his talk by exhorting all his subjects to continue to give alms freely and to perform as many good deeds as possible, that they might be reborn into that divine sumptuousness.

Eventually, the barber found several white hairs on King Nimi's head. As soon as the king saw the hairs, he announced his intention to renounce the world. He presented a village to the barber, gave the royal umbrella to his son, and donned an ascetic's robe. The prince asked why his father had decided to renounce the world, but Nimi simply intoned, "Lo, these gray hairs." Just as all the former kings had done, he left the city to dwell in the mango grove, where he practiced meditation and developed the Four Brahma Vihāras. When he passed away, he was reborn in the Brahma heavens.

King Nimi's son, Kalara-Janaka,[15] by not renouncing the world, broke the family tradition, which had lasted eighty-four thousand generations, and brought his line to an end. Thus, King Nimi had, indeed, rounded off his family.

Having concluded his story, the Buddha identified the birth: "At that time, Anuruddha was Sakka; Ānanda was Mātali; and I was King Nimi."

---

15 In the original, King Kalāra-Janaka also renounces the world and becomes an ascetic. The ending here seems more consistent with the rest of the story and agrees with the explanation given in the Makhādeva Sutta (Majjhima Nikāya, 83).

212

The Suggestion Is Obscene
Khandahāla Jātaka

It was while staying on Gijjhakūta near Rājagaha that the Buddha told this story about Devadatta.

In Rājagaha, Devadatta had impressed Prince Ajātasattu with his supernatural powers and had ingratiated himself to become the prince's teacher. Knowing that Ajātasattu had a willful, unruly nature and that he was impatient to become king, Devadatta incited him to usurp the throne and to kill King Bimbisāra, Ajātasattu's father. Then Devadatta approached King Ajātasattu and said, "Your Majesty has realized his desire, but mine has not yet been attained."

"Teacher, what is your desire?" Ajātasattu asked.

"I wish to have Gotama killed; then I myself will become the Buddha."

"Well, what do we have to do?"

"First, we must gather some archers."

The king assembled five hundred skilled archers from which he selected thirty-one. He ordered these men to report to Devadatta and to carry out whatever he commanded.

"My friend," Devadatta said to the chief archer, "the ascetic Gotama is staying on Mount Gijjhakūta. Every day, at a certain time, he walks back

227

and forth at a place where you can easily see him. Go to the mountain and watch. When you see him, shoot him with a poisoned arrow. Return to Rājagaha by the southern road, and report to me."

He summoned two other archers and instructed them, "Go to Gijjhakūta by the southern road. You will meet an archer coming from the mountain. You must kill him and return by the northern road. When you get back to Rājagaha, report to me."

In the same way, he sent four archers to kill those two, eight to kill the four, and sixteen to kill the eight. This strategy was intended to conceal his involvement in the plot to assassinate the Buddha.

The chief archer strapped on his sword, put a quiver of poisoned arrows on his back, took up his ram's-horn bow, and went to Gijjhakūta. Seeing the Buddha, he strung his bow, fixed the arrow, and pulled back the bowstring, but he could not shoot. He stood there immobilized, frozen with fear at what he had meant to do.

The Buddha saw the archer and spoke to him in a gentle voice, "Don't be afraid. Come here."

The archer threw down his weapons, fell at the Buddha's feet, and wept. "Lord, evil overpowered me like a child or a fool," he cried. "I didn't know your virtues. I came here to assassinate you because I was ordered to do so by that wicked Devadatta. Forgive me, I beg of you."

The Buddha comforted him and asked him to sit down at one side. As the Buddha taught the Dhamma, the archer attained the first path. The Buddha advised the archer to return by a safe road while he himself remained sitting at the foot of a tree.

Soon after that, the two archers, not having met the man they were supposed to kill, arrived at Gijjhakūta. When they saw the Buddha, they went up to him, paid their respects, and sat down.

The Buddha taught them, and they, too, attained the first path. Gratified by the teaching, they returned to the city. In the same way, the other groups of archers went to Gijjhakūta, met the Buddha, and attained the first path. The Buddha advised them, in turn, to return to Rājagaha by different roads, thus thwarting Devadatta's evil plans.

The archers reported their failures to Devadatta and praised the virtue and power of the Buddha. Devadatta was furious that his plan had failed. Later, when the men met together and discussed their adventures, they realized what Devadatta had tried to do and understood that they owed their own lives to the Buddha's great compassion. All of them decided to renounce the homelife and to become bhikkhus under the Buddha. In no long time, all of them became arahats.

As this incident became well known in the Sangha, the bhikkhus discussed how Devadatta, hating one person, the Blessed One, had plotted to kill thirty-one archers, and how they were all saved by the Teacher.

When the Buddha heard them talking about this, he said, "This is not the first time! Long ago, because he hated me, he tried to kill many people." Then he told this story of the past.

Long, long ago, when Bārānasi was called Pupphavatī, Vasavatti was reigning there. The Bodhisatta was born as the crown prince and was named Canda. The king's chief advisor was a brahmin named Khandahāla. The king had such a high opinion of Khandahāla's wisdom that he appointed him chief justice. Unfortunately, Khandahāla was a greedy man. Rather than objectively listening to arguments and deciding a case fairly, he invariably ruled in favor of the man who gave him the largest bribe. He very often took property from the real owners and gave it to those who were generous toward him, even though they had no legal claim to it.

One day, as Prince Canda was passing the court, a man threw himself at the prince's feet. "My good man," said the prince, "what troubles you so? How can I help you?"

"Your Highness," the man said with a quavering voice, "I have just lost a court case most unfairly. There is no justice under Khandahāla. Even though I gave him a small gift so that he would hear my case, he ruled against me because my opponent gave him a larger bribe. I implore you! Please help me."

"Take heart, sir," said the prince. "I will see what I can do."

The prince immediately reopened the case, examined the evidence, and restored the disputed property to the rightful owner. The people in the court applauded loudly and shouted their approval.

When the king heard the uproar, he asked one of his servants what was going on and was told, "Sire, people are rejoicing because Prince Canda has just reversed judgment on a suit which had been decided most unfairly by Khandahāla. Everyone is applauding because, at least in this case, justice has prevailed."

That evening, when the prince paid his respects to his father, the king said, "My son, they say that you have judged a case today. Is it true?"

"Yes, Sire," replied the prince.

On a whim, the king appointed the prince judge and told him that, from then on, he was to decide all lawsuits.

This appointment devastated Khandahāla, who was suddenly deprived of the major portion of his income. He soon came to loathe the honest prince and constantly looked for some way to eliminate him.

The king, to put it mildly, had little religious insight. One day, at dawn, just before waking, he dreamed of Tāvatimsa with its elaborately ornamented portico, its walls made of precious gems, and its streets of gold. As he strolled through the beautiful Nandana garden, enjoying the sight of the lakes and flowers, he marveled at the glory of the devas inhabiting that splendid realm.

His captivating dream left him with an intense longing to go there, and he thought, "When Khandahāla comes, I will ask him the way to that glorious realm of the devas. Whatever he says, I swear that I will do it and that I will get to heaven by that route."

When Khandahāla greeted him and asked whether he had slept well, the king immediately described his dream. "Teacher," he concluded, "you are a seer to whom all sacred learning is known. Tell me the road by which travelers rise up to heaven."

Of course, this question should be asked only of a Buddha, of one of his enlightened disciples, or, at the very least, of a Bodhisatta. The king, however, like a man who has been lost for a week but is seeking guidance from another lost for a fortnight, posed his question to Khandahāla.

"This is the chance I've been waiting for," Khandahāla thought, inwardly rejoicing.

Solemnly addressing the king, he said: "Sire, it is by sacrificing those who do not deserve to be slain that one makes the most excellent merit and thus reaches the bliss of heaven."

"What is this sacrifice? Who are those who do not deserve to be slain? I'll sacrifice the victims you say. Just tell me who you mean."

Khandahāla explained, "Your children and your queens must be offered. Then your great merchants, your choicest bulls, and your noblest steeds—the best that is yours. These are the victims which must be sacrificed."

Of course, what Khandahāla was explaining was the road leading straight to hell! He reasoned that, if he told the king to sacrifice Prince Canda alone, everyone would see that he was speaking out of hatred for the prince. By putting the crown prince together with many others, his personal vendetta wouldn't be suspected.

Rumors quickly spread through the palace about the king's intended sacrifice. The women of the royal household were filled with alarm. The cry went up, "Heaven help us! The princes and queens are doomed!" The entire royal family was shaken, like sal trees shaken by the wind that will end the world.[16]

---

16 The world can be destroyed in three ways: by water, by fire, or by wind. In the case of fire, the destruction reaches the heavens of radiance. In the case of water, the destruction reaches the heavens of glory. In the case of wind, the destruction reaches the heavens of great reward. During the period of destruction, all beings are reborn in the higher planes.

Even Khandahāla doubted whether the king could actually offer the sacrifices he demanded, so he questioned him.

"What do you mean, Teacher?" the king replied. "Of course, I can do it. After all, if I offer this sacrifice, I will be able to go to the realm of the devas that I want so much!"

"Sire, those who are timid and weak cannot do what is necessary. Only the strong and steadfast can do it," the brahmin said sternly. "You gather them all here in the palace, and I will make the offering for you in the sacrificial pit."

The brahmin took a group of workers to a site just outside the eastern gate of the city. He instructed them to dig a huge pit. They were to level the ground at the bottom of the pit and to erect a sacrificial post in the center. The pit was to be surrounded by a fence. In times past, brahmins had realized that such a fence was required to keep out any righteous ascetics who might try to stop the ceremony.

The king commanded that a proclamation be made throughout the city, "By sacrificing my children and my wives, I will go to the realm of the devas." Then he ordered courtiers to announce this to his family and to bring them to him. "Tell Prince Canda first, then the other princes, Bhaddasena, Sūra, and Suriya. Inform them of my command. They must all die. My mind is made up!"

The courtiers went to Prince Canda's apartment, paid their respects to the prince, and announced, "Prince, your father desires to sacrifice you in order to go to heaven. He has ordered us to seize you."

"Whose instructions is my father following in ordering me seized?"

"Khandahāla's."

"Does he want me alone or are others to be seized with me?"

"Others also. Your father wants to offer a sacrifice of the four kinds of victims."

Prince Canda thought, "Khandahāla has no quarrel with the others, but he needs to sacrifice them to kill me. He bears me a grudge because I have stopped him from cheating the people. It's my duty to talk with my father and to get the others released."

"Obey my father's command," he said calmly.

One of the courtiers escorted Prince Canda to the courtyard, and the others went to seize the other princes.

Next, the king ordered his courtiers to bring his daughters, Upasenī, Kokilā, Muditā, and Nandā.

As soon as the weeping princesses had been brought to the courtyard and confined with their brothers, the king turned again to his courtiers and com-

(See The Thirty-one Planes of Existence in the Appendix.)

manded, "Now, bring my queens, Vijayā, Sunandā, and Kesinī. Despite their beauty and charm, I will give them up. They all must die. I will not yield!"

The women wailed loudly as they were brought in and placed near the princes.

Next, the king ordered the arrest of the four great merchants, Punna-mukha, Bhaddiya, Singāla, and Vaddha. "They too must die. I am king, and it is my will."

The king's officers brought them to the palace. When the king's sons and wives were taken, the people were silent. The great merchants, however, had many relatives, so the whole city was upset when they were arrested. Their families protested loudly. The merchants, surrounded by their relatives, begged the king to spare their lives. "Make us your slaves if you wish, but do not kill us!" they cried, but there was no mercy in the foolish tyrant. The king ordered soldiers to force the people out of the courtyard and to drag the merchants to stand near the princes.

Turning to the next order of sacrifice, the king said, "Bring my mighty elephants, then my best stallions. They must all be sacrificed. My bulls will make a noble offering. Of course, the officiating priests will all be rewarded appropriately. The sacrifice will take place with proper ceremony at dawn. Everything must be made ready. That is my command. Let the princes feast and enjoy the last night of their lives."

When the king's elderly parents heard about this sacrifice, they hurried to the courtyard to confront the king. "My son," the queen mother cried, "is what I hear true? Do you really plan to make such a monstrous sacrifice? Surely, you cannot mean to execute your four handsome sons in this cruel way?"

"Mother, when I lose Canda, I lose everything, but I am resolved to give him up and all the rest, besides. By this difficult sacrifice, a heavenly dwelling will be mine."

"My son, sacrificing your own sons can never carry you to heaven's bliss! Don't listen to such lies. That road leads straight to perdition! You were taught to give alms and harm no living being. That is the true path to heaven."

The king would not be swayed. "I must obey my teacher's words. My sons, alas, must all be sacrificed. Of course, it is hard to part with them, but heaven's the prize and my reward."

Unable to dissuade her hardheaded son, the queen mother went away, weeping. Then the king's father came to remonstrate with him. "Unbeliev-able stories have reached me that your four sons will be put to death in some heinous ritual. Please reassure me that it isn't true."

The despot repeated his answer, and his father, unable to turn his son from his evil course, went away shaking his head. "Give generous alms and never harm a living thing, then, with your sons around you, protect our land from every danger! That is the path to heaven."

Hearing this, Prince Canda felt it was time to speak. "Father!" he cried. "We love you as much as you proclaim that you love us. If your intent is to make a sacrifice by depriving yourself of our love, send us into exile, banish us to foreign lands, or make us slaves to Khandahāla. We will gladly serve him, doing whatever he tells us. We will care for his horses and elephants. We will sweep his stables and work in chains. We will do anything he wants. Please spare our lives. Do not kill us. We love you as our father and respect you as our king. Please be merciful."

At last, the king was moved. "No one will kill my sons. I have no need of the realm of the devas. These pleas for mercy break my heart. Set them free! Release the princes. No more sacrifice for me."

The king's men immediately began releasing the whole multitude, beginning with the princes and ending with the tethered animals and caged birds.

A servant ran quickly to the eastern gate, found Khandahāla, and shouted, "You villain, Khandahāla! Why don't you go and kill your own sons and offer a sacrifice with the blood from their throats? The king has released all the victims and has cancelled the sacrifice!"

"What?" cried the brahmin in disbelief as he began running toward the palace.

"Sire!" Khandahāla shouted as soon as he reached the courtyard. "I warned you that this sacrifice would be grueling! How can you stop a rite that is so well begun? You swore that you were strong and steadfast! Have you suddenly become weak? Only those who can be strong in their resolve to fulfill this supreme sacrifice can be sure to reach the highest heaven."

The wishy-washy king changed his mind again. "My dear teacher! You are right! I must be strong. Continue with the preparations."

"Guards!" he shouted. "Bring back the captives!"

Once more a prisoner in the courtyard, Prince Canda reasoned gently with the king. "Father," he said, "if our fate was to be your innocent victims, why did brahmins bless us at birth? Why did you spare us as babies? It would have been better to have died without knowing what was happening. Now that we know the joys of youth, however, how can you say that we must die tomorrow? Dying in battle for our country would be noble, but to be butchered in a fruitless sacrifice is utterly vulgar. Father, since it is our greatest desire to serve you with our lives, how can you slay us like this at the whim of a foolish brahmin? Even wild birds love their young and tend them with loving care, yet you deign to slay your offspring. Do not imagine that your treacherous brahmin friend will spare your life when I am gone, dear Father. Your turn will soon come. Kings give these villainous brahmins whole villages, but they are parasites, preying on every family. Sire, brahmins are a faithless lot! They make a rich living but betray their own benefactors. If you were to examine this carefully, Sire, you would see that that is what is happening here."

Hearing Prince Canda's words, the king weakened. "My son is right! Release the princes and the rest. No more sacrifice for me. I'll do without a heavenly reward."

Khandahāla rushed up as before, renewed his expostulations, and once more swayed the king.

Prince Canda again spoke up. "Father," he said calmly, "if one who sacrifices his sons and loved ones is glorified when he dies, let this brahmin offer his own family. You could then trust him to be a capable guide. Why does he point the way to heaven but not follow it himself? It's clear to all and always has been common knowledge that those who slay such victims will go straight to hell."

The prince could see that his father was not paying attention to his words, so he turned to the multitude surrounding the king and addressed them, "My friends, you are yourselves fathers and mothers. You, too, have children whom you love dearly and who love you. How can you stand silently by and allow the king to carry out this heinous deed? I love the king, and I love our country. Is there none among you who will raise the protesting voice of reason and compassion?"

No one dared speak for fear of the tyrant.

Beginning to feel his helplessness, the prince lamented, "If I had had a common birth, if I had been born to a cobbler, a sweeper, or an outcaste, I could have lived my whole life in peace. I would not be dying now, the victim of a king's impulsive wish!" He turned to his wife and his sisters-in-law and pleaded, "Noble ladies, make your prayers, implore the king to spare his innocent sons, his beloved daughters, and his faithful wives. Fall at Khandahāla's feet and beg him for mercy. Tell him that you have never wronged him and that you are guiltless."

Selā, one of the king's younger daughters, not included in the sacrifice, fell at the king's feet and cried, "Father, please spare my brothers! How can you believe that such a cruel sacrifice will reward you with the prize of heaven you so dearly long for?"

The king ignored her pleas.

At this point, Prince Canda's little son, Vāsula, realizing that his father was in danger, toddled toward the king and sank at his feet, "Grandfather!"

he lisped in his childish voice. "Spare my father! He loves you as I love you. Do not take him from us!"

The king bent down and picked up his favorite grandchild. With tears in his eyes, he hugged the boy and stroked his head. "Dear heart," he wept, "be comforted. I will give your father back to you. Dear Vāsula, my darling boy, your words pierce my heart. Your father is free." To his soldiers he said, "Release the princes! No more sacrifice for me."

Again Khandhāla rushed up with his old remonstrances, and, once more, the king blindly yielded to his words and ordered that all the victims be recaptured.

Khandahāla thought, "This wishy-washy and tender-hearted king first arrests his sons, then frees them. I had best get him to the sacrificial pit."

"Sire," he said, "the sacrifice has been prepared. Let us go. Offer the sacrifice and claim your reward, the supreme joys of heaven."

The king gestured his approval, and the guards seized Prince Canda to lead him away. Again, a cry went up from all the ladies of the court. They tore their hair and wept until their eyes were red. "Prince Canda! Prince Suriya!" they cried, "Innocent victims in a senseless sacrifice! Breaking their mother's heart! Breaking all our hearts! Once these handsome young men rode gallantly on elephants; now they plod mournfully on foot to die. For what? For a mad king's mad dream!"

The guards escorted the victims toward the eastern gate, and the entire court followed. Then came the agitated populace. The gate was too narrow for the crowd to pass through quickly, so the brahmin, apprehensive of an uprising, ordered that it be closed, trapping the people inside.

Blocked from reaching the sacrificial pit, people gathered in a garden near the gate, and bewailed the fate of the victims. Looking up, they saw vultures circling overhead. "Birds of carrion!" they cried. "If it is flesh you want, you are in luck! Just outside Pupphavatī's eastern gate, our unhinged monarch is sacrificing his four brave sons. There you can feast on what was once our treasure!"

The crowd went in a solemn procession to circumambulate Prince Canda's palace. Their lamentations echoed throughout the city: "If this evil deed is done and our prince's blood is shed for no good reason, our country will be ruined, and our great city will become a jungle."

Outside the gate, the guards had arrived at the sacrificial pit and were leading Prince Canda down to the post. The chief queen, Gotamā, prostrated herself at the king's feet and begged for mercy. "Spare my sons' lives, My Lord. I will go mad from grief if you kill them!"

Unable to dissuade the king, she turned to Khandahāla. "Evil brahmin," she cursed, "may your mother one day suffer the agony which tears my heart. May your wife feel the bitter pain my daughters-in-law feel today. You destroy me when you slay my sons. May your mother and your wife see sons and husband slain, you savage priest. Today, you slay the glory of the world, these lion-hearted men of mine!"

From the sacrificial pit, Prince Canda appealed once more. "Sire, some women long for sons and offer prayers to heaven. We were born in answer to our mother's prayers. Do not sacrifice us in spite of all our mother's care. Do not murder us recklessly!"

Hearing no response from his father, Prince Canda bowed at his mother's feet. "Tenderly you nursed your son. Today you face the unbearable. Let me kiss your feet once more. All blessings to my father. Mother, I grieve to bring such bitter sorrow to your dear heart."

Prince Canda's wife, Candādevī, cried out, "How is it, Your Majesty, that you have no affection for your sons?"

"My sons are dear, myself is dear, and you are dear, as well," the king replied. "I sacrifice my sons because I wish to go to heaven."

"Sire!" she cried, "have mercy, and slay me first. I cannot bear to see my husband murdered. Kill us together. Let me go where Canda goes. Let all merit be yours, just let me die first!"

"Do not wish for death before its time." the king replied, throwing out a platitude; "there will be others to console you for the dear prince you lose now."

She beat her breast and threatened poison. Turning to the crowd, she screamed, "Does this king have no friends or counselors to keep him from doing this heinous thing!"

"Cut me in pieces, offer me in sacrifice, but spare my brave and lion-hearted husband, revered by the world!" she begged, to no avail.

"Dear wife," Prince Canda called from the pit, "grieve not. In the years we have spent together, I have given you many pearls and gems to show my devotion. Now from my body, take this last ornament," he said, removing the gold chain and royal pendant from around his neck and extending it toward the weeping princess.

Candādevī wept even more loudly as she took the gold chain from her husband's hands. "Oh, woe!" she cried. "Inexpressible woe! Soon the sword will sweep down upon that guiltless royal neck! Dear Canda goes to the sacrificial post."

Even as she spoke, guards led Prince Canda to the center of the pit, where he knelt beside the post with his neck bent forward. Khandahāla picked up the golden bowl and held it at the prince's throat to catch the blood. The brahmin raised his sword and announced, "In performing the sacrifice for our king, I will now sever his neck."

The princess pressed her palms together and raised them aloft, making a solemn asseveration. "I have no other refuge." she proclaimed. "I will bless my husband with all my power of truth. Just as truly as this brahmin, by a wicked and vicious plot, prepares to murder not only the prince but also many others while I, the daughter of the Pañcāla king, watch helplessly, so may I have my dearly loved lord restored to me by right. May all devas hear my truthful word. All devas who fill this place, I worship at your feet. Protect me in my helplessness, and, with mercy, protect my lord!"

Sakka heard this asseveration of truth and immediately realized that a terrible wrong was about to be committed. In an instant, appearing overhead, he held a blazing mass of iron in his right hand and whirled it around, terrifying the king. "Know me, tyrant! Know that I am Sakka! Mark well the weapon that I wield! Do not harm your innocent eldest son, that lion-hearted hero. Where has the earth seen a crime like this? How dare you dream of slaughtering all these innocent folk, your own sons, your noblest citizens! That killing these would make you worthy of entering my highest heaven—the suggestion is obscene!"

Khandahāla dropped his sword and fell on his knees before the king of the devas. While the guards quickly released all the innocent victims of the intended sacrifice, the frenzied crowd rushed to the center of the pit and attacked the brahmin with clubs, stones, and their bare hands. As soon as Khandahāla was dead, they started toward the king. They would have killed him, as well, but Sakka protected him and held back the mob.

"All right," the people relented, "we will spare his life, but we will no longer accept him as our king. He must leave the city and get by as best he can."

After Sakka had returned to his heaven, the people stripped the king of his royal garments and dressed him in a yellow robe, with a yellow cloth on his head. "Go!" they commanded him. "You are a pariah! Do not dare to enter our city ever again!"

As one, the multitude turned to Prince Canda and called upon him to be their king. All the captives returned safely to their homes, and the city began to make preparations for a magnificent coronation ceremony for King Canda. The reign of King Canda was a time of peace and prosperity for the kingdom of Pupphavatī.

King Canda made sure that all his father's wants were attended to, but the deposed king was never allowed to reenter the city. When his allowance was exhausted, he sometimes approached his son in public places. At those times, he never paid respect to his son, for he said to himself, "I am the true king." Instead, he said only "Live long, Master." King Canda, nevertheless, invariably gave him whatever he asked for.

Having concluded his story, the Buddha added, "Bhikkhus, this is not the first time that Devadatta has planned to kill many people in order to kill me. As you can see, he did the same before." Then he identified the birth: "At that time, Devadatta was Khandahāla, Queen Mahā-Māyā was Queen Gotamā, Rāhula's mother was Candādevī, Rāhula was Vāsula, Uppalavannā was Princess Selā, Mahā-Kassapa was Prince Sūra, Moggallāna was Prince Bhaddasena, Sāriputta was Prince Suriya, and I was King Canda."

213
Bhūridatta, the Nāga Prince
Bhūridatta Jātaka

It was while staying at Jetavana that the Buddha told this story about observing Uposatha.

On a full-moon day, some lay followers awoke early in the morning, took the eight precepts, offered alms to the bhikkhus on their rounds, and, after their own meal, took incense and flowers to Jetavana. When it was time to hear the Buddha teach the Dhamma, they sat respectfully at one side.

When the Buddha entered the hall, he considered the assembly and realized that a talk about former teachers would suit them, so he asked, "Lay-followers, are you observing Uposatha?"

When they answered in the affirmative, he said, "That is well done, but it is hardly surprising that you, with a teacher like me, are observing the Uposatha day. Consider how remarkable that the wise, long ago, without any teacher whatsoever, gave up wealth and glory and steadfastly observed the Uposatha days!"

The people were interested to learn more, and, at their request, the Buddha told this story of the past.

Long, long ago, when Brahmadatta was reigning in Bārānasi, he designated his son, of the same name, as the crown prince. Shortly thereafter, however, he noticed the prince's abilities and promise and began to worry that his handsome son might try to seize the throne. He summoned him and ordered him to leave the kingdom, going wherever he wanted, but not to return until after he, the king, had died, at which time he should take the throne as his birthright. Obedient to his father's wishes, the prince saluted him and departed. He walked to the Yamunā River and built a hut of leaves on a suitable spot between the river and the sea. He decided to live there, eating only roots and fruit which he collected from the forest.

One day, a young nāga widow, who was not happy in the nāga realm beneath the ocean, was wandering aimlessly along the seashore. She noticed the prince's footprints and followed them to his hut of leaves, but he was not there.

Entering the hut, she observed the simple furniture and thought to herself, "This is an ascetic's hut. I wonder whether or not this man is an ascetic from faith. If he is serious about his asceticism, he will reject my adorned bed; but, if he still loves pleasure, he will lie down on it. If his faith is weak, I will become his wife and stay here."

She hurried to the nāga realm and quickly returned with perfume and many beautiful flowers. After decorating the bed and scattering scented powder all around the hut, she went back to her home in the nāga realm.

When the prince returned, he was surprised to find his hut so beautiful. As he ate his fruit, he savored the pleasant aromas. In the evening, he lay down among the fragrant flowers and fell fast asleep. The luxury reminded him of the life he had enjoyed in his youth in the palace. Since he had not chosen to become an ascetic, he was still attracted to such pleasures.

The next day, the prince awoke at sunrise. Still wondering who had visited the day before, he went off to gather fruit without sweeping out his hut.

As soon as he left, the nāga widow returned. When she saw the crushed, withered flowers, she thought triumphantly, "This man is not a real ascetic. He is addicted to pleasure, so I will be able to captivate him." She completely cleaned everything, beautifying the bed and the hut with flowers even more lavishly than before. She even scattered blossoms along the covered walk as she left.

The prince was delighted to find his hut again so attractively decorated. He slept very soundly, enjoying the luxury of the flowers and the perfume. The next morning, he was determined to find out who was bringing the flowers, so, instead of going in search of fruit, he hid nearby and waited.

Soon, he saw the nāga carrying fresh blossoms and scattering scent along the path to the hut.

She was so lovely that the prince immediately fell in love with her. While she was again decorating the hut, he quietly entered and asked who she was.

"My Lord, I am a nāga," she replied.

"Are you married?"

"I am a widow. Who are you?"

"Prince Brahmadatta. I am the eldest son of the king of Kāsi. Why are you wandering in this forest, far from the nāga realm?"

"My Lord, I was not happy in the nāga realm. I have come this way looking for a husband."

"I see. Well, I may be living like an ascetic, but I am not an ascetic. My father drove me into exile. I will marry you, and we can stay here together."

The nāga woman was overjoyed, and they began living together very happily.

Using her magic power, she created a lovely house and filled it with fine furniture. The prince no longer had to eat roots and raw fruit but feasted on the delicious meals she prepared for him every day. After some time, a son was born, and they named him Sāgara Brahmadatta. He was followed by a daughter whom they called Samuddajā.

One day, a forester from Bārānasi happened to pass by, exchanged cordial greetings, and recognized the prince. As he was leaving, the forester promised to tell the king that he had met his son.

Before the forester reached the capital, however, the old king died. After the funeral, the royal advisors were lamenting, "A kingdom must have a king. Unfortunately, we have no idea where the crown prince is or even if he is still alive." When the forester heard this, he immediately informed the ministers about the prince. They followed him to the prince's hut, told him that his father was dead, and invited him to assume the throne.

Before the prince accepted their offer, he discussed it with his wife. "My dear," he said, "my father is dead. His ministers want me to take the throne. Let us go to Bārānasi, where you will be chief queen!"

"My dear husband, I cannot possibly go with you."

"Why not?"

"Like all nāgas, I possess a very strong venom. We are easily angered, even by trifles. If something were to irritate me, I might give an angry glance in someone's direction, which could be deadly. It is much too dangerous for me to go with you."

The prince repeated his offer again the next day, but his wife replied, "My dear, I love you, but under no circumstances will I go with you. Our children, however, are not nāgas. Because they are your children, they are human. If you love me, take them with you and look after them."

The prince agreed, and she continued, "Since the children have inherited something of a delicate and watery nature from me, they cannot endure travel by road, exposed to the wind and the sun. You must prepare a pool, fill it with water, and let them play in it as you go. In Bārānasi also, they will need to have a lake near the palace. With water near at hand, they will thrive."

She showed her esteem for the prince by walking around him respectfully with her palms pressed together. Then she embraced her children, kissed their heads, and entrusted them to him. With many tears, she vanished and reappeared in the nāga realm.

The eyes of the crown prince were also filled with tears. Overcoming his sorrow, he went to the waiting ministers and accepted their offer. They immediately anointed him king, and said, "Sire, let us return to the capital."

Before setting out, the king ordered that a pool, filled with water, be placed in the cart. "My little ones have a watery nature," he told the ministers. "Scatter flowers on the water so that they can play happily as we travel along."

When they arrived in Bārānasi, they found the capital lavishly decorated. The coronation celebration, with music and feasting, continued for seven days.

Again following his wife's suggestion, the king ordered his men to build a lake near the palace, where his children sported continually.

Some time later, a large sea turtle entered the lake. Unable to find his way out, he floated near the surface and poked his head above the water. When the children saw the great turtle's head, they were frightened and ran to their father. "Help!" they cried. "There's a terrible monster in the lake!"

The king ordered his men to seize the creature that had so frightened his children. They threw a net into the water and caught the unsuspecting turtle. As soon as the children saw it, they cried, "Look, Father! That is the monster!"

The king ordered that the animal be punished. One attendant recommended that the creature be beaten to death with a pestle. Another wanted to cook the turtle and eat it. One of the king's ministers, however, was himself terrified of water, and he suggested, "The worst possible punishment is to throw the beast directly into the whirlpool in the middle of the Yamunā. There it will be utterly destroyed!"

When the turtle heard this, he thrust his head out of his massive shell and cried out, "What wrong did I ever do to you that you suggest such a cruel punishment for me? I could endure any other fate, but yours is so excessively harsh that I can't bear to think of it!"

The king declared that throwing the turtle into the whirlpool was precisely the right penalty for the beast.

As the men carried the turtle toward the Yamunā River, he loudly lamented his miserable fate. At last, they threw him into the whirlpool. As soon as the turtle was safely in the water, he found a current which carried him toward the nāga realm.

Some impetuous young nāga princes, who were playing in that same current, saw the turtle and ordered their servants to seize him.

"Woe is me," thought the turtle. "I have just escaped from the king of Kāsi, and now I fall into the hands of these fierce nāgas! How can I get out of this predicament in one piece?" No sooner had he thought this, than he came up with a plan. "Why do you speak impolitely to a messenger?" he asked the princes. "My name is Cittacūla, and I bear a message to King Dhatarattha from the king of Kāsi. The king has sent me to offer his daughter to King Dhatarattha. Take me to your king!"

The nāga king agreed to see the turtle but complained that royal messengers should not be so ugly. The turtle defended himself, saying, "Sire, the important thing is the ability to carry out royal errands. The king of Kāsi has many messengers: men do his business on dry land, birds in the air, and I in the water. I am a favorite of the king. My name is Cittacūla, and I have my post, so do not scoff at me."

"What message does Brahmadatta have for me?" asked King Dhatarattha.

"The king said that, having gained the friendship of all the kings of Jambudīpa, he now wishes to gain the friendship of the nāga king Dhatarattha by giving his daughter Samuddajā in marriage. He has entrusted me with that message. Don't delay, Sire! Send a company back with me, name the day, and receive the maiden."

Highly flattered, the nāga king honored the turtle and chose four nāga youths to accompany him to Bārānasi. He ordered them to arrange a suitable day for the wedding and to return as soon as possible.

When they got near Bārānasi, the turtle spotted a lotus pond, which gave him his chance to escape. "My friends," he said to the nāga emissaries, "the king and queen asked me to bring them some lotuses and lotus roots. Let me gather some for them here. Please go on ahead. I will catch up with you shortly. If you reach the palace before me, just introduce yourselves to the king. I will see you there."

The nāgas believed his story and continued toward the city, and the turtle escaped. Before arriving at the palace, the nāgas transformed themselves into young men. The king received them with honor and asked who sent them.

"King Dhatarattha of the nāga realm, Your Majesty."

"What is your business?"

"Sire, we are messengers for King Dhatarattha, who asks after your health. He wants to give you whatever you desire—any jewel, any treasure he possesses—and, in return, he asks you to send your daughter Samuddajā to be his queen."

"That's outrageous!" cried the king. "No human has ever married his daughter to a nāga king. It's unheard of!"

"If an alliance with King Dhatarattha seems so unthinkable," the youths retorted, "why did you send your messenger, the turtle Cittacūla, to our king, offering your daughter Samuddajā in marriage? You sent that message, but you now scorn our king! We nāgas know how to respond to such an insult from a puny mortal!"

The king hastily tried to clarify his statement, saying, "Don't misunderstand me! It is not that I scorn your king, the renowned Dhatarattha. He is the rightful monarch of many nāgas. Still, as noble as he is, my daughter comes from a proud line of warriors. Her blood is much purer than his. She cannot marry him."

The nāga youths were infuriated and wanted to slay him with a blast of their venomous breath, but, since their orders had been to set the wedding day, they didn't dare kill him without a specific command. They simply replied, "We will depart and report this to our king," and vanished.

When King Dhatarattha asked the delegation whether they had brought the princess, they indignantly replied, "Your Majesty, you sent us there for no reason! That monarch insulted you and proudly extolled his daughter." Not worrying about the accuracy of the details, the youths described their meeting with King Brahmadatta in such a way as to arouse King Dhatarattha's fury.

The king responded to their report by shouting, "Summon all nāgas! Assemble an army! We march on Bārānasi." Then he added, "Once there, however, you are not to harm anyone."

Puzzled, the nāga commanders asked, "If we cannot harm anyone, what are we supposed to do there?"

"I want you to terrorize the populace. Infest the ponds, and hang from the trees. Drape yourselves over gates, and enter the palace. Show yourselves everywhere; spread your broad hoods. We will besiege the city by terrifying the citizens."

Following the king's orders, the nāgas appeared everywhere in Bārānasi and frightened the residents out of their wits. Whenever they spread their hoods, people shrieked in fear and ran frantically to get away, but they could not escape. Wherever they turned, they found more nāgas. The city of Bārānasi was immobilized.

The king had been asleep, but the uproar awakened him. The citizens begged him to protect them. "Save us from these fierce serpents!" they cried. "Give your daughter to the nāga king as he demands!" Realizing that he was helpless against the power of the nāgas, he relented and agreed to give Samuddajā to King Dhatarattha. As soon as the nāgas heard this, they withdrew from the city, set up a camp outside the walls, and dispatched an emissary with presents to King Brahmadatta.

The king accepted their gifts and promised to send his daughter to the nāga king as soon as possible.

He summoned his daughter, took her onto the balcony, opened a window, and said to her, "Daughter, behold our beautiful city. Soon, my dear, you will be the chief queen of a great king whose city is equal to this. It is not far away, my child, and, whenever you feel homesick, you may return for a visit, but this will no longer be your home. You must now go to stay in your husband's capital city."

As soon as Samuddajā was suitably dressed and adorned, she was taken in a covered carriage to the nāga realm. King Dhatarattha greeted her, paid her great honor, and sent her escorts back to their king with many lavish presents. The princess was taken into the palace and lodged in a splendid room with an elegant bed. She was waited on by young nāga women in the guise of human servants. The next morning, when she awoke, she asked her maids about the magnificent palace, which seemed so different from her own.

"My Lady," they replied, "this kingdom belongs to your lord. You must have great merit to have won such glory as this!"

King Dhatarattha ordered that no nāga was ever to show the slightest sign of a serpent-nature to Samuddajā, and, accordingly, none ever dared appear in snake form in front of her.

Samuddajā was very happy and comfortable in her new home. She loved her husband, and, never suspecting that he was a nāga, she believed that she was still in the realm of men. In time, she had a son, whom they named Sudassana. A second son, who was the Bodhisatta, was named Datta. Samuddajā had two more sons, who were named Subhaga and Arittha. Even after all these years, she did not know that she was living in the nāga realm.

One day, some young playmates told Arittha that his mother was a woman and not a nāga. Arittha decided to test her. While he was nursing at his mother's breast, he assumed his nāga form and struck her with his tail. When she saw his serpent-body, she screamed in terror and threw him down, accidentally striking his eye with her fingernail, causing him to bleed profusely.

Hearing his wife's screams, the king rushed in to find out what was the matter. When he learned what his son had done, he was furious and ordered servants to seize Arittha and to execute him.

Samuddajā tried to calm her husband's anger and pleaded for her son to be spared, "My Lord, I injured my son's eye! Please forgive him."

Helpless against his wife's maternal love, the king excused the lad.

Thus it was that Samuddajā learned for the first time that she was living in the nāga realm. Also, from that time on, Arittha was known as Kānārittha, "One-eyed Arittha."

The four princes grew up to be strong and handsome. When they came of age, their father gave each son his own kingdom. Possessing great glory and power, they were attended by retinues of nāga youths and maidens. Three of the sons visited their parents once a month, but Datta returned twice a month. During his visits, he regularly raised issues which had come up in the nāga realm and went with his father to discuss these matters with the supreme nāga ruler, Virūpakkha.

One day, Datta accompanied King Virūpakkha and other nāga leaders on a visit to the realm of the devas. As they were sitting in attendance at Sakka's court, a question arose among the devas, but none of the elders could answer it. To the admiration of all, Datta answered it clearly and comprehensively. Sakka himself honored him with celestial flowers and fruit, proclaiming, "Datta, you are endowed with deep wisdom. From now on, you will be called Bhūridatta."

After that, Bhūridatta went regularly to pay homage to Sakka in his heaven. So impressed was he with the splendor of the celestial realm that he yearned to reside there. "What is this frog-eating snake-nature to me?" he asked himself. "On my return to the nāga realm, I will observe the precepts and behave righteously," he vowed, "so that I may be reborn among the devas!"

When he informed his parents of his intention, they agreed, but, fearing for his safety outside the nāga domain, they begged him not to leave the kingdom.

Honoring their request, he began observing Uposatha in the parks and gardens of a deserted palace. He was hampered, however, by nāga maidens who kept trying to wait on him and to entertain him. "If I stay on here," he lamented, "my observance of Uposatha will never amount to anything. To accomplish my goal, I must go to the realm of men and practice there alone."

Anticipating objections from his parents, he informed only his wife. "On the bank of the Yamunā River," he told her, "stands a great banyan tree. Near it, there is an anthill. I will coil myself on the top of that anthill, and there I will observe the Uposatha day and keep the precepts. At dawn, the next morning, send ten of your servants with musical instruments to bring me back to our home."

Then Bhūridatta left the nāga realm and arrived at the place he had chosen in the human realm. Before coiling his body on the anthill, he announced loudly, "Let anyone who wishes, take my skin, my muscles, my bones, or my blood. Here I will keep the precepts."

The next morning at daybreak, lovely attendants came and conducted him back to the nāga realm, all the while playing beautiful music. In this way, Bhūridatta continued to observe Uposatha.

In those days, near Bārāṇasi, there was a destitute brahmin who had taken up hunting and made his living by selling the flesh of wild animals. Every day, this outcaste brahmin and his son, Somadatta, went to the forest to set traps and to hunt with bow and arrow.

One day, after they had failed to snare even a tiny lizard, the brahmin said to his son, "If we go home empty-handed, your mother will be furious. We must catch something!" Just then he noticed the hoof prints of deer going down to the Yamunā.

"My boy," he whispered, "there are deer about! Wait over there while I try to shoot a deer going to the river to drink." Stepping quietly to the foot of a tree, he held his bow ready to shoot and waited for a deer to appear.

At sunset, a deer warily approached the river. The brahmin shot and hit the deer, but the animal fled, blood flowing from the wound. Father and son chased the animal until it finally fell. They quickly skinned it, hoisted the carcass on their pole, and headed for home. They reached the great banyan tree just as night was falling.

"Son," the brahmin said, halting his steps, "this is a dangerous time to be out. We'd better not try to go further in the dark. Let us stay right here for the night." They safely stowed away their load of venison, climbed the tree, and settled down among the branches.

The brahmin woke at dawn and was listening for the sound of deer, when the nāga maidens appeared. He looked on as they prepared a beautiful couch of flowers for Bhūridatta, who changed his serpentine body into a splendid divine form, dressed in radiant and magnificent garments. The maidens honored him with garlands of flowers and heavenly music.

Having watched in fascination, the brahmin wondered who this remarkable creature could be. He tried to wake his son, but the boy was sound asleep, so he decided to climb down by himself. As soon as the nāga maidens saw him, they sank into the earth with their instruments and fled to their underwater abode. Bhūridatta was left alone.

Overcome with curiosity, the brahmin approached and asked him, "Creature, adorned with gold and jewels and waited on by ten lovely maidens, are you a deva, a nāga, or a yakkha?"

Bhūridatta understood that, because this man was a brahmin, he would easily believe that he was a deva, but, to keep the precepts pure, he must speak only the truth. "I am a mighty nāga," he declared. "My venomous breath and angry bite can destroy anyone I wish to kill. My mother's name is Samuddajā, King Dhatarattha is my father, and Bhūridatta is my name."

Bhūridatta instinctively realized that the brahmin was a cruel man, who might easily betray him to a snake-charmer, which would interfere with his observance of Uposatha. "Brahmin," he continued, without giving the man a chance to speak. "I would like to show you our nāga hospitality. Come to the pleasant land of the nāgas. Let us go at once."

"Sir," the brahmin answered, "my son Somadatta is here with me. If he agrees to go, so will I."

Bhūridatta urged him to fetch his son that they might leave as soon as possible.

The brahmin scurried up the tree and quickly returned with his son.

Standing on the bank of the Yamunā River, Bhūridatta told them not to be afraid, "The peacocks and herons call us to plunge beneath the dark blue waves of the beautiful water. Follow my directions, and you will safely reach my home, where you will be honored with the most cordial reception I can arrange." With his magic power, he conveyed father and son to his nāga palace. He showered them with precious gifts and provided each of them with four hundred lovely nāga maidens instructed to supply them with everything they could wish for.

In this way, Bhūridatta was able to continue observing Uposatha without interference. He still went every fortnight to pay his respects to his parents and to discuss the law. At that time, he also visited the brahmin and his son and inquired about their health. He encouraged them to enjoy themselves and told them to let him know immediately if anything was lacking.

After spending one year in the nāga realm, the brahmin, who had gained no merit in his previous lives, began yearning to return to the realm of men. In spite of all the opulence, he felt that he was in hell: the palace seemed like a prison, and the graceful nāga maidens like yakkhas.

When he told Somadatta how he felt, however, the boy answered, "Why are you so unhappy? We have everything we desire."

"I miss your mother and your brothers and sisters." he replied. "Come. Let's go home!"

Somadatta did not want to leave, but, because his father repeatedly nagged him, he finally gave in and agreed to go.

The brahmin knew, however, that, if he told Bhūridatta that he was dissatisfied, the nāga would grant him more privileges and honors, which would make it impossible to escape. He tried to devise a plan to trick his host into allowing him to leave.

The next time Bhūridatta came to ask how they were doing and whether everything was all right, the brahmin assured him that nothing was wanting. He praised Bhūridatta's prosperity, his palace with its magnificent furnishings, his jewels, the servants, and the serving maidens and observed that his every desire was satisfied. "In fact," he continued, "your glory surpasses even that of Sakka!"

"Brahmin, don't say that," Bhūridatta objected. "Comparing our glory to Sakka's is like comparing a mustard seed to Mount Sineru! You must understand that the reason I observe Uposatha on that anthill is that I aim to obtain heaven."

"Oh, Bhūridatta," the brahmin said, feigning remorse, "I have spent my life as a rough and wicked hunter, killing many living creatures. In fact, my son and I were hunting for deer when we strayed into that forest spot where we met you. Now our relatives and friends do not know whether we are alive or dead. Please let us go and see our families again."

Bhūridatta answered, "I would prefer you to stay with me and be happy here. Where in the realm of men can you find such comfort as you have here? Still, if you insist on leaving, go, see your family and friends, and be as happy as you can." Hoping that he could give the hunter enough wealth to prevent him from telling anyone about the nāga realm, he offered the man his precious wish-fulfilling gem and continued, "Please take this precious stone. The person who possesses this heavenly gem can see his children and his home. As long as you have this treasure, you will want for nothing, and you will never come to harm!"

The brahmin answered, "I understand your words full well, but I have grown old and will take up the ascetic's life on my return. Worldly pleasures are nothing to me now. I have no need of your precious gem."

"Very well," Bhūridatta said, "but, if you find that you cannot adapt to the ascetic life, come back to me, and I will give you everything your heart desires."

The brahmin thanked Bhūridatta for his kind offer and promised that, should the occasion ever arise, he would return to claim his assistance.

Seeing the brahmin's determination to leave, Bhūridatta ordered some young nāgas to accompany him to the realm of men.

Back in the forest, the brahmin excitedly pointed out places to his son, saying, "Somadatta, remember how we wounded that deer here? Over there we shot that big boar! Do you remember the size of it?" Then, spotting a lake, he suggested they bathe. They took off their fine garments and jewelry, laid them carefully in a bundle on the bank, and stepped into the water. At that moment, all their finery vanished and returned to the nāga realm. In place of their handsome things, their old tattered clothes appeared along with their bows, arrows, and spears. They were back exactly as they had been before.

"We are ruined, Father," wailed Somadatta.

"Don't worry, Son," his father comforted him, "As long as there are deer in the forest, we will manage to make a living somehow."

Somadatta's mother heard them coming and went to meet them. Without comment, she gave them something to eat and drink. As soon as the hunter had fallen asleep, she asked her son, "Where have you two been all this time?"

"Mother, we were taken to the great nāga realm by one of their princes named Bhūridatta. We have returned because Father was dissatisfied."

"Did you bring back any jewels?"

"None, Mother."

"Why didn't the nāga give you any? I thought they were always generous!"

"Mother, Bhūridatta offered Father a jewel which can grant all desires, but he would not take it."

"What? Why not?"

"He said he was going to become an ascetic."

"He said what? After abandoning me and the children to enjoy life in the nāga realm, he is now going to become an ascetic?" Flying into a rage, she hit her husband on the back with the rice ladle. "Wicked brahmin!" she cried. "What do you mean by saying that you are going to become an ascetic? How dare you refuse that precious jewel! Why come back here at all? Get out of my house right now!"

Roused from sleep, the brahmin tried to placate his irate wife. "My dear, don't be angry. As long as there are deer in the forest, I will support you and the children."

Meanwhile, somewhere in the Himavat, a giant garula left its home in a silk-cotton tree and flew to the ocean, where it stirred up the waters with the wind from its great wings. Wondering what was causing such a disturbance in the nāga realm, a nāga king swam near the surface. The sharp-eyed garula instantly swept down again and seized the nāga by the head with its sharp claws. On the way back to its mountain home, the garula stopped to rest in the top of a huge banyan tree, still clutching the nāga tightly in its claws. When the garula took to the air again, the nāga tried desperately to escape by wrapping his powerful tail around a stout branch of the tree. Unaware of this, the garula flew upwards. The garula held on tightly to the nāga, the nāga held on tightly to the branch, and, together, they uprooted the entire banyan tree, which dangled below as the garula flew towards his home.

As soon as he had arrived at his nest in the silk-cotton tree, the garula slit the nāga open with his beak and began eating the fat. Of course, when the nāga died, his tail released the great banyan tree, which fell with a great crash. "What was that noise?" wondered the garula. Then he looked down and saw the fallen tree. "Now where did I carry that off from?" he asked himself. "Oh, yes. I recognize it now. That was the banyan at the end of an ascetic's walk where I stopped to rest on my way here. I remember seeing him very often resting in that tree's shade. It was very useful to him. I wonder whether any harm will come to me because of this. I must go and ask him."

Disguising himself as a young student, the garula approached the ascetic's hut. The old man was smoothing down the earth where the great tree had been.

The garula greeted the ascetic respectfully and, pretending to know nothing about what had happened, asked what had once grown there.

"Until today," answered the ascetic, "a great banyan tree stood in this very spot. This morning, a garula, carrying a nāga, stopped here to rest. The great snake wrapped its tail around a branch of the tree, and, when the bird flew off, the whole tree was uprooted."

"That's very interesting," said the garula, still feigning ignorance. "You must have been very fond of that tree. What blame accrues to the bird for having done such a deed?"

"If he was not aware of what he did, it was only ignorance, not a fault."

"What about the nāga?"

"Since he did not seize the tree with an intent to hurt it, he also has no demerit."

Overjoyed to hear the ascetic's assurance that he would not suffer for what he had done, the garula revealed himself and bowed. "Thank you, sir, for your wise answers. As a fee for your lesson, I would like to give you the priceless serpent-quelling Ālambāyana spell, which will be helpful to you here in the forest. Please accept it."

"Thank you, but no. I already know enough spells. Please don't go to any trouble."

The garula continued to press the ascetic to accept the Ālambāyana spell, until, at last, he gave in. As soon as the garula had taught the powerful spell to the ascetic and instructed him in its use, he left, satisfied.

A few days later, a poor brahmin appeared at the hermitage. This brahmin had gotten himself deeply in debt in Bārānasi and, unable to face his angry creditors, had decided to go into the forest and die. He had wandered aimlessly until he chanced upon the ascetic, who welcomed him and invited him to stay. The brahmin proved to be so helpful and was so diligent in his work, that the ascetic decided to reward him by teaching him the spell which the garula had taught him.

"Brahmin," the ascetic said, "let me teach you the Ālambāyana spell."

"No, sir," the brahmin protested, "I have no need of any spell." The ascetic insisted, however, and, finally, the man consented. After he had learned the spell, the brahmin realized that he had acquired a means of livelihood as a snake charmer. A few days later, he pretended to have an attack of rheumatism, bade farewell to the ascetic, and left the forest.

The brahmin wandered from place to place, constantly repeating the Ālambāyana spell, lest he forget it. One morning, he arrived at the bank of the Yamunā River, where he saw a group of nāgas, sitting in a circle. These nāga youths, one thousand in number, had come from Bhūridatta's palace, carrying the marvelous jewel which grants all desires. All night, they had played in the water, illuminated by the radiance of the magical gem. At dawn, they had put on their garments and sat on the sand, guarding the magnificent stone.

When the nāgas heard the brahmin coming, they were afraid that he might be a garula in disguise and quickly plunged into the earth. Each thinking that another had picked up the gem, they unwittingly left it behind.

Assuming that his spell had chased the nāga youths away, the Brahmin was very pleased with himself. He joyfully picked up the beautiful gem and continued on his way.

Not long afterward, his wandering took him close to the spot where the outcaste brahmin and his son Somadatta were again hunting for deer. Seeing the jewel, the outcaste brahmin whispered, "Son, isn't that the same jewel that Bhūridatta offered us?" His son nodded his head in agreement.

"I'm going to trick that old fool and get the jewel for myself." the outcaste brahmin muttered.

"Father," Somadatta objected, "You refused the jewel before when Bhūridatta tried to give it to you. You'd better be quiet now. This brahmin will just cheat you, and we will be poorer than ever."

"Hush, my son. Watch me! You will see who can cheat better."

Stepping out from the bushes, the outcaste brahmin shouted, "Friend, that certainly is a beautiful gem you have. I think I recognize it. Where did you get it?"

"I found it lying on the sand not far from here," the brahmin answered. "Whoever had been guarding it ran away and left it."

"I see," the outcaste brahmin replied, pretending to examine the jewel. "I'm sure that that is a stone that I have seen before. It can bring its owner many good things if it is well taken care of, but, if the bearer shows any sign of disrespect or if he treats the stone the least bit carelessly, he will rue the day that he ever held it because it will bring him only misery. You'd be safer selling it to me. I'll even give you one hundred gold coins for it."

"In your dreams!" the brahmin retorted contemptuously. "I wouldn't part with this gem for any amount of gold! It is not for sale."

"All right, you won't sell it," the outcaste brahmin quickly responded, "but there must be something you would rather have than that stone."

"Actually," the brahmin answered just as quickly, "I would give this beautiful gem to any person who could tell me where to find the nāga king himself."

"Oh," the outcaste brahmin exclaimed, "you must be a garula in disguise, hunting nāgas."

"Not at all," the brahmin protested. "I am a brahmin doctor specializing in snakes and snake bites."

"What special power do you have, which makes you immune to the bite of poisonous snakes?" the outcaste brahmin asked curiously.

"In the forest, near the Himavat," the brahmin explained, "I served for several months under an old ascetic. For my service, he rewarded me by teaching me a serpent-quelling spell, called the Ālambāyana spell, which he had learned from a garula. Protected by that spell, I am not afraid of even the most dangerous snake. I am safe from the deadliest venom. I am now called 'Ālambāyana, the Snake Charmer.'"

The outcaste brahmin was delighted that it would be so easy to get the gem, but he hesitated. "Please wait a minute," he said to Ālambāyana. "Let me consult with my son." He drew Somadatta back into the bushes where they could talk privately.

"Dear Somadatta," he whispered, "let's be quick and get this magic gem. Let's not waste our luck this time!"

"Father," Somadatta cautioned again, "Bhūridatta showed us great hospitality even though we were complete strangers. I can't believe that you would turn around now and betray him, repaying his kindness with cruel ingratitude. If it is wealth you want, why don't we go to Bhūridatta and ask him? He will gladly give you anything you ask for."

"What are you saying, son? Do you want me to throw away what luck has brought my way? He who hesitates is lost. I'd be a fool not to jump at this chance now!"

"Father," Somadatta begged, "a traitor will be swallowed up by the earth and will burn in hell. If he is not sent to hell right away, the man who betrays his friend will die a slow death of starvation. All you have to do is ask Bhūridatta, and he will freely give you anything you wish. If you hand Bhūridatta over to his enemy, you will suffer for your sin."

"My boy, there's nothing to worry about," his father insisted. "For brahmins like us, a simple sacrifice can erase any sin. Come and help me."

"No, Father, I will never be part of your wicked plan. If you intend to return evil for the good our friend has done to us, I will leave you." He looked into his father's eyes and realized that his warnings were having no effect; his father was determined to betray their noble benefactor. Somadatta threw down his weapon, exclaimed in a voice so loud that it startled the deities residing in the vicinity, "I will not go with such a sinner!" and stalked away.

Ignoring his son's outburst, the outcaste brahmin thought, "No doubt, Somadatta will go back home to his mother." When he noticed that the other brahmin was growing impatient, he quickly said, "Don't mind my son, Ālambāyana. Come with me. I will take you to the nāga king."

He led Ālambāyana to the place where Bhūridatta was observing Uposatha. They stopped some distance away, and the traitor pointed. "There, asleep on that anthill is Bhūridatta, the nāga king. He is stretched out without a fear in the world. Seize him, and claim the priceless gem in his crown. Capture him now before he knows you are here!"

Hearing that familiar voice, Bhūridatta slowly opened his eyes. "Ah," he thought, "it is the brahmin hunter I took to my nāga palace. When he left, he refused the gem I offered him. Now he comes here with a snake-charmer. What treachery! Still, wretch though he be, I dare not get angry. I must preserve my moral character. My duty is to observe Uposatha. Even if this snake-charming brahmin cuts me into pieces or skewers me on a spit, I must not get angry."

Bhūridatta closed his eyes, made a supreme resolution to be forbearing, and lay perfectly motionless.

Distressed at Ālambāyana's hesitation, the outcaste brahmin shouted, "Friend, capture this nāga, and give me the gem!"

Ālambāyana, for his part, was so delighted to see the great nāga king that he had forgotten all about the wish-fulfilling jewel. Keeping his eyes intently on Bhūridatta, he mumbled, "Here you are," and carelessly tossed the gem toward the other's outstretched hands. The outcaste brahmin tried to catch the gem, but it slipped through his fingers. As soon as it touched the ground, the priceless jewel vanished and reappeared in the nāga realm.

In the space of a few minutes, the outcaste brahmin had lost three things: his own son, Bhūridatta's friendship, and the priceless gem. Left with nothing, he turned to go home, crying, "I am lost! I'm a fool! I'm an idiot! Why didn't I listen to my son?"

After leaving his father, Somadatta did not return home. He went to the Himavat, became an ascetic, practiced meditation with great seriousness, and, in time, was reborn in the Brahma heavens.

Completely ignoring the outcaste brahmin and his misery, Ālambāyana rubbed his own body with medicinal herbs and ingested a bit of a protective drug. Reciting the Ālambāyana spell, he drew near to Bhūridatta, seized him by the tail, forced open his mouth, and spat some of the drug into it. Then he violently shook the nāga, causing him to vomit the food he had swallowed the day before.

In spite of all this, Bhūridatta remained perfectly calm, not allowing himself to feel even the slightest anger. With all his might, he determined to keep his mind pure and not to violate his moral precepts.

The brahmin stretched Bhūridatta out full length on the ground and proceeded to beat him as hard as he could, crushing the serpent's bones. Grabbing the nāga again by the tail, he pounded him as if he were beating clothes on rocks at the river.

Of course, this caused Bhūridatta excruciating pain, but he continued to control his mind so that no anger arose.

Having rendered Bhūridatta completely helpless and proved himself the master, the brahmin stuffed the hapless nāga king into a rude basket of creepers that he had prepared. At first, the huge body would not fit in the basket, but Ālambāyana kicked and shoved until he was able to force the snake's coils inside and to seal the basket with its cover.

The brahmin picked up the basket and carried it to the first village he could find. Placing the basket in the center of the square, he shouted, "Come one! Come all! Gather round, and see a magnificent snake dance!" In a few minutes, the square was filled with excited spectators.

Inside the basket, Bhūridatta could hear the brahmin shouting orders to him and encouraging the crowd. He reflected, "It is best for me to dance and to please the crowd today. Perhaps, if this man gets enough money, he will be satisfied and will let me go. I will do whatever he tells me to do."

Ālambāyana opened the basket and shouted, "Come out, mighty snake, and assume your full size!" Bhūridatta instantly appeared and hovered above the square. The spectators gasped and shrank back in terror. The brahmin ordered Bhūridatta to make one hood, then five, then twenty, then one hundred. At every command, Bhūridatta obeyed immediately. The spectators were awed.

The brahmin ordered Bhūridatta to become blue, then yellow, then red, and then white. "Emit fire!" he shouted. "Smoke! Water!"

In spite of his exhaustion and the immense pain he was still suffering, Bhūridatta forced himself to do all of those things and to exhibit his dancing powers, as well. People showered Ālambāyana with gold coins, garments, and jewelry. At the end of just this one performance, he left the village with one hundred thousand coins.

Initially, Ālambāyana had planned to release the nāga as soon as he had earned one thousand coins, but that first performance brought in so much wealth that he became greedy. "Look how much money I got in this one little village!" he exulted. "If I take this nāga to a real city, I'll make a fortune!"

With this new wealth, Ālambāyana retrieved his family and settled them in a magnificent mansion. He also ordered an exquisite jeweled basket and threw Bhūridatta into it. He seated himself in a fashionable new carriage with the basket beside him and headed for the capital. On the way, he forced the nāga king to dance in every village, hamlet, and town they passed through. At every stop, he received more money than he could count.

Ālambāyana offered Bhūridatta honey and fried grain. He even killed frogs for him, but the nāga king refused all food, afraid that, if he ate, he would never be released from captivity. Even though he was weak from hunger, Bhūridatta forced himself to obey all the man's commands and to display his full powers in every performance. They arrived in Bārānasi, but the brahmin stayed near the city gates, performing every day.

In the morning of the full-moon day, Ālambāyana had it announced to the king that he would display the dancing powers of the great nāga king that very day for His Majesty's pleasure.

The king had tiers of seats erected in the palace courtyard and sent out town criers with drum attendants to gather spectators. Very soon, all the seats were filled, and the huge crowd eagerly awaited the spectacle.

On the day that Ālambāyana had captured Bhūridatta, Samuddajā, Bhūri-datta's mother, had dreamed that a black man with red eyes had sliced off her arm with a sword and was carrying it away, blood flowing from the severed limb. In terror, she leapt from her bed but, feeling her right arm, realized that it had been only a dream. Nevertheless, she feared that her evil dream was an omen of some misfortune to someone in her family. "Most of us are here, safe in the nāga realm," she reflected, "but Bhūridatta has gone to the human world to observe Uposatha. Could it be that a snake charmer or a garula has seized him?" Day and night, she fretted about her beloved son. When he failed to return, she became depressed and murmured to herself, "My son would not willingly stay away a whole fortnight without seeing me. I am sure that some evil has befallen him." Every morning, she sat watching the road, repeating, "Surely he is coming home now. I'm sure he will come home soon."

When her eldest son, Sudassana, came to visit, he left his attendants outside, entered the palace, and bowed before his mother. Although she saw him, Samuddajā was so preoccupied with thoughts of Bhūridatta, that she did not even greet him.

Surprised, Sudassana asked, "Is this the welcome you give me when I return from a foreign land?" Still, Samuddajā seemed not even to see her son.

"Mother," Sudassana cried, "what is the matter? Is something troubling you, or have I offended you in some way?"

"Oh, Sudassana," she finally said between sobs, "exactly one month ago today, I had an evil dream. As I lay sleeping, a man came and hacked off my arm. I could see him carrying it away. There was so much blood that I awoke in a cold sweat. Since then, I have not had a moment's peace. It has now been one month since my darling Bhūridatta, your little brother, has been home. I am sure something terrible has happened to him! My Bhūridatta is gone!" With that, she broke down.

Sudassana held his mother to comfort her and led her immediately to Bhūridatta's palace to inquire about him. Bhūridatta's wives had not worried about his absence because they had assumed he'd gone to pay a visit to his mother. When they learned that Samuddajā had also not seen him, they fell at her feet and joined her in weeping over him.

Bhūridatta's other brothers, Kānārittha and Subhaga, who were also visiting their parents, hurried in to find out what the commotion was about. When they saw their mother and learned why she was distraught, they tried to console her. "Mother," they said, "please be calm. If, indeed, he is dead, that is the fate of all who live. Change holds true in all things. All must pass from birth to birth, so you must not grieve."

"My children," Samuddajā replied, "I am well aware of that. Yes, death is the end of all who live, but I cannot bear to lose him. How can I live without Bhūridatta? He is so dear to my heart that, if I cannot see him again, I'm sure I will die this very night."

"Don't give way, dear Mother. I feel sure that Bhūridatta is still alive. We will find our brother," Kānārittha promised, "even if we have to search the whole world!"

"After we find him, we'll bring him back to you," added Subhaga. "We promise you that we will not fail."

"Give us ten days, and we will return with Bhūridatta, safe and sound," promised Sudassana.

The three nāga princes left their mother in the care of Bhūridatta's wives and withdrew to discuss how they should proceed. Sudassana thought, "It would be useless for the three of us go in the same direction. We must go to three different places—one to the realm of the devas, one to the Himavat, and one to the realm of men. Ah, but Kānārittha has a rather cruel nature. If he goes to the land of men and happens to find Bhūridatta, he might destroy a village or a town."

"Kānārittha," Sudassana said aloud, "You must go to the heavens. Perhaps the devas have carried our brother to their realm in order to learn the law from him. If you find him, bring him back to Mother."

"Subhaga," he continued, "please search for Bhūridatta in the Himavat, the land of the five rivers."

"I myself will go to the realm of men," he concluded, as he sent his brothers away. Then Sudassana thought, "No one will respect me if I go as a young man. Better that I go as an elderly ascetic for humans always welcome ascetics." Transforming himself accordingly, he bade his mother farewell, and set off.

The princes also had a half-sister named Accimukhī, who loved Bhūridatta very much. When she saw Sudassana setting out, she announced, "Brother, I am also very worried about Bhūridatta. I will go with you."

"Dear sister," Sudassana objected, "you cannot go because I am going disguised as an ascetic."

"Then I will become a little frog and ride in your matted hair."

Sudassana agreed, and Accimukhī transformed herself into a tiny frog and nestled in her brother's tangled locks.

Sudassana had asked Bhūridatta's wife where his brother usually spent the Uposatha day, and she had told him about the anthill near the banyan tree, so he began his search there. He wept as he examined the bloodstains on the ground where the Ālambāyana brahmin had beaten Bhūridatta and the scraps of creeper left from the rough basket he had made. Sudassana was sure that his brother had been taken by a snake-charmer. He followed Ālambāyana's trail with a heavy heart.

When he inquired in the first village he came to, he learned that, indeed, a snake charmer had given a magnificent performance exactly one month earlier.

"Did the man make any money from the show?" Sudassana asked.

"Certainly! He made more than one hundred thousand coins here. He became so rich that he settled his family in a great mansion in this very village."

"Is he here now?" Sudassana asked hopefully.

"Oh, no. He has taken his marvelous snake to Bārānasi. We heard rumors that they performed in every village on the way."

Sudassana hurried on. In every settlement, he heard the same story. Making very good time, he arrived in the capital at the moment that Ālambāyana, wearing a fine new tunic, was ready to begin the show.

The courtyard was overflowing with spectators, and the royal box had been prepared. The king himself had not yet appeared, but he sent a message that Ālambāyana should begin the performance without waiting for him. The crowd was breathless with excitement.

The brahmin's attendant placed the jeweled basket on an exquisite carpet in the middle of the courtyard. Ālambāyana stepped forward and intoned, "Come out, snake-king!"

Standing at the edge of the crowd, Sudassana could see Bhūridatta raise his head above the rim of the basket and survey the audience. Before they perform, nāgas always examine the crowd to see whether either a garula or an actor is present. If a nāga sees a garula, he will not dance for fear. If he sees an actor, he will not dance for shame.

Bhūridatta immediately recognized Sudassana. Slowly and silently, he slid from the basket and slithered toward his brother.

As the huge serpent came close, the spectators screamed and retreated in fear, leaving Sudassana standing alone. Bhūridatta stopped directly in front of Sudassana, laid his head on his brother's foot, and wept. Sudassana, too, could not hold back the tears.

Without saying a word, Bhūridatta lifted his head and returned to the basket.

"Don't worry, my friend," Ālambāyana called to the ascetic, trying to reassure him. "I'm sorry I let the snake slip from my grasp. Did he bite you? Don't worry. He is perfectly harmless."

Realizing immediately that Ālambāyana was a complete fake, Sudassana provoked him, "Of course, your snake can't harm me. I am more than a match for him. Search the world over, and you will find no one who can charm a snake as well as I can."

Stung by this insolence, Ālambāyana turned to the crowd and shouted angrily, "This braggart in ascetic's garb dares to challenge me! I accept his arrogant wager. Let the crowd be the judge as to who is the better snake charmer—this simple-minded ascetic or the great Ālambāyana!"

Sudassana calmly responded, "A frog will be my champion. Let a snake be yours. Five thousand coins will be the stake. I dare you to show whatever skill you think you have!"

"Rogue," Ālambāyana rejoined, "your challenge is met. I am, however, a man of means. Everyone knows that my money is as good as my word, and I cannot possibly lose. You, on the other hand, are a complete unknown, a wandering nobody. Who is going to back you? Let's see the color of your money!"

Unperturbed, Sudassana confidently entered the palace and approached the king. "Sire! May good fortune never leave you. Will you be my guarantor for five thousand coins?"

"My dear sir," the king responded, "that is a very large sum. Why are you asking me for such a loan? Is it to repay a debt left you by your father or, perhaps, one of your own?"

"No, it is nothing like that, Your Majesty. The snake-charmer Ālambāyana has accepted my challenge. He expects to defeat me, but I will humble him with my frog. Come, Your Majesty, with your court. Give me your support and watch me thoroughly defeat this miserable brahmin in a grand contest!"

Sensing something unusual about the demeanor of this ascetic, the king agreed and accompanied him to the courtyard.

When Ālambāyana saw Sudassana returning with the king, he grew nervous. "Perhaps," he thought, "this ascetic is a friend of the king." He approached Sudassana and said, "My dear sir, please don't misunderstand me. I do not want to embarrass you. I am not boasting, but you should not scorn this snake."

Sudassana replied, "Nor do I seek to humble you, Brahmin. I certainly do not discount your skill, but I wonder why you want to deceive these people with a snake you claim is harmless and cannot bite. If they could see through you as I can, you would be lucky to get even rice and curry for your show! You wouldn't dare talk of gold!"

"You bloody beggar in an ass's skin!" Ālambāyana retorted furiously. "You dirty, uncombed lout! How dare you insult my snake! Come near and see what it can do! Its bite will turn you into a stinking corpse!"

"Your snake is as harmless as a kitten," Sudassana mocked. "It may hiss, but it will not bite."

The snake charmer sputtered, "Many ascetics have told me that one who gives alms will go to heaven when he dies. I advise you to give quickly because, as soon as I open this basket, this snake will kill you! Don't waste your time! You have but a little left!"

Sudassana calmly replied "I, too, have heard that from ascetics, but it is you who must make haste to give gifts. My champion will put a stop to your boastful tone. This tiny frog is my half-sister, Accimukhī, daughter of the great nāga king. She can shoot fiery flames from her mouth, and her venom is the deadliest poison in the world."

"Accimukhī," he called, "come out of my matted locks!" and he held out his hand. When his sister heard his voice, she uttered three croaks, hopped to his shoulder, spat three drops of poison into the palm of his hand, and returned to his hair.

With his hand extended, Sudassana stood perfectly still and shouted, "This country will be destroyed! This country will be wholly destroyed! This country will be utterly destroyed!" His shout filled all Bārānasi.

Alarmed, the king asked what he meant.

"Your Majesty, I see no place where I can drop this poison."

"This earth is big enough. Drop it on the earth."

"That is not possible, Sire. If I drop it on the ground, the grass, the crops, and all plants and herbs will wither and perish."

"Well then, throw it into the sky."

"That is also impossible, Sire. If I throw it into the sky, no rain will fall for seven years."

"Then throw it into the water."

"That, too, is impossible, Sire. If it falls into the water, the fish, crabs, turtles, and other marine life will all die."

"Then, what can we do?" asked the king. "Is there no way to save our land from destruction?"

"Your Majesty," Sudassana replied. "You must immediately order three large pits to be dug here."

As soon as the pits were ready, Sudassana ordered the first to be filled with cow dung, the second with potent herbs, and the third with heavenly medicine. Then he let fall the drops of poison into the middle pit.

Suddenly, there was an explosion. Blinding fire and thick smoke filled the pit and completely consumed the herbs. The fire spread to the pit with the cow dung and to the pit with the medicine. When all of this fuel was consumed, the fire extinguished itself as quickly as it had started.

Ālambāyana was standing so near the pits that the heat of the poisonous flames struck him. In an instant he became a leper, and his skin turned a sickly white. Filled with terror, he shouted three times, "I will set the snake-king free!"

On hearing him, Bhūridatta emerged from the jeweled basket. Assuming a radiant form, dressed in magnificent garments and adorned with dazzling jewels, he appeared as glorious as Sakka. Sudassana and Accimukhī took their places beside him. Sudassana turned to the king and asked, "Sire, do you know whose children we are?"

"I have no idea," the king replied.

"Certainly, you remember that, many years ago, the king of Kāsi gave his daughter Samuddajā to King Dhatarattha."

"Of course, I know that very well. She was my younger sister."

"Uncle," Sudassana said, as the three bowed to the king. "We are her children."

Overcome with emotion, the king embraced them and kissed their heads. Then he took them into his palace and paid them great honor. While they feasted and rested from the ordeal in the courtyard, Bhūridatta satisfied the king's curiosity by relating the entire story of how Ālambāyana had managed to catch him in spite of his powerful venom. Then Sudassana instructed his uncle on the law and gave him good advice about ruling wisely.

At last, he said, "Uncle, when we left, our mother was distraught with worry over Bhūridatta. We must not keep her waiting any longer."

"You are right. You must go back to her immediately. Before you go, however, you must tell me how I can see my sister."

"Uncle," Sudassana replied, "where is our grandfather, the former king of Kāsi?"

"He was so deeply distressed at losing my sister that he lost interest in ruling and abdicated his throne to become an ascetic. He is now living deep in the forest."

"Let us meet you there, Uncle. Our mother will be delighted to see both you and our grandfather."

As soon as they had learned the location of the hermitage and set a date for the meeting, the three siblings returned to the nāga realm.

Samuddajā was overjoyed to see them return, but Bhūridatta was still so exhausted from the trials he had suffered that he took to his sickbed. Nevertheless, innumerable nāgas came to visit and to commiserate with him, and talking with them tired him even more.

When Kānārittha returned from the realm of the devas, he was appointed doorkeeper of Bhūridatta's sickroom because he was forceful enough to keep out the crowd of visitors.

Meanwhile, the traitorous outcaste brahmin heard the news that Ālambāyana had become a leper. He said to himself, "That brahmin was afflicted with leprosy because he tortured Bhūridatta, but what about me? I betrayed Bhūridatta, my friend and benefactor, because I craved that jewel. My crime will surely come back to me. Let me go to the sacred bathing-place in the Yamunā and wash away my treachery and guilt." Fearing that disaster might strike him at any moment, he hurried to the Yamunā River, muttering to himself that he must quickly wash away his sin.

At that precise moment, Subhaga, after searching the Himavat, as well as the great oceans and rivers, reached the same spot in the Yamunā and overheard the brahmin talking to himself. "So this is the vile brahmin who betrayed my brother for the gem!" he cried. "I will not spare him!" Coiling his tail around the brahmin's feet, he dragged him into the water and held him under. He relaxed his grip for a moment, and the brahmin bobbed up for air. Subhaga dragged him under again and again. Gasping for breath, the brahmin finally managed to speak. "What cruel yakkha is trying to kill me?" he shouted. "All I'm doing is bathing at this sacred spot."

Subhaga answered, "I am the son of that mighty serpent king who once made all of Kāsi quake with fear. Subhaga is my name."

The brahmin realized that no brother of Bhūridatta was going to spare his life, unless he could somehow soften his heart. Thinking quickly, he cried, "Heir of Kāsi's royalty, your mother came from that illustrious line. Surely, it would be beneath your exalted rank to let a mean slave like me drown beneath the ruthless waves!"

"Your praise is hollow," retorted Subhaga. "Think back to that day when you mercilessly shot the thirsty deer which approached the river to drink. When the animal fled in fear and pain, you followed it relentlessly. When it fell, deep in the forest, you happily tied it onto a pole and carried it away. Then, in the lovely wood, your cruel eye spotted my brother, who was relaxing there with his attendants. Despite his power, he never harmed you. He even showed you great hospitality, but, in your greed and malice, you betrayed him. You didn't care if he died. He was an innocent victim of your desire for that precious gem. Today, your sin comes back to you. Now you will suffer my vengeance! I will not spare your life."

Desperate to find a ruse to save his life, the hapless man cried, "Wait! I am a brahmin, so you must not destroy me. Study, prayers, and offerings to the sacred fire—these three things make a brahmin's life sacrosanct, no matter how angry you may be."

When Subhaga heard this, he became unsure of himself. "All right, worthless man," he relented. "I will take you to the nāga capital where the great Dhatarattha rules. There, my brothers will decide your fate."

Seizing the man by the neck, Subhaga violently shook him and carried him to the gate of Bhūridatta's palace. When Kānārittha saw Subhaga dragging the man along so roughly, he became very upset. In his previous birth, Kānārittha had himself been a brahmin. He remembered the sacrificial lore and retained some of those beliefs. He hurried to meet them. "Subhaga, do not hurt him," he urged his brother. "Brahmins are the sons of the great Brahmā. If Brahmā learned that we were hurting one of his sons, he might be angry and destroy our nāga realm. In the realm of men, brahmins are the highest and have great dignity. To them belong the Vedas and the sacrifice, which are worthy of esteem. No matter how worthless a brahmin may seem, it is his privilege to be honored. One who scornfully flouts this law not only will lose his wealth, but will forever live guilt-burdened and forlorn.

"Brother," Kānārittha continued, "do you know who created the world?"

"No," Subhaga answered, "I have no idea."

"When Brahmā made the world," Kānārittha explained, "he created brahmins to study and to offer sacrifice; khattiyas to fight and to rule; vessas to farm; and suddas to serve and to obey the other three. Therefore, brahmins have great influence. One who offers gifts to them can, at death, go directly to the realm of the devas.

"Kuvera, Soma, Varuna, Dhātā, and Vidhātā all gave plenty of offerings to their brahmin priests, and, because of their abundant gifts, they became devas. The greater the offering to the brahmins, the better the rewards. King Mucalinda, famous for worshiping fire with offerings of ghee, earned heaven as the reward for his piety. You have heard of Dujīpa, who lived one thousand years. He, too, had a great kingdom but later became an ascetic. Because of all his sacrifices, he went straight from his hermitage to heaven. The old stories tell of many more. In every tale, Brahmā the great creator, rewards those who make offerings to his brahmins and pay them due respect.

"Brother," Kānārittha went on, "do you know why the sea became salty and undrinkable?"

"I have no idea, Kānārittha."

"Of course, you don't," Kānārittha retorted. "You only know how to abuse brahmins! Listen and I will tell you. I have heard that a young brahmin once stood on the seashore. When he touched the sea, it swallowed him, and, from that day on, the sea has been undrinkable. Actually, all these brahmins have such power. When Sakka attained his royal throne, he gave his special favor to the brahmins, who earned great honor by carrying out their Vedic rituals."

Many of the nāgas who had come to visit Bhūridatta on his sick-bed were swayed by Kānārittha's sermon. They gathered around to listen, eager to learn more of the legends of the past.

Bhūridatta also heard his brother, but he was not at all impressed. He rose from his bed, bathed, put on his royal garments, gathered all the nāgas, and sent for his brother. "Kānārittha," he said sternly, "you speak falsely when you describe the brahmins and the Vedas. The sacrifice of victims according to these Vedic rituals is not worthy, and it does not lead to heaven! Your sham explanations are deceiving these impressionable nāgas. By studying the Vedas, a clever brahmin spins a web which lures his victims, whom he ruins! These stories are fantasies designed to snare the careless. Wise men avoid these traps. The Vedas have no secret power to save the wicked, the foolish, or the cowardly. The sacrificial fire, even though it is tended for many years, can offer no hope to the dolt who so carefully feeds it. Even if all the trees in the world were piled up to be offered as fuel, they could never satisfy fire's rapacity. If that is true, how could one ever dream of gratifying fire's hunger? Of course, it requires effort to make fire. If fire kindled itself, every forest would be burned to ashes. However, if the man who feeds the flame makes merit, then cooks, blacksmiths, and those who cremate the dead must be the best of all! We know that this is not so! No one, no matter how zealously he prays and heaps fuel to feed the flame, gains any merit by his mumbo-jumbo. There is nothing noble about fire. If fire were the honored deva that brahmins claim, why would it feed on garbage and carrion? Would Brahmā the creator worship something he himself created, something as lowly as a fire? Some people worship fire as a deva, while others think that water is divine. Neither is worthy to be called a deva. Fire is nothing but a galley slave, senseless, blind, and deaf to the believer's prayers.

"These crafty brahmins need to earn a living, so they tell us that only a brahmin is allowed to offer sacrifices. By making up their own absurd doctrines and rules, these brahmins try to gain power and wealth. They proclaim the rules and enforce them, too. They say, 'Brahmins were created for study and sacrifice; khattiyas were intended to fight and rule; vessas were made to farm; and suddas were created as servants to obey.' These self-serving brahmins take the best place for themselves and repeat their lies while fools swallow their fictions. Anyone with eyes can see this disgusting sight. If Brahmā is so great, why doesn't he set his creatures right? If Brahmā has unlimited power, why doesn't he comfort and bless his creations? Why are all beings condemned to sickness, old age, pain, and death? If Brahmā is so great, why doesn't he give them happiness, instead?

"Why does Brahmā allow fraud, lies, and ignorance to prevail over truth and justice? If Brahmā made this world with all its wrongs, he is wicked and unjust. It is savage to think that men are pure because they kill frogs, bees, snakes, and insects. If one who sacrifices living things is innocent and his victim goes to heaven, then let brahmins kill brahmins, and both will be happy! We do not see cattle begging to be sacrificed so that they can have a new and better life. Instead, they go unwillingly to their slaughter, vainly struggling against the blow and the knife. To disguise the horror of the scene, the brahmins use flowery rhetoric, promising that the sacrificial post will be like a cow of plenty to give you all your heart desires. How can any good come from such a wicked, heartless act? If a sacrifice could bring such rewards, they should offer it for themselves alone and keep the benefits within their own families. They are nothing but cruel cheats, who tempt others to offer their wealth and promise them their heart's fondest dreams. The donor brings his purse, and the brahmins gather around like vultures, ripping from him all he has, until he is stripped bare and bankrupt. The wealth which he possessed has been exchanged for promises, which no one can ever test. The sacred rites from days of old are bought and paid for with hard-earned gold, but their offers of heaven, health, and riches are a fake. If a person lives a life of sin, how can he dream of achieving heaven?

"Brother, you recounted the pernicious tale of a brahmin youth who was drowned while he was praying on the seashore. The legend tells us that the ocean was punished for this sin. Reflect a moment! From the beginning of time, rivers have drowned learned men by the hundreds, yet their water remains fresh. Rivers and streams flow on and never taste the worse. Why should the sea alone be cursed?

"As for who ranks the highest, all men started equal, but their various failures soon gave some an advantage over others. It was no lack of merit in the past, but present faults which make them first or last. Were a clever low-caste lad to use his wit and recite the sacred hymns, his head would not split as the brahmins threaten. The brahmins made up the Vedas and learned them by rote. Their obscurity is meant to catch the foolish, who cannot think for themselves and blindly swallow all that they are told. Actually, brahmins are not like beasts of prey; they are more like cows and oxen, dull and stupid.

"The brahmin's Vedas and the khattiya's arbitrary rule are but delusions. Both blindly grope along a path they pretend was dictated from on high. The entire notion of the four castes is absurd. Loss, gain, glory, and shame touch all four castes alike. In pursuing a livelihood, a man should do what suits him best. What's important is living righteously. If a king ruled righteously and lived in peace with all, conquering his passions instead of other kingdoms, imagine the happy lives his subjects would have!"

The assembly of nāgas was overjoyed to hear Bhūridatta refute his brother's faulty arguments. They heartily agreed with the doctrine he thus established. After he had finished, Bhūridatta conveyed the traitorous brahmin back to the realm of men, exercising great patience, and not even scolding him with disdainful words.

On the appointed day, King Brahmadatta led his entire army to the forest to visit his father. Near the hermitage, he met his sister Samuddajā and her four sons, and, together, they formed a great procession. The old ascetic was greatly surprised to hear the drums and conch shells. The first person he saw was a handsome youth wearing a golden coronet upon his head. His body was radiant, even though shaded by a golden umbrella. The ascetic was even more surprised when this young man, who resembled Sakka after defeating the asuras, took off his golden shoes and bowed low to pay his respects. The old ascetic asked who he might be.

King Brahmadatta stepped forward and paid his respects to his father. "These four are the sons of King Dhatarattha, the nāga sons of your daughter. They all revere Samuddajā as their mother, and the one resembling Sakka is called Bhūridatta," he said.

The other three nāga brothers stepped forward, bowed at the ascetic's feet, and sat down on one side. Finally, Samuddajā tearfully greeted her father.

After a short time, still weeping, Samuddajā returned with the other nāgas to their own realm. King Brahmadatta stayed with his father for a few days before returning to Bārānasi.

In time, Samuddajā died in the nāga realm. Bhūridatta continued keeping the precepts and scrupulously observing Uposatha and, at the end of his life, was reborn in heaven.

Having concluded his story, the Buddha added, "Thus, you can see, pious disciples, that the wise of former times, before there was a Buddha in the world, gave up the glory of the royal nāga state and rigorously observed the Uposatha days!" He then identified the birth: "At that time, my father and mother were the parents of Bhūridatta. Devadatta was the treacherous brahmin. Ānanda was Somadatta. Uppalavannā was Accimukhī. Sāriputta was Sudassana. Moggallāna was Subhaga, Sunakkhatta was Kānārittha, and I was Bhūridatta."

214
Wrong View
Mahā-Nārada-Kassapa Jātaka

It was while staying at Latthivana near Rājagaha that the Buddha told this story about abandoning a false doctrine.

The Buddha was staying there with Uruvela-Kassapa, his two brothers, and their one thousand followers. At that time, King Bimbisāra visited the garden with a large retinue, paid his respects to the Buddha, and seated himself to one side. King Bimbisāra had promised to present Veluvana, the Bamboo Grove, to the Buddha and the Sangha. There was disagreement among the courtiers, however, as to whether Uruvela-Kassapa had become a follower of the Buddha or the Buddha had become a follower of Uruvela-Kassapa. In order to resolve the issue and to show the truth to everyone, the Buddha asked Uruvela-Kassapa, "What did you see, Kassapa, that caused you, renowned for your austerities, to abandon your sacrificial fire?"

"Venerable Sir," Kassapa replied, "the goal of ritual sacrifices is the gratification of sensual desires, which is part of the material world. When I came to understand that those pleasures are of no more value than excrement, I lost all interest in sacrifices and rituals." He touched his forehead to the Buddha's feet and loudly proclaimed, "The Blessed One is my teacher, and I am his disciple." Then he rose into the air, to the height of a palm tree and descended to pay his respects at the Buddha's feet. He repeated this action, rising to the height of two, three, four, five, six, and seven palm trees. After descending the seventh time, he paid his respects to the Buddha and sat to one side.

At last, everyone understood that, although Uruvela-Kassapa had believed himself to be perfectly enlightened, he was, in this way, acknowledging that the Buddha was his teacher and that the Buddha had shown him his error, converted him, and led him to true arahatship. The entire assembly paid their respects to the Buddha and intoned, "Great is the power of the Buddha."

"It is hardly remarkable that I, who have now attained omniscience, was able to convert Uruvela-Kassapa," the Buddha said. "Far more noteworthy, indeed, was my convincing him of the falsity of his beliefs long ago, when I myself was still subject to passion." At the people's request, the Buddha told this story of the past.

Long, long ago, when King Angati, a just and righteous king, was reigning in Mithilā, all his wives were barren, except his chief queen. She conceived a daughter of great merit, who had aspired to virtue for one hundred thousand eons. When this child was born, she was truly fair and beautiful, and they named her Rujā.

The king adored his precious daughter, and, every day, he sent her twenty-five baskets of flowers, elegant clothing, and precious jewelry, asking her to beautify herself with them. He frequently sent her one thousand coins, encouraging her to give alms.

One night, on the festival of the full moon of the fourth month, the entire city was decorated as beautifully as Tāvatimsa. The king, having bathed and dressed in his robes of state, stood at a window of the palace with two of his ministers, Vijaya and Sunāma, and the commander-in-chief, Alāta. As the king was gazing at the full moon in the clear dark sky, he observed, "What a pleasant, clear night this is! How should we amuse ourselves?" he asked the three men.

"Let's call out the army for a battle and conquer new territory to enhance your kingdom," suggested General Alāta.

"All around Videha, Sire," Sunāma pointed out, "the other kings have already submitted to you and are behaving themselves properly. War hardly appeals to me tonight. You might summon your servants and have them prepare a great feast. You could enjoy yourself with music, dance, and song!"

"Such paltry pleasures, Sire," Vijaya suggested, "are always available to you. Entertainment of that kind is not nearly special enough to do justice to this splendid night. You might visit an ascetic or a learned sage from whom you might learn what should be the object of your desire."

"Excellent!" exclaimed the king. "Vijaya's idea is very good! Let's visit a teacher and ask about the most worthy desire. But what teacher should we visit? Who will be able to remove our doubts?"

"Sire," General Alāta said, "There is a naked ascetic staying in the royal deer park. His name is Guna-Kassapa, and I have heard that he is wise and that he has a large following. Let us visit him. He will surely remove your doubt."

The king immediately agreed and ordered everything to be readied. Mounted in his ivory chariot, which was decorated with silver and drawn by four white Sindh horses, King Angati, dressed in white, standing beneath the white umbrella, and illuminated by moonlight, shone like the full moon itself. The royal party reached the deer park in what seemed no more than a moment.

The king and his retinue dismounted at the gate, entered the park on foot, and sat down near the naked ascetic, Guna-Kassapa. The king paid his respects to the ascetic and asked, "Are your needs provided for? Are you living comfortably? Do you receive sufficient alms?"

"Yes, Sire, all my wants are provided for," Guna replied. "What about you, Your Majesty? Is your health as you wish? Is the kingdom peaceful?"

After acknowledging this kindly greeting, the king asked, "Sir, how should a man behave toward his parents, his teacher, his wife, and his children? How should he show respect to the elderly, ascetics, and brahmins? How should a king deal with his army and his subjects? How should we live so as to attain heaven and to avoid falling into hell?"

These are questions which ought to be asked of a Buddha, a Pacceka Buddha, a noble disciple, or a wise sage. Guna-Kassapa, the naked ascetic, however, was deluded and as blind as a newborn puppy. Like a man who beats his ox when it is already pulling nicely or one who throws garbage onto another's plate, he jumped at the chance to declare his own nihilistic doctrine with bluster and vehemence.

"Listen, Your Majesty, and I will proclaim a true and unerring doctrine," Guna-Kassapa began. "This world is all there is. No one has ever come back from the hereafter, so there is no reason to believe that there is anything hereafter. All beings are equal. There is no need to respect father, mother, or teacher. There is no one to honor, nor anyone who needs to honor another. There is no result whatsoever from following the law. There is no result whatsoever from violating the law. Strength, courage, heroism, and valor are mere words, puffs of air, illusions. Choice is a mirage. Each life follows a predetermined course just as certainly as the stern rope follows the ship. Since every mortal gets what he is fated to get, there can be no value in generosity.

"There are seven indestructible aggregates—fire, earth, water, air, pleasure, pain, and soul," Guna-Kassapa proclaimed arbitrarily. "None of these can destroy anything, nor be itself destroyed. Weapons pass harmlessly through these aggregates. The man who decapitates another with a sword does no damage to the aggregates, so, how can there be any consequence of his action? All beings become pure by passing through eighty-four great eons. Until that time has elapsed, no one can become pure, no matter how self-restrained. Righteousness and unrighteousness are of no consequence. We cannot pass beyond our destiny any more than the sea can pass beyond its shore."

"That makes perfect sense to me!" General Alāta immediately declared. "I remember my former birth when I was a violent, wicked man named Pingala. I committed many sins, killing innumerable creatures. I cheated, lied, stole, and behaved violently. In this life, I was born into a prosperous family, and I have become a general. Obviously, since I did not go to hell, there are no consequences of evil!"

Just outside the royal entourage clustered around Guna, stood a miserable slave in rags, named Bījaka, who was observing Uposatha. Suddenly, he burst into tears.

King Angati asked him why he was crying, and Bījaka replied, "I, too, remember a former birth, a happy one. I was a wealthy merchant. My name was Bhava, and I lived in Sāketā. I led an exemplary life. I was virtuous, generous, and kind to all my neighbors, and everyone respected me. I can't recall committing a single evil deed, but, when I died, I was conceived by a wretchedly poor prostitute and born into this miserable life. Now, despite my poverty, I share my food with others, I never harm living creatures, I never steal, and I observe the Uposatha days. It has always seemed that my good deeds bear no fruit. Now, I understand, from listening to Guna-Kassapa and General Alāta, that virtue is useless. Like an unlucky dice player, I have lost at the game of life, and General Alāta continues to win. No matter how virtuously I live, I will never reach heaven. That, Sire, is why I am crying."

"At last, I understand!" declared the king. "Everything depends on fate. There is no door to heaven. Happiness or misery is decided by destiny. In time, we will all reach deliverance through transmigration. We shouldn't be eager for the future. I, too, was fortunate in former births, but, I have been so busy administering the kingdom that I have had no enjoyment. I've been cheating myself of life's pleasures!

"Guna-Kassapa," the king continued, as he prepared to leave, "now I have a teacher! From now on, following your teaching, I will take my pleasure only in sensual delights. I won't even bother with lectures on virtue. Perhaps we may see each other again." The king and his entourage all departed.

When the king had first met Guna-Kassapa, he had respectfully saluted the naked ascetic and had asked his questions with great politeness. When he left, however, he went away without paying his respects. Because Guna-Kassapa taught that there was no point in respect or generosity, he received, appropriately enough, few salutations and even fewer alms.

The next day, the king summoned his ministers, advisors, and officers and announced, "Today I am turning over the administration of the kingdom to Vijaya, Sunāma, and General Alāta. Those three will be responsible for all state business, all matters requiring an official decision, and all cases of justice. From now on, I will devote myself entirely to pleasure. I want you to arrange matters so that I am constantly provided with good food, good wine, music, and various kinds of entertainment. In my presence, you must make sure that there is never a mention of any state business."

As the next full moon approached, Princess Rujā instructed her maids to dress her in her finest because she was going to see her father. Her maids adorned her with garlands, sandalwood, gems, pearls, and other jewelry, and sent her off to meet the king. Princess Rujā's radiant beauty was so dazzling that, when she entered the Candaka Palace with her entourage, it was as if lightning were flashing against a dark cloud. She approached her father, who was surrounded by his courtiers, saluted him, and sat down to one side on a golden seat.

The king was delighted to see her. "My darling child," he greeted her warmly, "do you enjoy yourself in the tank in the royal garden? Do the servants bring you enough delicious food? Do you and your companions gather flowers and make garlands? Is there anything further you want? Whatever you ask will be immediately provided, even if we have to go to the moon to get it!"

"Sire," Rujā replied, smiling, "through your generosity, every desire of mine is gratified. Tomorrow is the full-moon day. Please grant me one thousand coins so that I may offer alms to mendicants."

"My dear child," replied the king sharply, "ask for anything for yourself, but you have already wasted a great deal of money on these beggars. There is no benefit in it! Also, I don't see why you insist on keeping these pointless Uposatha days. Rujā, you should be enjoying all the good food our cooks prepare! Enjoy yourself all the time! Everything is decided by fate, so there is absolutely no point in depriving yourself in any way. This is the only world there is, dear girl, so we might as well just relax and take it easy!"

"Oh, Father!" Rujā exclaimed. "It seems that the rumors are true! I dared not believe them until I had talked with you myself. Now I know! I'm not surprised that deluded people like Alāta and Bījaka believe such foolishness,

273

but you, Sire, are a king. You're educated, wise, and skilled in managing affairs! How have you fallen for such a low and simplistic theory, fit only for toddlers? If the passage of time alone could purify a man, then Guna's own asceticism would be absurd! If, as he says, renunciation has no benefit, why has that idiot chosen to live as a naked ascetic? He should be living the life of comfort that he is recommending for you! It makes no sense! The false doctrine that everything will automatically be purified through transmigration is dangerous. Believers can do many thoughtless and wicked things, but later, when they are caught by the effects of their evil deeds, they will find it hard to escape, like the gullible fish trying to escape from the hook.

"Sire, take Alāta as an example. Your commander-in-chief is now enjoying his high position and his prosperity because of his virtuous deeds in the past, even though he doesn't remember them. The merit he made is being spent, and he is not replacing it. As a ship that's overloaded sinks into the sea, a man who accumulates the weight of many evil deeds will sink down to perdition. Alāta's present cargo is not the material wealth he is collecting. It is his action. If he persists in doing evil, he will go down to hell.

"When more weight is put in the pan, the beam of a scales swings higher. In the same way, when, little by little, merit is accumulated, a man improves his lot. That poor slave, Bījaka, is suffering the fruit of evil deeds of his distant past, but, since he is now devoted to good deeds, his past wrongs will melt away, and he will reach the heaven he so desires. Unless, that is, he falls for Guna-Kassapa's perverted teaching and loses everything!

"One who follows a child becomes like a child himself," Princess Rujā added emphatically. "The fool who associates with fools plunges into folly. Through the power of intimacy, a wicked companion affects his friend like a poisoned arrow defiles the quiver. Thus, the wise become friendly with neither the wicked nor the foolish. Tie up rotting fish with kusa grass, and the grass soon smells putrid. Tie up sandalwood in an ordinary leaf, and the leaf absorbs the fragrance. Follow the wise and good, Father, for they will lead you to heaven, whereas the wicked will lead to hell.

"Let me describe my own experience from previous births, Sire, and you will see how our actions have consequences. Seven births ago, I was the devilish son of a blacksmith in Rājagaha, and I had an evil companion. The two of us went about seducing the wives of other men. We didn't care how many families we destroyed for we thought that we were immortal and that nothing could touch us. When I died, the force of that evil lay dormant, like embers covered with ashes. Due to the effect of many wholesome deeds from a previous birth, I was born into a wealthy merchant's family in Kosambi. As the only son, I was well brought up and educated. I had a wise friend who was honest and devoted to generosity, and he grounded me in righteousness. I carefully observed the Uposatha days with fasting and wise reflection. All that virtuous action was laid up like treasure in water.

"After that, in successive births, I reaped the fruit of the evil deeds which I had committed in Rājagaha. First, I endured a painful and wretched birth in the Roruva Hell. Then I was born as a goat in Bhennakata. I was castrated and made to carry the small sons of the wealthy on my back and to pull them in a little cart. Next, I was born as a monkey in the jungle. Soon after my birth, the leader of the troop grabbed me and bit off my testicles. After that, I was born as a bull, castrated, and forced to pull a heavy wagon, but, at least, I was strong and well taken care of. Then I gained a human birth, and I was born into a Vajjian family, but I was a hermaphrodite, neither man nor woman. The suffering of those four births was the consequence of ruining other men's wives.

"Next, Sire, I was born as a deva in Tāvatimsa. Because of the merit that I gained in Kosambi, I became an attendant in Sakka's court. The force of that merit is continuing, and I have again had the great opportunity of this royal human birth. Thus, do our actions follow us through countless births, bringing good or evil. Actions are neither erased nor lost.

"One who wishes to rise from birth to birth must avoid evil by thought, word, and deed. By applying wisdom and being ever mindful in body, speech, and mind, a person, whether man or woman, will reap the highest good. One who enjoys honor, wealth, and happiness in this world can be sure that, in a previous life, he practiced virtue and that now he is reaping the fruit of that virtue. All beings abide supported by their own actions.

"Sire, what else but your own past virtuous deeds could have enabled you to live in this wonderful palace, surrounded by luxury and with all your beautiful wives? Father, do not listen to the words of a blind naked ascetic. Listen to the words of someone who cares about you. You know that I am your friend, and you must believe me when I declare that, in both this world and the next, there are consequences of our actions. Please do not go down the wrong road!"

Despite all of her pleading and her wise teaching, Princess Rujā could not dissuade her misguided father from his false doctrine. King Angati was pleased, of course, with the thoughtful attention she paid him, and he greatly enjoyed listening to her sweet voice (What parent does not love to hear his own dear child's voice?), but he would not accept anything she said. He neither considered her arguments nor gave up any of his foolish ideas.

Although she could not herself change his mind, the princess did not lose heart. As she bowed in the ten directions, she declared, "In this universe, there are righteous teachers, devas, and Brahmās. May one who is wise come and dispel the false doctrine that has blinded my father, the great King Angati of Videha! If not by his own power, let him come by the power of my virtue!"

At that time, there was, in the Brahma heavens, a Mahā-Brahmā named Nārada. As he was surveying the world, he heard the princess' plea and realized that he was the only one who could deliver her father from his heresy. He resolved to descend to the realm of men to grant the princess' wish and to bring happiness to the king and to his subjects. To do that, he decided to visit the king disguised as an ascetic.

Nārada assumed a human form with a golden complexion and placed a golden needle in his matted hair. He wore a bright red robe with a stunning silver antelope skin decorated with golden stars draped over one shoulder. His golden almsbowl and a coral water pot were hanging from strings of pearls around his neck, and, across his shoulder, was a golden carrying-pole. He entered the Candaka Palace like the radiant moon. As soon as Princess Rujā saw the divine sage, she bowed down and paid her respects to him.

The king was so awed by the ascetic's glory that he arose from his throne and stepped off the dais. "Sir, your features are divine! Please tell us where you have come from. What is your name and family? What are you called in the realm of men?"

"I come from the Brahma heavens. I am known as Nārada Kassapa."

"How is it, Nārada, that you can stand before me in this marvelous guise?" asked the king.

"Truth, righteousness, self-control, and generosity," Nārada replied; "those were my virtues in the past. Because I diligently followed those virtues, I can now go as swift as thought wherever I wish."

"You speak of other realms and of rewards for virtues practiced in the past, but my teacher has told me that these are mere illusions," protested the king. "Your presence fills my mind with many doubts, and I would ask you many questions."

"Ask me what you wish, Sire," Nārada told him. "I will assuredly resolve your doubts with reasoning and logic."

"All right, let me ask you," the king began, "are there other realms from which we have come and to which we go? Are there really rewards and consequences for our actions, good and bad?"

"Indeed, Your Majesty, there are other realms. Everything you do has consequences in those other realms. Because of greed and infatuation with pleasure, people are deluded into thinking that this realm is all there is."

The king laughed mockingly and replied, "If you believe in another realm, a dwelling place for the dead, then give me five hundred coins here, and I'll give you one thousand in the next realm!"

"Foolish king!" Nārada chided him in front of the entire court, "if I knew you to be honest and virtuous, I would gladly give you five hundred coins. In the next life, however, if you were roasting in hell, no one would demand repayment of the one thousand coins or even the original five hundred! In this realm, if a man is idle, cruel, and wicked, wise men do not lend money to him. There is no return from such a debtor. If, on the other hand, a man is skillful, active, and virtuous, many will lend him as much as he needs, knowing that he will faithfully repay his debt."

Soundly rebuked, but still unconvinced, the king made no answer.

The courtiers shouted in delight and praised the princess, whose virtue was rescuing the king from the dire consequences of his false doctrine. Indeed, everyone in Mithilā rejoiced as they listened to the teaching of the wise Nārada, who by his supernatural power was projecting his voice seven yojanas beyond Mithilā.

"Sire," Nārada continued, "if you refuse to abandon your false doctrine, you will surely go to hell! When you first arrive in the infernal regions, ravenous crows, vultures, and hawks will tear hunks of flesh from your body with their sharp beaks and razor-like talons. Who would go there to ask you for one thousand coins?

"From there you must wander through a vast region of utter emptiness, where no light has ever shone nor any sound been heard. The darkness is without relief. Who would go there to ask you for one thousand coins?

"Sire, if you refuse to abandon your false doctrine, you will surely be dragged from the infernal antechamber into one of the many hells that await. Let me describe something of the tortures you will endure.

"In Lokantara, the two fierce hounds, Sabala and Sama, hold a victim with their mighty jaws and shake him senseless, and with their iron teeth they rip his body to shreds again and again.

"In Kalupakala, the victim is pierced by arrows, spears, javelins, and heavy spikes which indefatigable wardens throw at him from above. Covered with blood, his entrails protruding from the slash across his belly, he stumbles on to suffer showers of burning coals and flaming streams of lava. Hotter even than these is the desiccating wind that blows without relief. Who would go there to ask you for one thousand coins?

"Some victims are yoked to wagons and forced to pull impossible loads over fiery ground, all the while being goaded on and whipped. Others are forced to climb a mountain studded with razors, while their bodies drip with blood. Still other are forced to climb a mountain of burning coals, and their bodies, charred beyond belief, never cease burning. Who would go there to ask you for one thousand coins?

"For adulterers, there is a towering silk-cotton tree, its trunk a mass of spikes, which they are forced to climb, driven by Yama's servants who prod them with spears. The victims cry out in pain as, with every step, their bodies are pierced, and they are showered with the blood from those above. Who would go there to ask you for one thousand coins?

"When a victim leaves those hells, he falls into the boiling river Vetarani, which is covered with burning lotuses whose leaves are as sharp as razors. Struggling against the rapid current, lest he fall to a worse fate, the swimmer's limbs are burned and slashed anew, and still the bloody water boils. Who would go there to ask you for one thousand coins?"

Nārada's description of these hells so frightened the king that he could barely speak. "I am trembling like a tree that is being cut down!" he cried. "I don't know which way to turn! Oh, wise Nārada! Be my refuge like a lamp in the darkness or like an island in a stormy ocean! I see that my past has been full of sins! Teach me the truth! Show me the path of purity, Nārada, that I may not fall into hell!"

"Consider the famous kings of the past," Nārada proclaimed. "Dhatarattha, Vessāmitta, Atthaka, Yāmataggi, Usinnara, and Sivi! All practiced righteousness and were reborn in Sakka's heaven. Like them, you should rule justly and be generous. Feed those who are hungry, give to those in need, and clothe the poor. Teach your people to care tenderly for their elders. Even aged oxen, horses, and elephants should be honored because they fulfilled their duty when young and strong."

"Think of your body as a chariot. Your mind is the charioteer. Non-harming is the axle. Generosity is the decorative covering. Absence of conceit is the yoke. Humility is the pole. The restraint of the five precepts is the rope. Detachment is the cushion. Right speech keeps the chariot running smoothly and prevents the wheels from rattling. Desire and lust are the evil path to hell, but, if the horses are well-trained, they will follow the straight path of self-control. As we rush through the sensory realm of forms, sounds, and smells, the mind holds the reins of steadfastness to guide the horses with wisdom and heedfulness, thereby avoiding pitfalls and staying on the path to heaven and away from hell."

Having completely dispelled the false doctrine, Nārada established King Anjati in the moral precepts. He further advised the king to eschew evil friends and to associate with the virtuous. He praised the wise Princess

Rujā and exhorted the entire court to live righteously. Having successfully accomplished his mission, Nārada returned to the Brahma heavens.

Having concluded his story, the Buddha identified the birth: "At that time, Devadatta was Alāta, Bhaddaji was Sunāma, Sāriputta was Vijaya, Moggallāna was Bījaka, Sunakkhatta was Guna-Kassapa, Ānanda was Princess Rujā, Uruvela-Kassapa was King Angati, and I was Nārada, the Mahā-Brahmā."

215
The Wise Vidhura-Pandita
Vidhura-Pandita Jātaka

It was while staying at Jetavana that the Buddha told this story about the Perfection of Wisdom.

One day, in the Hall of Truth, several bhikkhus were talking about the Buddha's wisdom. "Our Master's wisdom is so great," they said, "that he can shatter an opponent's arguments, overturn his subtlest questions, and reduce him to silence. By the time the Buddha finishes teaching, he has established his adversary in the refuges and precepts and has started him on the path which leads to Nibbāna."

When the Buddha heard what they were discussing, he said, "It is not remarkable, Bhikkhus, that the Tathāgata, who has perfected wisdom, should be able to overturn the arguments of his opponents and to convert them. He was able to do this even while he was still striving for supreme knowledge. Indeed, in the time of Vidhura-Pandita, on the summit of the Black Mountain, I converted the yakkha Punnaka and prevented him from committing a hideous mistake, which would have sent him to hell." At their request, the Buddha told this story of the past.

Long, long ago, in Bārānasi, the capital of Kāsi, there were four wealthy brahmins who renounced the world and retired to the Himavat to practice meditation. Once, as the rains were beginning, they left to get salt and vinegar and to find a place to spend the rainy season.

When the ascetics arrived in Campā, the capital of Anga, four men, living near each other, greeted them, offered them food, and invited them to stay in their gardens. The ascetics accepted, and each took up residence in one of the gardens. Every day, however, after taking their meals, the four ascetics, by means of their extraordinary powers, flew off and spent the day elsewhere. The first went to Tāvatimsa; the second, to the realm of the nāgas; the third, to the realm of the garulas; and the fourth, to Indapatta, the capital of Kuru. At the end of the day, the ascetics returned to their respective gardens, and each described to his patron the particular delights of his sojourn. The first praised the magnificence of Sakka and the Heaven of the Thirty-three; the second, the opulence of the nāga king and his palace; the third, the splendor of the garula king and his realm; and the fourth, King Dhanañjaya and his royal park. The king's chief advisor, the fourth ascetic said, was a wise man named Vidhura-Pandita. Vidhura-Pandita's voice was so sweet that kings visiting Indapatta, like elephants fascinated by the sound of a melodious lute, often extended their stay in the city just to hear his eloquent discourses.

At the end of the rainy season, the four ascetics returned to the Himavat. They continued practicing meditation and, when they died, were reborn in the Brahma heavens.

The four laymen continued practicing generosity and performing other good deeds in Campā. They had been strongly impressed by the ascetics who had stayed in their gardens. Each of the laymen was so attracted to the particular place which he had heard praised that, when he died, he was reborn there. The first was reborn as Sakka, the second was reborn as a nāga king named Varuna, the third was reborn as a king of the garulas, and the fourth was conceived by the chief queen of King Dhanañjaya.

When King Dhanañjaya died, that son, also called Dhanañjaya, became king and ruled well. He was famous for his skill at dice, but most important for the welfare of the kingdom was the fact that he retained his father's chief advisor, the wise Vidhura-Pandita.

Following Vidhura-Pandita's counsel, the young king gave alms, kept the precepts, and observed the Uposatha days. On one particular Uposatha day, unable to concentrate his mind in the palace, he retired to the royal park, seated himself in a pleasant spot, and began meditating. At the same time, Sakka, Varuna, and the garula king were also having difficulty meditating in their respective realms. All three descended on Indapatta, seated themselves in the royal park, and began meditating.

In the evening, having finished their meditation, the four happened to meet at the lake in the center of the park. Feeling affection from their previous lives, they exchanged pleasant greetings and sat down to talk.

"All four of us are now kings," Sakka began. "What is the preeminent virtue of each of us?"

"Even though this garula king is the traditional enemy of all nāgas," the nāga king replied, "when I see such a hostile foe, I feel no anger. One who feels no anger toward another who deserves anger, who never lets anger arise within him, and who, even when angered, does not allow his anger to be known, can truly be called an ascetic. This is my virtue, and I am certain that it is superior to all of yours."

"Ah, but this nāga is a garula's main diet," retorted the garula king. "Nevertheless, even though there is such food in front of me, I endure my hunger. One who bears the pangs of hunger, who, self-restrained, eats and drinks according to the rules, and who commits no evil for the sake of food, can truly be called an ascetic. This is my virtue, and I am certain that it is superior to all of yours."

"In order to maintain my virtue," Sakka said, "I left behind unsurpassed heavenly luxury and came to this vulgar realm of men. One who abandons all pleasure, who eschews pomp and sensual delights, and who utters no false word, can truly be called an ascetic. This is my virtue, and I am certain that it is superior to all of yours."

"In order to practice meditation in this garden today," King Dhanañjaya said, "I left my entire court, including sixteen thousand beautiful dancers. One who, with full knowledge, abandons all he owns, who relinquishes all lust, and who unselfishly practices self-restraint and strong determination, can truly be called an ascetic. This is my virtue, and I am certain that it is superior to all of yours."

As long as each continued to claim that his own virtue was the greatest, they could come to no agreement. Finally, the other three turned to King Dhanañjaya and asked, "Is there anyone here in your court wise enough to resolve this matter for us?"

"Certainly," King Dhanañjaya replied. "My chief advisor, Vidhura-Pandita, is exceedingly wise. He is fully competent and qualified to resolve our doubts. Let us go to him."

The four kings left the garden together and proceeded to the hall for religious assemblies. Vidhura-Pandita took his prescribed seat, and the four kings sat at his feet. "Wise sir," King Dhanañjaya began, acting as spokesman for the group, "we four kings find ourselves in disagreement. We would like you to listen and to resolve the issue for us. We would like to know which of us possesses the greatest virtue."

"Please state your positions. I will answer as best I can," Vidhura-Pandita responded.

"Well," King Dhanañjaya continued, "the nāga king upholds forbearance, the garula king upholds gentleness, Sakka upholds abstinence from sensual pleasure, and I uphold freedom from all hindrances."

"These virtues," Vidhura-Pandita declared, "are like spokes of a wheel. They are essentially the same, and none can be said to be superior to another. One who is endowed with these four virtues is unquestionably an ascetic supreme."

The four monarchs were delighted with this perceptive answer. "Incomparable!" they cried. "With your wisdom, you are both a knower and a guardian of the law. Instantly, you grasped the problem we posed, and you have completely eliminated our doubts."

To further express their appreciation, they each presented Vidhura-Pandita with a valuable gift. Sakka gave him a robe of heavenly silk, the garula king placed a golden garland around his neck, the nāga king offered him an exquisite gem, and King Dhanañjaya gave him one thousand head of cattle. Then each returned to his own palace.

As soon as the nāga king had returned to his palace, Vimalā, his queen, noticed that he was not wearing his special jeweled pendant, and she asked him where it was. "In the palace of the king of Kuru, I heard a discourse by Vidhura-Pandita, his wise advisor. The discourse was so pleasing that I immediately offered him the gem. I was not alone. Sakka gave him a heavenly robe, the king of the garulas gave him a golden garland, and King Dhanañjaya gave him one thousand head of cattle."

"He must be eloquent in preaching the law," Queen Vimalā replied.

"Lady, that is a great understatement! His speech is magnificent, and his wisdom is beyond compare. Kings from all over Jambudīpa are so enthralled by his voice that they flock to that court and forget to return home. They are like wild elephants fascinated by a melodious lute!"

Hearing this praise for Vidhura-Pandita, Queen Vimalā found herself longing to hear one of his discourses. She was sure that her husband would never agree to bring the advisor to the nāga realm or to take her to the human realm, so she wondered how she might contrive to hear him. As she performed her usual duties, she continued to think about this and, at last, devised a plan. She summoned her maids and took to her bed.

The king noticed the queen's absence and asked her attendants where she was. They replied that she was ill. He immediately visited her room, sat on the side of her bed, and massaged her back. "My dear," he said tenderly, "you seem pale and weak. What ailment has come upon you?"

"Dear husband," she replied, feigning weakness, "I am suffering a woman's affliction. It is called a craving. I long to have Vidhura-Pandita's heart brought here, but it must be done without any guile."

"Beloved!" the king cried unbelievingly. "You are longing for the moon or the wind. The very sight of Vidhura-Pandita is difficult to obtain. Who can possibly bring him here?"

"If I do not get what I crave," she sobbed, "I will surely die!" Pretending to be in great distress, she rolled over in her bed with her back to her husband and covered her face with her robe.

King Varuna was troubled by his wife's illness. He went to his own chamber, sat on his bed, and wondered what to do. He certainly did not want his wife to die, but he had no idea how he might get Vidhura-Pandita's heart.

At that moment, his daughter, the lovely Princess Irandatī, wearing her finest ornaments, entered the room to pay her respects to her father. Sensing that something was bothering him, she asked what the problem was.

"My dear," he replied, "your mother longs for the heart of Vidhura-Pandita, the chief advisor of King Dhanañjaya. Even to see that wise man is difficult. I cannot imagine how to bring him here or who could do it."

As Irandatī tried to comfort her father, he suddenly sat up straight. "Wait a minute!" he cried, looking her straight in the eye. "No one in my court can bring Vidhura here, but you can save your mother! Daughter, you must find a husband who can bring Vidhura-Pandita to our realm! Yes! That is what you must do!" he repeated as he sent her away. As soon as Irandatī had left, the king hurried to inform the queen of his plan.

Excited at the prospect of following her father's improper suggestion, Princess Irandatī gave free rein to her passionate nature. She gathered colorful, fragrant flowers from the Himavat, scattered them all around an elegant couch set up on a hilltop, and began a sensual dance. In an alluringly sweet voice she sang, "What magical being—yakkha, nāga, or man—will consent to be my husband and share this couch with me tonight?"

At that moment, a yakkha general named Punnaka, the nephew of the great yakkha king, Vessavana, was on his way to an assembly. As he was passing over Black Mountain on his magical Sindh horse, he recognized the princess' sweet voice as one he had heard in a previous life, and it pierced him like a spear, penetrating to the very marrow. He instantly turned his horse and shouted in response to her song, "Be comforted, peerless lady! I will be your husband! I will do whatever you ask, and you will be my wife!"

"Come with me to my father," Irandatī invited him, drawing upon the experience of wooing in a previous life. "You can discuss this matter with him."

As Punnaka approached the hilltop where she was standing, she took his hand and led him into her father's presence. After formal greetings, Punnaka declared, "Your Majesty, I wish to marry your daughter, and I will offer fitting presents for the fair Irandatī. A dowry of one hundred elephants, one hundred horses, and one hundred wagons filled with precious gems—all this will I give for your daughter's hand!"

"Something done in haste leads afterwards to regret," King Varuna replied. "Please wait while I consult with my relatives."

When he told Queen Vimalā of Punnaka's offer, she reminded him of his instructions to Irandatī. "Our daughter is not to be won by treasure. Her husband must be the one who can, by his own honest effort, bring the sage's heart to us. Only in that way can he win Princess Irandatī. We want no further treasure than that."

The nāga king returned to where Punnaka was patiently waiting and announced, "We have no need of your treasure. We ask but one task in return for our fair Irandatī. If you can bring to us the heart of a sage, you will have won the princess, and we will ask no more."

Punnaka replied, "Your Majesty, the man which some call a sage others will call a fool. Who is this sage whose heart you so desire?"

"I speak of Vidhura-Pandita, the chief advisor of King Dhanañjaya in Indapatta, the capital of Kuru. Bring that sage's heart to Queen Vimalā, and Irandatī will be your lawful wife."

Delighted at the prospect, Punnaka ordered his attendant to bring him his magnificent Sindh steed and sped away toward the yakkha realm to notify his uncle, King Vessavana, of his intentions and to obtain his permission. When Punnaka arrived, his uncle was very busy settling a dispute between two young devas who were both claiming a palace. Without interrupting and fully aware that King Vessavana was not listening to him, Punnaka softly but eloquently described the glories of the land of the nāgas and the beauty of Princess Irandatī. "So, you see," Punnaka concluded, "Queen Vimalā desires the heart of the sage Vidhura-Pandita. I will take it to them, Sire, and they will give me Princess Irandatī for my wife."

As Punnaka was talking, he was also carefully following the progress of the case his uncle was judging. When Punnaka concluded his speech, he moved to stand close to the disputant who was certain to win. King Vessavana turned to the young deva to declare his decision and, looking directly at both the deva and Punnaka, said, "Go then, and live in your palace." As soon as the word "Go" had been uttered, Punnaka called some other young devas. "You are my witnesses," he said to them. "You heard my uncle tell me to go as he sent me on my mission! Thank you!" Then, saying, "Thank you!" once more, he bowed to his uncle and jumped on his faithful steed.

As he was flying through the air, he pondered, "Vidhura-Pandita has a great retinue. Obviously, he cannot be taken by force, and Queen Vimala has stipulated that the sage must be gained honestly. What to do? Ah! I've heard that King Dhananjaya likes gambling and is very proud of his skill. All I need to do to take Vidhura-Pandita from him is beat him in a game of dice. Now what could I offer as my stake? The king already has so many treasures in his palace that he won't play for just anything. I need something of great rarity and value. Yes! I've got it!" he shouted as he quickly turned his steed toward Vepulla Mountain. From the top of this mountain near Rājagaha he plucked an enormous, unique gem, which sparkled like lightning in the night sky. Clutching the gem and confident of success, he flew to Indapatta.

Dismounting in the courtyard of the palace, the fearless yakkha shouted his challenge to the warriors gathered there: "Who wants to win the prize of kings from us? Or perhaps we ourselves will win a peerless jewel!"

Excited at the thought of a new gambling opponent, King Dhananjaya looked out the window. "Who are you?" he asked. "We can tell by your speech that you are not from Kuru. You surpass us in appearance, and your boldness is remarkable. Where are you from? What kingdom do you represent?"

"If I tell the king who I really am," Punnaka thought, "he will look down on me as no more than a servant." Aloud he replied, "Sire, I am named Kaccāyana," recalling his identity in the previous birth. "I come from a noble family of Anga. I have come here for the sake of a game of chance."

"What do you propose to wager, friend Kaccāyana?"

"I have here a priceless jewel, a magnificent stone which can bring untold wealth to its owner. The gambler who defeats me can also claim this peerless steed on which he could defeat any enemy."

"Young man!" the king laughed scornfully. "What is one jewel to us? Our treasure house is overflowing with the finest gems. And what is one thoroughbred, however fine? Our stables are full of steeds, all as swift as the wind!"

"Sire," Punnaka replied, "I beg your pardon, but you are wrong. There is one horse, and there are one hundred thousand horses. All the world's horses together are not equal to this one. Watch this!"

Punnaka quickly mounted his horse, flipped the reins, and flew to the top of the city wall. Suddenly, it seemed that the rampart was surrounded by horses racing neck and neck. As his speed increased, neither the horse nor rider could be distinguished. Only the bright red sash tied around Punnaka's waist was visible as a single red line running around the city.

Dismounting once more in the courtyard, Punnaka sent the incredible horse toward the lotus pond, where it galloped over the surface of the water without getting its hooves wet. Then he made the horse walk gently on the leaves of the lotuses. Finally, he clapped his hands and stretched out his arm. The marvelous horse instantly leapt up and stood serenely with all four hooves on the palm of his hand.

"This, Sire, is indeed a jewel of a horse!"

"Indeed it is, young man!"

"Now, Sire, behold this precious gem. Within this stone, you can find the entire world. Everything that exists is in this jewel.

"Here are kings, elephants, horses, and an entire army.

"Created in this jewel is a complete city with gates and walls, streets and crossroads, buildings and palaces with gardens and ponds, markets, shops and merchants, garland weavers, cooks, jewelers, and gold workers.

"Behold within this priceless gem wrestlers, jugglers, poets, and barbers, as well as crowds of men, women, and children.

"Here you can see flocks of swallows, parrots, warblers, eagles, herons, cranes—birds of every species.

"On the mountain slopes, look at all the deer, wild boar, rhinos, buffaloes, antelopes, lions, tigers, bears, wolves, hyenas, and rabbits. In fact, all kinds of beasts are created in the jewel.

"Now see the four quarters of the earth. Here are all the lakes, covered with birds and abounding with fish. Here are all the oceans, interspersed with great mountains, jungles, deserts, and plains.

"Watch the sun and the moon, shining on the four sides, as they go around Mount Sineru inside this jewel.

"Not only Sineru but also the Himavat and the heaven of the Four Great Kings are all created in this gem.

"Here you will find Tāvatimsa, including Sakka's incomparable Sudhamma Hall, his elephant Erāvana, and the Pāricchattaka tree in full bloom

"Behold within this magnificent gem all the heavens—Tāvatimsa, Yama, Tusita, Paranimmita, and more—with all their celestial palaces covered with lapis lazuli and all the devas dwelling there.

"Behold this gem, Your Majesty. This incomparable jewel, perfect in all its facets, will grant any wish to its owner. This is the prize I offer. If I lose, I will give you my magnificent horse and this precious jewel. If I win, what will you give me?"

Overwhelmed by the power of the gem, the king replied, "I will wager everything I own, except myself and my white umbrella."

"Very well, Sire. Let's not delay. I have come a great distance. Let the gaming room be got ready."

The king ordered his ministers to spread a carpet in the gambling hall for his throne, to prepare a suitable seat for Punnaka, and to arrange chairs for the one hundred visiting kings.

"My jewel is worth much more than what you are wagering," Punnaka warned, "but let us play fairly, without violence. When you have lost, you must pay up."

"Young man, have no fear," the king replied. "Although I am the ruler here, all gambling will be completely fair, with neither force nor violence."

Punnaka called on the other kings to witness that the game was to be played fairly, without cheating, and all proceeded to the gambling hall, where golden dice were placed on the silver board.

"Your Majesty," Punnaka said graciously, "there are twenty-four throws of the dice. Choose the one that pleases you the most."

King Dhanañjaya announced his choice, and Punnaka chose a different throw.

"Young man, you throw first," said the king.

"Sire, the first throw does not belong to me. You play first."

The king consented and picked up the dice.

The secret to the king's great gambling success was that his mother in a previous existence had become his guardian deity. Whenever the king played a game of dice, she was close by, and it was because of her power that the king always managed to win. As the king rubbed the dice in his cupped hand, he remembered her and hummed a tune. Then he confidently threw them into the air.

Punnaka used his power to make the dice fall so that the king would lose, but the king, with his keenness and visual acuity, immediately recognized that the dice were falling against him and seized them before they hit the board. He carefully rubbed them in his hand and tossed them once more into the air. Again, he could tell that they were going against him, and he caught them before they could touch the board.

Punnaka wondered how the king was able to know that he would lose and to catch the dice before they fell. As he gazed around the room, he recognized the guardian deva and gave her a fierce look, which so frightened her that she fled trembling to the top of Mount Cakkavala.

When the king threw the dice the third time, he knew that they would fall against him, but, without his guardian to help and restrained by Punnaka's formidable power, he could not catch the dice, and they hit the board.

Punnaka gleefully seized the dice and threw a winning combination.

As soon as the dice fell, Punnaka clapped his hands loudly and cried, "I have won! I have won! I have won!" That shout was heard throughout Jambudīpa.[17]

King Dhanañjaya could not believe that he had lost so quickly. As he sat bewildered, staring at the dice board, Punnaka declared, "Your Majesty, in any contest, there is always both victory and defeat. Unfortunately, you have lost a great prize. Now, Sire, please pay what you wagered!"

"Elephants, oxen, horses, chariots, gold, and jewels," the king solemnly intoned. "Take my wealth, and go where you wish!"

"Elephants, oxen, horses, chariots, gold, and jewels," Punnaka repeated. "These are common. I have no need of them. Of all that you own, your advisor, Vidhura-Pandita, is the best. He is the prize I claim. Give him to me!"

"Sir! Vidhura-Pandita is my minister, my refuge, my shelter, my fortress, and my defense. My advisor is not to be weighed against wealth. He is my family, my very life. Furthermore, he is not mine to give."

"Not yours, you say! We could debate long about this, but let us go to him and have him decide the matter. We can both abide by his judgment."

"Yes, by all means. That is fair and just. Let us go immediately and ask him. In that way, we will both be satisfied."

The entire assembly hurried to the Hall of Justice, where they found the royal advisor. Punnaka at once addressed him, "Wise Vidhura-Pandita, your reputation has spread throughout the entire world. Everyone knows that you are resolute and just and that you would not lie, even to save your life. Today, let us see whether you really are as honest as your fame implies. Are you a relative of the king, or are you his property?"

"In this world there is no protection like the truth," Vidhura-Pandita said to himself. Aloud he proclaimed, "Young man, some are born servants, some become servants for money, some choose freely to be servants, and some do so from fear. As for me, I am the king's servant, his slave, his property. He may dispose of me as he wishes."

Punnaka clapped his hands once more and shouted, "This is my second victory today, Sire! Your advisor has answered your question." Then, seeing a note of hesitation on the king's face, he continued, "But, Sire, can it be that

17 Four great sounds that were heard throughout Jambudipa were made by Mahā-Kanha (Tale 181), Ālavaka (q.v. in The Glossary of Personal Names in the Appendix), Kusa (Tale 206), and Punnaka.

you, the best of kings, are unjust? The decision has been made, but, perhaps, you will not surrender him to me."

"Obviously, you have little regard for your king," King Dhanañjaya snarled at his advisor. "Surely, you must want to follow this young man who has caught your eye!" Turning to Punnaka, he said, "If Vidhura-Pandita is indeed a slave, take him, and go. My chief advisor has answered your question to your liking. Take Vidhura, whom I regard as the best of treasures, and go wherever you wish!"

Almost immediately, the king reflected on what he had said. "This youth will soon take away the great man. After he is gone, I will no longer be able to hear his sweet discourses on holy matters. While I still have the chance, let me ask him to resolve all my questions."

"Sage," he said aloud, "I have been hasty. After you have gone, I will no longer be able to discuss important matters with you or to hear your sweet voice. Would you be so kind as to take your proper place and to expound to me for one last time about the householder's life?"

"Certainly, Your Majesty," Vidhura-Pandita agreed as he seated himself on the dais. "Let me tell you how a householder can have a prosperous life, how he can be free from suffering, and how he can escape sorrow in the next world.

"To have harmony at home, let there be understanding between husband and wife. The householder should avoid wasting time in vain conversation for this does nothing to increase wisdom. The wise person is virtuous, faithful to his duties, careful, humble, kind, compassionate, gentle, skilled in winning friends, and always ready to give. He is open-handed toward those in need and toward those who deserve—the ascetics and the learned. In this way, he will lead a prosperous life at home, and he will be well-regarded by others. Thus, he will not only avoid suffering in this life, but he will have a fortunate rebirth and escape sorrow in the next world."

Having concluded his discourse, Vidhura-Pandita stepped down from the dais and saluted the king. The king paid great honor to his wise advisor and retired with his guests.

Punnaka, who had all this time been waiting patiently, signaled to Vidhura-Pandita and said, "Come. I am ready to leave. You were given to me by the king, so it is your duty to come with me."

"Young man," the sage replied, "I know that you defeated the king and that I have been given to you. I will gladly go with you, but I must prepare my sons for my going. Please let me lodge you for three days in my home before we go."

Punnaka realized that this was only proper. Furthermore, he felt that staying with the wise man would be of great benefit to himself, as well. He would have agreed even if the sage had asked for a week or a fortnight.

"Let us both take advantage of these three days," he said aloud. "Do whatever needs to be done at home. Prepare your family for your leaving. Instruct your sons and your wife so that they can manage without you."

Vidhura-Pandita had a chamber prepared for the yakkha and ordered delicious food and drink. Attendants were assigned to look after him, and accomplished women played musical instruments and danced to entertain him.

Having arranged everything to make the yakkha comfortable, Vidhura-Pandita escorted him into the presence of his wife Anujja and said, "Fair lady, call your sons here."

Anujja turned to her daughter-in-law and ordered, "Please call the family together."

When all the sons and daughters had gathered, she announced, "Your father wishes to give you an exhortation. This will be your last chance to see him."

Dhammapala, the eldest son, immediately began to cry and ran to embrace his father. Vidhura-Pandita pressed his eldest to his heart, but, quickly surrounded by all his other sons, he was unable to maintain his composure. His eyes swelled with tears and he kissed each one on the head.

Then, asking them to return to their places, he sat on a couch on a raised platform and gave them his parting advice.

"I have been given by the king to this young man. From now on, I am subject to him, but he has granted me this time to be with you. Indeed, how could I go without giving you some final instruction?

"If you should be asked what your father taught first and foremost, let it be that you should not grieve. All material things are impermanent, and all success ends in failure!

"Now, let me tell you how to obtain favor in a king's court. A man does not win honor if he is unknown nor if he is foolish, thoughtless, or a coward. When a monarch learns of a man's moral qualities, his wisdom, and his purity of heart, he may come to trust him and may confide his secrets to him. When one is asked to carry out some business for the king, he must not hesitate. If one is willing to undertake any burden and to do the king's business at any time of day or night, he may succeed in a king's court.

"To serve his king, one must not enjoy the same pleasures as the king, and he must let the king lead in everything while he himself follows respectfully behind.

"To succeed in a king's court, a man must not dress like the king or even use the same tone of voice.

"Even if the king jokes with his ministers or his wives, let the courtier make no allusion to the royal ladies. Only a man who is prudent, who controls his senses, and who possesses insight and resolution may succeed in a king's court.

"In serving the king, a man must never speak with the king's wives nor take money from the treasury. He must not be concerned about his own sleep nor touch a drop of alcohol. Such a man may succeed in a king's court.

"Never, not even for a moment, should one sit on the throne or on the king's elephant. Never should he step into the royal chariot. Never let him regard himself as a privileged person. He must prudently stay neither too near to nor yet too far from the king.

"The king should not be regarded as an ordinary person, nor should he be compared to anyone else. Kings are easily irritated. A king can be as sensitive as an eye brushed by a barley bristle.

"The wise man must never feel confident that he is trusted or honored by his king. Not placing his trust in the king, he is always alert and on his guard, as in the case of fire. Such a man may succeed in a king's court.

"When the king gives presents or increases wages, the wise man says nothing to interfere. Like a fish, he has no tongue. He keeps his belly small and bends easily like bamboo. If a man never goes against the king, he may survive in a king's court.

"One must be careful to keep his distance from a spy. Looking to his own lord alone, he must owe allegiance to no other. Such a man may succeed in a king's court.

"A man must neither speak too much, nor stay too silent. He should speak neither idly nor foolishly. When it is necessary to speak, his words should be concise, measured, truthful, and gentle. One must never let himself be given to anger nor be quick to take offence. He should neither gossip nor utter any slanderous remarks. Such a man may succeed in a king's court.

"If one is educated, skillful, self-controlled, experienced in business, moderate, and careful, he may succeed in a king's court.

"If one is humble, respectful of the elderly, compassionate, pleasant to live with, and ready to obey, he may succeed in a king's court.

"Let him pay his respects to ascetics and teachers who are virtuous and learned, waiting carefully on them and generously offering them gifts. Such a man may succeed in a king's court.

"One must be virtuous, wise, energetic, and free from greed. Devoted to his king, he must seek only his king's interest. Such a man may succeed in a king's court.

"If asked to make his salutation to a jar full of water or to offer reverential greeting to a crow, he must do so. Such a man may succeed in a king's court.

"Generous to all petitioners, he will give away his bed, his garments, his carriage, and his house. Like a cloud, he will shower blessings on all beings. Such a man may succeed in a king's court.

"My sons," he concluded, "this is how a man must behave to obtain favor and honor and to succeed in a king's court. Heed my advice that you may be successful and gain for yourselves great honor."

The three days with his sons, members of his household, friends, and neighbors passed quickly. Early in the morning of the last day, Vidhura-Pandita went to the palace to take his leave of the king.

Accompanied by kinsmen and friends, he bowed to the king, stood on one side, and uttered his final words of counsel: "The young man who beat you at dice is taking me away now. Please look after my sons and whatever property I have so that my family does not perish. When the earth is firm, all on it remains firm, but, when the earth trembles, that which is on it also trembles. I am afraid that, when I leave, my kin will fall. This is my great failing. I depend on you to support them."

"Wise sage, please do not go!" King Dhanañjaya pleaded. "You don't have to go. I will summon the young man on some pretext, and we can kill him. No one need know."

"Sire!" Vidhura-Pandita exclaimed. "Such an intention is not worthy of you! Do not allow such an unrighteous thought to enter your mind. It would be an ignoble and sinful act, which would send the doer straight to hell! I have no hatred for him, nor should you. Devote yourself to goodness, both worldly and spiritual. Farewell."

After bidding farewell to the king's household and court, Vidhura-Pandita turned and left. Many in the court burst into tears. A great cry went up from the streets as the sage walked away. Some, however, remembered what he had taught them and said calmly, "The wise Vidhura-Pandita told us that we must not sorrow. All material things are transitory. Let us be zealous in almsgiving and in other good deeds."

Vidhura-Pandita found Punnaka already mounted on his horse and announced that he was ready to do as his new master wished.

"Don't be afraid," Punnaka told him. "Just take hold of the tail of my noble steed. This will be your last sight of the realm of the living."

"Why should I be afraid?" Vidhura-Pandita asked. "How can I come to misfortune when I have done no evil to anyone by body, speech, or thought?"

With strong determination, he wrapped his robe tightly around himself and grasped the horse's tail firmly, pressed his feet against the horse's thighs, and said calmly: "I have hold of the tail. Do as you wish."

At once, the marvelous horse bounded into the sky.

Seeing the sage being thus carried away, Vidhura-Pandita's sons and many townsfolk rushed to the king's palace and shouted, "Sire, now we know that that was no ordinary youth, but a yakkha in disguise who has carried off Vidhura-Pandita. How can we live without the sage? If he does not return within seven days, we will collect cartloads of wood, build a fire, and throw ourselves into the flames."

"Fear not!" said the king. "With his honeyed speech, the sage will soon captivate the youth. As soon as that yakkha hears one of his religious discourses, he will fall at the feet of the sage and bring him back to us. Don't worry! The sage is wise, learned, and skillful. He will quickly free himself, and we can live peacefully and happily once more."

When Punnaka reached Black Mountain, he set Vidhura-Pandita on top of the mountain and pondered what to do. It was only the sage's heart that he needed, so he had to kill him, take his heart back to Queen Vimalā in the nāga realm, and claim the lovely Irandatī as his bride. Rather than kill the sage with his bare hands, he thought it would be better to frighten him to death. Punnaka assumed the form of a hideous yakkha, seized Vidhura-Pandita with his fangs, and made as if to devour him. Vidhura-Pandita was unfazed; not a single hair on his head was disturbed.

Punnaka attacked him as a ferocious lion and as an enraged elephant, but Vidhura-Pandita still displayed no fear. Transforming himself into a gigantic cobra, Punnaka hissed and coiled his body around the sage, but this made no impression whatsoever on him. Punnaka created a wind as strong as a cyclone which would have destroyed an entire village, but Vidhura-Pandita never flinched. In the form of a mighty bull elephant, Punnaka shook the mountain as though it were a wild palm tree, but the sage evinced not a single sign of fear. Punnaka crawled inside the mountain and created a tremendous roar which filled heaven and earth, but Vidhura-Pandita seemed not even to hear it, for he knew that all these forms and phenomena were transformations of the yakkha and nothing more.

"Obviously I can't frighten him to death," Punnaka declared. "I will have to kill him outright."

Punnaka went to the foot of the mountain and suddenly penetrated to the very center, like thread passing through the eye of a needle or a perforated jewel. With a ferocious roar, he exited like an arrow from the top of the mountain, seized Vidhura-Pandita by the feet, and whirled him around, preparing to fling him headfirst into the abyss.

Hanging there, with his head downwards, as if he were on the rim of hell, Vidhura-Pandita spoke calmly to Punnaka. "You are base by nature, although you assumed, for a time, a noble form. Now you are committing a cruel and monstrous deed. Why do you want to kill me by throwing me off this precipice? Your appearance suggests something superhuman. Tell me, what kind of deva are you?"

Punnaka paused to answer: "You may have heard of the yakkha Punnaka, nephew of King Vessavana. I am he. I have fallen in love with the beautiful Irandatī, daughter of the mighty nāga king, Varuna. To win the hand of Irandatī, I must kill you."

"What does my death have to do with your marriage?"

"When I asked King Varuna for the hand of his daughter, he told me that I could have her as my bride if I brought Queen Vimalā your heart, fairly obtained. They asked for no other gifts. Nothing has been misunderstood. That is why I have to kill you. After I have thrown you from this mountain, I will take your heart to Queen Vimalā."

In an instant, Vidhura-Pandita understood exactly what had happened. He realized that Queen Vimalā was not actually asking for his heart but for his teaching and that Punnaka's misunderstanding could end in disaster.

"Young man," Vidhura-Pandita said, "I know the law as followed by good men. Please put me down and listen to the law. After that, you may do what you will."

"This law has never before been declared to devas or men," Punnaka reflected. "This is indeed a rare chance, which I should not miss." Deliberately and carefully placing the sage back on the mountain top, he said, "Teacher, I need your heart, but I have brought you back from this precipice, so please teach me the law of good men."

"Certainly," Vidhura-Pandita replied, "but my body is dirty. I must bathe before I speak."

Punnaka agreed and brought water, celestial garments, and perfumes. While Vidhura-Pandita bathed, the yakkha arranged a heavenly meal.

After Vidhura-Pandita had finished eating, he sat on the prepared seat and began teaching. "Young man, follow the path already traversed; do not burn the innocent hand; never be treacherous to your friends; do not fall into the power of unchaste women."

Punnaka could not understand the meaning of these four rules so concisely stated. "How does one follow the path already traversed?" he asked. "What is the innocent hand one should not burn? Who is treacherous to his friend? Who is the unchaste woman? Please, sir, tell me the meaning clearly."

Vidhura-Pandita elaborated, "When a man is invited, as a stranger, into another's house, he should let his host's actions be his guide. This is what the wise call following in the path already traversed. If a man stays, even for one night in another's house, receiving hospitality, food, and drink from him, he must not conceive any evil thought against his host. This is what the wise call not burning the innocent hand. A man must not break even a bough of the tree that gives him shade, nor cause any harm to one who supports him. This is what the wise call not being treacherous to one's friends. Even if a man gives the entire earth with all its riches to a woman, she may still despise him. A man should avoid such a woman. This is what the wise call not falling into the power of unchaste women. To be a righteous man, abandon all unrighteousness."

When Punnaka heard Vidhura-Pandita declare these four duties of a good man, he thought, "In stating these four truths, the sage has made a strong case for preserving his own life. He welcomed me kindly even though I was a stranger. I stayed in his home for three days, receiving great honor and hospitality from him. Here am I, proposing to do him great wrong for a woman's sake! I am being treacherous to my friends! If I kill this sage, I will be going against all the duties of a good man. I must carry Vidhura-Pandita back to Indapatta and gladden the sorrowful faces of the citizens."

"Sage!" he cried aloud. "I stayed three days in your house, where I was treated with great kindness. Teacher of excellent wisdom, you are my friend. I will let you go. I have had enough of the nāga maiden. I should have nothing to do with the nāga realm. I must respect your wisdom and your eloquence."

"Young man," Vidhura-Pandita replied, "do not take me back to my own home just yet. We must go together to the nāga realm. Take me to your future father-in-law. Let me show you the royal nāga palace which you have never really seen.

"Sir!" Punnaka objected. "The wise should not look for trouble! Why do you want to go to your enemies?"

"I understand your fear," Vidhura-Pandita answered calmly, "but I have never committed any evil deed, so I have no fear of death. Furthermore, my talk softened you, even while you were planning to slay me so cruelly. It changed you so much that you could even say, 'I have had enough of the nāga maiden.' My task now is to soften the heart of the nāga king. Take me there immediately!"

"All right!" Punnaka agreed. "Let's go and see that glorious realm where the nāga king lives surrounded by lovely music and rare pleasures. It is, indeed, a wondrous realm!"

Showing Vidhura-Pandita great respect, Punnaka placed the sage behind him on his wonderful horse, and, together, they rode to the palace of the nāga king.

After they dismounted in the courtyard, Vidhura-Pandita stood behind Punnaka. The nāga king greeted the yakkha and said, "You went to the realm of men seeking the sage of unequaled wisdom. Have you returned successfully with his heart?"

"The one you desire is here," Punnaka replied. "He is my guardian, my teacher, won by righteous means. Conversation with the good brings happiness."

"You do not speak to me," King Varuna said, addressing Vidhura-Pandita. "You must be afraid of death. This is not the behavior of a wise man."

Vidhura-Pandita replied mildly, "I am not terrified of death, Your Majesty. I am not silent from fear. The victim should not address his executioner, nor should the latter ask his victim to address him."

"Sage, you speak the truth," the nāga king agreed, praising Vidhura-Pandita's wisdom.

"Let me ask you a question, Your Majesty," Vidhura-Pandita continued. "This splendor, this glory, this palace, and your nāga birth are impermanent and subject to death. How did you obtain all this? Was it gained without a cause or as the result of a previous condition? Was it made by yourself or given to you by the devas?"

"It was not gained without a cause," the nāga king answered thoughtfully, "nor was it the result of a previous condition. It was neither made by myself nor given by the devas. It was won by my own virtuous deeds."

"What vow was it, what practice of sanctity? What good action had this splendor, glory, and power as its fruit?"

"My wife and I, in the realm of men, were virtuous, generous, and full of faith. Our house was always open to ascetics and teachers. We offered food and drink, robes, medicine, garlands, and perfumes. That was my vow and my practice of sanctity. This is the fruit of that good conduct. This splendor, this glory, this great palace, and my nāga birth—all spring from those good deeds."

"Having gained all this, you know about rebirth and the fruit of holy actions. Therefore, practice virtue with all diligence so that you may again live in a palace."

The nāga king was troubled and said, "Sage, there are no ascetics here to whom we may give food and drink. There are none to receive hospitality and gifts. Tell me, how can I live rightly so as to again live in such glory?"

Vidhura-Pandita instructed him, saying, "There are many nāgas born here. There are wives, sons, daughters, relatives, and friends aplenty. Toward them commit no sin in word or deed at any time. Be generous to all. By living thus, innocent and virtuous in action and speech, when you depart from here, you will pass to the realm of the devas where you will also live in splendor."

King Varuna was overjoyed to hear these words from Vidhura-Pandita. He took the sage by the hand and led him to his wife, "My dear," the king called, as they entered the queen's chamber, "the one because of whom you grew pale and ill is now here. It is a great honor to have him here, and you will never again have such a chance. Please listen closely to his wise discourse."

As soon as Queen Vimalā saw the sage of great wisdom, she pressed her palms together in reverence. Although her whole soul was full of delight, she spoke to him brusquely, attempting to continue her ruse. "This mortal, seeing me for the first time, does not speak. Can it be that he is overwhelmed with the fear of death? This is not the behavior of a wise man."

"I am not terrified of death, Your Majesty. I am not silent from fear. The victim should not address his executioner, nor should the latter ask his victim to address him."

"You are indeed as wise as your reputation suggests," the queen replied. "Please tell us, great sage, how you came to be in the power of this young man. He was instructed to obtain you without guile. Did he conquer you in a contest? Did he win you fairly? Please tell us how it came about."

"This young man challenged my former master, King Dhanañjaya, to a game of dice. When my master lost, he gave me to the youth as a prize. I was won fairly and not by treachery. I now present myself to you. Whatever use this body or my heart may be to you, I will submit to, according to your wishes."

"The heart of a sage is his wisdom," Queen Vimalā proclaimed. "We are delighted with your wisdom, and, today, I have received my heart's desire."

King Varuna, also thoroughly satisfied with all that had transpired, announced, "This young man has indeed fulfilled his task. Let him take the fair Irandatī as his bride today." Then, turning to Vidhura-Pandita, he continued, "Surely, that best of kings who depends upon you is mourning your absence. You must return to quell his distress. Let my son-in-law escort you back today."

Punnaka was overjoyed at this turn of events. Paying the greatest respect to Vidhura-Pandita, he cried, "Great sage, you earned me my wife, and I will do what should be done. Allow me to present to you this peerless jewel and to return you to King Dhanañjaya."

"May your friendship with your beloved wife be unfailing," Vidhura-Pandita replied. "I gratefully accept your gem and your offer to carry me back to Indapatta."

After the sage and the royal couple had exchanged farewell greetings, Punnaka placed Vidhura-Pandita in front of him, and, together, they rode to Indapatta. They flew even more swiftly than thought itself. "Look below!" Punnaka shouted, almost immediately after they had left. "There is your city, with its pleasant mango groves and graceful neighborhoods. I have gained a wife, and you are regaining your home."

Early that very morning, King Dhanañjaya had had a dream in which he saw a great tree standing at the door of his palace. Its trunk was wisdom, its branches were virtues, and its fruit was the five products of the cow.[18] The tree was covered with saddled horses, mighty elephants, and glorious jewels. A huge crowd of people, with their palms pressed together, were worshiping it with great reverence. Suddenly, a dark man, dressed in red, wearing earrings of red flowers, and carrying weapons in both hands, stepped up and cut down the tree, despite the pleas and protestations of all the worshipers. The man dragged away the tree and disappeared. Then, suddenly, he returned carrying the great tree which he replanted in exactly the same spot where he had cut it down. Then he departed.

When the king awoke, he remembered his dream and immediately understood its meaning. "The sage Vidhura-Pandita," he said to himself, "is that great tree. The youth who carried him off is the dark man. My subjects are the worshipers who protested. Obviously, the young man will come back, place our sage at the door of the Hall of Justice, and depart. We will see Vidhura-Pandita again today!"

King Dhanañjaya joyfully ordered that the city be decorated and that a pavilion with a dais be erected in front of the Hall of Justice. He seated himself on the dais and, along with the one hundred visiting kings, waited for the sage's return. "Be of good cheer!" he said repeatedly to the crowd which had gathered. "Today you will see the sage again. He will be here very soon."

Before long, Punnaka descended and escorted the sage to the dais where the king was waiting. Without saying a word, he remounted his incomparable steed and sped away to fetch Irandatī from the nāga realm and to carry her to his own celestial city.

18 Milk, curd, buttermilk, butter, and ghee.

Overjoyed to behold his wise advisor once more, the king sprang from his seat and warmly embraced Vidhura-Pandita, led him to a special throne which had been prepared, and seated him at the head of the entire assembly.

"Everyone in the kingdom rejoices at seeing you again," the king proclaimed. "Great sage, we rely upon your wise guidance. Please tell us how you gained your freedom from that young man. Why did he let you go?"

"Your Majesty," Vidhura-Pandita replied, "the one you call 'young man' is no common man. He is the yakkha Punnaka, nephew of King Vessavana. He fell in love with Princess Irandatī, daughter of King Varuna of the nāga realm. He was scheming to kill me in order to win the hand of the princess. In the end, he obtained his wife, presented me with this peerless jewel, and brought me safely back."

To make this amazing story clear to everyone, Vidhura-Pandita told it in detail, beginning with the visit of the nāga king to Indapatta. In conclusion, he presented the magnificent wish-fulfilling gem to King Dhanañjaya.

For his part, the king recounted his marvelous dream. When he had finished, he turned to the assembly and shouted, "Let us all pay homage to this tree!" At once, the multitude raised their voices in praise of the sage. "To all prisoners in my realm, I grant freedom and full amnesty," the king proclaimed. "Just as this tree has been delivered from its captivity, let all others be released from bondage. Let all in the kingdom hang up their plows and spend a month in holiday. Let all my subjects enjoy themselves with feasts and festivals for one full cycle of the moon. I urge all of you to keep careful watch so that, during this celebration, none may injure his neighbor. Let us pay homage to this tree!"

For the rest of his life, Vidhura-Pandita fulfilled all his duties. When he passed away, he was reborn in heaven. Abiding by the sage's teaching and following the glowing example of their king, all the inhabitants of the Kuru kingdom practiced generosity and virtue so that, at the end of their lives, they too went to swell the hosts of heaven.

Having concluded his story, the Buddha added, "Not only now, but also formerly, did I possess the wisdom to convert opponents and to show them the way to accomplish their goals." Then he identified the birth: "At that time, Rāhula's mother was the sage's wife Anujja, Rāhula was Dhammapala, the eldest son, Sāriputta was King Varuna, Moggallāna was the garula king, Anuruddha was Sakka, Ānanda was King Dhanañjaya, and I was the wise Vidhura-Pandita."

216
Mahosadha's Incomparable Ingenuity
Mahā-Ummagga Jātaka

It was while staying at Jetavana that the Buddha told this story about the Perfection of Wisdom.

One day, in the Hall of Truth, bhikkhus were talking about the Buddha's great wisdom. "Bhikkhus, the Buddha's wisdom is vast, ready, swift, and sharp. He has crushed heretical doctrines and converted the brahmin Kutadanta, the ascetic Sabhiya, the murderer Angulimāla, the yakkha Ālavaka, Sakka, Baka-Brahmā, and many others. He has ordained a vast multitude in his Sangha and has established them on the paths.

When the Buddha heard what they were discussing, he said, "Not now only am I wise. Long ago, even before my knowledge was completely mature, I was full of wisdom." Then he told this story of the past.

Long, long ago, when Vedeha was reigning in Mithilā, he had four advisors, named Senaka, Pukkusa, Kavinda, and Devinda.

One morning, just before sunrise, the king had a vivid dream. He saw four columns of fire, one in each corner of the royal courtyard. While these columns were blazing, each as high as the palace wall, a tiny flame arose in the middle of the court. At first, it was only about the size of a firefly, but it soon grew much taller than the other four columns. It continued growing until it reached the realm of the devas and illuminated the entire earth so that even a tiny mustard seed lying on the ground could be clearly seen. A huge crowd of both humans and devas passed through the fire as they worshiped with garlands and incense, but not a single hair on any head was singed.

The king awoke in terror and sat mulling over the meaning of his dream, waiting for the dawn.

When the four advisors came into the royal chamber, they asked the king whether he had spent a comfortable night.

"How could I sleep well when I had a dreadful dream?"

After the king had described what he had seen, Senaka replied, "Don't worry, Your Majesty. It is an auspicious dream. It means that you will prosper! Your Majesty, a fifth sage will be born who will surpass the four of us. We are like the four columns of fire, but, in the midst of us, there will arise one who will be unparalleled and will fill a post unequaled in the realms of both devas and men."

At each of the four gates of Mithilā there was a market town. At the moment the king was having his dream, the Bodhisatta descended from Tāvatimsa and was conceived in the womb of Sumanadevī, the wife of a wealthy merchant named Sirivaddhaka, who lived in the eastern town. At the same time, one thousand other devas left Tāvatimsa and were conceived by wives of wealthy merchants in that same town.

Just before the Bodhisatta's birth, in order to make this important event known to the world, Sakka placed a medicinal herb in the baby's hand. As the baby emerged from her womb, Sumanadevī did not feel the slightest pain. His birth was as easy as pouring water from a ceremonial water pot. The new-born baby was the color of gold. As soon Sumanadevī saw him, she asked, "Dear baby, what do you have in your hand?"

"It is a medicinal herb, Mother," he replied as he placed it in her hand. "Please give it to anyone who is afflicted with a sickness."

Sumanadevī immediately told her husband about this. They were both overjoyed at the auspiciousness of the child being born holding the herb and being able to speak. It so happened that, for seven years, Sirivaddhaka had been suffering from a terrible headache. "Medicine given by a being of such incredible merit must possess great efficacy!" he thought. He ground the herb in a mortar and mixed it with water to make a paste. No sooner had he smeared a little of the paste on his forehead than his headache, which has been throbbing incessantly for seven years, disappeared like water running off a lotus leaf. "It's a miracle!" he exclaimed, overjoyed to be, at last, free of pain. The news that Sirivaddhaka's baby had been born with the miraculous herb quickly spread, and many sick people crowded around, begging for some of the medicine.

Sirivaddhaka gave a little of the herb paste to everyone who came. The medicine cured every disease and every affliction as quickly, as easily, and as thoroughly as it had cured Sirivaddhaka's headache. Happy patients went away proclaiming the marvelous virtues of the medicine.

Rather than naming the child after any of his relatives or ancestors, Sirivaddhaka chose to give him the name Osadha, which means "medicine."

Sirivaddhaka also surmised that a son of such great merit would not have been born alone. He made inquiries throughout the town and learned about the one thousand other boys who had been born at the same time. To each boy he sent clothes and a nurse, resolving that these boys would be Osadha's companions. As they grew up, they all played together. Even as a young boy, Osadha was as handsome as a golden statue.

While the children were playing, elephants and other animals sometimes passed by and disturbed their games. At other times, rain or severe heat spoiled their fun.

One day, when the boys were seven years old, there was a sudden downpour, and the boys all ran to a nearby house for shelter. In their rush, they tripped over one another and bruised their knees and elbows. "We need a proper place for play," Osadha said to his companions. "Let's build a hall here, where animals won't bother us and where we can enjoy ourselves even when it's windy, hot, or rainy. Each one of us should bring one coin."

Osadha collected the one thousand coins and hired a carpenter. The young boy told the carpenter that he wanted a hall built on that spot. The carpenter leveled the ground and cut the posts. Then he admitted that he did not really understand what Osadha was describing. "If you don't know more than this," Osadha chided him, "how can you build a hall for us?" Osadha drew the plans for the hall, and showed the carpenter how to measure the area for the foundation. "Can you do the rest of the work on your own?" he asked the carpenter.

"I'm afraid not, sir," the carpenter replied.

"Will you be able to follow my instructions?" Osadha asked.

"I will indeed, sir."

Osadha continued supervising the work until it was finished. He had to show the carpenter everything that needed to be done, but the carpenter was able to follow the boy's directions perfectly, and the hall, when it was finished, was a marvel.

There were separate apartments for travelers, the homeless and destitute, ascetics, and foreign merchants. Each apartment had an entrance from the outside. The hall also included a gymnasium for sports activities, a court of justice, and a hall for religious gatherings. When the construction work was completed, Osadha summoned painters and ordered them to decorate all the walls as though it were a heavenly palace.

On one side of this magnificent hall, he laid out a garden as beautiful as Nandana in Tāvatimsa. The tank in the center was surrounded by flowering trees. There were steps for bathers, and the water was covered with lotuses. Nearby was an alms-hall, where food was distributed to mendicants.

News of this great hall built by such a young boy spread throughout the kingdom, and everyone wanted to see the remarkable structure. Every day crowds of people thronged the hall. Sometimes, Osadha himself, whom people now called Mahosadha, "Great Osadha," sat in the Hall of Justice to listen to petitions which citizens brought, seeking his judgment.

About this time, King Vedeha recalled the prediction that a sage would be born who would surpass his four advisors in wisdom. Figuring that the boy would have to be about seven years old, the king wondered where he was. He sent out four servants, one by each of the city gates, to search for the boy.

The servants returned from the north, the south, and the west with no information at all. The servant who went out by the eastern gate, however, saw the great hall and was sure that only a wise man could have built it. When he asked the townspeople who the architect was, they told him that it had been designed and built by the young Mahosadha, son of the merchant Sirivaddhaka.

When the servant heard that Mahosadha was only seven years old, he thought, "This fulfils the king's dream!" He immediately sent a messenger to inform the king of what he had found and to ask whether he should escort Mahosadha to the palace.

The king was delighted at this news. He immediately summoned Senaka, gave him the servant's account, and asked whether he should send for the young sage.

Being jealous of his position, Senaka brushed off the suggestion. "Your Majesty," he replied, "a person is not to be called a sage merely because he has built one hall! Anyone can do that! It's a trifling accomplishment!"

The king wondered why Senaka objected so strongly to sending for the boy, but he remained silent. He sent a message to the servant, however, instructing him to stay in the town, to observe the youth, and to keep the palace informed.

It was not long before the servant witnessed an example of Mahosadha's wisdom.

One day, as Mahosadha and his companions were entering the great hall to play, they saw a hawk swoop down and snatch a piece of meat from a butcher's block. Some of the boys ran after the bird and began throwing stones, trying to make it drop the meat. To elude the stones, the hawk zigzagged in different directions, and the boys tried to follow it, but they ended up getting dizzy and tripping over each other. Soon, they were exhausted and gave up.

"I can make him drop it!" Mahosadha announced. The other boys begged him to do it.

Mahosadha looked up and gauged where the hawk was and which way it was flying. Then, with the swiftness of the wind, he ran until he stood in its shadow. He clapped his hands and shouted as loud as he could. His cry was so piercing that the hawk felt as though it had been struck with an arrow. Terrified, it dropped the piece of meat. Mahosadha saw the shadow of the meat and caught it before it touched the ground. Not only the boys, but a great crowd of townspeople who had stopped to watch, cheered and clapped their hands.

The servant reported this incident to the king, who, again, asked Senaka whether he should summon Mahosadha to the palace.

"As soon as this young sage appears," Senaka thought, "I will lose my glory. The king will forget my very existence! I must not let him come here!" Aloud he said, "Making a hawk drop a piece of meat is really a minor matter, Your Majesty. Just for that, he is not a sage!"

Again, the king wondered why Senaka objected so strongly, but he still remained silent. He told the servant to continue watching and to keep the palace informed.

One day, a man, who lived in a small village near the eastern town, bought some cattle from another village and took them home. The next day, he took the cattle to a field to graze. He was so tired that he soon fell asleep under a tree. While he was dozing, a thief began leading the cattle away. The man suddenly woke up, and noticed that his cattle were gone. He hurried down the path and saw the thief. "Stop!" he shouted. "Where are you taking my cattle?"

"These are my cattle," the thief retorted, "and I am taking them where I want."

The argument soon attracted a large crowd, who followed the two men.

When Mahosadha heard the shouting, he sent for the two men. As soon as he saw them, he could tell from their behavior which was the thief and which was the real owner. He knew, however, that he had to prove the case, so he asked them what they were quarreling about.

The owner said, "I bought these cattle yesterday from a farmer in the next village and took them home. Today, I brought them to graze in a field near here. This thief noticed that I was not watching and drove them off. I ran after him and finally caught up with him, but he would not give me back my cattle. The villagers all know that I bought these cattle."

The thief said, "None of that is true. These cattle were born on my farm, and I have reared them there."

Mahosadha told them that he could decide the case fairly and asked whether they would accept his decision. The two men both agreed.

First, he asked the thief what he gave the cattle to eat and drink.

"I gave them sesame flour and kidney beans to eat," he replied, "and rice gruel to drink."

Then he asked the real owner the same question.

"My Lord," the owner replied, "where would a poor man like me get rice gruel, sesame flour, and kidney beans for my cattle? They ate nothing but grass, and they drank from the stream."

Mahosadha ordered someone to bring panic seeds, which were ground in a mortar, mixed with water, and given to the cattle. When the cattle vomited, it was only grass they threw up. Mahosadha let everyone see this and asked the thief how he could explain it. The thief confessed his crime and apologized to the owner.

Mahosadha told him never to do such a thing again and established him in the five precepts.

The servant reported this incident to the king and asked whether he should escort Mahosadha to the palace.

The king again summoned Senaka and asked for his advice.

"That was a simple case of cattle ownership, Your Majesty," Senaka replied. "Anybody could have decided it. Let us wait a little longer."

The king still remained silent and told the servant to continue watching. The servant observed several more remarkable instances of Mahosadha's wise judgment. After each one, he reported to the king, but each time Senaka objected, and the king told the servant to continue watching.

One day, a poor woman went to the tank beside the great hall to take a bath. She was wearing a necklace she had made herself. This was simply several strands of different-colored thread twisted together, but she liked it very much and wore it often. Before stepping into the water, she carefully removed the necklace and laid it on her clothes. While she was bathing, a young woman picked up the necklace and said, "Mother, this is a beautiful necklace. How much did it cost to make? I would like to make one like it for myself. May I try it on to check the size?"

"Of course, my dear," replied the poor woman from the water.

The young woman tied the necklace around her neck and ran off. The poor woman hurried out of the water, threw on her clothes, and ran after her. Grabbing the young woman by her sari, she cried, "Give me back my necklace!"

"What are you talking about?" protested the other. "I haven't taken anything of yours. This is my necklace!"

"No, it isn't!" cried the poor woman. "I made that necklace myself!" The two women continued arguing as a large crowd gathered around them.

Mahosadha was playing with his friends nearby and asked what the noise was. Some passers-by told him, and he sent for the two women. As soon as he saw them, he could tell which was the rightful owner, but again, he needed proof. He asked the women whether they would abide by his judgment. They agreed, and he asked the young woman, "What scent do you use for this necklace?"

"I always use sabbasamharaka."[19]

He asked the older woman the same question, and she replied, "How could a poor woman like me get sabbasamharaka? I always scent it with cheap perfume made of piyangu flowers."

Mahosadha asked for a bowl of water and put the necklace in it. Then he sent for a perfume-seller and asked him to determine the scent of the water. The perfume-seller smelled the water and immediately identified it as piyangu.

Mahosadha confronted the young woman. She confessed her crime, and the crowd shouted their approval. Mahosadha's wisdom became even more widely known.

A little later, a woman who watched cotton fields was returning home with some fine cotton thread which she herself had spun and wound into a perfectly round ball. As she was passing the great hall, she decided to bathe in the tank. She placed the cotton ball on her clothes and stepped into the water. Another woman picked up the ball and exclaimed, "What a lovely ball of thread! Did you make it yourself?" Before the first woman could answer, the second woman walked away with the ball. The first woman scrambled out of the water, threw on her clothes, and rushed after the thief. An argument ensued, and the two women were taken before Mahosadha.

Mahosadha asked the thief, "When you made the ball, what did you put inside?"

"A cotton seed," she replied.

To the same question, the other woman replied, "A timbaru seed."

19   An expensive mixture of many kinds of incense.

When the ball of cotton was unwound, the timbaru seed was revealed, and Mahosadha made the thief admit her guilt. Again, the crowd shouted their approval.

Another day, a woman took her infant son to the tank to bathe. After she had washed him, she laid him on her clothes and went back to take her own bath. Just then, a yakkhinī, disguised as a woman, noticed the child and looked at him hungrily. She picked him up and said, "Friend, this is a fine child. May I play with him?" The mother agreed, and the yakkhinī began playing with the baby. After a few minutes, she stood up and ran off with him.

The mother scrambled out of the tank, dressed hurriedly, and raced after them. The mother grabbed the other woman and shouted, "Where are you taking my baby?"

"What do you mean, your baby?" the yakkhinī replied. "This is my child, and I am taking him home!" As they continued fighting, they passed by the door of the hall, and Mahosadha asked what the problem was.

They told him that they both claimed the baby, and they agreed to abide by his decision. Although Mahosadha immediately recognized that one of the women was a yakkhinī, he wanted her to reveal herself. He drew a line between the two women and placed the child on it. He directed the women to take hold of the baby—one by the hands and the other by the feet.

"Now pull!" he said. "The baby surely belongs to the one who can pull it over the line."

The two began pulling, and the frightened baby screamed in pain.

Immediately, the mother released her child and began weeping herself.

"Whose heart is tender towards a child," Mahosadha asked the crowd, "a mother's or a stranger's?"

"Of course, a mother's," everyone replied.

"Who showed greater compassion, the one who kept pulling the baby or the one who let go?" he asked.

"The one who let go!" the crowd shouted.

"Who is the mother?" he asked.

"The one who let go!" the crowd shouted again.

"Do you know who the one who stole the baby really is?" he asked.

"We have no idea," everyone replied.

"She is a yakkhinī disguised as a woman."

"How do you know?" the crowd asked.

"I recognized her at once because of her unblinking eyes and lack of shadow, and she just proved herself by her heartlessness. She wouldn't care even if the baby died, for her intention was to eat him!" The crowd gasped. Mahosadha turned to the yakkhinī and said, "You are a blind fool! In the past you committed evil deeds and were reborn as a yakkhinī as a result. Now you are continuing your wickedness!" Overcome with shame, the yakkhinī admitted her guilt and asked for forgiveness. Mahosadha showed her great compassion and established her in the five precepts.

The grateful mother blessed Mahosadha, wished him long life, and went away hugging and caressing her baby.

Near the eastern town, there was a man nicknamed Golakāla, or "dark ball," because his skin was very dark and he was very short. Golakāla had worked for a family and had received no wages, but, after seven years, they had given him a wife named Dīghatālā.

After they had been married some time, Golakāla said, "Wife, prepare some snacks and some curries. We're going to visit your parents."

"What use are parents to me now?" she protested.

Golakāla insisted, however, and she finally agreed. Taking provisions, some freshly baked cakes, and a present, they set out on the journey to her hometown.

On the way, they came to a swift-flowing stream. They were both afraid of the water and dared not try to cross it. They stood on the bank and wondered how to get to the other side.

At that moment, a tall man named Dīghapitthi approached along the same path they had just traveled. "Excuse me, sir," Golakāla said. "Do you know whether this steam is deep or shallow?"

Seeing that the couple were already afraid, Dīghapitthi answered maliciously, "Oh, my goodness! This stream is very deep and full of crocodiles!"

"How will you get across?" Golakāla and Dīghatālā asked.

"I have struck up a friendship with the crocodiles in the stream," he replied. "They do not hurt me."

"Will you please take us with you?" they begged, offering him some of their food. Dīghapitthi agreed to carry them across and accepted the offer of a meal. After he had finished eating, he asked which he should carry first.

"Take your sister first and then come back for me," suggested Golakāla.

Dīghapitthi hoisted Dīghatālā onto his shoulders, picked up all their bags and stepped into the water. As he waded across, he gradually crouched lower and lower to make it look as though the water were very deep.

"Oh, dear!" Golakāla thought, as he watched Dīghapitthi. "Look at how deep this stream is! I'm glad I didn't try to wade across! I never would have made it!"

When Dīghapitthi reached the middle of the stream, he said to Dīghatālā, "Lady, marry me, and I will give you fine clothes, servants, and every comfort. What can that poor black dwarf do for you? Leave him, and come with me!"

Dīghatālā was excited at the possibility of having such a tall, handsome, and strong man for a husband and, infatuated with the stranger, replied, "Sir, if you promise not to abandon me, I will gladly go with you."

Dīghapitthi continued walking in his bent posture to the other side of the stream. He carefully put Dīghatālā down and sat on the bank beside her. In full sight of Golakāla, the scheming man ate all the food. Then he and Dīghatālā walked away, leaving Golakāla stranded on the other side.

Realizing that his wife was leaving him for the stranger, Golakāla ran back and forth in agitation. Several times he stepped into the water, but, each time, he anxiously drew back. At last, his anger overcame his fear, and he made a desperate leap into the river, not caring if he drowned. He quickly discovered how shallow the water was and hurried across.

"Wicked thief!" Golakāla shouted as he ran after the couple. "Where are you taking my wife?"

"Your wife?" Dīghapitthi shouted back. "This is my wife!" He grabbed Golakāla by the neck and threw him down.

Golakāla jumped up and caught hold of Dīghatālā's hand. "Stop!" he pleaded. "Where are you going? You are my wife! I worked seven years to get you! Why are you leaving me?"

They were still arguing when they arrived in the eastern town, and their shouting attracted a crowd of people. They were taken before Mahosadha, and he asked whether they would abide by his decision. All three of them agreed.

Mahosadha announced that he would interview each of them separately. He sent Golakāla and Dīghatālā into separate rooms. Then, in front of the assembly, he told Dīghapitthi to state his name and his wife's name. The scoundrel had failed to ask her, so he blurted out the first name that came into his head. Mahosadha next asked him about his parents, and he answered promptly. When Mahosadha asked about his wife's family, he, again, made up names.

Next, Mahosadha called Golakāla and sent Dīghapitthi back to the room where Golakāla had been waiting. In the same way, Mahosadha told Golakāla to state his own name, his wife's name, and the names of her parents. Golakāla confidently did so.

Finally, Mahosadha called Dīghatālā and sent Golakāla to the room where she had been waiting. He told Dīghatālā to state her name and the names of her parents, and she did so. When he asked what her husband's name was, she hesitated for a moment and gave a common name, hoping it was right. Then Mahosadha asked for her husband's parents' names, and she hesitated again before making up some names for them, too.

Mahosadha called the two men, and, with the three standing in front of the crowd, he asked, "Do Dīghatālā's answers agree with Dīghapitthi's or with Golakāla's?"

"With Golakāla's!" Everyone shouted in unison.

"Obviously, Golakāla is her rightful husband, and Dīghapitthi is an imposter! Is that true?" Mahosadha questioned Dīghapitthi and Dīghatālā. They admitted that it was true, and the crowd cheered the wise judgment.

In order to make even more people aware of Mahosadha's greatness, Sakka himself instigated another case. One day, as a man was driving his chariot past the tank, Sakka disguised himself as a laborer, grabbed the back of the chariot and followed behind.

The driver looked back and shouted, "What do you want?"

"I want to work for you," Sakka answered.

"All right, hold the reins," the driver agreed, as he climbed down to answer the call of nature.

Sakka quickly jumped into the chariot, whipped the horse, and drove away.

"Stop! Stop! Where are you taking my chariot?" shouted the driver as he raced after the thief.

"Your chariot?" Sakka shouted back at him. "This is my chariot!"

As they continued shouting and arguing, they arrived in front of the hall. As soon as Mahosadha saw them, he recognized Sakka, and he knew that the chariot belonged to the other man.

To prove the case, he asked another skillful driver to drive the chariot at full speed while the two disputants held on behind. "I'm sure that the real owner will hold on to the chariot longer," he told the two men.

After the horse took off, the owner ran a little way, but the speed was too great for him, and he was forced to let go. Even though the horse increased its speed, Sakka held on and kept on running with the chariot until it circled back to the place where it had started.

"Look!" Mahosadha said to the crowd. "This man ran a little way, but was forced to let go. The other kept on running, but he isn't even perspiring or panting. He is not at all exhausted. This is not human! In fact, this is not a man at all. This is Sakka! Is that true?" he asked the one dressed as a laborer.

"Yes, it is," the king of the gods admitted. "I am Sakka!"

"Why did you come here?" Mahosadha asked him.

"I have come to display your wisdom to the world!" Sakka replied. "Mahosadha, I wanted everyone to witness another wise judgment from such a wise boy!"

The king's servant went himself to the palace and reported that Mahosadha could detect even Sakka in disguise. "Sire, why don't you recognize this boy's superiority?" the servant asked.

"What say you now, Senaka?" the king asked. "Shall we bring the sage here?"

"Your Majesty," Senaka replied, "it takes more than that sort of trick to make one a sage. Let me test him myself." Not wishing to go against his chief advisor, the king agreed.

Senaka cut a piece, about a span in length, from an acacia pole, and had both ends nicely smoothed so that they looked identical. He sent this piece to the eastern town with this message: "We understand that the people of the eastern town are very clever. Let them find out which end of this stick is the top and which is the root. If they fail, there will be a fine of one thousand coins."

The townspeople had no idea how to determine which end was which. They appealed to the headman, and he suggested that Mahosadha might know how to figure it out. They called him from the playground, showed him the stick, and explained the problem.

"Surely, the king does not expect the townspeople to solve this puzzle," he thought. "Undoubtedly, this has been sent as a test for me."

As soon as he had grasped the stick, he knew which was the top and which the root, but, to demonstrate the matter, he sent for a pot of water. He tied a string around the stick at the exact center between the two ends. He balanced the stick over the pot of water and lowered it to the surface. When it touched the water, one end of the stick sank a little more than the other.

"Which part of a tree is heavier," he asked the townspeople, "the root or the top?"

"The root," they replied.

"Do you see how this part sinks more?" he asked. "This is the root."

The headman sent the pole back to the king clearly indicating which end was the root.

The king was pleased and asked who had solved the puzzle.

"The wise Mahosadha, son of Sirivaddhaka," the messenger answered

"Well, Senaka, shall we send for him now?" the king asked.

"Let's give him another test," the insecure advisor replied.

Senaka sent two skulls to the eastern town, demanding that they be returned with identification as to which was a man's and which a woman's. In case of failure, the town would be fined one thousand coins. Again, the townspeople appealed to Mahosadha.

"This is very simple," he told them. "The sutures in a man's skull are straight, and in a woman's, crooked." He showed them that the sutures in the two skulls were different, thereby distinguishing one from the other. When the king received the skulls with this answer, he was again pleased and wanted to call for Mahosadha, but Senaka insisted on another test.

This time, he sent two snakes, a male and a female, demanding that the townspeople determine the sex of each. There was the usual penalty for failure. Mahosadha explained that this was very easy to do because the male snake's tail was thicker, while the female's head was longer. The king was pleased, but Senaka insisted on another test.

He demanded that the eastern town send the king a pure white bull with horns on its legs and a hump on its head and which sang with three notes, one short, one middling, and one long. There was the same penalty for failure. The puzzled townspeople again appealed to Mahosadha. The sage chuckled and said, "The king is asking for a rooster. The horns on its legs are the spurs; the hump on its head is his comb; and its early morning crow has three notes—long, middling, and short. Send the king a white cock, and he will be happy!" The king was pleased, but Senaka insisted on another test.

King Vedeha had inherited the exquisite Verocanamani which Sakka had given to King Kusa. This was an octagonal gem with a tiny hole for a string. Unfortunately, the old string had been broken off inside, and no one could remove it or put in a new one. Senaka sent this gem to the eastern town with an order for it to be restrung. There was the usual penalty for failure. The townspeople again appealed to Mahosadha. The sage asked for some honey, which he smeared around both sides of the hole in the gem. He twisted a wool thread, smeared one end with honey, and pushed that end a little way into the hole. Then he put the gem in a place where there were plenty of ants. As soon as the ants smelled the honey, they came out of their hole and swarmed all over the gem. After eating away the old thread, they took hold of the end of the new wool thread and pulled it all the way through the gem and out at the other end. The king was delighted to see the gem strung on its new thread and to hear how the task had been accomplished, but Senaka insisted on another test.

For the next test, the royal bull was given a rich diet for several months so that its belly swelled. Then it was rubbed with oil and covered with turmeric. Senaka sent the bull to the eastern town with the message that the bull was pregnant and that the townspeople were to deliver the calf and return both animals to the palace. There was the same penalty for failure. The perplexed townspeople again appealed to Mahosadha. The sage told them to find a bold man who could go to the palace and confront the king. They found a man confident enough to do this, and Mahosadha told him what to do.

"Loosen your hair and go to the palace," the sage instructed him. "Stand in front of the palace gate, weeping and wailing, and tell the guards that you will speak to no one but the king. When you meet the king, he will ask you why you are crying. You must reply, 'Your Majesty, for the past seven days, my son has been in labor, but he cannot give birth. Help me! Tell me how I can deliver his baby!' The king will tell you that that is impossible because men do not bear children. Then you must say, 'If that is true, how can the people of the eastern town deliver a calf of your royal bull?'"

The man did exactly as he was told, and the king asked who had thought of the counter-question. When told that it was Mahosadha, he was very pleased, but Senaka insisted on another test.

Senaka demanded that the people of the eastern town deliver boiled rice to the palace. He stipulated that this rice must meet eight conditions. It was to be cooked (1) without rice, (2) without water, (3) without a pot, (4) without an oven, (5) without fire, and (6) without firewood; (7) it was to be delivered to the palace by neither a man nor a woman; and (8) it was not to be carried along a road. There was the usual penalty for failure. The townspeople again appealed to Mahosadha.

"This is again very simple," Mahosadha told them. "Use broken rice, which is not accepted as rice. Use snow, which is not water. Use an earthen bowl, which is not a pot. Make an enclosure of wood blocks, which is not an oven. Create a flame by rubbing two sticks together, rather than bringing fire. Use leaves and brush, instead of firewood. Have the rice delivered by a eunuch, who is neither man nor woman. Have the eunuch travel to the palace by a footpath, instead of the main road. This will meet all eight of the king's conditions."

The king was pleased, but Senaka insisted on another test.

Senaka ordered that the people of the eastern town replace the broken rope of the king's swing with a new rope of sand. There was the same penalty for failure. The townspeople again appealed to Mahosadha.

Mahosadha immediately realized that a counter-question was required. He summoned several clever speakers and told them what to do. "Go to the palace," he instructed them, "and say to the king, 'Your Majesty, the people of the eastern town do not know whether the sand-rope is to be thick or thin. Please send them a bit of the old rope, no more than four finger lengths. With this sample, they will twist a rope of the same size.' The king will tell you that there is no sand-rope in the palace and that there never has been such a thing. Then you must reply, 'If Your Majesty has never seen a sand-rope, how can you expect the villagers to make one?'"

The men did exactly as they were instructed, and the king was very pleased, but Senaka insisted on another test.

Senaka informed the people of the eastern town that the king wanted to amuse himself in the water and ordered that they deliver a new tank complete with water lilies and lotuses to the palace. There was the usual penalty for failure.

Mahosadha realized that, again, a counter-question was required. Again, he summoned several men and told them what to do. "Go to a pond, and splash around until you are completely soaked and covered with mud. Then, with your hair and clothes still wet, go the palace, carrying ropes, sticks, and clods of earth. Tell the guards that you must speak with the king. When you see him, you must say, 'Your Majesty, we were bringing the tank to you, but, because she was so used to her life in the forest, she ran away when we got near the city. It seems that she was frightened by the crowds, tall buildings, and all the commotion. We tried to restrain her, but she broke the ropes and escaped. Please give us your old tank to use as a decoy to lure the new tank back to the capital.'"

The men did exactly as they were instructed, and the king broke up with laughter. Senaka insisted on another test.

Senaka ordered that the people of the eastern town deliver a new park to the king to replace his old one. Mahosadha suggested that they solve this problem in the same way they had done with the tank, and his strategy was again successful.

"Well, Senaka," the king asked his advisor, "shall we send for the sage now?"

"Your Majesty," Senaka replied, "there is more to being a sage than we have seen. The youth has not yet proved himself. We must wait."

The king was not pleased. "The sage Mahosadha has shown great wisdom since he was seven years old," he thought. "He has given ingenious solutions to all the puzzles, trials, and dilemmas he has faced. I am very interested in him, but Senaka keeps stalling and won't let me summon him. What do I care about Senaka's opinion? I will bring him here myself!"

Accompanied by his attendants, the king set out from the palace on his royal horse and headed toward the eastern town. On the way, however, his horse stepped in a hole and broke its leg, and the king was forced to turn back.

Senaka asked him, "Sire, were you going to fetch Mahosadha from the eastern town yourself?"

"Yes, I was," replied the king.

"Your Majesty," Senaka chided him, "you act as if my advice has no importance. I begged you to wait, but you went off in a hurry, and your royal horse broke its leg. You should listen to me!"

The king had no answer to this.

Some time later, he again asked his advisor, "Shall we send for the sage now, Senaka?"

"All right, Your Majesty," Senaka replied. "If you insist, we'll summon him, but you must not go yourself. Send a messenger to the eastern town to say, 'Sage, as I was on my way to fetch you, my horse broke his leg. Send us an excellent horse followed by a better one.' Let us see how he solves this problem."

When Mahosadha received the message, he went to see his father and, after greeting him, said, "Father, the king wishes to see both you and me. You should go first with one thousand attendants. You must not go empty handed. Take a sandalwood casket, filled with fresh ghee as a gift for the king. When the king offers you a seat, sit in an appropriate place. I will come later, and the king will offer me a seat. When I look at you, that is your cue to stand up and offer me your seat. This will allow me to solve the king's riddle."

Sirivaddhaka prepared the gift, gathered his attendants, and went to the palace, where the king greeted him cordially. After he had presented the ghee, the king asked about his son, the wise Mahosadha.

"He's coming after me, Your Majesty," Sirivaddhaka replied.

The king, pleased to hear that, offered Sirivaddhaka a seat, and he sat in a suitable place.

Mahosadha, dressed in his finest robes and attended by his one thousand companions, had left the eastern town in a magnificent chariot just behind his father. On the way, he saw an ass in a ditch. He ordered some of his strong companions to muzzle the animal so that it would make no noise, to put it in a huge bag, and to carry it to the palace on their shoulders.

As he passed through the city with his entourage, the citizens thronged the streets and cried out his praises: "This is the wise Mahosadha, son of the merchant Sirivaddhaka!" "He was born holding a miraculous herb!" "He can solve every puzzle he is given!"

As scheduled, he arrived shortly after his father, and the king summoned him immediately.

Mahosadha saluted the king and stood to one side. The king greeted him cordially and asked him to take a seat. Mahosadha looked at his father, and Sirivaddhaka immediately stood up and offered his seat to his son.

Many in the court, led by the king's four advisors, Senaka, Pukkusa, Kavinda, and Devinda, mockingly clapped their hands and laughed loudly.

"This is the arrogant fool they call wise!" they sneered. "He made his father get up, and he is ready to sit there himself! He has no respect. How can he be called a sage at all?"

The king was crestfallen.

"Sire, why do you look so sad?" Mahosadha asked.

"My son," the king replied, "I am sad because, after having heard so much about you, I am now not happy to see you."

"Why is that?"

"I feel that my advisors are right. You show a definite lack of respect in making your father rise from his seat so that you could sit there yourself."

"Your Majesty," Mahosadha countered, "I believe that you told me to send an excellent horse followed by a better one. Is that correct?"

"Yes, it is," replied the king.

"Your Majesty, do you believe that the sire is always more worthy than the son?" Mahosadha asked.

"Of course!" the king replied quickly.

Mahosadha asked his companions to bring in the ass and to place it before the king. "Sire," he said, "how much is this ass worth?"

"If it is a serviceable beast," the king replied, "it is worth eight coins."

"Well, Your Majesty, if we breed this ass with a thoroughbred Sindh mare, how much will its mule offspring be worth?"

"Such a colt would be priceless!" the king replied.

"How can you say that, Your Majesty? Didn't you just say that the sire is always more worthy than the son? Now you say that the mule is worth more than the ass. Is not the ass the sire of the mule? Your Majesty, if you believe that the sire is better than the son, take my father into your service. I believe that my father is an excellent man, and I fully respect him, but, if you can agree that I am wiser than he is, take me."

The king was delighted with this presentation, and everyone in the court, except, of course, the four jealous advisors, applauded Mahosadha's wisdom, waved their scarves, and shouted their praise. The four royal advisors simply looked abashed.

To show his approval, the king filled a golden vase with scented water, and, as he poured the water over Sirivaddhaka's hand, he declared, "Enjoy the eastern town as a royal gift!" The king also sent many precious necklaces, bracelets, rings, and earrings to Sumanadevī, Mahosadha's mother.

The king was awed by Mahosadha's wisdom, not only in this case, but in all the cases he had judged and the puzzles and riddles he had solved. He told Sirivaddhaka that he wanted to adopt the boy as his own son.

"Sire, my son is still very young," Sirivaddhaka protested. "As soon as he is old enough to leave home, I shall send him to you."

The king insisted so adamantly, however, that finally Sirivaddhaka relented. Mahosadha comforted his father and told him not to worry about him. Sirivaddhaka embraced his son and gave him some parting advice. Then he paid obeisance to the king and returned to the eastern town.

The king asked Mahosadha whether he would prefer to take his meals in the palace or outside. The boy replied that, since his entourage was large, it would be better for him to take his meals outside the palace. The king accepted that decision and gave him a suitable house and everything else he might need. The king also provided for the maintenance of Mahosadha's one thousand companions. From that time on, Mahosadha served the king as advisor.

One day, the king summoned Senaka and said, "Men have told me that there is a jewel in the lake near the southern gate. How can we get it out?"

"Surely, Sire," Senaka replied, "the best way would be to drain the water from the lake."

"Do what must be done!" the king instructed him. Senaka went with the men to investigate. They showed him the jewel, and he ordered them to drain the lake. After the water had been drained, they searched the mud, but no jewel could be found. As soon as they refilled the lake, the jewel was again visible. Senaka ordered them to drain the lake once more, but still they could not find the jewel.

The king sent for Mahosadha and said, "There is a jewel in the lake near the southern gate. Senaka had the lake drained twice and searched the mud, but he could not find it. As soon as the lake was refilled, the jewel reappeared. Can you get it for me?"

"Of course, Your Majesty," Mahosadha replied. "That is not a hard task. I will certainly get it for you."

Pleased at this promise, the king led his great retinue to the lake to observe Mahosadha's wisdom in action.

Mahosadha stood on the shore and asked the men to show him the jewel. As soon as he saw it, he realized that they were seeing only a reflection. "There is no jewel in the lake!" he announced to the king.

"What do you mean?" asked the king. "We can all see it! It must be there!"

Mahosadha asked for a pail which he filled with water from the lake. He tilted the pail toward the king and said, "Look, Sire! Now the jewel appears to be in the pail. It is only the reflection visible both in the lake and in the pail." Pointing at a tall talipot palm tree standing beside the lake, he explained, "The jewel itself is wedged in the bottom of a crow's nest in that tree. Send a man up to the nest and have the jewel brought down."

A servant quickly climbed the tree and retrieved the jewel for the king. The crowd applauded and shouted their approval. "Senaka's men dug in the mud," they cried, mocking the advisor, "to find a gem in a tree! An advisor should be wise like Mahosadha!"

The king was so pleased that he gave Mahosadha the priceless string of pearls from his own neck. He also gave a string of pearls to each of Mahosadha's companions. The king also granted all of them the privilege of visiting the palace at any time.

Another day, as the king was going with Mahosadha to the park, a chameleon that lived in the arched gateway, seeing the king approach, hurried down and lay flat on the ground.

The king was puzzled and asked, "What is that chameleon doing, wise sir?"

"Paying its respects to you, Sire."

"If that is so, its service should not be unrewarded. Give it a gratuity."

"Sire, a tip is of no use to the chameleon, but it would appreciate something to eat."

"What do chameleons eat?"

"Meat, Sire."

"How much should we give?"

"A small coin worth a half a grain of gold would be ample, Sire."

"A half a grain of gold is hardly a royal gift!" exclaimed the king, and he ordered a servant to give the chameleon a piece of meat worth two and a half grains of gold everyday.

The servant began giving meat to the chameleon every day, and, every day, the chameleon descended from the archway and paid its respects to the king. This continued for some time, but, on the full-moon day, when no animals were butchered, the servant couldn't find any meat for the chameleon. Instead, he drilled a hole through a piece of gold weighing two and a half grains, strung it on a thread, and tied it around the chameleon's neck.

That afternoon, as the king was going to the park, the chameleon saw him approach, but, instead of descending to pay its respects to the king, it remained motionless on the archway.

"Wise sir," the king asked Mahosadha, "why doesn't the chameleon come down today as usual?"

Mahosadha saw the piece of gold on the chameleon's neck and realized immediately what had happened. "Today is a full-moon day, Sire. The servant, not finding any meat in the market, gave the chameleon a piece of gold worth two and a half grains. Now the chameleon has become proud and thinks itself your equal."

The king checked with the servant and learned that Mahosadha's speculations were correct. This made the king even happier with the sage, since it seemed that he understood even the thoughts of animals! As a reward, he gave Mahosadha the revenue from the four gates. Piqued by the chameleon's ingratitude, however, the king wanted to discontinue the ration of meat, but Mahosadha dissuaded him, saying that it was unworthy of the king to renege on his promise for such a slight offense.

At about the same time, a young man from Mithilā named Pinguttara finished his studies under a famous teacher in Takkasilā. As he was preparing to return to Mithilā, his teacher announced that his beautiful daughter had just come of age, and, according to family tradition, she was to be given in marriage to his senior student, who happened to be Pinguttara.

All his life, Pinguttara had been extremely unlucky, and he expected that he would always be so. On the other hand, the teacher's daughter had always been extremely lucky, and she expected that she would always be so. When Pinguttara saw his future wife, he was not in the least attracted to her, but, not wanting to offend his teacher, he hid his feelings and agreed to the marriage, which was performed with great ceremony.

On the wedding night, Pinguttara lay down on the lavishly decorated bed, but, as soon as his new wife lay down beside him, he began groaning, got up, and stretched out on the floor. When she got out of bed and lay down beside him, he immediately climbed back into bed. She got up and lay beside him again, but he retreated again to the floor. Of course, the reason for this was that good luck and bad luck make a poor match. Eventually, the woman tired of this game and stayed on the bed, leaving Pinguttara on the floor. They slept this way for the seven days of their honeymoon. After all the formalities had been concluded, Pinguttara bade farewell to his teacher and left with his wife for Mithilā.

The journey was miserable for both of them, and they exchanged not a word. Not far from Mithilā's city gate, Pinguttara noticed a fig-tree laden with fruit. Feeling hungry, he climbed the tree, sat in the branches, and began eating figs. His wife was also hungry, so she stepped to the foot of the tree and called out, "Throw down some fruit for me, too."

"What?" retorted Pinguttara, "don't you have hands and feet? If you want some of this luscious fruit, climb up and get it yourself!"

As soon as she was in the tree, Pinguttara climbed down and piled thorns and brambles all around the tree. "At last, I have gotten rid of that miserable creature!" he exclaimed and fled. Unable to get down safely, she remained sitting in the tree.

That evening, as the king was returning to the city on his royal elephant, after enjoying himself in his pleasure garden, he caught sight of the woman and immediately fell in love with her. He sent a courtier to ask if she had a husband.

"Yes," she answered, "my parents gave me to a man, but he has abandoned me."

When the king heard this, he exclaimed, "Treasure lost and found belongs to the king!"

The young woman was helped out of the tree, seated on an elephant, and conveyed to the palace, where she was consecrated as the king's queen consort. Because she was found in a fig tree (udumbara), she was called Queen Udumbarā.

Some time later, the king ordered some of the men who lived near the city gate to repair the road to the pleasure garden. One of the men who was pressed into service was Pinguttara. One day, while the work was going on, King Vedeha and Queen Udumbarā passed by in the royal chariot. The men, covered with dirt and sweat and with their dhotis tucked up, were toiling in the hot sun. The queen recognized Pinguttara and smiled.

When the king saw her smile, he became intensely jealous and demanded to know why she was smiling.

"My Lord," she said, "that laborer over there, half-naked, covered with grime, and working like a slave, is my former husband. He is the one who made me climb the fig-tree, piled thorns around it, and abandoned me. When I recognized him, I could not help but smile at my great fortune and his wretched luck."

"I don't believe you!" the king shouted, drawing his sword. "You were smiling at someone else. I will kill you for being unfaithful to me!"

"Sire!" the queen cried in fear for her life. "It's the truth! Ask your advisors!"

Barely lowering his sword, the king asked Senaka whether he believed her.

"No, My Lord," Senaka replied. "I do not believe her story at all. Who would leave such a beautiful woman if he had had the good fortune of marrying her?"

The queen became even more frightened. "Please, My Lord!" she begged.

"What does Senaka know?" the king wondered, as he lowered his sword a little more. "I had better ask Mahosadha." Aloud he said, "Mahosadha, if a woman is both virtuous and fair, is it possible for a man to cast her aside? What do you think, sage? Can you believe the queen's story?"

"Your Majesty," Mahosadha replied, "it is possible, and I believe her story. Look at that man. He is certainly an unlucky wretch, whereas the queen is the most fortunate of women. I am sure that things happened exactly as she has said, for good luck and bad luck make a poor match."

His words completely quenched the king's anger, and his heart became calm. "Mahosadha, you are very wise!" the king exclaimed. "If you had not been here, I would have listened to that fool Senaka, and I would have lost this precious woman. You have saved my queen!" He rewarded the sage with a gift of one thousand coins.

Filled with gratitude for Mahosadha's wisdom, the queen respectfully said to the king, "Sire, this sage has saved my life. Please allow me to treat him as my younger brother."

"Certainly, my queen! I gladly grant you this boon."

"Sire," the queen continued, "I would like to be able to share all delicacies with my brother. Please grant that I be free to send him sweets and fruit, unhindered, at any time."

"This boon also I gladly grant, my dear," the king replied. Thus, did the young Mahosadha become foster brother to the queen.

In the palace compound, there was a billy goat that had discovered the abundance of lush grass in the elephant stables. Whenever the elephant-keepers saw the mischievous goat eating the elephants' grass, they drove it off. One day, a fierce mahout caught the goat eating and chased it away, but not satisfied with that, he grabbed a big stick and hit the goat's back as hard as he could. The poor goat, suffering great pain, lay down on a bench by the palace wall.

That same day, the royal cook had finished preparing the food early, had dished it up, and was standing outside, wiping the sweat off his brow. A dog, overcome by the temptation of the savory meat dishes, sneaked into the kitchen, knocked the cover off a large pot, and began to devour the roasted meat. When the cook heard the noise, he ran into the kitchen, saw the dog, and gave it a fierce blow with a stick. The dog dropped the piece of meat and ran, yelping, to the courtyard. Arching its back with pain, it limped to the place where the goat was lying.

"Friend, why are arching your back like that?" the goat asked.

"I've just been beaten for trying to eat a little of the extra meat in the kitchen," the dog replied. "What about you, friend? It looks like your back is also in pain."

"It is," replied the goat. "A mahout just beat me for helping the elephants dispose of the grass that their keepers are always throwing at them."

As they related their stories to each other and commiserated that neither could, for fear of his life, ever return to the scene of his punishment, the goat brightened up. He had an idea.

"Tell me what you are thinking!" the dog pleaded.

"Well," the goat began, "I can't go to the stables any more, but you can. You can't go to the kitchen any more, but the cook does not know me. If you go into the stables every day and bring back several mouthfuls of grass for me, I will saunter into the kitchen and grab some meat for you. No one will ever suspect either of us."

"That's a great plan!" exclaimed the dog. "It's a deal!"

Thereafter, the two animals became the greatest of friends. Every day each brought food for the other, and they ate together in the courtyard.

One morning, as the king was pacing up and down in a corridor after breakfast, he glanced into the courtyard and saw the two animals lying side by side and eating. "How remarkable!" he thought. "Here are two natural enemies living peacefully together. It looks like they are even sharing their food! How can such a thing be? I'll use this to test my advisors. Any unable to figure it out should be banished! Well, it is too late today. I'll ask them about it when they come tomorrow morning."

The next day, when the advisors went to wait upon the king, he announced, "Two natural enemies, who never could stand to be within seven paces of each other, have become friends and are now inseparable. What is the reason? You must solve this question for me before noon. If you don't, you will be banished! I have no need of ignorant men."

Mahosadha, who was sitting furthest from the king, thought, "The king is not clever enough to have thought this up by himself. He must have seen something. I could solve the riddle if I had a day to work on it." The other four advisors were completely in the dark. Senaka, who was sitting closest to the king, looked at Mahosadha for help and could see by the way the younger sage was looking at him that even he did not know the answer. Senaka understood, however, that Mahosadha wanted him to ask the king for a day's grace and wondered how to obtain this from the king.

Senaka laughed loudly to reassure the king and said, "Sire, are you saying that you will banish us all if we cannot answer your question?"

"Yes, I am!" responded the king promptly.

"Sire, this is a knotty question," Senaka countered. "It cannot be solved in a hurry because it needs serious reflection. With so many people around, our minds are distracted. We must think it over in silence. Give us one day, and we will solve this problem for you. If you will allow it, we will bring the answer to you tomorrow."

"All right, I'll grant you one day," the king replied, obviously not happy with this excuse, "but I warn you, if any one of you fails to figure this out, I will banish him!"

The four senior advisors left the palace, and Senaka said to the others, "Friends, this is an extremely difficult question, and I'm afraid that we are in serious trouble. Ponder on it for a while, and, if you come up with anything, be sure to share it with the rest. Together we must try to work it out!" Each of them went to his own home to consider the problem.

Mahosadha, however, went to visit Queen Udumbarā. "Your Highness," he asked her, "where did the king spend a good deal of time yesterday and today?"

"Brother," answered the queen, "he walked back and forth in the corridor, looking out of the windows at the courtyard."

"Thank you, Your Highness," Mahosadha replied happily. "That's it! He must have seen something there." He went straight to the corridor and gazed out the windows. After a few minutes, he saw the dog coming from the elephant stables, carrying a mouthful of grass. Then he saw the goat coming from the kitchen, carrying a piece of meat. The two animals lay down side by side and began eating the food which the other had brought. "This must be what the king saw," Mahosadha thought as he continued watching. "Of course!" he exclaimed triumphantly, having understood the friendship between the two and figured out exactly how it had happened. "The king's question is solved!" Completely satisfied and confident, he went home.

Later that day, Pukkusa, Kavinda, and Devinda visited Senaka. "Have you found the answer to the problem?" he asked them.

"No, Master," they replied.

"What are you going to do if the king banishes you?" he challenged them.

"What about you?" they asked. "Have you figured it out?"

"Well," he replied awkwardly, "I've thought a lot about it."

"If you can't find the answer, how can you expect that we would?" they cried. "When you said, 'Give us one day, and we will solve this problem,' we were confident that you would find the answer. We depended on you! Now what are we going to do? The king will be furious!"

"Obviously, this question is beyond us," Senaka admitted. "No doubt, Mahosadha has already solved it in one hundred ways."

"What are we waiting for?" the other three cried. "Let's go and see him!"

The four advisors hurried to Mahosadha's house. After greeting him politely, they asked, "Well, sir, have you figured out the question?"

"If I haven't, who will? Of course I have."

"Then tell us, too," they pleaded.

Mahosadha thought, "If I don't help them, the king will banish them and honor me. I do not want to be responsible for the downfall of these fools." Aloud he said, "All right, I will help you." He sat them down on low seats, and, rather than telling them what the king had seen and what had happened, he taught each of them one piece of the answer. "When the king asks you for the solution, if each of you recites your verse correctly, the king will be satisfied," he said and sent them away.

The next morning, when all the advisors went to wait on the king, he asked, "Senaka, have you solved my problem?"

"Sire, if I don't know the answer, who does?" Senaka replied.

"All right, then tell me," ordered the king.

"Young beggars and young princes enjoy goat meat, but neither eats dog meat," Senaka recited, not understanding a word of what he was saying, "still there may be friendship between a goat and a dog."

The king assumed that Senaka had figured out the secret, and he was pleased. "Pukkusa," he said, addressing his second advisor, "have you solved my problem?"

"Am I not a wise man?" Pukkusa asked in response.

"We shall see," the king replied.

"Men use a goatskin to cover a horse's back, but no one would use a dog-skin that way," Pukkusa recited, also not understanding a word of what he was saying. "Nevertheless, there may be friendship between a goat and a dog."

The king assumed that Pukkusa had also figured out the secret, and he was pleased. "Kavinda," he said, addressing his third advisor, "have you solved my problem?

"A goat has twisted horns, but a dog has none. One eats grass, and the other meat," Kavinda recited, also not understanding a word of what he was saying. "Nevertheless, there may be friendship between a goat and a dog."

The king assumed that Kavinda had also figured out the secret, and he was pleased. "Devinda," he said, addressing his fourth advisor, "have you solved my problem?"

"A goat eats grass and leaves; a dog eats neither, but feasts on rabbit and cat," Devinda recited, also not understanding a word of what he was saying. "Nevertheless, there may be friendship between a goat and a dog."

The king assumed that Pukkusa had also figured out the secret, and he was pleased. "My son," he said, addressing Mahosadha, "have you solved my problem?

"Sire, who, between the lowest hell and the highest heaven, could understand this question better than I?"

"No one, I am sure," replied the king. "Please tell me the answer."

"From the kitchen, a goat carries meat; from the stable, a dog carries grass. Banished from their natural places, these enemies have made a pact of friendship and serve each other well. From the corridor these two can be seen exchanging their bounty in the courtyard below."

The king, unaware that Mahosadha had coached the others, was delighted that all five had discovered the solution to his riddle. "How fortunate I am to have such wise men in my palace!" he exclaimed. "All of you have successfully solved this difficult riddle. I am very pleased, indeed! To each of you I give a chariot, a mule, and a village!"

Queen Udumbarā realized that Mahosadha had told the others what to say, and she was not at all satisfied that the king had rewarded all equally. As soon as she was alone with the king, she asked him, "Sire, who discovered the solution to your riddle?"

"Why, my dear," the king replied in surprise, "my five advisors did. You heard each of them give his very clear answer."

"How do you think they solved it?" she asked.

"I have no idea."

"Sire, your four senior advisors are fools!" she told him. "Mahosadha alone solved the problem. He didn't want the others to be banished, so he taught each of them one little piece. They had no idea what they were saying. It is most unfair that you gave all of them the same reward. You should acknowledge Mahosadha's much greater wisdom."

The king was pleased that Mahosadha had neither ridiculed the others nor divulged his role in helping them. Instead of revising the rewards he had given, however, the king decided to pose another problem and to bestow greater honor on Mahosadha when he solved it.

Not long afterwards, the opportunity arose. One morning, when the five advisors had come to wait upon him, the king said, "Senaka, I will ask a question."

"Please do so, Sire," Senaka replied.

"Wise and poor or rich and foolish! My question is this: is it better for a man to be endowed with wisdom and bereft of wealth, or endowed with wealth and bereft of wisdom? Which of these conditions, Senaka, should be considered the higher?"

The answer to this question had been handed down in Senaka's family for generations, so, without hesitation, he replied, "Your Majesty, wise men and fools, the educated and the illiterate, all provide service to one who is wealthy. They may be well-bred, and he may be illegitimate, but it doesn't matter. If he is rich, they serve him. Having seen that this is the way the world is, I declare that wisdom is lowly and that wealth is higher."

Without paying any attention to the other three, the king turned to Mahosadha and asked, "Mahosadha, how would you answer the same question?"

"Your Majesty," Mahosadha replied, "A fool, filled with false pride, commits many evil deeds; he sees this world but not the next, and he suffers for it in both. Beholding this, I declare that the poor wise man is superior to the wealthy fool."

"What do you say to that, Senaka?" asked the king.

"Your Majesty," Senaka replied, "Mahosadha is still a child. What does he know? Neither learning nor good looks can guarantee a comfortable life, but even an idiot, if he is wealthy and lucky with his money, is catered to by everyone. Having seen that this is the way the world is, I declare that wisdom is lowly and that wealth is higher."

"What do you say to that, my son?" the king asked Mahosadha.

"Your Majesty," Mahosadha replied, "what does Senaka know? He is like a crow pecking at scattered rice or a frog trying to lap up milk. He sees himself but not the stick which is about to fall on his head. The man of small wit, when he gets money, becomes intoxicated. When he is struck by misfortune, however, he is stupefied and writhes like a fish out of water. Beholding this, I declare that the poor wise man is superior to the wealthy fool."

"Your Majesty," Senaka retorted, "what does he know? In the forest, it is the sturdy tree full of fruit which the birds seek out. In the same way, the rich man attracts many friends among the powerful and influential. Having seen that this is the way the world is, I declare that wisdom is lowly and that wealth is higher."

"Your Majesty," Mahosadha countered, "what does this potbelly know? The rich fool may use his wealth to seek glory by violence, and he may roar loudly, but he is sorely mistaken. He will be dragged off to hell. Beholding this, I declare that the poor wise man is superior to the wealthy fool."

"Your Majesty," Senaka retorted, "look at all the rivers and streams that pour into the Gaṅgā. All lose their identity in that great river. When the Gaṅgā flows into the sea, it, too, can no longer be distinguished. In the same way, the wealthy absorb all those around them. Indeed, the world is devoted to wealth. Having seen that this is the way the world is, I declare that wisdom is lowly and that wealth is higher."

"Your Majesty," Mahosadha replied, "This mighty ocean, which Senaka has foolishly mentioned, beats incessantly on the shore. However mighty it may be, it cannot pass beyond that boundary for very long. So it is with the chattering of the fool. Even his prosperity cannot overcome the wise. Beholding this, I declare that the poor wise man is superior to the wealthy fool."

"Your Majesty," Senaka replied, "a wealthy man can easily gain a high position of influence and power so that, even if he lacks self-control, whatever he says has weight among his friends and in a court of law. In this case, money speaks, and wisdom alone is weak. Having seen that this is the way the world is, I declare that wisdom is lowly and that wealth is higher."

"Your Majesty," Mahosadha replied, "what does stupid Senaka know? For another's sake or for his own, when the fool speaks falsely, in this world, he is put to shame in front of others, and, in the next, he suffers even greater misery. Beholding this, I declare that the poor wise man is superior to the wealthy fool."

"Your Majesty," Senaka replied, "elephants, cattle, horses, and jewelry are found only in rich families. Because of these things, the rich man can enjoy life to the full. Having seen that this is the way the world is, I declare that wisdom is lowly and that wealth is higher."

"Your Majesty," Mahosadha replied, "The fool who performs thoughtless acts and speaks foolish words is cast off by fortune as the worn-out skin is cast off by a snake. Beholding this, I declare that the poor wise man is superior to the wealthy fool."

"Your Majesty," Senaka replied, "what can this little boy know? The five of us are wise, but, nonetheless, we all wait upon you with respect. Like Sakka, you are our lord and master. Having seen that this is the way the world is, I declare that wisdom is lowly and that wealth is higher."

"Your Majesty," Mahosadha replied, "this fool is looking only at himself and does not see the excellence of wisdom. When questions of this kind arise, it is the sage who finds the answers. Without the wise, the wealthy fall into confusion. Beholding this, I declare that the poor wise man is superior to the wealthy fool."

"What do you say to that, Senaka?" asked the king.

Senaka was disturbed. Like one who had used up all the corn in his granary, he sat there speechless and unable to answer. Seeing that his opponent was defeated, Mahosadha concluded, "Verily, Your Majesty, wisdom is esteemed by the virtuous, whereas wealth is respected only by those who are devoted to base sensual pleasures. Wealth can never surpass wisdom."

"I hereby declare Mahosadha the victor!" proclaimed the king. "He has refuted every opposing argument and answered every question. Whatever problem I have posed, he has wisely solved. To show my pleasure, I grant this sage one thousand cows, a bull, an elephant, ten chariots, each drawn by thoroughbreds, and sixteen prosperous villages."

From that day on, there was no question as to the wisdom of Mahosadha. The sage's glory continued to increase, and he was looked after by Queen Udumbarā. When he became sixteen, she thought, "My younger brother has grown up. Now we must find a wife for him." She mentioned this to the king, and he agreed.

When the queen broached the subject to Mahosadha, he told her that he wanted to get married, but he was sure that he would not be satisfied with a wife that she and the king chose, so he asked her not to do anything for a few days while he himself searched for a suitable bride. The queen had no objection to this and agreed to inform the king that he would be absent for a few days.

Mahosadha disguised himself as a tailor and went to the northern town. As he was approaching the town, he saw a lovely young woman carrying a pot of rice gruel. "I can see that that young woman is wise and that she has all the auspicious signs," he thought. "If she is not married, she must become my wife."

When she saw Mahosadha, she thought, "If I could live in the house of such a man, I would be able to restore my family's fortune."

Stopping a short distance in front of her, Mahosadha clenched his fist. The young woman understood that he was asking whether or not she had a husband, and she held out her open palm.

Mahosadha was pleased. He went up to her and asked her name.

"My name is that which for any being does not exist, never has been, and never will be," she replied.

"Sister," Mahosadha replied, "all beings are subject to death, so your name must refer to the deathless. Is it Amara?"

"You have spoken correctly, Master," she replied.

"For whom do you carry that gruel?" he asked.

"It is for the deva of former times," she replied.

"The devas of former times are one's parents," he said. "No doubt, you mean your father."

"You have spoken correctly, Master," she replied.

"What is your father doing?"

"He is making two out of one."

"He must be plowing."

"You have spoken correctly, Master," she replied.

"Where is your father plowing?"

"Near the place where one goes, never to return."

"He must be plowing near a charnel ground."

"You have spoken correctly, Master," she replied.

"Will you come back today?"

"If it comes, I will not come. If it does not come, I will come."

"Your father must be plowing on the other side of a river. If the river floods, you will not return. If it doesn't flood, you will."

"You have spoken correctly, Master," she replied, and she offered him some gruel.

Thinking it would be discourteous to refuse, he accepted.

As she put the pot of gruel on the ground, he thought, "If she offers it to me without first washing the jar and giving me water to wash my hands, I will leave her."

Amara poured a little water in a jar, swished it around and offered it to him to wash his hands. Then she placed the empty jar on the ground, and, after stirring the gruel, she put some of it into the jar, saving enough for her father. She handed the jar to him, and he noticed that the gruel was very weak.

"There is not enough rice in this gruel," he said.

"There was no water, Master." she replied.

"During the growing season, you must not have had enough water for irrigation," he said.

"You have spoken correctly, Master," she replied.

When he had finished drinking the gruel, he rinsed his mouth and said, "Sister, I would like to go to your house. Please tell me the way."

"Past the cakes and the gruel, beyond the double-leaf tree in bloom, along the way of the hand with which one eats. Avoid the way of the hand with which one does not eat. My parents' house lies there."

Mahosadha thanked her and took his leave. He entered the town and walked past a cake shop. A little further, he passed a gruel shop and an orchid tree in full bloom. He turned right and easily found her parents' house. He could see that they were poor but that they had once been wealthy merchants. Amara's mother welcomed him and offered him a seat.

"Will you have some gruel, Master?" she asked.

"Thank you, Mother," he replied, "but I received some from Sister Amara." The woman understood at once that he had come on her daughter's account.

"Mother, I am a tailor," Mahosadha announced. "Do you have anything to mend?"

"Yes, Master, but we cannot pay," she replied.

"There is no need to pay, Mother. Just bring whatever you have."

She gave him some old clothes, and the sage quickly mended them all.

Then he said to her, "Please announce my presence to the people in the street."

She went from house to house in the neighborhood and announced that a tailor had come to her house. By the end of the day, Mahosadha had earned one thousand coins.

At noon, Amara's mother served him lunch, and, in the evening, she asked how much food she should prepare.

"Cook enough, Mother, for all those who are staying in this house," he replied.

The woman understood that he would be staying. Late in the afternoon, Amara returned from the forest, bearing a bundle of wood on her head and a basket of leaves on her hip. She left the wood near the front door, put the basket of leaves in its proper place, and entered by the back door. Her father returned at sunset.

Mahosadha enjoyed a delicious meal of rice and curry. Amara served her parents before she herself sat down to eat. After they had finished, Amara washed her parents' feet. Then she washed Mahosadha's feet. Mahosadha stayed with the family for several days, observing Amara's behavior.

One day, to test her, he said, "My dear Amara, take half a measure of rice and prepare some gruel, a cake, and some boiled rice for me."

Without the slightest hesitation, she agreed and measured out the exact amount of rice he had stipulated. After husking the rice, she separated it into three small portions. With the big grains, she made gruel; the middling grains she boiled, and, with the small pieces, she made a cake.

She served Mahosadha the gruel, and its exquisite taste sent a thrill through his body. Nevertheless, to test her, he spat it out and said, "Sister, if you don't know how to cook, why did you spoil my rice?"

Without the least bit of anger, she gave him the cake and said, "Master, since the gruel is not good, please eat the cake."

He did the same with the cake, and, again, the same with the boiled rice. Then, pretending to be angry, he mixed the remains of all three together and smeared it all over her face and body. "Go and sit by the door!" he ordered her.

"Very good, Master," she replied and went to sit by the door.

Thus, Mahosadha saw that there was no pride in her, and he called, "Sister, come here."

Amara returned and knelt before him, and he removed from his bag a beautiful silk sari which he had brought from the palace. He placed it in her hands and said, "Sister, please bathe and come back wearing this." After she had come back, magnificently adorned, Mahosadha gave her parents the money he had earned tailoring and an additional one thousand coins which he had brought with him. Then he returned with her to the city.

To test her further, he left her in a room of the gatekeeper's house. After secretly informing the gatekeeper's wife of his scheme, he went to his own house.

He summoned several of his companions and said to them, "There is a beautiful woman in the gatekeeper's house at the northern gate. Here are one thousand coins. Please go and enjoy yourselves with her."

The young men cheerfully took the money and offered it to Amara, but she scorned them. "That is not worth the dust on my master's feet," she cried, sending them away.

Satisfied that she had passed that test, Mahosadha sent several others of his companions to seize Amara and to carry her to his house without telling her anything. Meanwhile, he dressed himself in his finest robes. The men carried her in and placed her before Mahosadha, who was sitting in the shadows, so, of course, she did not recognize him. She looked at the sage and smiled. Then she began weeping.

Disguising his voice so that she still would not recognize him, he asked her why she had smiled and why she was weeping. "Sir, when I beheld your magnificent robes, I could see that your glory is certainly due to some good deed you did in a previous life. I smiled in appreciation of your good fortune. Then I realized that you are about to commit a great sin against one who is pledged to another and that, for that, you will go to hell. I wept in pity for the misery you will suffer."

Firmly convinced of her purity, he sent her back to the gatekeeper's house. Later, he returned there himself in his guise as a tailor and spent the night.

The next morning, he went to the palace and told Queen Udumbarā everything that had happened, and the queen joyfully informed the king. The queen sent a magnificent sari and exquisite jewelry for Amara to wear. Then, standing the bride in a royal chariot so that all could see her, the queen ordered a procession around the city to carry her to Mahosadha's house, where the wedding ceremony was performed with great pomp. The king and the queen each gave the young couple a gift worth one thousand coins, and every citizen of Mithilā sent a wedding present, as well. Amara accepted half of each gift, but graciously returned the other half. In this way, she gained the respect of everyone in the kingdom.

Not long afterwards, Senaka remarked to the other three senior royal advisors, "Friends, we cannot compete with this commoner's son, Mahosadha, and now he has a wife as clever as he is. We must find a way to drive a wedge between him and the king."

"What can we do?" they asked Senaka. "We'll follow your suggestion, teacher!"

"All right, here is my plan. I will steal the jewel from the royal crown. Pukkusa, you take the king's golden necklace. Kavinda, you take his woolen cape. Devinda, you take his golden slippers. Then all we have to do is to smuggle them into Mahosadha's house." During the next few days, they managed to steal these things from the palace.

Senaka put the royal jewel in a pot of dates. He gave the pot to a servant girl and told her to pretend to be selling them but not to give them to anyone except someone from Mahosadha's house.

The girl walked back and forth in front of the sage's house, crying, "I have dates! Who needs dates?"

Amara noticed that the girl was not going anywhere else and suspected something. After ordering her own servants to stay inside, she herself stepped out and called, "Come here, young woman. I would like some dates." Amara called for her servants, but, of course, none responded, so she sent the girl to fetch them.

While she was gone, Amara put her hand into the pot, felt around, and found the jewel.

The girl returned, saying that she could not find any servants.

"It doesn't matter," Amara said. "Please tell me whose servant you are, dear?"

"I have come from the house of the sage Senaka, madam," the girl replied.

After also asking her name and her mother's name, Amara said, "Very well, give me some dates."

"Please, madam, take the pot and all," the girl insisted. "I need no payment."

"Thank you," Amara said, taking the pot of dates. "You may go."

After the girl had left, Amara wrote on a leaf that Senaka, on that date, had sent the royal jewel in a pot of dates, carried by that girl and indicated her mother's name, as well.

In the same way, Pukkusa sent the golden necklace hidden in a casket of jasmine flowers, Kavinda sent the woolen cape hidden in a basket of vegetables, and Devinda sent the golden slippers hidden in a bundle of straw.

Amara accepted each gift in the same way, carefully recording the details each time. She put the leaves in a safe place and told everything to her husband.

One day, the four senior advisors mentioned that it had been a time since they had seen the king with his royal regalia.

"So it has!" replied the king, and he ordered servants to fetch his crown, his golden necklace, his woolen cape, and his golden slippers. The servants went to the treasure house to retrieve these things but quickly returned to announce that the jewel from the crown was gone and that they could not find the other three items at all.

"Your Majesty," the advisors said, "we think that we have seen these things in Mahosadha's house. It seems that he is using them himself in secret. Undoubtedly, the honor you have bestowed on that young son of a commoner has made him so proud that now he is your enemy." The king believed them and was furious.

Some of Mahosadha's companions, who happened to overhear this, went to warn Mahosadha, who replied, "I will go to the king myself and find out."

As soon as it was proper, he went to the palace, but the king shouted, "I don't know Mahosadha! What is he doing here?"

Mahosadha left the palace, but the king ordered officers to arrest him. Again, his friends sent him a warning. He told his wife that the time had come and immediately left the city in disguise. In the southern town, he took up residence with a master potter and served as his apprentice. Soon, the city was filled with rumors that the great sage had fled in disgrace.

Senaka, Pukkusa, Kavinda, and Devinda each secretly sent a message to Amara: "Do not worry that Mahosadha has gone. After all, I am also a wise man!"

Amara graciously accepted the messages and invited the advisors to visit her. As soon as each one arrived, Amara had her servants seize him, shave his hair and beard, beat him, roll him in a straw mat, and put him in the outhouse. When she had taken care of all four, she announced to the king that she would like to see him.

She had her servants place the four advisors, still rolled up inside the mats, in a cart and proceeded to the palace with the royal regalia. After servants had dumped the mats in the courtyard, Amara announced to the king, "Your Majesty, my husband, the wise Mahosadha is not a thief! Senaka stole the jewel, Pukkusa stole the golden necklace, Kavinda stole the woolen cape, and Devinda stole the golden slippers. Here are the records indicating when each item was sent to our house and who carried it. Here, also, are the thieves," she said, pointing to the four mats, "who have shamed themselves by seeking my favors. Take back what is yours, and throw these scoundrels out!"

The king was extremely confused by this turn of events, and, without Mahosadha to advise him, he did not know what to do. He simply told the four advisors to bathe and to go home.

The deva that lived in the royal umbrella missed hearing Mahosadha's sweet voice advising the king and wondered where he was. When she learned that the king had chased him away, she resolved to bring him back. That night, she appeared to the king and posed four riddles, demanding a solution. Of course, the king could not answer, but he told the deva that he would ask his advisors and give her the answers the next day.

The next morning, he summoned the four advisors, but they sent messages in reply that they were ashamed to show themselves in the street, shaven as they were. The king sent them skullcaps and ordered them to appear in court.

When they finally arrived, the king told them, "Last night, the deva of the royal umbrella appeared to me and demanded that I solve four riddles. You must give me the answers."

"Of course, Your Majesty," they replied. "You have but to recite these riddles, and we will solve them for you."

"The first riddle," the king began, "is this: 'He strikes with hands and feet and beats upon the face; yet he is dear and grows dearer than a husband.'"

"Uh, strikes how? Strikes whom?" Senaka stammered, without understanding a word. The other three just stared dumbly at the king. In shame, they left the king without answering or even asking about the other three riddles.

That night, the deva returned and asked the king for the answers. The distressed king replied, "I asked my four advisors, the wisest men in my court, but even they could not answer."

"Those fools?" the deva cried. "Your Majesty, when you want fire, don't blow on a firefly! When you want milk, don't squeeze a horn. No one but the wise Mahosadha can solve these riddles. I will give you one more day! If you do not find the solution to these riddles, I will split your head with my fiery sword! Do what you know you must do!" The king cowered in fear when he heard the deva's dreadful threat.

Early the next morning, he sent out four courtiers, one in each direction, to find Mahosadha, to show him all honor, and to bring him back as quickly as possible. The courtier who went to the western town found nothing at all. The one who went to the northern town talked with Amara's family, but they had not seen or heard anything from the sage. The courtier who went to the eastern town searched throughout the great hall but found no trace of him. The courtier who went to the southern town happened to see Mahosadha sitting on a bundle of straw at the potter's shop, eating his lunch of rice balls and soup. He was completely covered with dirt since he had been digging clay and turning pots on his master's wheel all morning.

When Mahosadha saw the courtier, he knew that the king had sent for him, that he would be reinstated, and that he would soon be enjoying choice food prepared by Lady Amara. He put down the ball of rice he was eating, stood up, and rinsed his mouth.

The courtier, who happened to be a follower of Senaka, said sarcastically, "Wise teacher, what a surprise to see you here, covered with clay and eating poor rice and thin soup! Is this how your wisdom serves you? It seems that Senaka was right! Wisdom is lowly, and wealth is higher."

"Blind fool!" retorted the sage. "By the power of my wisdom, I will restore my prosperity when I choose. I am here of my own free will. When the time is ripe, I will make an effort, and you will see that the poor wise man is superior to the wealthy fool. Why have you come?"

"Wise sir," the courtier replied, "the deva in the royal umbrella has posed four riddles to the king, but none of the four wise men could solve them. The king has sent me to fetch you. Please dress and come with me." The courtier presented Mahosadha with clean clothes and one thousand coins, all of which had been sent by the king.

During this exchange, the master potter had been listening attentively. He was shocked to learn that his apprentice was actually the great sage. When Mahosadha turned toward him, he immediately fell to the ground and prostrated himself. "Do not be alarmed, Master," Mahosadha said. "You have no need to worry. You have been of great help to me. Please accept this gift." Mahosadha gave him all the money he had just received from the king. Then, taking the time neither to bathe nor to change clothes, he stepped into the chariot and said to the courtier, "Come! Let us go to see the king!"

When they arrived at the palace, the courtier asked Mahosadha to wait and hurried in to announce his success to the king.

"Where did you find the sage, my son?" asked the king.

"Your Majesty," the courtier replied, "he was working as an apprentice to a potter in the southern town. As soon as I told him that you wanted to see him, he gave the money you sent to his master and mounted the chariot. Although he was covered with clay, he neither bathed nor put on the exquisite clothes you sent. He hurried to the palace and is waiting outside."

"If he were my enemy," the king thought, "he would have come with an army. He is certainly not after my throne."

"Tell the sage to go to his home, to bathe, and to dress," the king commanded the courtier. "When he is properly attired, he is to return to the palace with due ceremony."

When Mahosadha returned to the palace, the king greeted him warmly. Then, as the sage stood to one side, the king said, "Sir, some wealthy men commit no evil deeds in order to protect their wealth. Some avoid evil for fear of blame. Some, because they are ignorant. Some, because they are completely incapable. You are wise and extremely competent. You could, if you wished, seize control of all of Jambudīpa. Pray, tell me, why do you do me no harm? Why have you not tried to kill me and to seize my throne?"

"Your Majesty," Mahosadha replied, "Wise men never commit evil deeds for the sake of the pleasure that wealth provides. The virtuous never deviate from the right, not because of misfortune, nor because of friendship, nor because of hatred."

"It is often said," interjected the king, "that, if a man raises himself from poverty to a position of wealth and respect, he will always walk the path of righteousness."

"Sire," Mahosadha replied, "if a man has rested beneath a tree and benefited from its shade, it would be treachery to cut a branch from that tree. How much worse would it be for a person to harm or to kill his benefactor? Your Majesty gave my father great wealth. You have shown me favor and bestowed great honor upon me. How could I entertain any thoughts of betrayal or injury to you?"

Having assuaged and pleased the king with this avowal of loyalty, Mahosadha took it upon himself to teach the king and to reprove him for the ill-treatment he had received. "Sire," he continued, "when a man has been shown the right or has had his doubts cleared by another, he becomes the protector and the refuge of that other. A wise man will not forsake that trust. A virtuous layman is restrained by the moral precepts. A virtuous ascetic is restrained by his practice. A virtuous king must be restrained by justice. Only a bad king would decide a case without examining the evidence from both sides. Anger is never justified. The king who makes well-pondered judgments will always enjoy fame, respect, and honor."

When he heard this, the king stood up and invited Mahosadha to sit on the throne under the royal umbrella. He himself sat down on a lower seat and said, "Wise sir, the deva of the royal umbrella gave me four riddles. I consulted my four other advisors, but they could find no answers. Please solve these riddles for me, my son."

"Sire, let me hear the riddles, and I will give you the answers you desire."

"The first riddle," the king began, "is this: 'He strikes with hands and feet and beats upon the face; yet he is dear and grows dearer than a husband.'"

"Your Majesty," Mahosadha replied, "This is as clear as the moon in the night sky. When a child is on his mother's lap, he playfully kicks her, beats her face, and pulls her hair. With a broad smile, she asks, 'Little rogue, why do you beat me so?' and she presses him close to her breast. Unable to restrain her affection, she kisses him, and, at such a time, he is dearer to her than his father."

"The riddle is well solved!" cried the deva with her sweet voice as she emerged from the royal umbrella showing half her body. She presented the sage with a precious casket full of heavenly perfume and flowers and disappeared. The king was pleased and also rewarded him.

"The second riddle is this," said the king. "She abuses him roundly, yet wishes him to be near, and he is dearer than a husband.'"

"Sire," Mahosadha replied, "when a boy is seven years old, he is able to do his mother's bidding. Supposing she tells him to go to the bazaar, he may retort, 'If you will give me that snack, I will go.' After she gives it to him, he may eat it and say, 'Why should I go out in the sun to do your work while you just sit there in the cool shade?' If he says this, makes a face, and mocks her, she may get angry, pick up a stick, and cry, 'How dare you eat what I give you without doing anything for me!' When he runs off, she may shout, 'Run, you rascal! I hope thieves chop you up into little bits!' She sounds so angry that he may stay away playing the whole day, and, in the evening, afraid to go home, he may go to an uncle's house. Meanwhile, his mother has forgotten her anger and is watching the road for him. When he doesn't return, she realizes that he was frightened, and her heart is full of pain. With tears streaming down her face, she searches the houses of her relatives. When she finally finds her son, she hugs and kisses him, and cries, 'My darling son! Did you take my words seriously?' In the hour of anger, a mother loves her son even more, and, at such a time, he is dearer to her than his father."

Both the deva and the king again rewarded him.

"The third riddle is this," said the king. "She reviles and reproaches him with neither cause nor reason; yet he is dearer than a husband.'"

"Sire," Mahosadha replied, "when a pair of lovers are secretly enjoying their love's delights, the woman may say to the man, 'You don't care for me! Your heart is elsewhere, I know!' As she coquettishly accuses him and as they quarrel thus, they, in fact, grow dearer to each other."

Both the deva and the king again rewarded him.

"The fourth riddle is this," said the king. "They take food and drink, clothes and lodging; in fact, they carry them off; still, they are dearer than a husband.'"

"Sire," Mahosadha replied, "this refers to religious mendicants. Pious devotees, believing that giving alms offers a reward in the next world, delight in giving. When they see these ascetics accepting their offerings and carrying them away, they are overjoyed, and this increases their affection and respect for the ascetics."

When the last question had been answered, the deva presented Mahosadha with a golden casket filled with the seven precious things, and the king appointed him commander-in-chief. Mahosadha's glory became even greater than before.

Once again, the four senior advisors found themselves eclipsed. "What can we do?" they grumbled to each other as they watched Mahosadha's star rising higher and higher in the court.

"I have a plan," Senaka told them. "Mahosadha, unlike us, was not born among nobility. He is a country bumpkin and does not know the ins and outs of court life. If we can make it look like he is secretly scheming something, we can discredit him with the king, and that will be the end of him. Let's go and talk to him!"

The four went to Mahosadha's house and greeted him. "Wise sir," Senaka said, "we would like to ask you a few questions."

"Ask away," he consented.

"Wise sir," Senaka said, "in what should a man be firmly established?"

"In the truth," Mahosadha promptly answered.

"Having established himself in the truth, what should he do next?" Senaka asked.

"He should make his fortune," Mahosadha replied.

"Having made his fortune, what should he do next?" Senaka asked.

"He must learn from wise advisors," Mahosadha replied.

"Having learned from the wise, what should he do next?" Senaka asked.

"He must be careful not to divulge his secrets to anyone," Mahosadha replied.

"Thank you very much, sir," the four of them said together, as they stood up and took their leave. Once outside, they gloated to each other, "Now we have him! We must report this to the king!" They went to their own homes, satisfied that they were about to see the last of the sage.

The next day, as soon as they arrived at the palace, they announced to the king, "Sire, Mahosadha is a traitor!"

"I do not believe you!" the king replied. "My son would never betray me."

"Sire, you must believe us! The sage is scheming something. He is guarding some mysterious secret. He trusts no one. If you do not believe us, ask him yourself. Sometime, you might ask him to whom a secret might be told. If he says, 'To no one,' you can be sure that he is scheming something against your royal person and that he is afraid to let anyone know about it."

A few days later, the king had the opportunity and said, "An interesting question has occurred to me, and now that you five wise men are together, I would like to hear your opinions. If one has an important secret, whether good or bad, to whom should he confidently reveal this secret? What do you think?"

Senaka was delighted that the king was bringing this up, but, to make sure that the king was with them, he said, "Sire, each of us has his own thought on this matter, but it would help us to see the matter clearly, if you would express your opinion first."

The king, not being the brightest of men, answered, "If a man has a wife who is virtuous, faithful, affectionate, and supportive, that man can confidently tell his wife his secret, whether good or bad."

"The king is on my side!" thought Senaka joyfully.

"What say you, Senaka?" asked the king.

"If a man has a friend, Sire," Senaka said, "who cares for him when he is sick and who is his refuge in distress, that man can confidently tell his friend his secret, whether good or bad."

"What say you, Pukkusa?" asked the king.

"If a man has a brother, Sire," Pukkusa said, "who is virtuous and loyal, that man can confidently tell his brother his secret, whether good or bad."

"What say you, Kavinda?" asked the king.

"If a man has a son, Sire," Kavinda said, "who is obedient and wise, that man can confidently tell his son his secret, whether good or bad."

"What say you, Devinda?" asked the king.

"If a man has a mother, Sire," Devinda said, "who fondly cherishes him, that man can confidently tell his mother his secret, whether good or bad."

Finally, the king turned to the sage and asked, "What say you, Mahosadha?"

Mahosadha answered, "Sire, the value of a secret is its secrecy. Once it is revealed to anyone, that value is compromised. As long as the secrecy of a situation, an idea, or a scheme is important, a wise man would hesitate to divulge that secret to anyone. Once the situation changes, once the idea becomes a reality, or once the scheme is accomplished, he may speak freely."

Mahosadha immediately sensed that the king was displeased with his answer and noticed that the king and Senaka exchanged glances. He guessed that the four had once again slandered him to the king and that it must have been a trick question. "How unpredictable this king is!" he thought. "No one can guess where this might lead. I had better leave at once!" He stood up, paid his respects to the king, and left the hall.

He continued thinking about what the others had said. "Each of the four said that a secret could be revealed. One said to a friend, another said to a brother, another said to a son, and the last said to a mother. There must be something behind all that. I wonder how I can find out what it is."

The sun had set, and the lamps had been lit, so Mahosadha realized that the other advisors would also soon be leaving. He knew that, when the four left the court, they usually sat for a few minutes on an overturned stone trough and discussed their plans before going home. He had his servants lift the trough and spread a carpet on the ground. He lay down on the carpet, had his servants replace the trough, and instructed them to let him out once the four advisors had gone away.

As soon as Mahosadha had left, Senaka said to the king, "Sire, what do you think? Do you believe us now?"

"How could I not believe you, wise Senaka? He said exactly what you said he would say! Now what must we do?"

"Sire, there is no time to wait," Senaka replied. "He must be killed."

"No one looks after my interests as well as you do, Senaka," said the king, feeling very reassured. As he handed Senaka his royal sword, he continued, "When Mahosadha comes to the palace tomorrow morning, you and your friends must be waiting at the gate. Strike the traitor with this sword, and save me!"

"Very good, Your Majesty," Senaka replied, accepting the sword. "Have no fear. We will do your bidding."

As the four left the court, they whispered to each other, "Well done! At last, we will be rid of him!" Feeling triumphant, they sat down on the trough to gloat over their success. "Who will strike the fellow?" Senaka asked.

"It is your plan, master," the others said. "You should do it."

"All right," Senaka agreed. "Now, tell me, friends. I'm curious about what you said to the king. Why did you say that you can confidently reveal a secret to a brother, a mother, or a son?"

"What about you?" they asked. "First tell us why you said that a secret can be confidently revealed to a friend."

"What does that matter to you?" Senaka asked.

"Why won't you tell us?" they asked in reply. "Aren't we your friends?"

"Well, I have a secret," Senaka relented, "but if the king ever heard about it, he would have me killed."

"Don't worry, master," they assured him. "You can trust us, and there is no one else here."

"What if," he asked, tapping the trough, "that bumpkin were under here?"

"What a joke!" they cried, laughing. "He is so proud of himself that he would never crawl into such a dirty place! He is intoxicated with his own glory! Come on! Tell us!"

"All right," Senaka began. "Do you remember the famous courtesan who used to live near here?"

"Of course, we do!" they replied.

"Have you seen her recently?" Senaka asked.

"No. Come to think of it, we haven't."

"Well, some time ago, I had my pleasure with her in the sal grove of the royal park. When she fell asleep, I killed her and tied her jewelry in a bundle, which is now hanging from an elephant's tusk in an upper room of my house. Of course, I dare not do anything with it until it's safe. The only other person I've told this to is my best friend. I'm sure that he has not told anyone else. That's why I said that a secret may be confidently revealed to a friend."

"Well, I have a secret, too," Pukkusa admitted. "On my thigh, there is a spot of leprosy. No one knows about this except my younger brother. Every morning, he washes it and puts salve and a bandage on it. Sometimes, when the king wishes to rest, he calls me and lays his head on my thigh. If he ever found out about my leprosy, he would kill me. I am sure that my brother will never tell a soul. That's why I said that a secret may be confidently revealed to a brother."

"Well, I have a secret, too," Kavinda admitted. "Every month, on the night of the new moon, a deva named Naradeva takes possession of me, and I bark like a mad dog. I told my son, and, whenever he sees the condition coming on, he locks me in a back room. In order to hide the noise of my barking, he throws a party with lots of music. He has vowed never to tell anyone about this. That's why I said that a secret may be confidently revealed to a son."

"Well, I have a secret, too," Devinda admitted. "As you know, I am the inspector of the king's jewels. One day, I stole the magnificent Verocanamani, the gem which Sakka gave to King Kusa, and I gave it to my mother. Every morning, as I leave home to go to court, my mother hands me the gem, and I hold it for a few seconds. Just from touching that jewel, I am blessed with good fortune all day in the palace. The king always greets me first, and he gives me money every day. If he ever finds out that I have that gem, he will have me killed, but I know that my secret is safe with my mother. That's why I said that a secret may be confidently revealed to a mother."

The four advisors stood up and bade each other farewell. "Be sure to come early tomorrow," Senaka reminded them. "First thing in the morning, we will kill the churl!" With the greatest of confidence, each went to his own home.

As soon as the four had left, Mahosadha's men lifted the trough and released their master. After he had washed and eaten supper, he told a servant that he was expecting an urgent message from Queen Udumbarā and lay down on his bed.

That evening, the king was extremely upset. He lay in bed tossing and turning with pangs of guilt. "Mahosadha has served me since he was seven years old," he thought, "and he has never done me any wrong. The deva would have split my head if he hadn't solved the riddles for me. I never should have believed Senaka and the others. They just want revenge. Why did I give them my sword? Now I will never see the peerless sage again! What a fool I was!"

Queen Udumbarā noticed his restlessness and asked, "What is troubling you, Sire? Have I done anything to displease you?"

"No, my dear, you have done nothing wrong, but I have made a great mistake. Senaka and the other advisors told me that Mahosadha was scheming against me, and I believed them. I even gave them my sword so that they could kill him tomorrow morning. I can't bear to think about losing the wise sage, and I sorely regret that I have condemned him to death."

The queen was devastated to hear this, and she immediately began thinking of ways to save the sage. "First," she thought, "I must console the king. As soon as he is asleep, I will send a message to my brother." Aloud she said, "Sire, don't be upset. You really had no choice. Your first consideration has to be your own safety. After all, the sage is just a commoner's son. You raised him to a position of power and made him commander-in-chief. You shouldn't be surprised that all that honor has gone to his head and that he has indeed become your enemy. Just put it out of your mind, and go to sleep."

The king was greatly relieved to hear her say this, and he soon fell fast asleep.

The queen then went to her own chamber and wrote a letter informing Mahosadha of the danger. She explained that the king had given the four advisors his sword and that they would be waiting early in the morning. "Do not come to the palace tomorrow unless you have the entire city behind you," she concluded.

She put the letter in the center of a cake, tied it with a string to conceal it, and put the cake into a jar. She sealed the jar and gave it to a servant, instructing her to hand it directly to Mahosadha. The servant walked straight to the sage's house. No one hindered her because they knew she was carrying delicacies from the queen, and all the guards had been informed that the queen had been given the privilege of sending food to Mahosadha at all hours of the day or night.

As soon as the servant arrived at the sage's house, a man woke Mahosadha and told him that a present had arrived from the queen. Mahosadha accepted the jar and dismissed the girl, who informed Her Highness that she had accomplished her mission. The sage opened the jar, read the message, and perfectly grasped the situation. After a few minutes of deliberation, he returned to bed.

Early the next morning, the four advisors concealed themselves just inside the palace gate and waited. Senaka held the sword above his head, ready to strike Mahosadha down as soon as he stepped through the gate, but the sage never arrived. Finally, they gave up. Humiliated that they had failed at their task, they went to see the king.

Mahosadha, however, had not been idle. By sunrise, he had positioned guards at strategic points and had gained control of the entire city. Gathering many of his companions around him, he mounted a chariot and proceeded with great pomp to the palace. Since he was very familiar with the king's schedule, he timed his arrival so that the king would be in his chamber and looking out the window. Mahosadha stepped out of the chariot and saluted the king. "If he were my enemy," the king thought, "he would not salute me!" The king descended to the throne room with the queen and summoned the sage. Mahosadha entered and sat in his usual seat. The other four advisors were also sitting in their seats.

Pretending that he had done nothing wrong, the king said, "My son, yesterday you left us abruptly. This morning you have come quite late. Why are you treating me so negligently?"

"Sire," Mahosadha replied, "I did not come to the palace early this morning because I knew that you had ordered your four advisors to kill me as I entered the gate. Perhaps you recall mentioning this secret to your wife last night."

The king glared angrily at his queen.

"Your Majesty," Mahosadha continued, "why would you be angry with the queen? I know many secrets. Perhaps I learned your secret from your wife, but do you think that I have talked with Senaka's friend, Pukkusa's brother, Kavinda's son, and Devinda's mother to learn their secrets? I know all their secrets! I know everything, past, present, and future." As the four advisors gasped, Mahosadha said, "Sire, let me tell you a few secrets.

"In the sal grove, Senaka killed the famous courtesan of Mithilā and stole her jewelry, which he has hidden in his house. I ask you, Sire, which of us is your enemy?"

"Is this true, Senaka?" the king asked.

"Yes, Your Majesty," Senaka replied meekly, and the king ordered guards to arrest him.

"Your Majesty often rests his head on Pukkusa's thigh. What you find so soft is actually the bandages which cover a leprous spot which he conceals there."

"Is this true, Pukkusa?" the king asked.

"Yes, Your Majesty," Pukkusa replied reluctantly, and the king ordered the guards to arrest him, too.

"Every month, Your Majesty, on the night of the full moon, Kavinda is possessed by a deva. He crawls on all fours and barks like a dog."

"Is this true, Kavinda?" the king asked.

"Yes, Your Majesty," Kavinda replied, barely audibly, and the king ordered the guards to arrest him, too.

"Perhaps Your Majesty has not yet noticed that the precious octagonal gem which Sakka presented to King Kusa, your illustrious ancestor, is missing. Some time ago, your trusted Devinda stole it and gave it to his mother."

"Is this true, Devinda?" the king asked.

"Yes, Your Majesty," Devinda replied timidly, and the king ordered the guards to arrest him, too.

"Thus, you can see, Your Majesty, that it is never wise to divulge a secret, not to a wife nor to anyone else. These four, who declared that a secret can be confidently revealed to a friend, a brother, a mother, and a son, have come to utter ruin. The value of a secret is its secrecy. When one discloses a secret to another, he becomes the slave of that person. As many as there are who know a man's secret, so many are that man's anxieties."

The king was furious. "These four advisors," he shouted, "defamed the wise Mahosadha and tried to turn me against him, but they are themselves wretched traitors! Take them to the southern gate and cut off their heads!"

Guards bound the hands of the four hapless advisors behind their backs and marched them through the streets, beating them at every crossroads.

"Your Majesty," Mahosadha interceded, "these men have been your advisors for many years. It is not right that you should now order their execution. Please reconsider and grant them your clemency."

The king consented, and turned them over to Mahosadha to be his slaves. The sage immediately gave them their freedom. "In that case," cried the king, "they cannot live in the kingdom. I banish them from my realm!"

Mahosadha again appealed to the king, asking him to pardon their blind folly and to restore them to their former positions. The king was so impressed and pleased with the sage's compassion that he agreed. "If my son has this much gentle mercy for his enemies, what must he feel toward others!" thought the king.

From then on, however, the four advisors were like snakes defanged. The king began to regard the wise Mahosadha as his chief and most trusted advisor. Mahosadha, for his part, reflected, "I have, indeed, become the king's white umbrella. Because I manage the kingdom, I must be vigilant."

Mahosadha set about preparing the city for possible dangers and fortifying it against enemies. He ordered a great rampart to be built around the city. This great wall had elaborate gates and hundreds of watchtowers. The wall was surrounded by three moats, a water moat resplendent with the five kinds of lotuses and infested with man-eating fish and crocodiles, a mud moat, and a dry moat. Inside the city, he ordered that all dilapidated, abandoned buildings be torn down and that, in their place, tanks be dug and filled with water. All storehouses were stocked with grain. Ascetics were asked to bring white mud and water lily seeds from the Himavat when they returned to the city. Canals and waterways were dredged and repaired. The towns around the city were also cleaned, and old buildings were restored.

Traveling merchants who visited the city were given warm hospitality and were gently questioned as to conditions in their own countries and the tastes of their kings. Having gathered this information, Mahosadha sent soldiers to each of the one hundred one other kingdoms in Jambudīpa with gold and jeweled accessories as gifts. Each gift was designed to the taste of that particular king, and each was engraved with the name "Mahosadha," but the engraving was skillfully done in such a way that it would not become visible until the time was right. These soldiers, who were, in fact, spies, were instructed to take up residence and to enter the service of their respective kings. They were to observe conditions and to send back any useful information they gathered. Mahosadha promised them that their families would be well cared for during their absence.

From the kingdom of Ekabala, the spy sent a message that King Sankhapāla was mysteriously assembling a great army. As soon as Mahosadha had received this message, he brought out the clever parrot Māthara, fed him honey and grain, and gave him sweet water to drink. He anointed the joints of the bird's wings with oil which had been refined one thousand times and said, "My friend, find out what King Sankhapāla is doing in Ekabala. Then fly all over Jambudīpa and bring me the news." He released the bird from the eastern window and watched him fly toward Ekabala. Māthara did not find anything worrisome in that kingdom, but, when he reached Uttarapañcāla, the capital of Kampilla, he discovered something very important.

The king of Kampilla was Cūlani-Brahmadatta, and his advisor was a shrewd brahmin named Kevatta. One morning, when Kevatta awoke at dawn, he looked around his magnificent chamber and thought, "All this splendor belongs to King Cūlani-Brahmadatta. A king possessing such riches ought to be the emperor of all of Jambudīpa, and I should be his chief advisor."

Early that morning, he went to the king and, after the usual greetings, said, "Your Majesty, there is something I wish to say."

"Speak, then, Teacher," replied the king.

"Sire, a secret cannot be told in the town. We should go to the royal park."

"Very well," replied the king. "Let's go to the park."

Māthara was perched in a tree in the courtyard and heard this, so he followed them to the royal park and hid among the leaves of a sal tree above the king's stone seat.

At the entrance to the park, the king ordered his retinue to wait outside while he and Kevatta went alone inside. The king sat down and asked, "Now what do you wish to say to me, Teacher?"

"Sire, bend your ear this way," Kevatta said softly. "I don't want anyone else to hear this. I have a plan to make you emperor of all of Jambudīpa."

The greedy king listened eagerly and replied, "Just tell me what to do, and I will do it."

"Sire, let us raise an army and attack the capital of one of the small kingdoms on your border. With the city surrounded, I will enter the city and tell the king that there is no use in resisting. If he joins us, we will let him stay on as a figurehead. If he resists, we will utterly destroy him. In either case, with the combined armies we will attack another kingdom, and then another and another, until we have gained dominion over all of Jambudīpa. Then we will invite the one hundred one other kings to Uttarapañcāla to drink the cup of victory. We will serve them poisoned liquor and throw their bodies into the Gangā. With all of them out of the way, you will declare yourself the unrivaled emperor of Jambudīpa."

"An excellent plan, Kevatta!" cried the king. "How shall we begin?"

Kevatta was about to answer when Māthara let fall a messy dropping on the brahmin's head.

"What's that?" he asked, looking up with his mouth wide open. Māthara dropped another right into the advisor's mouth and flew away, crying, "Kevatta, you think your plan is for four ears only, but now it is for six! Soon it will be for eight, and then for hundreds of ears!"

"Catch that parrot!" the king and Kevatta shouted, but, as swift as the wind, Māthara flew away, straight back to Mithilā and through an open window in Mahosadha's house.

Māthara was well-trained. Whenever he returned, if the news he had was for the sage's ears only, he would perch on Mahosadha's shoulder. If Lady Amara was also to be privy to it, he would perch on Mahosadha's lap. If the news was intended for everyone, he would land on the floor. When all those present saw the bird land on the sage's shoulder, they immediately withdrew.

With the bird still on his shoulder, Mahosadha climbed to the top story and asked him, "Well, my dear Māthara, what have you seen? What have you heard?"

"My Lord," the bird replied, "I found no danger in any other kingdom in all of Jambudīpa, but in the city of Uttarapañcāla there is a gathering threat. Kevatta, chief advisor to King Cūlani-Brahmadatta, took the king to the royal park and told him of his plan to conquer all of Jambudīpa. He warned the king that what he had to say was for four ears only and that no one else should hear, but I perched on a branch overhead and heard everything. As I was leaving, I dropped a piece of dung into the brahmin's mouth, so he knows that I heard, but he does not know that I was there on your orders." Then he told the sage the details of Kevatta's scheme.

"Did the king agree to the plan?" Mahosadha asked.

"Yes, he did, and they plan to get started right away," Māthara replied.

Mahosadha made sure that Māthara was well fed and returned him to his golden cage. "Kevatta does not know that I am the wise Mahosadha," he thought. "I will prevent him from carrying out this evil plan!"

Over the next few days, Mahosadha summoned all the rich and powerful families of the kingdom and settled them in the capital. As an extra precaution, he gathered even more grain and stored it in the city.

Following Kevatta's plan, King Cūlani-Brahmadatta began attacking the neighboring kingdoms, and, just as the brahmin had predicted, every king surrendered. It took Cūlani-Brahmadatta exactly seven years, seven months, and seven days to conquer every kingdom in Jambudīpa, except that of King Vedeha. As each kingdom was attacked and fell, the spy in that capital informed Mahosadha of what was happening. To each message, the sage replied, "I am on my guard! Continue to be alert yourself!"

"Teacher," King Cūlani-Brahmadatta said to his advisor, "the time has come for us to seize the kingdom of Vedeha. Let's attack Mithilā!"

"Sire," Kevatta replied, "Mithilā is home to the wise Mahosadha. He is so cunning and clever that I am afraid we will never be able to gain possession of that city as long as he is there, but, after all, Vedeha is a very small kingdom. Certainly, we don't need to bother with it. The rest of Jambudīpa should be enough for us."

This satisfied King Cūlani-Brahmadatta, but the one hundred other kings protested, "We will drink no cup of victory unless Vedeha is brought into the union. All of Jambudīpa must be included!" Disgruntled, they prepared to return to their own capitals.

"Come back!" Kevatta urged them. "Why should we bother about Vedeha? Mahosadha may be clever, but the king can easily be persuaded to join with us later. We'll just need a little patience. Let's all go to Kampilla and celebrate with a victory banquet!" The kings accepted this argument and set out for Uttarapañcāla with King Cūlani-Brahmadatta.

As this was taking place, Mahosadha's spies were sending messages to Mithilā. The first message was that an attack was imminent. The next message was that all the kings were returning home. Finally, the spies reported that the victory celebration would, indeed, take place in Uttarapañcāla. When Mahosadha received this message, he thought, "With a wise man like me alive, it is not reasonable that so many kings should be killed. I will save them!" He told his spies to let him know as soon as the date for the festivities had been set.

When King Cūlani-Brahmadatta and Kevatta arrived in Uttarapañcāla, they began making preparations for the victory banquet. Choosing an auspicious day, they ordered servants to decorate the royal park, to prepare an array of delicious meat and fish dishes, and to set out one thousand jars of wine. All this was reported to Mahosadha.

The sage sent for his one thousand companions and told them that he wanted them to go to Uttarapañcāla. "King Cūlani-Brahmadatta is going to hold a victory celebration," he said. "You must go to the royal park and, as soon as the one hundred other kings have arrived, you must claim the seat of honor next to Cūlani-Brahmadatta. Before any of them have had a chance to eat or drink anything, you must shout, 'This is for King Vedeha!' There will be a great outcry, and they will shout, 'For seven years, seven months, and seven days, we were conquering kingdoms, and, not once, did we see your king! What kind of king is this Vedeha? Go find him a seat at the end of the table!' Then you must shout, 'Except for Cūlani-Brahmadatta, no king is above our king! If you will not allow our king to sit here, we will not allow you to eat or drink!' Then you must rush around and break every pot of wine. Scatter the food so that it is unfit to eat. Shout in your loudest voices, 'We have been sent by the wise Mahosadha of Mithilā! Catch us if you can!' When everything has been spoiled, escape from the park, and come back here."

The men did exactly as the sage had instructed them, and King Cūlani-Brahmadatta was furious that his cunning plan had failed. The kings, for their part, were disappointed and angry that they had been deprived of the delicious food and drink.

King Cūlani-Brahmadatta summoned the kings and urged them, "Let us go with our combined armies to Mithilā and teach King Vedeha a lesson. We will cut off his head and trample on it. Then we can come back and enjoy our great victory banquet. Prepare your armies! Let's leave immediately!"

Kevatta had no illusions about their chances of conquering Mithilā. He foresaw only failure, disappointment, and disgrace. "Sire," he pleaded, "King Vedeha is weak, but the city and the kingdom are managed by the sage Mahosadha, and he is very powerful. We can neither conquer nor outwit Mahosadha, nor can we take Mithilā as long as he is in control. Don't even think of fighting him! We shall only be disgraced!"

King Cūlani-Brahmadatta would not listen to his advisor. Thrilled by the prospect of becoming emperor of all Jambudīpa, he refused to be deterred.

The combined armies of the one hundred one kings rode out of Uttarapañcāla and headed for Mithilā. Kevatta had no choice but to go along.

Mahosadha's warriors made it back to Mithilā in a single night and reported everything to the sage. His undercover agents, based all over Jambudīpa, sent word that Cūlani-Brahmadatta was marching on Mithilā with the one hundred kings and their combined forces to take King Vedeha.

The next morning, Mahosadha received updated reports from his spies informing him of the armies' progress. By the time they arrived, the sage was fully prepared. Guards were posted throughout the city to make sure that no invader could get inside.

King Cūlani-Brahmadatta threw a cordon of elephants, another of chariots, and a third of horses around the city. At regular intervals he placed infantry battalions.

There were so many torches that, as night fell, it seemed that Mithilā was encircled by a ring of fire. The elephants, horses, and soldiers created a deafening din. The four royal advisors had no idea what was happening and rushed to the king. King Vedeha had heard rumors that Cūlani-Brahmadatta was on his way and told the advisors that he had probably arrived.

When King Vedeha looked out the window, however, he was shocked at the size of the regular army encamped outside the city wall. "This is dreadful!" he cried. "Tomorrow morning, Cūlani-Brahmadatta will undoubtedly slay us all!"

At that moment, Mahosadha entered. The king had never been so glad to see him. "No one but Mahosadha can save me from this calamity!" he thought, as the sage greeted him and stood respectfully at one side. "Cūlani-Brahmadatta has come with an infinite army of foot-soldiers, archers, chariots, horses, and elephants!" the king cried. "Our royal city of Mithilā is surrounded by the armed forces of all the kings of Jambudīpa who have come under his sway! Think, Mahosadha! What can we do? How can we defeat this monarch who is advised by ten wise men, skilled in strategy, and by his mother[20] who is the wisest of all?"

20 Her reputation came from the following incident:

One day, a man started to cross a river, but, in midstream, he was caught in the current and could go no further. Afraid of drowning, he called to several men on the bank, "Help! I have here a bundle of husked rice, a portion of boiled rice wrapped in a leaf, and one thousand coins. I will give whichever of these I like to the man who will take me across!"

One of the men, who was very strong, quickly tied up his dhoti, dived into the water, and pulled the other man safely to the far side of the river.

"There you are!" said the strong man. "Now, pay me!"

"Certainly!" replied the other man. "Here is the husked rice."

"What? I risked my own life to save you! I don't want rice! Give me the

"The hungry man seeks refuge in food," Mahosadha thought; "the thirsty man, in water. The sick man's refuge is the physician, but I alone am the refuge of this king who trembles in fear for his life. I had better soothe his mind." Aloud he said, "Have no fear, Sire. Your royal power is secure. Everything is ready for this pretender's attack. I will scatter that mighty host as a farmer scares crows with a stone."

Mahosadha issued a proclamation which was read throughout the city accompanied by a drum: "Citizens! Have no fear! I, the wise Mahosadha, declare seven days of celebration! Let everyone enjoy food, drink, and all sorts of entertainment. Let there be music and dancing in every neighborhood.

---

money."

"My good man, I told you that I would give you whichever I liked. I choose to give you the husked rice. Take it, and be satisfied."

The strong man complained to a bystander, but he opined that the man he'd saved was giving what he liked and that the rescuer should just take it.

Dissatisfied, the strong man complained before the court, but the judges all decided against him. As a last resort, he complained to the king, but even the king agreed with the man he'd saved.

When the king's mother, Queen Talatā, heard about the case, she asked the king whether he had carefully considered the evidence.

"Mother," the king replied, "I did the best I could. If you think you can judge the case any better, go ahead!"

"All right, I will," she declared.

She summoned the man who had been saved and said, "Friend, place here, for me to see, the three things you were carrying when you were in the water."

The man placed the bundle of husked rice, the leaf of boiled rice, and the one thousand coins on the floor in front of the queen.

"Very good," said the queen. "Now tell me, when you were in the water, afraid of drowning, exactly what you said."

I shouted, 'Help! I have here a bundle of husked rice, a portion of boiled rice wrapped in a leaf, and one thousand coins. I will give whichever of these I like to the man who will take me across!'"

"All right," the queen said. "You may go. Take away whichever of these you like."

The man picked up the money and started to walk away.

"One moment!" called the queen.

The man stopped and turned around.

"Do you like the money?" the queen asked him.

"Yes, Your Highness."

"Did you or did you not say that you would give your rescuer whichever of these you liked?"

"That is what I said."

"Then you must give this man the money!" declared the queen.

Reluctantly, he surrendered the cash. While he wept and grieved at his loss, the assembly applauded the wisdom of the queen mother.

Dress up in your holiday best. Decorate the city with garlands and perfume. Everything is being offered as a gift from me. I will bear all expenses."

When King Cūlani-Brahmadatta heard the music and laughter, he summoned his advisors and asked, "What is the meaning of this? We have surrounded this city with our armies, but the population shows no fear or anxiety. They are enjoying themselves as if we were not even here! How can this be?" Mahosadha's spies told the king, "Sire, we had to go inside the city on business, and we asked the citizens this same question. They told us that, when their king was a boy, he had a wish to hold a festival when all the kings of Jambudīpa were besieging the city. Now that the one hundred one kings are indeed attacking, to fulfill that wish, he has proclaimed a public festival, and he himself is celebrating inside the palace."

This news infuriated King Cūlani-Brahmadatta. He ordered a division of his army to attack, to destroy the gate towers, to break down the walls, to enter the city, to slaughter the inhabitants, and to bring King Vedeha's head to him as a trophy.

A battalion of warriors, in full battle gear, marched to the gate and the wall, but guards posted atop the wall assailed them with arrows, javelins, spears, clubs and rocks. As the soldiers tried to break through, the guards held up skewers of meat and fish. "If you can't conquer us, at least have a bite to eat!" they shouted as they gobbled the food themselves and shot more arrows at the invaders. At last, the soldiers were forced to retreat. "Sire," they reported to the king, "no one but a magician could get into that city!"

King Cūlani-Brahmadatta waited five days, but still he could not see any way to conquer Mithilā. He summoned Kevatta. "Teacher," he cried, "we cannot take the city! None of our soldiers can even get near it! What's to be done?"

"Don't worry, Your Majesty," Kevatta replied. "The city gets its water from outside. All we have to do is cut the water supply. If we set up a blockade, they will soon be so thirsty that they will have to open their gates."

"Brilliant!" cried the king, and he ordered soldiers to make sure no water got into the city.

As had been arranged, the sage's spies wrote messages on leaves, fastened them to arrows, and shot them into the city. In this way Mahosadha was continuously informed of all that was happening outside the walls.

"Cūlani-Brahmadatta and his advisors have no idea what I can do!" Mahosadha thought. He ordered men to fetch long pieces of bamboo. The men split the bamboo, removed the joints, and filled each piece with the mud and water lily seeds that the ascetics had brought from the Himavat. Then they rejoined the pieces and sealed them with mud. The lilies quickly sprouted, the stalks emerged from the ends of the bamboo, and the flowers bloomed.

The sage had the lilies pulled out of the bamboo. Men tossed the magnificent flowers with their gigantic leaves and elongated stalks over the wall. "Hey, you servants of Brahmadatta," they shouted, "are you hungry? Here you are! Eat these stalks, and use the flowers to adorn your helmets!"

One of the sage's spies picked up one of the lilies and took it to King Cūlani-Brahmadatta. "Look at this, Your Majesty," he said. "Have you ever seen such a long stalk before?"

"Measure it!" ordered the king. The spy pretended to measure it and told the king that it was twice as long as it really was.

"Where did that grow?" asked the king.

"Inside the city, Sire," the spy replied. "Some of the guards threw these flowers over the wall this morning. Last week, being thirsty for a little toddy, I sneaked into the city and saw people in boats gathering flowers like this in great tanks."

The king was astonished. He summoned Kevatta and said, "Teacher, it is useless to try to cut off their water. Give up that tactic! What else can we do?"

"Well," said the brahmin, "let's starve them out. They have to get food from outside. We'll cut off their food supply."

"An excellent plan!" replied the king.

As soon as Mahosadha learned of this stratagem, he had mud laid along the top of the city wall and rice seedlings transplanted there. The rice quickly grew tall and was visible above the ramparts.

"What is that green above the wall?" King Cūlani-Brahmadatta asked.

One of the spies replied, "Sire, Mahosadha, the son of a farmer, foreseeing danger, collected grain from all the farmers in the kingdom. After filling all the granaries, men threw the surplus rice over the wall. Undoubtedly, this rice fell atop the wall and, soaked in the rain and warmed by the sun, grew up there on its own. Recently, when I was in the city on some business, I picked up a handful of this rice, and people laughed at me. 'If you're hungry,' they said, 'take as much as you want. We have more than we'll ever need.'"

Again, the king was astonished. He summoned Kevatta and said, "Teacher, it is useless to try to starve them out. Give up that tactic! What else can we do?"

"Well," said the brahmin, "let's cut off their supply of fuel. They will have to get fuel from outside to cook their rice."

"Good idea!" replied the king.

Mahosadha ordered that firewood be piled on the top of the wall so that it towered over the rice. Guards threw logs down on the invading soldiers. "Use these to cook your rice!" they jeered.

"Is that firewood showing above the rampart?" the king asked.

"Yes, it is, Your Majesty," replied one of the spies. "The farmer's son, foreseeing danger, collected firewood and stored it in the sheds behind the houses. What was left over was stacked just inside the wall."

Again, the king was astonished. He summoned Kevatta and said, "Teacher, it is useless to try to cut off their fuel. Give up that tactic! What else can we do?"

"Well, Sire, I have another plan," replied Kevatta.

"What plan, Teacher?" asked the king. "I see no end to your plans. Vedeha cannot be taken; let's go back to our city."

"Sire," Kevatta pleaded, "if word gets out that Cūlani-Brahmadatta with one hundred other kings could not take Vedeha, we'll be disgraced. Mahosadha is not the only wise man; I am another. Let me think a moment. I have it! Let's propose a Battle of the Law!"

"What do you mean by that?" the king asked.

"A Battle of the Law, Sire, is a contest between the two sages of the kings. Whichever one bows to the other, loses. It's as simple as that. No armies need fight at all. Of course, Mahosadha will not understand what this is, and, being much younger than I, when we meet, he will bow to me in respect. You will declare me the winner, and Vedeha will be ours! We can return home with honor and hold the victory celebration."

King Cūlani-Brahmadatta was overjoyed. He immediately sent a message to King Vedeha; "Tomorrow there will be a Battle of the Law between our two sages. If you refuse to send your sage, you will be declared vanquished!"

Of course, Mahosadha had learned all the details of this stratagem even before the king received the challenge.

King Vedeha immediately sent for the sage. "My son," he announced, "Cūlani-Brahmadatta has challenged us to a Battle of the Law between our two sages. What is that, and what does it mean?"

"Sire," Mahosadha replied with a chuckle, "this is just a simple-minded game thought up by that foolish brahmin, Kevatta. It is nothing to worry about. Let us prepare for this Battle of the Law near the western gate. We will gather there tomorrow morning."

"Excellent!" replied the king, very much relieved.

"Oh, one more thing, Your Majesty," said Mahosadha. "I will need to borrow your eight-sided Verocanamani gem."

"Of course, my son," replied the king. "By all means, take it."

Early the next morning, Kevatta positioned himself in front of the western gate to wait for Mahosadha. Not knowing what was going to happen, the one hundred kings surrounded Kevatta to protect him. Mahosadha bathed in sweet-smelling water, put on a magnificent robe of the finest silk from Kāsi, took the gem, and mounted his chariot. Accompanied by his one thousand companions, he proceeded slowly to the western gate. When he arrived, he ordered that the gate be opened.

By this time, the sun had risen high in the sky, and Kevatta was sweating. As soon as he saw the crack in the doors, he began craning his neck to catch sight of his rival. Cool and unruffled, Mahosadha rode through the gate behind his great white horses. After crossing the moats, he stopped the chariot and stepped down, as majestic as a lion. As he deliberately strode forward, the one hundred kings were so impressed by his stately bearing that they called out, "Here comes the sage Mahosadha! Here is Sirivaddhaka's son, who has no equal for wisdom!"

Kevatta, also, was unable to restrain himself. He advanced and said in a loud voice, "Sage Mahosadha, we are both wise men. Although I have been living quite near to you for some time, you have never sent me even a token. Why is this?"

"Wise sir," Mahosadha replied softly, holding up the incomparable gem and allowing the sun's rays to reflect from its facets, "I have been searching for a gift which would be worthy of you. At last, I have found something. There is nothing like it in the whole world."

Kevatta was awestruck by the dazzling jewel. He held out his hands and cried, "Give it to me!"

Mahosadha dropped the gem onto the tips of Kevatta's fingers. The brahmin was unprepared for the weight of the huge stone, and it slipped from his fingers and fell at Mahosadha's feet. In his greed, the surprised brahmin stooped to pick it up.

Mahosadha quickly put one hand on the brahmin's shoulder and pushed him to the ground. With his other hand on the brahmin's back, he firmly held him down. "Rise, Teacher, rise!" he shouted. "I am younger than you, young enough to be your grandson! Do not pay obeisance to me. It is not proper! It is not right!" As he said this, Mahosadha ground the brahmin's forehead into the gravel until it was bloody. In a whisper so that only the brahmin could hear, he spat out his disdain, "You blind fool, did you really think that I would pay obeisance to you?" He released the brahmin and shoved him away. Kevatta regained his balance and ran off.

Before Kevatta had straightened up, the kings and soldiers had seen him bow, and the shout went up, "The brahmin Kevatta is paying obeisance at Mahosadha's feet!"

King Cūlani-Brahmadatta was devastated. "My sage," he cried, "has paid obeisance to Mahosadha! We are vanquished!" He turned his chariot around and fled. The one hundred kings saw this, and they, too, began running away.

As they passed Kevatta, they vilified him, "Scoundrel! Wretched brahmin! Having declared a Battle of Law, you bowed down to someone young enough to be your grandson! What a disgrace!"

"Wait!" Kevatta cried. "I didn't bow to him! He tricked me with a gem! You must believe me! Stop!" No one bothered to listen to him. He jumped on a horse and rode after the kings, wiping the blood from his forehead as he went.

To tumultuous applause from all the troops of Mithilā, Mahosadha returned to the city.

After some time, Kevatta was able to convince the kings to rally the shattered army. This army was so huge that, had each man taken a handful of dirt and thrown it into a moat, they could have filled it in, but none of the soldiers showed the least initiative. They simply returned to their former positions and waited.

"What are we to do, Teacher?" King Cūlani-Brahmadatta asked Kevatta.

"Your Majesty," the brahmin replied confidently, "let's completely seal the city. Let neither anyone nor anything enter or leave the city. Eventually, the people will get so discouraged that they will have to open the gate. Then we storm the city and destroy it."

"Very well," replied the king.

Mahosadha knew of the plan almost before the king had replied. "This army is really a nuisance," he thought. "I must find a way to get rid of these pesky kings and their soldiers!" He told his companions that he needed a clever and stout-hearted man, and they brought him a man named Anukevatta, who perfectly suited his requirements.

"What am I to do, wise sir?" Anukevatta asked.

"Listen carefully," Mahosadha began. "Stand on the rampart, and, when the guards pretend to look the other way, let down cakes, fish, meat, and other food to Brahmadatta's men. Say to them, 'Here, eat this good food, and don't be discouraged. The people inside the city are beginning to feel like hens in a coop. If you can hold out and stay here a few more days, they will throw open the gates themselves. Then you'll be able to capture both the king and that villain of a farmer's son.' Then our guards will shout, 'Traitor!' and seize you. In plain sight of Brahmadatta's soldiers, they will bind you hand and foot and beat you with bamboo sticks. They will tie your hair in knots, daub you with brick dust, and put a foul garland of kanavera flowers around your neck. I'll ask them not to beat you too severely, but they will have to raise some welts on your back to convince the enemy. Then they will lower you down outside the wall and shout, 'Go, traitor! Good riddance, double-crosser!'

"My spies will take you before Brahmadatta, and he will ask what happened. You must say to him, 'Your Majesty, I once enjoyed a high position in King Vedeha's court, but Mahosadha denounced me as a traitor and robbed me of everything. I vowed revenge on that son of a farmer. Inside the city, the people are starving and almost ready to give up. In order to encourage your soldiers, I stole as much food as I could find in the palace and dropped it over the wall. When the sage's guards found me, they beat me as you can see. Your own soldiers saw this and can tell you that it is all true.' The king will believe you and take you into his confidence. Once you are sure he trusts you completely, say to him, 'Sire, I am sure that the people inside the city are ready to give up. They no longer support the king and that farmer's son. Now is the time for you to launch an attack. I know the strong places and the weak places of the city wall. I know where the crocodiles are and how to cross the moat. I can lead your army into the city and deliver it into your hands.'

"The king will believe you, and he will let you lead the army. When you take the men to the moat, they will refuse to go across because they are afraid of the crocodiles. Then you must return and tell the king that the soldiers refuse to follow your orders. Suggest to him that the one hundred other kings, their armies, and even the brahmin Kevatta, have all been bribed by the farmer's son and can no longer be trusted. Convince him that you alone are loyal and true! Say 'If you don't believe me, summon the kings in full dress! Examine their belts and other accessories! You will see that they were all given to them by the farmer's son!' King Cūlani-Brahmadatta will summon the one hundred kings, and he will find that all the accessories are inscribed with my name. This will fill the king with so much fear of betrayal that he will abandon them all. Then he will you ask what is to be done. You must reply, 'Sire, you must trust me. Even Kevatta has betrayed you. He may have a scar on his forehead, but he tricked you so that he could get the Verocanamani gem. Once he had the gem, he got you to retreat for three yojanas. Then he lied and regained your confidence. You can't trust him. Now, without an army, there is no way for you to capture the city. The farmer's son is too resourceful. If you stay here any longer, he will turn your army against you and they will deliver you to him. Your only hope is for the two of us to escape tonight. In the middle watch, you and I should take horses and flee so that we do not die by our enemies' hands.' Of course, he will follow your advice.

"While the king is resting, you must rig the reins so that the more they are pulled, the faster the horse goes. You can pretend to leave with the king, but he will soon be gone, and you can come back inside. Is all of that clear?"

"Good sir," Anukevatta replied, "I understand perfectly, and I will do exactly as you have instructed."

"Well, I'm afraid you will have to suffer a few blows," Mahosadha warned.

"Wise sir, do what you will with my body," Anukevatta replied. "Only spare my life and my limbs."

Mahosadha ordered that Anukevatta's family be well taken care of in his absence and sent his trusty agent with food to the top of the rampart. Anukevatta proved himself a most worthy actor, and the scheme was carried out perfectly and went precisely as planned.

As Anukevatta was returning toward the city, he shouted, "King Cūlani-Brahmadatta has fled!" Mahosadha's spies repeated the cry in every battalion. The guards on the ramparts began shouting and clapping their hands and led the citizens inside in a chorus of cheers so that the whole city was in an uproar.

The one hundred kings were sure that Mahosadha had opened the gates and was attacking them. All of them fled as fast as they could, without bothering to take any of their valuables. As soon as the officers and common soldiers realized that their leaders were fleeing, they, too, dropped everything they had and escaped. Before the sun rose, the entire invading force had disappeared.

When King Vedeha's soldiers opened the gates, they found the field strewn with booty. They asked Mahosadha what to do with it all. "Everything they left is ours," he replied. "That which belonged to the kings should be given to our king. That which belonged to Kevatta should be given to me. As for the rest, soldiers and citizens may take what they like." Everyone rejoiced at the unexpected windfall. In recognition of his service, Anukevatta was given great honor.

When King Cūlani-Brahmadatta held a meeting in Uttarapañcāla with the one hundred kings, he discovered how he had been completely deceived by Mahosadha's plan, and he was ashamed.

One year later, when Kevatta looked in a mirror, he saw the scar on his forehead and thought, "That is the doing of the farmer's son! He made me a laughing-stock in front of King Cūlani-Brahmadatta and the other one hundred kings! What can I do to get revenge? I must bring down both him and King Vedeha! What to do? I've got it! Princess Pañcālacandī, King Cūlani-Brahmadatta's daughter, is peerless in beauty, like a deva. If King Vedeha hears of her beauty, he will be undone by desire like a fish that has swallowed a hook. With her as bait, I will trap both king and sage, kill them, and drink the cup of victory!"

He immediately went to King Cūlani-Brahmadatta and said, "Your Majesty, I have an idea."

"Really?" the king replied with sarcasm. "An idea of yours once left me without a rag to cover myself with. Whatever you have to propose now would be better left unspoken."

"Sire," Kevatta insisted, "there has never been a plan equal to this."

"All right," relented the king, "tell me what it is."

"Sire," Kevatta whispered, "we two must be alone."

"So be it," replied the king, and he led the brahmin up the stairs to the royal bedchamber.

"Your Majesty," Kevatta began conspiratorially, "I will arouse King Vedeha's desire, lure him here, and kill him."

"That sounds good, Teacher," replied the king, "but how are you going to arouse his desire?"

"Sire, your daughter Pañcālacandī is without equal in beauty. We will have poets celebrate her charms in verse. When these poems are sung in Mithilā, the king will become so intoxicated with her beauty that he won't be able to get her out of his mind. He will be so obsessed with the thought of possessing her that he will think, 'If I cannot get this pearl of maidens, of what use is my kingdom?' At that point, I will go to Mithilā and propose the match. The king will be overjoyed, and we will fix the day. When he and the farmer's son come to Uttarapañcāla, they will be like fish that have swallowed hooks. All we have to do is kill them."

"You've hatched a fine plan, Teacher!" replied the king. "Let's carry it out!"

The king called for skillful poets and acquainted them with his daughter. He asked them to compose poems celebrating her face, her hair, her figure, and her voice and supported them while they worked. When they had finished, they recited to the king what they had written. He was very pleased and rewarded them handsomely. Next he summoned musicians, who learned the poems from the poets and set them to enchanting music. The king sent the musicians to all parts of Jambudīpa to sing the songs in every public place. Soon, everyone was singing the praises of the princess, and every king longed for her.

King Cūlani-Brahmadatta again sent for the poets, and said, "My sons, your poems have been very effective! Now I need new poems which express in the most beautiful language that a princess like my daughter is too good for any king in all Jambudīpa, except King Vedeha of Mithilā. Your poems must extol both my daughter's beauty and His Majesty." The king was again delighted with their work and paid them well. After the poems had been set to music, troubadours went to Mithilā and sang the songs on every street corner. Wherever they sang, people applauded and threw coins. At night, the troubadours climbed into the trees and tied bells on the roosting birds sleeping there. In the morning, as the birds flew away, the little bells tinkled in the air, and the troubadours sang their songs. The effect was of a heavenly chorus of devas singing the praises of their king and the foreign princess. King Vedeha sent for the musicians and asked them to perform in the palace. He was overjoyed to learn that King Cūlani-Brahmadatta was, in effect, offering him the princess, and he paid the troubadours handsomely. They returned to Uttarapañcāla and reported everything to Kevatta and King Cūlani-Brahmadatta.

"Sire," Kevatta advised, "it is time for me to go to Mithilā to fix the date and to bring King Vedeha back to Uttarapañcāla."

"Very good, Teacher," replied king. "Take appropriate gifts and go."

When Mahosadha had first heard the songs about the princess and King Vedeha, he had become suspicious. He asked his spies in Uttarapañcāla for an explanation, but they replied, "We do not know what all this means. We know only that the king and Kevatta went secretly to the royal bedchamber to discuss something shortly before the poems and songs starting appearing. There is a female mynah bird who lives in that chamber. She surely knows what they discussed, but we have no access to the bird." The sage sent Māthara, the clever parrot, back to Uttarapañcāla to discover what secrets he could pry from the mynah.

When Mahosadha heard that Kevatta would be visiting Mithilā, he thought, "Our enemies must not be given any advantage. Kevatta must not be allowed to see the city!" He ordered that lattice work be erected on both sides of the street between the city gate and the palace. This was covered with beautifully painted mats. The road was strewn with flowers, and jars of drinking water were placed at regular intervals. Overhead, flags and banners fluttered in the breeze.

The citizens of Mithilā, however, had no suspicions. "At last, King Cūlani-Brahmadatta and King Vedeha will settle their quarrel!" they shouted. "Brahmadatta will give his daughter to our king! Kevatta is here to make the match!"

As Kevatta passed through the city, of course, he could not see any houses, shops, storerooms, or tanks, but he assumed that the king had decorated everything in his honor. He entered the palace, offered his gifts to the king, and sat down at one side. After a proper reception, he announced, "Your Majesty, a king who wishes for your friendship has given you these precious gifts. He sent me as an ambassador to offer you an excellent and beautiful princess to unite the people of Kampilla and Vedeha. Please come back with me, Sire, to Uttarapañcāla to receive this princess of peerless beauty."

The king was flattered by this proposal, but he hesitated to accept right away. "Teacher," he replied, "there was a quarrel between you and the wise Mahosadha at the Battle of the Law. Go now, and see my son. You two wise men must resolve your differences. After you've had a talk with him, come back." Kevatta agreed and went to see the sage.

Mahosadha had already decided not to talk with the wicked Kevatta. Early that morning, he had his servants remove all the chairs and seats from his chamber, leaving only one narrow couch for himself. Then he ordered them to smear wet cow dung on the floor and to cover the pillars with oil. He drank some ghee and instructed his servants, "When Kevatta comes, tell him that I have taken a dose of ghee and that he must not speak to me. When I start to speak, stop me, and say, 'My Lord, you have taken a dose of ghee. You must not talk." Finally, he lay down on his couch and covered himself with a red robe.

Kevatta arrived at the house and asked for Mahosadha. A servant told him that their master was in his chamber. "Brahmin," he continued, "do not make much noise; if you wish to go in, go silently. Today, the sage has taken ghee, and he cannot stand any noise." As Kevatta passed through the house, he was told the same thing at each door.

The seventh door led to Mahosadha's chamber. Kevatta entered, but, as he approached the sage, the dung oozed through his toes. He furtively looked around for a place to sit, but, finding none, continued standing uncomfortably and rubbing one foot against the other leg in a vain attempt to scrape off the filth. Mahosadha made as if to speak, but his servants told him to stay silent because he had taken a dose of ghee, adding, "Why should you talk with this wretched brahmin anyway?"

Kevatta noticed that the servants were staring at him. One rubbed his eyes, another lifted his eyebrows, and a third scratched his head and yawned. This rude behavior annoyed Kevatta, and he said, "Wise sir, I am going."

"Wretched brahmin," one of the servants snarled at him, "didn't we tell you to be quiet? If you make another sound, I'll break your bones!" Startled, Kevatta looked up, and another servant hit him with a bamboo stick. A third caught him by the throat and pushed him. Yet another slapped him on the back. Barely able to stand, but aghast at the thought of falling in the muck, Kevatta hurried away as best he could, like a fawn fleeing a panther.

While the king was waiting for Kevatta to return to the palace, he imagined how pleased Mahosadha would be to hear his happy news. He was sure that the two wise men were having a wonderful conversation, and he thought, "Today, they will be reconciled, and I will be the winner!"

As soon as he saw Kevatta, he asked, "How was your meeting with Mahosadha? Were you reconciled? Was he pleased?"

"Sire," Kevatta replied, "you may think that he is a wise man, but there is no man worse than he! He is ignoble, disagreeable, and obstinate, and he has a foul disposition! I went in to meet him, but he said not a word to me!"

This displeased the king, but he remained silent. He provided Kevatta and his attendants with all that they needed and told them to go and rest. After they left, the king thought, "My son is wise and has good manners. Still, he refused to speak courteously to this brahmin. Undoubtedly, he suspects something. My son must see some mischief in this visit. He must think that Kevatta has come here for no friendly purpose. Perhaps the brahmin is trying to lure me to Uttarapañcāla so that Cūlani-Brahmadatta can capture me there. I wonder whether Mahosadha foresees some danger in this venture." As he was turning these thoughts over in his mind, the four other advisors entered.

Turning to Senaka, the king asked, "Do you think I should go to Uttarapañcāla to marry King Cūlani-Brahmadatta's daughter?"

"Sire, what a question! When good luck comes along, who would drive it away? King Cūlani-Brahmadatta knows that all the other kings of Jambudīpa are his vassals and that you alone are his equal. Obviously, that is why he wants to give you his peerless daughter. By going to Uttarapañcāla to marry the princess, you will unite the two greatest families, and all of Jambudīpa will be one great realm. Of course, we, too, will be rewarded." The other three advisors were of the same opinion.

While they were conversing, Kevatta arrived. "Sire," he announced, "I cannot linger here any longer. I must return to my own capital. I hope you will accept our hospitality and join us soon in Uttarapañcāla." The king spoke a few friendly words and let him leave.

When Mahosadha heard of Kevatta's departure, he bathed, dressed, and went to wait on the king.

The king, addled by passion, disregarded his own misgivings and ignored his regard for Mahosadha's insight, and asked, "Well, my son, all my other advisors think I should go to Uttarapañcāla. What do you think?"

"Oh, dear," the sage thought, "this greedy king is still foolishly listening to those four idiots. I wonder whether he will believe me when I warn him of the danger." Aloud he said, "Your Majesty, King Cūlani-Brahmadatta is powerful and ruthless, and he wants to kill you. His daughter is the bait on a hook, and, like a hungry fish, you are rushing to grab it. Go to Uttarapañcāla, and you will find yourself caught in a deadly trap like that which the hunter sets for the unsuspecting deer."

"How insulting!" thought the king. "Instead of offering me congratulations, he compares me to a deer and a fish! Does he think that I am so stupid as to fall into a trap? Haven't I sought the advice of four other wise men? Why is he trying to deprive me of the most beautiful woman in the world, the daughter of the most powerful king in Jambudīpa?" Aloud he said, "It seems, sir, that I was foolish to consult a farmer like you on important matters of state! How could you be expected to understand such things when you grew up hanging on to a plow?" Raising his voice, he cried, "This clodhopper is spoiling my good luck! He is trying to deprive me of a rare jewel! Take him by the neck and throw him out." The king was shouting in anger, but he still respected the sage enough not to demand that any of his attendants carry out his command.

Mahosadha realized the danger he was in. Not wanting to be shamed by being manhandled, he saluted the king and returned to his house.

Meanwhile, after Mahosadha had released Māthara from the eastern window for the second time, the parrot flew directly to King Cūlani-Brahmadatta's palace in Uttarapañcāla and landed in the royal bedchamber. "Hello, my dear," he said to the sweet-voiced mynah. "I hope all is well with you? Are you happy in your fine cage? Does your master give you enough parched corn with honey?"

"All is well with me, sir," the surprised mynah replied, "and I am, indeed, happy. Yes, Mister Parrot, my master gives me enough parched corn with honey every day, but please tell me who you are, why you have come, and why you speak to me in this way. I don't believe that I have ever seen you before, nor have I ever heard of you."

"If I tell her I am from Mithilā, she will never trust me," Māthara reflected. On the way, he had noticed a town called Aritthapura in Sivi, so he said, "Until very recently, I was King Sivi's own chamberlain, but that righteous king set all prisoners, including me, free."

"Sir, you have come a long way," she replied, as she gave him some of the delicious corn and honey which had been served to her in a golden dish. "What has brought you here?"

"I once had a wife," he told her, "a sweet-voiced mynah, but, one day, right in front of my eyes, a hawk killed her."

"Oh, dear!" she cried. "How did that happen?"

"One day, the king invited us to a party at the tank in the royal garden. My wife and I had a joyous time playing in the water. In the evening, after we had returned to the palace, my wife and I flew out of a window and sat on the top of a pinnacle to dry our feathers. Suddenly, a hawk swooped down at us. I was able to fly away, but my wife's feathers were still very wet and heavy. The hawk easily snatched her in his sharp talons and carried her off. I saw that wretched brute of a bird tear her body apart and eat it. It was more than I could bear. When the king learned of this, he comforted me and urged me to look for another wife.

"Why should I wed another?' I asked him. 'Better to live alone!'

"He insisted and finally said, 'Friend, I know a lovely mynah, as virtuous as your late wife. She lives in King Cūlani-Brahmadatta's royal chamber. Go and court her. If she accepts your proposal, come and tell me, and my queen or I will bring her to Sivi with great pomp.' Thus, here I am."

Although his words pleased her, she didn't show her feelings. Instead, she asked, "Is it natural for a parrot and a mynah to mate?"

The parrot was pleased that she was not rejecting his advances. He felt confident that she was just being coy, so, hoping to gain her trust, he persisted. "When two beings are in love, caste has no meaning, but all are equal. In love there is no distinction. Consider Vāsudeva, king of Dvāravatī and the eldest of ten Andhakavenhu brothers. One day, as he was going to the royal park, he saw a stunningly beautiful girl standing by the roadside and immediately fell in love with her. Even though he was a khattiya and she was a candāla, when he learned that she was unmarried, he turned back, took her home, surrounded her with precious things, and made her his chief queen. This candāla woman, Queen Jambāvatī, was the mother of King Sivi. If even a great king had no qualms about marrying a candāla woman, why should we, who are mere animals, worry? If we wish to mate, there is no more to be said."

To strengthen his case, he gave another example, citing the story of Rathavatī, a kinnarī, who married an ascetic named Vaccha.

"My dear, perhaps you have heard of Vaccha, who renounced the world and became an ascetic in the Himavat. Not far from his hut of leaves, there was a cave inhabited by a number of kinnaras. Also in that cave lived a powerful and hideous spider, which caught the kinnaras in its web. The poor kinnaras were helpless against the spider and appealed to the ascetic for help. Vaccha refused, saying that he could never take the life of a living being. The kinnaras tempted him with a beautiful kinnarī named Rathavatī, and, as soon as Vaccha saw her, he fell in love with her. He took her as his mate, killed the dreadful spider with a club, and spent the rest of his life with her. They had many children and were devoted to each other. Vaccha was a human, and Rathavatī was a kinnarī, but we are both birds, so we can certainly do the same."

"My Lord," the mynah replied, "I am not a steady creature. I'm actually very passionate, and, if we were to become intimate and you ever left me, I'm afraid my heart would break."

"Well, my dear," the parrot replied in as captivating a manner as he could manage, "if you are so afraid of love that you want me to leave, I will just go on my way. Obviously, dear, sweet-voiced mynah, you don't really care for me."

"No!" the mynah cried. "Don't say that! Wise parrot, act in haste and repent at leisure! Please remain here a little longer. You must meet our king and enjoy the splendors of our court." The parrot stayed and lived with the mynah long enough that he was sure of her confidence. One day, after he had become certain that she would not hide the secret from him, he said, "My dear!"

"What is it, My Lord?" she asked.

"I want to ask you something. May I speak?" he asked.

"Please do, My Lord."

"Oh, never mind," he replied. "Today is a festival. It can wait for another day."

"If what you have to ask is not unsuitable for a festival, please ask it now, My Lord," she insisted.

"Actually, it is about a festival day."

"Then speak."

"Well," he began, pretending reluctance, "I keep hearing a rumor, all over the country, that the daughter of your king, who is now our king, that is to say the mighty king of Uttarapañcāla, a beautiful young girl, who is as bright as a star, is going to be given to King Vedeha of Mithilā and that a great festival will be held to proclaim their wedding."

"My Lord," the mynah squawked, shivering her wings and ruffling her feathers, "on a festival day, you have said something most inauspicious!"

"What do you mean?" asked the parrot. "I thought that this marriage was most auspicious for everyone. How can something this joyous be unlucky?"

"My Lord," the mynah replied, suddenly clamming up, "I dare not say."

"Madam," the parrot responded, moving slightly away, "if you refuse to tell me what you mean, our happy union will come to an end! If you don't trust me, how can I marry you?"

"Don't say that, darling!" she cried. Then, lowering her voice, she said, "All right, I will tell you. You would not wish such a wedding on even your worst enemy! There will never be an unluckier match than this one between the kings of Kampilla and Vedeha."

"Why do you say such a thing, my dear?" he whispered, taking a cue from her.

"Listen, and I will tell you." she answered softly, revealing the entire plot to the parrot.

"This Kevatta is certainly clever and resourceful!" the parrot replied. "That's a perfect plan to kill the king and that haughty sage as well. I am very impressed! Nevertheless, such things mean nothing to us! We need not concern ourselves with anything so unlucky as that! Silence is best."

That night, he was particularly affectionate toward her to make sure that she did not suspect anything. The next morning, he announced, "My dear, I must return to Sivi and tell the king that I have found a loving wife. Please allow me to be gone for just one week. As soon as I have finished my business, I will return to you."

The mynah didn't want him to leave, but she could not refuse. "I give you permission to be away for seven nights, my darling, but, if you do not return to me in a week, I will die."

"My dear, how could I live for more than seven days without seeing you?" he asked, but what he really meant was, "What do I care whether you live or die?"

He flew through the window, and she watched him fly toward Sivi, never suspecting that he had no interest in that kingdom. Without once stopping to rest, he flew all the way to Mithilā and through the window of Mahosadha's house. He landed on the sage's shoulder, and everyone else in the room immediately got up and left. When the two of them were alone, the parrot revealed everything he had learned from the mynah.

Mahosadha thanked Māthara, fed him, and returned him to his golden cage.

"It's just as I suspected," Mahosadha thought. "The king is in great danger. He is an utter fool and has no notion of his own welfare. Blinded by his desire for the princess, he has no idea of the disaster awaiting him. He is determined to go to Uttarapañcāla and refuses to listen to my advice. Nevertheless, he is my great benefactor, and I should neither bear a grudge nor let his words bother me. If he goes unprotected, he will be destroyed. If I fail to protect him, I will be disgraced. As long as he has me to guard him, he is safe. I will go ahead of him, see the place, and arrange everything. Once more, I will outwit Kevatta and Cūlani-Brahmadatta. I will snare the princess for our king, even while being besieged by all the kings of Jambudīpa and their armies. I will perform a great feat, which only I can do. I will save our king, as the moon is released from the jaws of Rāhu. I will bring him home safe and sound. His safe return is in my hands alone." As he made this resolve, joy pervaded his body, and he declared, "A man should always work for the interests of his patron."

After bathing and putting on his formal robes, he went to the palace. "Sire, have you decided to go to Uttarapañcāla?" he asked the king.

"Yes, I have," the king replied. "If I cannot win Pañcālacandī, what is my kingdom to me? My son, don't desert me! Come with me. By going there, I will gain two benefits. I will marry the most precious of women, and I will make friends with the king."

"Your Majesty," Mahosadha replied. "Allow me to go ahead. I will prepare a suitable place for you to stay and fix the date for the wedding. As soon as all the arrangements are completed, I will send word, and you can arrive in great ceremony."

"An excellent idea!" exclaimed the king, delighted that Mahosadha was not abandoning him, after all. "What do you need to take with you?"

"An army, Sire."

"Take as many men as you wish, my son."

"Thank you, Sire, I will begin recruiting the men I need, but I would also like to take all the men who are in your prison."

"Of course, my son," the king consented. "Do as you will. I give you a free hand!"

Mahosadha went to the prison and offered all the prisoners their freedom if they would follow him to Uttarapañcāla and obey his orders. They all agreed. He next asked the skilled shipwright, Ānandakumāra, to join him. Then he recruited eighteen different crews, composed of masons, blacksmiths, carpenters, painters, and men skilled in many other arts and crafts. They carried with them all the tools they would need. Accompanied by all these workers, the released prisoners, and his one thousand companions, the sage left Mithilā for Uttarapañcāla.

All along the route, Mahosadha had the men build villages at intervals of one yojana. In each village, he left a courtier with orders to prepare elephants, horses, and chariots to defend the king and to facilitate his return to Mithilā with his new bride, Princess Pañcālacandī.

When Mahosadha reached the Gaṅgā, he summoned Ānandakumāra and told him to take three hundred carpenters upriver, where they were to procure choice timber and to build three hundred ships. They were to fill these ships with lumber and return as soon as possible.

With the rest of his army, Mahosadha crossed the river. From the landing, he began choosing sites and pacing distances. "The great tunnel will be dug here. This is where we will build the city walls," he mused, "and the palace will be here," he continued as he walked toward Uttarapañcāla. "The small tunnel will extend this way into the city." Having decided the layout for his construction, he mounted his chariot and entered the capital.

King Cūlani-Brahmadatta was extremely pleased to hear that Mahosadha was, at last, arriving. "My cherished dream will soon be realized!" he gloated. "King Vedeha will follow him shortly. Then, after I have killed the two of them, I will control Vedeha, and I will be emperor of all Jambudīpa!"

As soon as the sage appeared, people flocked into the streets to see him. "Here is the wise Mahosadha!" they cried. "He put to flight the one hundred one kings like crows scared by a clod of earth!" The citizens of Uttarapañcāla could not help but admire Mahosadha's handsome features as he proceeded to the palace.

The king greeted him and asked, "My son, when will King Vedeha come?"

"When I send for him, Your Majesty," Mahosadha replied.

"Why have you come alone?"

"I must build a place for our king to stay, Sire."

"Good, my son." He settled Mahosadha in a beautiful mansion and provided everything necessary for his entourage. "Please make yourself at home while you are here," he said. "I'm sure you will be quite busy, but, if you find anything in our palace or capital which needs to be done, we would be delighted to have your assistance."

As soon as Mahosadha had entered the palace, he noticed the staircase leading to the royal chambers and thought, "This is where we should construct the entrance to the small tunnel, but we must be careful that the stairway doesn't collapse while we are digging." Aloud he said, "Your Majesty, as I passed by the great staircase, I noticed that there is a fault in its construction and that it is in danger of collapse. If I may be allowed, I could easily reinforce it to make it safer for you and your family."

"By all means, my son," replied the king. "We would be very grateful. Please do it!"

After placing curtains all around the staircase so that no one could see what was happening, Mahosadha dismantled the entire structure, excavated the ground beneath it, and built a sturdy wooden platform to support the staircase and to serve as the entrance to the small tunnel. Then he quickly installed a secret door and replaced the stairs. When he was finished, it looked exactly the same as it had before. The king was delighted that Mahosadha was so filled with goodwill and concerned for the welfare of his hosts.

Having completed that project, Mahosadha approached the king and said, "Sire, if I could know where our king is to stay, I could arrange everything for him."

"Very good, wise sir," replied the king. "You may choose for your king any place in the city, except my palace."

"Sire," Mahosadha continued, "we are strangers here. If we were to take over the house of one of your favorites, there would be an uproar, which would be very unpleasant for you and for us."

"Wise sir," the king insisted, "pay no attention to any objections. I give you leave to choose whatever place pleases you the most."

"Thank you, Sire." Mahosadha replied. "We will bother you no more. May I post guards to prevent people from disturbing you about this?"

"Of course, my son!" agreed the king. "That would be very kind of you."

Mahosadha placed his own guards at the bottom of the stairs, at every door, and at every gate of the palace, with orders that no one be admitted to see the king.

The sage first sent his men to the palace of Talatā, the queen mother, to act as if they were going to pull the entire building down.

As soon as they began chipping at the walls and foundation, the queen mother appeared and shouted, "Who are you, and what do you mean by tearing down my house?"

"Mahosadha, the great sage, wants to build a new palace for his king on these grounds," the men replied as they continued working.

"But this is a perfectly good palace," insisted the queen mother. "If you must have it, your king may live here as long as he likes."

"Our king's retinue is very large, Madam. This house is much too small. We must tear it down and build a much larger palace."

"Obviously, you do not know who I am!" she shouted indignantly. "I am the queen mother! I will go to my son and see about this!"

"Your Highness," they replied calmly, "we are acting on the king's orders. Go ahead and ask him if you want."

The queen mother stormed off angrily, but Mahosadha's guards would not let her enter the palace.

"What do you mean by this?" she cried. "I am the king's mother!"

"We know who you are, Your Highness," the guards replied, "but the king has ordered us not to let anyone enter. He does not want to be bothered. Please go away!"

She sullenly returned and watched the men beginning to destroy her elegant palace.

"What are you doing back here?" shouted one of the workers as he grabbed her and threw her to the ground. "Go away, and let us get on with our work!"

"This really must be the king's orders," she thought, as she stood up and dusted herself off. "Otherwise, they would never dare do this. I must go and see the sage himself."

She hurried to Mahosadha's residence, but he insisted that he was too busy to talk with her and suggested that she file a complaint with his foreman.

"My son," she pleaded with the foreman, "why are your men tearing down my palace?"

"Didn't they tell you, Madam?" the foreman asked her. "We must build a new palace for King Vedeha."

"In this great city," she said, "there must be many other good places where you can build a suitable palace. "Here!" she cried, placing several bags of money in front of him. "Accept this gift of one hundred thousand coins and leave my palace alone. Build a glorious palace for your king on some other spot."

"Madam!" the foreman replied with a look of surprise. "We will accept this generous gift and leave your palace only if you promise that you will not reveal to anyone that you have given this money to us. If others learn of this, they might also try to bribe us in order to spare their own houses."

"My son," she whispered, "if word ever got out that the queen mother bribed you, the shame would be mine! You can be sure that I will tell no one."

The foreman returned with her to her palace and told his workers to stop. She thanked him and went inside.

Mahosadha next sent his men to Kevatta's house. Of course, the advisor was also upset and hurried to the palace. The guards barred his entry and beat him with bamboo sticks until his back bled. He also offered one hundred thousand coins to the foreman.

In this way, Mahosadha's men crisscrossed the entire city and collected nine crores of coins. He went himself to the palace, thanked his guards, and sent them away. Then he went in to see the king.

"Did you find a suitable place?" the king asked him.

"Sire," the sage replied, "we looked at many houses, and all the owners were willing to cooperate, but, as soon as we started working, they were stricken with regret and asked us to stop. We do not wish to be the cause of any unpleasantness or hard feelings. However, outside the city, not far from the gate, between the city and the Gangā, there is a suitable place where we could build a palace for our king without disturbing anyone."

The king was extremely pleased with this suggestion. "Fighting an enemy's army inside the city would be difficult" he thought. "It would be hard to distinguish friend from foe. Outside the city, we could easily defeat Vedeha." Aloud he said, "Excellent, my son! Build your palace in the place you have seen."

"Thank you, Sire." Mahosadha replied. "We would like to request that none of your subjects come onto the construction site, looking for firewood, herbs, or such things. If they do, there might be quarrels, and that would be unpleasant for everyone."

"Of, course, my son. I will tell everyone to stay away from your construction site."

"One more thing, Your Majesty. Our elephants like to frolic in the river. We hope that none of your subjects complain that the water has gotten too muddy. Please tell them to let the water settle a little longer before using it, and it will be clean enough for bathing and drinking."

"Let your elephants play," the king replied.

The king had it proclaimed throughout the land: "No one is to enter the site where the sage Mahosadha is constructing a palace for King Vedeha. Violators will be fined one thousand coins. No one is to complain that the water is too muddy. This is a temporary inconvenience."

Mahosadha led his army of workers to the bank of the Gangā and showed them where to erect the wall of the new city to be called Upakāri. He also indicated the location of the palace for the king, the houses for all the courtiers who would be coming, and the layout of the streets. While they were leveling the site, the three hundred ships which he had commissioned arrived, carrying not only the lumber that was needed but also all the furnishing for the palace and the houses. As soon as the ships were unloaded, Mahosadha had the sailors conceal them in a secure place from which they could be summoned at short notice.

On the other side of the Gangā, he ordered men to build a village where he would station the elephants, horses, chariots, cattle, and oxen.

Then he called sixty thousand men to begin digging the great tunnel, which extended from the palace in Upakāri to the bank of the Gangā. As they excavated, the dirt was carried to the river in leather sacks and dumped into the water. Elephants trampled it as they sported in the water, and the Gangā became muddy. As Mahosadha had predicted, citizens were upset that the water was unfit for use, but they dared not complain.

Seven hundred men began digging the small tunnel which extended from the great tunnel, under the new palace to King Cūlani-Brahmadatta's palace. The dirt from that excavation was also brought out in leather sacks, but it was mixed with straw and water, and used for constructing walls.

The main door of the great tunnel was eighteen hatthas high. In all, there were eighty great doors and sixty-four smaller ones. All of the doors were cleverly fitted with mechanisms so that they could be opened and closed simultaneously with the turn of a single handle.

The sides of the great tunnel were brick, covered with stucco and polished with lime. The ceiling was wooden planks, polished white with powder from conch shells. Built into the walls were hundreds of cells for lamps. The doors of these cells were also mechanically fitted so that one switch opened or closed them simultaneously. Along both sides of the great tunnel, doors led to one hundred one chambers. Each chamber contained a bed with a multi-colored cover, a throne over which was raised a white umbrella, and a statue of a beautiful woman, so realistic that, without touching it, no one could tell that it was not warm and breathing. The doors of these rooms were also controlled by a central device.

On the walls of the great tunnel, skillful artists had painted all manner of scenes—the splendor of Sakka, majestic Mount Sineru, the seas and the ocean, the four continents, the Himavat, Lake Anotatta, Manosila, the sun and the moon, the heaven of the Four Great Kings, and more. The ceiling was painted with lotuses, and pure white sand covered the floor. Bouquets of flowers were hung here and there. The tunnel, indeed, resembled the divine hall of Sudhamma.

Four months from the beginning of construction, Upakāri was finished. The small tunnel, the great tunnel, the palace and all the other houses were completed. The wall around the city had been erected, and three moats had been dug. It was truly a wonder to behold. Mahosadha sent a messenger to summon King Vedeha, who eagerly set out with a great retinue.

Mahosadha met him on the bank of the Gangā, and escorted him to the palace in Upakāri. After eating a delicious meal and resting, the king sent a message to King Cūlani-Brahmadatta: "Sire, I have come to pay my respects and to receive your beautiful daughter, full of grace and charms, to be my wife."

Naturally, King Cūlani-Brahmadatta was delighted. "There is no way my enemies can escape me now!" he thought. "I will split open both of their skulls and drink the joyous cup of victory!" He treated the messenger with respect and sent this reply, "Welcome, Vedeha! Please ascertain from your astrologers the most auspicious time, and I will give you my dear daughter, attended by her handmaidens, in marriage."

King Vedeha immediately sent a return message: "What day and time could be more auspicious than now?"

As soon as King Cūlani-Brahmadatta had received this message, he summoned the most trusted palace guards and ordered them to take his mother, Queen Talatā; his consort, Queen Nandā; his son, Prince Pañcālacanda; and his daughter, Princess Pañcālacandī; as well as their retainers to a secure apartment inside the palace and to protect them there. To King Vedeha, however, he sent the message: "I give you my daughter, the most beautiful and graceful of women, to marry now, at this very auspicious hour." He sent a completely different message to the one hundred kings: "Prepare for battle! The time has come for us to besiege the new city of Upakāri and to slay our two worst enemies, King Vedeha and the sage Mahosadha. Then we can drink the cup of victory together." With that, King Cūlani-Brahmadatta led his army and the forces of all the other kings in an attack on the new city of Upakāri.

As soon as Mahosadha was sure that King Cūlani-Brahmadatta had left his palace, he summoned three hundred of his companions and told them: "Go swiftly through the small tunnel to the palace in Uttarapañcāla. Go up the staircase to the apartment where the queen mother, the king's consort, his son, and his daughter are staying. Bring them to the main tunnel and make them comfortable until I arrive with the king. When you hear us in the tunnel, escort them to the great hall at the other mouth of the great tunnel, on the bank of the Gangā."

The men hurried through the great tunnel and the small tunnel and quietly opened the secret door at the foot of the staircase. They quickly seized the guards who had been stationed there and bound and gagged them without anyone else in the palace suspecting what was happening. After enjoying some of the king's food, they mounted the staircase and found the royal chamber.

The queen mother was surprised to see these strange guards and asked what was happening. "Your Highness," Mahosadha's men replied excitedly, "your son has been victorious! King Vedeha and Mahosadha have been slain! Our king is now the ruler of all of Jambudīpa. He asked us to escort you to the field where he is preparing to drink the cup of victory with the one hundred other kings. Please come, all of you!"

Without any misgivings, the royal family followed the guards to the foot of the staircase. As they were entering the small tunnel, they asked one another, "Have you ever been here before? Do you remember this street?"

"This is a special route," the guards answered. "Because today is such a special day, the king told us to fetch you this way."

As soon as they were in the tunnel, others of Mahosadha's companions roamed through King Cūlani-Brahmadatta's palace, overcoming the guards and pillaging the valuables. They even broke into the treasury and took away as much as they could carry.

When the royal family reached the large tunnel, they could not believe their eyes. "When did my son build this?" asked the queen mother as she admired the paintings.

"This is the most beautiful hallway I have ever seen!" exclaimed the queen.

"These beds are magnificent!" exclaimed the princess.

"Look at these statues!" cried the prince. "They are so lifelike!"

They were completely at ease as they settled down in a well-furnished chamber to await the summons of the king. One of the sage's companions went to inform Mahosadha that they had arrived.

Meanwhile, King Vedeha was in his palace, impatiently awaiting his bride. Becoming restless, he wandered to the window and gazed out. "What is this?" he cried when he saw the torches blazing all around the city. "Why are all those soldiers and cavalry out there? What does this mean?"

"Sire," Senaka reassured him, "don't worry. I am sure that Cūlani-Brahmadatta is bringing his daughter to you. It is dark, so, of course, the escorts have lit the way with torches."

"No doubt he has sent a special honor guard to welcome you," Pukkusa added.

Not satisfied with these foolish opinions, the king remained at the window. Listening carefully, he could hear voices. "Put a detachment here!" someone shouted. "Set a guard there!" shouted another. "Be vigilant!" shouted a third. He was sure that he could see thousands of fully armed soldiers. Quaking with fear, he turned to Mahosadha. "What is the meaning of that great army?" he asked the sage. "Please assure me that we are not in grave danger!"

"Let me shock some sense into this blind fool of a king!" Mahosadha thought. Aloud he said, "Sire, as you can see, we are surrounded by the mighty army of King Cūlani-Brahmadatta and the other kings. Tomorrow morning, Brahmadatta will kill you. He never intended to give you his daughter."

The advisors began quaking so much that they could barely stand. The king's mouth became dry, and his hair stood on end. "My temples are throbbing!" he cried. "My mouth is parched, and my heart has turned to ice!"

"Your Majesty," Mahosadha continued, "in Mithilā, you ignored my advice. Now let your clever advisors save you if they can. I clearly warned you that coming here would bring disaster. A king who ignores his most faithful servant deserves what he gets. You insisted on satisfying your desires. Like a greedy fish, you were so eager for the bait that you didn't notice the hook hidden in the lure. Now that you are caught, you recognize that hook which promises death. Blinded by lust, you mocked my good advice and failed to recognize the king's daughter as your own downfall. Accusing me of trying to deprive you of a beautiful maiden, you called me a farmer and ordered your men to take me by the neck and throw me out. Well, Sire, since I am a mere clodhopper, how could I possibly know what to do in a case like this? Ask Senaka and your other advisors. Counseling kings is not my trade. Let these sages rescue you from the deadly army that surrounds you."

The king recognized his faults, but he was confident that Mahosadha had arranged for his safety. "My son," he replied softly, "do not throw the past in my face. What you are doing is like spurring a horse still hitched to a post! If you see an escape, save me! Please stop scolding me!"

"It is too late for me to do anything, Sire. If you have a flying elephant or a magical horse, ride it, and escape. I can do nothing for you. You must manage on your own."

"Mahosadha," Senaka begged, "when a man lost in the mighty ocean finds a foothold, he is filled with joy. You, wise sir, are firm ground to stand on. Best of counselors, please rescue us from this disaster!"

"I have told you that it is too late." Mahosadha replied. "There is nothing I can do. Senaka, save your king and yourself!"

The king was ashamed to plead with Mahosadha. He turned to Senaka and said, "You see the great peril we are in, Senaka. What should we do?"

"Your Majesty, let us set fire to the door!" Senaka suggested, unable to come up with anything positive. "Let us take swords and slay one another! That would be better than letting Brahmadatta kill us by slow torture."

"You fool!" the king shouted angrily. "You seem to be ready for your own funeral, but I am not! What do you suggest, Pukkusa?"

"Sire," Pukkusa replied, terribly shaken, "we had better all take poison and die peacefully. Cūlani-Brahmadatta certainly is planning to kill us most painfully!"

"Idiot!" cried the king. "Poison may be good enough for you and your wife, but I am not ready to lie down and die! What do you suggest, Kavinda?"

"Sire," Kavinda replied, "the situation is very grave. Let us hang ourselves from the rafter and die quietly. Who knows what this king has in store for us?"

"Dolt!" cried the king. "You and your relatives may hang themselves as high as you please, but I am not interested in that! What do you suggest, Devinda?"

"Sire," Devinda replied, "I agree with Senaka. We could set fire to the palace and throw ourselves on our swords. However, there is one other possibility, which is really our only hope. Your Majesty, we are no more than fireflies compared to the bright flame of Mahosadha! Only he can save us. Rather than wasting your time and your breath asking us what to do, Your Majesty should be pleading with Mahosadha to rescue you from this peril! His wisdom is great!"

The king, however, recalling how badly he had treated the sage, could no longer even look him in the face. "We are like the man who sought heartwood in a banana plant!" he moaned. "We have found no solution to our misery!

Here I am in mortal danger but surrounded by worthless men who know nothing! My heart is pounding, and I see nothing but darkness!"

"Your Majesty, let your heart cease its pounding," Mahosadha consoled him. "Do not despair! As long as I am here, you have nothing to fear. I will set you free, as one frees the moon when it has been seized by Rahu. As one frees an elephant sunk in the mud, a snake shut in a basket, or a fish caught in a net, I will release you from this trap! You, your advisors, your courtiers, and your army—all will be safe. I will chase away your enemies as one scares the crows with a clod. Of what use is your sage's wisdom if it cannot extract you from such difficulties as these?"

"My son!" cried the king, much relieved. "I feel alive again! With you to help us, I know that we are safe!"

"Wise sir, I am sure that you truly can save us," Senaka declared, "but how will you manage to spirit us away from this danger?"

"You will escape through an elaborate tunnel. Prepare yourselves!"

He ordered one of his men to turn the handle, and the door of the great tunnel swung open. Everyone gasped when they saw the blazing lights before them.

"Come, Your Majesty," Mahosadha beckoned. "It is time to go."

Senaka, who was standing behind the king, took off his turban and loosened his gown. "What are you doing?" Mahosadha asked him.

"Wise sir," he replied, "in a tunnel, a man must take off his headdress and wrap his clothes around himself tightly."

"Senaka," Mahosadha said, correcting him, "in this tunnel, there is no need to crawl on your knees, nor will you even need to stoop. If you wished, you could ride through on an elephant! This lofty tunnel is eighteen hatthas high, with a wide door. Wear what you like, and go in front of the king."

Senaka and the other advisors went first, the king followed them down the stairs, and Mahosadha was right behind the king. As they walked through the great tunnel, the advisors were constantly pointing and exclaiming, "Look at that!" "How beautiful!" "What a marvel!" The king, dazzled by the splendor of it all, repeatedly stopped to stare at the paintings on the walls and the ceiling. Mahosadha gently urged him on. The entire entourage relished the plentiful rice, curries, and delicacies piled on the tables against the walls, as well as the delicious beverages in innumerable pots.

When the guards learned that their king and his entourage had entered the great tunnel, they escorted King Cūlani-Brahmadatta's family out the other end and seated them in the main hall on the bank of the river. When the four royals saw King Vedeha and Mahosadha emerge from the tunnel, they shrieked in fear. "We're in the hands of our enemies!" they cried. "Those were the sage's soldiers who came for us! We've been captured! Help!"

At that moment, King Cūlani-Brahmadatta, who was about halfway between Upakāri and the Gangā, heard their cries. He clearly recognized the voice of his queen but dared not say anything for fear that his soldiers would scoff at him for imagining things.

Mahosadha seated Princess Pañcālacandī on a great heap of treasure and performed a wedding ceremony by sprinkling her with lustral water. "Here, Sire, is the prize for which you came to Uttarapañcāla!" he proclaimed. "Let her be your queen!"

The three hundred ships silently glided up to the pier beside the great hall. The king, the new queen, her mother, her grandmother, and her brother boarded one of the richly decorated vessels.

"Pañcālacandī was born a royal princess, Sire," Mahosadha advised the king from the bank of the river. "Respect her as your queen. Protect Prince Pañcālacanda as your brother. Treat Queen Nandā as your esteemed mother-in-law. As long as I am safe, let no harm come to them." Mahosadha did not feel that it was necessary to mention the queen mother because she was an elderly matron.

"Of course, my son," replied the king, "but what do you mean, 'as long as I am safe?' Why are you still standing on the riverbank? Come aboard quickly. We have escaped from great danger. It is time to go. Surely, you are coming with us!"

"No, Sire," the sage replied, "I cannot go with you. We still must confront King Cūlani-Brahmadatta, who is besieging your new city. I cannot abandon our army. The men who came with you are weary from travel. My men are fatigued from all the construction work they have been doing for the last four months. I will return with all of them, with the consent of Cūlani-Brahmadatta himself. Go, Sire, with all speed! Do not tarry at any point. I have stationed relays of elephants and chariots all along the route. Return quickly to Mithilā!"

"Yours is a small army against a great one. How can you prevail?" asked the king, greatly concerned for the safety of the sage.

"A small army with wise leadership can easily conquer a huge force that has none," Mahosadha replied, "just as the rising sun dispels the darkness." Mahosadha saluted the king and signaled for the ships to leave.

As he sailed across the river, the king reflected on how he had been saved from the hands of his enemies and how, by winning the princess, he had gained his fondest wish. He also reflected on the sage's virtues. "True happiness comes, Senaka," he declared, "from living with the wise."

When the ships arrived on the other side of the Gaṅgā, elephants, horses, and chariots were waiting. At the end of each day, having traveled one yojana, they arrived in a village, where fresh elephants, horses, and chariots had been prepared. At every point, food and drink for the royal party and water and fodder for the animals was amply provided. Thus, they reached Mithilā refreshed, yet without delay.

Still on the bank of the Gaṅgā, Mahosadha turned and walked back toward the great tunnel. At the entrance, he took off his sword and buried it in the sand. Then he entered the tunnel and walked to Upakāri. After bathing in scented water, he ate supper and retired to his bed, satisfied that he had accomplished what he had set out to do.

The next morning, King Cūlani-Brahmadatta, mounted on his most powerful elephant, which was a sixty-year-old tusker, ordered his combined army to attack Upakāri. "Storm the palace, but take King Vedeha alive!" he shouted. "Even if Vedeha could fly like a bird, he would not be able to escape from me now!"

Inside the city, the army of Vedeha and Mahosadha's companions, who had not been given orders to fight and did not know that the king was gone, were unsure what to do. They rushed to protect the sage. Mahosadha had awakened unperturbed, completed his toilet, and was leisurely having his breakfast. When his companions informed him that King Cūlani-Brahmadatta was at the gates of the palace, he mindfully put on his robe of Kāsi silk worth one hundred thousand coins and his golden slippers, took up his formal staff inlaid with precious jewels, and stepped onto the terrace.

"Welcome to our city, Sire," he said to King Cūlani-Brahmadatta. "You look very happy, as if you have achieved a great success. Put down your bow and arrows and come in. Why are you goading your elephant so fiercely?"

"Don't mock me, you clodhopper!" cried the king. "You speak with a smile on your face, but you and your king have a rendezvous with death this very day!"

The soldiers of the combined army were struck by the sage's handsome visage, and they strained to hear his words.

"You do not know what I am capable of doing. Have you forgotten that I am the wise Mahosadha? I will not allow you to kill me, nor to kill my king. The plan which you and Kevatta devised has been thwarted. Last night, King Vedeha crossed the Gaṅgā with all his courtiers and attendants."

King Cūlani-Brahmadatta could not imagine how such a thing was possible, but he instinctively knew that Mahosadha was not lying. He was furious to think that he had again been outsmarted. He was doubly furious to have been made a fool a second time. "Seize him!" he shouted to his soldiers. "Cut off his hands and feet, slice off his ears and his nose. Because of him Vedeha has slipped away! Cut off his flesh and cook it on skewers!"

"Sire," Mahosadha called out in a loud, convincing voice, "Let your men cut off my hands, my feet, my ears, and my nose. You can be sure that King Vedeha will deal with your family in the same way. If you cut off my flesh and cook it on skewers, my friends in Mithilā will roast Princess Pañcāla-candī, Queen Nandā, and Prince Pañcālacanda in the same way. This was our agreement when he left."

"What do you mean, you damned yokel? My wife, my daughter, and my son are closely guarded in my palace! Are you so afraid to die that you resort to foolish, empty threats?"

"Are you sure, Sire? Send some of your men to go and look. Let them tell you that your inner apartments are empty and that your guards are in bonds. Your wife, your daughter, your son, and your mother were spirited quite willingly out of the palace through a secret tunnel. They were given to King Vedeha, and they left with him last night."

For a moment, the king was speechless. "Could it be that what I heard truly was the voice of Queen Nandā?" he wondered. "This sage speaks with such confidence! Who knows what he is capable of?" Aloud he shouted to the soldier next to him, "Go! Hurry to my palace to see whether my family is still in the upper apartment! Tell me that the sage is lying!"

The messenger galloped off. Dismounting and rushing through the palace, he found the guards bound, gagged, and hanging on hooks. Broken vessels were scattered about, and the doors of the treasury were open. The inner apartments were deserted. As fast as he could, the soldier rode back to report all of this to the king. When he heard the messenger confirm what Mahosadha had said, the king began trembling with grief.

Mahosadha could see that the king's grief was developing into anger directed at him. To protect himself, Mahosadha stepped back from the edge of the terrace and began praising Queen Nandā. "Last night, Sire, the most beautiful woman, adorned with sparkling jewels, stood on the bank of the Gaṅgā. Around her slender waist she wore a golden belt. Her supple limbs swayed beneath dark silk as she gracefully walked across the courtyard. Her lips were ruby red, her eyes sparkled like a pigeon's, and her long black hair curled slightly at her waist. When she spoke, she charmed the world with music. The beauty of the queen was like a flame in winter."

As the king listened to Mahosadha's description of his wife, a great long-ing arose in him, not only for his wife, but for his children, as well. Then, with the realization that only the sage could return them to him, he was filled with sorrow.

"Don't be troubled, Sire. Your queen, your son, and your mother will all come back safely to you. The only condition is my safe return to Mithilā."

"Mahosadha," King Cūlani-Brahmadatta called, still sitting on his elephant, "My palace in Uttarapañcāla was closely guarded. The armies of the one hundred kings had Upakāri surrounded. Still, you were able to abduct my queen, my daughter, my son, and my mother right from under my nose and to send them off with King Vedeha. How did you do it? Are you a master of magic?"

"Sire," Mahosadha replied, "you might say that I do, indeed, know magic. A wise man must be constantly on his guard to understand what is happening so that, when danger arises, he can save both himself and others. I have many young companions who are clever at overcoming obstacles, so, when I saw the threat which was coming, I was able to summon them. I devised secret passages, and, with the help of my companions, we whisked your family and our king to the Gangā and on to Mithilā."

"Where are these secret passages?" asked the king. "Did my wife and mother crawl through tunnels all the way from the palace to the river?"

"Come with me, Sire," Mahosadha replied, "and you will see my great tunnel. There is no need to crawl. It is brightly illuminated and large enough for an elephant. Bring your army and come into the city of Upakāri. Let me show all of you my tunnel."

The sage ordered that the city gate be thrown open, and King Cūlani-Brahmadatta entered, followed by the one hundred other kings. Mahosadha left the terrace, saluted the king, and led the entire party into the tunnel.

When the main door opened, the king felt that he was standing before the gate of Sudhamma Hall in Tāvatimsa. The light from the thousands of torches blinded him. The tunnel was larger than any palace he had ever seen. He was sure that the paintings had been done by the devas themselves. As Mahosadha led him through the tunnel and explained its many features, the other kings helped themselves to the delicious food and drink. Each king discovered that there was a chamber arranged especially for him and entered it. "How blessed is King Vedeha," thought King Cūlani-Brahmadatta, "to have so wise a sage in his service!"

Mahosadha led the king back to the entrance and turned a handle. Suddenly all the doors closed, and the one hundred kings were locked in their chambers. He turned another handle, and the lamp niches also closed, plunging the tunnel into utter darkness. The kings cried out in terror.

Before King Cūlani-Brahmadatta knew what was happening, Mahosadha recovered the sword he had hidden the night before, grabbed the king's arm, and shouted, "Sire, to whom belong all the kingdoms of Jambudīpa?"

"To you, wise sir!" cried the king. "Spare my life!"

"You have nothing to fear, Sire," Mahosadha assured him. "I did not brandish my sword to harm you. I only wished to impress upon you my wisdom! Take it, Sire!" he continued, handing the sword to the king. "If you still feel anger and hatred toward me, kill me!"

"Never, wise sir!" cried the king. "You have nothing to fear from me. I promise you your safety."

Standing there at the entrance to the tunnel, with the sword between them, the king and the sage pledged their friendship.

"Wise sir," the king asked, "with wisdom such as yours, why have you not seized the kingdom and declared yourself king?

"Sire," Mahosadha replied, "if I wished, I could certainly conquer all the kingdoms of Jambudīpa and destroy all rivals, but it is not in the nature of a wise man to gain glory by killing others."

Suddenly, the king remembered the other kings. "Wise sir," he cried, "the kings must be frightened to death trapped in the tunnel. Please open the doors and spare them!"

Mahosadha turned a handle, and the tunnel became a blaze of light once more. He turned another handle, and all the doors swung open. The one hundred kings rejoiced as they emerged from the tunnel.

"Wise sir," they cried, "you have saved our lives!"

"My Lords," Mahosadha replied, "this is not the first time I have saved your lives."

"What do you mean?" they asked in unison. "When did you save us before, wise sir?"

"After King Cūlani-Brahmadatta had conquered all the kingdoms of Jambudīpa except Vedeha, you were all gathered in Uttarapañcāla. You were planning to celebrate by drinking together the cup of victory. Do you recall that occasion?" he asked.

"Yes, of course, wise sir," they all answered.

"At that time," Mahosadha explained, "this king, along with Kevatta, had poisoned the drinks, intending to murder you all. I did not want you to die such repugnant and unjust deaths, so I sent my men to break the vessels before you drank a drop. I thwarted their plan and saved your lives."

The one hundred kings gasped in disbelief and turned to King Cūlani-Brahmadatta, asking whether this was true.

"The sage speaks the truth," the king admitted, shamefacedly.

The one hundred kings crowded around Mahosadha and praised him for saving them. Each gratefully offered him a treasured talisman.

"Sire," Mahosadha reassured King Cūlani-Brahmadatta, "your fault was in associating with a wicked man. Ask forgiveness from these kings."

"My friends," the king cried, "it is true that I was under the influence of that wicked advisor when I committed that evil deed. Nevertheless, it was my own fault. Please forgive me! I promise that I will never do such a base thing again!"

Not only did all one hundred kings express their forgiveness, but they also confessed their own faults. At last the one hundred one kings pledged enduring friendship to each other.

King Cūlani-Brahmadatta ordered a banquet, with savory dishes and delicious drinks. To honor the one hundred kings he placed a garland around the neck of each one. For seven days, they all feasted and reveled in the tunnel, honoring the sage. At the end of this festival, they ascended to the palace in Upakāri, and the king sat on his new throne. Summoning Mahosadha, he said, "Wise sir, I offer you honor and support, a double allowance of food and wages, and many other great boons, as well. I beg you not to return to King Vedeha!"

"Your Majesty," Mahosadha replied, "to desert a patron for the sake of gain is a disgrace to all concerned. As long as King Vedeha is alive, I can neither serve another nor live in another kingdom."

"Well spoken, wise sir!" declared the king. "Promise me that, when your king is no more, you will come to serve me."

"If I am alive, Sire, I will come." Mahosadha agreed with a formal bow.

After another week of feasting and ceremonies, King Cūlani-Brahmadatta presented Mahosadha with a large quantity of gold, eighty villages in Kāsi, four hundred servants, and one hundred wives. He then granted the sage permission to return to Mithilā with his army.

"I will now take my leave!" Mahosadha agreed. "Do not worry about your family, Sire. Before my king left, I sprinkled your daughter with lustral water and solemnized their marriage. I told him to treat Queen Nandā as his own mother and Prince Pañcālacanda as his younger brother. I will send back your wife, your son, and your mother."

The king was thoroughly pleased at this and sent a proper dowry of gold, precious jewels, elephants, horses, and servants for his daughter. He also presented gifts to all of Mahosadha's men.

Accompanied by his companions, his army, and all his spies, Mahosadha set out for Mithilā. On the way, he sent men to collect the revenues from the eighty villages.

In Mithilā, Senaka had stationed a man to keep watch for Mahosadha's return. When this man saw the sage a full three yojanas away, he hurried to alert the palace.

As King Vedeha kept watch from the window, he saw the massive army approaching and was frightened. "Senaka," he cried, "Mahosadha's company was small. Surely this is King Cūlani-Brahmadatta himself, coming with a great army to attack us. Who else would be marching with elephants, horses, chariots, and foot soldiers?"

"On the contrary, Your Majesty," Senaka insisted, "this is indeed Mahosadha returning with his men. King Cūlani-Brahmadatta must have been so pleased with the sage that he gave him a large company." Convinced, the king ordered that the city be decorated to welcome the sage.

When Mahosadha entered the palace, the king rose to embrace him. "My son!" he exclaimed. "We left you like a corpse in the charnel ground. How did you escape?"

"I overcame the scheme, Sire, by a counter-scheme," Mahosadha answered. "I encompassed King Cūlani-Brahmadatta as the ocean encompasses Jambudīpa."

To the delight of the king, the sage explained all that had happened and described the many gifts he had received.

"Happiness truly comes from living with the wise," declared King Vedeha. "Like birds from a closed cage, like fish from a net, Mahosadha set us free from the hands of our enemies."

"You have spoken true, Sire," Senaka agreed. "Mahosadha is indeed our savior."

The king ordered a seven-day festival to honor the great sage. The entire population joined in the celebration. Overjoyed at the sage's return, everyone waved scarves and showered Mahosadha with gifts and great honor. At the end of the festival, Mahosadha told the king that it was time to send King Cūlani-Brahmadatta's wife, son, and mother back to Uttarapañcāla, and the king agreed.

Before sending them back, Mahosadha paid them great honor and entertained them lavishly. Not only did he assemble an army to escort them home, but he returned the four hundred servants and one hundred wives he had received from King Cūlani-Brahmadatta.

When this great company reached Uttarapañcāla, the king asked his mother whether she had been treated well in Mithilā.

"My son, how can you ask?" she exclaimed. "King Vedeha treated me as if I were a deva." She assured her son that the king had also respected Queen Nandā as a mother and Prince Pañcālacanda as a younger brother.

King Cūlani-Brahmadatta was so pleased to hear this that he sent a rich gift to King Vedeha, and, from that time on, the two monarchs lived in friendship and amity.

Queen Pañcālacandī was very dear to King Vedeha, and, two years later, she bore him a son. When the child was ten, King Vedeha died, and Mahosadha raised the white umbrella over the prince. The sage asked permission to go to Uttarapañcāla, but the young king begged him to stay. "Wise sir," the boy said, "do not leave me in my childhood. I will honor you as a father."

"Please do not go, wise sir," the queen mother Pañcālacandī also begged. "If you leave, there will be no one to protect us!"

"My promise was given," the sage insisted. "I have no choice but to go."

The entire population of Mithilā cried in lamentation as Mahosadha and his entire household left for Uttarapañcāla. King Cūlani-Brahmadatta welcomed him with great pomp, presented him with many more gifts, and gave him a fine residence.

Queen Nandā, however, had never forgiven the sage for having separated her from her husband. She summoned five women that she could trust and told them to watch Mahosadha closely and to report to the king anything that might cause a breach between the two. The women accepted the task and kept a close eye on everything that the sage did.

Also living in Uttarapañcāla at that time was a learned female ascetic named Bherī, who took all her meals in the palace. She and Mahosadha had never met, but they had heard about each other.

One day, as Bherī was leaving the palace after her meal, she caught sight of the sage on his way to wait on the king. They saluted each other and stood still.

"They say this is a wise man." Bherī thought. "Let me see whether or not he is really wise."

She held out her open hand.

Mahosadha clenched his fist.

Bherī rubbed her head.

Mahosadha rubbed his stomach.

Mahosadha and Bherī were both pleased with this silent communication. They saluted each other again and went their separate ways.

The queen's confidantes observed this pantomime from a window of the palace and hurried to the king. "Your Majesty," they said, "Mahosadha is conspiring with Bherī to seize your kingdom."

"How do you know this?" asked the king.

"Sire, as Bherī, the ascetic, was going out after her meal, she and Mahosadha confronted each other.

"We saw her open her hand, asking, 'Can't you crush the king flat like the palm of the hand and seize the kingdom for yourself?'

"Mahosadha clenched his fist, replying, 'In a few days, I will cut off his head and take power.'

"She rubbed her head, saying, 'Cut off his head!'

"He rubbed his stomach, saying, 'I will cut him in half.'

"Be vigilant, Sire! Mahosadha is your enemy! He should be put to death before he can harm you!"

The king thanked the women for their information and sent them away. "I dare not harm my sage," the king thought. "These charges don't make sense. Let me question the ascetic."

The next day, after the ascetic had finished her meal, the king approached her and asked, "Madam, have you seen wise Mahosadha?"

"Yes, Sire," she replied, "I met him yesterday as I was going out after my meal."

"Did you talk with him?"

"I did not exactly talk with him," she replied. "I had heard of his wisdom, so I decided to test him by conversing with hand gestures.

"I asked him, by showing my open hand, whether you were treating him generously.

"He replied, by clenching his fist, that he had come in fulfillment of a promise, but that now you gave him little.

"By rubbing my head, I asked why, if he was dissatisfied, he did not become an ascetic.

"He rubbed his stomach to reply that, since he had many to support and many bellies to fill, he was not free to become an ascetic."

"In your opinion, Madam," the king asked, "is Mahosadha a wise man?"

"Yes, indeed, Sire," she replied. "In all the world there is no equal to him in wisdom."

The king paid his respects to the ascetic and returned to his chamber.

When Mahosadha came to the palace, the king asked him, "Sir, have you seen the ascetic, Bherī?"

"Yes, Sire," the sage replied, "I saw her yesterday on her way out."

"Did you talk with her?" the king asked.

"We conversed with hand gestures, Your Majesty." He related the incident exactly as Bherī had done.

The king was so pleased with the sage that he appointed him commander-in-chief, raising him to a position second only to his own.

"I wonder why the king has suddenly rewarded me," Mahosadha reflected. "Kings often do something like that when they are getting ready to destroy a presumed rival. I must find out whether or not the king has genuine goodwill toward me. Only the ascetic Bherī is wise enough to do that. I'm sure that she will find a way."

He prepared a large offering of flowers and incense and went to visit the ascetic. After paying his respects, he said to her, "Madam, after you praised me to the king, he rewarded me with great honor. I wonder, however, whether his show of respect is sincere. I would be very grateful if you could find out the king's real intentions." She willingly agreed to try to do so.

"I don't want to look like a spy," Bherī thought, "but, just by posing an intellectual question to the king, I will be able to discover how he feels about the sage."

The next day, after she had finished her meal, the king again approached her, greeted her, and sat down on one side. "If, indeed, the king bears ill-will toward the sage," she thought, "it would not do for him to express this in front of other people. I should ask him when we are alone."

"Sire," she said, "I wish to speak to you in private."

The king sent away all the attendants.

"There is an interesting question I would like to pose to Your Majesty," Bherī began.

"Ask, Madam," said the king, "and, if I can, I will reply."

"This is called the Question of Dakarakkhasa," she continued. "Imagine, Sire, that you are traveling on the ocean with your mother, Queen Talatā; your wife, Queen Nandā; your brother, Prince Tikhinamanti; your friend, Dhanusekha; your advisor, Kevatta; and the sage, Mahosadha. Suddenly, your ship is seized by a yakkha, who demands a human sacrifice. Whom would you offer to be eaten?"

The king promptly answered, "I would give my mother."

Without commenting, the ascetic asked, "If, on the next day, the yakkha asked for another victim, whom would you offer?

"My wife," replied the king.

"On the third day?" asked the ascetic.

"My brother," replied the king.

"On the fourth day?"

"My friend."

"On the fifth day?"

"My advisor."

"On the sixth day?"

"Myself. I would never give up the sage Mahosadha!" declared the king.

In this way, Bherī discovered the king's goodwill towards Mahosadha, but she felt that, if the king were to extol the merit of Mahosadha publicly, the sage's virtue would shine like the full moon in the night sky.

The next day, when all the members of the inner palace were gathered, Bherī repeated her question, and the king answered in the same way. "Sire, you say that you would first give your mother, but a mother is of great merit, and Queen Talatā has indeed been your great protector. When King Chambhī sought to have you killed, she bravely and wisely saved you by arranging for you to be spirited out of the country.[21] Why would you so readily give your mother to the yakkha?"

---

21   While Cūlani was still young, his mother committed adultery with a brahmin advisor named Chambhī. She poisoned her husband Mahā-Cūlani and made Chambhī king.

One day, she gave Cūlani some molasses. While he was eating, flies swarmed around the molasses. The boy cleverly dropped a little molasses on the ground and drove the flies away from his bowl. The flies all settled on the molasses on the ground. The boy ate in peace, washed his hands, and rinsed his mouth. Chambhī saw this and thought: "If Cūlani could so easily get rid of the flies, when he grows up, he will take the kingdom from me. I should kill him now."

He told Queen Talatā, and she replied, "Very good, My Lord. I killed my husband for love of you. What is the boy to me? Nevertheless, let us kill him secretly."

She sent for the cook and said to him, "Friend, my son, Prince Cūlani, and your son, Dhanusekha, were born on the same day, and they have grown up together. Chambhī wants to kill my son, so I must ask you to save his life. Let my son stay in your house and sleep with you in the kitchen. After a few days, put some sheep's bones in your bed, set fire to the house, and flee with the two boys to another country. Here is enough gold to sustain you for many years. Please take care of my son, but do not tell anyone that he is a prince."

The cook agreed, and, several days later, there was a great outcry throughout the city: "The cook, his son, and Prince Cūlani have perished in a fire!" Queen Talatā showed King Chambhī the sheep's bones and assured him that his wish had been fulfilled.

The cook had escaped to Sāgala, where he became cook for the king of Madda, and the two boys played in the palace. After some time, Cūlani and the king's daughter, Nandā, fell in love. As they played together, Cūlani often told the princess to fetch his ball or to give him a toy. If she refused, he hit her on the head and made her cry. When the king or one of the nurses asked her why she was crying, for fear that Cūlani would be punished, she never let them know what he had done. One day, the king saw Cūlani hit the princess and thought, "This lad is fearless and handsome. I don't believe that he is the cook's son." He commented to the cook that his two sons were not at all alike, and the cook replied that they had different mothers.

The king doubted this, so he kept watching Cūlani. Several days later, the nurses gave some food to the princess. She offered it to the other children, and all of them, except Cūlani, knelt to accept it from her. Cūlani, however, never put down his toy but stood before her and held out one hand. The king noticed this, too, and wondered. At another time, Cūlani's ball rolled under the king's couch. The boy ran to get the ball, but, when he saw where it had gone, he used a stick to retrieve it. The king saw this and immediately understood that Cūlani was refusing to kneel in front of the seat of a foreign king. The king summoned the cook again and said, "My good man, I am sure that Cūlani is not your son."

"Your Majesty," the cook replied, "he is my son."

Drawing his sword, the king threatened, "Tell me the truth, or I will strike you down!"

"Sire," the cook replied, trembling with fear, "I will tell you, but I must I ask you for secrecy."

The king answered, "My mother has many virtues, and I acknowledge all she has done for me, but she has her faults. Although she is now advanced in years, she still wears cosmetics and jewelry like a young woman. She shamelessly flirts with every man in the palace. She writes letters in my name to foreign kings, extolling her charms as though she were an available maiden. That is why I would allow the yakkha to take her."

"So be it, Sire," said the ascetic. "Next, you would give your wife. Sire, Queen Nandā has been dear to you since childhood. She is completely devoted and clings to you like a shadow. She is prudent and exceedingly gracious of speech. Rarely showing her anger, she is always concerned about your well-being. Why would you so readily give your wife to the yakkha?"

"Queen Nandā has many virtues, but her sensual attractions have made me liable to evil influences. She sometimes makes unreasonable requests for her sons. She is haughty in front of my other wives and unkind when they receive my favors. She is so greedy for herself and her sons that, when I give presents to her or to them, I often come to regret my generosity. That is why I would allow the yakkha to take her."

"So be it, Sire," said the ascetic. "Next, you would give your younger brother. Sire, Prince Tikhinamanti has been extremely generous to you. When you were living in exile, he brought you back and gave you the kingdom.[22] He is a peerless archer and a great hero. Why would you so readily give your brother to the yakkha?"

The king agreed, and the cook told him the truth. Not at all angry, the king adorned his daughter and gave her to Prince Cūlani in marriage.

22 By the time Tikhinamanti was born, Queen Talatā had killed his father and was living with the brahmin Chambhī. When the prince was old enough, the brahmin presented the boy with a sword.

One day, one of the courtiers told the boy that the brahmin was not his father. "While you were in your mother's womb," the courtier said, "your mother, Queen Talatā, murdered your father, King Mahā-Cūlani, and made Chambhī king."

Tikhinamanti became angry and resolved to kill the brahmin. He secretly called two servants. He gave his sword to one of them and told them to begin quarreling loudly in the courtyard over the ownership of the sword.

As the prince was sitting with the brahmin, they heard the ruckus, and the prince sent a servant to find out what it was. The servant returned and said that two men were arguing about the prince's sword.

"What sword is that?" Chambhī asked.

"Father," Tikhinamanti asked, "did the sword you gave me belong to anyone else?"

"What do you mean, son?" retorted the brahmin.

"Well," replied the prince, "it seems that these men are having a serious argument about a sword. Would you recognize that sword if you saw it?"

"Of course, I would!" declared the brahmin.

"When Tikhinamanti was young, he did indeed give me the crown, and I am grateful," replied the king. "Nevertheless, recently he has become proud. Thinking, 'I made my brother king, I gave the kingdom its prosperity, I am a peerless bowman, and I am my brother's wisest advisor,' he no longer comes to wait on me. That is why I would allow the yakkha to take him."

"So be it, Sire," said the ascetic. "Next, you would give your childhood friend. Sire, Dhanusekha has been devoted to you all his life. You were born on the same day and grew up together. It was his father who saved you from the wicked brahmin. He has been zealous in his service to you. Why would you so readily give this friend to the yakkha?"

"It is true that Dhanusekha and I have shared many joyous times together for many years. I am very grateful for his father's courageous act and loving care for me as a young boy. Nevertheless, Dhanusekha has recently begun to take liberties. Sometimes, when I have been speaking privately with my wife, he has barged in unannounced. There have been instances where he has acted not only disrespectfully but shamelessly. That is why I would allow the yakkha to take him."

"So be it, Sire," said the ascetic. "Next, you would give your advisor. Sire, Kevatta has been your trusted advisor for many years. His skill in interpreting omens, signs, and dreams is known throughout Jambudīpa. He understands the stars and can predict the future. He is a master at devising schemes for augmenting your power. Why would you so readily give your advisor to the yakkha?"

"Often, while I am attending to court business, Kevatta rubs his forehead and stares at me with eyes like a yakkha's. He puckers his eyebrows and scares me out of my wits. Even in company, he stares at me with wide open eyes. That is why I would allow the yakkha to take him."

"So be it, Sire," said the ascetic. "Now you say that, despite your great glory, you would give yourself to the yakkha rather than the sage Mahosadha. Why do you honor him more than your own person?"

"Since Mahosadha came to me," declared the king, "I have not seen this steadfast man do even a trifling wrong. His conduct is impeccable and his wisdom is incomparable. This man neither sins nor errs. Should I die before

---

The prince told the servant to bring him the sword. As the servant handed it to him, the prince drew it from the scabbard and, making as if to show it to the unsuspecting brahmin, cut off his head.

He ordered that the palace be cleaned and the city decorated and proclaimed himself king. When his mother informed him that his elder brother, Cūlani, was living in Madda, Tikhinamanti went himself to Sāgala, brought his brother back, and gave him the crown.

he does, I would be confident that he would bring happiness to my sons and my grandsons. I would never give him to the yakkha."

"This gathering is too small," Bheri thought, "to demonstrate adequately Mahosadha's virtues." She prepared a throne in the courtyard and seated the king amidst the entire populace. Once more, from the beginning, she posed the Question of Dakarakkhasa so that everyone could hear the king's answer. When he had finished, she proclaimed, "Our great king, Cūlani-Brahmadatta would sacrifice not only his mother, his wife, his brother, his friend, and his advisor but also himself, before allowing the wise Mahosadha to be harmed. Marvelous is the power of wisdom, not only for good in this world, but for happiness in the next." In reply, the great assembly shouted in praise of the sage.

Indeed, in all of Jambudīpa, as well as in all the heavenly realms, the citizens praised, honored, and glorified the wisdom of the sage Mahosadha.

Having concluded his story, the Buddha identified the birth: "At that time, Uppalavannā was Bherī, Suddhodana was Sirivaddhaka, Mahā-Māyā was Sumanādevī, Rāhula's mother was Amarā, Ānanda was the parrot Māthara, Sāriputta was King Cūlani-Brahmadatta, Devadatta was Kevatta, Culla-Nandikā was Queen Talatā, Sundarī was Princess Pañcālacandī, Yasassikā was Queen Nandā, Ambattha was Kāvinda, Potthapāda was Pukkusa, Pilotika was Devinda, Saccaka was Senaka, Ditthamangalikā was Queen Udumbarā, Kundalī was the mynah bird, Lālūdāyī was King Vedeha, and I was the wise Mahosadha."

217
Prince Vessantara
Vessantara Jātaka

It was while staying at Nigrodhārāma near Kapilavatthu that the Buddha told this story about an extraordinary shower of rain.

After spending a winter in Rājagaha, the Buddha proceeded to Kapilavatthu, capital city of his father's kingdom, attended by twenty thousand bhikkhus. The Sākyan princes were very eager to see the chief of their clan. They went to inspect the residence where he would be staying and declared, "This Banyan Grove is a delightful place, worthy of Sakka himself." Then they went with flowers to greet the Buddha, accompanied by all the young princes and princesses and many children.

The Sākyans were a notoriously proud people. The older princes thought to themselves, "Suddhodana's boy is younger than we are. He is merely our little cousin, our nephew, our grandson!" After the Buddha was seated in the appointed place, surrounded by all the bhikkhus, they sent the younger princes to pay obeisance to him, while they, in their pride and stubbornness, sat toward the back without bowing.

The Buddha realized their intention and thought, "My relatives do not pay me proper respect as a Buddha, but I will make them do so." He concentrated his mind, rose into the air, and, as though shaking the dust from his feet on

393

to their heads, caused fire and water alternately to stream from his body, which is called the Twin Miracle.

When King Suddhodana saw that wonder, he exclaimed to his son, "Soon after your birth, when I saw your feet placed on the head of the brahmin Asita, I bowed to you for the first time. On the day of the Plowing Festival, as you sat on the royal seat in the shade of a jambu tree whose shadow had not moved, I bowed to you for the second time. Now I see this glorious miracle, and I bow to you for the third time."

As soon as the Sākyan princes saw the king paying reverence, they were compelled to do likewise. Satisfied, the Buddha came down and sat again on the appointed seat. All who were there became calm with peace in their hearts. Suddenly, the skies opened and released a refreshing shower of rain. However, the rain fell on only those who wanted to get wet. Not a single drop fell on those who wished to remain dry.

"Look at this miracle!" everyone cried. "What power the Buddha has to make such a rain fall on his kinsmen!"

The Buddha said to them, "This is not the first time that such a great shower of rain has fallen upon my relatives because of me." At their request, he told this story of the past.

Long, long ago, a king named Sivi reigned in his capital city of Jetuttara in the kingdom of Sivi. King Sivi had a son named Sañjaya. When Prince Sañjaya came of age, the king chose for his bride Princess Phusatī, daughter of King Madda.

Here are Phusatī's connections in the distant past. In the ninety-first eon before this, a Buddha named Vipassi arose in the world. While Vipassi Buddha was staying in a deer park in King Bandhuma's realm, another ruler sent King Bandhuma a golden wreath worth one hundred thousand coins, along with a gift of precious sandalwood. King Bandhuma had two daughters, so he gave the sandalwood to his elder daughter and the golden wreath to the younger. Since neither young woman wanted such a present for herself, they both decided to offer the precious gifts to the Buddha. When they announced their intention to their father, he readily consented.

The elder sister powdered the sandalwood and put it in a golden box. The younger princess had the golden wreath made into a necklace which she laid in another golden box. Together they went to the hermitage in the deer park. The elder sister reverently sprinkled the Buddha with some of the sandalwood and scattered the rest around his hermitage with the prayer, "Sir, in the future, may I be the mother of a Buddha like you." The younger princess reverently placed the golden necklace on the Buddha, praying, "Sir, until I attain liberation, may I always wear such an ornament as this."

After that life was over, the sisters were reborn in the realm of devas. In the time of Kassapa Buddha, they were both reborn as daughters of King Kiki. The younger sister was born with the likeness of a necklace traced upon her neck and shoulders, as delicate as though drawn by an artist, and her name was Uracchadā. When she was only sixteen, she heard Kassapa Buddha teach and attained the first path. On that same day, she also attained arahatship, became a bhikkhunī, and entered Parinibbāna.

King Kiki had seven other daughters besides Uracchadā. Their names were Samanī, Samanā, Guttā, Bhikkhudasikā, Dhammā, Sudhammā, and Sanghadāsī. In the lifetime of our Buddha, these sisters became Khemā, Uppalavannā, Patācārā, Kisāgotamī, Dhammadinnā, Queen Mahā-Māyā, and Visākhā, respectively.

Sudhammā had been the elder daughter of King Bandhuma. By the power of her offering of sandalwood to Vipassi Buddha, her body was always fragrant, as if freshly sprinkled with precious sandalwood, so she was called Phusatī. Passing back and forth between the realms of men and of devas, she eventually became Sakka's chief queen.

When her lifetime in Tāvatimsa was nearly over, the signs of impending demise appeared. Immediately realizing what was happening, Sakka escorted her with great ceremony to the Nandana pleasure grove. As she reclined on a lavish seat, he sat beside her and said, "Dear Phusatī, I grant you ten boons. Choose!"

Phusatī was shocked by his words. She asked Sakka what fault she had committed that she had to leave that lovely place.

Sakka reassured her that she was still dear to him and that she had done nothing wrong. He explained that, since her merit was used up, she would soon pass away from that heaven. Her future life, however, would be blessed with the ten favors he was offering her. She should hurry and choose before she died.

Phusatī understood, calmed herself, and began enumerating her wishes. She wished to live in Sivi's realm, to be chief queen, to have dark eyes and dark eyebrows, to be named Phusatī, to have a son who loved giving, to keep her figure, to remain youthful so as to keep the king's affection, to have soft skin, not to become gray, and to be able to save those who had been condemned.

As soon as she had spoken her tenth wish, she passed away from that realm and was conceived in the womb of King Madda's queen. Again, she was named Phusatī, and, by the time she was sixteen, she was the most beautiful woman in the world.

As soon as Sañjaya and Phusatī were married, King Sivi abdicated and handed the kingdom over to his son. King Sañjaya loved his wife dearly.

Sakka remembered the boons he had granted Phusatī and noted that one remained unfulfilled. "She asked for a good and generous son," he thought. "I will send him to her."

At that time, the Bodhisatta was in Tāvatimsa, and his time there was ending. Sakka approached him and said, "Venerable Sir, you must be reborn in the realm of men. Now is the time for you to be conceived by Queen Phusatī, consort of the king of Sivi." The Bodhisatta agreed and descended to earth. At the same time, sixty thousand other devas from that heaven were conceived by the wives of the king's courtiers.

As soon as Queen Phusatī had conceived, she expressed the desire to have six alms-halls built, one at each city gate, one in the city center, and one at her own door so that every day she could distribute six hundred thousand coins in alms.

When the king learned that his queen was expecting, he consulted his fortune tellers, who said, "Your Majesty, your wife is pregnant with one who will be so devoted to generosity that he will never be satisfied with giving." The king was pleased with their prediction, and he, too, made a practice of generosity. Because of the king's goodness, other rulers from all over Jambudīpa sent him presents. There seemed to be no limit to the king's revenue.

After ten months, the queen informed the king that she wished to tour the capital. He ordered the city decorated, seated his queen in a royal chariot, and made a procession around the city. When they reached Vessa Street, the merchant quarters, the queen went into labor. The king had a lying-in chamber prepared, and she gave birth to a son right there.

The Bodhisatta was born free from impurity, with his eyes wide open. Immediately after he was born, he held out his hand to his mother and said, "Mother, I wish to make some gifts. Is there anything for me to give?"

She dropped a purse with one thousand coins into his outstretched hands and said, "Yes, my son. Give as you wish!"

Because he was born on Vessa Street, he was called Vessantara. On the same day, in the royal stables, a beautiful white elephant was born. This was regarded as an auspicious omen, and, because the elephant would be essential to the prince when he grew up, it was named Paccaya, which means "support."

The king appointed nurses for Vessantara and for the sixty thousand boys born at the same time. Vessantara grew up surrounded by these companions.

When the prince was four years old, the king ordered jewelers to make a precious necklace for him at a cost of one hundred thousand coins. He presented it to his son, but Vessantara immediately gave it to his nurses. They tried to return it to him, but he refused to take it back. When the nurses reported this, the king answered, "What my son has given is well given." He then had another necklace made, but the prince gave that away too. This happened nine times in all.

When Vessantara was eight years old, he thought to himself, "Everything that I give comes from outside. This does not satisfy me. I wish to give something of my very own. If someone should ask for my heart, I would tear it out and give it. If someone asked me for my eyes, I would pluck them out and give them. If someone asked for my flesh, I would cut off every bit from my bones and give it." As he pondered these thoughts in the depths of his heart, the great earth shook like a mad elephant. Mount Sineru, the highest of mountains, bowed like a sapling in the direction of the city of Jetuttara. Thunder rumbled, lightning flashed across the sky, and the seas churned as in a storm. Sakka clapped his hands, and Mahā-Brahmā signaled his approval. The entire universe was in an uproar.

By the age of sixteen, Vessantara had mastered all the arts and sciences. His parents chose his first cousin, Maddī, as his bride. On the appointed day, the young girl arrived from her father's palace with a full retinue of attendants. The grand ceremony was both their wedding and the investiture of Vessantara as crown prince.

In time, Maddī gave birth to a son who was named Jāli because he was first placed in a golden hammock. Later she had a baby girl, who was named Kanhajinā because, right after birth, she was placed on a black skin.

From the time Vessantara became heir apparent, he gave away six hundred thousand coins every day. Six times each month, mounted upon his magnificent white elephant, Paccaya, the prince visited his six alms-halls to supervise donations and to make offerings with his own hand.

It so happened that there was a severe drought in the kingdom of Kālinga. When the crops failed, there was a terrible famine. Many people were reduced to begging to escape outright starvation. In desperation, the people crowded into the king's courtyard. They cried out for help and blamed him for their troubles. "What is it, my children?" the king asked. When the people told him about conditions in the kingdom, he promised that he would bring rain. For the next seven days the king strictly observed the precepts, but no rain fell.

On the eighth day, King Kālinga appeared before the people and announced, "My loyal subjects, although I have strictly kept the precepts for seven days, I have not been able to bring any rain. What more can I do?"

One citizen spoke up, saying, "Sire, if you yourself cannot bring rain, King Sañjaya's son, Vessantara, in the city of Jetuttara, has a glorious white elephant, and, wherever that elephant goes, rain falls. We have heard reports that the prince is devoted to generosity. Send brahmins to ask for that elephant and to bring it back here to Kālinga."

Accepting that suggestion, the king promptly selected eight brahmins, gave them provisions for the journey, and sent them to fetch Vessantara's elephant.

When the eight brahmins reached Jetuttara, they were given hospitality in an alms-hall. On the full-moon day they went to the eastern gate to wait for a chance to ask for the elephant.

Early that morning, Vessantara bathed with perfumed water and ate breakfast. Mounting his noble, richly adorned elephant, he proceeded to the alms-hall at the eastern gate. From the knoll where they were standing, the brahmins could see the prince giving alms, but they had no chance to speak to him. They hurried to the southern gate.

When the prince reached the southern gate, the brahmins stretched out their hands and cried, "Victory to the noble Vessantara!"

"Brahmins, what is it that you desire?" Vessantara asked.

The brahmins replied, "We crave a precious thing, great prince. We ask for your marvelous elephant with tusks like poles."

When Vessantara heard this, he thought, "Here am I, willing to give anything that is asked for, including my head, my flesh, and my heart, but all they want is a mere possession. Of course, I'll give it to them." In a loud voice he declared, "I give and never shrink from giving. This noble beast, this mighty tusked elephant, is given freely to these brahmins who have asked for it." He climbed down from the elephant's back and presented the magnificent animal to the brahmins. The noble elephant Paccaya was fully adorned with precious ornaments. The gold and jewels decorating his tusks alone were worth hundreds of thousands of coins, and the magnificent howdah on his back was beyond price. When the prince relinquished this incomparable elephant and its priceless accessories, along with the grooms and stablemen to attend the great beast, the earth shook.

The brahmins immediately climbed on the elephant's back and rode down the main street of the city. When the crowd saw them, they shouted, "Hey, brahmins, why are you mounted on our elephant? Where are you taking our elephant?"

The brahmins shouted back, "The great prince Vessantara has given the elephant to us. What's it to you?" Then, with derogatory gestures to the crowd, they continued riding through the city and out the northern gate.

The people were outraged.

"When the great elephant was given away," one man cried out, "I'm sure I felt an earthquake!"

"Yes," shouted another, "and I heard a horrible noise!"

A raging mob rushed to the palace in protest. "The kingdom is ruined!" someone shouted to the king. "Why did Vessantara give away our elephant!" another asked. Others cried out, "How dare he make a present of our precious elephant!" "Let him be satisfied by giving food, clothing, jewelry, or horses to those rude brahmins." "Why did the prince do this?" "Explain your son's actions or we'll deal with him ourselves!"

The people sounded so angry that the king was afraid they wanted to kill Vessantara. "Let me be king no more," he shouted over the din. "I will not harm an innocent prince. No matter what you say, I could never kill him. He is my true-born son."

A spokesman from the crowd shouted in reply, "Sire, we are not demanding that Prince Vessantara be killed or even that he be imprisoned. Still, when he gave away our elephant he went too far! He must be banished from the kingdom. Send him into exile on Mount Vanka!"

Unable to appease the crowd in any other way, the beleaguered king capitulated to the people's will, but he asked that his son be allowed one happy night before he had to leave the capital. The people accepted that condition, and the king sent a message to his son, informing him of the people's anger and of his banishment. Unaware of any offense he might have committed, Vessantara asked the messenger why the people were so angry. The messenger told him that the people of Sivi were outraged at his gift-giving and were demanding that he be banished to Mount Vanka, the traditional place of exile.

"My good man," the prince replied, "since I would willingly give away my own eyes and my own heart, there should be no question of my giving mere gold and treasure. If anyone asked me, I would give away my own right hand without hesitation. My delight is in gifts! Even if the people banish me or kill me, I will never stop giving! I have committed no crime, but I will leave the city by the criminals' gate. Even though I am being banished for the gift of the white elephant, I am not through with giving. Please ask the citizens to grant me a reprieve of an additional day. Before I go, I want to make one more offering. Tomorrow I would like to give the great Gift of the Seven Hundreds, and the following day I will leave."

The messenger returned and reported everything to the people. As soon as the man had left, Vessantara summoned his servants and ordered them to arrange everything so that he could give away seven hundred of each of the following: elephants, horses, chariots, cows, male servants, and female servants. Leaving all the preparations to them, he went to see Maddī.

He sat on a couch and spoke gently to his wife, "You must find a safe place for the wealth and presents that I have given you in the past and for your father's dowry, too. Hide all this treasure well."

"Where should I find a place to hide these things, my husband?"

"Give your wealth in gifts to those who are deserving. I know of no better or safer place than that, my dear."

"Of course, that is true, My Lord, but ..."

"Take good care of your children and your husband's parents," the prince continued. "Take good care of him who will be your new husband. If no one comes forward to marry you when I'm gone, seek a husband for yourself. Don't languish all alone."

"My Lord," Maddī cried, not understanding at all, "why are you saying these things that make no sense to me?"

Vessantara answered, "Lady, the people of Sivi are angry with me for the gift of the white elephant. They are banishing me from the kingdom. Tomorrow I will give the Gift of the Seven Hundreds, and the next day I will leave. I will go to the dark and dangerous forest, full of fierce beasts of prey. Who can predict whether or not I will be able to survive there? Nevertheless, the day after tomorrow, I must go."

Understanding at last Vessantara's meaning, Maddī cried with all earnestness: "No, My Lord, I will not let you go alone! Wherever you go, I will go. Given the choice to die with you or to live apart from you, death will be my choice. I'll follow wherever you lead. The children and I will stay with you. I promise that you will never find me a burden. When you see your darling children playing and hear them prattling in our new forest home, you will forget that you were born to be king. When you hear the trumpeting of the elephants, the crying of the screech owls, and the roaring of the rivers, you will forget that you were born to be king."

Neither Vessantara nor Maddī knew that Queen Phusatī was overhearing their conversation. Distraught at the news of the banishment, she had gone to visit her son, but, finding him alone with Maddī, she hesitated to interrupt. "Better I should drink poison or leap off a cliff and die," she moaned to herself. "Why are they banishing my unoffending son, Vessantara, who is so respected, so free from greed, so generous to all who ask, so beloved by family, by friends, and by everyone in the kingdom! Why banish my innocent son, Vessantara?"

The queen hurried to the king and pleaded, "Please, Sire! Do not banish Vessantara just because some people are shouting! If this blameless boy is banished," she warned the king, "your kingdom will fall like an overripe mango. You will be like the crippled wild goose when the pond is dry—deserted by your courtiers and living alone."

"My dear," the king replied, "by sending your son into exile, I fulfill my royal duty, which is dearer than life itself."

"My son! My son!" the queen cried in despair. "Once hosts of men escorted him with banners as he rode in a chariot, but soon he'll trudge unattended on foot. And Maddī—she is used to being carried in a palanquin. How can she, with her delicate hands and feet, go into the rough forest?

"I am like an eagle that finds its nest empty, its young chicks all slain. I cannot bear the emptiness they will leave behind. How I shall endure the pain of never seeing my son again? If my innocent son is banished, my life will be over!"

Alerted by the devas, people from all over Jambudīpa flooded into Jetuttara and, as dawn was breaking, Vessantara began giving his gifts. In addition to the Gifts of the Seven Hundreds, he gave freely of every other imaginable thing; everyone received what he desired. He gave food to the hungry and even strong drink to those who required it. He was still distributing his gifts when evening fell. Banishing Vessantara from the kingdom was like cutting down a veritable wishing tree!

Having finished his great donation, the prince returned to his apartments to prepare for his departure. Then he and Maddī went to bid farewell to his parents.

Bowing to his father, he announced, "I go now to Mount Vanka. Having wronged my people by giving bounty from my hand, I accept this sentence of exile. I will atone for my mistake, but I will continue to do good."

Turning to the queen, he said, "Mother, I take leave of you as an outcast."

"I give you permission to go," Queen Phusatī replied, "and I give you my blessing, but, please, I beg you to leave Maddī and the children behind. She is unsuited for the forest. Why should she go with you?"

The prince replied, "I wouldn't even take a slave away against his will. If Maddī wishes, let her come. If not, let her stay."

"Princess," the king urged his daughter-in-law, "please stay with us. Rough bark cloth does not suit you. You are suited for fine Bārānasi silk. Your nature is very delicate. Forest life is too hard for you."

"Without Vessantara," Maddī answered calmly, "I have no desire to go on living."

The king persisted by explaining the hardships of forest life, with all its biting and stinging insects, frightening noises, deadly snakes, and fierce beasts. Maddī listened and replied, "I willingly accept all the terrible things you describe. I am resolved to go. I will forge my way through the thickest forest without complaining. Any wife who loves her husband must do her duty. The wife who shares her husband's lot, whether it is rich or poor, is praised even by the devas. Your Majesty, I will go into exile with your son. He is my joy and my very life."

"Go if you will," the king relented, "but leave your two little ones behind. What can they do in the forest? Let us keep them here with us where they will be well cared for."

"My Jāli and Kanhajinā are dearest to my heart," Maddī answered. "They will live with us in the forest and ease the pain of exile."

"These children have always eaten the finest rice and meat," the king insisted. "How can they survive if they are forced to eat wild fruit and berries? They have lived in beautifully painted rooms, safely guarded at night. How can they sleep at the roots of trees, on a bed of grass, bothered by mosquitoes and flies? It will be more than they can bear."

Even as they talked, dawn came. An elaborate carriage with a team of four Sindh horses was brought. Maddī paid her respects to her husband's parents and entered the carriage with her two children. "Do not worry," she said to the king. "Wherever we go, we will care for the children."

Vessantara also bowed to his parents and climbed into the carriage. As they drove in the direction of Mount Vanka, he shouted, "A blessing on my relatives. Farewell!"

"If my son desires to give," the queen announced as they drove away, "let him give." She sent two carts with him, each loaded with all sorts of precious things, but, in a short time, he had distributed everything to beggars he met on the road. Before they left the city, he had given away even all the jewelry he was wearing. Vessantara turned around to take one last look at his ancestral home in all its loveliness and ordered the people who had followed them to turn around and to return to the city. Then the carriage continued on its journey.

As soon as the prince had left the city, four brahmins arrived, asking about the Gift of the Seven Hundreds. When they were told that the ceremony was over and that the prince had left, they asked if he had taken anything with him. Learning that he had a coach and horses, they rushed after him.

Vessantara had asked Maddi to watch for other beggars, and, when she saw the four, she said, "Mendicants, My Lord." The prince immediately stopped the carriage. When the brahmins asked for the horses, he gave one horse to each.

Instantly, four devas, disguised as red deer, appeared and yoked themselves to the carriage. Vessantara, realizing who they were, smiled and said,

"Look, Maddī! It's a miracle!" Before they had gone very far, a fifth brahmin approached and asked Vessantara for his carriage, which he gave willingly.

"Maddī," Vessantara instructed, "you take Kanhajinā for she is light. Jāli is a heavy boy, so I'll carry him myself." With the two children on their hips, they proceeded on foot, talking together happily and asking the way of people they met. Other travelers, touched by the sight of the little family, told them that Mount Vanka was a long way off and that they still had a hard task ahead.

The children became hungry and cried when they saw all the different kinds of fruit on the tall trees beside the road. Because of Vessantara's virtue, the trees bowed down so that the parents could reach the ripe fruit. Maddī marveled at this wondrous event.

Out of pity for the children, the devas shortened the way. That evening, the family arrived in the kingdom of Ceta, which was ruled by one of Vessantara's uncles. The prince chose to rest in a hall outside the city gate, without entering the city itself. Maddī brushed the dust off his feet and rubbed them. Then she went toward the gate, intending to announce her husband's arrival. Some local women recognized her and wondered why this princess, who should have been riding in a palanquin, appeared on foot. Realizing that Vessantara, Maddī, and the children had all come in this unbecoming manner, they hurried to inform the king.

As soon as the princes of Ceta heard of the royal family's peculiar arrival, they went to meet Vessantara. "What has happened to your kingdom, mighty prince?" they asked. "Where is your army? Where is your royal carriage? Why are you without a chariot or even a horse? You've come a long way. Were you defeated by an enemy? Is that why you are here without an entourage?"

"Thank you, sirs," Vessantara answered. "My father is well, but misfortune has befallen me. The other day, some brahmins came and asked for my great elephant because their kingdom was having a drought, so I gave them the elephant and all his trappings. This made the people of Sivi so angry that they called for my banishment, and my father was forced to accept their demands. Now I am on my way to Mount Vanka. Though I am only an exile, please show me a place to stay in the meantime."

The royal cousins welcomed Vessantara warmly, gave him many presents, and prepared a delicious feast for the family. They even offered Vessantara their own kingdom, and asked him to stay.

Vessantara accepted their gifts but insisted that he had to continue on to Mount Vanka to live in exile. "You must not even inform my father that I was here," he told the princes. "I must go away a banished man. If the people of Sivi knew that you had asked me to become your king, they would be furious. I would hate to start a quarrel."

Vessantara refused even to enter the city, so the princes furnished and decorated the hall where he was going to sleep and made it comfortable. Vessantara, Maddī, and the children stayed two nights in Ceta. When they left early the next morning, the princes accompanied them for fifteen yojanas.

"You must continue for another fifteen yojanas," they told Vessantara. "That rocky mountain in the distance is Mount Gandhamadana. You, your wife, and your children may safely pass that way. From there, go straight northward, and you will see Mount Vepulla, a pleasant place with many shady trees. When you get there, you will find the Ketumati River, whose fresh, sweet water is full of fish. Bathe and rest there, and let the children play. After that, you will see Mount Nalika, which is full of songbirds and kinnaras. Continuing north, you will find Lake Mucalinda with blue and white water lilies. A little further along, you will come to a thick forest with lots of fruit trees and flowers. Follow the mountain cataracts to their spring, and you will see a lotus-covered lake. Build yourself a hut a little to the north. There is plenty of food nearby. It should be a safe haven for you." Not satisfied with just giving directions, however, before returning to their capital, the princes assigned a trustworthy forester from that region to watch over Vessantara and his family.

When the family reached the Ketumati River, they took the princes' advice and stopped to bathe and to rest. The forester prepared a delicious lunch for them and Vessantara gave him a golden hairpin. As they crossed the river, Vessantara's mind became very calm. The family rested under a banyan tree and ate some of its fruit. Then they proceeded to Mount Nalika and to Lake Mucalinda. They walked along the northeast shore of the lake and entered the thick forest by a narrow footpath.

Sakka looked down and saw that Vessantara had entered the Himavat. He immediately called Vissakamma, chief architect among the devas, and ordered him to build a suitable place for Vessantara to stay. Vissakamma built two lovely hermitages, with sleeping rooms and day rooms, connected with covered walks, lined by banana plants and flowering shrubs. Then he drove away all unfriendly devas and all harsh-voiced animals and birds. At the entrance to the settlement he posted a sign saying, "All of this is for anyone who wishes to become an ascetic."

When Vessantara saw the path, he felt sure it would lead to a settlement of ascetics. As soon as he saw the empty hermitage and the sign, he knew that Sakka had provided it for him. Accepting the gift of the hermitage, Vessantara took off his royal robe and put on the rough garb of an ascetic.

When Maddī saw him dressed like that, she could not keep herself from crying, but, following his example, she also changed her clothes and the children's. At that moment, because of Vessantara's compassion, all beings within a radius of three yojanas, even the fiercest carnivores, stopped their violence and began treating each other gently. None even thought of hunting or hurting another.

Maddī suggested that Vessantara stay with the children during the day so that she could gather food, and he agreed. Vessantara told his wife that he also had a request. He asked her to stay apart from him so that they might maintain the modesty appropriate to their new ascetic life.

Every morning, Maddī arranged drinking water, food, and toothsticks. After sweeping out the hermitage, she left the children with their father and went to the forest with a basket, a pruning hook, and a trowel to find fruit, roots, berries, and flowers. She returned in the evening and bathed the children. Then the four of them sat at the door of the hermitage to eat their meal. At night, Maddī took the children to her own cell to sleep. For seven months, they lived peacefully in this way deep in the mountains.

At that time, in the kingdom of Kālinga, in the village of Dunnivittha, there was a brahmin by the name of Jūjaka. In the past, Jūjaka had collected one hundred coins in donations. He had left this fortune in the safekeeping of a family in the village and had gone off in search of more. He stayed away such a long time, however, that the family assumed that he would never come back, and they spent the money. When Jūjaka finally returned, he was furious to discover that his savings were gone. Too poor to replace the money, the couple gave Jūjaka their daughter, Amittatāpanā, instead.

Amittatāpanā took very good care of Jūjaka. In fact, some young men said to their wives, "Look at Amittatāpanā. See how well she cares for that old man while you are careless of your young husband!" Naturally, this infuriated the other women, and they decided to drive Amittatāpanā out of the village.

At every opportunity, the women mocked her and made her life miserable. When they went to the river with their pots to get water, they teased her: "How your parents must have hated you to give you to an ugly, decrepit old man like that! How can you bear to look at that hideous old man? You are a young girl! How could that old dotard give you any happiness? Why don't you go back where you came from?"

This abuse upset Amittatāpanā very much, and she usually returned home in tears.

One day, Jūjaka saw her crying and asked, "What is wrong, my dear?"

"I can't fetch water anymore. Whenever I go out, the other women make fun of me."

"Don't worry. You don't have to carry water. From now on I'll fetch it myself."

"That is impossible. That would just make things worse! If you did that, I would be ashamed to stay with you. You must get a slave to do the work."

"My dear, how can I get a slave? I have no money. Don't be angry; I'll do your work myself."

"Now, listen to me! I've heard that Prince Vessantara is staying on Mount Vanka. People say he is devoted to giving. Go and ask him for a slave. He will certainly give you what you want."

"I'm an old man, and Mount Vanka is far away. The road there is rough. Please don't be unreasonable; I'll do the work myself."

"So! You're going to give up without even trying! I'll say it once more: if you don't get a slave to do the work for me, I'll leave you. You'll soon see me in someone else's arms," she taunted him, "and then you'll be sorry! You'll miss me so much, your gray hairs will multiply, and you will be miserable and lonely in your old age."

Terrified that his young wife would carry out her threat and leave him, Jūjaka gave in. "All right! All right!" he cried, "I'll go and return with a pair of slaves who will wait on you hand and foot."

While his wife prepared the provisions for his journey, Jūjaka laid in a supply of wood and water so that she would be safe and comfortable until he returned. "Don't go out after dark," he warned her. "Be careful until I return. I promise not to be gone long." Then, with tears in his eyes, he set out.

As soon as he reached the capital city of Sivi, he asked where he could find Prince Vessantara. He was shocked that his question provoked such anger. Everyone he asked shouted at him and pushed him away. "It's people like you," they said, "who ruined our prince. Because of giving to you beggars, he has been banished from the kingdom. It's your fault that he had to leave with his wife and children to live on Mount Vanka." Some people were so angry that they threw sticks and stones at Jūjaka to chase him away.

The devas, however, guided the brahmin and set him on the right road to Mount Vanka. He soon reached the forest, but then he got hopelessly lost and whined loudly, "Does anyone know where Vessantara, the great and generous prince, is staying? Won't someone tell me how to find Prince Vessantara?"

When the forester who had been assigned to look after Vessantara heard Jūjaka, he thought, "This man is up to no good. I'll bet he wants to ask for Maddī or the children. I cannot let that happen. I will kill him!"

The forester drew his bow and approached Jūjaka. "Because of men like you," he shouted at the brahmin, "Prince Vessantara has been exiled.

You worthless fool! Rather than let you harm his wife and children, I'll kill you myself!"

Shaking with fear, Jūjaka quickly devised a bold lie. "My friend," he said as sweetly as he could, "you cannot kill a messenger. That's an ancient rule! I am an ambassador from the king of Sivi. The people have come to repent their hasty anger with Prince Vessantara. The king misses his son, and the queen is pining away. I have come to escort Vessantara back to the capital. If you know where I can find him, it is your duty to help me."

The forester was delighted to hear this wonderful news. He quickly put down his bow, called off his hunting dogs, and invited Jūjaka to a feast of roast leg of deer and a pot of honey. Completely taken in by Jūjaka's deceit, the forester described Vessantara's peaceful hermitage and gave detailed directions to get there.

Jūjaka was so pleased that he offered the forester a piece of his homemade barley bread, but the forester refused, insisting that he was fully provisioned. To make sure Jūjaka would not make a mistake, the forester explained the path once more.

Further along, Jūjaka came upon an ascetic by the name of Accuta. "Holy man," the brahmin greeted the ascetic, "I trust that you are prosperous and well, with plenty of roots and fruit, that you are not bothered by flies or gnats or creeping things, and that wild beasts leave you alone."

"Thank you, brahmin", the ascetic replied. "Yes, I am quite well, and there is plenty of fruit here. I am not troubled by insects or animals. As a matter of fact, in all the years I've lived here, I have never been bothered by any sickness whatsoever. Please wash up, and rest from your journey. Have some tender leaves and ripe fruit. This water is from a cave up the hill. It is very cool and refreshing."

Jūjaka wasted no time in explaining his errand. "I am looking for Vessantara, King Sañjaya's son, who was banished by the people of Sivi. If you know where he is, please tell me."

"I'm afraid your intentions are not good," the ascetic replied suspiciously. "No doubt, you have come to ask for his wife or to take his children as your servants. The prince has no wealth or property here."

Jūjaka quickly protested. "No, no, you misunderstand me! I have only the best of intentions. It is a joy to be able to visit a good man. I have never met this prince before. I have just come here to see him; that's all. If you know where he is, please tell me."

"All right then," Accuta answered, also taken in by the brahmin's honeyed words. "Stay with me tonight, and tomorrow I'll tell you how to get there."

The next morning, the ascetic pointed out the route to Vessantara's hermitage, and Jūjaka set out. By evening, he had reached the lake. He thought to himself, "Vessantara's wife will be returning from the forest. Women are always in the way, so, tomorrow, after she has gone out to gather fruit, I will approach Vessantara and ask him for the children. I'll get them and be on my way before she comes back." Satisfied with his plan, he climbed a small hill and lay down to sleep in a pleasant spot.

Just before dawn, Maddī dreamed that a black man, wearing yellow robes and with red flowers in his ears, came into the leaf hut. He grabbed her by the hair, dragged her out, and threw her down. As she lay shrieking on the ground, he gouged out her eyes, lopped off her arms, cut open her breast, and tore out her heart, which he carried off, dripping with blood. She awoke in terror. "What an unspeakably evil dream!" she cried. "I must ask Vessantara to tell me what it means. Surely he will understand it."

Although it was still dark, she hurried to Vessantara's hut and knocked at the door. "Who is it?" Vessantara asked.

"It is I, My Lord," Maddī answered.

"Why have you come at this hour?" Vessantara asked, without opening the door. "Are you not breaking our agreement?"

"I am very sorry, but I am not coming out of desire. I have had an evil dream, and only you can explain it."

"I see," Vessantara replied, opening the door. "Please tell me what you saw."

As soon as Maddī had explained the nightmare, Vessantara understood its meaning. "My generosity will soon be perfected," he thought. "Today someone will come and ask for the children. I must comfort Maddī and let her go back to bed."

Aloud he said, "Your mind must have been disturbed by indigestion. Don't worry."

Reassured by his words, Maddī returned to her own hut, but the dream continued to haunt her so much that she could not get back to sleep. When it finally became light, she emerged and prepared things as she did every day. As she hugged and kissed the children, she told them that she had had a bad dream and warned them to be careful. She asked Vessantara to look after the children with extra care. Then, wiping away her tears, she picked up her basket and tools and went to the forest to gather food.

Jūjaka waited until he was sure that Maddī would be out of the way. In joyful anticipation, Vessantara had come out of his hut and was sitting on a stone slab. "Now the supplicant will come!" he thought. As the children played at his feet, he eagerly watched the road. As soon as Vessantara saw the brahmin approaching the hermitage, he sensed that his seven idle months were at an end. He once again took up the burden of generosity and called out happily, "Welcome, brahmin! Come here!"

"Jāli," he called to his son, "stand up! Here comes a brahmin! Isn't it wonderful? It's just like old times!"

"Yes, Father," the boy answered. "I see him too. It looks like he wants to ask a favor. Let's welcome him." Jāli quickly ran to meet the brahmin and offered to carry his bag.

"This must be Jāli, the prince's son," Jūjaka thought. "I must start out by treating him roughly." He snapped his fingers at the lad and snarled under his breath, "Get back! Get away!"

"What a harsh man this is!" thought the boy.

To Vessantara, however, Jūjaka was extremely polite. He greeted him warmly, inquired after his health, and asked about the family's welfare.

"We are all faring quite well, thank you," Vessantara replied. "We have plenty of food and good water, the surroundings are comfortable, and no wild animals annoy us. Please have some of our fruit, and drink some of the delicious cold water from a cave on the hill."

As soon as Jūjaka was seated comfortably, Vessantara addressed him directly, "Tell me, good sir, why you have come to this deep forest. What business do you have here?"

"You are like a great flood which never fails," Jūjaka replied, praising Vessantara's virtues. Then just as directly as the question had been posed, he answered, "I have come to ask for your children. Please give them to me."

Vessantara was delighted. "I give them to you without hesitation," he announced. "You will be their master. But, sir, my wife went a little while ago to collect food. She'll be back this evening. Please stay here tonight. My wife will wash the children and garland them with flowers. Tomorrow morning, we will send you on your way with them."

"No, great prince," Jūjaka answered, "I must go. I do not want to stay. I'll leave right away to make sure that nothing happens to delay me. Women are not generous givers. Give me your children now. There is no need for them to see their mother's face. No need at all!"

"If you don't want to meet my wife—and a faithful wife she is, indeed," Vessantara said, "take Jāli and Kanhajinā to their grandfather. As soon as my father sees them, he will give you a fortune."

"Oh no, my friend," Jūjaka answered quickly. "I'm sure your father, the king, would punish me, perhaps even kill me. I want the children to serve my wife, and I'll take them away right now."

When the children heard this, they ran to hide in the bushes behind the hut, but they were so frightened that they couldn't keep still. They scampered here and there, looking for a safer place. Finally, in desperation, they jumped into the lake and hid among the lotus leaves.

Jūjaka looked for the children but could not find them.

"Vessantara!" he cried. "You're nothing but a liar and a fraud! You said that you would give me the children, but as soon as I told you that, instead of taking them to the capital, I was going to take them home and make them my wife's servants, you signaled to them to hide. And now you just sit there, looking so innocent!"

"Don't worry," Vessantara said calmly to Jūjaka. "They have probably just run away. I'll get them." Seeing their footprints behind the hut, he started walking toward the lake, calling, "Jāli, my beloved son! Please come and fulfill my perfection now by following my will. You will be the ship to carry me across the sea of existence beyond the realms of devas and men. Through you, I will be free."

When the boy heard his father, he pushed aside the lotus leaves and came out. "Let that old brahmin do what he wants with me," he sobbed as he embraced his father's feet. "I will never disobey my father."

"My boy, where is your sister?" Vessantara asked.

"Father," Jāli answered, "in times of danger, all creatures take care of themselves."

Realizing that the children had made a pact, Vessantara called again, "Kanha, my beloved daughter! Please come and fulfill my perfection now by following my will. You will be the ship to carry me across the sea of existence beyond the realms of devas and men. Through you, I will be free."

"I will not quarrel with my father," Kanhajinā resolved as she too emerged from the water. Falling beside her brother at her father's feet, she grasped Vessantara's left ankle and wept. As Vessantara stood looking down at his two young children, his own tears fell upon their backs. "My dear, dear children," he said, lifting them up and comforting them, "don't you know that I have gladly given you away so that my desire may attain fulfillment? Now you must go with this brahmin.

"Jāli, my son, if you wish to become free, you must pay him one thousand coins, but your sister is very beautiful. Should a person of low birth give the brahmin money to free her, it would break her noble birthright. No one but a king can pay the price of the one hundreds. Therefore, for your sister to be free, the brahmin must be paid one hundred elephants, one hundred horses, one hundred bulls, one hundred coins, one hundred male servants, and one hundred female servants."

Then he led the children back to the hermitage and called the brahmin. Vessantara took his water pot and poured water, signifying that his gift was freely given. "Dearer than my son one-hundredfold, one-thousandfold, one-hundred thousandfold," he declared, "is omniscience!"

As he handed the brahmin the precious gift of his beloved children, his mind was filled with joy, and the earth trembled at the greatness of his gift.

Impatient to be off, Jūjaka tied the boy's right hand to the girl's left hand with a vine and dragged them away. As the children staggered forward, he beat them until they bled. When they came to a very rough place in the road, the old man stumbled and fell. Instantly the children slipped off their bonds and ran back to Vessantara.

"Father! Father!" they cried, "please let us wait until Mother returns! Don't send us away before she comes back. Let the brahmin sell us or kill us, but please let us see our mother again. His hands are rough; his nails are torn; he's covered with spots and wrinkles; and he has squinty eyes. He's cruel and inhuman; maybe he's even a cannibal."

"Father!" Jāli cried. "I appeal to you on behalf of my dear sister. Let her stay! She has never known such harshness before."

When Vessantara did not answer, Jāli continued, lamenting, "I'm not afraid of death; I know that we all must die. What I regret is that I will never see my mother's face again. Never again will I see my beloved father. I know how much they, too, will grieve. How they will weep after my sister and I have gone! Now we must leave our playground and our toys. No more will we wear these lovely flowers, nor eat this delicious fruit. Farewell to all the animals that we have loved in this forest home!"

Jūjaka roughly retrieved the children, tied their wrists together again, and drove them away even more roughly.

"Father!" Jāli cried. "Give Mother all our toys. They will ease her grief."

Seeing the children treated like this and hearing their plaintive cries, Vessantara trembled violently. When he thought of never seeing his son and daughter again, he began to weep uncontrollably. "Who will feed my children when they are hungry?" he cried, as he entered the hut alone. "How could that brahmin strike my defenseless, innocent children in front of me? Has he no shame? No man with any decency would treat even the lowliest slave like that! Though I can no longer see them, I know that he is scolding and whipping my darlings while I am here, helpless and unable to protect them."

As he stood alone in the hut, his love for the children welled up in his mind. The vision of the brahmin beating them was more than he could bear. He felt an urge to follow Jūjaka, to kill him, and to bring the children back. He even picked up his bow and started for the door.

"No!" he thought, restraining himself with great effort. "To give a gift and then to regret it would be a great sin. That is not the way of righteousness.

Although the children are suffering, I cannot ask for them back. It's wrong to rescind a gift once given. I must not even allow myself to feel any pain."

Jūjaka hurried the children along, beating them the whole while.

"Now I understand," Jāli cried, "what people mean when they say that a child who has no mother is fatherless, as well. Without mother and father, life is nothing to us. We might as well be dead, Kanha. We are nothing more than the chattel of this horrible, greedy man. Farewell, beautiful forest! Good-bye, lovely home! Oh, Kanha, everything is lost!"

Once again, the clumsy old brahmin fell and dropped the cord. As fast as they could, the children ran back to their father.

Jūjaka became very angry. He got up quickly and followed them back to the hut. "You two are clever at running away, but I'll fix that!" he shouted. He tied the cord even tighter than before and led them away a third time.

Kanhajinā turned back and called to her father, "Father, this man beats me as if I were a slave. Brahmins are said to be upright men. He cannot be a brahmin. He must be a yakkha, taking us away to eat us. How can you just stand there and watch us being dragged away to be a yakkha's meal?"

This plaintive cry from his beloved daughter was like a flame burning Vessantara's heart. Tears welled up in his eyes and rolled down his cheeks like drops of blood. Then he thought, "All this pain comes from affection and not from any other cause. I must quiet this affection and become calm." By the power of this insight, he overcame his sorrow and was able to sit perfectly still.

"My feet are very sore and the road is very hard," Kanhajinā continued lamenting. "It's already evening, but still this hateful brahmin drives us on. To devas that dwell in these hills and forests, we bow in greeting. Devas of this lake, keep our mother well. She's been gone a long time. She must have gathered a lot of wild fruit and roots by now. When she sees our empty hut, she'll cry! Perhaps she will follow us. If she does, I hope she hurries. If she had met this cruel man and given him fruit and honey, he never would have treated us so cruelly."

When Vessantara gave his dearly beloved children to the brahmin, the earth resounded so loudly that the sound reached the Brahma heavens and touched the hearts of all the deities dwelling there. When those devas heard the sobs of the children being beaten by the brahmin, they thought, "When Maddī returns to the hermitage, she will ask Vessantara about the children. As soon as she learns that they have been given away, if it is still daylight, she will run after them. This would not be right." They assigned three devas to assume the shapes of a lion, a tiger, and a leopard. They were told to keep

Maddī from returning before sunset, to guard her from other wild animals, and to allow her to come back only by moonlight.

All day, Maddī had been thinking about the evil dream she had had. She wanted to gather food very quickly and to return early to the hermitage. She tried to hurry, but, as she became more flustered and worried, her hand trembled, she dropped her trowel, and the basket slipped from her shoulder. She could no longer tell the barren trees from those laden with fruit. Her head began throbbing, and the whole world felt upside down. "Why do I feel so strange?" she asked herself. "What can be the meaning of this? Look!" she cried. "It's time for dinner. My children are waiting for me. They are hungry and thirsty." She turned to go, but she found the three wild animals standing in front of her. "What is this? The only path blocked! Oh, mighty beasts, mighty monarchs of the wood," she pleaded, "please let me pass. I am royal, too! A banished prince's wife. When you return home this evening, you can see your children. Let me return to my Jāli and Kanhajinā. My father is a king; my mother, a queen. Be brothers now in righteousness, and let me pass."

Although she continued pleading, the three great beasts refused to move. They remained there, watching her until the moon was shining overhead. Then they got up and silently moved away, finally allowing Maddī to return to the hermitage.

By the time she reached the end of the covered walk, it was dark, except for the light of the full moon. When she reached the entrance to the hermitage, she cried out, "My children, all dusty from their play, like little fawns with their ears pricked up, always wait for me here. Today I cannot see Jāli and Kanhajinā. My head is spinning. My children must be dead! Why is the hermitage so quiet? Even the crows and songbirds are silent!"

Confused and frightened, she approached Vessantara and set down the basket of fruit. "Why are you so quiet?" she asked, trembling. "Where are the children? That nightmare comes back to me! Have my children been carried off by some beast of prey? Have they wandered off to play? Are they asleep?"

Vessantara said nothing.

"My husband, why don't you speak to me? What have I done wrong? That I cannot find my children is pain enough, but, if you do not speak to me, I will die from grief!"

"Maddī, royal princess whose glory is great," Vessantara said slowly, "you went for food early in the morning. Why are you so late?"

"Didn't you hear the lion, the tiger, and the leopard roaring? I had so much trouble in the forest. I kept dropping my spade, and my basket kept slipping off my shoulder. My head was spinning, and the dream haunted me all day. I bowed to all four quarters, praying that no harm should come to my daughter or my son. Then, when I tried to come home, those three fierce animals blocked my path. That is why I am late."

Vessantara did not answer.

"I have tended my husband and my children night and day," Maddī cried, becoming more and more distracted. "I have brought wild fruit and roots from the forest. Here is a lily for our daughter, and here is one for Jāli. Let's give them these flowers and see them dance. Call them, Sivi, call them! Oh, mighty monarch, since we were banished, we have shared all our joy and sorrow. Please tell me now where my beloved Kanhajinā and my Jāli are. What have I done to offend the devas so that I cannot see my darlings?"

Vessantara remained perfectly still and silent.

Trembling, Maddī ran from the hut to look for the children. By the light of the full moon she could see the jambu trees, the great banyan, and all the other places where they played. She found some fruit half-eaten, flowers they had cast off, and toys they had been playing with, but there was no trace of the children. After searching all through the hermitage again, she returned to where Vessantara was sitting. He had not moved since she arrived.

"You haven't split the kindling or lit the fire," she said to him. "You haven't even carried water. Why are you sitting here idly? When I return at the end of the day, I would like to rest, but, today, I cannot find Jāli and Kanhajinā!"

Vessantara neither moved nor spoke.

Maddī ran back to search again in every corner of the hermitage, fearing that she might have overlooked some hiding place.

"Husband!" she wept. "I cannot find my children, nor can I see how they have died!"

Still Vessantara said nothing.

Unable to accept the possibility that the children were not there, Maddī frantically searched a third time in all the same places.

"I have searched everywhere for them or for a sign of what has happened to them, but I can find nothing! Silence hangs over this hermitage like a great black cloud. I can endure no more!" she cried, as she stretched out her arms and fell in a swoon.

"Oh no! She's dead!" thought Vessantara, becoming agitated. "This is not a fit place for Maddī to die. If she had died in Jetuttara, there would have been great splendor. Two entire kingdoms would have mourned. Here in the forest, I am alone. What should I do? What can I do?"

Recovering his presence of mind, he knelt beside her and felt her pulse. Her heart was still beating, and her body was still warm. Although they had lived as ascetics for seven months, Vessantara tenderly laid her head upon his lap, sprinkled her with water, and, with tears in his eyes, rubbed her face and her bosom, trying to revive her. After a few minutes, Maddī opened her eyes. As soon as she had regained her senses, she asked, "My husband, where have the children gone?"

"I have given them to a brahmin," he answered softly.

"My dear, if you gave the children to a brahmin, why didn't you tell me? Why did you let me weep and carry on?"

"I didn't want to cause you pain," Vessantara answered. "This morning, a poor old brahmin came begging for the children. I gave them to him." Before Maddī had a chance to say anything, he continued, "Don't worry, Maddī. Please don't grieve too much. Look at me. Breathe again. We'll get them back, and we'll be happy again. When asked, good men should give whatever they can—grain, cattle, wealth, and even sons. Maddī, rejoice with me! There is no greater gift than one's children."

"I do rejoice!" Maddī reassured him. "I know that there is no greater gift than one's children. Set your mind at ease. My dear husband, in a world of selfish men, you give gifts with a lavish hand. Your generosity does you credit. I pray that you may always give like that!"

"Maddī," he said, greatly relieved and overjoyed that she agreed with him, "if I had not been able to give away my children and, thus, to gain this sublime peace of mind, these great miracles would not have happened." He told her that, when he gave the children to Jūjaka, he had felt a great earthquake, the sky was filled with thunder and lightning, and a great cry arose from the devas.

"Yes," Maddī cried, "I, too, felt the earthquake. I saw the lightning and heard the thunder. Of course, both the Brahmās in the highest heavens and the devas in Tāvatimsa rejoiced. There is no greater gift than one's children."

From their arrival in the forest, Sakka had been watching over Vessantara and the hermitage. While Vessantara and Maddī were talking, Sakka thought, "Vessantara willingly gave his children to Jūjaka. It is very possible now that some vile creature will come and ask him for the incomparable and virtuous Maddī. It would not do for an undeserving beggar to take her away, leaving the prince alone, helpless and destitute. I must prevent that. I will prevent it, and in so doing, I will enable Vessantara to attain the supreme height of perfection!"

At dawn the next morning, another brahmin appeared at the hermitage and politely greeted Vessantara, inquiring as to his health and well-being.

"Thank you, brahmin," Vessantara replied. "I am prosperous and well. There are abundant roots and wild fruit here. There are neither annoying insects nor wild beasts of prey to trouble me. I've lived here seven months, and you are the second brahmin to visit. Welcome. Please make yourself at home. Wash your feet, and enjoy the simple hospitality I can offer. Taste this sweet fruit, and drink some of this cool water which comes from a cave hidden high on a hill."

After they had spoken pleasantly for a few minutes, Vessantara asked the brahmin why he had come to the remote forest.

"Mighty prince," the brahmin answered, "you are like a great flood which never fails. I am old, but I have come here to ask for your wife Maddī. Please give her to me."

Vessantara thought, "Yesterday, I let another take both Jāli and Kanhajinā. Now it is Maddī, my dear devoted wife. I cannot say that I do not love my children or that I do not treasure my faithful wife, but dearer than these is wisdom. Above all, I love perfect knowledge."

He answered the brahmin without hesitation, "I will not hide that I am weary, but gifts delight my heart. Good sir, of my own free will, and with an open hand, I offer you my wife." As he poured water from a pitcher to consecrate the gift, the earth again shook and lightning flashed.

As Maddi listened to this conversation, she neither frowned nor showed surprise. Holding her head erect, she thought, "Vessantara knows best what he is doing." When Vessantara looked at her to see her reaction, she said, as clearly as if a lion were roaring, "From childhood, I have been his wife, and he is my husband still. Prince Vessantara is free to give me to whomever he wishes."

Delighted with her composure and her resolution, the brahmin praised Maddī for her fortitude. He affirmed that the earthquakes and the lightning had been the result of Vessantara's mighty gifts and of his overcoming obstacles, both human and divine. "It is hard to do as good men do," he proclaimed, "and to give as they can give. Virtuous and generous men like you go to heaven, while the evil and stingy fall into hell."

"Now, good prince," he continued, "I give Maddī, your good and lovely wife, back to you. The two of you are perfectly matched to live together harmoniously. Since both of you are of one mind in all things, it is fitting that you stay on here in this forest hermitage and continue doing good."

Then, rising into the air like the morning sun, the brahmin identified himself. "I am Sakka!" he declared. "I have come to test you, and I am satisfied. Eight boons I grant to you. Choose what you will."

"First," Vessantara began, "I wish to be reconciled with my father. Let him call me back and set me on the throne.

"My second wish is that I may never condemn any man to death, even the guiltiest. Instead, let me be able to release from death those who have been condemned.

"May all people—young, middle-aged, and elderly—feel free to look to me for help. This is my third wish.

"Fourth, may I always be contented with my own wife, never straying, never unfaithful.

"My fifth wish, Sakka, is that you grant long life to my beloved son, that he may conquer the world with righteousness.

"Every morning may I receive celestial food. This is my sixth wish.

"My seventh wish is that the means of giving may never fail me and that I may always give whole-heartedly and gladly.

"Finally, may I, at the end of my life, be reborn straightway in heaven."

"These eight boons I grant," Sakka declared. "Very soon, your beloved father will long to see you and will send for you." Then the king of the gods disappeared and returned to his heaven. Confident after having received Sakka's blessing, Maddī and Vessantara resumed their ascetic life.

Meanwhile, Jūjaka and the children were trudging through the forest. Every night, Jūjaka tied the children with vines and left them lying on the ground. He himself was so terrified of wild beasts that he climbed a tree to sleep safely in the branches. Devas, however, were constantly watching over the children. As soon as Jūjaka was gone, they appeared, disguised as the children's parents, and released the bonds. The devas gently massaged the children's hands and feet, washed and fed them, and placed them on a heavenly couch. At dawn, when Jūjaka came down from his tree, he would find the children just as he had left them. He never knew that anything had happened. In this way, the children journeyed onward unharmed.

The devas were also guiding Jūjaka. He thought he was headed for his home in Kālinga, but, after fifteen days of walking, he had walked sixty yojanas and arrived, instead, in Jetuttara.

The night before they arrived, King Sañjaya had a dream. He dreamed he was sitting on his throne when a man came and handed him two beautiful flowers. He hung the blossoms over his ears, and pollen fell from them, covering his chest. When he awoke, he asked his advisors what the dream meant. "Some noble warriors, Sire, who have been absent for a long time, will return to your kingdom."

After breakfast, the king went to the audience hall, sat on his throne, and waited. The devas guided Jūjaka to the courtyard of the palace. As soon as the king saw the children, he asked, "Whose faces are those, shining like gold? Who can those children be? The boy looks like Jāli, and the girl very much resembles Kanhajinā! They are as beautiful and as golden as two little lion cubs." Excitedly, he sent a courtier to bring them to him.

"Good sir," he said to the brahmin, "tell me where you have brought these children from?"

Jūjaka replied, "Two weeks ago they were given to me by one who was quite pleased with his gift."

"By what sort of speech did you manage to get them?" the king asked. "From whom did you receive these children, greatest of all gifts?"

Jūjaka replied, "From Prince Vessantara, who, like the great earth, gives without discrimination. He gave me his own children as slaves."

When they heard this, the courtiers heaped scorn upon Vessantara. "That is outrageous!" they cried. "We banished him for giving away his elephant, but now he goes beyond all decency and gives away his children! A man might well give servants, a horse, a mule, a cart, or even an elephant; but how could anyone give away his own children to become slaves? It certainly is good that we got rid of him; he is not fit to be king!"

"Grandfather!" Jāli cried, when he heard his father thus wrongly criticized. "What they are saying is not fair! How could my father have given slaves, a horse, a mule, a cart, or an elephant? He has nothing at all!"

"Children, I praise your father's gift," the king quickly reassured them. "I have no words of blame for him. But, tell me, how did he feel? What was in his heart when he gave you to this brahmin?"

Jāli replied, "His heart was burning, and it seemed that it would break. His eyes were red, and tears rolled down his cheeks."

"Grandfather," Kanhajinā said, speaking out for the first time since they arrived, "this brahmin enjoys beating us with creepers as if we were slaves. He is not really a brahmin, but a yakkha pretending to be a man!"

"My dears," the king said gently, "you used to climb up on my lap. Why are you standing over there so far away?"

Jāli answered, "We may be children of a king and queen, but now we are this brahmin's slaves, so we must stay where we are."

King Sañjaya was greatly shaken by their answer. "My dearest children, don't say that. You will break my heart. Come, let me buy you back, and you'll be slaves no more! Tell me what price your father set when he gave you away."

Jāli replied, "My price was set at one thousand coins, but, to free my sister, you will have to pay the price of the one hundreds, that is, one hundred each of elephants, horses, bulls, coins, male servants, and female servants."

The king immediately ordered his steward to pay Jūjaka the one thousand coins for Jāli as well as the full price of the one hundreds for Kanhajinā. He also had them prepare a seven-story mansion in which Jūjaka could keep all his newly-acquired treasure.

Thoroughly gratified by this unexpected outcome, the old brahmin retired to his new residence to enjoy his wealth. He reclined on a luxurious couch and let himself be served plate after plate of rice, with servings of succulent meat and spicy curries. He indulged his appetite without restraint.

Servants took the children, bathed them, and provided them with fine clothes. After Jāli and Kanhajīnā had been properly fed, they returned to their grandparents. The king took one in his lap, and the queen held the other.

"My dear boy," the king said to Jāli, "tell me how your parents are doing. We trust they are both well. Do they have enough to eat? Are they bothered by insects and wild beasts in the forest?"

"Thank you, Sire, for your concern," Jāli answered. "Our parents are both well. They are not troubled by insects, nor do wild beasts disturb them. Every day, Mother finds plenty of herbs, nuts, and fruit for us, but she has grown very thin. The exposure to the sun, the heat, and the wind has aged her and darkened her skin. Every night, she sleeps on animal skins spread on the ground."

He paused for just a moment, but, before his grandfather could ask more questions, he continued, "It is customary in the world for a man to love his son, but it seems that you have failed at this. You have not loved my father adequately."

"Yes, my boy. You are right." the king admitted reflectively. "It was wrong of me to drive your father away. I knew that he was innocent. I should not have listened to the people's angry cries. Seeing the error of my decision, I am now ready to bestow upon him my title, all my wealth, and all my power. Let Vessantara, your noble father, come and rule the kingdom of Sivi."

"But, Grandfather," Jāli quickly replied, "he will not return at my word. You yourself must go and personally give him your blessing."

"Again you are right, dear boy!" Turning to his commander-in-chief, King Sañjaya ordered, "Prepare my elephants, my horses, and my chariots! Mobilize the entire army! Prepare armor, shields, and banners! Summon all my brahmins and advisors! Invite all my loyal subjects! Let us proceed to Mount Vanka to find Prince Vessantara and to invite him back to the capital!"

The king commanded that the road from Jetuttara all the way to Mount Vanka be leveled and widened to accommodate the procession. He instructed the people to decorate the roadside and to prepare music, entertainment, and refreshments along the entire length of the thoroughfare by which his son would return.

Caught up in the festive atmosphere of these preparations, Jūjaka ate so much rich food that his stomach burst, and he died. Although his death was

proclaimed throughout the city, no relative could be found, so all his newly acquired property reverted to the king, who arranged a funeral for the brahmin.

In seven days, everything was ready. The king seated himself upon Paccaya, the great white elephant, which had been returned by the grateful
king of Kālinga after rains ended their kingdom's drought. The elephant
trumpeted loudly with joy at the prospect of being reunited with his master,
Vessantara, once more, and the grand procession set out from Jetuttara with
Jāli as a guide. The chariot wheels and the horses created a thundering din
as the army marched in a cloud of dust toward Mount Vanka. They entered
the forest and continued marching for one more day and one more night.
On the shore of Lake Mucalinda, Prince Jāli suggested that a camp be built.

From the hermitage, Vessantara heard the noise of horses and elephants and
wondered what it was. "Have they killed my father and come here after me?"
he asked Maddī. The two of them climbed the hill to see what was going on.

"Can they be hunters looking for wild animals?" Vessantara wondered.
"Are they enemies who have come to kill us?"

Maddī looked more carefully and saw that it was the army of Sivi. "Do
not worry," she said to her husband. "All will be well. Your enemies could
no more hurt you than fire could overcome the sea."

Reassured by these words, Vessantara returned with her to the hermitage.

King Sañjaya called Queen Phusatī and said, "My dear, if we all go together, it will be a great shock for the prince. I will go first, alone. Give me
time to greet him. After a few minutes, when you are sure that Vessantara
and Maddī are calm and reassured, please bring the children, and come with
the rest of the company."

Accordingly, the king posted guards at each entrance to the camp, mounted
his royal elephant, and set out for the hermitage. His heart filled with delight when he beheld his handsome son sitting fearless and self-composed
in front of the hut of leaves. As soon as the prince and Maddī saw the king,
they went forward to greet him. Maddī knelt and embraced the king's feet,
weeping with joy to see him again.

"I trust, my son, that you are prosperous and well, with plenty of
food," the king greeted Vessantara. "Have you been bothered by insects
and wild beasts?"

"Sire," Vessantara answered, "it is a wretched life that my wife and I
lead here, eating what can be gleaned from the forest. Adversity breaks in a
man just as a charioteer breaks in a horse. Adversity has tamed us, and the
separation from our parents has made us thin and gaunt, as you can see. Our
greatest hardship, however, is that Jāli and Kanhajinā, your hapless heirs,
are no longer here. Even now, I fear, they are being goaded and abused by

a merciless brahmin. If you know anything of our royal children, please tell me. If you can, please ease my mind."

"Both Jāli and Kanhajinā, your lovely children, have been released. I myself paid the brahmin the price you set. Let your heart rest easy, my son, for all is well."

"Father," Vessantara said, greatly relieved to hear this wonderful news, "I hope that you are also well. I would like to hear that my mother has recovered from her sorrow and that she no longer weeps for us."

"Thank you, my son," the king replied. "Both your mother and I are well."

"Is the kingdom peaceful and prosperous?" Vessantara continued.

As the king was about to answer, Queen Phusatī appeared with a great company. Vessantara and Maddī went to greet her, and Maddī embraced her mother-in-law's feet. As soon as Jāli and Kanhajinā saw their mother, they raced forward. The instant Maddī saw the children, she, likewise, ran to meet them. As they threw their arms around each other, laughing and crying, a great quake shook the earth, and lightning flashed across the sky. The entire party swooned, overwhelmed by great emotions of love and joy.

When Sakka saw these six royal personages and their attendants lying senseless on the ground, he sent a gentle shower of rain to revive them. This was, however, a miraculous rain which wetted only those who desired to be wet. When the rain fell on those who wished to remain dry, it rolled off as water rolls off a lotus leaf.

When the courtiers and citizens realized all that had happened, they clamored for Vessantara and Maddī to become their king and queen.

Vessantara turned and faced the king. "Your Majesty," he said, addressing his father, "when I was a royal prince, even though I was behaving right-eously, you and the people banished me from the kingdom."

"I was wrong to condemn an innocent man!" the king proclaimed. "I made a grievous mistake in heeding the heated and ill-considered opinion of the populace. I erred in driving my virtuous son into exile."

In a contrite voice, the king spoke pleadingly to his son, "To relieve the suffering of his father and mother, a son should not hesitate to give even his very life, let alone forgiveness of their faults."

Having heard himself exonerated and having regained the respect of the people and of his father, Vessantara agreed to accept the throne his father sought to abdicate.

"Come, Your Majesty!" the people cried to their new king. "It is time to bathe and to wash off the dirt of the forest."

"Wait a moment," Vessantara answered. He went into the hut, took off his ascetic's clothes, and put them away. When he came out, wearing his royal robes, he announced, "This is the place where I have spent nine and a half months in ascetic practices. It was here that I attained the summit of the Perfection of Generosity. Here the perfection of my giving caused the earth to quake."

He silently circumambulated the hut clockwise three times and performed the five-point prostration in front of it, touching the earth with knees, forearms, and forehead. At last, he allowed the courtiers to wash and trim his hair and beard and to pour lustral water over him. As the newly-consecrated king, Vessantara shone in all his glory. When he mounted his richly caparisoned white elephant, surrounded by his sixty thousand courtiers in gorgeous array, joyous music filled the air.

Meanwhile, women attendants bathed Maddī and dressed her in fine robes. As lustral water was sprinkled on her head, the people shouted, "May Vessantara protect our queen!"

Maddī stood beside the children, beaming with joy. "While you were gone, I ate only one meal a day," she told them, "and I slept upon the bare ground. That was the vow of love I made for you. Now that you are safely back, I pray that you may always be protected by whatever good your father and I have done!"

"Let my daughter-in-law wear these robes and jewels," Queen Phusatī proclaimed as she presented innumerable boxes to Maddī. So magnificent were these adornments that, when Maddī was dressed, she was as beautiful as a nymph from Tāvatimsa. Maddī mounted another noble elephant and rode beside Vessantara back to the camp.

The royal party and all the courtiers stayed in the forest for a month, enjoying various games and sports, but, by the glorious virtue of Vessantara, no animal or bird suffered any injury during that time, and no creature harmed another. When it was time for Vessantara to leave the forest, all the birds and beasts came together to pay their respects. When he finally left the woods, it seemed that all the sounds of joy were gone, and only silence remained.

The return journey of sixty yojanas took two months. All along the way, the royal road was adorned with flowers and bunting. When they arrived in Jetuttara, they found the city richly decorated, and all the citizens came out to welcome the new king and queen.

King Vessantara commanded that all creatures in the realm be set free, even cats, dogs, birds, and fish. Soon after entering the city, he thought, "Tomorrow morning, supplicants who have heard of my return will come to ask me for gifts. What can I give them?" As a result of this noble thought, Sakka's throne grew hot. As soon as the king of the devas understood the reason, he caused a shower of the seven precious things to fall upon the city, filling the palace grounds waist-high and the city streets knee-deep in precious gems. Vessantara allotted certain areas to various families, but most of the jewels were collected and deposited in a vault in the palace so that he would always have enough to distribute in the future. For the rest of his life, King Vessantara continued giving unstintingly, and, when he died, he was reborn in Tusita heaven.

Having concluded his story, the Buddha identified the birth: "At that time, Devadatta was Jūjaka, Ciñcā-Mānavikā was Amittatāpanā, Channa was the forester, Sāriputta was the ascetic Accuta, Anuruddha was Sakka, King Suddhodana was King Sañjaya, Queen Mahā-Māyā was Phusatī, Rāhula's mother was Queen Maddī, Rāhula was Prince Jāli, Uppalavannā was Princess Kanhajinā, my followers were the rest of the people, and I was King Vessantara."

Glossary of Terms

Abhidhamma: Abstract Teaching; the collection of texts in which the underlying doctrinal principles presented in the Suttas are reworked and reorganized into a systematic framework that can be applied to an investigation into the nature of mind and matter. The Abhidhamma Pitaka is the third division of the Tipitaka.

aggregate: See five aggregates.

Ājīvika: a sect of naked ascetics; followers of Makkhali Gosāla.

anumodana: a Dhamma teaching given by the Sangha following an offering, meant to encourage the donor, to rejoice in the donation, to dedicate the merit made, and to invite others to share in it.

arahat: a fully-enlightened one, who, having freed his mind of all defilements, has attained Nibbāna and is not subject to further rebirth.

Asadisadāna: the unmatched offering which occurs only once for each Buddha.

Āsālha: the eighth month of the Indian lunar calendar; the beginning of the rains retreat.

asseveration of truth (saccakiriya): a statement of truth, the force of which is used to obtain a desired result.

asura: a class of pugnacious, but cowardly and perpetually angry, beings, roughly equivalent to Titans. Sakka evicted the deva-asuras from Tāvatimsa while they were drunk. They continue to maintain a heavenly existence in a place outside, but equal to, Tāvatimsa. There are, quite distinct from this, beings called asura-kāya, sometimes referred to as peta-asuras and niraya-asuras. These beings lead a miserable life in the third woeful realm. Their suffering is very similar to that of the peta and niraya realms.

bael a Bengal quince; a woodapple.

bhikkhu: a fully ordained monk in the Buddha's order; a man who has left the household life to seek the end of suffering. He lives a life of discipline in accordance with the Vinaya.

bhikkhunī: a fully ordained nun in the Buddha's order; a woman who has left the household life to seek the end of suffering. She lives a life of discipline in accordance with the Vinaya.

Bodhi tree: the tree under which a Supreme Buddha attains Enlightenment. Within the Sāsana of that Buddha, saplings from that tree, wherever they are planted, are respected. For Gotama Buddha, the Bodhi tree was the pipal tree (Ficus religiosa).

Bodhisatta: one striving for Buddhahood; "a Buddha-to-be." The term is used to describe someone from the time he makes his aspiration and receives confirmation from a living Buddha until his full Enlightenment.

Brahmā: a deva in the non-sensual heavens of form or formlessness which are called the Brahma heavens.

Brahma heavens (Brahma-loka): the highest heavens, where beings enjoy blissful existence. Birth in these realms is achieved by practicing concentration meditation, particularly on the Four Brahma Vihāras to the point of attaining jhāna.

Brahma Vihāra: See Four Brahma Vihāras.

brahmin (brāhmana): a member of the highest caste in Indian society, respected as such and qualified to perform rituals and sacrifices. Rejecting the caste system, the Buddha used the term to refer to one who was worthy of respect, not because of birth, but because he had reached the goal and had become an arahat.

Buddha: one who attains full Enlightenment on his own. A Supreme Buddha is one who, having discovered for himself the liberating path of Dhamma, after its having been forgotten by the world for a tremendously long period of time, teaches others so that they, too, may attain Enlightenment. There have been and will continue to be innumerable Supreme Buddhas. The Bodhisatta made his aspiration to become a Buddha at the time of Buddha Dīpankara. From that time until he became the Buddha Gotama, there were twenty-four Supreme Buddhas, the last being Kassapa Buddha. The next Buddha will be Mettaya Buddha.

catumadhu: literally, four sweet things. This mixture of ghee, oil, honey, and jaggery is allowable as medicine for members of the Sangha in the afternoon.

candāla: an outcaste; an untouchable; someone born outside (below) the four castes.

caste: the system of social class in traditional India. The four main castes, said to have been created by Brahmā, are: brāhmana, brahmin, teacher, priest; khattiya, warrior, king, ruler; vessa, businessman, artisan, farmer; sudda, worker, servant to the others

cetiya: a stupa; a pagoda; a monument, originally a mound, enshrining the relic of an enlightened one or commemorating a great event. The term can also be used for a funerary mound, particularly in pre-Buddhist times.

craving (tanhā): the longing for sense pleasures, for existence, and for non-existence; the origin of suffering. Craving is the second of the Four Noble Truths.

crore: ten million.

defilement (kilesa): any of ten unwholesome, mind-defiling qualities. These are: 1. greed (lobha); 2. hatred; (dosa); 3. delusion (moha); 4. conceit (māna); 5. speculative views (ditthi); 6. skeptical doubt (vicikicchā); 7. mental torpor (thīna); 8. restlessness (uddhacca); and 9. shamelessness (ahirika); 10. lack of moral dread (anotappa). The first three are considered the root defilements from which all the others arise.

determination (adhitthāna): the resolute will-power which forces all obstructions out of one's path, such that, no matter what may come in the form of grief or disaster, one's eyes never turn from the goal. Determination is the eighth of the Ten Perfections.

deva: a heavenly being; a deity. This can be a resident of one of the heavens or a guardian or spirit of a tree, a hill, a doorway, or some other entity.

Dhamma: the Buddha's Teaching. Dhamma-vinaya is the Buddha's own term for the religion he founded.

dhutanga: the ascetic practices allowed by Buddha to be voluntarily undertaken. They are: 1. wearing only rag robes; 2. having only one set of robes; 3. eating only almsfood; 4. not skipping any house on almsrounds; 5. eating only one meal a day; 6. eating only from the bowl; 7. refusing any further food; 8. staying in the forest; 9. staying under a tree;

10. staying in the open (without a roof or a tree for shelter); 11. staying in a charnel ground; 12. accepting whatever accommodation is offered; and 13. never lying down.

Discipline: See Vinaya.

eight precepts: See precepts.

energy (viriya): the mental vigor or strength of character, which is the persevering effort to avoid or to overcome evil and unwholesome things and to develop and to maintain wholesome things. Energy is the fifth of the Ten Perfections.

Enlightenment (bodhi): the state of complete understanding, the supreme awakening from the stupor caused by the mental defilements, and the perfect comprehension of the Four Noble Truths; Nibbāna.

eon (kappa): a world-cycle; a world-age; the period between the formation and the destruction of the world.

equanimity (upekkhā): maintaining an even balance in times of happiness and adversity in the face of praise or blame; discerning rightly, viewing justly, and looking impartially, with neither attachment nor detachment, with neither favor nor disfavor; not to be mistaken for indifference or callousness. Equanimity is the tenth of the Ten Perfections and the fourth of the Four Brahma Vihāras.

first path: See four stages of Enlightenment.

five aggregates (pañca khandha): the five aspects or factors of clinging; the physical and mental components of the personality and of sensory experience, which make up individual existence: 1. form (rūpa), 2. feeling (vedanā), 3. perception (saññā;), 4. mental formations (sankhāra), and 5. consciousness (viññāna).

five extraordinary powers: the powers attainable by perfecting mental concentration. They are: 1. magical power (iddhi-vidha); 2. divine ear (dibba-sota); 3. penetration of the mind of others (ceto-pariya-ñāna);); 4. divine eye (dibba-cakkhu); and 5. remembrance of former existences (pubbenivāsānussati).

five precepts: See precepts.

Glossary of Terms

five symbols of royalty: sword, umbrella, crown, slippers, and fan.

Four Brahma Vihāras: also called the Four Divine Abidings; the four sublime abodes that are attained through the development of meditation on: 1. loving-kindness (mettā), 2. compassion (karunā), 3. sympathetic joy (muditā), and 4. equanimity (upekkhā).

four elements (dhātu): the four physical properties which are the ultimate constituents of all matters. They are: 1. earth, solidity (pathavi); 2. water, cohesiveness (āpo); 3. heat, fire (tejo); and 4. air, wind (vayo). All four are present in every material object, though in varying degrees of strength. Sometimes, the Buddha spoke of five or six elements, in which case, space (ākāsa) or space and consciousness (viññāna) are included.

Four Foundations of Mindfulness (satipatthāna): the bases for maintaining moment-by-moment mindfulness and developing mindfulness through meditation. They are: 1. contemplation on the body; 2. contemplation on feelings; 3. contemplation on the mind; and 4. contemplation on mental objects.

Four Great Kings (cātummahārājikā): the four powerful devas who reign over the lowest plane of heaven and serve as guardians of the four quarters. They are: Vessavana of the north, Dhatarattha of the east, Virūlhaka of the south, and Virūpakkha of the west. Their retinues consist of, respectively, yakkhas, gandhabbas, kumbhandas, and nāgas. Life in this realm lasts ninety thousand years, and beings are reborn here because of various acts of faith, prompted by rather unrefined motives. Their realm is located mid-way up Mount Sineru.

Four Noble Truths (cattāri ariya saccāni): 1. All forms of existence are subject to suffering. 2. The origin of suffering is craving. 3. The extinction of suffering, Nibbāna, is possible by eliminating craving. 4. The Noble Eightfold Path is the way to bring about the extinction of suffering.

four stages of Enlightenment: the four levels of progress on the path to Nibbāna. They are: 1. stream-enterer (sotāpanna), one who has attained the first path and who will undergo no more than seven rebirths, none of which will be lower than a human being; 2. once-returner (sakādagāmi), one who has attained the second path and will be reborn only once more in the human world and will attain Nibbāna in that life; 3. non-returner (anāgāmi), one who has attained the third path and will attain Nibbāna without being reborn in any sensuous realm; 4. fully-enlightened one (arahat), one who has attained the fourth path, Nibbāna, and will not be reborn again.

fourth path: See four stages of Enlightenment.

gandhabba: the lowest form of deva, inhabiting the realm of the Four Great Kings. The Buddha described gandhabbas as dwelling in the fragrance (ganda) of plants and flowers.

Gang of Six (chabbaggiya): the six bhikkhus frequently mentioned as being guilty of various Vinaya offences. These bhikkhus—Assaji, Punabbasu, Panduka, Lohitaka, Mettiya, and Bhummaja—were notorious for causing trouble.

Gaṅgā: the modern Ganges River.

garula (Sanskrit, garuda): an enormous supernatural bird; the implacable foe of the nāgas.

gavuta: one-fourth of a yojana.

generosity (dāna): a virtue which confers upon the giver the double blessing of inhibiting the immoral thoughts of selfishness and of developing the pure thoughts of selflessness. Generosity is the first of the Ten Perfections and the first of the ten duties of a king. Dāna often refers to giving alms to ascetics and members of the Sangha or to the alms thus given.

good deeds (kusala kamma): the wholesome, skillful, and meritorious actions which are bound to result eventually in happiness and a favorable outcome, whereas bad deeds (akusala kamma) lead to unhappiness and unfavorable results.

Great Renunciation (abhinikkhamana): Prince Siddhattha's act of leaving home in search of Enlightenment.

hattha: a hand; a measurement, similar to a cubit; namely, the distance from the elbow to the end of the middle finger.

Himavat: the region of the Himalaya Mountains. It is said to be three hundred thousand yojanas across with eighty-four thousand peaks, the highest being five hundred yojanas tall. The region includes seven great lakes—Anotatta, Kannamunda, Rathakāra, Chaddanta, Kunāla, Mandākinī, and Sīhappapātaka. Its forests have always been the refuge for ascetics. The region includes a mountain called Mahāpapāta where Pacceka Buddhas traditionally pass into final Nibbāna. The Himavat is inhabited by many supernatural creatures, and female nāgas go there to give birth.

impermanence (anicca): the doctrine that anything that has arisen will pass away. All conditioned things are in a constant state of flux and are of the nature to decay. Impermanence is the first of the Three Characteristics.

insight (vipassanā): the intuitive understanding of the reality of existence.

Jain: a sect of naked ascetics, followers of Nigantha Nātaputta.

jambu: a rose apple; a pink and green fruit. See Jambudīpa.

Jambudīpa: Land of the Rose Apple; the traditional name for the Indian subcontinent.

jhāna: mental absorption; a state of strong concentration in which the mind becomes fully immersed and absorbed in the chosen object of attention. There are eight jhānas (atthasamāpattiyo): four fine-material (rūpa jhāna) and four immaterial (arūpa jhāna).

kadamba: a tree with bright orange or yellow flowers, thought to reunite separated lovers.

kanavera: Indian oleander, a shrub with foul-smelling red flowers. A garland of these flowers (vajjhāmālā) was hung around the neck of a criminal on his way to execution.

kasina: an external device used to develop meditative concentration. There are ten kasinas in all: the elements—earth, water, fire, and air; the colors—blue, red, yellow, and white; and space and consciousness.

kathina: the ceremony marking the end of the rains retreat, when laypeople gather to express gratitude to the Sangha and to make a special offering of gifts, particularly new robes. Traditionally, the Sangha of a monastery receives an offering of cloth from laypeople and gives it to one of its members, who then dyes, cuts, and sews it into a robe before dawn of the following day.

Kattikā: in the Indian lunar calendar, the last month of the rainy season. It also refers to the constellation of Pleiades and to a traditional festival.

khattiya: See caste.

kinnara (female, kinnarī): a creature, half-bird and half-human, which lives in the Himavat.

kumbhanda: a low form of deva inhabiting the realm of the Four Great Kings. The name refers to a gourd or a pot (kumbha). They are so called, perhaps, because their bellies are like pots.

kuti: a bhikkhu's residence.

loving-kindness (mettā): a great regard, much deeper than goodwill, friendliness, or kindness, for all beings in all realms. It is the universal love through which one neither fears nor instills fear in any other being. Loving-kindness is the ninth of the Ten Perfections and the first of the Four Brahma Vihāras.

lower realms (apāya): woeful realms; states of deprivation; the four lowest planes of existence into which a being is reborn because of past unwholesome actions. They are: hell, the peta realm, the asura realm, and the animal realm. Of course, none of these states is permanent.

meditation (bhāvanā): mind training; mind development. There are two distinct types of meditation: tranquility (samatha) and insight (vipassanā). Tranquility meditation, which was practiced even before the Buddha's time, involves focusing the mind on an external object. Through this concentration, one can attain extraordinary powers and the jhānas. There are forty subjects suitable for tranquility meditation. Insight meditation requires concentration, but the goal is to develop purity of mind and insight into the Three Characteristics, which leads to Nibbāna. Meditation is the second section of the Noble Eightfold Path.

merit (puñña): the quality which purifies and cleanses the mind as the result of wholesome action. Accumulated merit can be shared with other beings, whenever that intention is expressed. There are ten meritorious actions: 1. generosity; 2. morality; 3. meditation; 4. reverence; 5. helping others; 6. sharing one's merit with others; 7. rejoicing in the merit of others; 8. teaching the Dhamma; 9. listening to the Dhamma; and 10. correcting one's views.

mindfulness (sati): self-collectedness; bare attention; the clear and single-minded awareness of what is actually happening in us and to us at the successive moments of perception.

morality (sīla): restraint through the precepts. For a layman, this means keeping the five or eight precepts. For an ascetic, there are additional rules, and, for a bhikkhu or a bhikkhunī, there are many more. Morality also includes all wholesome action of body, speech, and mind. Morality is the second of the Ten Perfections, the second of the ten duties of a king, and the first section of the Noble Eightfold Path.

nāga: a great supernatural serpent, capable of assuming the form of a human or a deva. The traditional enemy of the nāga is the garula. Sometimes a nāga swallows stones, hoping that, in that way, it will be too heavy to be carried away by a garula.

neem: a tree common in South Asia, considered beneficial for its medicinal properties. All parts of the tree are extremely bitter. Neem twigs are commonly used to make toothsticks for cleaning the teeth.

Nibbāna: Enlightenment; arahatship; the fourth path; liberation; the freeing of the mind from defilements (kilesas); the end of the round of rebirth (samsāra). The term refers to the extinguishing of a fire, so it also connotes stilling, cooling, and peace.

Nikāya: division, group. A group of texts within the Sutta Pitaka, the Collection of Discourses, of the Tipitaka.

Noble Eightfold Path (ariya magga): the Fourth Noble Truth. The factors are: 1. Right View; 2. Right Intention; 3. Right Speech; 4. Right Action; 5. Right Livelihood; 6. Right Effort; 7. Right Mindfulness; and 8. Right Concentration; This Path can be divided into three sections: Morality, 3–5; Meditation, 6–8; and Wisdom, 1–2.

non-self (anattā): the doctrine that neither within nor outside of the bodily and mental phenomena of existence can be found anything that, in the ultimate sense, can be regarded as a self-existing, real ego-entity, soul, or self. Non-self is the third of the Three Characteristics.

Pacceka Buddha: a fully enlightened Buddha who has attained perfect insight, but neither creates a Sangha nor establishes a Sāsana. Offerings to a Pacceka Buddha are of great efficacy. A Pacceka Buddha can also grant boons and make predictions.

panic: a type of millet which was made into a gruel. It was also used as a medicine.

Parinibbāna: a synonym for Nibbāna, though often used to refer to the passing away of a fully-enlightened one, particularly of a Supreme Buddha or a Pacceka Buddha.

path and fruit (magga-phala): the attainment (path) of one of the four stages of Enlightenment and the result (fruit) thereof.

patience (khanti): forbearance which includes enduring any suffering inflicted upon oneself by others. Patience is the sixth of the Ten Perfections and the ninth of the ten duties of a king.

Pātimokkha: the code of discipline for bhikkhus and bhikkhunīs, which is recited at every full and new moon.

Perfection (pāramī): See Ten Perfections.

peta: a hungry ghost; a miserable being born in the peta realm, one of the four lower realms. Petas are often depicted with huge bellies and tiny mouths which do not allow them to eat enough to ease their hunger. They are completely dependent for food and clothes on merit shared with them.

Plowing Festival: a festival in ancient India in which the king used a ceremonial plow to mark the beginning of the plowing season. Once, when Prince Siddhattha was a boy, he sat under a jambu tree during this festival and, for the first time, practiced meditation. The shadow of the tree continued to provide shade all day. Seeing this, King Suddhodana paid obeisance to his son.

precepts (sīla): virtue; morality; the training rules voluntarily undertaken to restrain one from doing unwholesome actions.

(a) five precepts (pañcasīla): 1. to abstain from killing, 2. to abstain from stealing, 3. to abstain from sexual misconduct; 4. to abstain from lying; and 5. to abstain from taking alcohol and drugs which cloud the mind. These are considered by Buddhists to be the minimum code of morality for a human being.

(b) eight precepts (atthasīla): the five precepts, except that the third becomes "to abstain from all sexual activity," plus 6. to abstain from eating after noon; 7. to abstain from indulging in music, singing, and dancing and from adorning the body; and 8. to abstain from using a large or high bed or chair. These are usually undertaken by laypeople on Uposatha days.

rains retreat (vassa): the period from July to October, corresponding roughly to the monsoon rainy season, when every bhikkhu and bhikkhunī is required to stay in a single place, without traveling, unless there is an urgent reason to do so.

rebirth (punabbhava): renewed existence in samsāra; the arising of a new group of the five aggregates after death. The consciousness arising in the new person is neither identical to nor different from the old consciousness, but is part of a causal continuum with it. Rebirth, which is conditioned by intentional action (kamma), may take place on any plane. [See The Thirty-one Planes of Existence]

renunciation (nekkhamma): giving up certain luxuries and worldly pleasures. Ultimately, renunciation, which implies freedom from sensual lust, is withdrawal from worldly life and pleasures by adopting the ascetic life to practice meditation and to make spiritual attainments. Renunciation is the third of the Ten Perfections.

requisites: (a) eight requisites (attha parikkharāni): the things which a member of the Sangha should have. They are: three robes, an almsbowl, a razor, a needle, a belt, and a water strainer.

(b) four requisites (cattāro paccaya): the things a member of the Sangha needs to sustain himself or herself. They are: robes, food, a dwelling place, and medicine.

Sakka's throne: the marble seat of the king of the devas, located in Sudhammā Hall. It grows hot and begins to shake for two different reasons. The first is the occurrence of a great injustice which requires Sakka's intervention. The second is that someone is performing an extremely meritorious act, which indicates, perhaps, that that person is striving to be reborn as Sakka in Tāvatimsa, in which case Sakka would be on the verge of losing his office.

sāmanera: a novice monk (sāmanerī, a novice nun), who keeps ten precepts, which are the eight precepts, with the seventh split into two, plus (10) to abstain from accepting gold and silver (money). A sāmanera or a sāmanerī is a candidate for higher ordination as a bhikkhu or a bhikkhunī.

samsāra: the round of existence through rebirth.

Sangha: the Buddha's order of bhikkhus and bhikkhunīs.

sāsana: dispensation; the legacy of a Supreme Buddha; the Buddhist religion. [See Dhamma]

second path: See four stages of Enlightenment.

seven precious things: gold, silver, pearls, gems, lapis lazuli, diamonds, and coral.

silk-cotton tree: a very large tree related to the kapok tree.

sudda: See caste.

suffering (dukkha): the doctrine that all phenomena and all experience are inherently unsatisfactory and lead to mental anguish. Suffering is the first of the Four Noble Truths and the second of the Three Characteristics.

Sutta: Discourse; a sermon attributed to the Buddha or to one of his closest disciples. The Sutta Pitaka, the Discourse Collection, is the second division of the Tipitaka. It is divided into five Nikāyas. The first four Nikāyas contain most of the actual discourses, or suttas. The Jātakas are included in the last Nikāya, Khuddaka Nikāya, or Minor Texts.

sympathetic joy (muditā): taking delight in the happiness or good fortune of others. Sympathetic joy is the third of the Four Brahma Vihāras.

tank: a man-made reservoir, usually rectangular, often with stone steps leading to the water for bathers.

Tathāgata: literally, "Thus Come One," an epithet which the Buddha used to describe himself.

Tāvatimsa: the Heaven of the Thirty-Three; the realm of Sakka, king of the devas.

ten courses of unwholesome action (dasa-akusala-kamma-patha): 1. killing any being; 2. stealing; 3. committing adultery; 4. lying; 5. slandering; 6. using harsh speech; 7. engaging in frivolous gossip; 8. being covetous; 9. having ill-will; and having wrong view. Abstaining from these constitutes the ten courses of wholesome action (dasa-kusala-kamma-patha).

ten duties of a king: the ten qualities a king must have to be considered a righteous ruler. They are: 1. generosity (dāna); 2. morality (sīla); 3. sacrifice (pariccāga), willingness to sacrifice everything—comfort, fame, even his life—for the people; 4. honesty (ajjava), integrity—neither fearing some nor favoring others and never taking recourse in any crooked or doubtful means to achieve one's ends; 5. kindness (maddava), gentleness which tempers firmness, so that a ruler is neither harsh nor cruel; 6. austerity of habits (tapa), self-control, shunning indulgence in sensual pleasures, and keeping the five senses under control; 7. freedom from ill-will (akkodha), bearing no grudge against anyone and acting with forbearance and love; 8. harmlessness (avihimsa), non-violence and a commitment to peace; 9. patience (khanti); and 10. non-opposition or uprightness (avirodha), ruling in harmony with the people, not opposing their will, and cultivating the spirit of amity among the people. (A different list is given in the text of Tale 210.)

Ten Perfections (dasa pāramī): the ten qualities of character which must be developed completely for one to attain Buddhahood, but of which the partial development is meritorious for any being. They are: 1. generosity (dāna); 2. morality (sīla); 3. renunciation (nekkhamma); 4. wisdom (paññā); 5. energy (viriya); 6. patience (khanti); 7. truthfulness (sacca); 8. determination (adhitthāna); 9. loving-kindness (mettā); and 10. equanimity (upekkhā). Each of these is given a separate entry in this glossary.

third path: See four stages of Enlightenment.

thirty-two parts of the body: one of the meditation subjects taught by the Buddha. They are: 1. hair of the head (kesa); 2. hair of the body (loma); 3. nails (nakha); 4. teeth (danta); 5. skin (taco); 6. flesh (mamsa); 7. sinew (nahāru); 8. bone (atthi); 9. marrow (atthimiñja); 10. kidneys (vakka); 11. heart (hadaya); 12. liver (yakana); 13. membrane (kilomaka); 14. spleen (pihaka); 15. lungs; (papphāsa); 16. intestines (anta); 17. mesentery (antaguna); 18. stomach (udariya); 19. feces (karīsa); 20. brain (matthalunga); 21. bile (pitta); 22. phlegm (semha); 23. pus (pubba); 24. blood (lohita); 25. sweat (seda); 26. lymph (meda); 27. tears (assu); 28 serum (vasa); 29. saliva (khela); 30. nasal mucous (singhānika); 31. synovial fluid (lasika); and 32. urine (mutta).

Three Characteristics (ti-lakkhana): the three basic facts of existence which are inherent in all conditioned phenomena. They are: 1. impermanence (anicca); 2. suffering (dukkha); and 3. non-self (anattā).

tinduka: an Indian persimmon.

Tipitaka: (literally, "Three Baskets"), the Buddhist canon; the collection of primary texts which form the doctrinal foundation of Buddhism. The three divisions are: 1. Vinaya Pitaka, Book of Discipline; 2. Sutta Pitaka, Book of Discourses; 3. Abhidhamma Pitaka, Book of Abstract Teaching. After the Buddha's Parinibbāna, the Teaching was arranged as the Tipitaka at the First Buddhist Council, a gathering of five hundred arahats. All the texts were memorized and, for about five hundred years, were transmitted and preserved orally. They were first written down in Sri Lanka about 100 B.C.E. when, due to hardship and famine, the number of bhikkhus declined to the point that it was feared that the Teaching would be lost.

toothstick: See neem.

Triple Gem (ti-ratana): the Teacher (Buddha), the Teaching (Dhamma), and the Order (Sangha).

truthfulness (sacca): keeping one's word and fulfilling a promise at any cost. It is said that a Bodhisatta may, at times, violate the other precepts but that he never tells a lie nor forsakes truthfulness. Truthfulness is the seventh of the Ten Perfections.

twenty-one wrong means of livelihood (ekavisati anesana): practices which bhikkhus are forbidden to perform. They are: 1. medical practice; 2. acting as a messenger; 3. doing things at the behest of laymen; 4. lancing boils; 5. giving oil for medical application; 6. giving emetics; 7. giving purgatives; 8. preparing oil for nose-treatment; 9. preparing oil for medicine; 10. presenting bamboos; 11. presenting leaves; 12. presenting flowers; 13. presenting fruits; 14. presenting soap-clay; 15. presenting toothsticks; 16. presenting water for washing the face; 17. presenting clay-powder; 18. using flattering speech; 19. speaking half-truths; 20. fondling children; and 21. running errands.

Uposatha: a day reserved for religious observance, corresponding to the phases of the moon (one, two, or four). In Buddhist practice, on Uposatha days, lay people gather to listen to the Dhamma and to observe eight precepts. On the new-moon and full-moon Uposatha days, bhikkhus assemble to recite the Patimokkha rules.

Veramba wind: a strong wind which blows at a great height.

vessa: See caste.

Verocanamani: the octagonal gem which Sakka gave to King Kusa (Tale 206). It is mentioned twice in Tale 216.

Vinaya: Discipline; texts concerning the rules of conduct governing the Sangha. The Vinaya Pitaka, the Collection of Discipline, is the first division of the Tipitaka. The Vinaya Pitaka also includes the story behind the origin of each rule. The rules are summarized in the Pātimokkha. There are 227 rules for bhikkhus and 311 for bhikkhunīs. Dhamma-vinaya is the Buddha's own term for the religion he founded.

water of donation (dakkhinodaka): water which the donor pours over the right hand of the recipient when a gift is made, indicating that the gift is freely given and dedicating the merit gained.

wisdom (paññā): right understanding of the real nature of the world; seeing things as they really are; ultimately, insight into the Three Characteristics. Wisdom is the fourth of the Ten Perfections and the third section of the Noble Eightfold Path.

yakkha (female, yakkhinī): a demon; an ogre; a superhuman being, often hostile to man. Some yakkhas resemble devas, but others resemble petas. They have strange characteristics; for example, they have red eyes, they cannot wink, and they cast no shadow. Sometimes, they are said to be repelled by palm leaves and iron. Their king is Vessavana, one of the Four Great Kings.

yojana: the distance a team of oxen can travel in one day; about twelve miles.

Glossary of Personal Names

This glossary includes those who were contemporaries of the Buddha. It does not include the innumerable characters who appear in the stories of the past. The two exceptions are Kassapa Buddha and Vipassi Buddha. (The numbers in parentheses at the end of each entry indicate the tales in this anthology in which the individual appears.)

Ajātasattu: the son of Bimbisāra, king of Magadha. Prince Ajātasattu became a generous supporter of Devadatta, who encouraged Ajātasattu to kill his father and to usurp the throne. Ajātasattu also aided Devadatta in his attempts to kill the Buddha. After Devadatta's death, King Ajātasattu repented and became a devoted follower of the Buddha, but his parricide prevented him from making any attainments. After a long rule, Ajātasattu was killed by his own son, Udāya, who had been born on the day that Bimbisāra died. According to the commentaries, Ajātasattu was reborn in hell, where he will suffer for 60,000 years, eventually becoming a Pacceka Buddha. (56, 62, 94, 130, 132, 179, 193, 212)

Ajita Kesakambala: one of the six teachers who were contemporaries of the Buddha. He taught materialism, stating that all is annihilated at death. (62)

Ālavaka: a yakkha in Ālavi, thirty yojanas from Sāvatthī. Vessavana, king of the yakkhas, had given him permission to eat anyone who stepped into the shade of the huge banyan tree near his mansion. The king of Ālavi, while hunting, did so, but avoided death by promising to send one victim daily. For twelve years, he sent prisoners, and later children. Finally, the only offering available was the king's own son. With compassion for the prince, the king, and the yakkha, the Buddha went there, but Ālavaka was away. When the gatekeeper went to inform Ālavaka, the Buddha entered the mansion and began teaching the yakkha's wives. Ālavaka returned and tried to kill the Buddha, first by frightening him and then by exhausting him. After going out from and reentering Ālavaka's house three times, the Buddha refused to leave again. Ālavaka then asked the Buddha a series of questions which had been handed down to him from Kassapa Buddha. The Buddha easily answered all of them. Ālavaka was delighted. He understood everything the Buddha said and attained the first path. The next morning, the king's men arrived and gave the prince to the yakkha. Ashamed of his former practices, Ālavaka handed the child to the Buddha. The king gave the reformed yakkha a special house, and the people gave regular vegetarian offerings. His conversion is one of the Eight Great Victories of the Buddha referred to in the Jayamangala Gāthā. (181, 216)

Ambattha: a brahmin, proud of his lineage and his learning, and the follower of another teacher. When the Buddha taught the Ambattha Sutta (Dīgha Nikāya, 3), Ambattha's teacher and other students were converted, but not Ambattha himself. According to the commentary, the Buddha knew that Ambattha would not benefit and, therefore, wasted no time on him. (216)

Ānanda: an eminent bhikkhu; the last personal attendant of the Buddha [See Tale 177]; "Treasurer of the Teaching." He was a Sākyan prince and a first cousin of the Buddha. Soon after ordaining, Venerable Ānanda attained the first path, but it was only after the Buddha's Parinibbāna, just in time to attend the First Buddhist Council, that Venerable Ānanda attained arahatship. Most suttas begin "Thus have I heard" because, at that council, Venerable Ānanda recited each discourse as he had heard it from the Buddha.

Venerable Ānanda was foremost among the bhikkhus in 1. having heard many of the Buddha's discourses; 2. having a good memory; 3. having mastery over the sequential structure of the teachings; 4. being steadfast in study; and 5. being the Buddha's attendant.

Venerable Ānanda was accomplished in seven ways: 1. in the doctrine; 2. in knowledge; 3. in knowledge of causes; 4. in investigation; 5. in having an eidetic memory with penetrative comprehension; 6. in applied attention; and 7. in the potentiality of Buddhahood. (5, 6, 8, 10, 14, 15, 16, 17, 20, 30, 32, 33, 34, 36, 40, 42, 55, 60, 61, 63, 65, 66, 67, 68, 73, 75, 77, 80, 82, 88, 91, 94, 95, 96, 98, 99, 104, 105, 106, 109, 112, 113, 116, 119, 121, 126, 130, 136, 144, 145, 147, 148, 150, 152, 153, 154, 155, 156, 157, 158, 160, 162, 163, 165, 170, 171, 172, 173, 175, 176, 177, 179, 181, 182, 183, 185, 187, 188, 189, 190, 196, 197, 198, 199, 203, 206, 207, 208, 210, 211, 213, 214, 215, 216)

Anāthapindika: a wealthy merchant, the great patron of the Buddha who built Jetavana Monastery near Sāvatthī. He appears in the occasions for many of the stories and attained the first path, but he is not mentioned in the identifications. (1, 10, 21, 22, 36, 98, 105, 108, 134, 136, 161, 182,)

Angulimāla: a bhikkhu. He was a serial murderer who was converted by the Buddha and became an arahat. [See Tale 207] His conversion is one of the Eight Great Victories of the Buddha referred to in the Jayamangala Gāthā. (29, 147, 181, 207, 216)

Anuruddha: an eminent bhikkhu; a Sākyan prince and first cousin of the Buddha. He was foremost among bhikkhus endowed with the divine eye. [See Tale 8] (8, 81, 95, 102, 167, 170, 190, 191, 197, 207, 210, 211, 215, 217)

Asita: a brahmin ascetic. A few days after Prince Siddhattha was born, Asita went to the palace. Instead of paying respect, the baby turned and touched the ascetic's head with his feet, signifying that he was the nobler. Asita smiled and then wept. He smiled because he knew that Prince Siddhattha would become a Buddha. He wept because he was too old to live to become his disciple. (217)

Baka-Brahmā: a deva in the Brahma heavens. Correcting his wrong view is one of the Eight Great Victories of the Buddha referred to in the Jayamangala Gāthā. [See Tale 151] (136, 151, 181, 216)

Bandhula: a son of a chieftain of Malla, who became commander-in-chief of King Pasenadi of Kosala. His wife's name was Mallikā [See Tale 179] (179)

Bhaddaji: a bhikkhu. He was the son of a wealthy merchant of Bhaddiya, a city in Anga. The Buddha went there to teach him. After hearing the Buddha's discourse, Bhaddaji attained arahatship. When the Buddha explained to Bhaddaji's father that, on that day, Bhaddaji had either to ordain or to pass away, the merchant let his son ordain. (This is related in the occasion to Jātaka 264, which is not included in this collection) This is one of the few instances in which a layman became an arahat. [See Suddhodana] (214)

Bhaddakaccānā: See Yasodharā.

Bhaddā-Kāpilānī: an eminent bhikkhunī. She was the daughter of a brahmin in Sāgala, a city in Madda. She was married, but the marriage was never consummated. (This took place very much as in Tales 129 and 206.) Her husband was named Pippali-mānava. They left the home-life together. He ordained as Venerable Mahā-Kassapa, and she lived as an ascetic until the bhikkhunī order was established. Soon after ordaining as a bhikkhunī, she attained arahatship. She was foremost among bhikkhunīs who could recall former lives. (210)

Bhaddiya: an eminent bhikkhu. He was a Sākyan prince. He was foremost among the bhikkhus of aristocratic birth. [See Tale 8] (8)

Bimbisāra: the king of Magadha and a strong supporter of the Buddha. He attained the first path. He was killed by his son Ajātasattu. (62, 132, 188, 193, 212, 214)

Channa: a bhikkhu. He was born on the same day as Prince Siddhattha and became his charioteer. He accompanied the prince at the time of the Great Renunciation, but returned to Kapilavatthu. Refused permission to leave the household life, he did not ordain until the Buddha returned to Kapilavatthu. Because of his closeness to the Buddha, he became conceited and could neither overcome his pride nor fulfill his monk's duties. He was chastised and punished for his obstinacy several times, the last instance being just before the Buddha's Parinibbāna. When Venerable Ānanda informed him of the Buddha's declaration that he was to be shunned by the Sangha, he was completely tamed and attained arahatship, at which point the penalty automatically expired. (142, 198, 217)

Ciñcā-Mānavikā: a female ascetic in Sāvatthī. At the instigation of rival ascetics, she accused the Buddha of making her pregnant. Exposing her lie is one of the Eight Great Victories of the Buddha referred to in the Jayamangala Gāthā. [See Tale 182] (80, 182, 217)

Citta: a merchant in Macchikāsanda, a town in Kāsi. When Venerable Mahānāma visited Macchikāsanda, Citta built a monastery in his garden, Ambātakārāma, which he presented to the Sangha. While listening to Venerable Mahānāma teach the Dhamma there, Citta attained the third path. He was foremost among laymen in teaching the Dhamma. (190)

Culla-Nandikā: nothing further seems to be known. (216)

Dabba: an eminent bhikkhu. He was the son of a Mallan family in Anupiya. He was born while his dead mother was being cremated on the funeral pyre. He heard the Buddha teach when he was seven years old and asked to be ordained. Attaining arahatship at the age of seven, he had extraordinary powers. He assumed the post of meals' designator and was very good at it. He was foremost among bhikkhus in assigning lodgings. [See Tale 5] (5)

Devadatta: one of the Buddha's cousins. He became a bhikkhu along with the other Sākyan princes. [See Tale 8] He was a rival of the Buddha, and tried to kill him several times. He also created a schism in the Sangha. Finally, he was swallowed by the earth and fell into hell. The origin of the implacable enmity which Devadatta felt toward the Bodhisatta and the Buddha is related in Tale 3. (1, 3, 8, 9, 10, 13, 18, 28, 32, 44, 51, 54, 56, 57, 62, 68, 71, 81, 85, 90, 91, 93, 94, 95, 115, 118, 128, 130, 135, 140, 141, 153, 164, 173, 182, 183, 187, 193, 198, 199, 201, 204, 212, 213, 214, 216, 217)

Dhammadinnā: an eminent bhikkhunī. She was the wife of Visākha of Rājagaha. When Visākha heard the Buddha teach, he attained the third path. On returning home, he gave his consent for his wife to ordain. She became a bhikkhunī, stayed in a nunnery near Rājagaha, and soon attained arahatship. Later, she returned to Rājagaha to revere the Buddha and taught the Dhamma to her former husband. She was foremost among bhikkhunīs in teaching the Dhamma. (217)

Dhanuggaha-tissa: a bhikkhu. He was an officer in King Pasenadi's army. No more is known of him. [See Tale 193] (193)

Ditthamangalikā: no one with this name can be identified at the time of the Buddha. (195, 216)

Gotama: the clan name of Prince Siddhattha. After leaving home, the Bodhisatta was called Gotama the Ascetic during the six years before his Enlightenment. Even after his Enlightenment, he was called Gotama the Ascetic by followers of other teachers. The Buddha is called Gotama Buddha to distinguish him from other Buddhas.

Jīvaka: the physician to King Bimbisāra and to the Buddha. He became a prominent lay follower of the Buddha and built a monastery for the Buddha in his mango grove in Rājagaha. After the death of King Bimbisāra, Jīvaka continued serving King Ajātasattu. (4, 62, 199)

Kāludāyi: an eminent bhikkhu. He was the son of a Sākyan minister. He was born on the same day as Prince Siddhattha and grew up with him. After King Suddhodana learned of his son's Enlightenment, he sent ministers to invite him to Kapilavatthu. The first nine times, the messengers ordained, became arahats, and forgot the king's request. Finally, the king ordered Kāludāyi to make the invitation, but allowed him to join the Sangha beforehand. Kāludāyi became a bhikkhu and attained arahatship, but, at the proper time, he informed the Buddha of his father's request. Kāludāyi was foremost among bhikkhus at reconciling families. (190)

Kassapa Buddha: the twenty-fourth Buddha and the third Buddha of the present eon. (23, 79, 95, 169, 181, 207, 217)

Khemā: an eminent bhikkhunī; one of the two chief female disciples of the Buddha. As the chief consort of King Bimbisāra, she was so proud of her golden skin and her beauty that she would not visit the Buddha. Finally, the king persuaded her to go to Veluvana. The Buddha conjured up the image of a woman as beautiful as a deva, who stood facing him. As Khemā gazed at this woman, whose extraordinary beauty far exceeded her own, the woman passed from youth to extreme old age and died. This so dismayed Khemā that, when the Buddha preached to her on the vanity of lust, she attained arahatship. With the consent of Bimbisāra, she entered the Sangha. She was foremost among bhikkhunīs in insight. (138, 209, 217)

Khujjuttarā: a slave woman belonging to Queen Sāmāvatī, who was one of the wives of King Udena. When Khujjuttarā heard the Buddha teach, she attained the first path and, subsequently, taught the queen. She was foremost among laywomen for her extensive knowledge. It is her record of the Buddha's teaching that forms the Itivuttaka, part of the Khuddaka Nikāya. (138, 190, 206)

Kisāgotamī: an eminent bhikkhunī. She came from a poor family in Sāvatthī but married into a rich family. She was disdainfully treated until she bore a son. When the boy died, just as he became old enough to run about, Kisāgotamī was so distraught with grief that she carried his body here and there, seeking medicine to revive him. People laughed at her, but one wise man directed her to the Buddha. The Buddha asked her to bring him a handful of mustard seed from a house where no one had ever died. In the course of her search, she grasped the truth, laid the child's body in the charnel ground, and requested admission to the Sangha. She attained the first path, and, soon after, became an arahat. She was foremost among bhikkhunīs in wearing coarse robes. (217)

Kokālika: a bhikkhu. The commentaries differ on his identification. In some sources there are two bhikkhus with this name, so they are called Culla-Kokālika and Mahā-Kokālika. In other sources, all references are to the same person.

Culla-Kokālika was one of the chief supporters of Devadatta and a great friend of the bhikkhunī Thulla-Nandā, who also supported Devadatta. Once, Culla-Kokālika complained that he had never been allowed to recite the Dhamma. When the monks gave him the chance, he put on brightly colored robes and went to the assembly. He tried to speak, but perspiration poured from his body, and he babbled incoherently. His confusion proved that his learning was a sham. (57; though Kokālika is not mentioned, the same incident is related in 9, 44, 68, and 183)

Mahā-Kokālika quarreled with Venerable Moggallāna and Venerable Sāriputta and, as a result, fell into hell. [See Tale 88] (88, 101, 131, 186)

Kosala-Devī: the sister of King Pasenadi, a wife of King Bimbisāra, and the mother of King Ajātasattu. (132, 193)

Kumāra-Kassapa: an eminent bhikkhu. He became a sāmanera at the age of seven. He was foremost among bhikkhus in eloquence. [See Tale 10] (10)

Kundalī: a bhikkhunī with the name Bhaddā-Kundalakesā. She was the daughter of a wealthy merchant in Rājagaha. One day, she saw a young man being led to his execution and fell in love with him. Her father bribed a guard and had the man released to her. From that point on, her life parallels Tale 161. (His name was also Sattuka.) After pushing Sattuka over the cliff, Kundalī joined the order of Ajivikas (a group of naked ascetics). At her ordination, all her hair was pulled out with a comb. It grew back curly (kundali), hence her name. She left the Ājīvikas and wandered from city to city, seeking debates, in the manner described in Tale 111. In Sāvatthī, Venerable Sāriputta challenged her and converted her in the same way as in that tale. Venerable Sāriputta sent her to the Buddha, who taught her a discourse, and she attained arahatship. She was foremost among bhikkhunīs in swift intuition. (216)

Kutadanta: a learned brahmin of Magadha. The Buddha arrived in his village while Kūtadanta was making preparations for a great sacrifice, and, wishing this sacrifice to be successful, Kūtadanta consulted the

Jātaka Tales of the Buddha

Buddha. The Buddha taught the Kūtadanta Sutta (Dīgha Nikāya 5) to him, and he attained the first path. The conversion of Kūtadanta is considered one of the great spiritual victories of the Buddha. (216)

Lakuntaka: an eminent bhikkhu. He was born in a wealthy family in Sāvatthī. Though extremely short (lakuntaka = dwarf), he was very handsome and had a beautiful voice. Taking the body as the object of meditation, he achieved insight and attained arahatship. He was foremost among bhikkhus in having a sweet voice. (84)

Laludāyi: a bhikkhu, notorious for saying the wrong thing at the wrong time and place and for arguing with learned bhikkhus. He is cited as an example of a person who did no good either to himself or to others. (5, 47, 87)

Losaka Tissa: a bhikkhu who attained arahatship, but failed to receive enough to eat. [See Tale 23] (23)

Madhuvasettha: a brahmin of Sāketā in Kosala. His son, Mahānāga, became a bhikkhu and attained arahatship. (190)

Mahā-Brahmā: a great deva. This refers not only to a particular being, as indicated in Tale 195, but, perhaps, to any resident of the highest Brahma heavens. (195)

Mahā-Kappina: an eminent bhikkhu, He was the king of Kukkutavata, a large kingdom northwest of Takkasilā. Every morning, he sent men to question travelers about news of distant lands. One day, when traders from Sāvatthī were asked for news, they replied, "Sire, we cannot tell you with unwashed mouths." After rinsing their mouths and clasping their hands, they reported the appearance of the Buddha. Mahā-Kappina rewarded the traders, renounced the world, and went to find the Buddha. With an asseveration of truth, he and his companions crossed three rivers without getting the horses' hooves wet. The Buddha perceived them with his divine eye and met them on the bank of the Candabhāgā River, where he taught them the Dhamma, and they all became arahats. Venerable Mahā-Kappina was foremost among bhikkhus in teaching other bhikkhus. (181)

Mahā-Kassapa: an eminent bhikkhu. He was born a brahmin named Pippali in the village of Mahātittha in Magadha. He didn't want to marry, but was finally wed to a like-minded woman, Bhaddā-Kāpilānī. (This took place very much as in Tales 129 and 206.) Never consummating their marriage, they slept separated by a chain of flowers and left the home-life together, When they came to a crossroads, they agreed that it was not proper to stay together and went in opposite directions. The earth trembled at their virtue. The Buddha felt the earthquake, understood its meaning, and traveled three gavutas to meet Pippali. Seated under a tree, Pippali listened to the Dhamma and was ordained as Mahā-Kassapa, On their way to Rājagaha, the Buddha wanted to sit, so Venerable Mahā-Kassapa folded his outer robe as a seat. The Buddha felt the robe and praised its softness. Venerable Mahā-Kassapa offered it to him. "And what would you wear?" asked the Buddha. Venerable Mahā-Kassapa requested the Buddha's rag robe, saying that he would prize it above the whole world. Venerable Mahā-Kassapa was foremost among bhikkhus in upholding minute observances of form. After the Buddha's Parinibbāna, Venerable Mahā-Kassapa called together five hundred arahats for the First Buddhist Council in Rājagaha. (102, 124, 126, 168, 175, 181, 190, 191, 207, 210, 212)

Mahā-Kosala: the king of Kosala and father of King Pasenadi. (132, 193)

Mahā-Māyā: the mother of Prince Siddhattha and the wife of King Suddhodana. As the mother of a Bodhisatta in his last life, she died seven days after the baby was born. She was reborn in Tusita heaven. After the Twin Miracle, she descended to Tāvatimsa to listen to the Buddha teach the Abhidhamma. [See Tale 188] (7, 20, 65, 83, 102, 163, 176, 188, 202, 206, 207, 209, 212, 217)

Mahā-Pajāpati-Gotamī: the first bhikkhunī. She was Mahā-Māyā's sister and was also married to King Suddhodana. After Mahā-Māyā's death, Mahā-Pajāpati-Gotamī nursed and cared for Prince Siddhattha. After having attained the first path, she requested ordination, but the Buddha refused twice. Finally, after Venerable Ānanda interceded, the Buddha agreed and ordained her as the first bhikkhunī, and she soon attained arahatship. She was foremost among bhikkhunīs in seniority and experience. (91, 141)

Mahānāma: a Sākyan king. He was the elder brother of Anuruddha and a great patron of the Buddha and the Sangha. He sent Vasabbha-Khattiyā, his daughter by a slave woman, to King Pasenadi. [See Tale

179] The Buddha declared that Mahānāma was foremost among laymen in giving choice alms to the bhikkhus. (7, 72, 179)

Makkhali Gosala: one of the six teachers who were contemporaries of the Buddha. He taught fatalism, stating that man is powerless in the face of predestination. (62)

Mallikā (1): the chief queen of King Pasenadi. She was the daughter of a garland maker in Kosala (mala = garland). At age sixteen, on the day she offered a portion of sour gruel to the Buddha, King Pasenadi made her his chief queen. She was always devoted to the Buddha, and, in her knowledge of the Dhamma, she was wiser than the king. She was one of the Buddha's outstanding female lay disciples. (33, 114, 119, 160, 197, 200)

Mallikā (2): the wife of Bandhula, who was King Pasenadi's commander-in-chief. [See Tale 179] (179)

Mantidatta: a bhikkhu. He was an officer in King Pasenadi's army. No more is known of him. [See Tale 193] (193)

Māra: a deva. Residing in the highest heaven of the sensuous worlds, he is the lord of the world of passion. He attacked the Bodhisatta with a great army hoping to prevent his Enlightenment under the Bodhi tree. Māra's elephant is named Girimekhala. The Buddha's victory over Māra is one of the Eight Great Victories of the Buddha referred to in the Jayamangala Gāthā. (22, 71, 204)

Mātali: Sakka's charioteer. (16, 95, 175, 181, 211)

Moggallāna: an eminent bhikkhu; one of the two chief disciples of the Buddha. He was born as Kolita in a village near Rājagaha on the same day as Sāriputta. The two were childhood friends and ordained together. Venerable Moggallāna was foremost among bhikkhus in extraordinary powers. [See Sāriputta] (9, 21, 32, 34, 57, 63, 64, 68, 85, 88, 101, 121, 128, 142, 149, 175, 185, 188, 189, 190, 191, 209, 212, 213, 214, 215)

Nālāgiri: an elephant from the royal stables of Rājagaha. In an attempt to kill the Buddha, Devadatta instructed the mahouts to give Nālāgiri extra alcohol and to release him on the street while the Buddha was going on his almsrounds. As Nālāgiri was charging, Venerable Ānanda stepped in front to protect the Buddha. Using his extraordinary power, the Buddha forced Venerable Ānanda aside and extended loving-kindness toward the elephant. Tamed by that loving-kindness, Nālāgiri knelt at the Buddha's feet, and the Buddha taught him the Dhamma. If Nālāgiri had not been an animal, he would have attained the first path. The townspeople were so impressed that they threw their ornaments and jewels on the elephant, completely covering him. From then on, he was called Dhanapāla (Treasurer). The Buddha's taming of Nālāgiri is one of the Eight Great Victories of the Buddha referred to in the Jayamangala Gāthā. (91, 130, 141, 198)

Nanda: an eminent bhikkhu. Being the son of King Suddhodana and Mahā-Pajapati-Gotamī, he was the Buddha's half-brother. When the Buddha returned to Kapilavatthu, he gave his bowl to Nanda to carry. Although Nanda was to marry that day, the Buddha asked him to ordain, and he could not refuse. Nanda ordained and became an arahat. He was foremost among bhikkhus in self-control. [See Tale 76] (76, 90, 102)

Nigantha Nātaputta: one of the six teachers who were contemporaries of the Buddha; now known as Mahāvīra, the founder of Jainism. He taught a doctrine of extreme restraint in order to avoid suffering, which is the result of wrong action. (62, 133)

Pakudha Kaccāyana: one of the six teachers who were contemporaries of the Buddha. He taught eternalism, stating that matter, pleasure, pain, and the soul are eternal and do not interact. (62)

Pārileyya: an elephant. Once, when two groups of bhikkhus refused to settle their quarrel, the Buddha went to stay alone in the forest near Kosambi. While he was there, Pārileyya and a monkey carefully looked after him. This incident is mentioned in Tale 143. It was on this occasion that the Buddha also told Tale 155. (190)

Pasenadi: the king of Kosala. Quite early in the Buddha's ministry, King Pasenadi became his follower. His devotion to the Buddha lasted until the king's death. (7, 10, 23, 28, 33, 40, 63, 82, 83, 98, 104, 114, 119, 132, 158, 160, 162, 179, 193, 197, 200, 205, 207)

Patācārā (1): a bhikkhunī. She had three sisters and a brother, Saccaka. Their parents were both wandering debaters, who had been encouraged by the Licchavi princes to marry and to settle in Vesāli. Patacara and her sisters became wandering debaters, too, but they were defeated by Venerable Sāriputta. They became bhikkhunīs, and Venerable Patācārā attained arahatship. [See Tale 111] (111)

Patācārā (2): an eminent bhikkhunī. She was the daughter of a rich merchant of Sāvatthī and eloped with a servant. When her first baby was due, she wanted to return to her parents' house. She and her husband set out, but, after she delivered on the way there, they went back home. The second time she became pregnant, she again went into labor on the road. When a storm arose, her husband went to get branches to make a shelter and was killed by a snake. After Patācārā found his body, she continued to Sāvatthī with her two sons. She was weak after childbirth, but she had to cross the flooded Aciravatī River. Carrying her newborn baby across, she laid him down and started back for her elder son. In midstream, she saw a hawk swoop down and snatch the baby. She shouted to scare the bird away, but her shouts were misunderstood by the toddler, who thought she was calling him and ran toward her. Before she could reach him, he fell into the water and was swept away. Devastated by her triple loss, she reached Sāvatthī, only to learn that her parents and brother had also been killed when their house collapsed in the storm. Seeing their funeral pyre, she went mad and began raving with grief and wandering naked though the city. (Patācārā means "garment walker.") Eventually, she reached Jetavana, where, restored to presence of mind by the Buddha's Teaching, she attained the first path. She was ordained and attained arahatship. She was foremost among bhikkhunīs in knowledge of the Vinaya. (217)

Pilinda Vaccha: an eminent bhikkhu who was well-known for his extraordinary powers. He was a brahmin with some magical abilities, but when the Buddha appeared, he lost his powers. Hearing that the Buddha knew a greater magic, he became a bhikkhu in order to learn it. The Buddha gave him some meditation subjects, and he attained arahatship. King Bimbisāra built a monastery for him and provided a village with five hundred attendants to support it. It was in this village that the incident related in Tale 152 took place. He was foremost among bhikkhus in being dear and delightful to the devas. (152)

Pilotika: a Paribbājaka, a religious wanderer. He often served the Buddha and the Sangha. His conversation with Jānussoni, another Brahmin who was an eminent follower of the Buddha, was expanded upon by the Buddha to form the Culla-hatthipadopama Sutta: The Shorter Elephant Footprint Simile (Majjhima Nikāya, 27). In the third century B.C.E., when Emperor Ashoka's son, Venerable Mahinda, arrived in Sri Lanka, it was this sutta which he first taught to King Devānampiyatissa. (216)

Pindola: an eminent bhikkhu. He was the son of the chaplain of King Udena of Kosambi and became a successful teacher in Rājagaha. Seeing the gifts bestowed on the Buddha's disciples, he became a bhikkhu, but continued to be greedy. By following the Buddha's advice, he conquered his greed and became an arahat. Then, with a lion's roar (a bold and thunderous declaration of his power), he announced his readiness to answer the questions of any doubting bhikkhus. He was foremost among the bhkkhus in making a lion's roar. (188, 195)

Potthapāda: a Paribbājaka, a religious wanderer, who was converted by the Buddha. (216)

Punna: an eminent bhikkhu. He was born in Kapilavatthu and was ordained by his uncle, Venerable Kondañña, one of the first five bhikkhus. He became an arahat and was close to Venerable Sāriputta. It was after hearing a discourse by Venerable Punna that Venerable Ānanda attained the first path. He was foremost among bhikkhus in teaching the Dhamma. (102, 190)

Purāna Kassapa: one of the six teachers who were contemporaries of the Buddha. He taught amoralism, which denies both reward for good deeds and punishment for bad.

Rāhu: an asura chieftain. He is jealous of the devas of the sun and the moon and stands in their path with his mouth wide open. Eclipses are said to occur when those orbs fall into his mouth. (152, 165, 207, 216)

Rāhula: an eminent bhikkhu. He was the son of Prince Siddhattha and was born on the day that the Bodhisatta left the household life. When the Buddha visited Kapilavatthu, Rāhula's mother sent the boy to the Buddha to ask for his inheritance, and the Buddha asked Venerable Sāriputta to ordain him. When his grandfather, King Suddhodana, heard of this, he objected, and the Buddha declared that no young man should be ordained without the consent of his parents. Venerable Rāhula became an arahat and was foremost among bhikkhus in being eager for training. (83, 109, 123, 129, 134, 138, 154, 156, 163, 172, 189, 209, 212, 215, 217)

Rāhula's mother: See Yasodharā.

Sabhiya: a bhikkhu. As a Paribbājaka, a religious wanderer, he was famous as a dialectician. From a list he had received from his mother, he devised twenty questions which he put before ascetics and brahmins, but none could answer them. He visited the Buddha in Veluvana, and, at the end of the discussion, he entered the Sangha and attained arahatship. (216)

Saccaka: a Nigantha of Vesāli. His clan name was Aggivessana. He was teacher of the Licchavis and the brother of Patācārā. After the Buddha defeated him in a debate, he became a follower. His conversion is one of the Eight Great Victories of the Buddha referred to in the Jayamangala Gāthā. (111, 216)

Sakka: the king of the devas. His realm is Tāvatimsa. Rather than belonging exclusively to a particular being, Sakka refers to the office of king which is held by different beings in succession. [See Sakka's throne in Glossary of Terms] (16, 22, 34, 60, 76, 78, 81, 84, 90, 95, 100, 102, 108, 110, 111, 114, 134, 138, 146, 156, 159, 167, 169, 170, 173, 175, 180, 181, 182, 188, 190, 193, 197, 201, 203, 204, 206, 207, 208, 209, 210, 211, 212, 213, 214, 215, 216, 217)

Sañjaya Belatthiputta: one of the six teachers who were contemporaries of the Buddha. He taught an evasive doctrine, denying both existence and non-existence. (62)

Sāriputta: an eminent bhikkhu; one of the two chief disciples of the Buddha; "Captain of the Teaching." He was born in a village near Rājagaha. His name was Upatissa, and he had a childhood friend named Kolita. One day, Upatissa met Venerable Assaji, one of the first five bhikkhus, heard him recite two lines of a verse, and attained the first path. He hurried to Kolita and, repeating the lines he had heard, established his friend in the first path. Together, they invited their former teacher, Sañjaya Belatthiputta, to visit the Buddha, but Sañjaya refused to go. Upatissa and Kolita (Moggallāna) ordained together. Venerable Moggallāna attained arahatship in seven days, but it took Venerable Sāriputta two weeks longer. He was foremost among the bhikkhus in wisdom. Venerable Sāriputta's wisdom was second only to the Buddha's. (6, 9, 21, 23, 32, 33, 57, 63, 64, 65, 68, 76, 79, 85, 86, 88, 90, 91, 98, 101, 102, 109, 110, 111, 113, 118, 119, 120, 121, 128, 136, 139, 142, 145, 146, 149, 150, 157, 160, 174, 175, 177, 178, 179, 182, 185, 188, 189, 190, 191, 194, 198, 201, 207, 208, 209, 212, 213, 214, 215, 216, 217)

Sātāgira: a yakkha. He was present at the birth of Prince Siddhattha and at the First Sermon of the Buddha. At the latter, he was distracted because he was searching for his friend Hemavata. Later that day, when he met Hemavata in Rājagaha, Hemavata suggested that they hurry to the Himavat because the region was covered with flowers. Sātāgira explained that the reason for the flowers was the appearance of the Buddha and enumerated the Buddha's qualities. Together, they went to Isipatana to hear the Buddha. Their conversation in Rājagaha was overheard by a laywoman named Kāli-Kuraragharikā, and, through it, she attained the first path. Sātāgira and Hemavata also happened to be in Ālavi when the Buddha converted Ālavaka. Unable to pass over the yakkha's mansion and perceiving the reason, they went inside and congratulated the Buddha on his victory. Kāli-Kuraragharikā was foremost among laywomen who achieved insight from hearsay. (190)

Siddhattha: the personal name of Gotama Buddha. He was born in Kapilavatthu, the capital of Sākya, as the son of King Suddhodana and Queen Mahā-Māyā. At twenty-nine, on the day that his son Rāhula was born, despite King Suddhodana's precautions, Prince Siddhattha saw the Four Sights—an old man, a sick man, a corpse, and an ascetic—which prompted him to leave home and to become an ascetic.

Suddhodana: the Sākyan king and the father of Prince Siddhattha. Mahā-Māyā was his chief queen, and, after she died, her sister Mahā-Pajāpatī-Gotamī took that position. King Suddhodana tried to prevent his son from leaving the world by shielding him from unpleasantness and surrounding him with luxury. Later, King Suddhodana invited the Buddha to Kapilavatthu. [See Kāludāyi] When the Buddha walked for alms in Kapilavatthu, King Suddhodana reproached him for begging, but the Buddha replied that going on almsrounds was the custom of all Buddhas. Hearing that, King Suddhodana attained the first path. Much later, on hearing the Buddha teach to him again, he attained arahatship just before he died. This is one of the few instances in which a layman became an arahat. In such a case, the person must, on that day, either ordain or pass away. [See Bhaddaji] (7, 20, 83, 143, 174, 202, 206, 207, 208, 209, 216, 217)

Sunakkhatta: a Licchavi prince of Vesāli. He became a bhikkhu but disrobed to follow other teachers. He publicly defamed the Buddha, complaining that the Buddha had neither performed any miracles nor shown him the beginning of things. The Buddha scolded him, enumerating his own extraordinary powers and saying that he had not promised to explain the beginning of things. The Buddha pointed out that he taught only suffering and the end of suffering. (214)

Thulla-Nandā: a troublesome bhikkhunī who was close to Devadatta. Although she was an eloquent speaker, she was also greedy and was accused of misappropriating gifts given to other bhikkhunīs. She enjoyed men's company and went out unattended. She was jealous of other bhikkhunīs and frequently quarreled with them. Her misdeeds led to the establishment of quite a few of the Vinaya rules. (52)

Upāli: an eminent bhikkhu. He was the barber of the Sākyan princes and ordained with them. [See Tale 8] He attained arahatship and was foremost among bhikkhus in Vinaya. (8, 188)

Uppalavannā: an eminent bhikkhunī; one of the two chief female disciples of the Buddha. She was extremely beautiful and had been sought by kings and commoners from all of Jambudīpa, but her father suggested that she ordain, and she readily agreed. One day, while she was sweeping the Ordination Hall in Jetavana, she concentrated on the flame of a lamp as a fire-kasina, attained jhāna, and became an arahat. She was foremost among bhikkhunīs in extraordinary powers. (102, 111, 138, 154, 171, 190, 198, 208, 209, 210, 212, 213, 216, 217)

Uruvela-Kassapa: a bhikkhu. He was an ascetic in Uruvela and had five hundred disciples. His brothers, also named Kassapa, were also ascetics and had three hundred and two hundred disciples, respectively. The Buddha spent an entire rainy season with them, performing many miracles and trying to convert them. Even after the Buddha had overcome two powerful nāgas, the Kassapas were unconvinced, and Uruvela-Kassapa still believed himself to be an arahat and the Buddha's superior. Finally, the Buddha was able to convert him, and the three brothers, with their one thousand followers, were ordained. A little later, the Buddha taught the Fire Sermon (Ādittapariyāya Sutta), and they all attained arahatship. Uruvela-Kassapa was foremost among bhikkhus in having a large following. (214)

Vessavana: one of the Four Great Kings. His kingdom is in the north, and he is king of the yakkhas. (6, 147, 168, 202, 215)

Glossary of Personal Names

Vidūdabha: the son of King Pasenadi and Vāsabha-Khattiyā. [See Tale 179] (7, 179)

Vipassi Buddha: nineteenth of the twenty-four Buddhas. (217)

Visākhā: the chief laywoman disciple of the Buddha. When she was seven years old, she heard the Buddha teach in Anga and attained the first path. Later, her family moved to Sāketā in Kosala. She moved to Sāvatthī when she married into a family that followed the Niganthas. After she converted her father-in-law, Migāra, she became known as "Migāra's mother" (Migāramātā). In Sāvatthī, she built Migāramātupāsāda, a monastery in the Eastern Park (Pubbārāma), and gave it to the Buddha. She was foremost among laywomen who ministered to the Sangha. (10, 98, 182, 203, 217)

Vissakamma: a deva. He is Sakka's chief architect and builder. (188, 202, 208, 210, 217)

Yama: the king of hell. (93, 188, 206, 210, 214)

Yasodharā: the wife of Prince Siddhattha and the mother of his son, Rāhula. She was also called Rāhula's mother (Rāhulamātā), and Bimbādevī. After Prince Siddhattha left home, she showed her loyalty by abandoning luxury, wearing yellow robes, and taking only one meal a day. After the bhikkhunī order was established, she ordained as Venerable Bhaddakaccānā and attained arahatship. (83, 102, 109, 129, 134, 154, 156, 163, 172, 201, 206, 212, 215, 216, 217)

The Thirty-One Planes of Existence

	Level	Realm	Inhabitants	Cause of rebirth there
		**The Immaterial World (*Arūpa-loka*)**		
	28–31	*Arūpa*	Devas of the formless realms. Mind only; no body	Four immaterial jhānas
		The Fine-Material World (*Rūpa-loka*)		
Brahma Heavens (*Brahma-loka*)	23-27	*Suddhāvāsa*	Devas of the Pure Abodes. Beings who have attained the path of non-returning are reborn and attain arahatship here. Brahmā Sahampati resides here.	Fourth jhāna
	22	*Asaññasattā*	Non-percipient Devas. Body only; no mind	
	21	*Vehapphala*	Devas of Great Reward	
	20	*Subhakinha*	Devas of Refulgent Glory	Third jhāna
	19	*Appamānasu-bha*	Devas of Limitless Glory	
	18	*Parittasubha*	Devas of Limited Glory	
	17	*Abhassara*	Devas of Brilliant Radiance	Second jhāna
	16	*Appamānābha*	Devas of Limitless Radiance	
	15	*Parittābha*	Devas of Limited Radiance	
	14	*Mahā-Brahmā*	Great Brahmā. Often refers to the first resident of this heaven, but all beings here and above can be called Mahā-Brahmā	First jhāna
	13	*Brahmā-purohita*	Brahmā's Ministers	
	12	*Brahmā-parisajja*	Members of Brahmā's Retinue	

The Sensuous World (*Kāma-loka*)			
Level	Realm	Inhabitants	Cause of rebirth there
11	*Paranimmita-vasavattī*	Devas who wield control over the creations of others. Abode of Māra	Ten courses of wholesome action, generosity, morality, and wisdom
10	*Nimmānarati*	Devas who delight in creation	
9	*Tusita*	Contented Devas. Bodhisattas are reborn here prior to their final human birth	
8	*Yāmā*	Comfortable Devas. Devas who live in the air, at ease, free of all difficulties	
7	*Tāvatimsa*	The Thirty-three Devas. Abode of Sakka. Large numbers of attendant nymphs also live here	
6	*Catumahārājika*	The Four Great Kings, who guard the four qauarters. Yakkhas, gandhabbas, kumbhandas, nāgas, and deva-asuras also live here. This realm and all the above are divine heaven realms, *deva-loka.*	
5	*Manussa*	Humans	
4	*Asura*	Asura-kāya	Ten courses of unwholesome actions
3	*Peta*	Petas (Hungry ghosts)	Lack of virtue, holding to wrong views
2	*Tiracchāna*	Animals	Behaving like an animal
1	*Niraya*	(The hells, of which there are eight, *Roruva* is the fourth highest. *Avīci* is the lowest and worst. *Ussada* is the collective name for lesser hells that surround each of the great hells.)	Killing one's parents, killing an arahat, injuring the Buddha, creating a schism in the Sangha

Happy Realms (*Sugati*) — Levels 5–11

Woeful Realms (*Apāya*) — Levels 1–4

Map of Jambudīpa

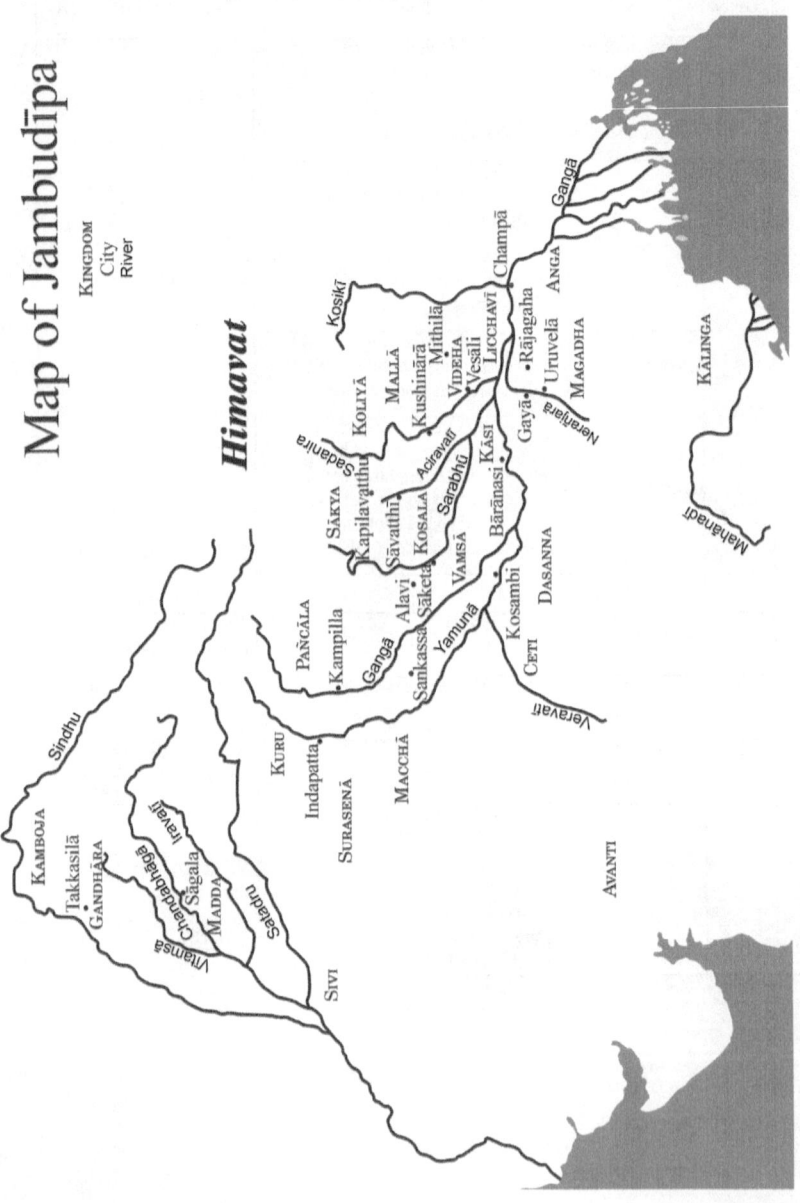

Table of Correspondence
Jātaka Numbers from the Pāli

JTB = Jātaka Tales of the Buddha (This Anthology)
PTS = The Jātaka or Stories of the Buddha's Former Births, Pāli Text Society
Book = Nipāta, Division of the Pāli in which the Jātaka is included

JTB	PTS	Book	JTB	PTS	Book	JTB	PTS	Book
1	1	I	36	83	I	71	168	II
2	2	I	37	87	I	72	177	II
3	3	I	38	89	I	73	178	II
4	4	I	39	91	I	74	179	II
5	5	I	40	92	I	75	181	II
6	6	I	41	96	I	76	182	II
7	7	I	42	107	I	77	183	II
8	10	I	43	109	I	78	186	II
9	11	I	44	113	I	79	190	II
10	12	I	45	115	I	80	193	II
11	14	I	46	118	I	81	194	II
12	18	I	47	123	I	82	195	II
13	20	I	48	124	I	83	201	II
14	22	I	49	125	I	84	202	II
15	28	I	50	128	I	85	206	II
16	31	I	51	131	I	86	207	II
17	32	I	52	136	I	87	211	II
18	33	I	53	137	I	88	215	II
19	34	I	54	139	I	89	218	II
20	35	I	55	140	I	90	220	II
21	37	I	56	141	I	91	222	II
22	40	I	57	143	I	92	234	II
23	41	I	58	144	I	93	240	II
24	43	I	59	146	I	94	241	II
25	46	I	60	148	I	95	243	II
26	48	I	61	149	I	96	251	III
27	50	I	62	150	I	97	252	III
28	51	I	63	151	II	98	254	III
29	55	I	64	153	II	99	257	III
30	63	I	65	156	II	100	267	III
31	67	I	66	157	II	101	272	III
32	73	I	67	159	II	102	276	III
33	77	I	68	160	II	103	278	III
34	78	I	69	161	II	104	282	III
35	80	I	70	166	II	105	284	III

JTB	PTS	Book	JTB	PTS	Book	JTB	PTS	Book
106	286	III	144	379	VI	182	472	XII
107	288	III	145	385	VI	183	474	XIII
108	291	III	146	386	VI	184	475	XIII
109	292	III	147	398	VII	185	476	XIII
110	300	III	148	400	VII	186	481	XIII
111	301	IV	149	401	VII	187	482	XIII
112	302	IV	150	402	VII	188	483	XIII
113	305	IV	151	405	VII	189	486	XIV
114	306	IV	152	406	VII	190	488	XIV
115	308	IV	153	407	VII	191	490	XIV
116	309	IV	154	408	VII	192	491	XIV
117	312	IV	155	409	VII	193	492	XIV
118	313	IV	156	411	VII	194	493	XIV
119	314	IV	157	412	VII	195	497	XV
120	315	IV	158	413	VII	196	498	XV
121	316	IV	159	417	VIII	197	499	XV
122	318	IV	160	418	VIII	198	501	XV
123	319	IV	161	419	VIII	199	503	XV
124	321	IV	162	420	VIII	200	504	XV
125	322	IV	163	421	VIII	201	506	XV
126	323	IV	164	422	VIII	202	510	XV
127	324	IV	165	425	VIII	203	512	XVI
128	326	IV	166	427	IX	204	514	XVI
129	328	IV	167	429	IX	205	520	XVI
130	329	IV	168	432	IX	206	531	XX
131	331	IV	169	439	X	207	537	XXI
132	338	IV	170	440	X	208	538	XXII
133	339	IV	171	442	X	209	539	XXII
134	340	IV	172	443	X	210	540	XXII
135	342	IV	173	445	X	211	541	XXII
136	346	IV	174	447	X	212	542	XXII
137	352	V	175	450	X	213	543	XXII
138	354	V	176	455	XI	214	544	XXII
139	356	V	177	456	XI	215	545	XXII
140	357	V	178	462	XI	216	546	XXII
141	358	V	179	465	XI	217	547	XXII
142	359	V	180	467	XII			
143	371	V	181	469	XII			

Bibliography

Burlingame, E.W., translator, Buddhist Legends, London, The Pali Text Society, 1921, reprinted in 1990 and 1995; a complete translation of Dhammapada Commentary. About sixty of the stories are shared with the Jātakas.

Chandavimala, Ven. Rerukane, Analysis of Perfections, translated by A. G. S. Kariyawasam, Kandy, Sri Lanka, Buddhist Publication Society, 2003; a succinct treatment of the Ten Perfections and how they can be developed.

Cowell, E. B., editor, The Jātaka or Stories of the Buddha's Former Births, London, The Pali Text Society, 18951907, reprinted in 1990; a complete translation of the Jātaka Commentary, including all 547 stories.

Harischandra, D.V.J., Psychiatric Aspects of Jātaka Stories, Galle, Sri Lanka, Upuli Offset, 1998.

Karunaratne, David, translator, Ummagga Jataka (The Story of the Tunnel), Colombo, Sri Lanka, M.D. Gunasena & Co. Ltd., 1962.

Malalasekera, G. P., Dictionary of Pāli Proper Names, London, The Pali Text Society, 1938, reprinted 1960 and 1974.

Na-Rangsi, Dr. Sunthorn, The Four Planes of Existence in Theravada Buddhism, Kandy, Sri Lanka, Buddhist Publication Society, 2006.

Recommendations for Further Reading

Bhikkhu Bodhi, Editor, In the Buddha's Words, An Anthology of Discourses from the Pali Canon, Somerville, Massachusetts, U.S.A., Wisdom Publications, 2005; a collection of suttas selected to serve as an introduction to the Buddha's Teaching.

Dhammapāla, Ācariya, A Treatise on the Pāramīs, A Discourse from the Majjhima Nikāya, translated from the Pali by Bhikkhu Bodhi, Wheel No. 409/411, Kandy, Sri Lanka, Buddhist Publication Society (BPS), 1996; a lucid translation of a sixth-century discussion of the Ten Perfections, drawing from both Theravada and Mahāyana texts.

Dhammika, Ven. S., Middle Land, Middle Way: A Pilgrim's Guide to the Buddha's India, Kandy, Sri Lanka, BPS, 2008; A description of the sites important to the life of the Buddha.

Gunaratana, Ven. Henepola, Mindfulness in Plain English, Somerville, Massachusetts, U.S.A. Wisdom Publications, 1992; a practical and straightforward guide to vipassanā meditation and its benefits for everyone.

Kawasaki, Ken and Visākhā, Strive on with Diligence, The Buddha and His Teaching, Kandy, Sri Lanka, Buddhist Relief Mission, 2002; www.brelief.org; a multi-media presentation in DVD and VCD format, presenting the life of the Buddha and basic Dhamma through art and scenes from around the world.

Nyanaponika Thera and Hellmuth Hecker, Great Disciples of the Buddha, Their Lives, Their Works, Their Legacy, edited by Bhikkhu Bodhi, Kandy, Sri Lanka, BPS and Somerville, Massachusetts, U.S.A., Wisdom Publications, 2003; biographies of many of the Buddha's disciples who appear in the Jātakas.

Piyadassi Thera, The Buddha's Ancient Path, Kandy, Sri Lanka, BPS, 1974; a clear explanation of the Buddha's Teaching.

U Pandita, Sayadaw, In This Very Life, Liberation Teachings of the Buddha, Kandy, Sri Lanka, BPS, 2007; a guide to vipassanā meditation and an analysis of the workings of the mind.

ABOUT PARIYATTI

Pariyatti is dedicated to providing affordable access to authentic teachings of the Buddha about the Dhamma theory (*pariyatti*) and practice (*paṭipatti*) of Vipassana meditation. A 501(c)(3) non-profit charitable organization since 2002, Pariyatti is sustained by contributions from individuals who appreciate and want to share the incalculable value of the Dhamma teachings. We invite you to visit www.pariyatti.org to learn about our programs, services, and ways to support publishing and other undertakings.

Pariyatti Publishing Imprints

Vipassana Research Publications (focus on Vipassana as taught by S.N. Goenka in the tradition of Sayagyi U Ba Khin)

BPS Pariyatti Editions (selected titles from the Buddhist Publication Society, co-published by Pariyatti in the Americas)

Pariyatti Digital Editions (audio and video titles, including discourses)

Pariyatti Press (classic titles returned to print and inspirational writing by contemporary authors)

Pariyatti enriches the world by

- disseminating the words of the Buddha,
- providing sustenance for the seeker's journey,
- illuminating the meditator's path.

www.ingramcontent.com/pod-product-compliance
Lightning Source LLC
Chambersburg PA
CBHW020501020726
47493CB00001B/124